FROM THE #1 *NEW YORK TIMES* BESTSELLI

RAINA TELGE

DRAMA

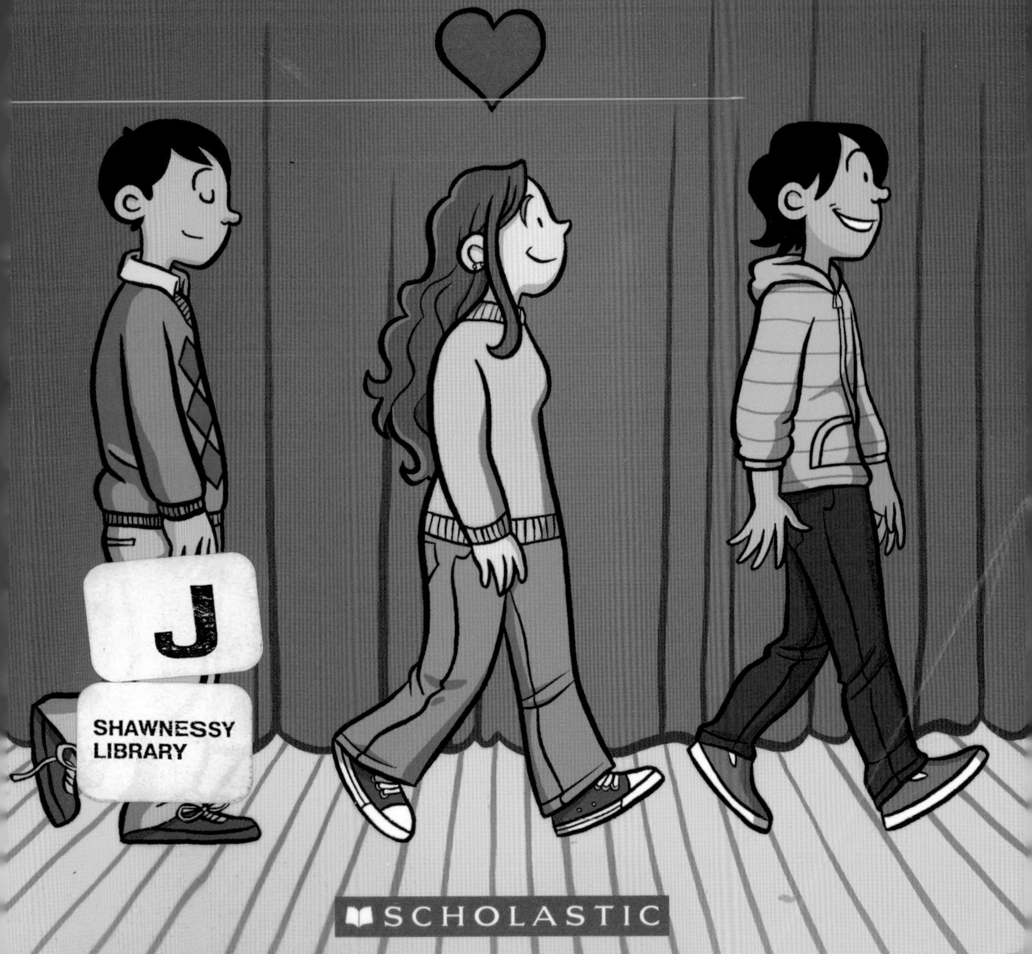

SCHOLASTIC

RAINA TELGEMEIER

DRAMA

WITH COLOR BY GURIHIRU

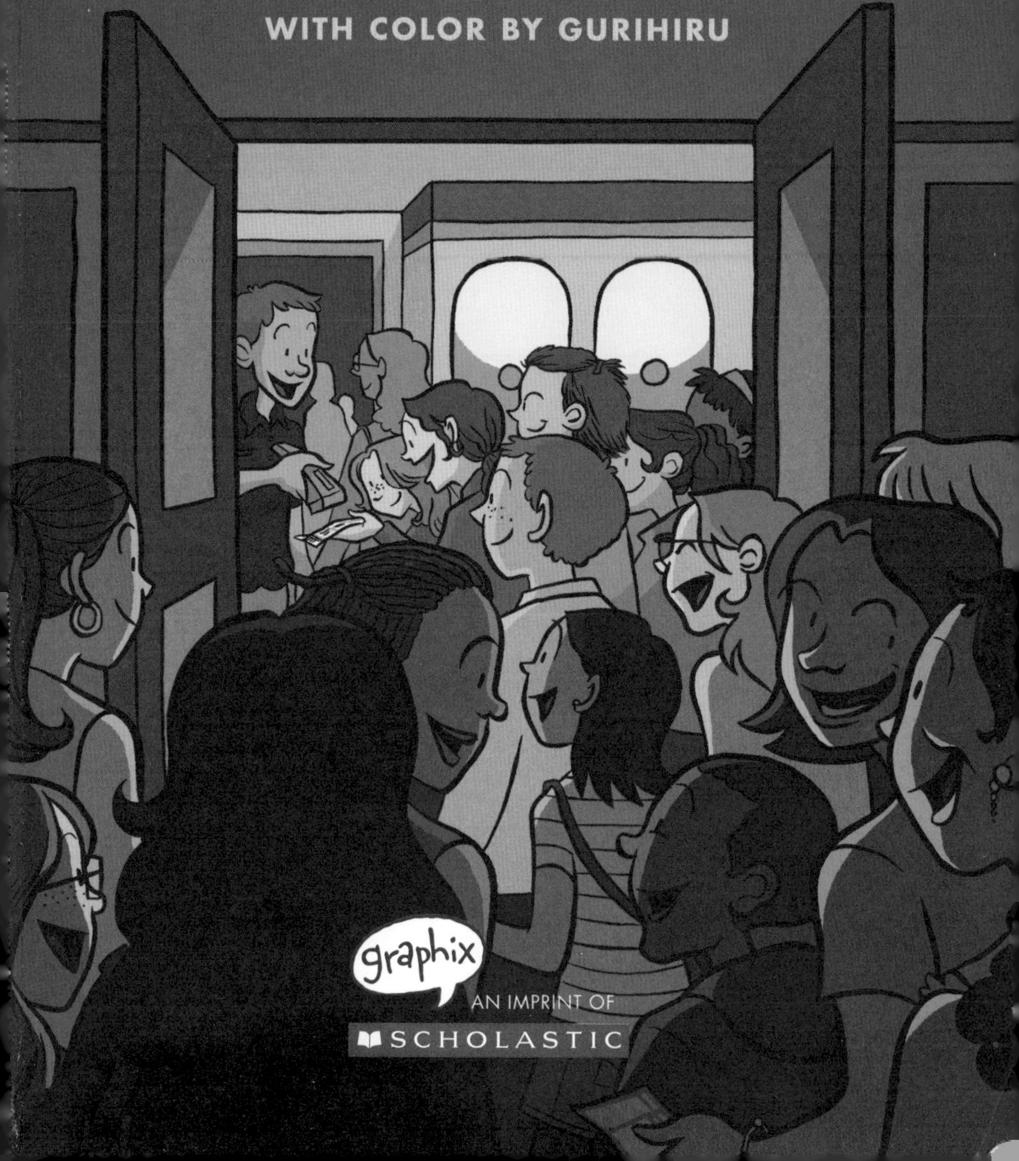

graphix
AN IMPRINT OF
SCHOLASTIC

For Jake and Jeff, who continue to inspire me.

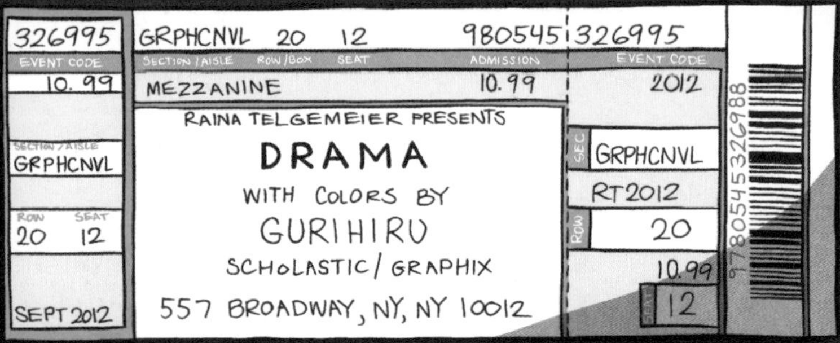
326995
EVENT CODE
10.99
SECTION / AISLE
GRPHCNVL
ROW SEAT
20 12
SEPT 2012
GRPHCNVL 20 12 980545 326995
SECTION / AISLE ROW / BOX SEAT ADMISSION EVENT CODE
MEZZANINE 10.99 2012
RAINA TELGEMEIER PRESENTS
DRAMA
WITH COLORS BY
GURIHIRU
SCHOLASTIC / GRAPHIX
557 BROADWAY, NY, NY 10012
SEC GRPHCNVL
RT2012
ROW 20
10.99
SEAT 12
9780545326988

Library of Congress Cataloging-in-Publication Data

Telgemeier, Raina.
Drama / Raina Telgemeier ; with color by Gurihiru. — 1st ed.
p. cm.
Summary: Callie rides an emotional roller coaster while serving on the stage crew for a middle school production of *Moon over Mississippi* as various relationships start and end, and others never quite get going.
ISBN 978-0-545-32698-8 (hardcover)
ISBN 978-0-545-32699-5 (paperback)
1. Graphic novels. [1. Graphic novels. 2. Theater—Fiction. 3. Interpersonal relations—Fiction. 4. Middle schools—Fiction. 5. Schools—Fiction.] I. Gurihiru. II. Title.
PZ7.7.T45Dr 2012
741.5'973—dc23
2011040748

20 18 19/0

First edition, September 2012
Edited by Cassandra Pelham
Lettering by John Green
Book design by Phil Falco
Creative Director: David Saylor
Printed in Malaysia 108

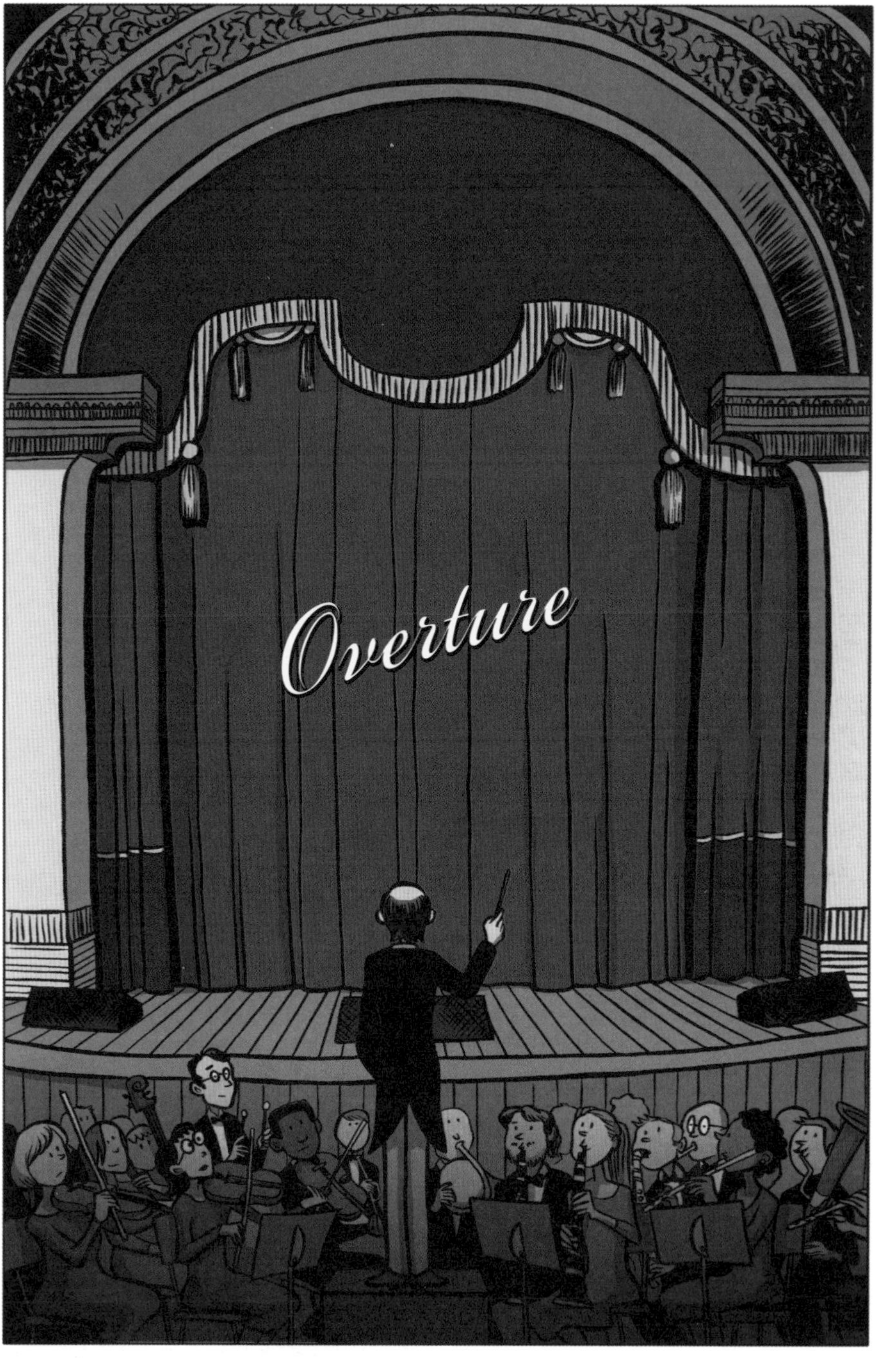
Overture

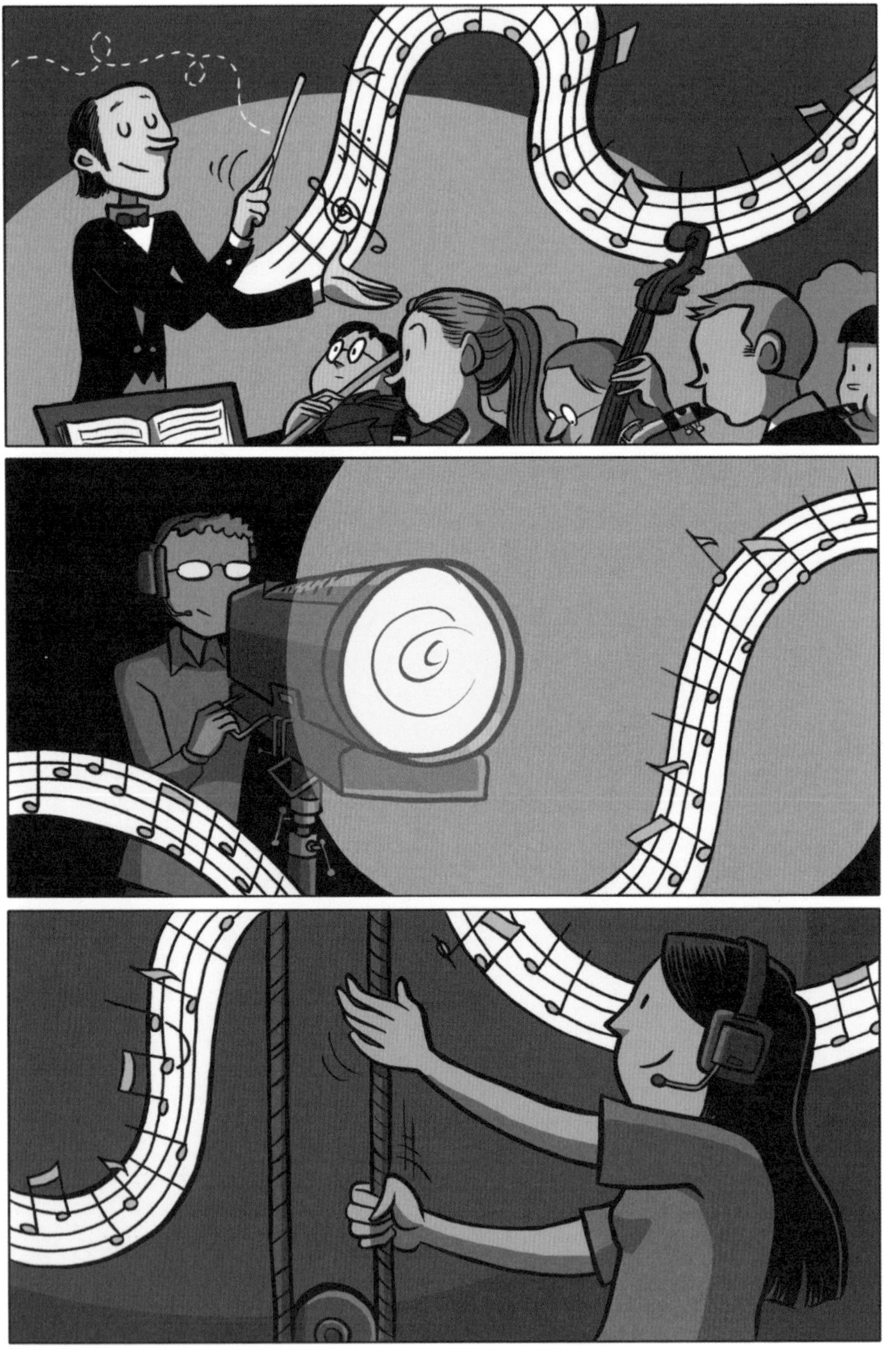

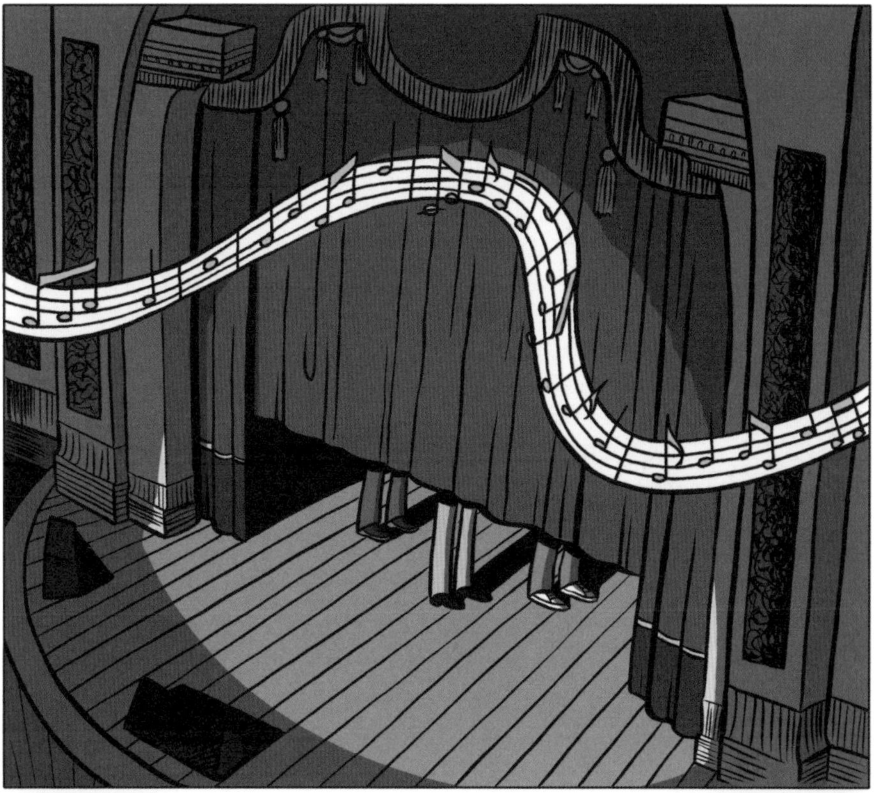

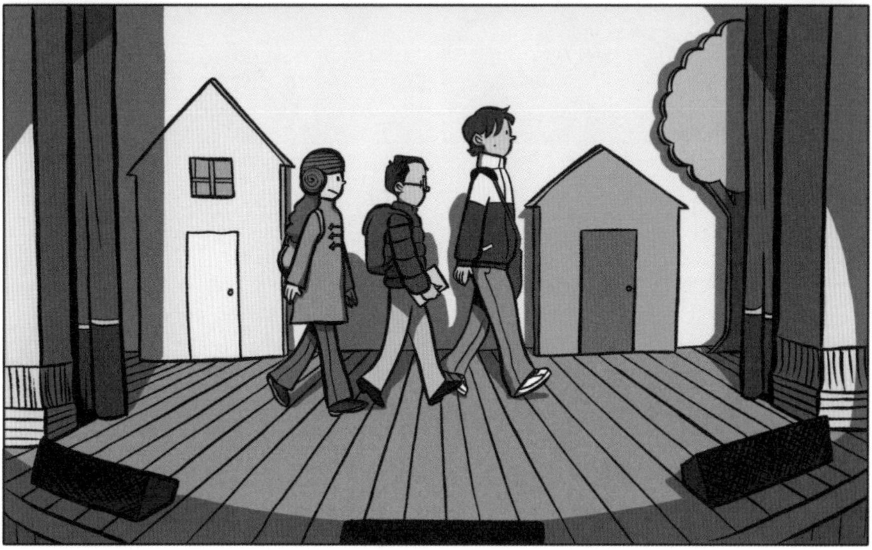

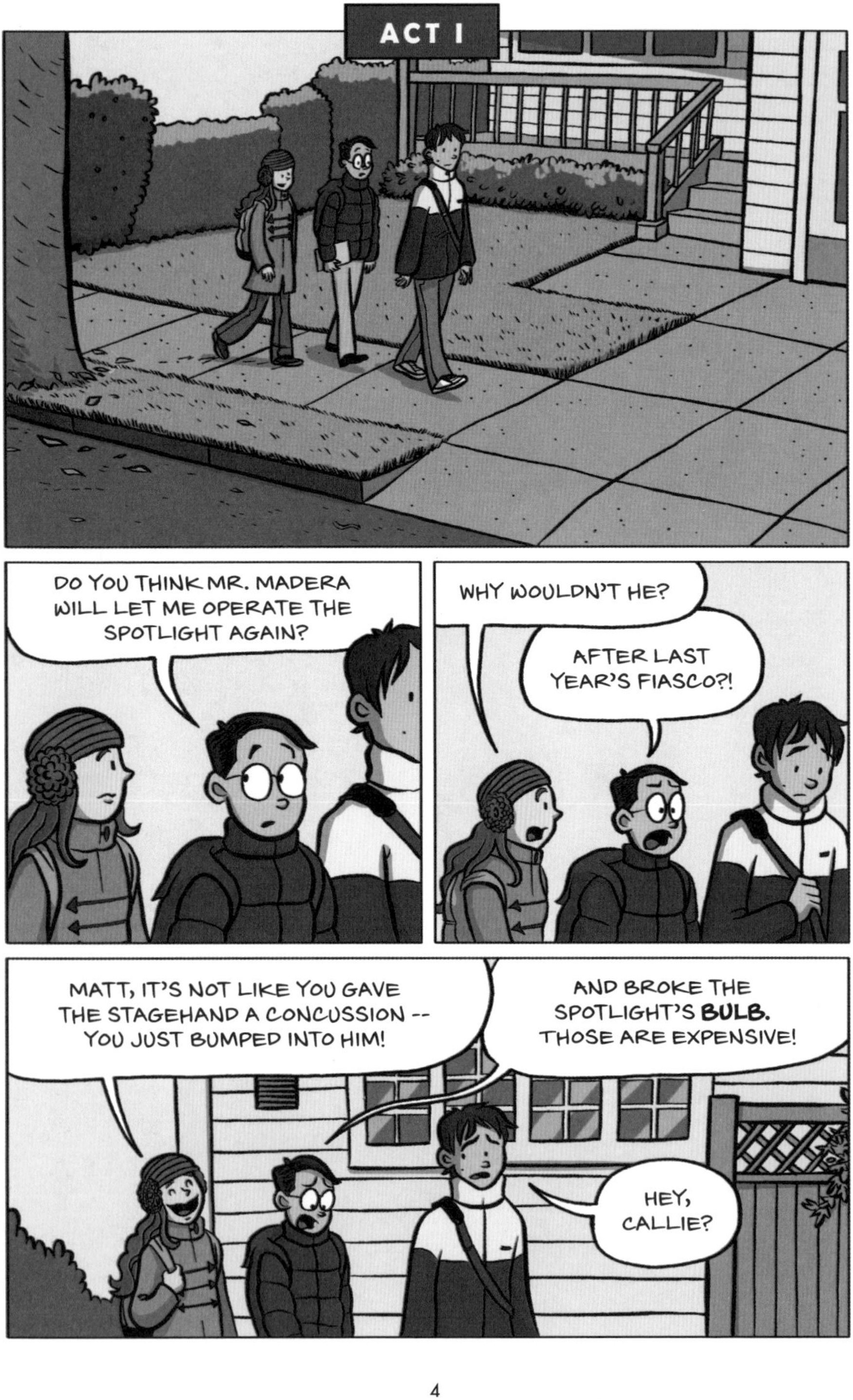
ACT I
DO YOU THINK MR. MADERA WILL LET ME OPERATE THE SPOTLIGHT AGAIN?
WHY WOULDN'T HE?
AFTER LAST YEAR'S FIASCO?!
MATT, IT'S NOT LIKE YOU GAVE THE STAGEHAND A CONCUSSION -- YOU JUST BUMPED INTO HIM!
AND BROKE THE SPOTLIGHT'S **BULB.** THOSE ARE EXPENSIVE!
HEY, CALLIE?

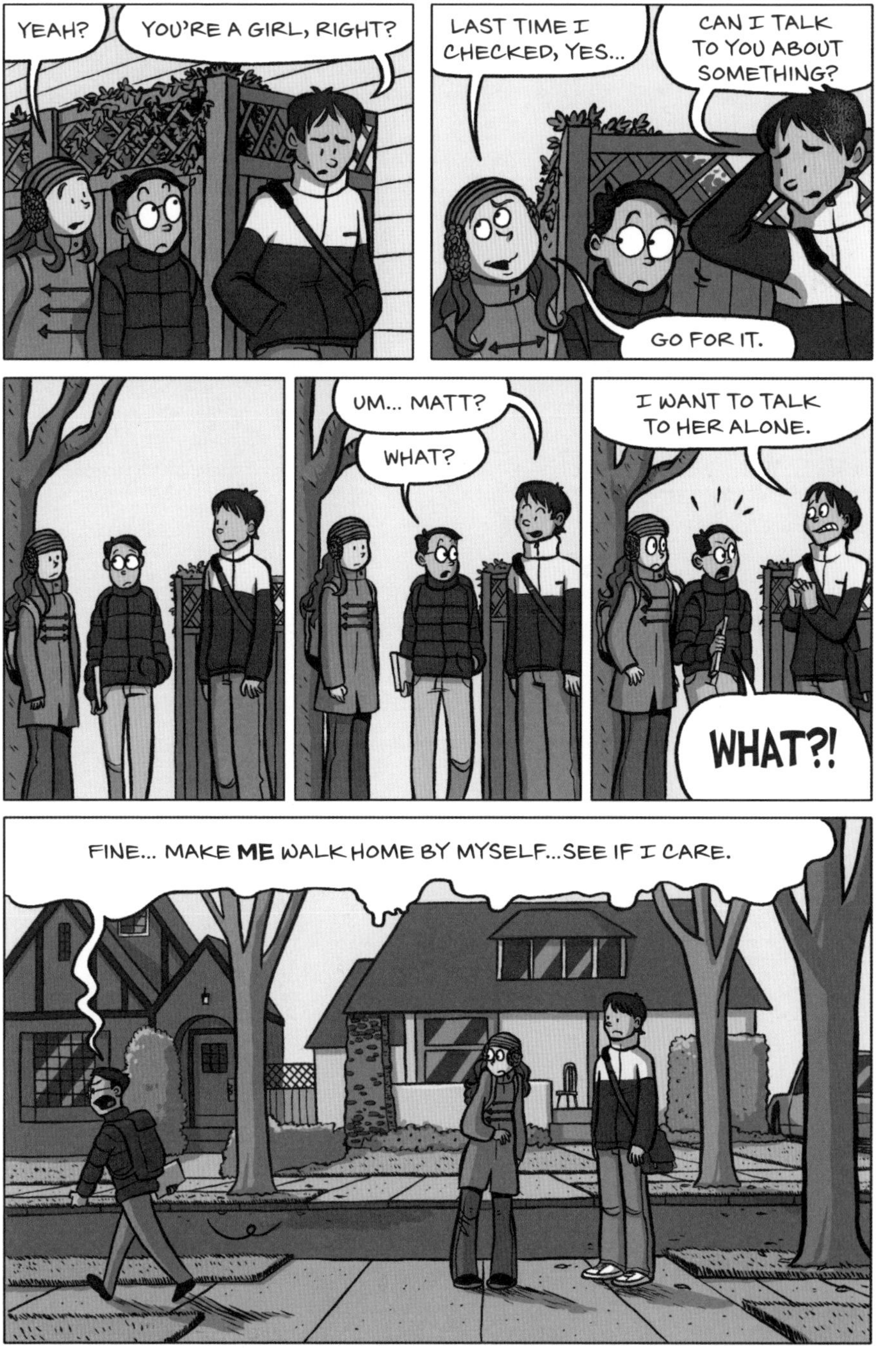
YEAH?
YOU'RE A GIRL, RIGHT?
LAST TIME I CHECKED, YES...
CAN I TALK TO YOU ABOUT SOMETHING?
GO FOR IT.
UM... MATT?
WHAT?
I WANT TO TALK TO HER ALONE.
WHAT?!
FINE... MAKE **ME** WALK HOME BY MYSELF...SEE IF I CARE.

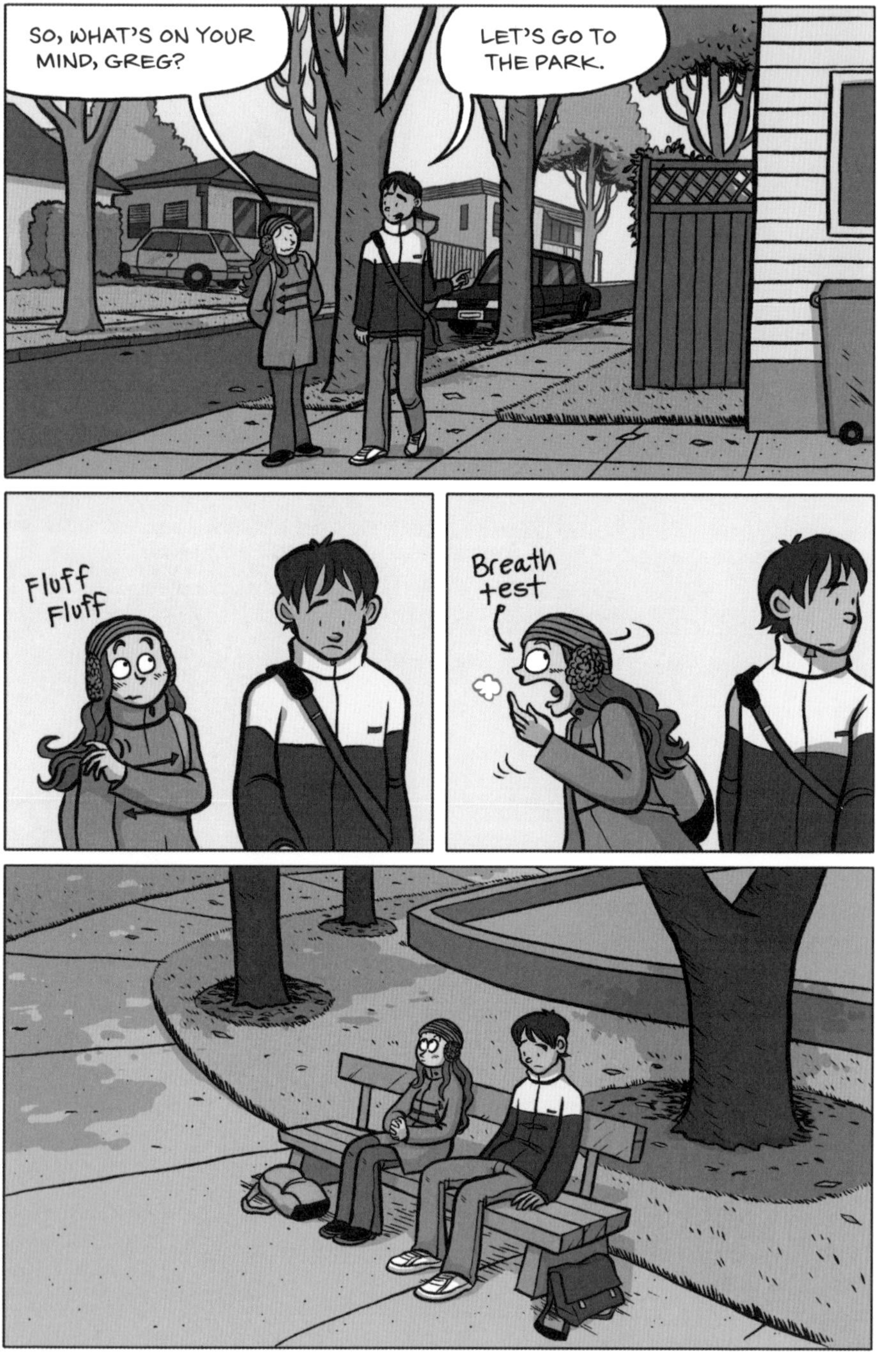
SO, WHAT'S ON YOUR MIND, GREG?
LET'S GO TO THE PARK.
Fluff Fluff
Breath test

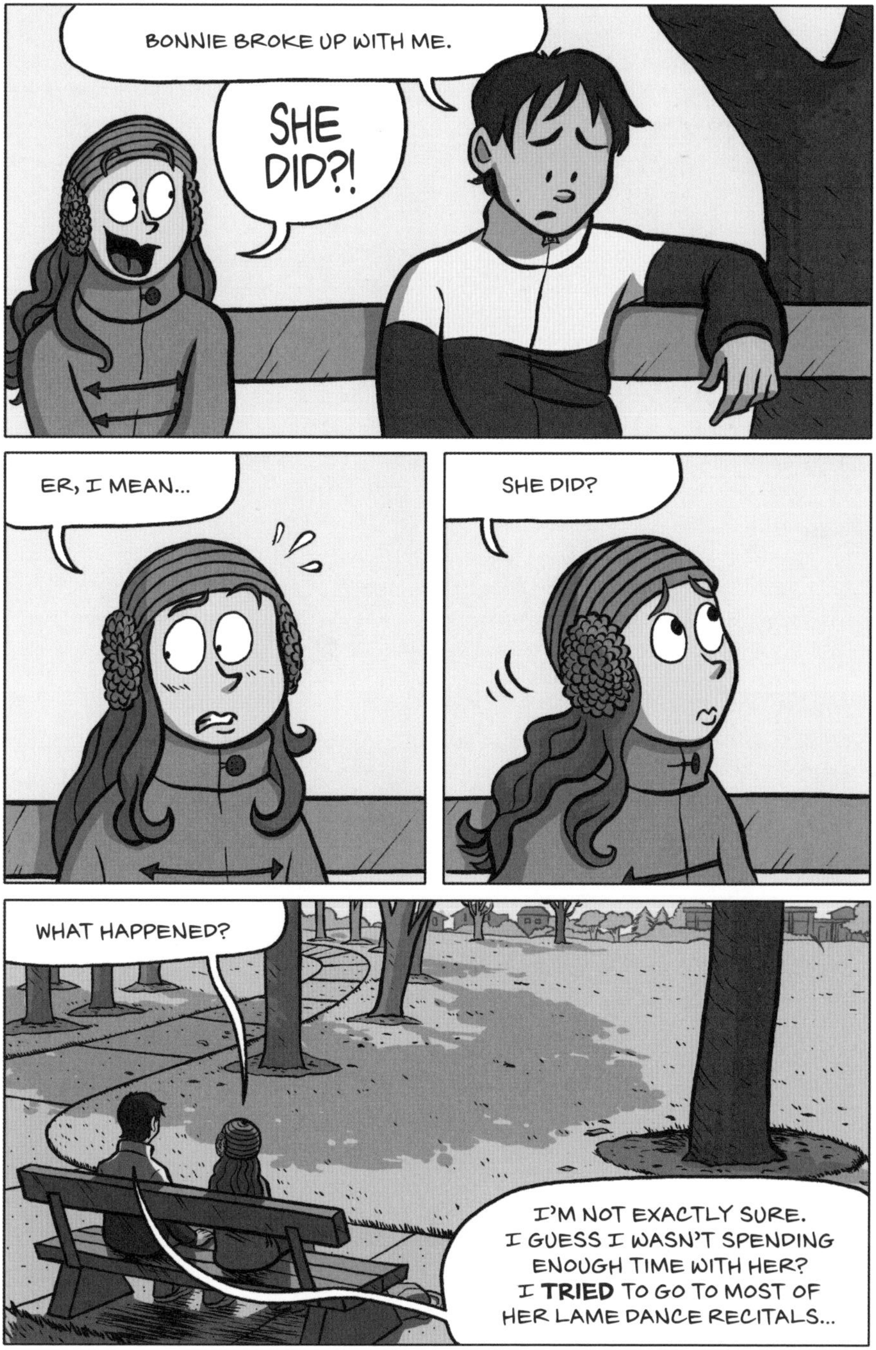
BONNIE BROKE UP WITH ME.
SHE DID?!
ER, I MEAN...
SHE DID?
WHAT HAPPENED?
I'M NOT EXACTLY SURE. I GUESS I WASN'T SPENDING ENOUGH TIME WITH HER? I **TRIED** TO GO TO MOST OF HER LAME DANCE RECITALS...

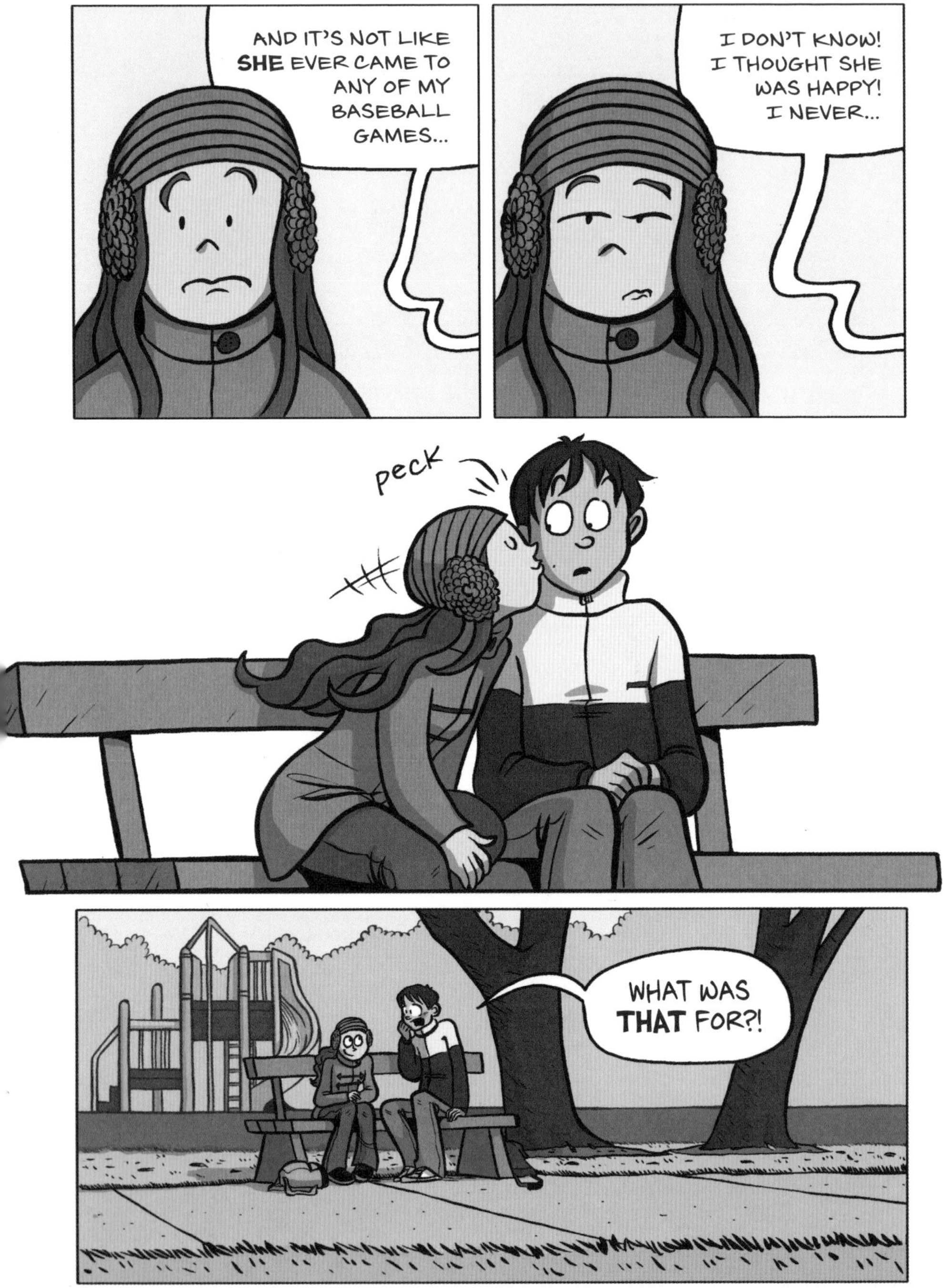
AND IT'S NOT LIKE **SHE** EVER CAME TO ANY OF MY BASEBALL GAMES...
I DON'T KNOW! I THOUGHT SHE WAS HAPPY! I NEVER...
peck
WHAT WAS **THAT** FOR?!

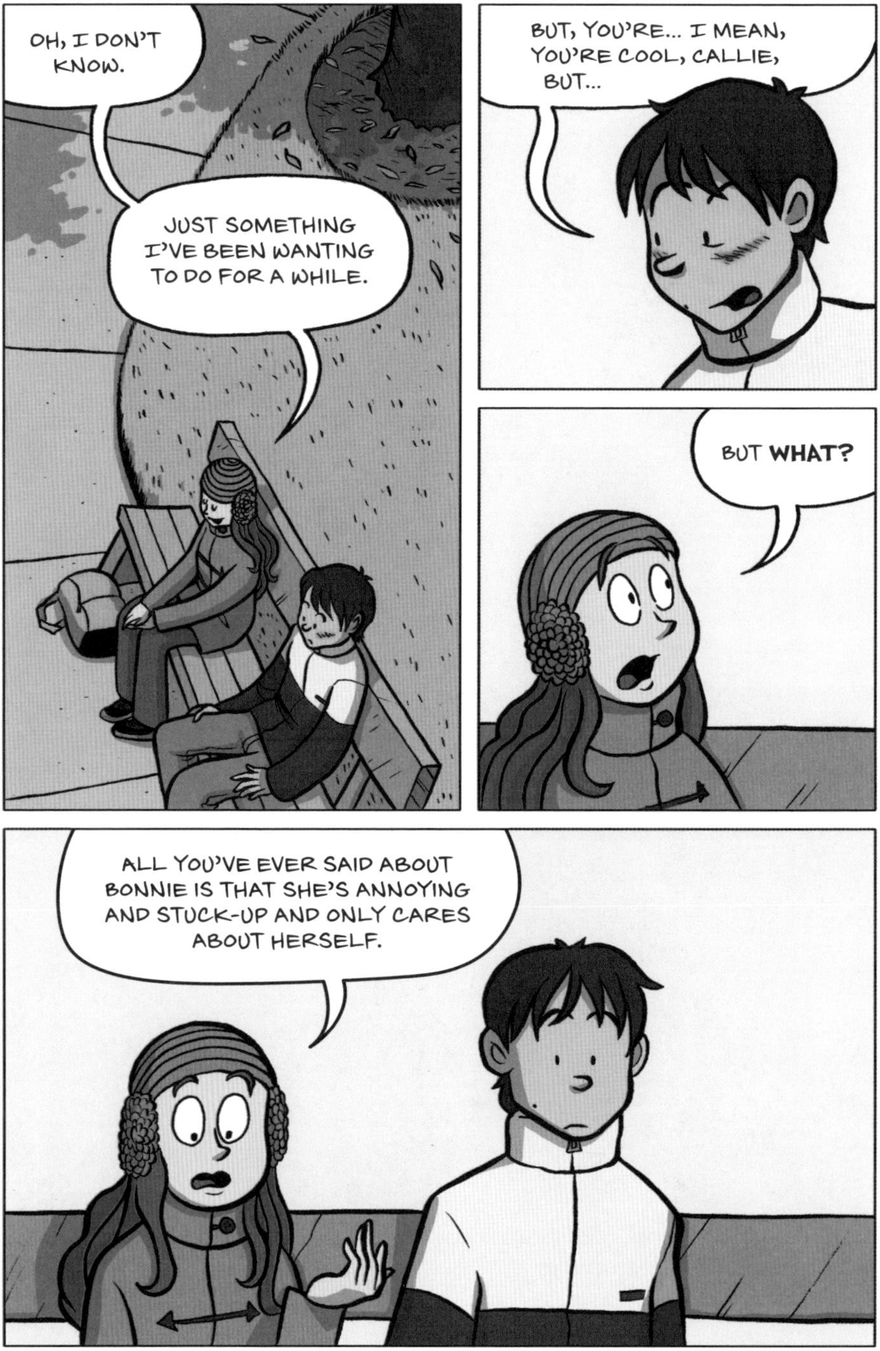
OH, I DON'T KNOW.
JUST SOMETHING I'VE BEEN WANTING TO DO FOR A WHILE.
BUT, YOU'RE... I MEAN, YOU'RE COOL, CALLIE, BUT...
BUT **WHAT?**
ALL YOU'VE EVER SAID ABOUT BONNIE IS THAT SHE'S ANNOYING AND STUCK-UP AND ONLY CARES ABOUT HERSELF.

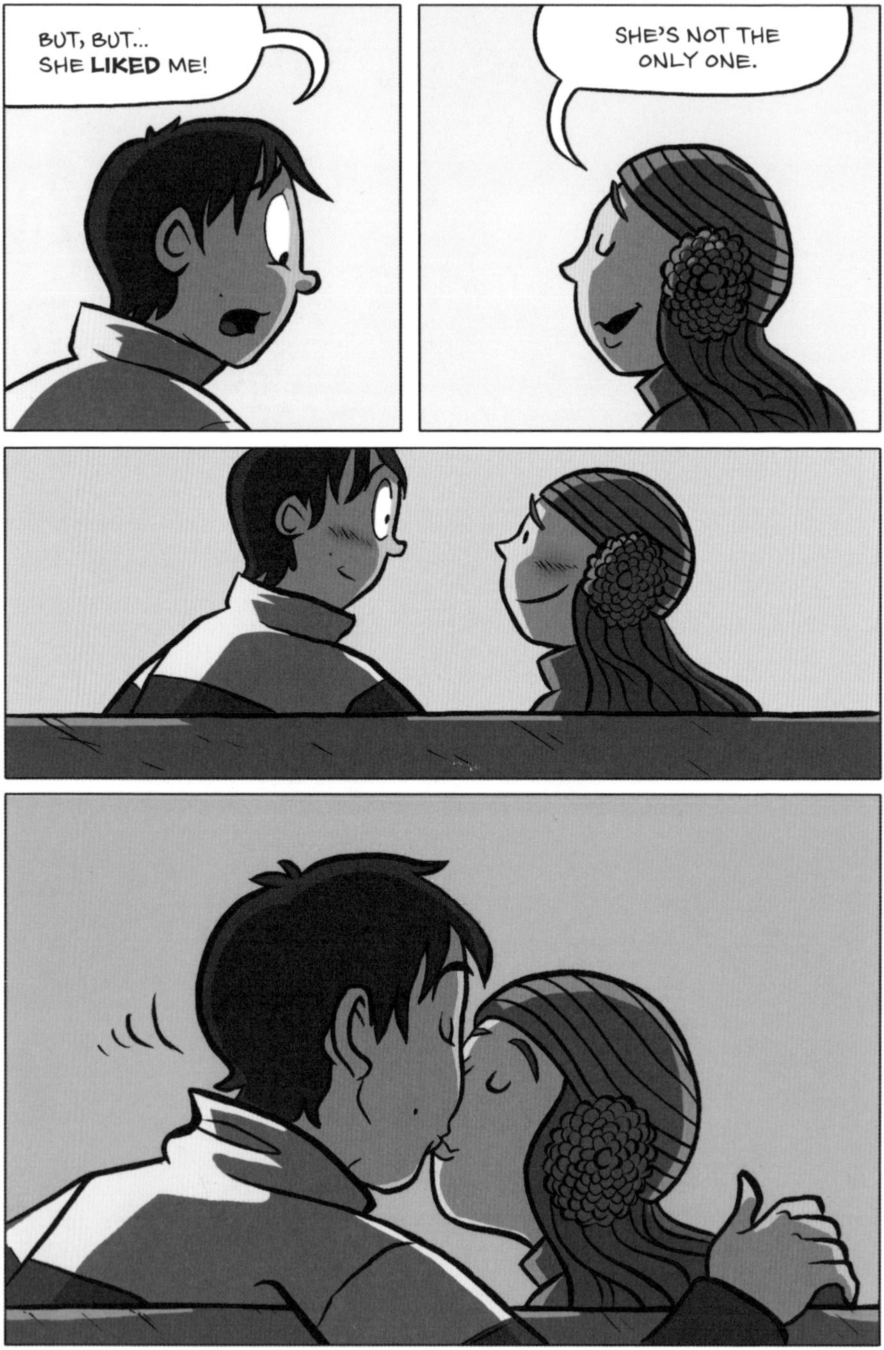
BUT, BUT...
SHE LIKED ME!
SHE'S NOT THE
ONLY ONE.

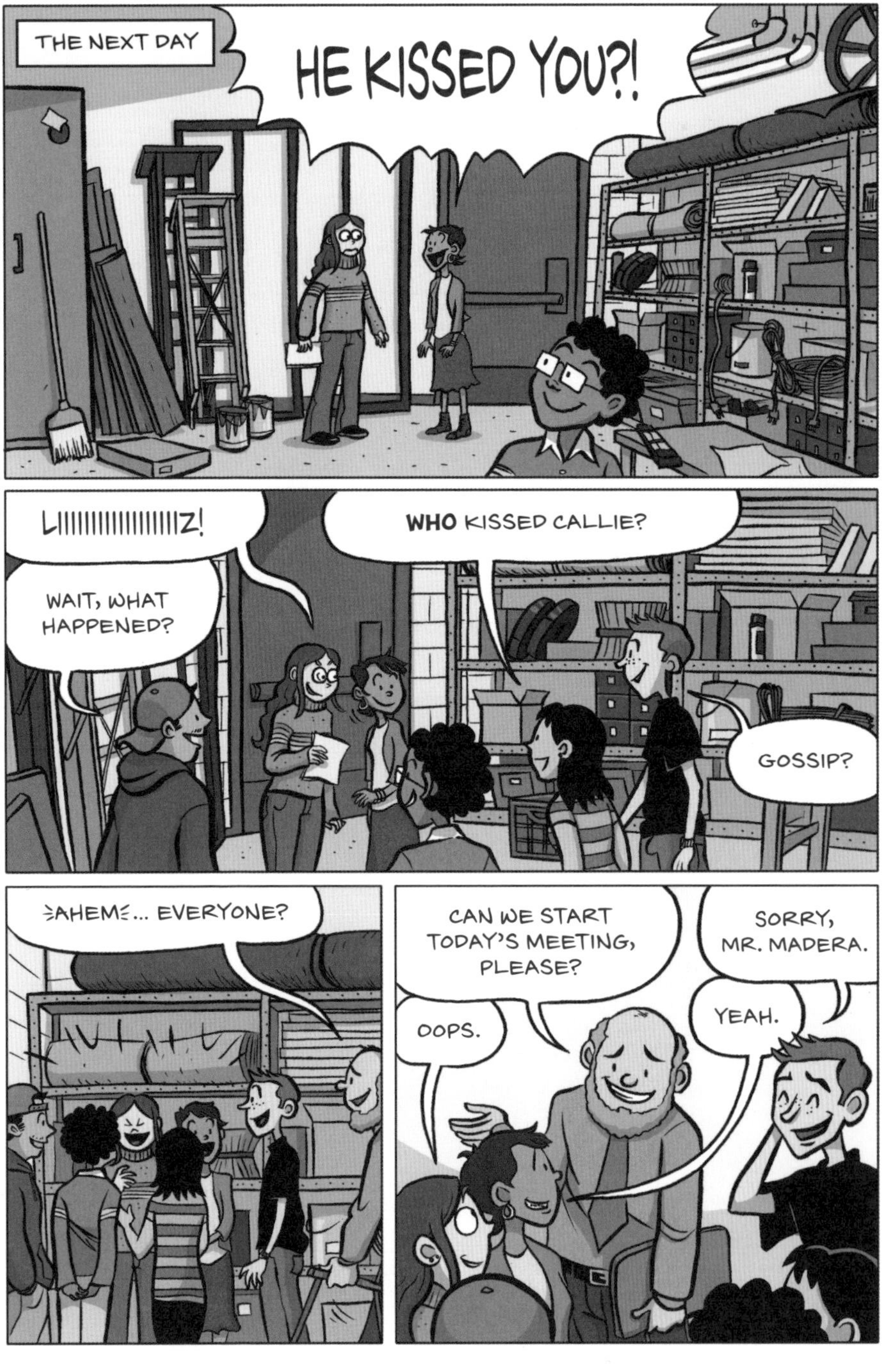
THE NEXT DAY
HE KISSED YOU?!
LIIIIIIIIIIIIIIIIZ!
WHO KISSED CALLIE?
WAIT, WHAT HAPPENED?
GOSSIP?
AHEM... EVERYONE?
CAN WE START TODAY'S MEETING, PLEASE?
SORRY, MR. MADERA.
OOPS.
YEAH.

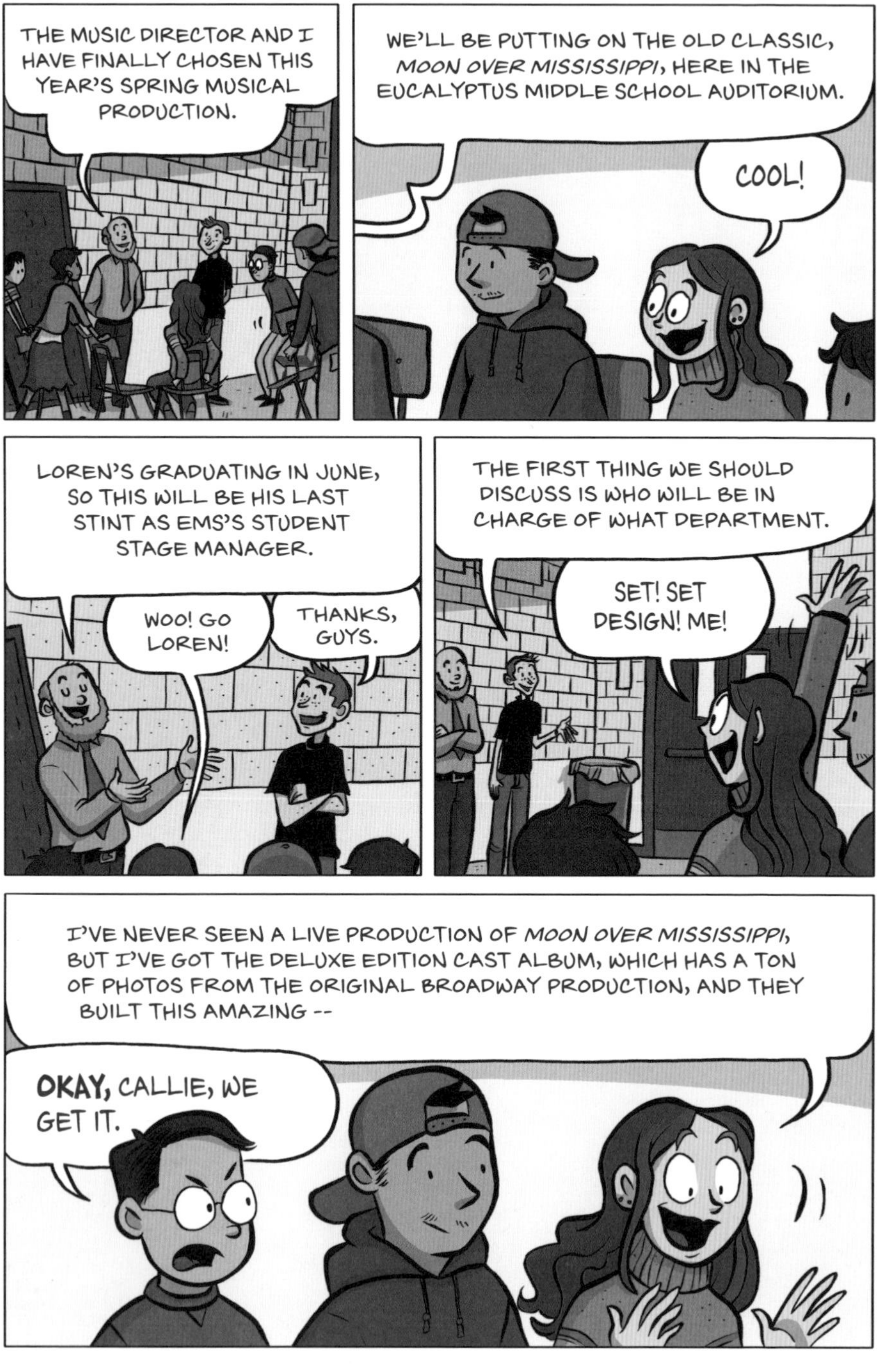
THE MUSIC DIRECTOR AND I HAVE FINALLY CHOSEN THIS YEAR'S SPRING MUSICAL PRODUCTION.
WE'LL BE PUTTING ON THE OLD CLASSIC, *MOON OVER MISSISSIPPI*, HERE IN THE EUCALYPTUS MIDDLE SCHOOL AUDITORIUM.
COOL!
LOREN'S GRADUATING IN JUNE, SO THIS WILL BE HIS LAST STINT AS EMS'S STUDENT STAGE MANAGER.
WOO! GO LOREN!
THANKS, GUYS.
THE FIRST THING WE SHOULD DISCUSS IS WHO WILL BE IN CHARGE OF WHAT DEPARTMENT.
SET! SET DESIGN! ME!
I'VE NEVER SEEN A LIVE PRODUCTION OF *MOON OVER MISSISSIPPI*, BUT I'VE GOT THE DELUXE EDITION CAST ALBUM, WHICH HAS A TON OF PHOTOS FROM THE ORIGINAL BROADWAY PRODUCTION, AND THEY BUILT THIS AMAZING --
OKAY, CALLIE, WE GET IT.

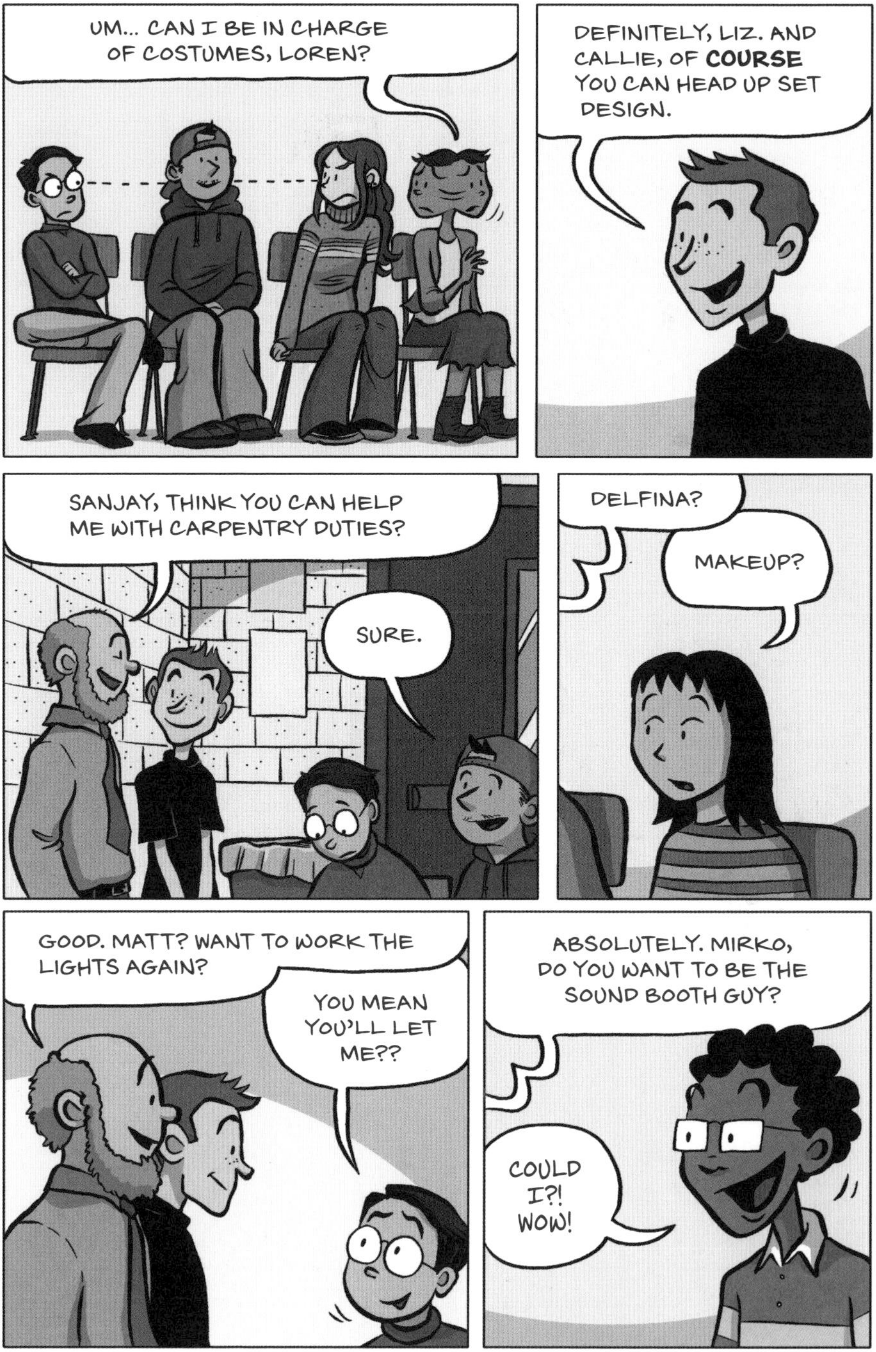
UM... CAN I BE IN CHARGE OF COSTUMES, LOREN?
DEFINITELY, LIZ. AND CALLIE, OF **COURSE** YOU CAN HEAD UP SET DESIGN.
SANJAY, THINK YOU CAN HELP ME WITH CARPENTRY DUTIES?
SURE.
DELFINA?
MAKEUP?
GOOD. MATT? WANT TO WORK THE LIGHTS AGAIN?
YOU MEAN YOU'LL LET ME??
ABSOLUTELY. MIRKO, DO YOU WANT TO BE THE SOUND BOOTH GUY?
COULD I?! WOW!

THERE'S ABOUT FOURTEEN WEEKS TILL OPENING NIGHT. DON'T FORGET THAT BY WEEK ELEVEN, WE'LL PRETTY MUCH BE HERE EVERY DAY.

I'M **STOKED** -- HOW ABOUT YOU GUYS?!

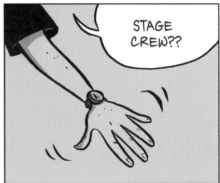

STAGE CREW??

STAGE CREW!!!

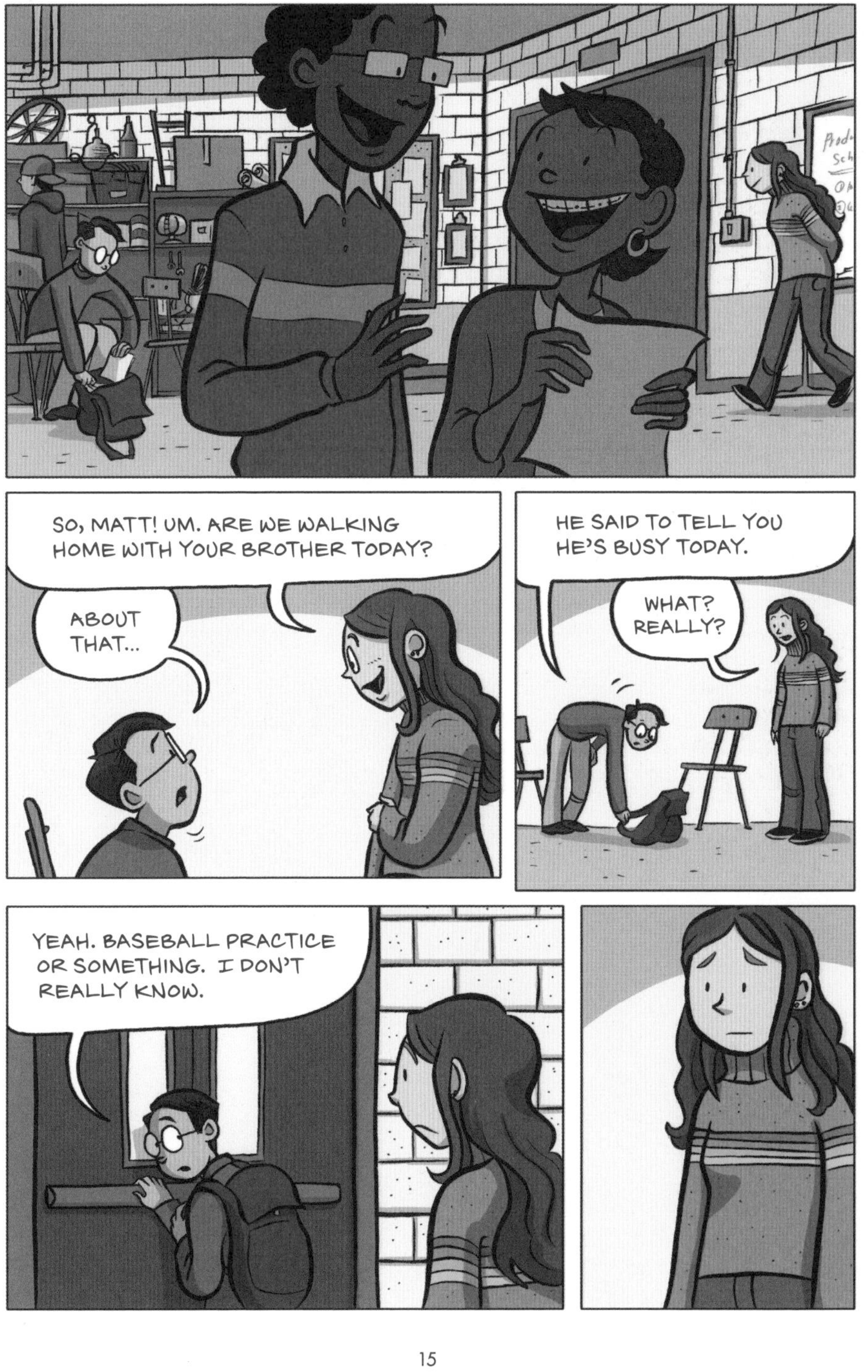
SO, MATT! UM. ARE WE WALKING HOME WITH YOUR BROTHER TODAY?
ABOUT THAT...
HE SAID TO TELL YOU HE'S BUSY TODAY.
WHAT? REALLY?
YEAH. BASEBALL PRACTICE OR SOMETHING. I DON'T REALLY KNOW.

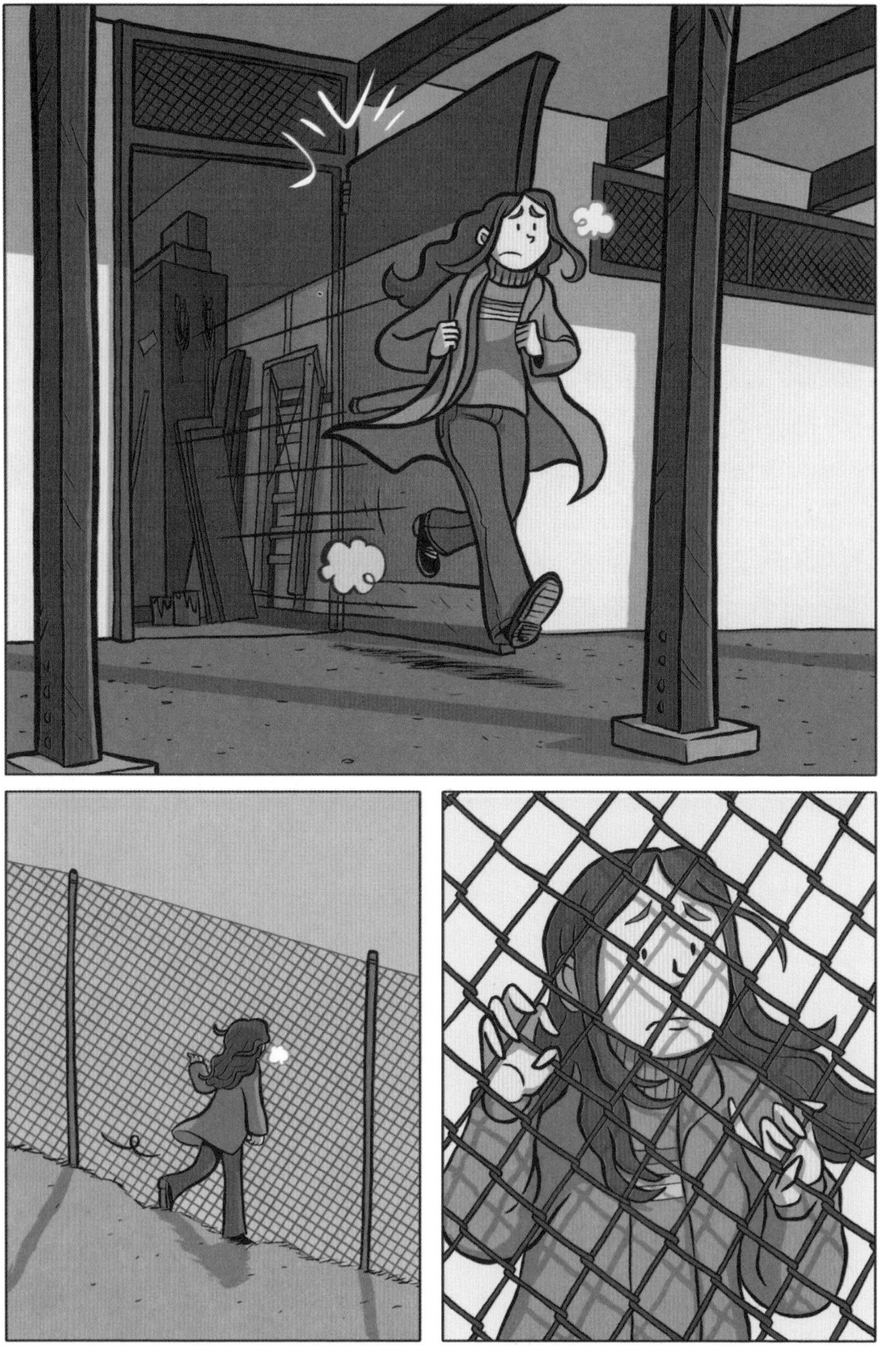

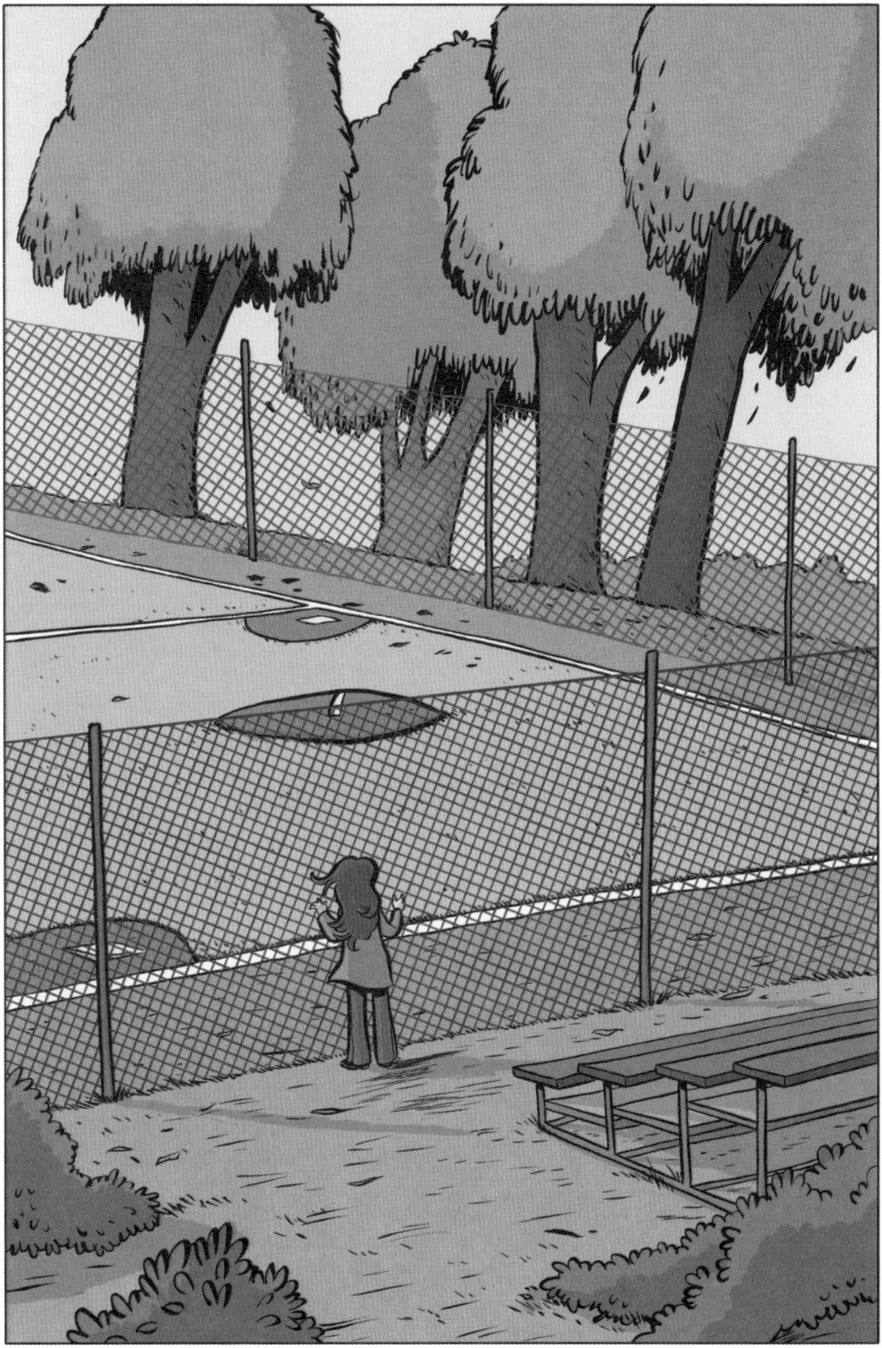

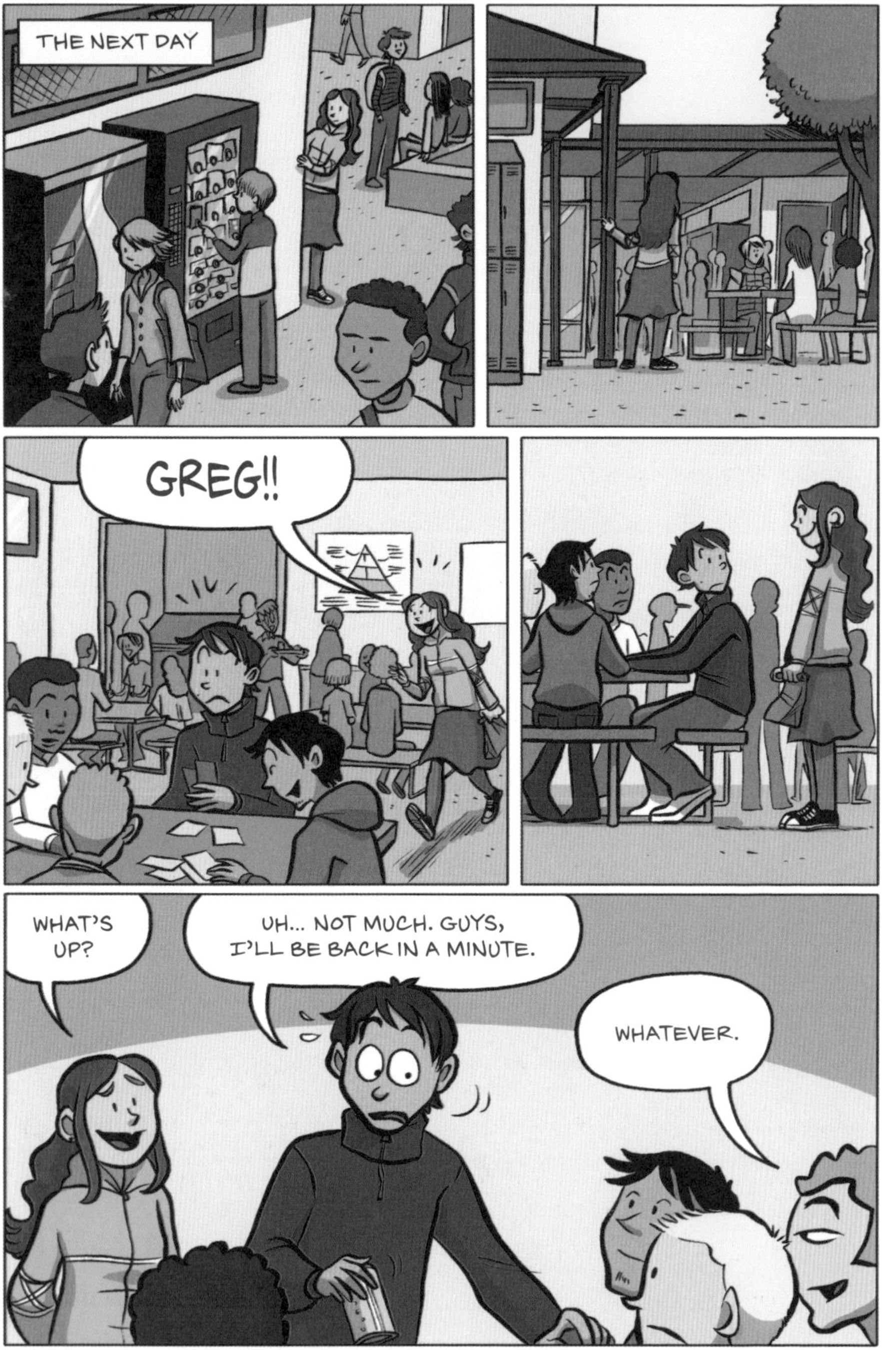
THE NEXT DAY
GREG!!
WHAT'S UP?
UH... NOT MUCH. GUYS, I'LL BE BACK IN A MINUTE.
WHATEVER.

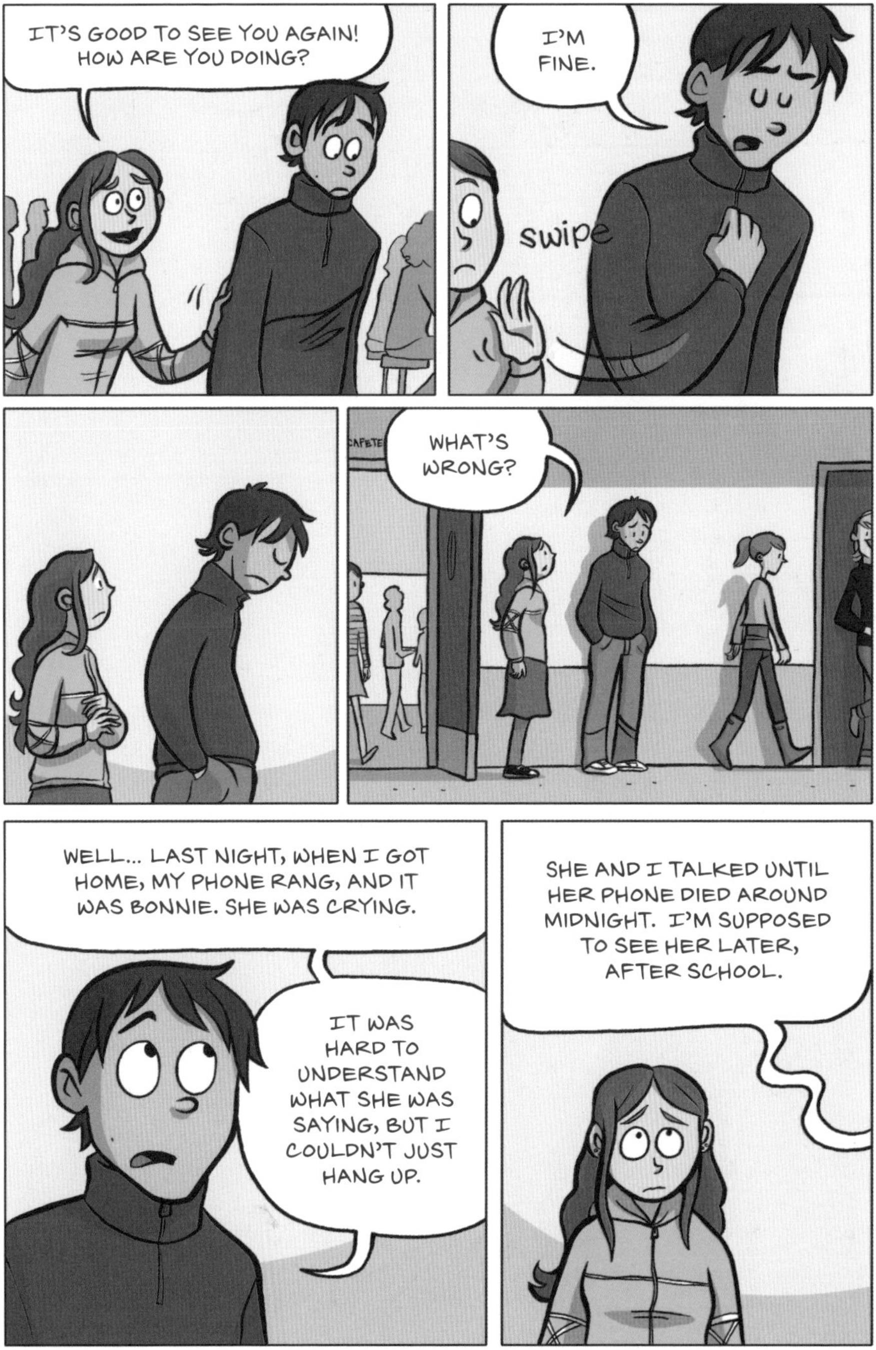
IT'S GOOD TO SEE YOU AGAIN! HOW ARE YOU DOING?
I'M FINE.
swipe
WHAT'S WRONG?
WELL... LAST NIGHT, WHEN I GOT HOME, MY PHONE RANG, AND IT WAS BONNIE. SHE WAS CRYING.
IT WAS HARD TO UNDERSTAND WHAT SHE WAS SAYING, BUT I COULDN'T JUST HANG UP.
SHE AND I TALKED UNTIL HER PHONE DIED AROUND MIDNIGHT. I'M SUPPOSED TO SEE HER LATER, AFTER SCHOOL.

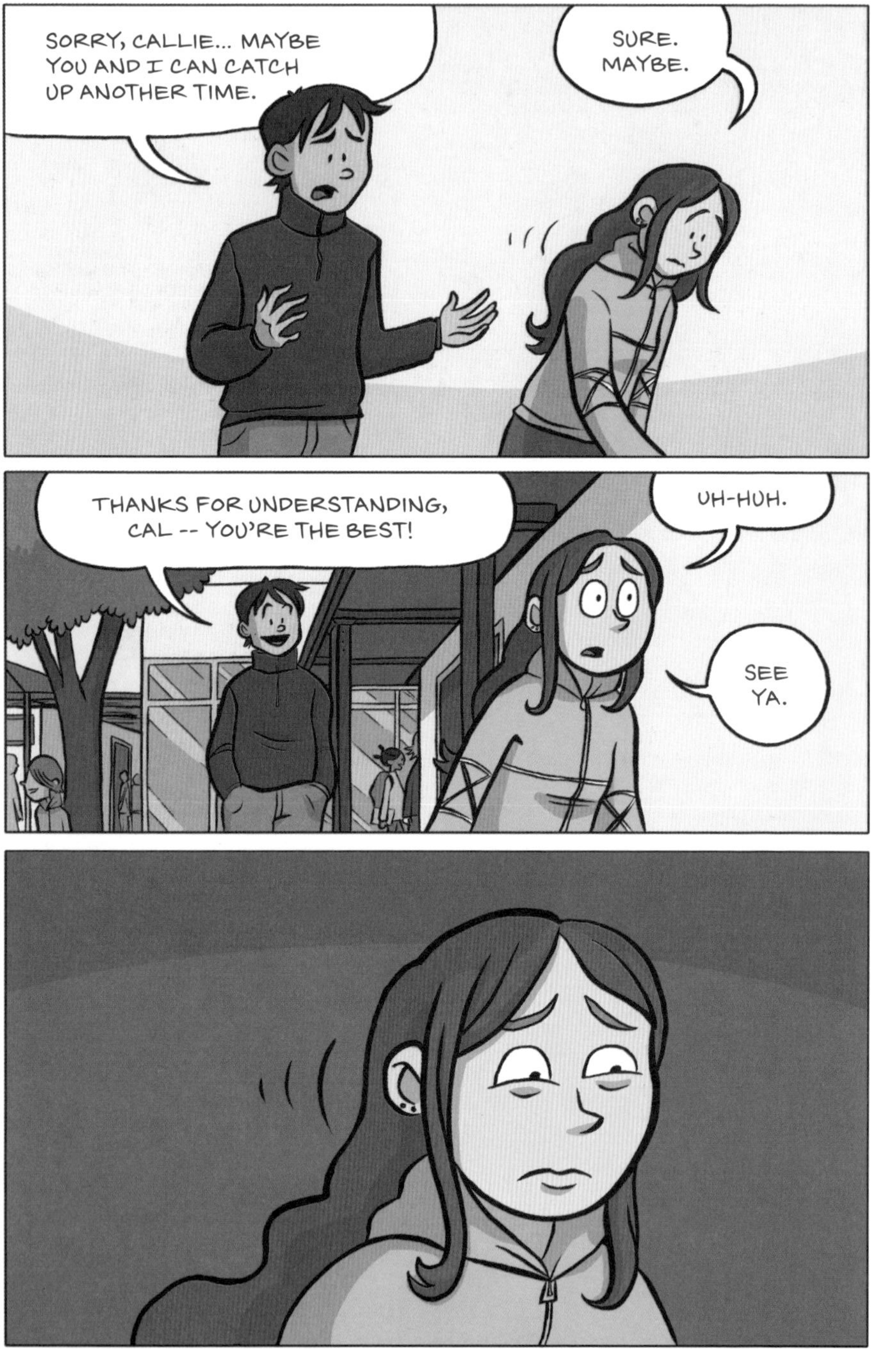
SORRY, CALLIE... MAYBE YOU AND I CAN CATCH UP ANOTHER TIME.
SURE. MAYBE.
THANKS FOR UNDERSTANDING, CAL -- YOU'RE THE BEST!
UH-HUH.
SEE YA.

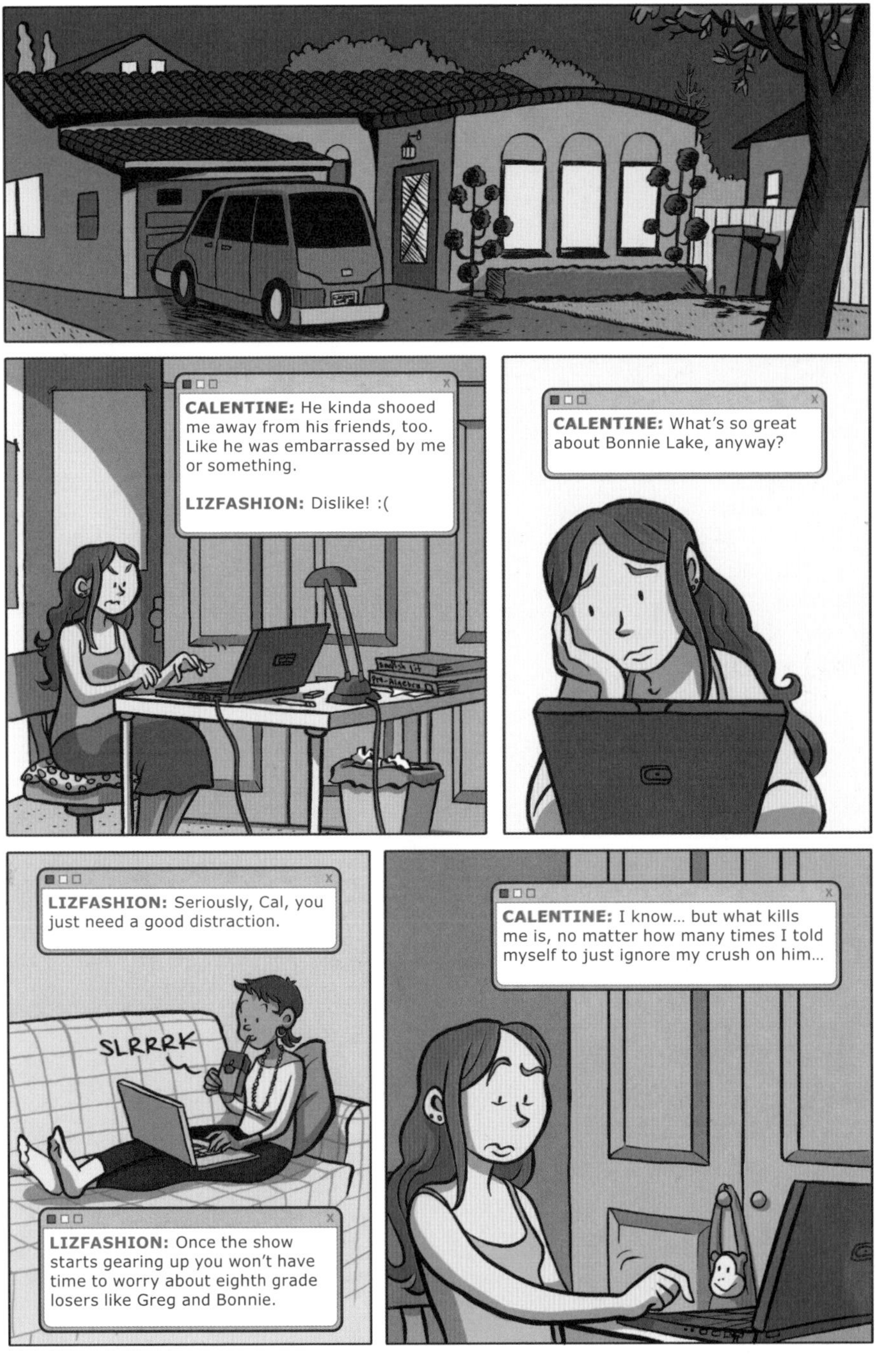
CALENTINE: He kinda shooed me away from his friends, too. Like he was embarrassed by me or something.
LIZFASHION: Dislike! :(
CALENTINE: What's so great about Bonnie Lake, anyway?
LIZFASHION: Seriously, Cal, you just need a good distraction.
SLRRRK
LIZFASHION: Once the show starts gearing up you won't have time to worry about eighth grade losers like Greg and Bonnie.
CALENTINE: I know... but what kills me is, no matter how many times I told myself to just ignore my crush on him...

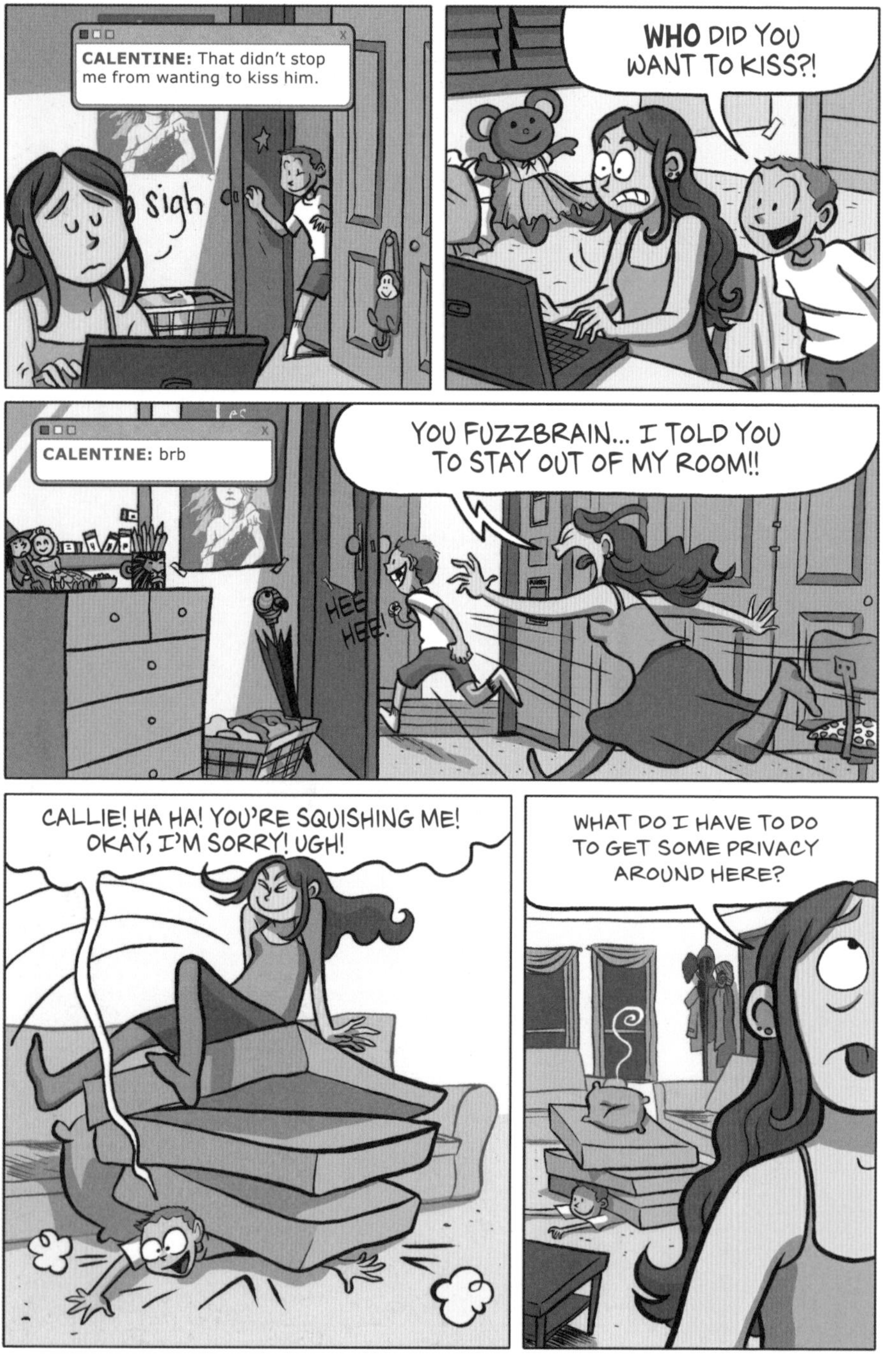
CALENTINE: That didn't stop me from wanting to kiss him.
sigh
WHO DID YOU WANT TO KISS?!
CALENTINE: brb
YOU FUZZBRAIN... I TOLD YOU TO STAY OUT OF MY ROOM!!
HEE HEE!
CALLIE! HA HA! YOU'RE SQUISHING ME! OKAY, I'M SORRY! UGH!
WHAT DO I HAVE TO DO TO GET SOME PRIVACY AROUND HERE?

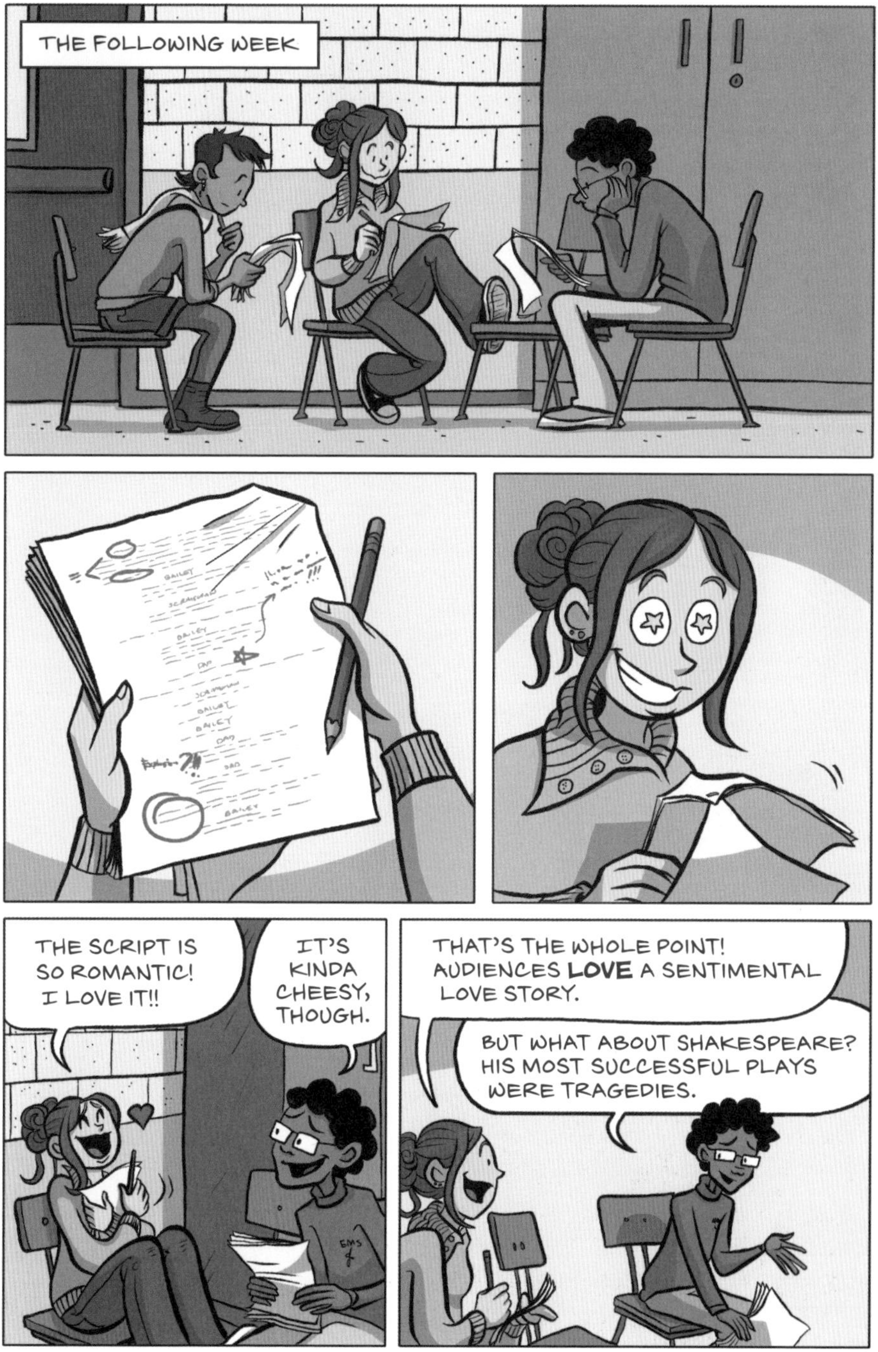
THE FOLLOWING WEEK
THE SCRIPT IS SO ROMANTIC! I LOVE IT!!
IT'S KINDA CHEESY, THOUGH.
THAT'S THE WHOLE POINT! AUDIENCES **LOVE** A SENTIMENTAL LOVE STORY.
BUT WHAT ABOUT SHAKESPEARE? HIS MOST SUCCESSFUL PLAYS WERE TRAGEDIES.

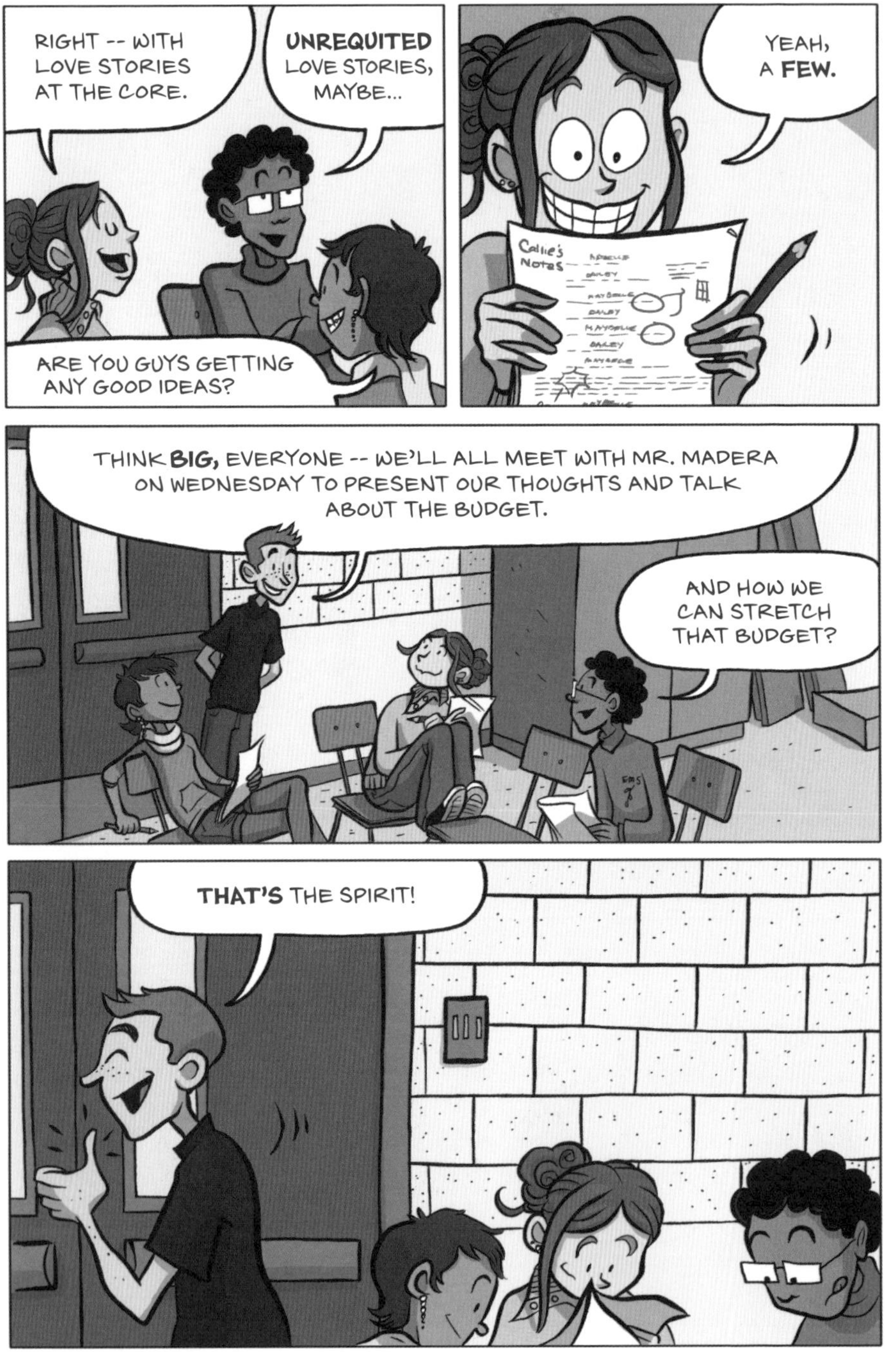
RIGHT -- WITH LOVE STORIES AT THE CORE.
UNREQUITED LOVE STORIES, MAYBE...
ARE YOU GUYS GETTING ANY GOOD IDEAS?
YEAH, A FEW.
Callie's Notes
THINK BIG, EVERYONE -- WE'LL ALL MEET WITH MR. MADERA ON WEDNESDAY TO PRESENT OUR THOUGHTS AND TALK ABOUT THE BUDGET.
AND HOW WE CAN STRETCH THAT BUDGET?
THAT'S THE SPIRIT!

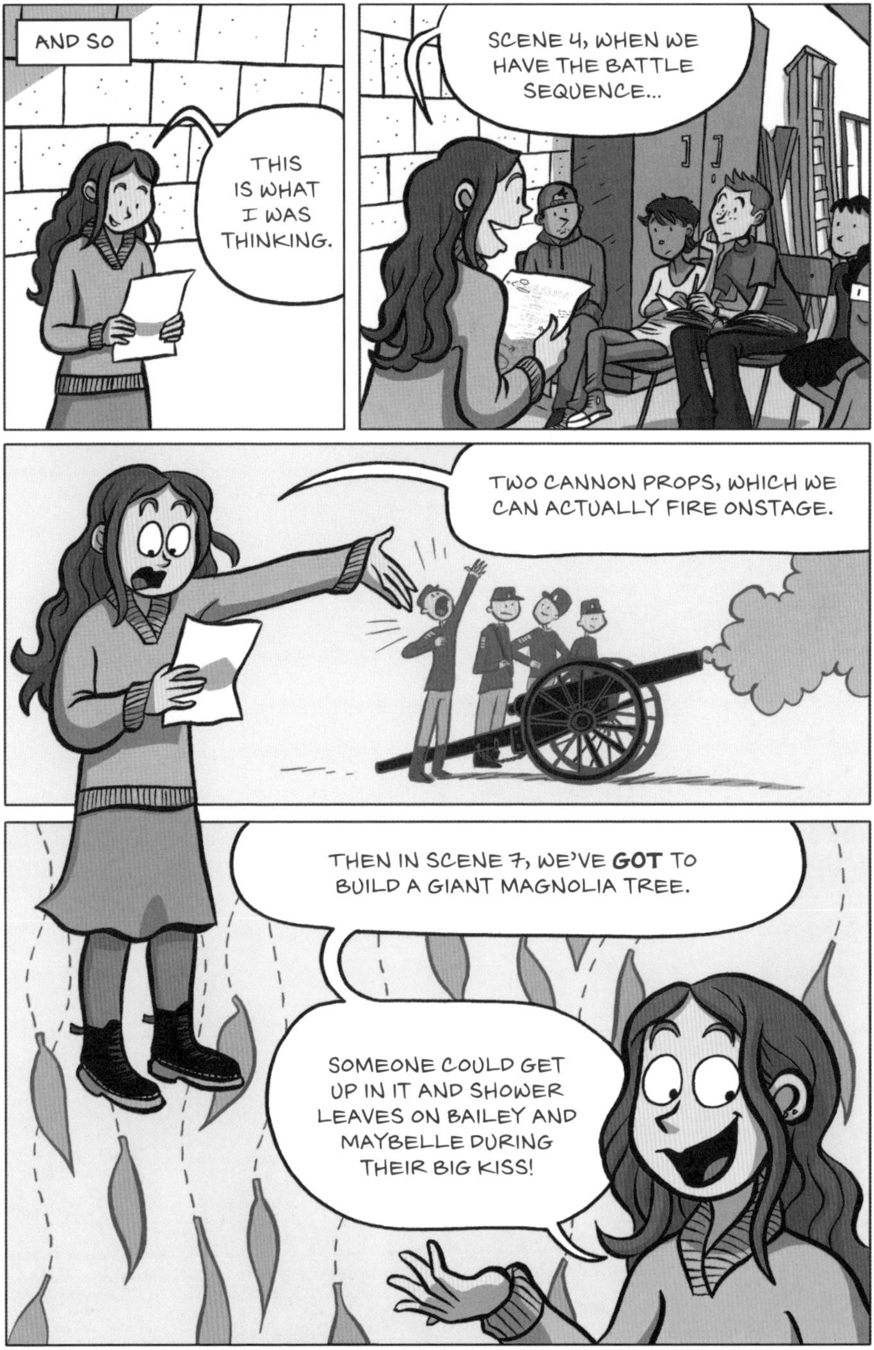
AND SO
THIS IS WHAT I WAS THINKING.
SCENE 4, WHEN WE HAVE THE BATTLE SEQUENCE...
TWO CANNON PROPS, WHICH WE CAN ACTUALLY FIRE ONSTAGE.
THEN IN SCENE 7, WE'VE GOT TO BUILD A GIANT MAGNOLIA TREE.
SOMEONE COULD GET UP IN IT AND SHOWER LEAVES ON BAILEY AND MAYBELLE DURING THEIR BIG KISS!

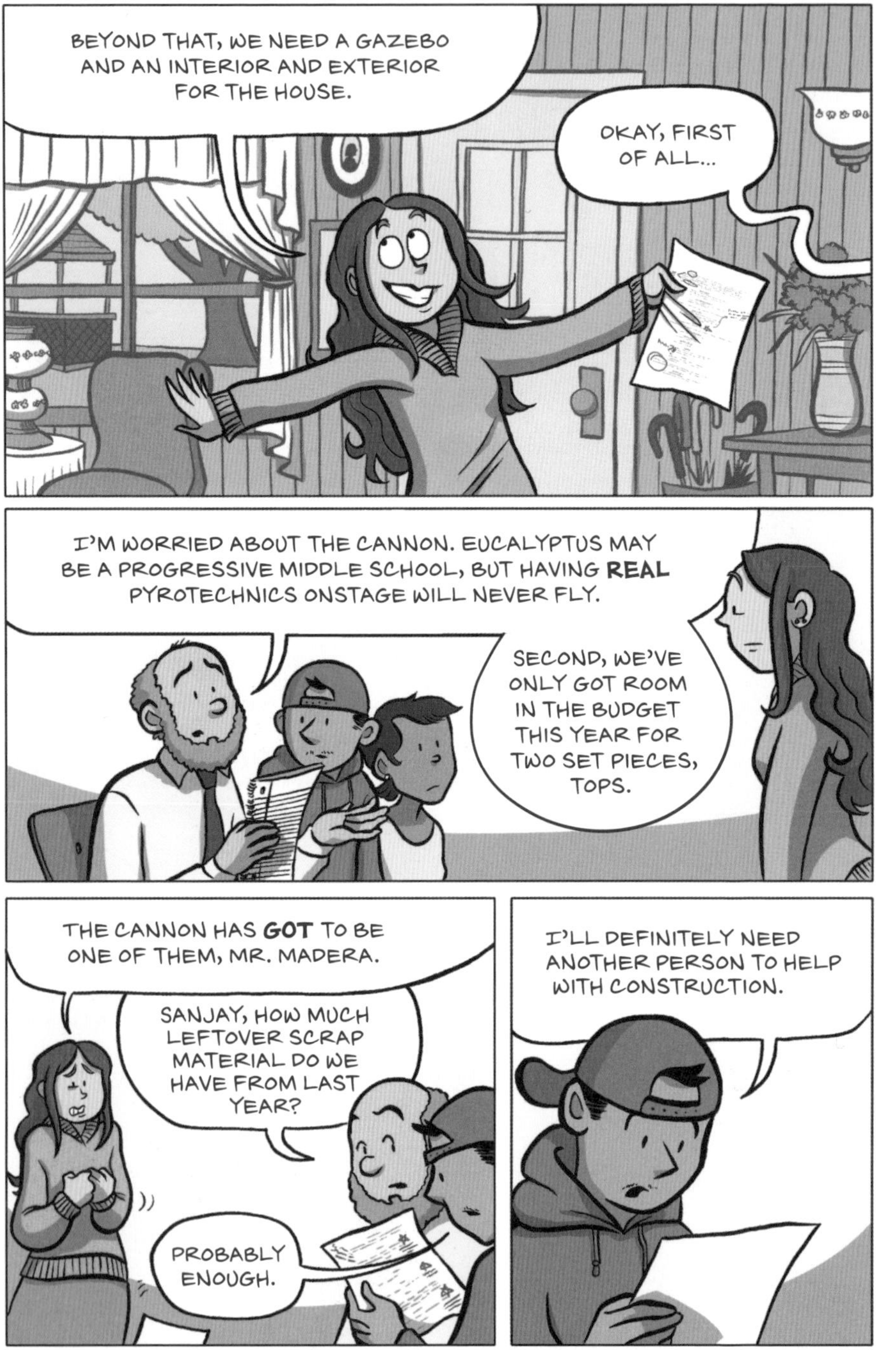
BEYOND THAT, WE NEED A GAZEBO AND AN INTERIOR AND EXTERIOR FOR THE HOUSE.
OKAY, FIRST OF ALL...
I'M WORRIED ABOUT THE CANNON. EUCALYPTUS MAY BE A PROGRESSIVE MIDDLE SCHOOL, BUT HAVING **REAL** PYROTECHNICS ONSTAGE WILL NEVER FLY.
SECOND, WE'VE ONLY GOT ROOM IN THE BUDGET THIS YEAR FOR TWO SET PIECES, TOPS.
THE CANNON HAS **GOT** TO BE ONE OF THEM, MR. MADERA.
SANJAY, HOW MUCH LEFTOVER SCRAP MATERIAL DO WE HAVE FROM LAST YEAR?
PROBABLY ENOUGH.
I'LL DEFINITELY NEED ANOTHER PERSON TO HELP WITH CONSTRUCTION.

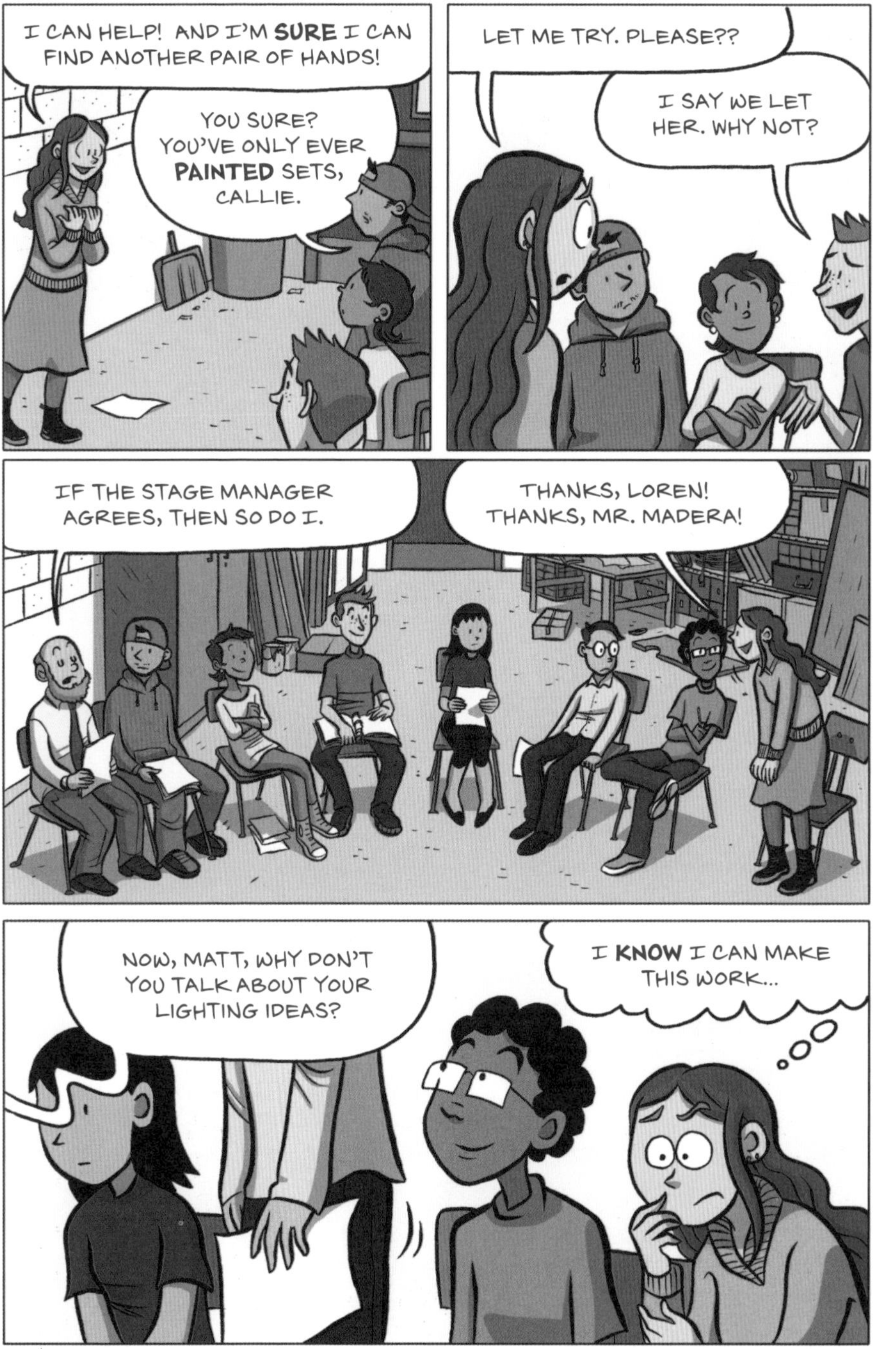

I CAN HELP! AND I'M **SURE** I CAN FIND ANOTHER PAIR OF HANDS!
YOU SURE? YOU'VE ONLY EVER **PAINTED** SETS, CALLIE.
LET ME TRY. PLEASE??
I SAY WE LET HER. WHY NOT?
IF THE STAGE MANAGER AGREES, THEN SO DO I.
THANKS, LOREN! THANKS, MR. MADERA!
NOW, MATT, WHY DON'T YOU TALK ABOUT YOUR LIGHTING IDEAS?
I **KNOW** I CAN MAKE THIS WORK...

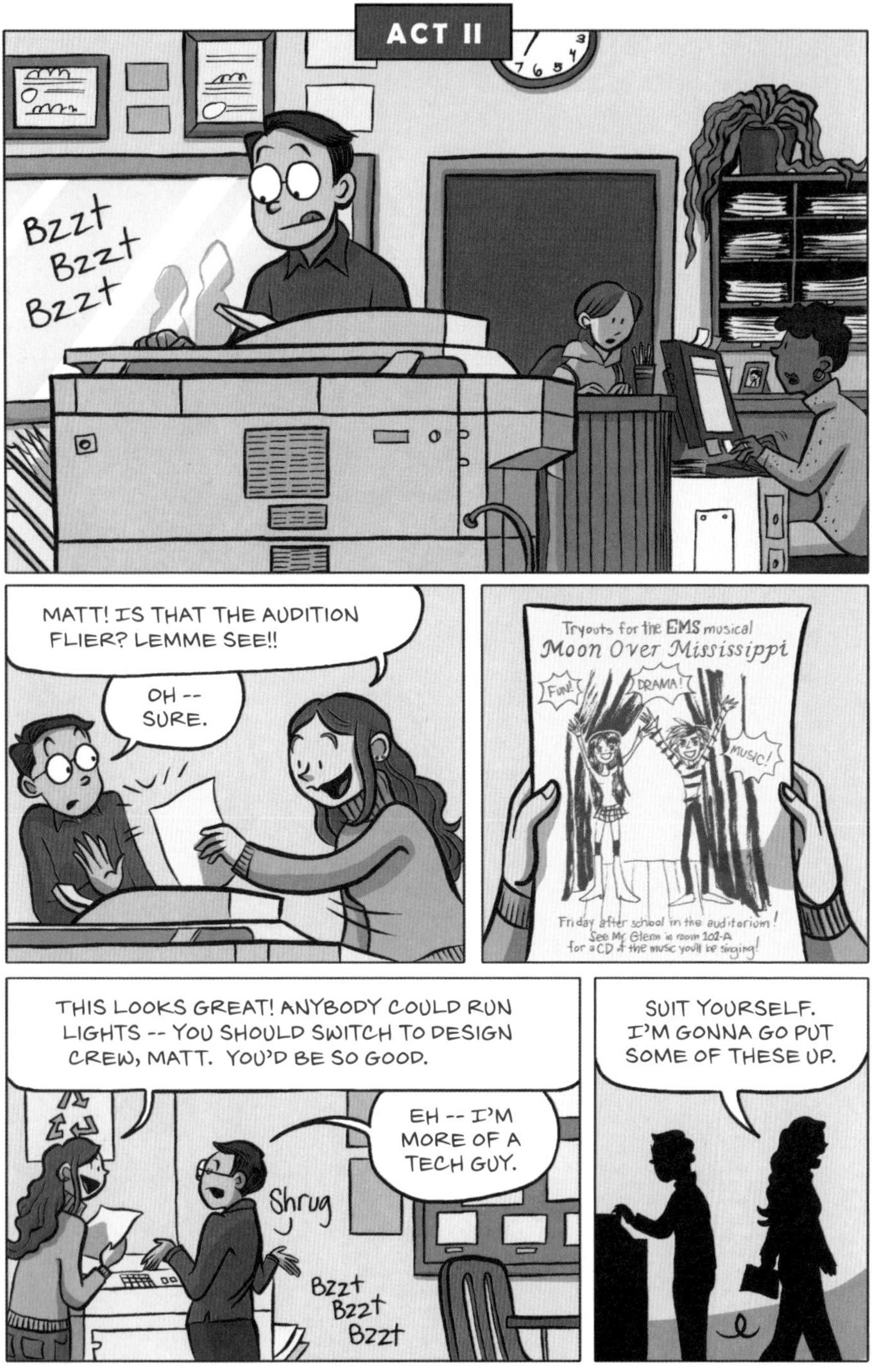
ACT II
Bzzt
Bzzt
Bzzt
MATT! IS THAT THE AUDITION FLIER? LEMME SEE!!
OH -- SURE.
Tryouts for the EMS musical
Moon Over Mississippi
FUN!
DRAMA!
MUSIC!
Friday after school in the auditorium!
See Mr. Glenn in room 102-A
for a CD of the music you'll be singing!
THIS LOOKS GREAT! ANYBODY COULD RUN LIGHTS -- YOU SHOULD SWITCH TO DESIGN CREW, MATT. YOU'D BE SO GOOD.
EH -- I'M MORE OF A TECH GUY.
Shrug
Bzzt
Bzzt
Bzzt
SUIT YOURSELF. I'M GONNA GO PUT SOME OF THESE UP.

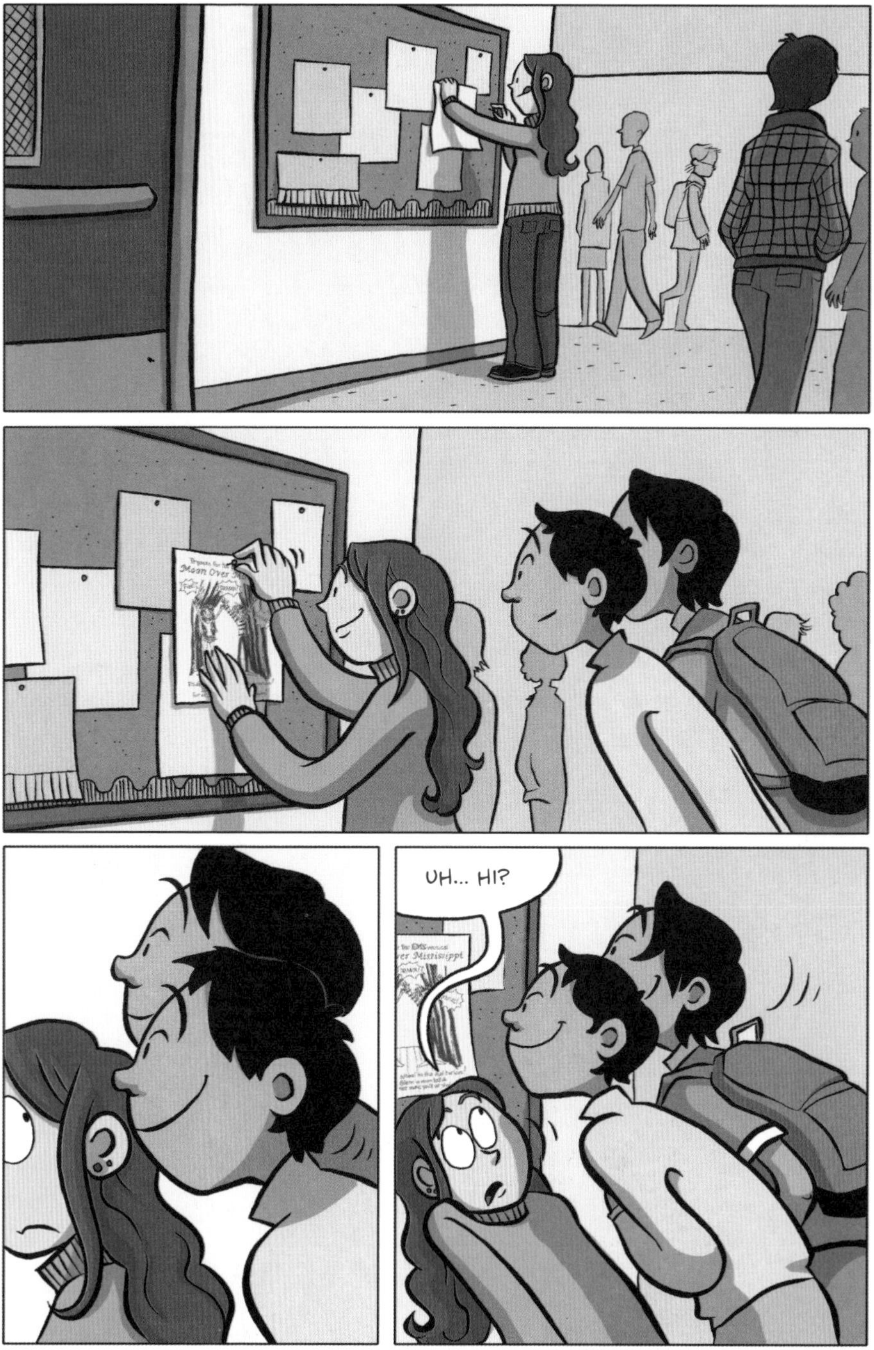
Moon Over
UH... HI?

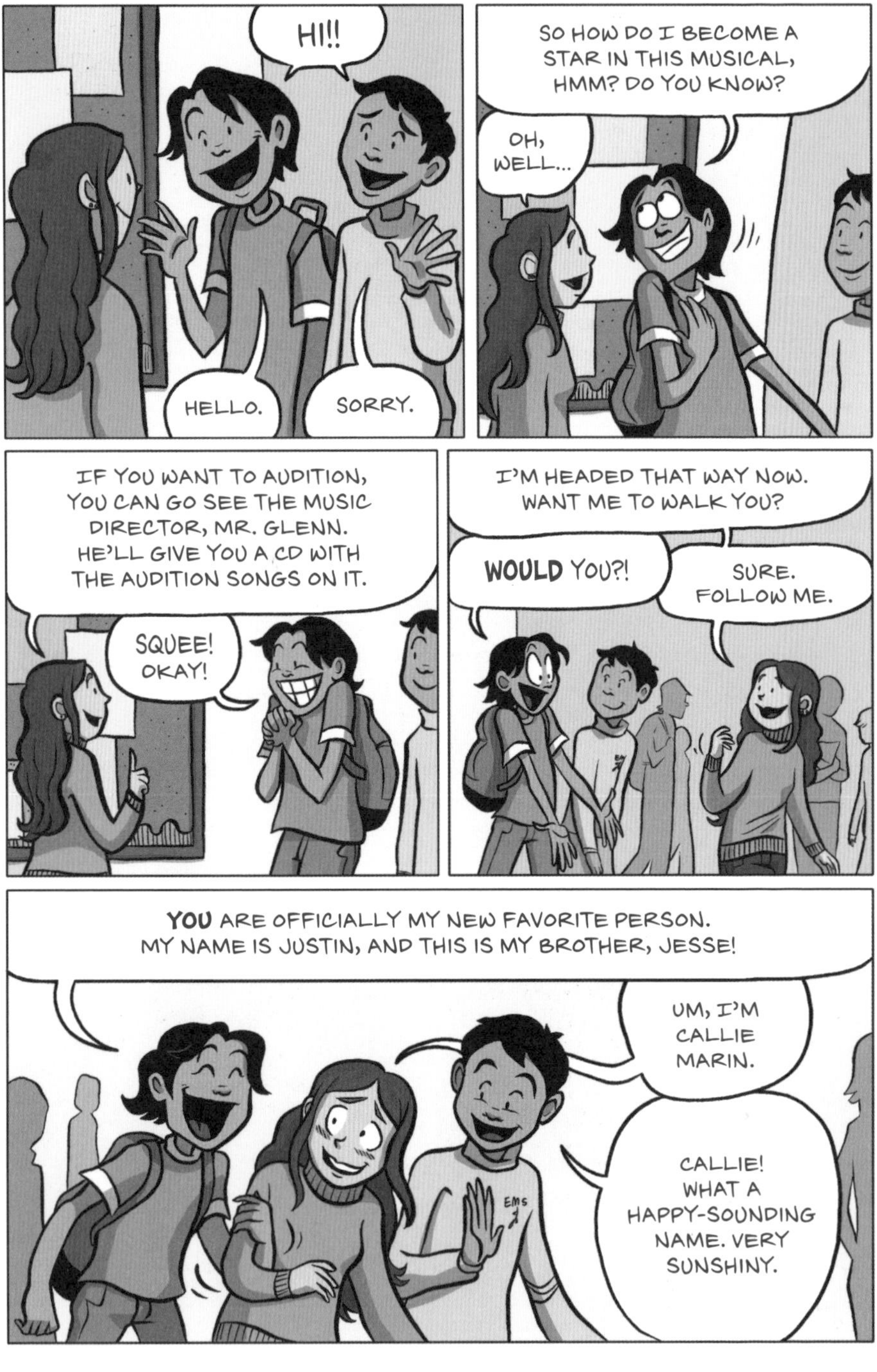
HI!!
HELLO.
SORRY.
SO HOW DO I BECOME A STAR IN THIS MUSICAL, HMM? DO YOU KNOW?
OH, WELL...
IF YOU WANT TO AUDITION, YOU CAN GO SEE THE MUSIC DIRECTOR, MR. GLENN. HE'LL GIVE YOU A CD WITH THE AUDITION SONGS ON IT.
SQUEE! OKAY!
I'M HEADED THAT WAY NOW. WANT ME TO WALK YOU?
WOULD YOU?!
SURE. FOLLOW ME.
YOU ARE OFFICIALLY MY NEW FAVORITE PERSON. MY NAME IS JUSTIN, AND THIS IS MY BROTHER, JESSE!
UM, I'M CALLIE MARIN.
CALLIE! WHAT A HAPPY-SOUNDING NAME. VERY SUNSHINY.

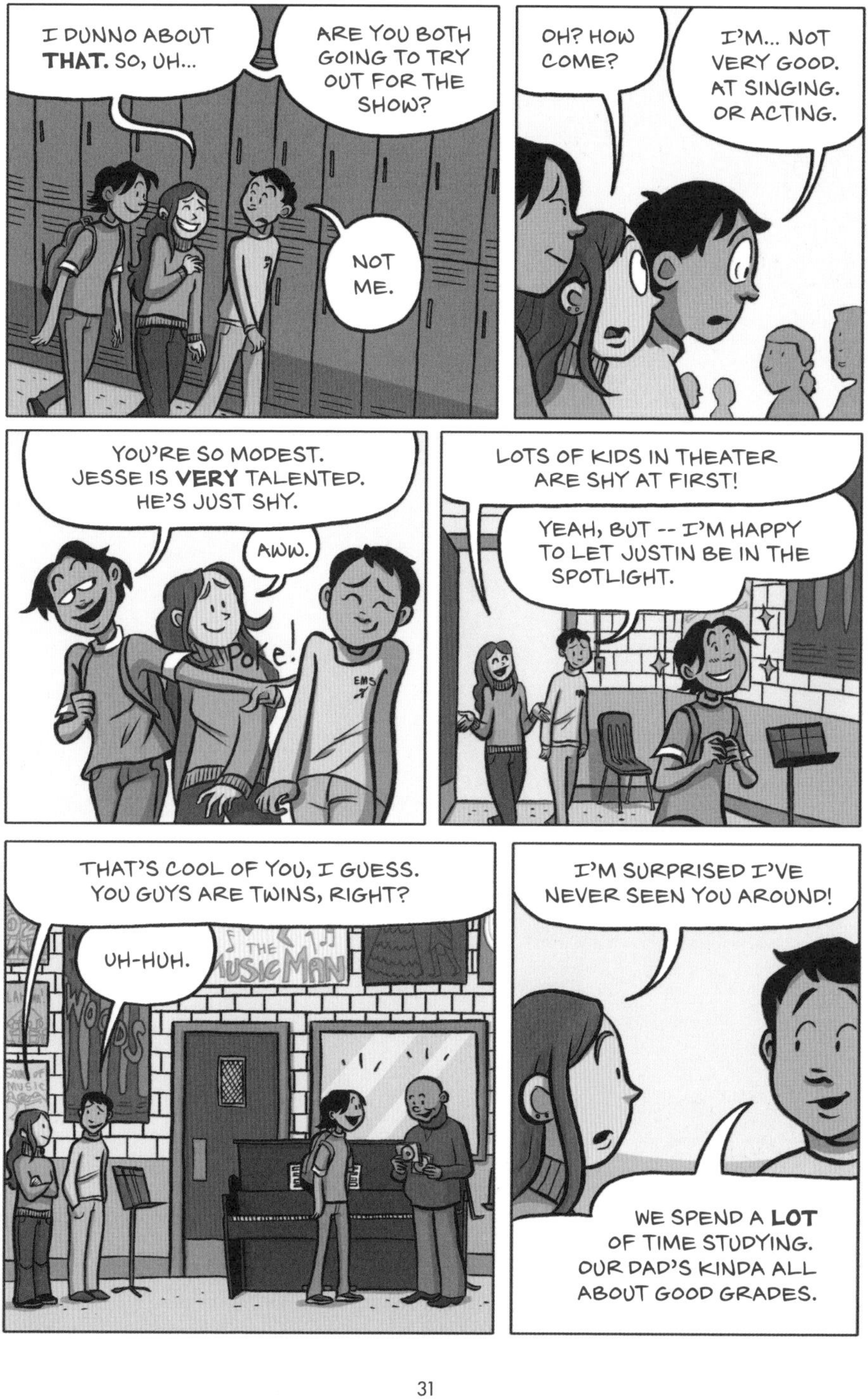

I DUNNO ABOUT **THAT.** SO, UH...
ARE YOU BOTH GOING TO TRY OUT FOR THE SHOW?
NOT ME.
OH? HOW COME?
I'M... NOT VERY GOOD. AT SINGING. OR ACTING.
YOU'RE SO MODEST. JESSE IS **VERY** TALENTED. HE'S JUST SHY.
AWW.
POKE!
EMS
LOTS OF KIDS IN THEATER ARE SHY AT FIRST!
YEAH, BUT -- I'M HAPPY TO LET JUSTIN BE IN THE SPOTLIGHT.
THAT'S COOL OF YOU, I GUESS. YOU GUYS ARE TWINS, RIGHT?
UH-HUH.
I'M SURPRISED I'VE NEVER SEEN YOU AROUND!
WE SPEND A **LOT** OF TIME STUDYING. OUR DAD'S KINDA ALL ABOUT GOOD GRADES.

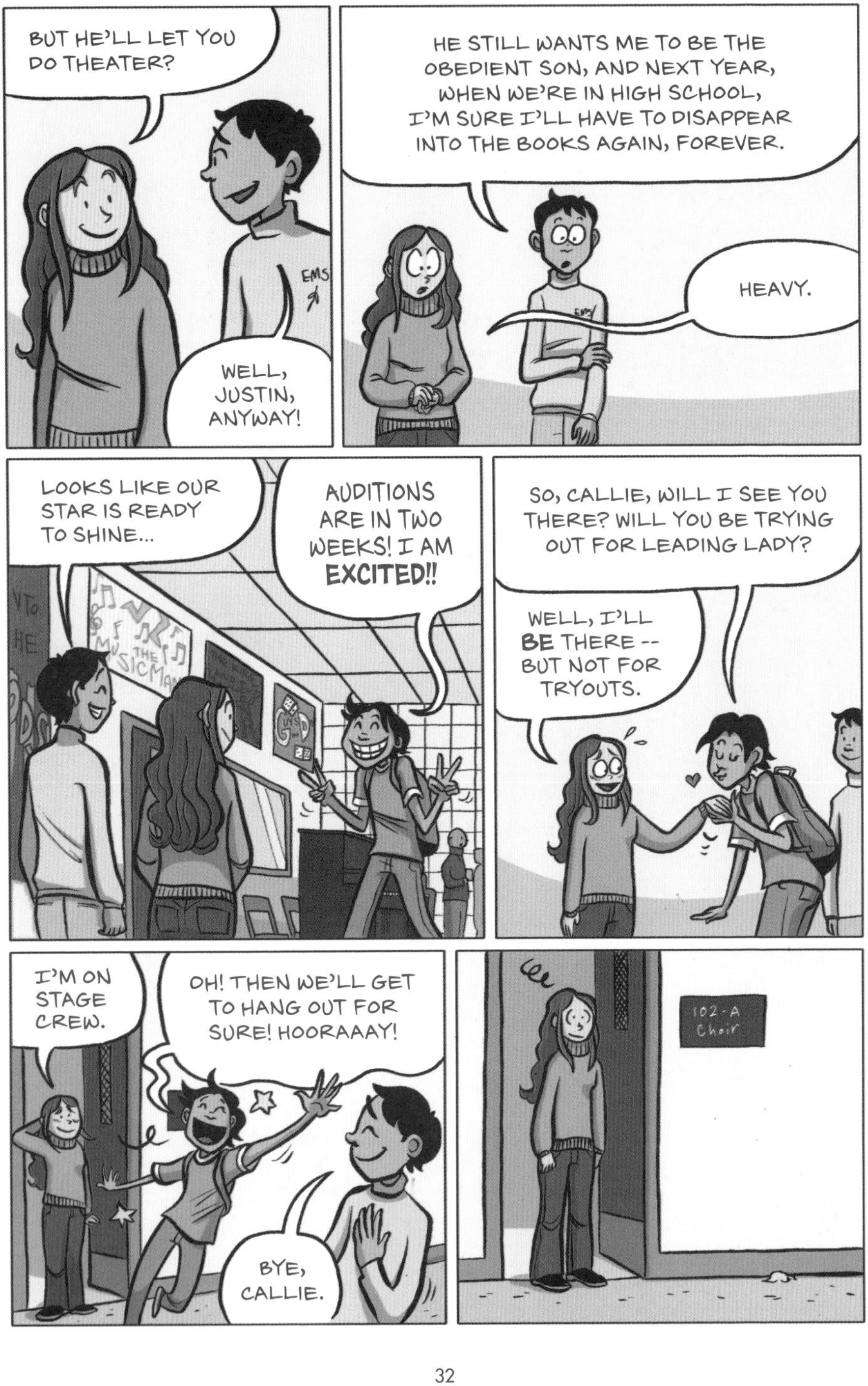
BUT HE'LL LET YOU DO THEATER?
WELL, JUSTIN, ANYWAY!
EMS
HE STILL WANTS ME TO BE THE OBEDIENT SON, AND NEXT YEAR, WHEN WE'RE IN HIGH SCHOOL, I'M SURE I'LL HAVE TO DISAPPEAR INTO THE BOOKS AGAIN, FOREVER.
HEAVY.
LOOKS LIKE OUR STAR IS READY TO SHINE...
AUDITIONS ARE IN TWO WEEKS! I AM **EXCITED!!**
THE MUSIC MAN
SO, CALLIE, WILL I SEE YOU THERE? WILL YOU BE TRYING OUT FOR LEADING LADY?
WELL, I'LL **BE** THERE -- BUT NOT FOR TRYOUTS.
I'M ON STAGE CREW.
OH! THEN WE'LL GET TO HANG OUT FOR SURE! HOORAAAY!
BYE, CALLIE.
102-A Choir

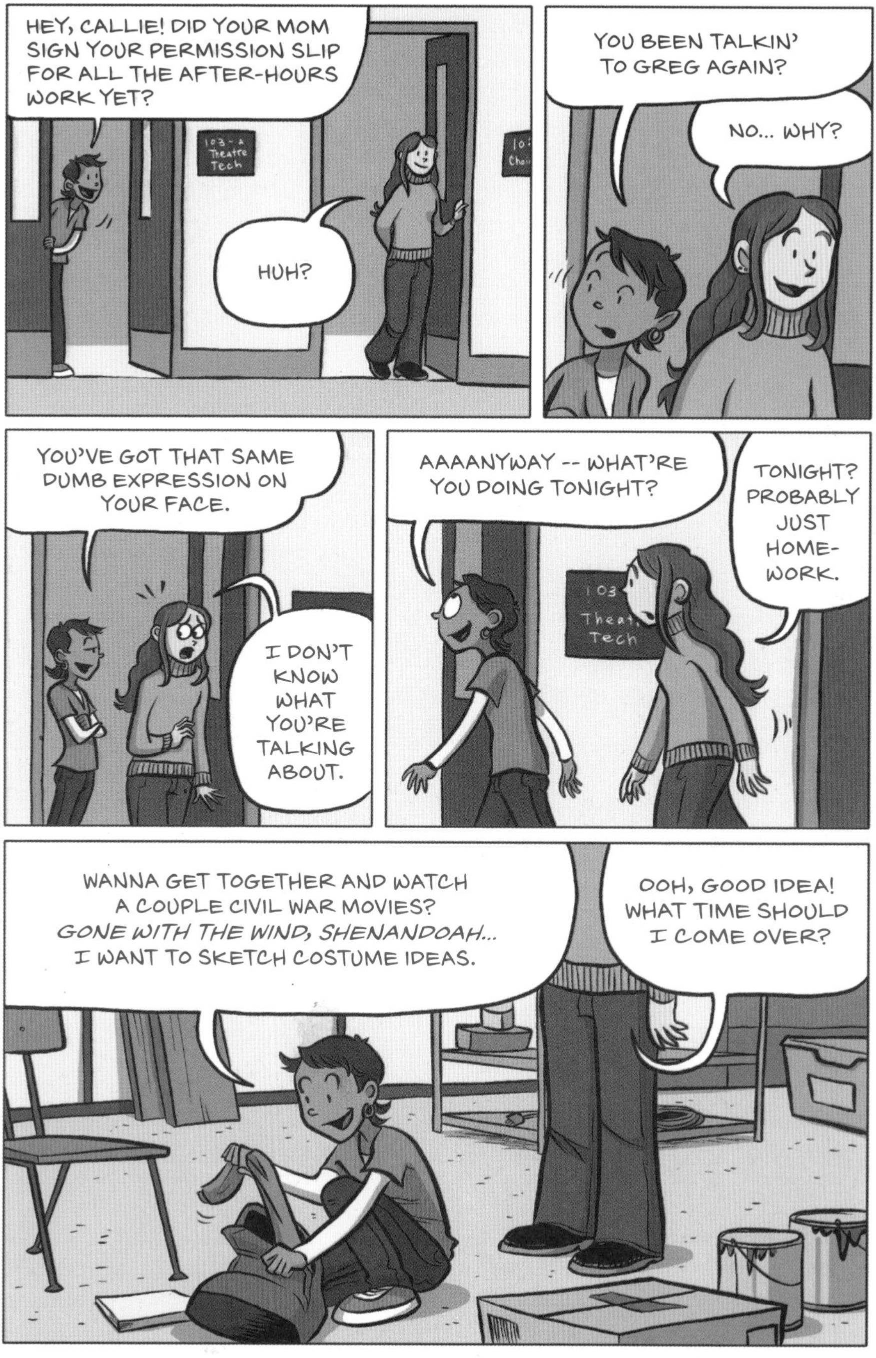
HEY, CALLIE! DID YOUR MOM SIGN YOUR PERMISSION SLIP FOR ALL THE AFTER-HOURS WORK YET?
103-A Theatre Tech
HUH?
YOU BEEN TALKIN' TO GREG AGAIN?
NO... WHY?
YOU'VE GOT THAT SAME DUMB EXPRESSION ON YOUR FACE.
I DON'T KNOW WHAT YOU'RE TALKING ABOUT.
AAAANYWAY -- WHAT'RE YOU DOING TONIGHT?
TONIGHT? PROBABLY JUST HOME-WORK.
WANNA GET TOGETHER AND WATCH A COUPLE CIVIL WAR MOVIES? *GONE WITH THE WIND, SHENANDOAH*... I WANT TO SKETCH COSTUME IDEAS.
OOH, GOOD IDEA! WHAT TIME SHOULD I COME OVER?

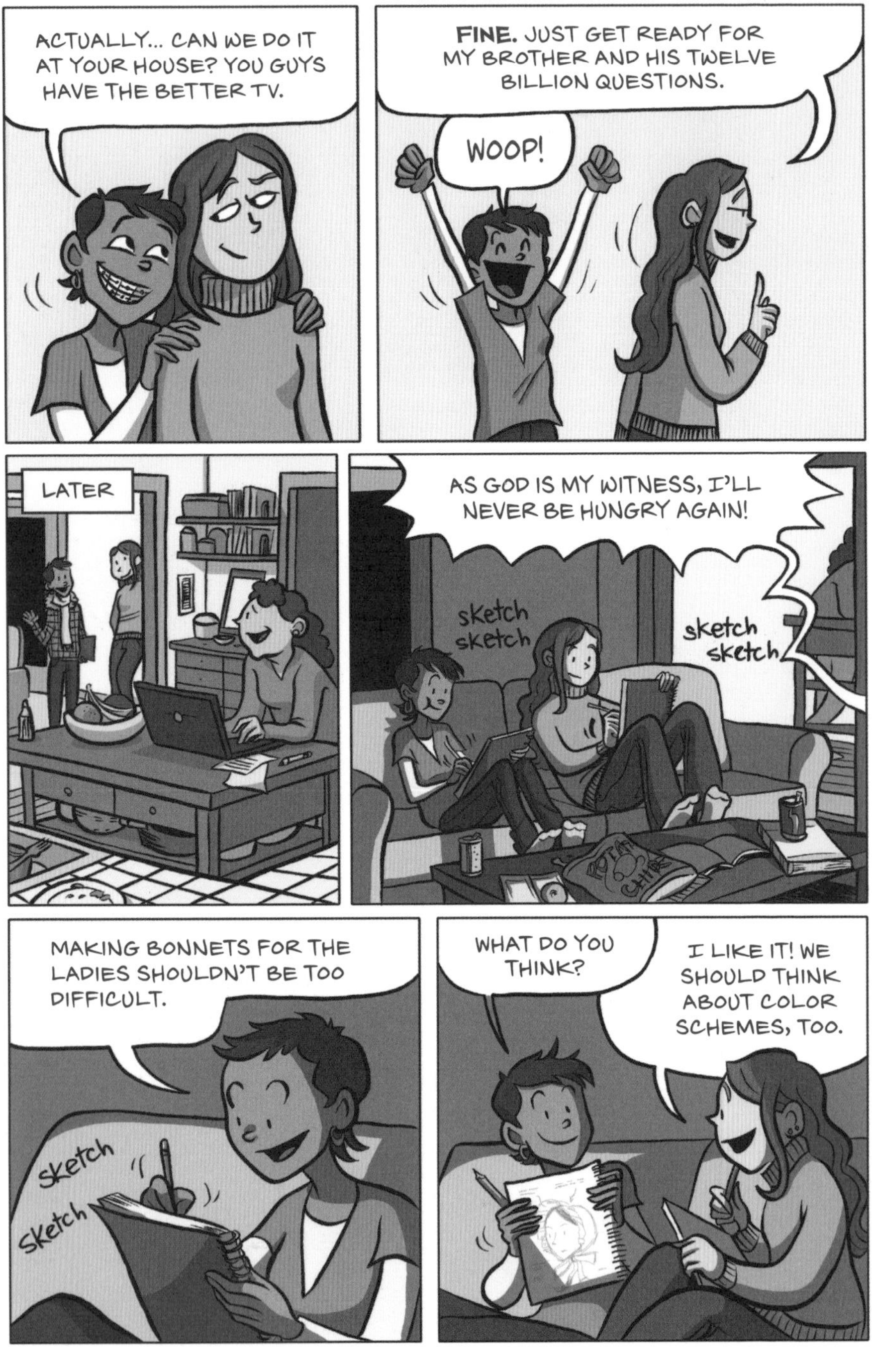
ACTUALLY... CAN WE DO IT AT YOUR HOUSE? YOU GUYS HAVE THE BETTER TV.
FINE. JUST GET READY FOR MY BROTHER AND HIS TWELVE BILLION QUESTIONS.
WOOP!
LATER
AS GOD IS MY WITNESS, I'LL NEVER BE HUNGRY AGAIN!
sketch sketch
sketch sketch
MAKING BONNETS FOR THE LADIES SHOULDN'T BE TOO DIFFICULT.
sketch sketch
WHAT DO YOU THINK?
I LIKE IT! WE SHOULD THINK ABOUT COLOR SCHEMES, TOO.

LIKE, IF ALL THE SETS END UP BEING YELLOW AND ORANGE, THE COSTUMES SHOULD BE BLUES, GREENS, AND PURPLES SO THAT THEY STAND OUT.

OKAY, BUT YOU'RE MAKING A GARDEN SET TOO, RIGHT?

HMM, YEAH.

WHAT'S UP WITH THAT LADY'S DRESS? I LIKE HIS MUSTACHE! WHATCHA GUYS DRAWIN'? CAN I WATCH THIS MOVIE, TOO?

GREAT BALLS OF FIRE!

DID YOU KNOW CALLIE HAS A DRESS THAT LOOKS LIKE A PRINC... F... PLAYER, BUT LAST YEAR MOM TOLD ME SHE DIDN'T HAVE TIME TO MAKE ME A FULL BASEBALL PLAYER... OUTFIT, SO SHE... ME TO THE STORE AND I... O CHOOSE A... D JERSEY...

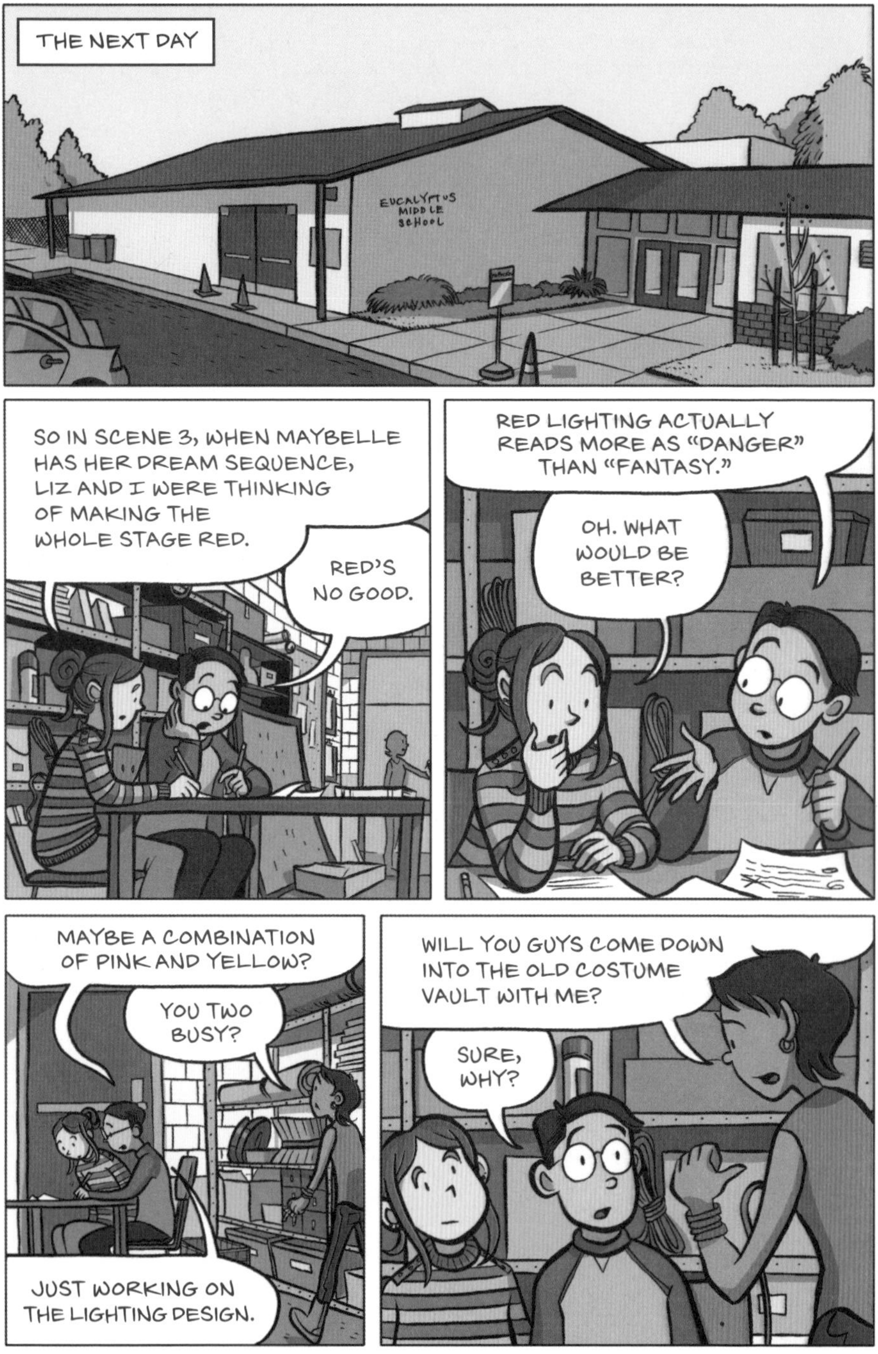
THE NEXT DAY
EUCALYPTUS MIDDLE SCHOOL
SO IN SCENE 3, WHEN MAYBELLE HAS HER DREAM SEQUENCE, LIZ AND I WERE THINKING OF MAKING THE WHOLE STAGE RED.
RED'S NO GOOD.
RED LIGHTING ACTUALLY READS MORE AS "DANGER" THAN "FANTASY."
OH. WHAT WOULD BE BETTER?
MAYBE A COMBINATION OF PINK AND YELLOW?
YOU TWO BUSY?
JUST WORKING ON THE LIGHTING DESIGN.
WILL YOU GUYS COME DOWN INTO THE OLD COSTUME VAULT WITH ME?
SURE, WHY?

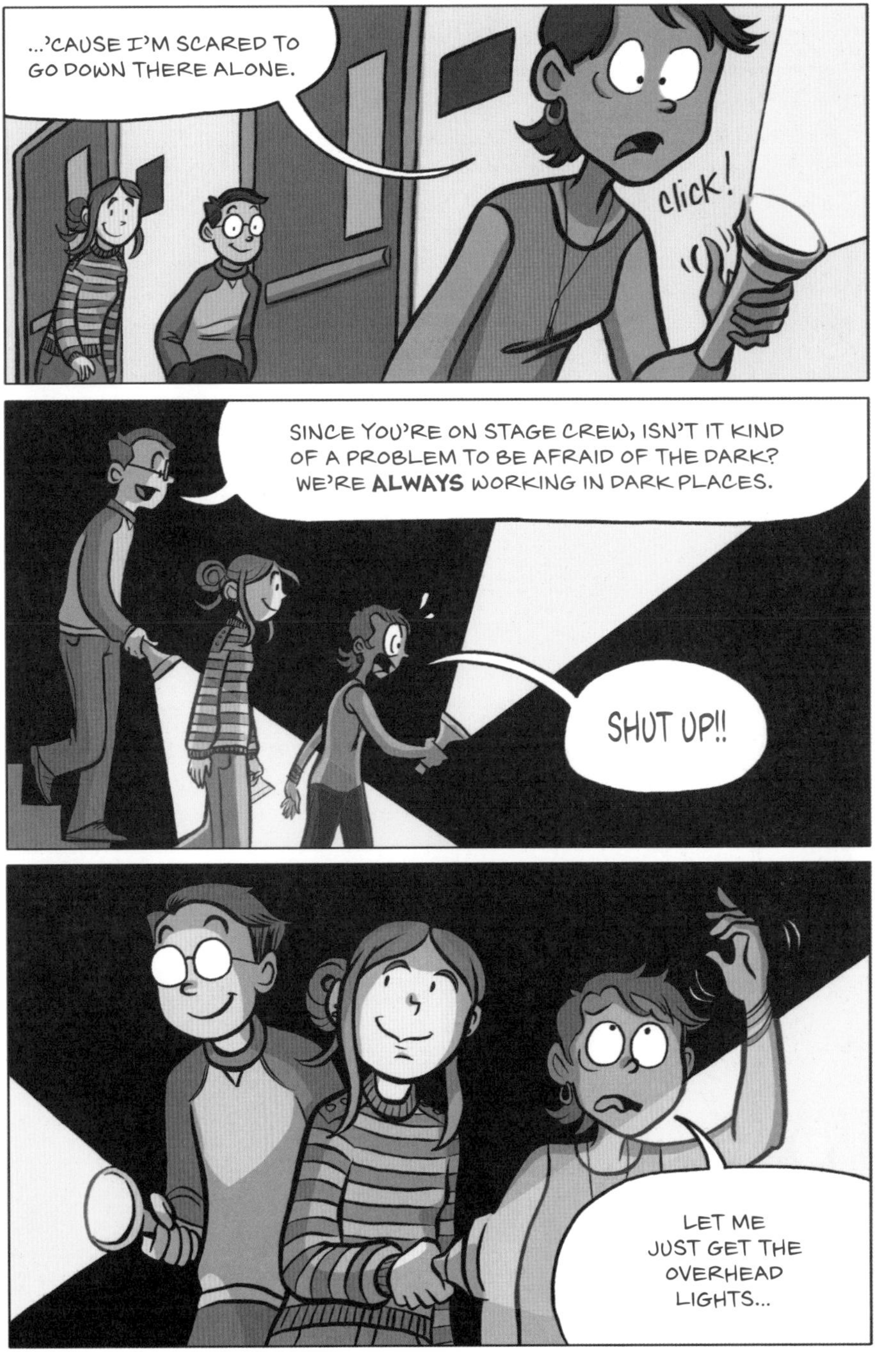
...'CAUSE I'M SCARED TO GO DOWN THERE ALONE.
CLICK!
SINCE YOU'RE ON STAGE CREW, ISN'T IT KIND OF A PROBLEM TO BE AFRAID OF THE DARK? WE'RE **ALWAYS** WORKING IN DARK PLACES.
SHUT UP!!
LET ME JUST GET THE OVERHEAD LIGHTS...

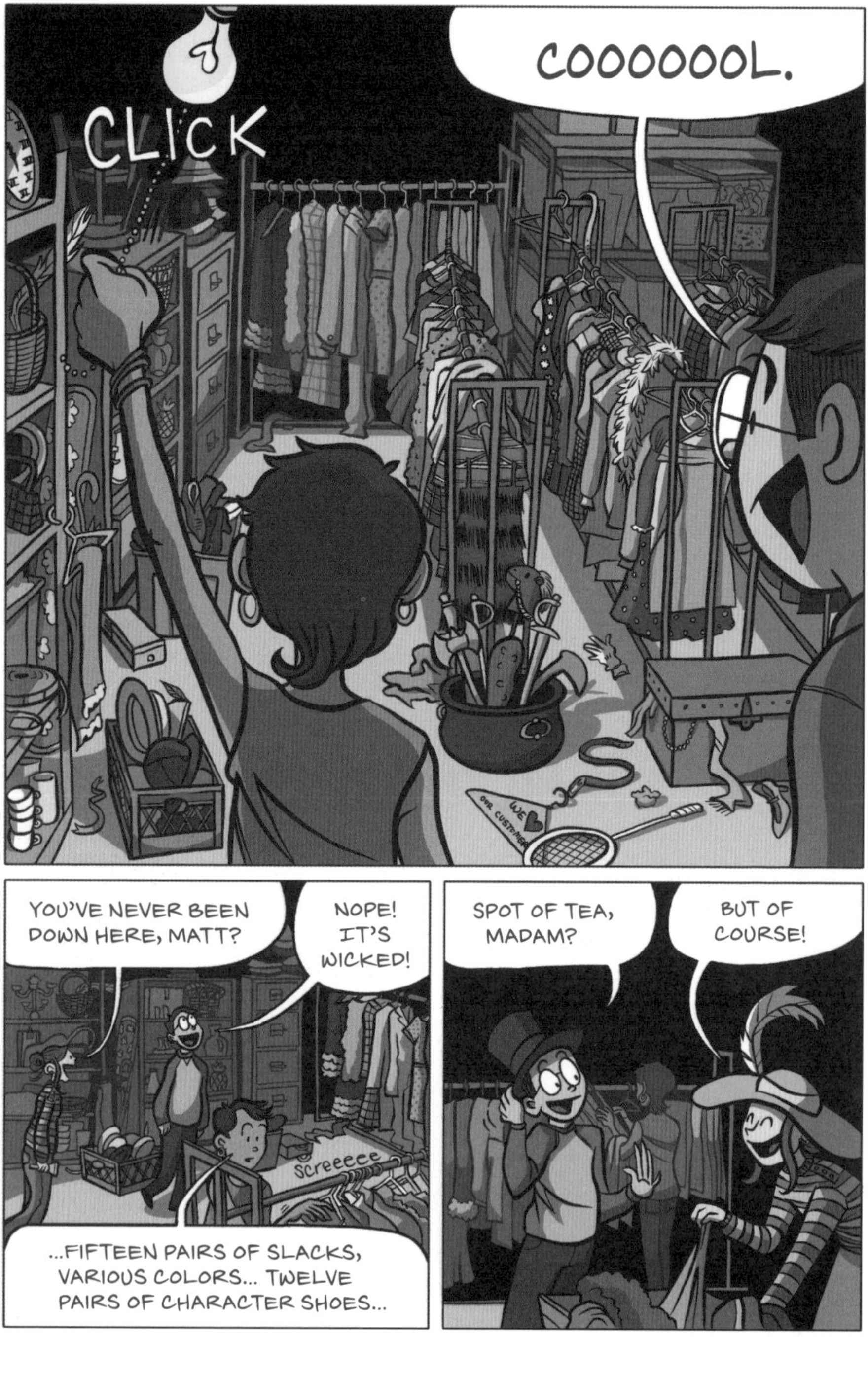
CLICK
COOOOOOL.
YOU'VE NEVER BEEN DOWN HERE, MATT?
NOPE! IT'S WICKED!
SCREEEEE
...FIFTEEN PAIRS OF SLACKS, VARIOUS COLORS... TWELVE PAIRS OF CHARACTER SHOES...
SPOT OF TEA, MADAM?
BUT OF COURSE!

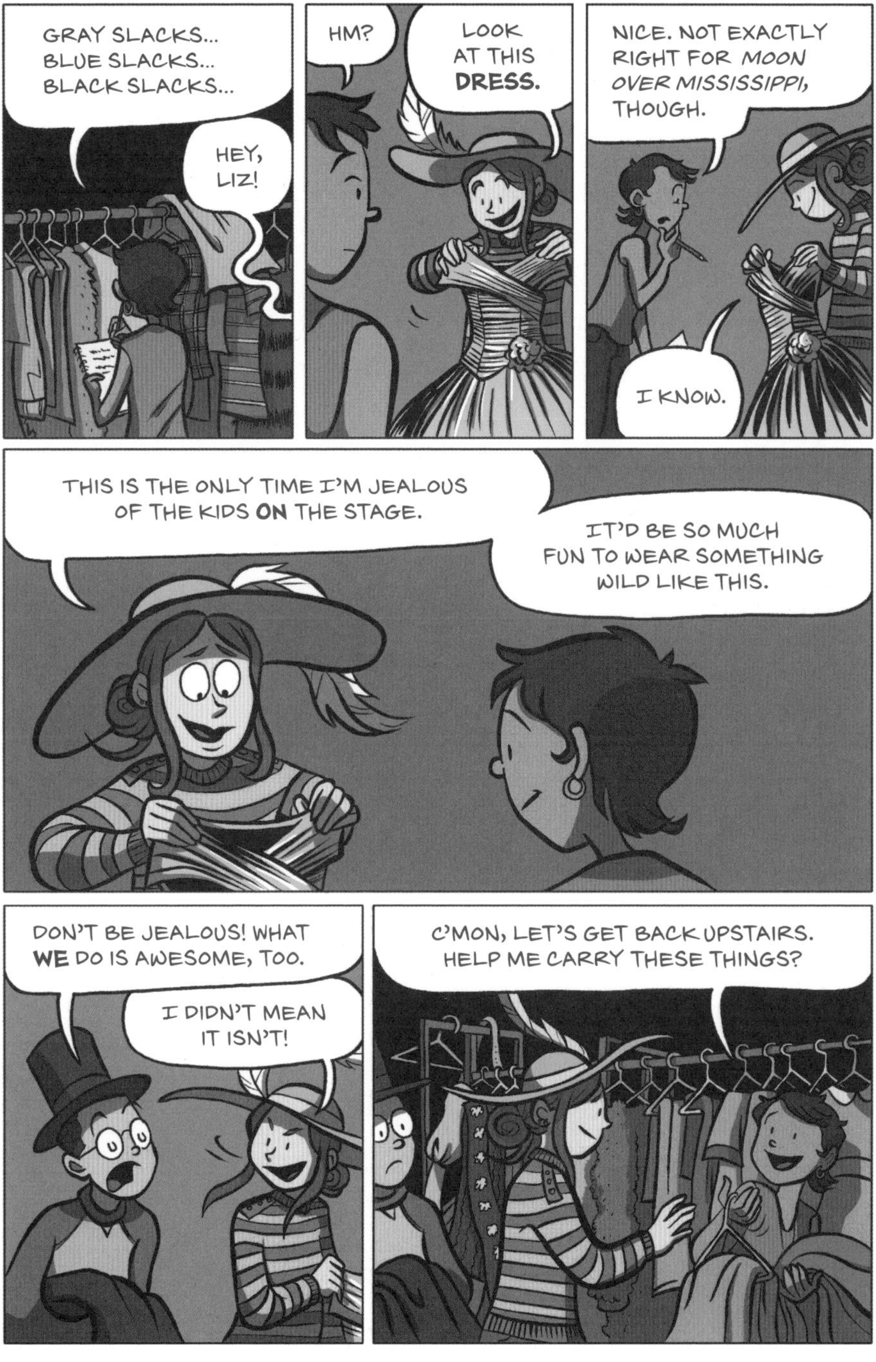
GRAY SLACKS... BLUE SLACKS... BLACK SLACKS...
HEY, LIZ!
HM?
LOOK AT THIS **DRESS.**
NICE. NOT EXACTLY RIGHT FOR *MOON OVER MISSISSIPPI,* THOUGH.
I KNOW.
THIS IS THE ONLY TIME I'M JEALOUS OF THE KIDS **ON** THE STAGE.
IT'D BE SO MUCH FUN TO WEAR SOMETHING WILD LIKE THIS.
DON'T BE JEALOUS! WHAT **WE** DO IS AWESOME, TOO.
I DIDN'T MEAN IT ISN'T!
C'MON, LET'S GET BACK UPSTAIRS. HELP ME CARRY THESE THINGS?

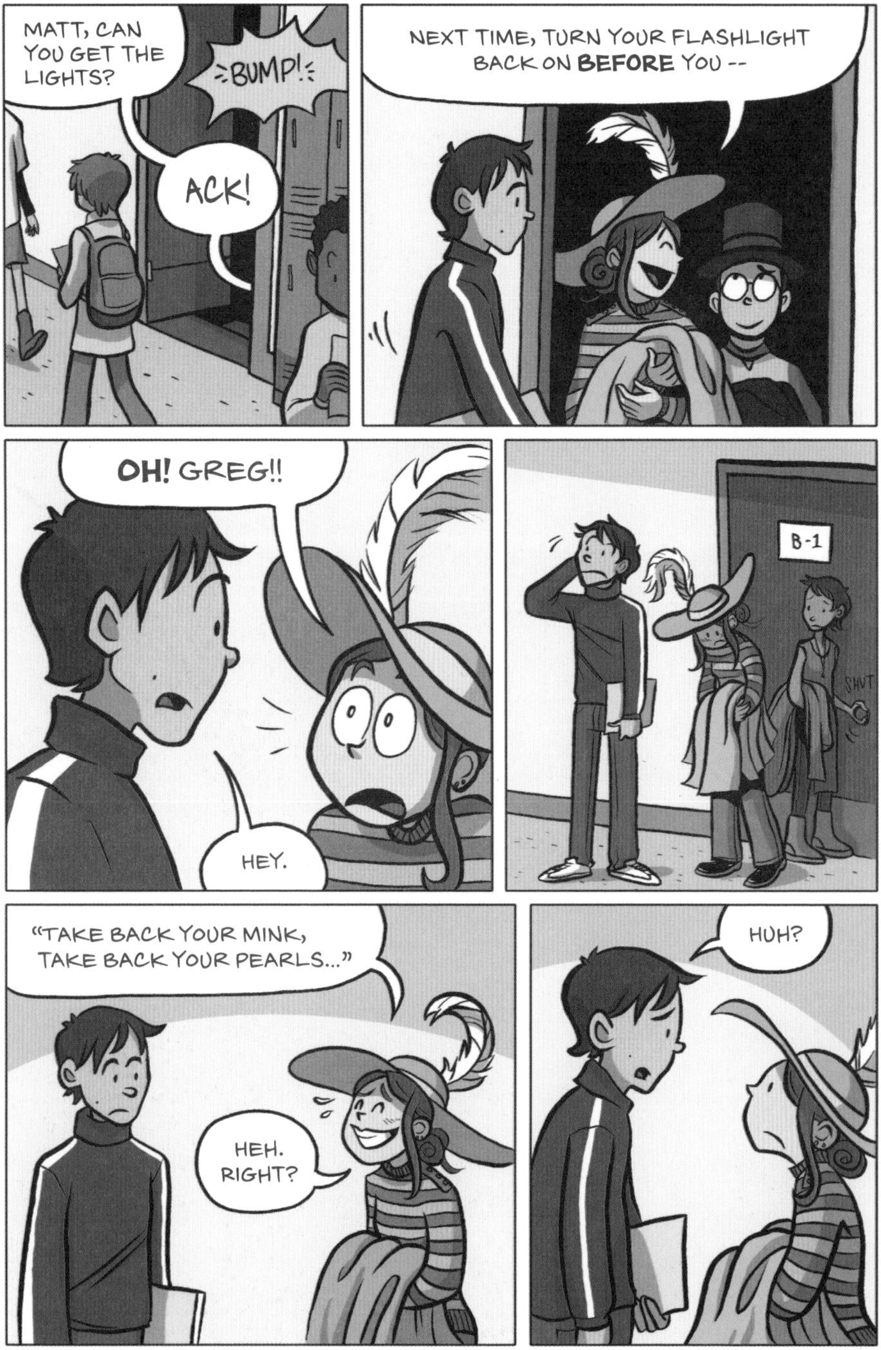
MATT, CAN YOU GET THE LIGHTS?
BUMP!
ACK!
NEXT TIME, TURN YOUR FLASHLIGHT BACK ON **BEFORE** YOU --
OH! GREG!!
HEY.
B-1
SHUT
"TAKE BACK YOUR MINK, TAKE BACK YOUR PEARLS..."
HEH. RIGHT?
HUH?

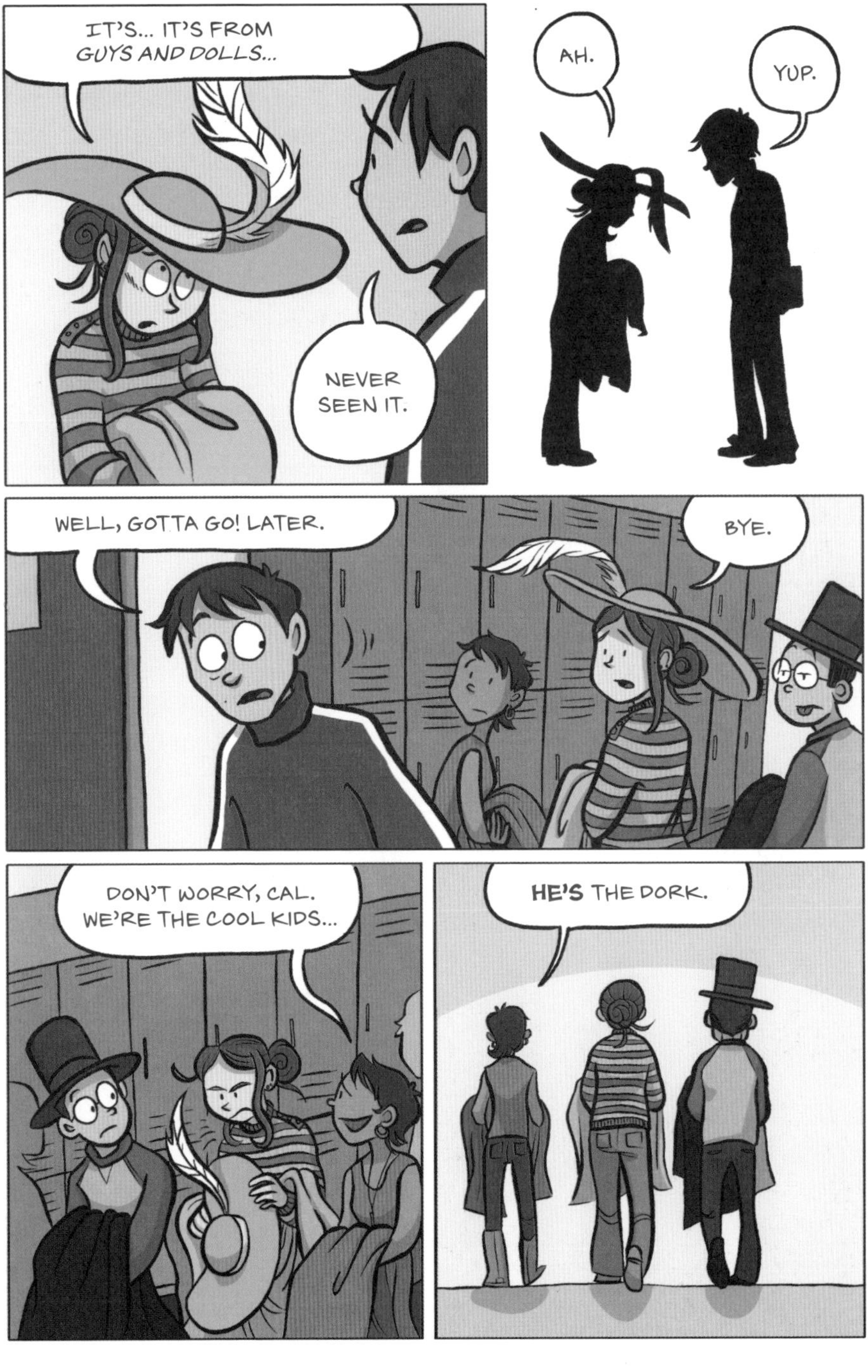
IT'S... IT'S FROM *GUYS AND DOLLS*...
NEVER SEEN IT.
AH.
YUP.
WELL, GOTTA GO! LATER.
BYE.
DON'T WORRY, CAL. WE'RE THE COOL KIDS...
HE'S THE DORK.

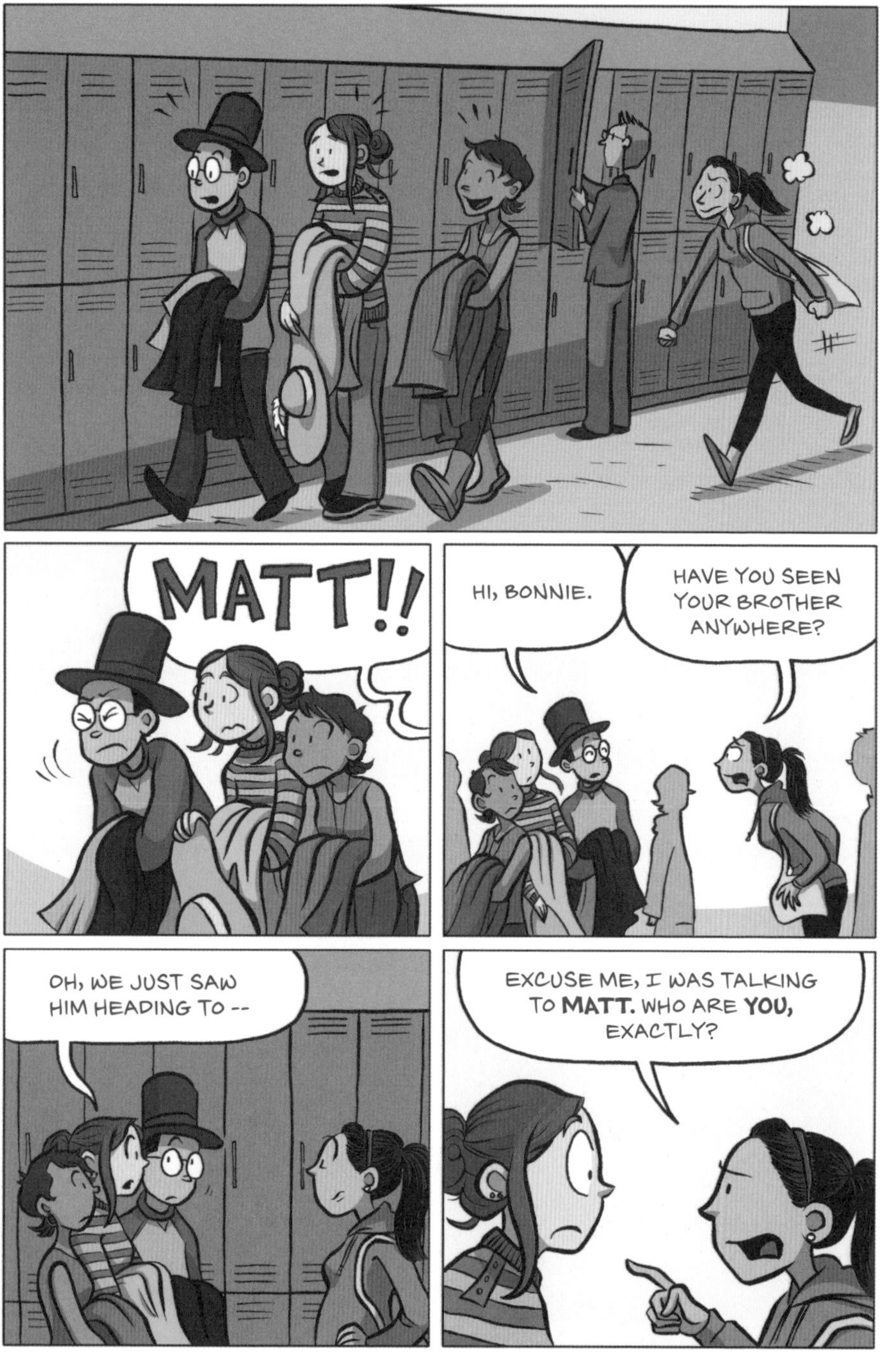
MATT!!
HI, BONNIE.
HAVE YOU SEEN YOUR BROTHER ANYWHERE?
OH, WE JUST SAW HIM HEADING TO --
EXCUSE ME, I WAS TALKING TO **MATT.** WHO ARE **YOU,** EXACTLY?

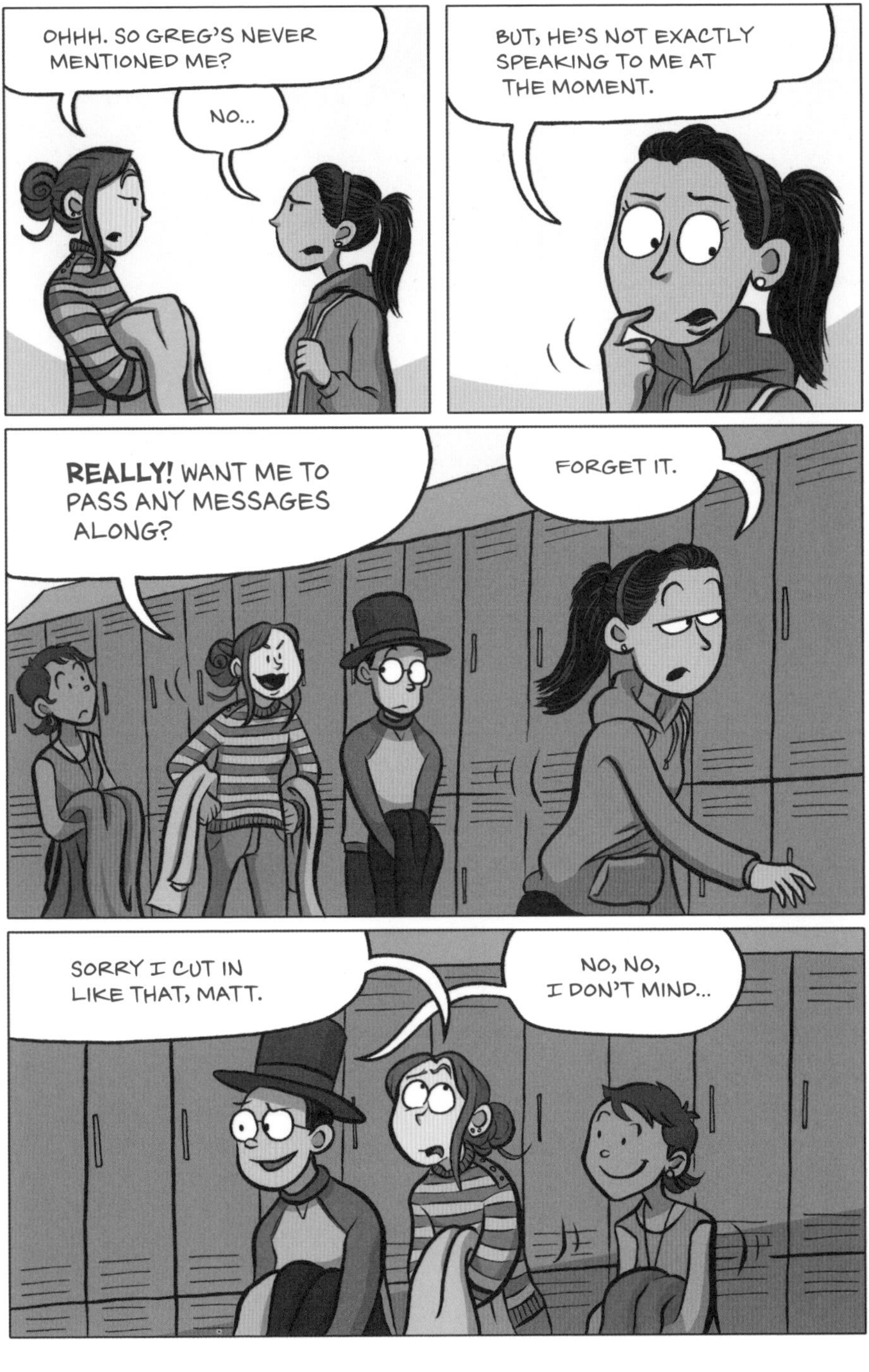
OHHH. SO GREG'S NEVER MENTIONED ME?
NO...
BUT, HE'S NOT EXACTLY SPEAKING TO ME AT THE MOMENT.
REALLY! WANT ME TO PASS ANY MESSAGES ALONG?
FORGET IT.
SORRY I CUT IN LIKE THAT, MATT.
NO, NO, I DON'T MIND...

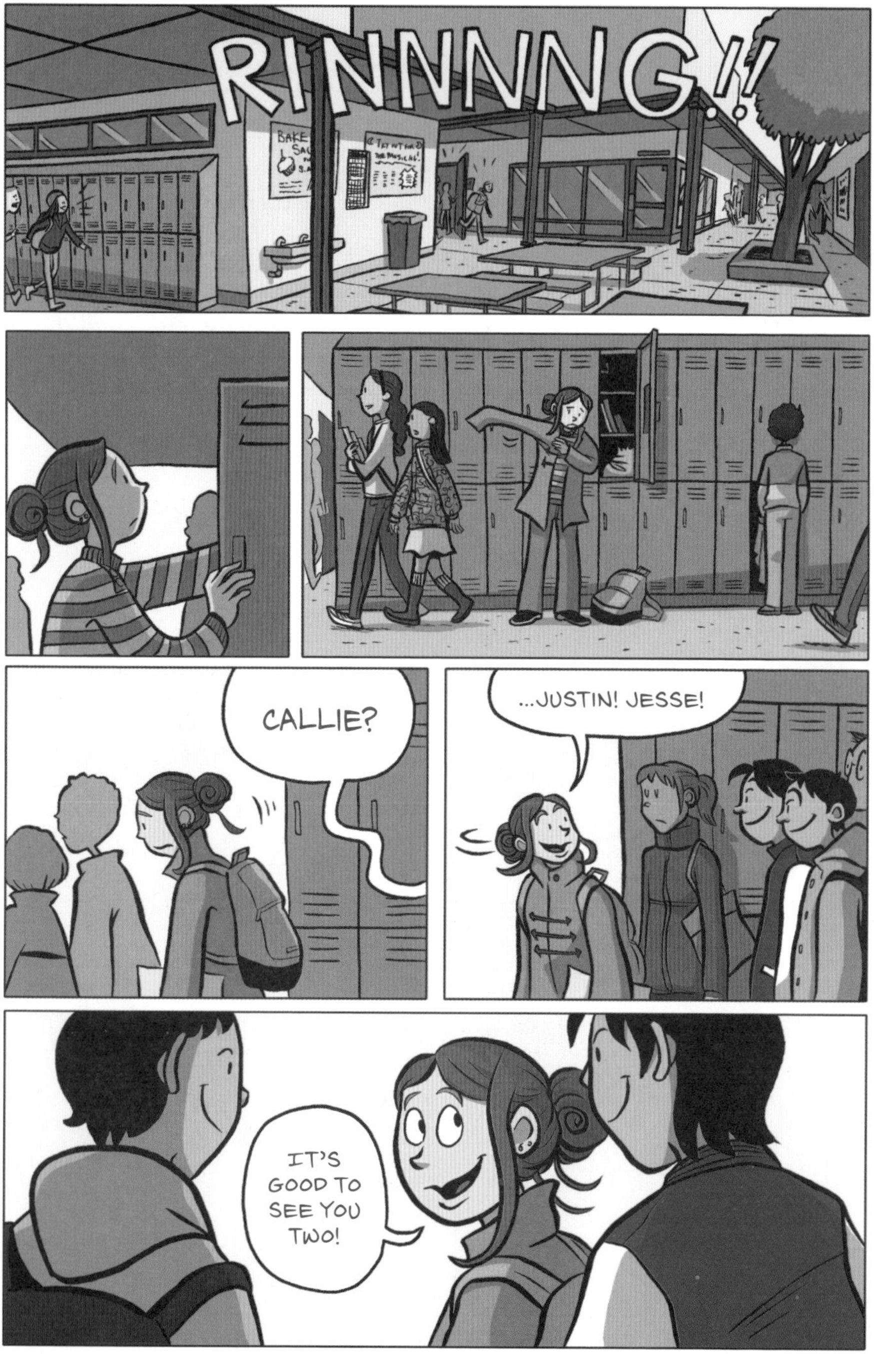
RINNNNG!!
CALLIE?
...JUSTIN! JESSE!
IT'S GOOD TO SEE YOU TWO!

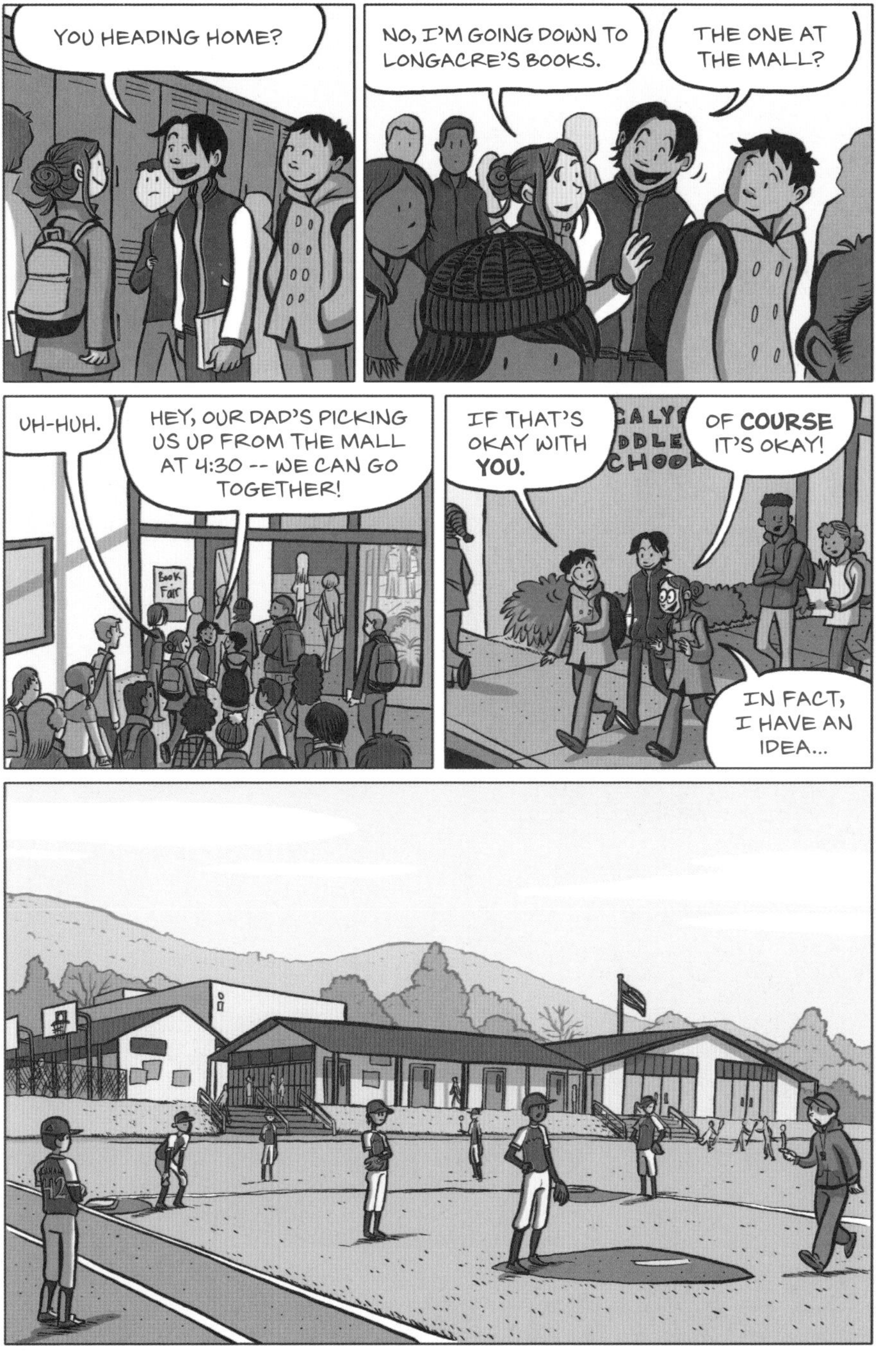
YOU HEADING HOME?
NO, I'M GOING DOWN TO LONGACRE'S BOOKS.
THE ONE AT THE MALL?
UH-HUH.
HEY, OUR DAD'S PICKING US UP FROM THE MALL AT 4:30 -- WE CAN GO TOGETHER!
BOOK FAIR
IF THAT'S OKAY WITH **YOU.**
OF **COURSE** IT'S OKAY!
IN FACT, I HAVE AN IDEA...

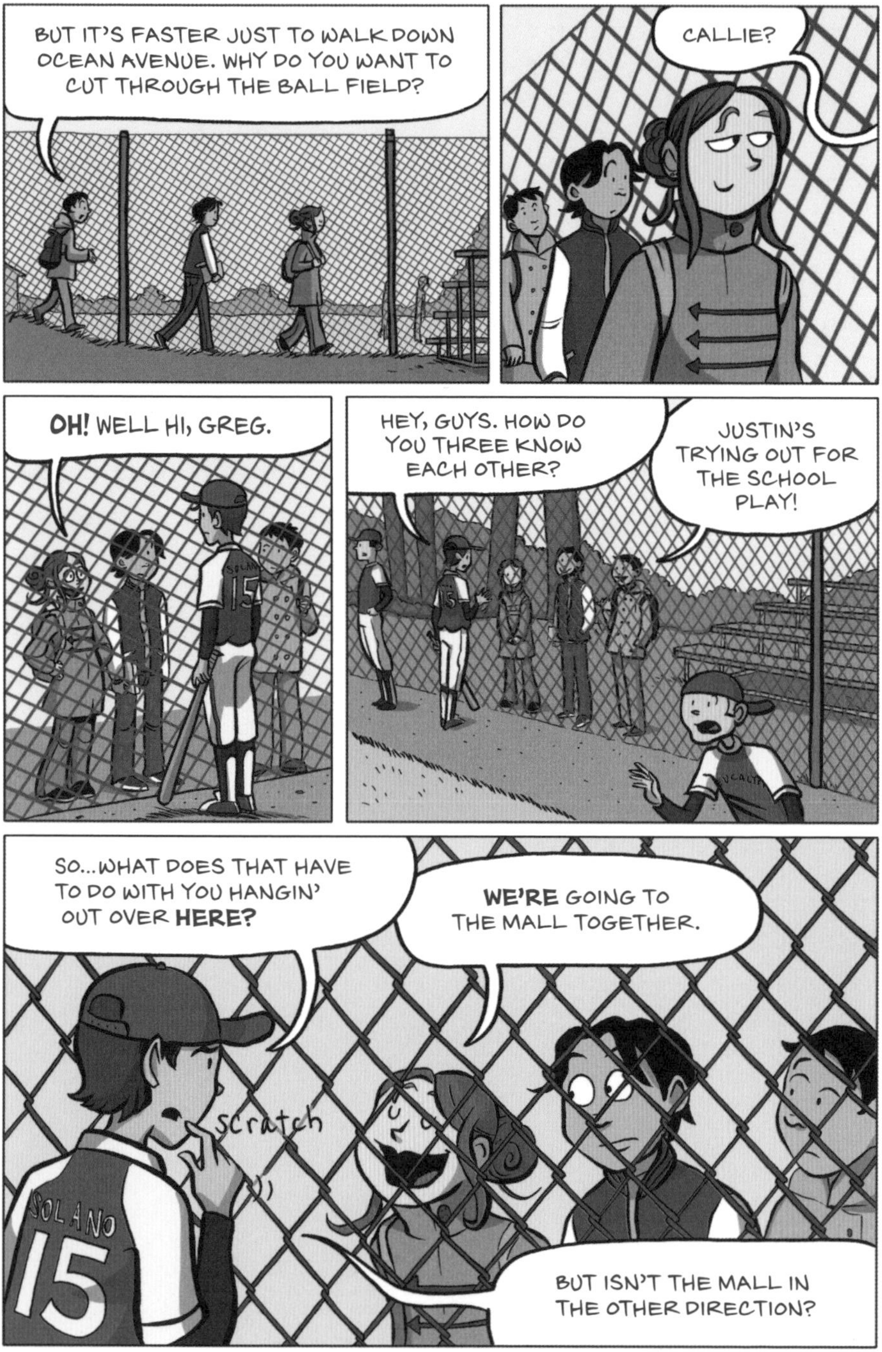
BUT IT'S FASTER JUST TO WALK DOWN OCEAN AVENUE. WHY DO YOU WANT TO CUT THROUGH THE BALL FIELD?
CALLIE?
OH! WELL HI, GREG.
HEY, GUYS. HOW DO YOU THREE KNOW EACH OTHER?
JUSTIN'S TRYING OUT FOR THE SCHOOL PLAY!
SO...WHAT DOES THAT HAVE TO DO WITH YOU HANGIN' OUT OVER **HERE?**
WE'RE GOING TO THE MALL TOGETHER.
scratch
SOLANO
15
BUT ISN'T THE MALL IN THE OTHER DIRECTION?

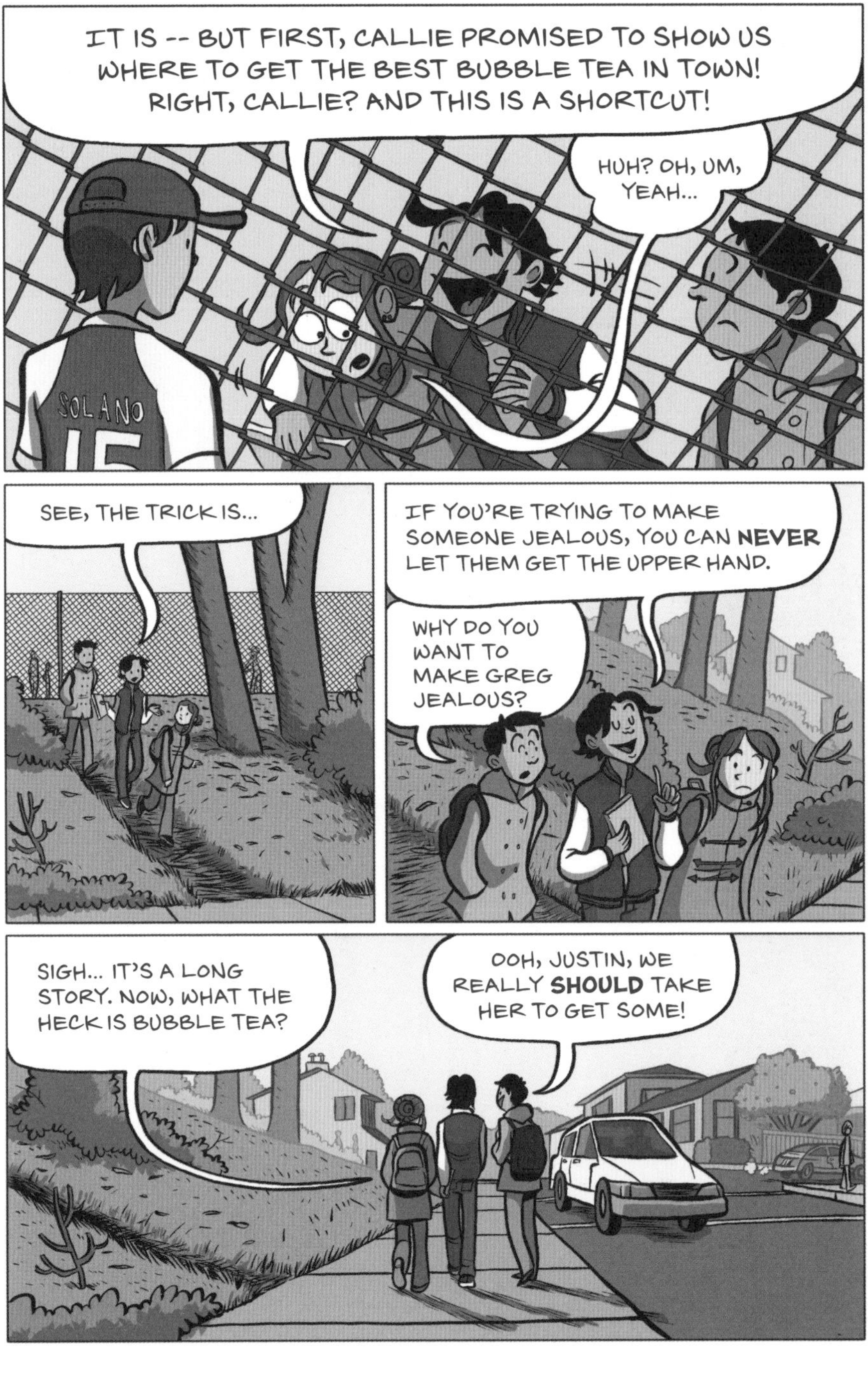
IT IS -- BUT FIRST, CALLIE PROMISED TO SHOW US WHERE TO GET THE BEST BUBBLE TEA IN TOWN! RIGHT, CALLIE? AND THIS IS A SHORTCUT!
HUH? OH, UM, YEAH...
SOLANO
15
SEE, THE TRICK IS...
IF YOU'RE TRYING TO MAKE SOMEONE JEALOUS, YOU CAN **NEVER** LET THEM GET THE UPPER HAND.
WHY DO YOU WANT TO MAKE GREG JEALOUS?
SIGH... IT'S A LONG STORY. NOW, WHAT THE HECK IS BUBBLE TEA?
OOH, JUSTIN, WE REALLY **SHOULD** TAKE HER TO GET SOME!

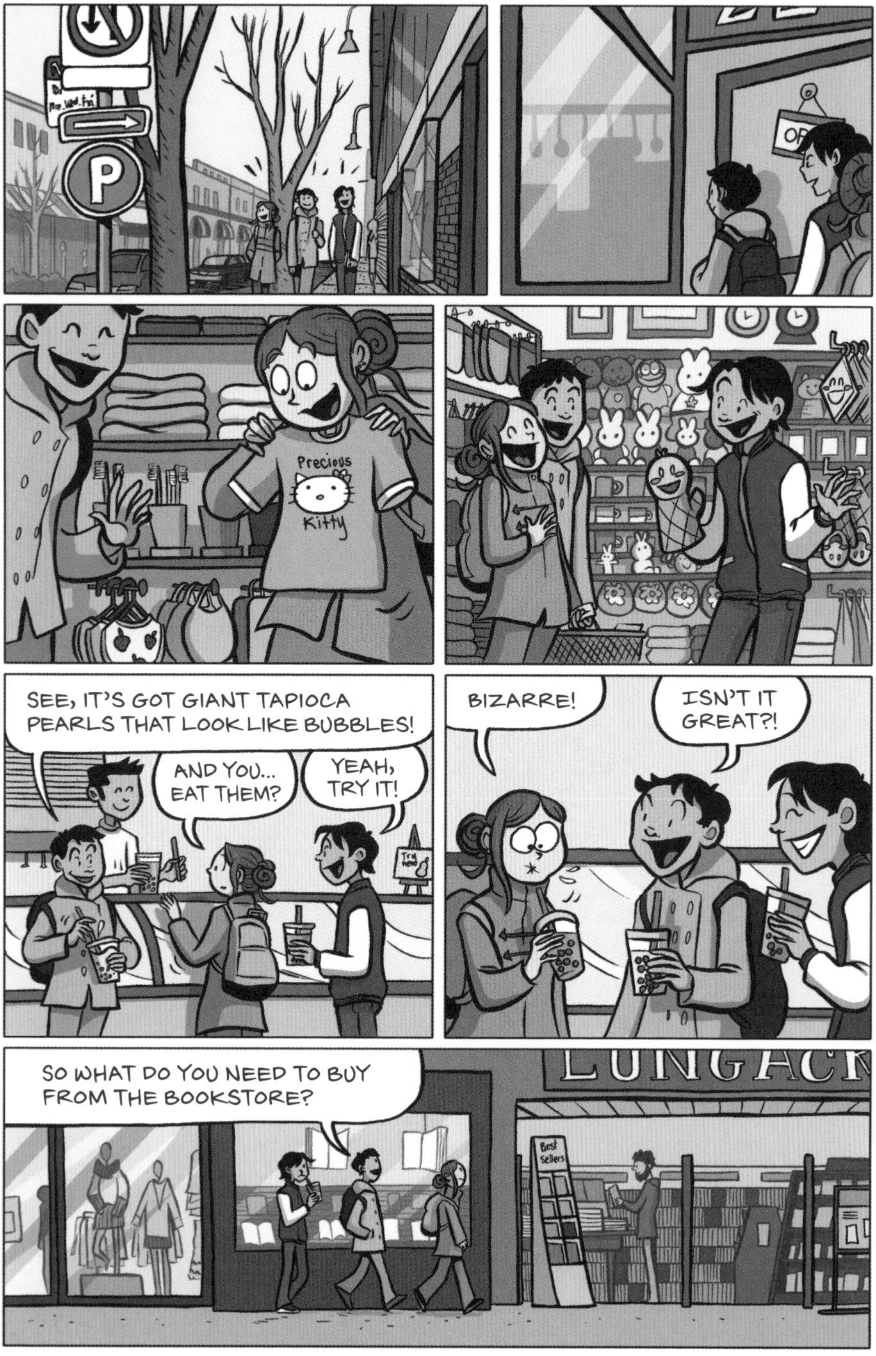
Precious
Kitty
SEE, IT'S GOT GIANT TAPIOCA PEARLS THAT LOOK LIKE BUBBLES!
AND YOU... EAT THEM?
YEAH, TRY IT!
BIZARRE!
ISN'T IT GREAT?!
SO WHAT DO YOU NEED TO BUY FROM THE BOOKSTORE?
LUNGACK
Best Sellers

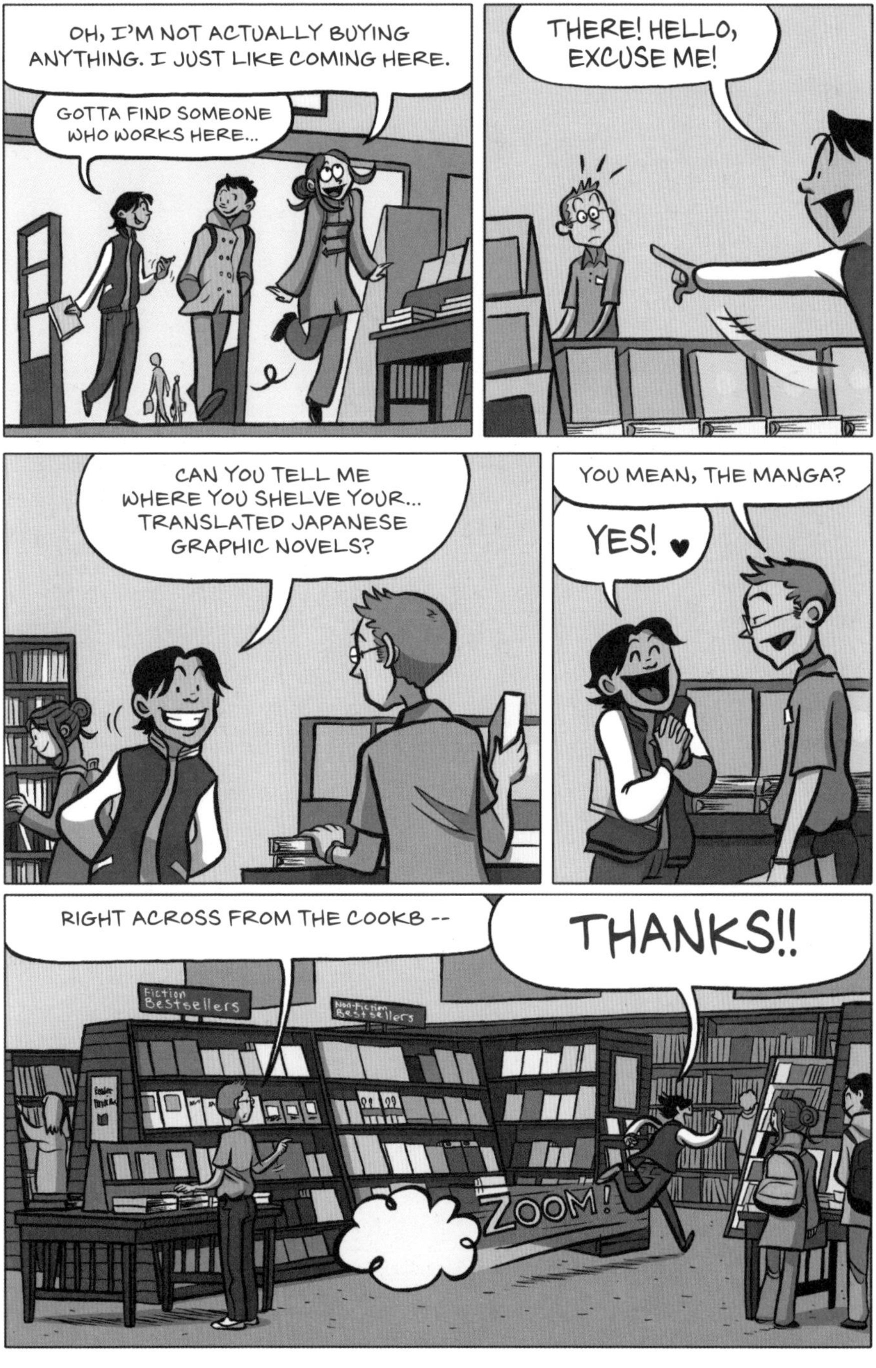
OH, I'M NOT ACTUALLY BUYING ANYTHING. I JUST LIKE COMING HERE.
GOTTA FIND SOMEONE WHO WORKS HERE...
THERE! HELLO, EXCUSE ME!
CAN YOU TELL ME WHERE YOU SHELVE YOUR... TRANSLATED JAPANESE GRAPHIC NOVELS?
YOU MEAN, THE MANGA?
YES!
RIGHT ACROSS FROM THE COOKB --
THANKS!!
Fiction Bestsellers
Non-fiction Bestsellers
ZOOM!

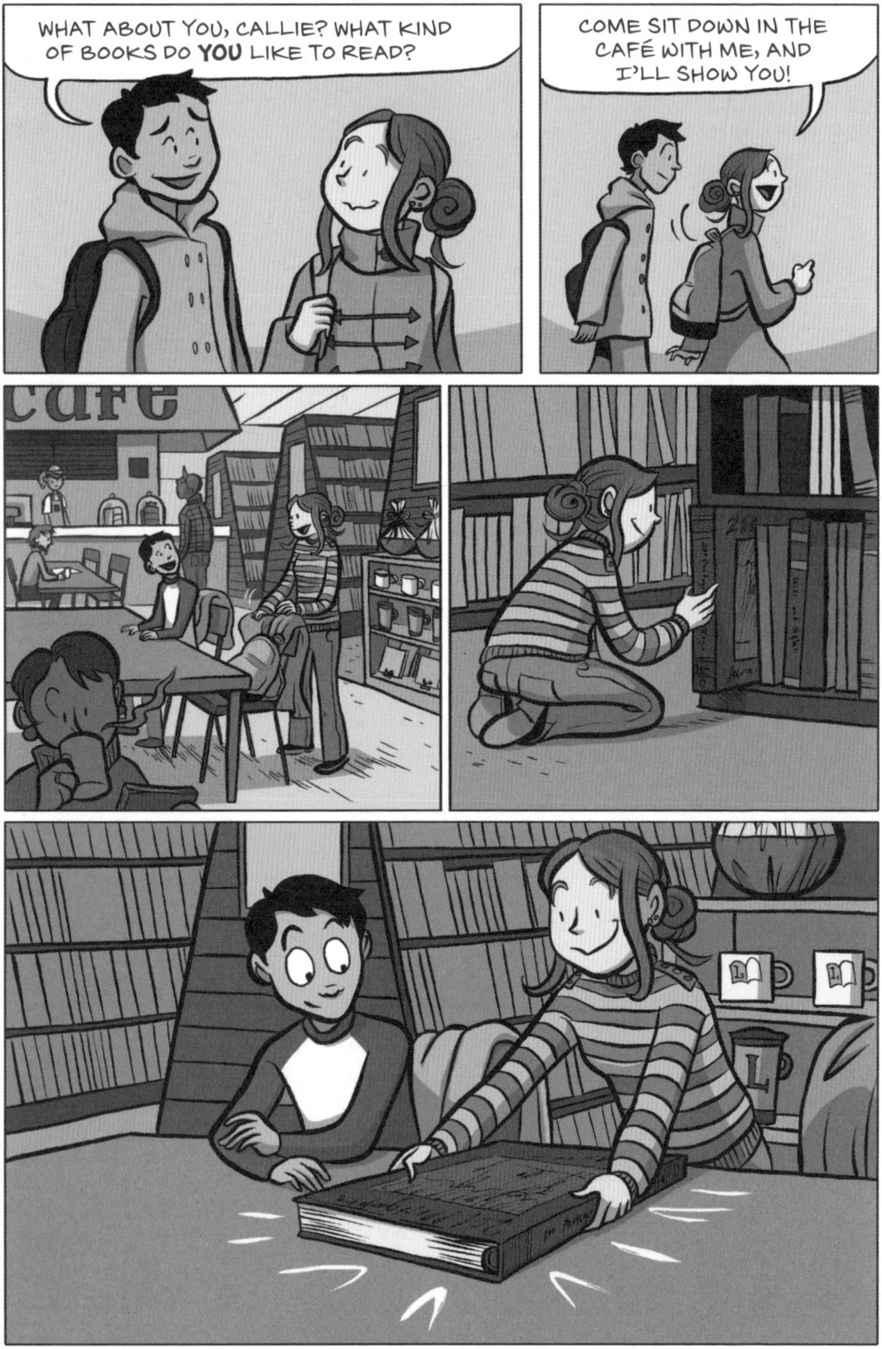
WHAT ABOUT YOU, CALLIE? WHAT KIND OF BOOKS DO **YOU** LIKE TO READ?
COME SIT DOWN IN THE CAFÉ WITH ME, AND I'LL SHOW YOU!
cafe

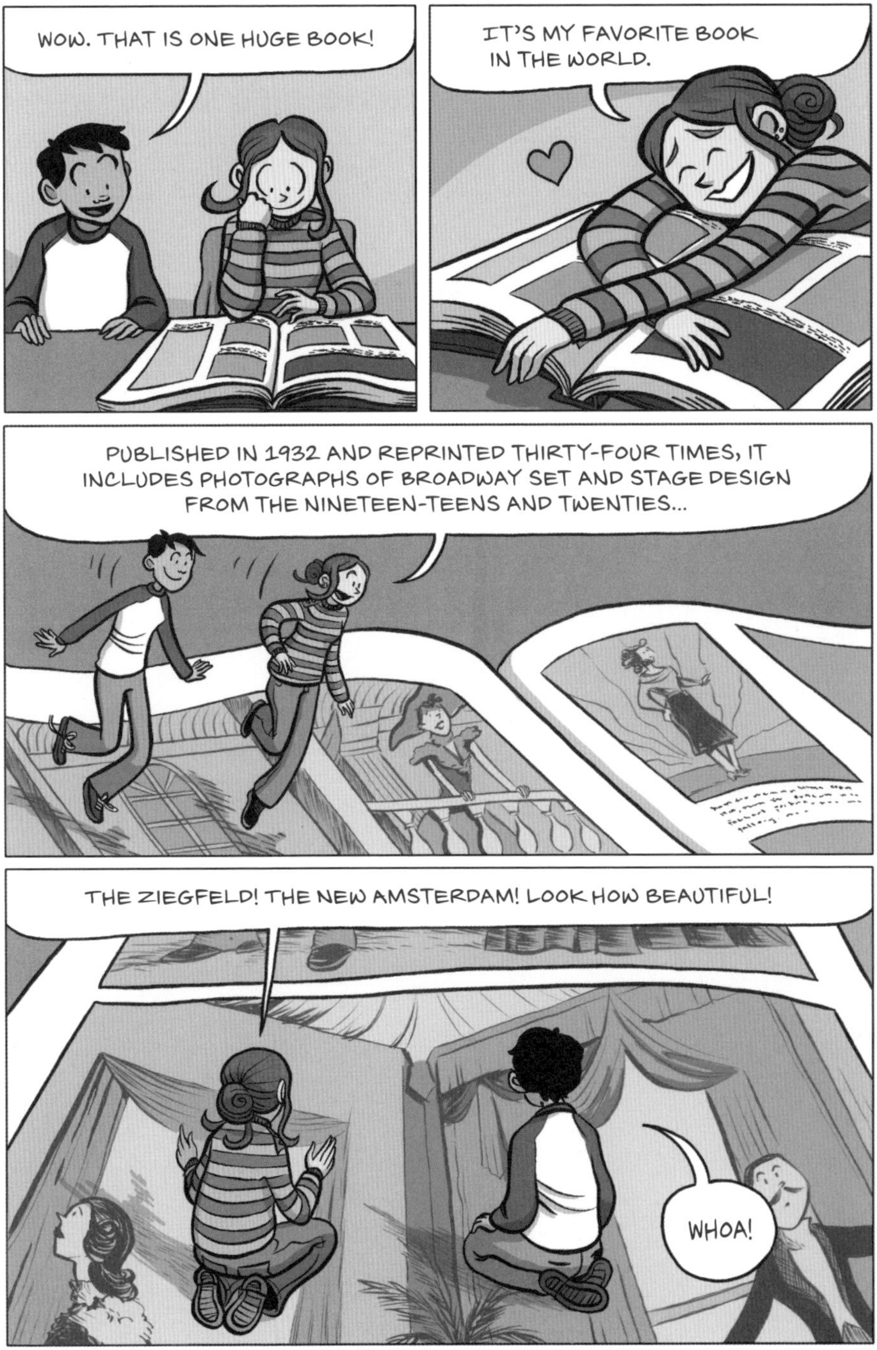
WOW. THAT IS ONE HUGE BOOK!
IT'S MY FAVORITE BOOK IN THE WORLD.
PUBLISHED IN 1932 AND REPRINTED THIRTY-FOUR TIMES, IT INCLUDES PHOTOGRAPHS OF BROADWAY SET AND STAGE DESIGN FROM THE NINETEEN-TEENS AND TWENTIES...
THE ZIEGFELD! THE NEW AMSTERDAM! LOOK HOW BEAUTIFUL!
WHOA!

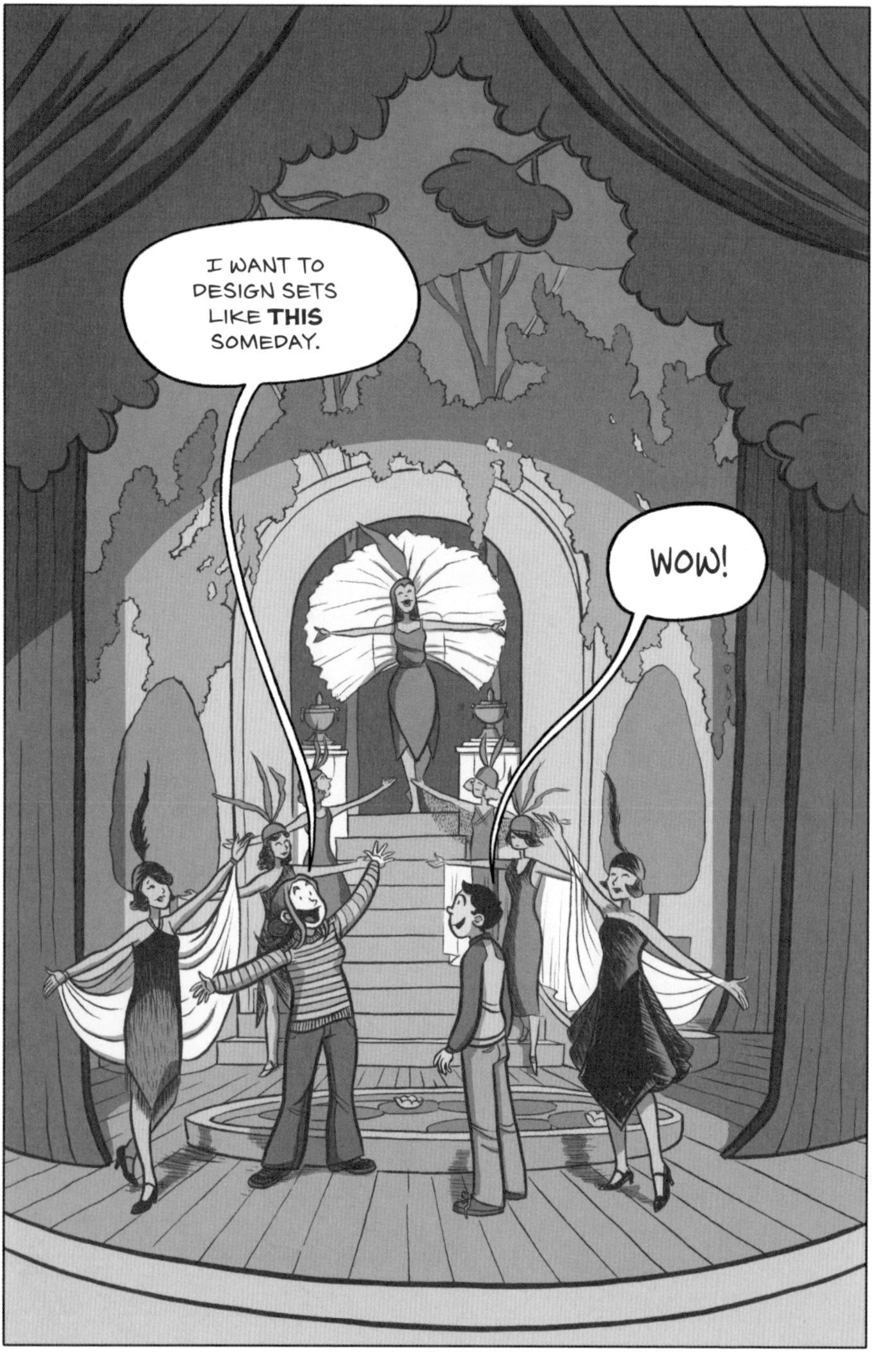
I WANT TO DESIGN SETS LIKE **THIS** SOMEDAY.
WOW!

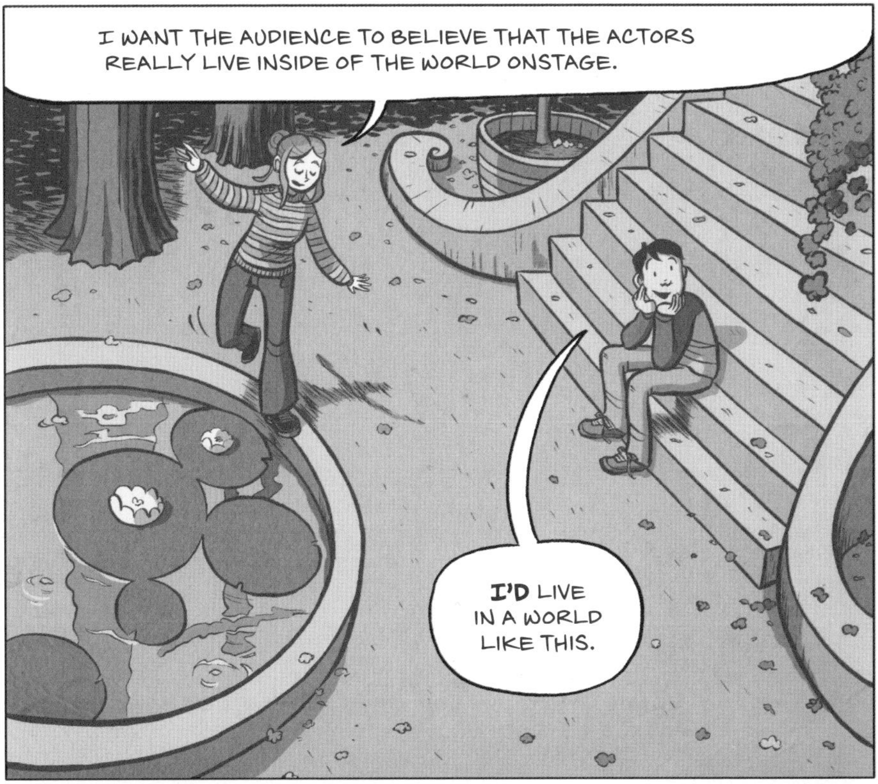
I WANT THE AUDIENCE TO BELIEVE THAT THE ACTORS REALLY LIVE INSIDE OF THE WORLD ONSTAGE.
I'D LIVE IN A WORLD LIKE THIS.

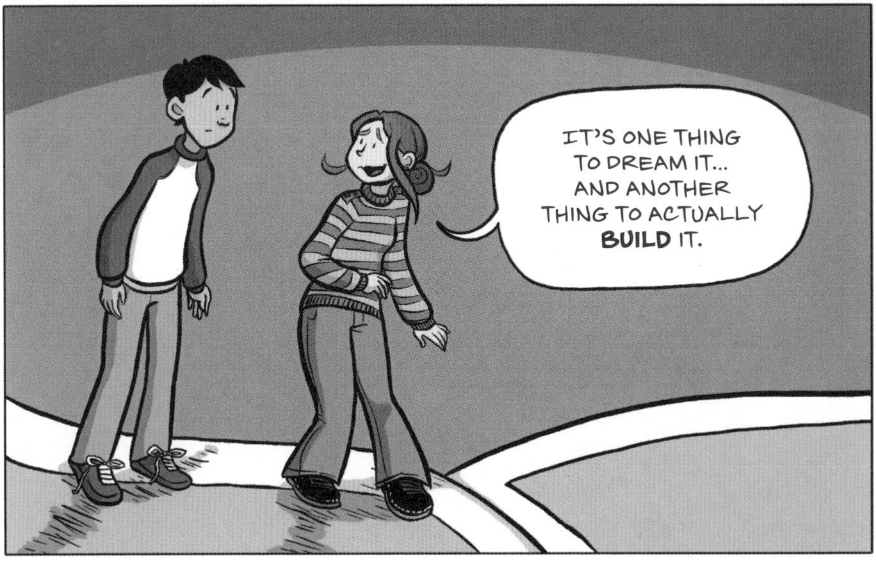
IT'S ONE THING TO DREAM IT... AND ANOTHER THING TO ACTUALLY **BUILD** IT.

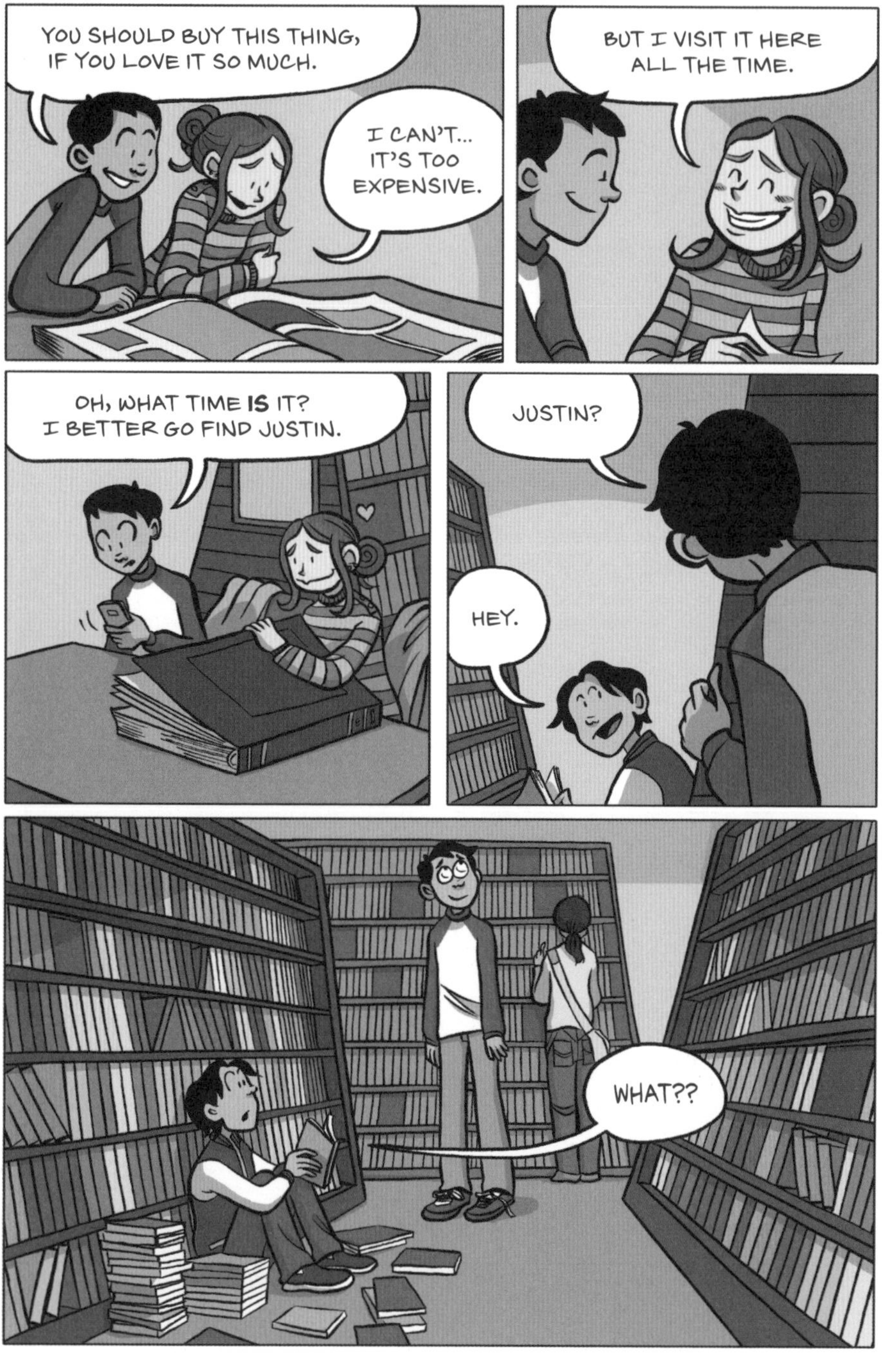
YOU SHOULD BUY THIS THING, IF YOU LOVE IT SO MUCH.
I CAN'T... IT'S TOO EXPENSIVE.
BUT I VISIT IT HERE ALL THE TIME.
OH, WHAT TIME **IS** IT? I BETTER GO FIND JUSTIN.
JUSTIN?
HEY.
WHAT??

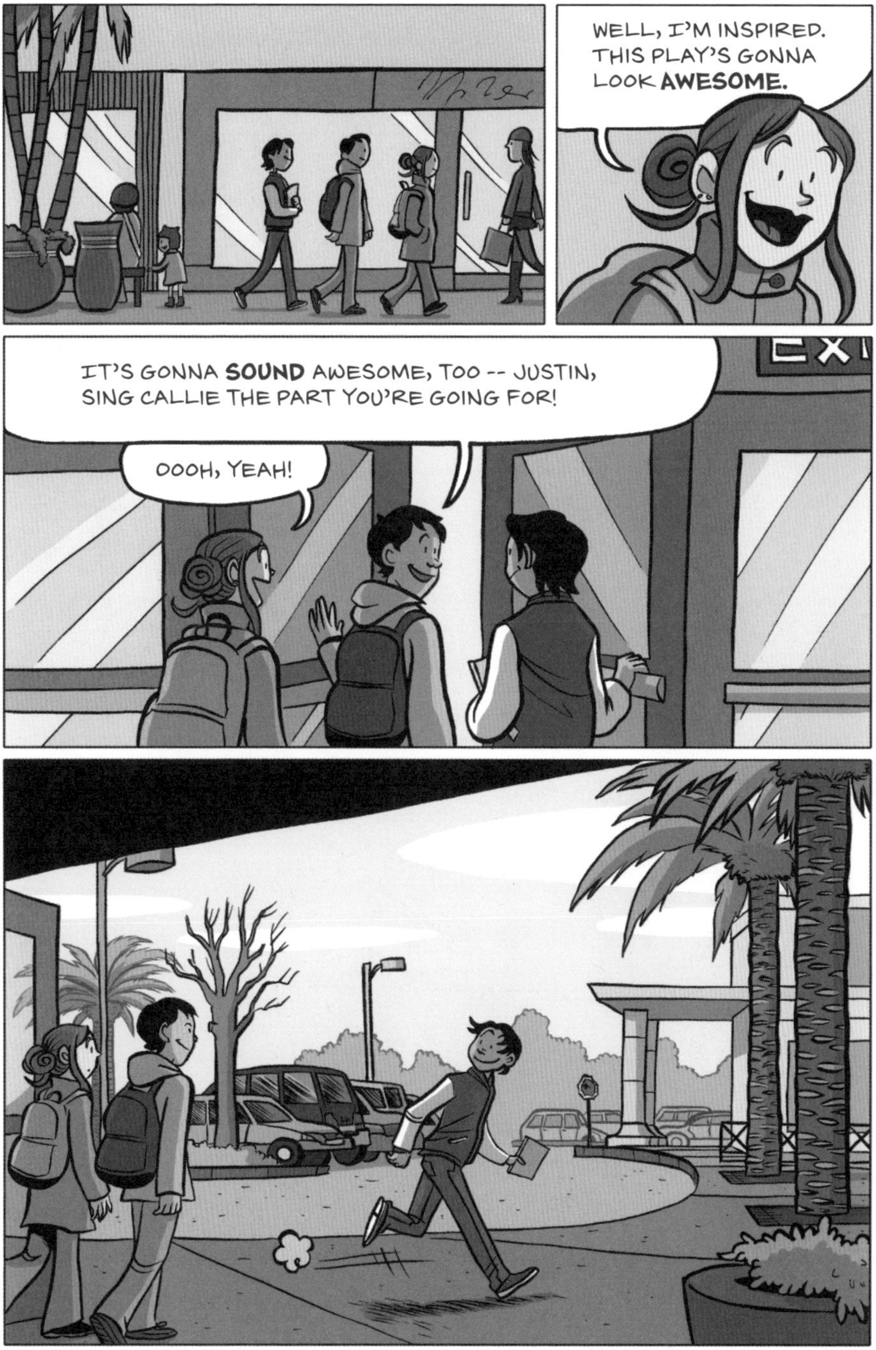
WELL, I'M INSPIRED. THIS PLAY'S GONNA LOOK **AWESOME.**
IT'S GONNA **SOUND** AWESOME, TOO -- JUSTIN, SING CALLIE THE PART YOU'RE GOING FOR!
OOOH, YEAH!

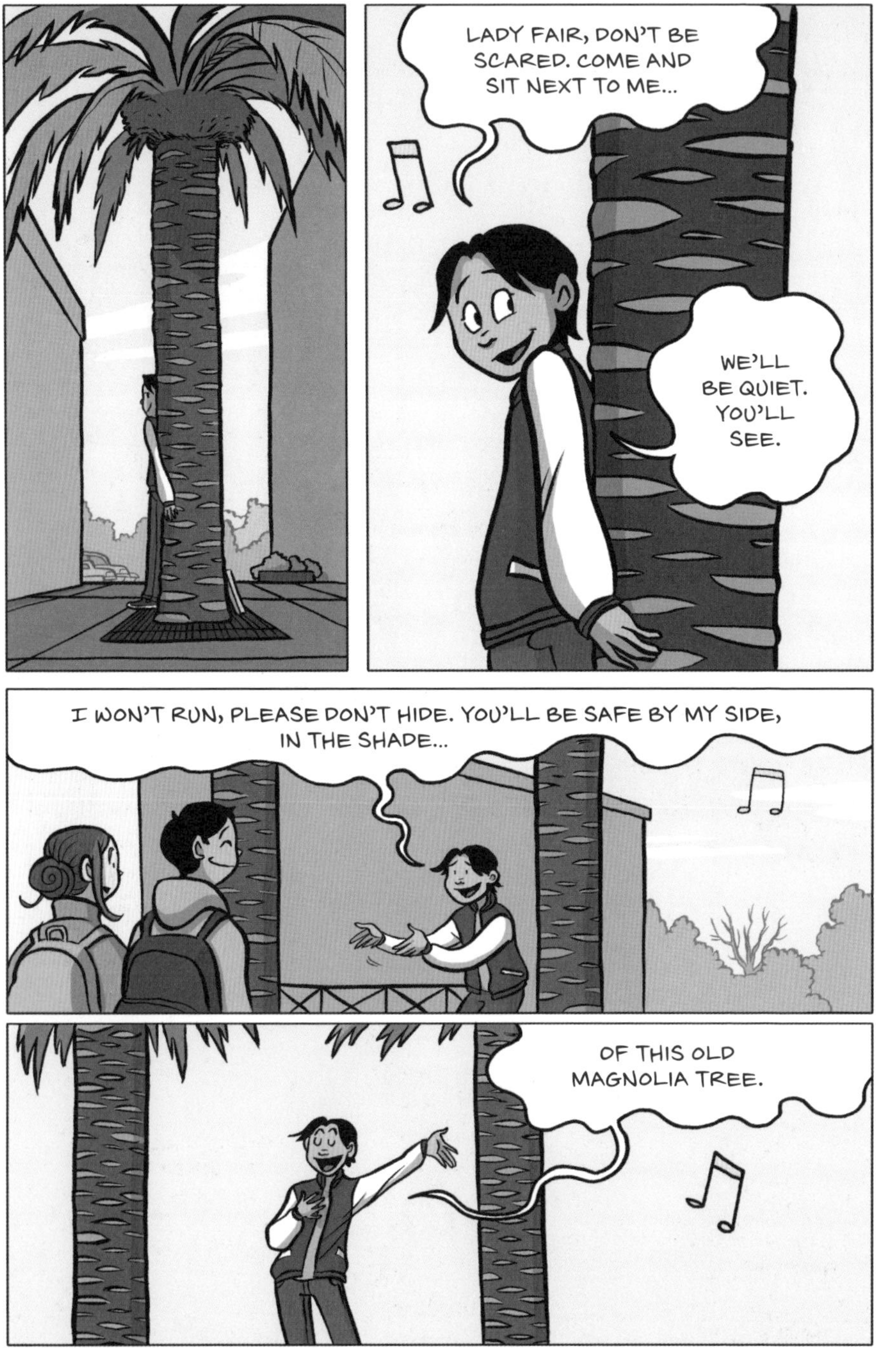
LADY FAIR, DON'T BE SCARED. COME AND SIT NEXT TO ME...
WE'LL BE QUIET. YOU'LL SEE.
I WON'T RUN, PLEASE DON'T HIDE. YOU'LL BE SAFE BY MY SIDE, IN THE SHADE...
OF THIS OLD MAGNOLIA TREE.

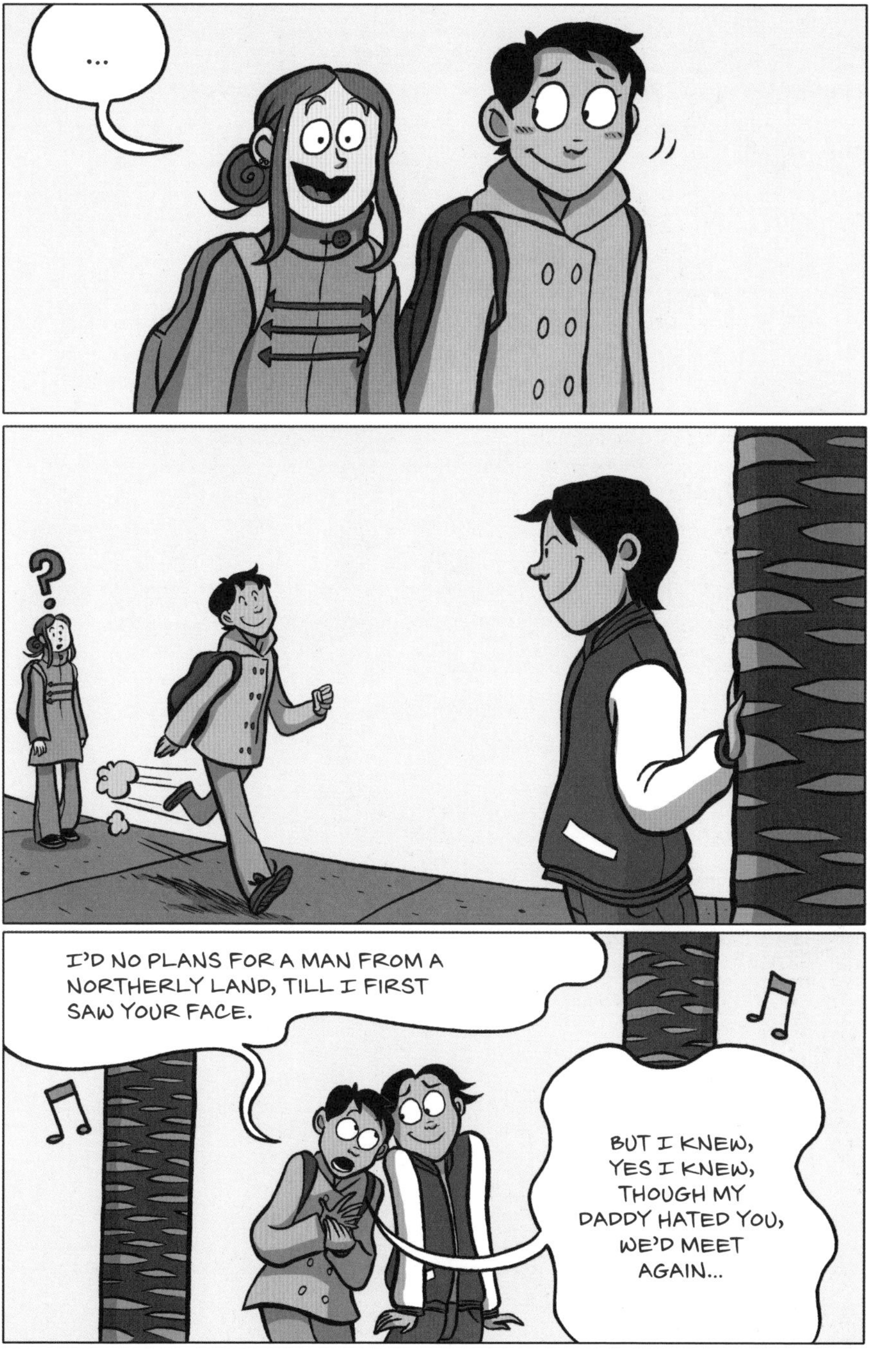
...
?
I'D NO PLANS FOR A MAN FROM A NORTHERLY LAND, TILL I FIRST SAW YOUR FACE.
BUT I KNEW, YES I KNEW, THOUGH MY DADDY HATED YOU, WE'D MEET AGAIN...

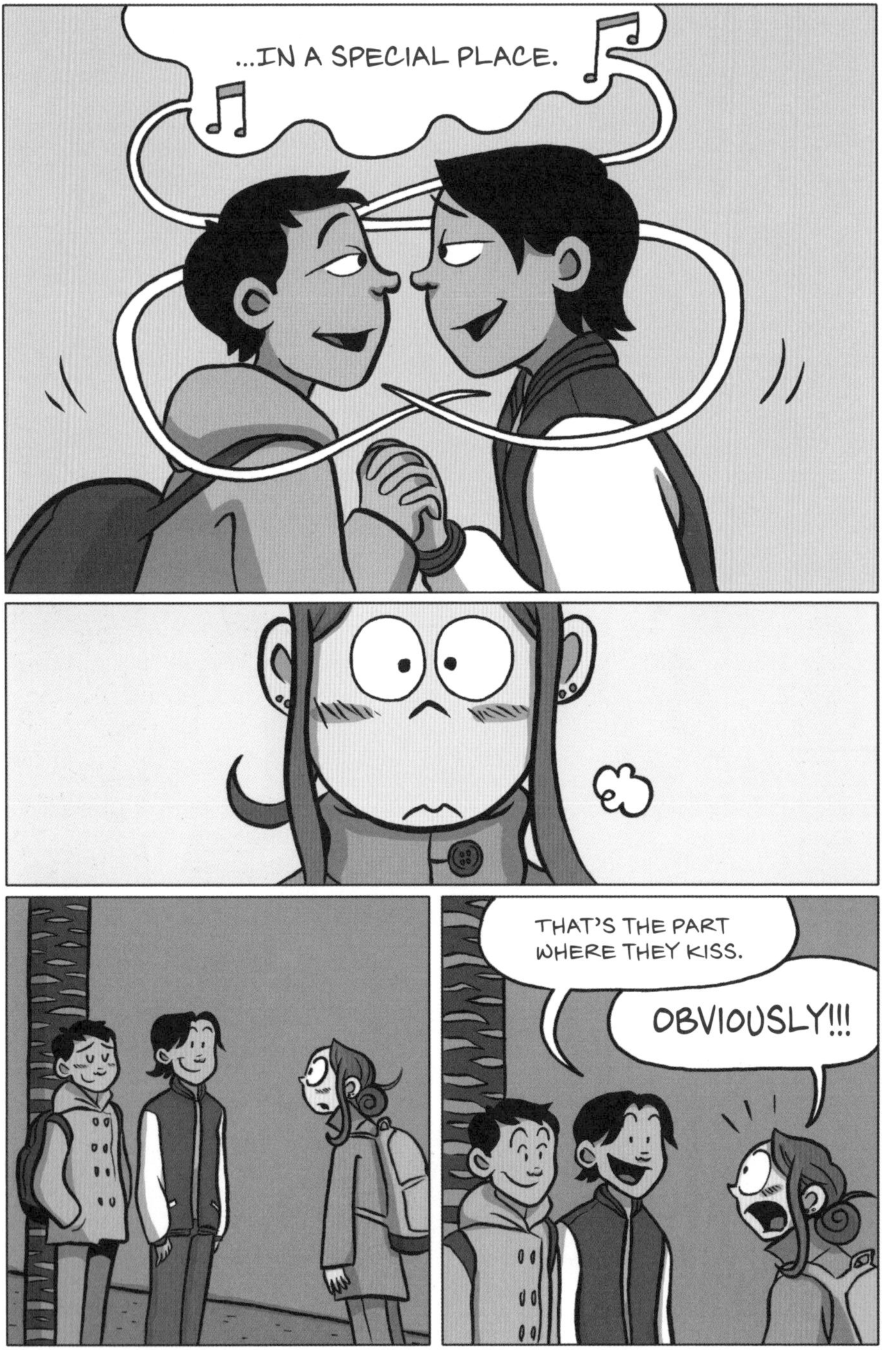
...IN A SPECIAL PLACE.
THAT'S THE PART WHERE THEY KISS.
OBVIOUSLY!!!

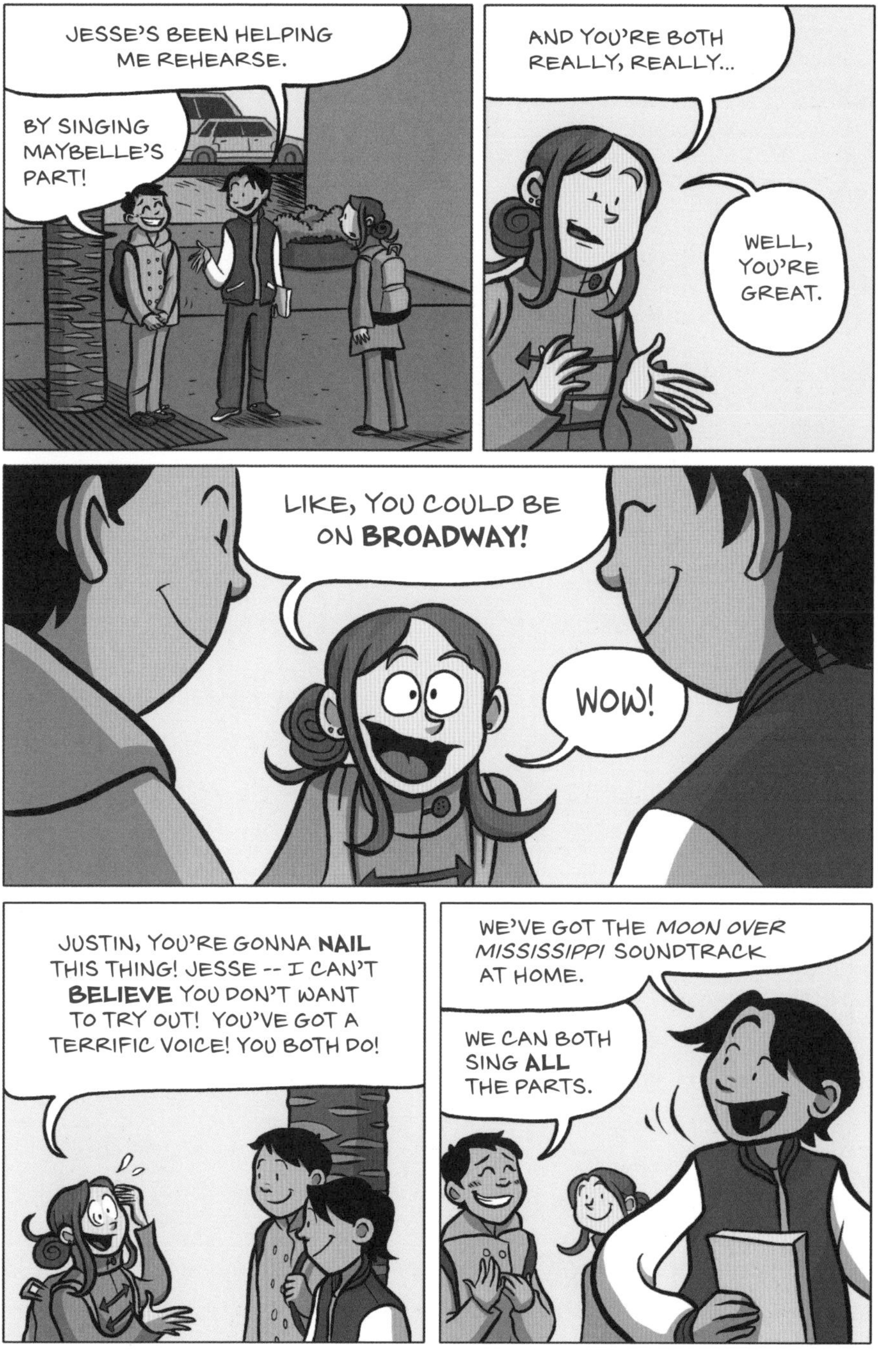
JESSE'S BEEN HELPING ME REHEARSE.
BY SINGING MAYBELLE'S PART!
AND YOU'RE BOTH REALLY, REALLY...
WELL, YOU'RE GREAT.
LIKE, YOU COULD BE ON BROADWAY!
WOW!
JUSTIN, YOU'RE GONNA NAIL THIS THING! JESSE -- I CAN'T BELIEVE YOU DON'T WANT TO TRY OUT! YOU'VE GOT A TERRIFIC VOICE! YOU BOTH DO!
WE'VE GOT THE MOON OVER MISSISSIPPI SOUNDTRACK AT HOME.
WE CAN BOTH SING ALL THE PARTS.

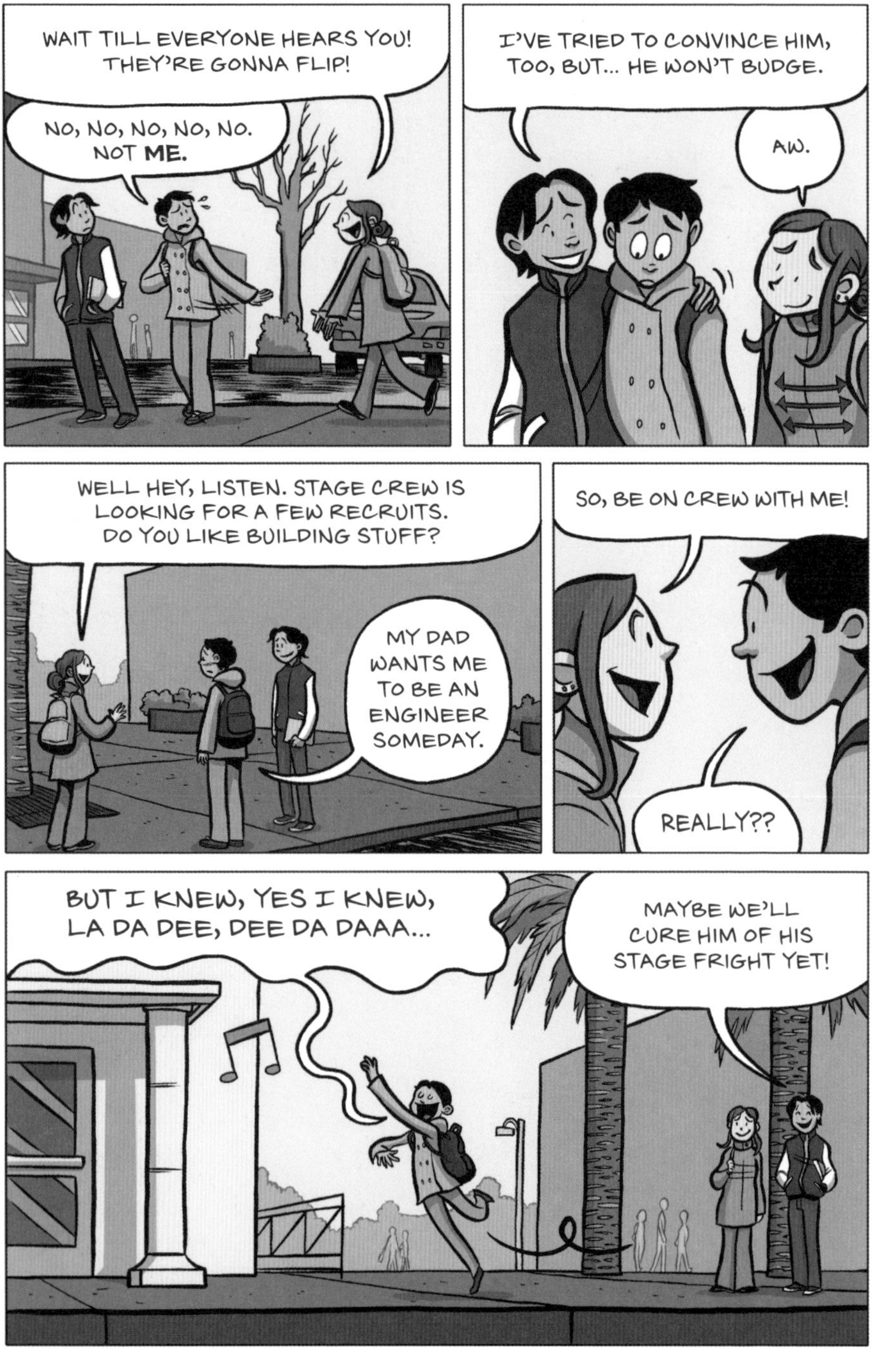
WAIT TILL EVERYONE HEARS YOU! THEY'RE GONNA FLIP!
NO, NO, NO, NO, NO. NOT **ME.**
I'VE TRIED TO CONVINCE HIM, TOO, BUT... HE WON'T BUDGE.
AW.
WELL HEY, LISTEN. STAGE CREW IS LOOKING FOR A FEW RECRUITS. DO YOU LIKE BUILDING STUFF?
MY DAD WANTS ME TO BE AN ENGINEER SOMEDAY.
SO, BE ON CREW WITH ME!
REALLY??
BUT I KNEW, YES I KNEW, LA DA DEE, DEE DA DAAA...
MAYBE WE'LL CURE HIM OF HIS STAGE FRIGHT YET!

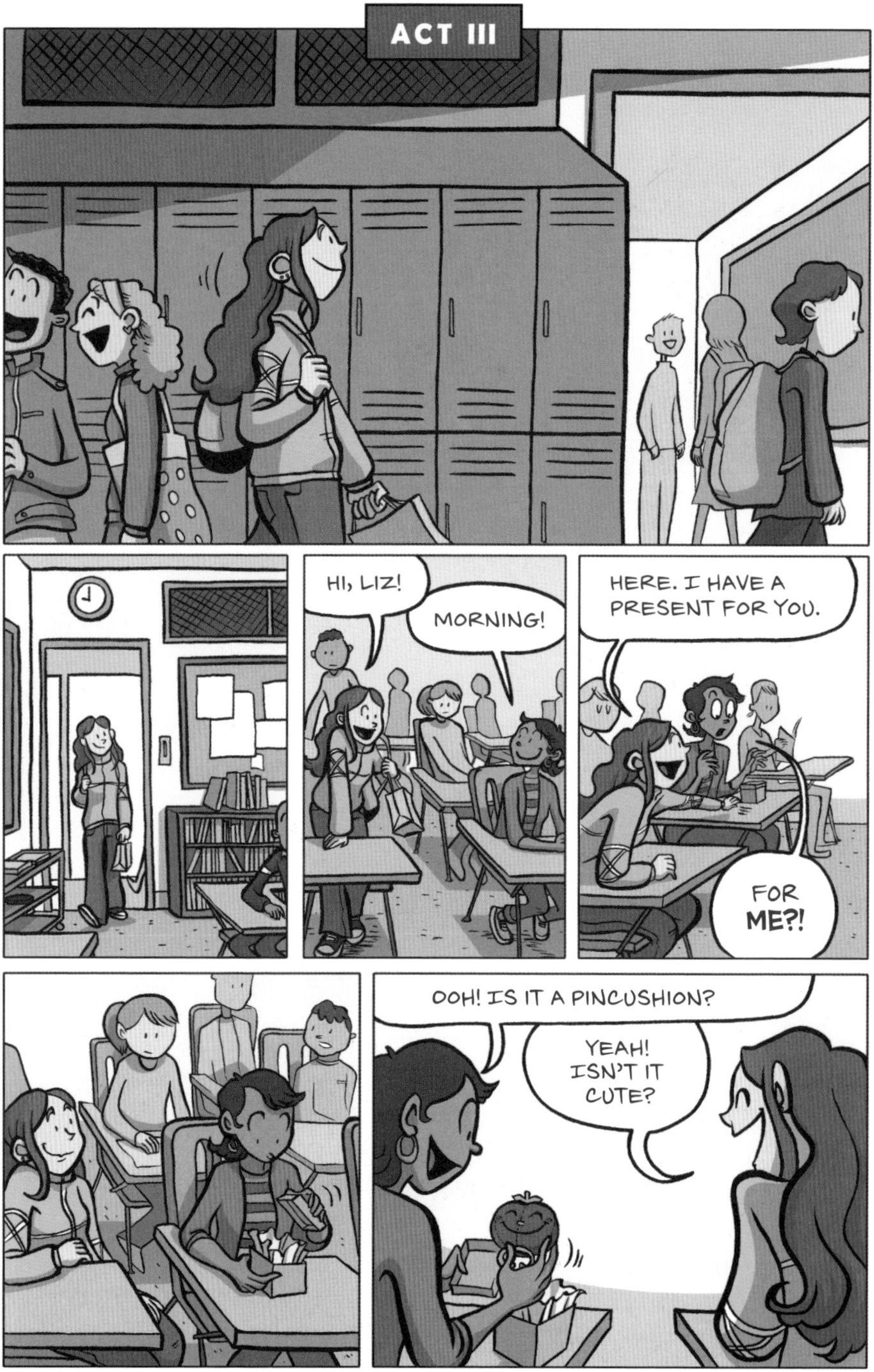
ACT III
HI, LIZ!
MORNING!
HERE. I HAVE A PRESENT FOR YOU.
FOR **ME?!**
OOH! IS IT A PINCUSHION?
YEAH! ISN'T IT CUTE?

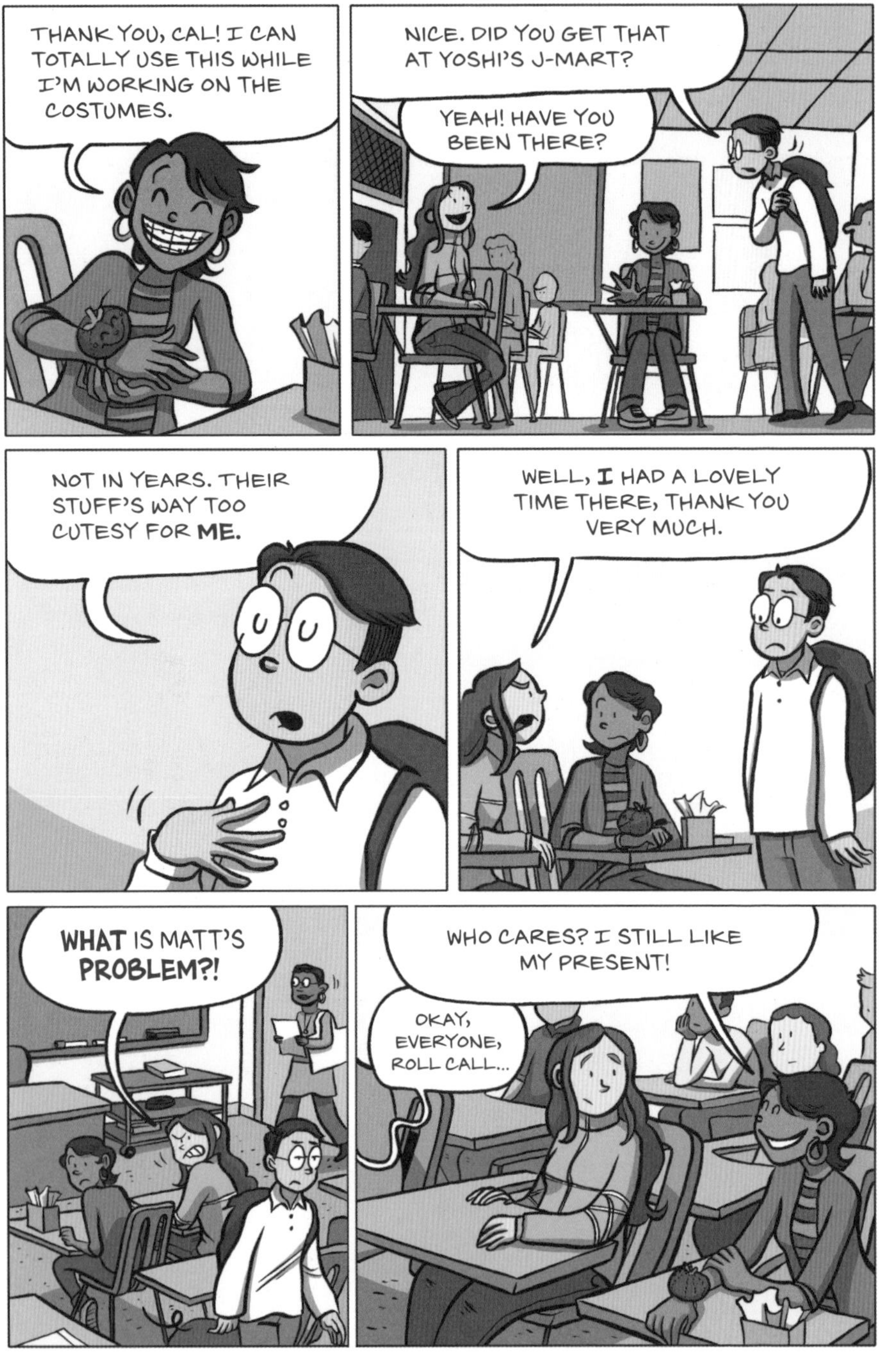
THANK YOU, CAL! I CAN TOTALLY USE THIS WHILE I'M WORKING ON THE COSTUMES.
NICE. DID YOU GET THAT AT YOSHI'S J-MART?
YEAH! HAVE YOU BEEN THERE?
NOT IN YEARS. THEIR STUFF'S WAY TOO CUTESY FOR **ME.**
WELL, **I** HAD A LOVELY TIME THERE, THANK YOU VERY MUCH.
WHAT IS MATT'S **PROBLEM?!**
WHO CARES? I STILL LIKE MY PRESENT!
OKAY, EVERYONE, ROLL CALL...

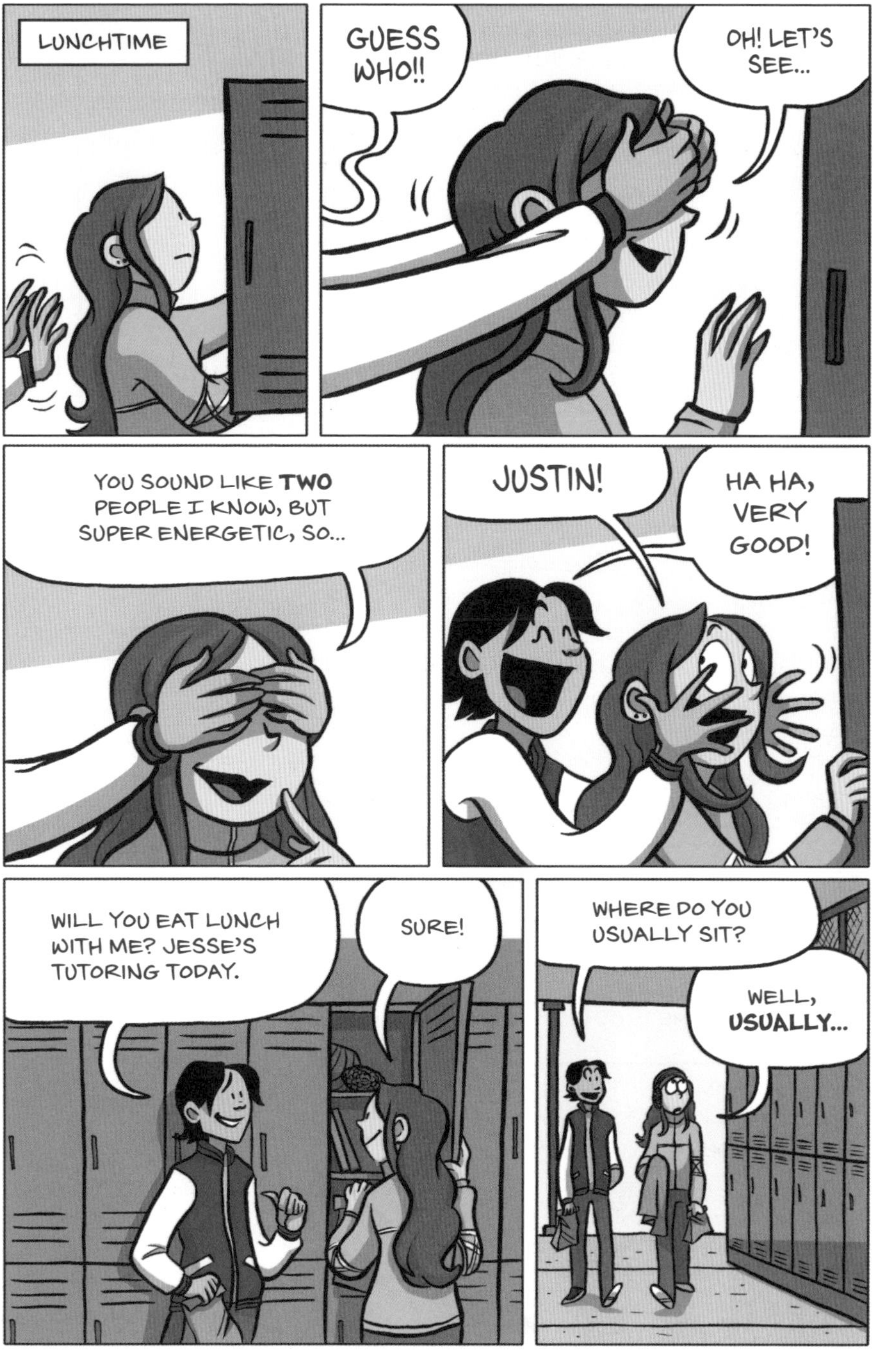
LUNCHTIME
GUESS WHO!!
OH! LET'S SEE...
YOU SOUND LIKE **TWO** PEOPLE I KNOW, BUT SUPER ENERGETIC, SO...
JUSTIN!
HA HA, VERY GOOD!
WILL YOU EAT LUNCH WITH ME? JESSE'S TUTORING TODAY.
SURE!
WHERE DO YOU USUALLY SIT?
WELL, **USUALLY...**

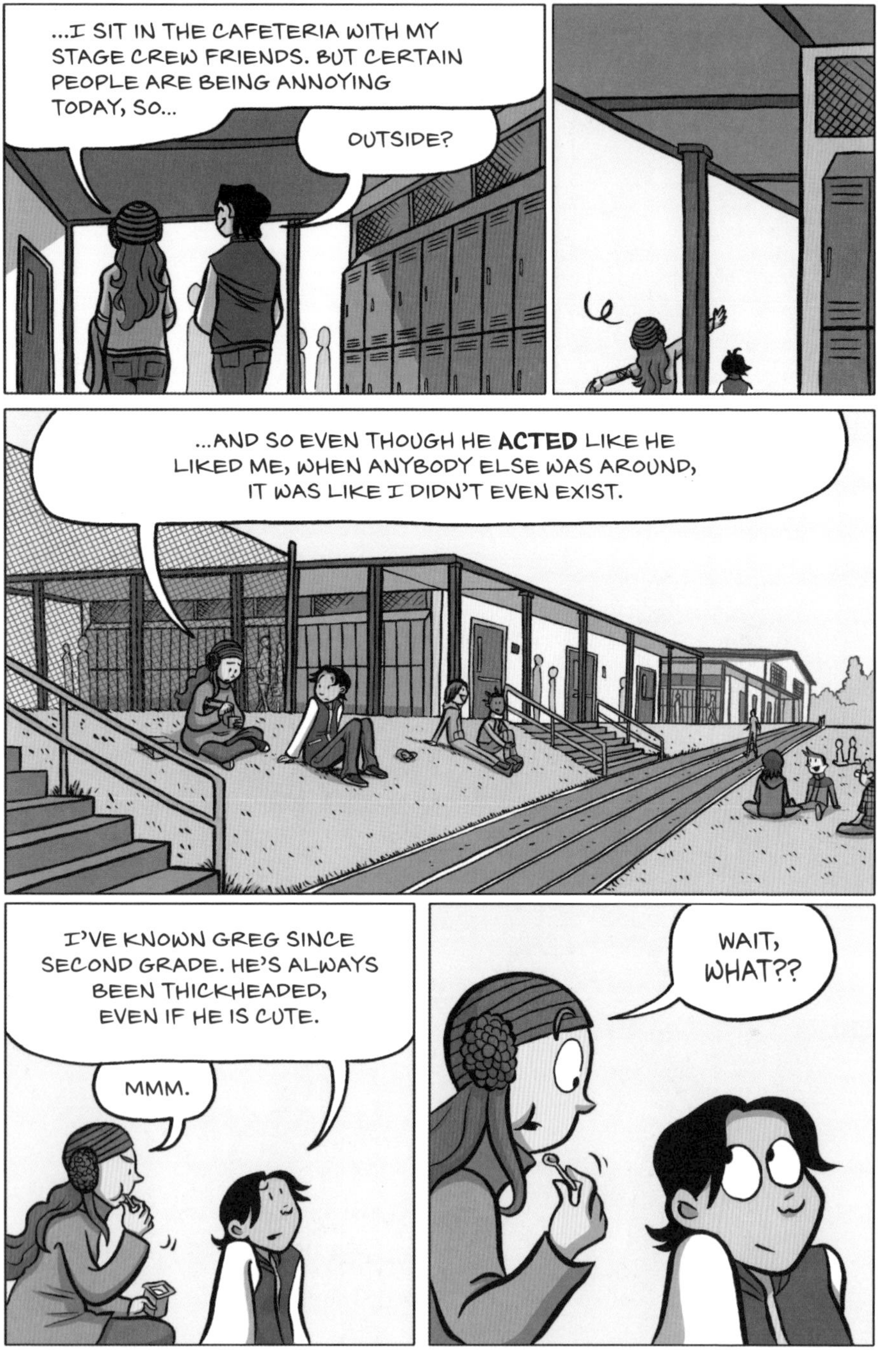
...I SIT IN THE CAFETERIA WITH MY STAGE CREW FRIENDS. BUT CERTAIN PEOPLE ARE BEING ANNOYING TODAY, SO...
OUTSIDE?
...AND SO EVEN THOUGH HE ACTED LIKE HE LIKED ME, WHEN ANYBODY ELSE WAS AROUND, IT WAS LIKE I DIDN'T EVEN EXIST.
I'VE KNOWN GREG SINCE SECOND GRADE. HE'S ALWAYS BEEN THICKHEADED, EVEN IF HE IS CUTE.
MMM.
WAIT, WHAT??

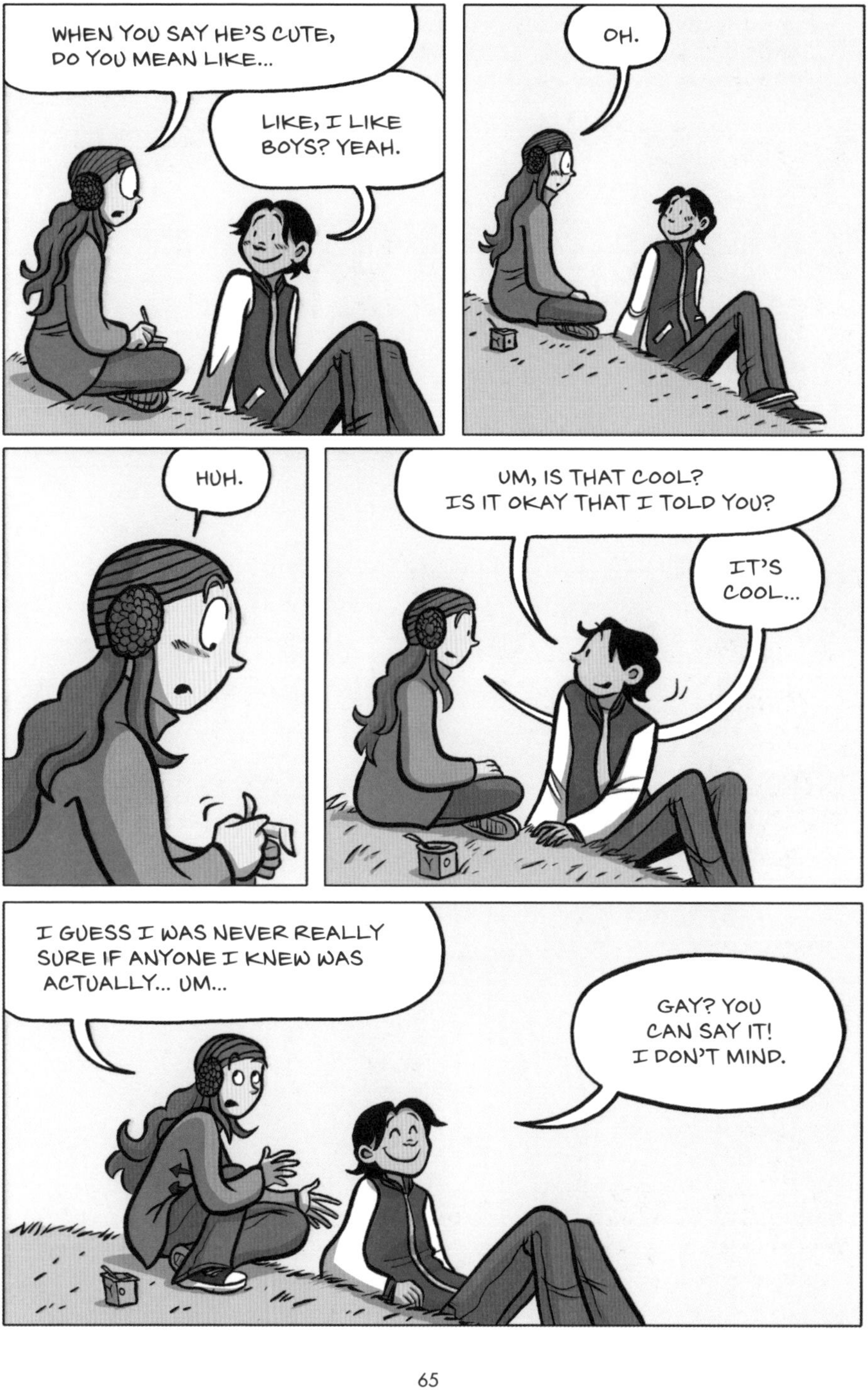
WHEN YOU SAY HE'S CUTE, DO YOU MEAN LIKE...
LIKE, I LIKE BOYS? YEAH.
OH.
HUH.
UM, IS THAT COOL? IS IT OKAY THAT I TOLD YOU?
IT'S COOL...
I GUESS I WAS NEVER REALLY SURE IF ANYONE I KNEW WAS ACTUALLY... UM...
GAY? YOU CAN SAY IT! I DON'T MIND.

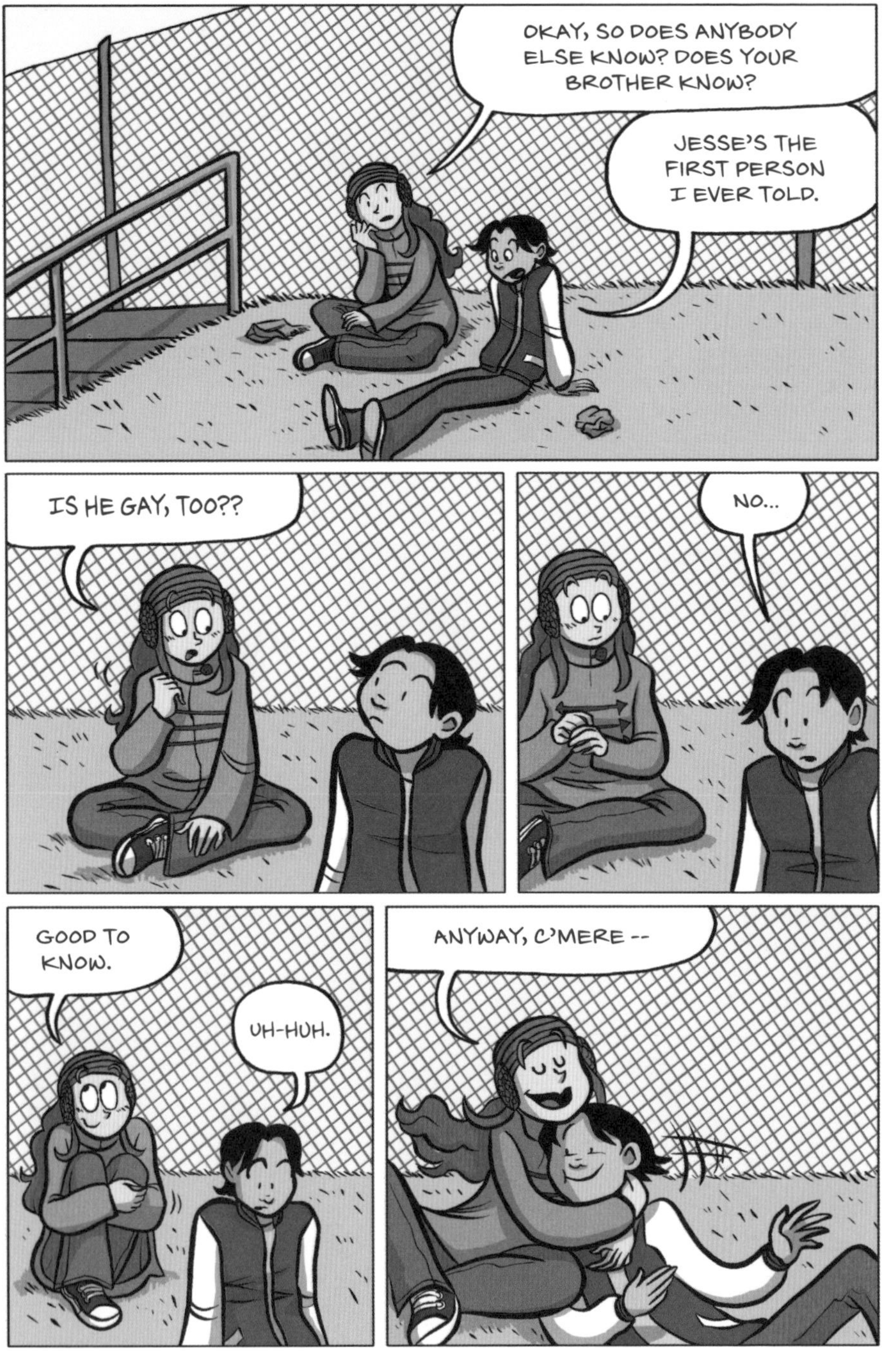

OKAY, SO DOES ANYBODY ELSE KNOW? DOES YOUR BROTHER KNOW?
JESSE'S THE FIRST PERSON I EVER TOLD.
IS HE GAY, TOO??
NO...
GOOD TO KNOW.
UH-HUH.
ANYWAY, C'MERE --

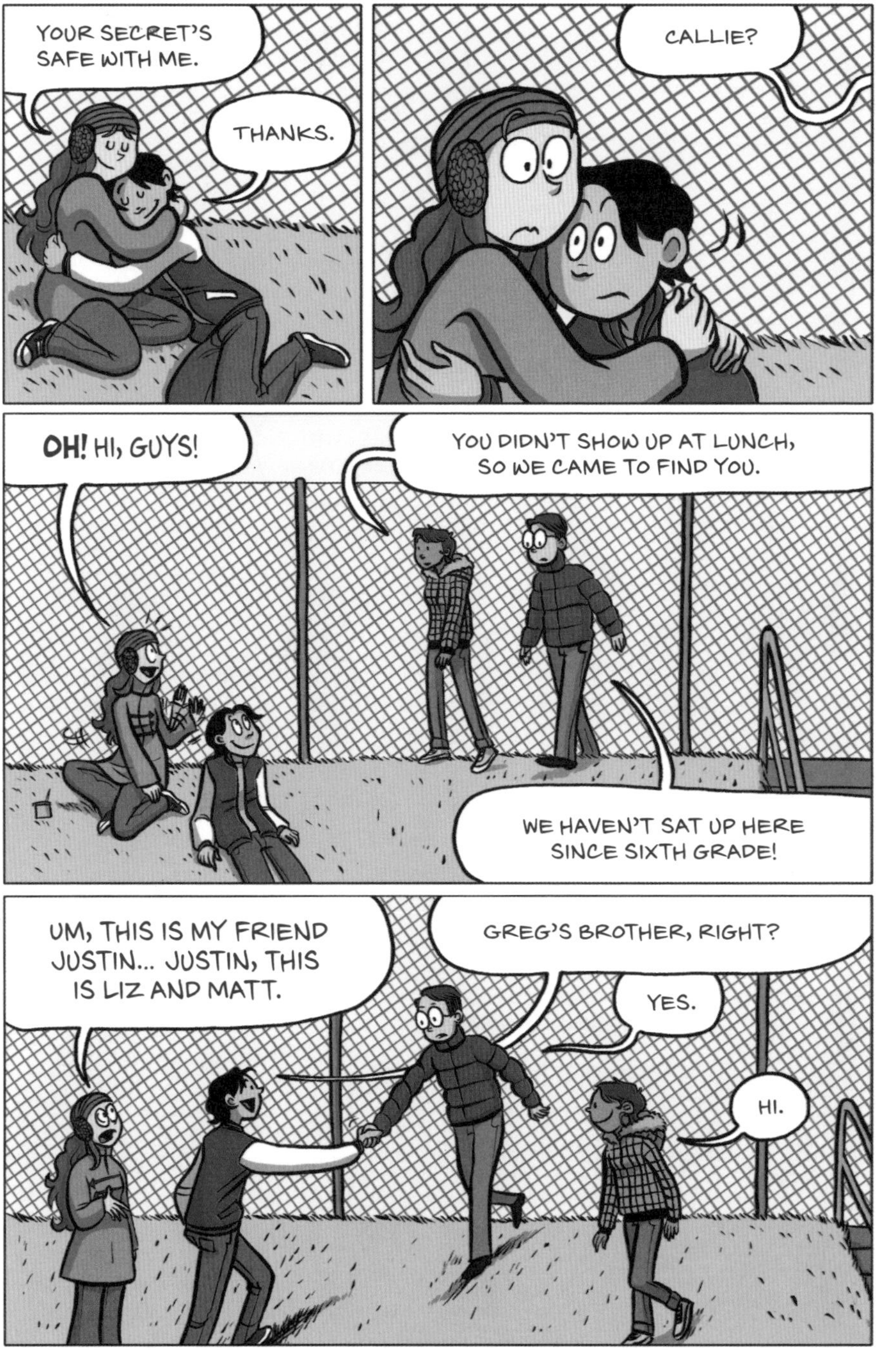
YOUR SECRET'S SAFE WITH ME.
THANKS.
CALLIE?
OH! HI, GUYS!
YOU DIDN'T SHOW UP AT LUNCH, SO WE CAME TO FIND YOU.
WE HAVEN'T SAT UP HERE SINCE SIXTH GRADE!
UM, THIS IS MY FRIEND JUSTIN... JUSTIN, THIS IS LIZ AND MATT.
GREG'S BROTHER, RIGHT?
YES.
HI.

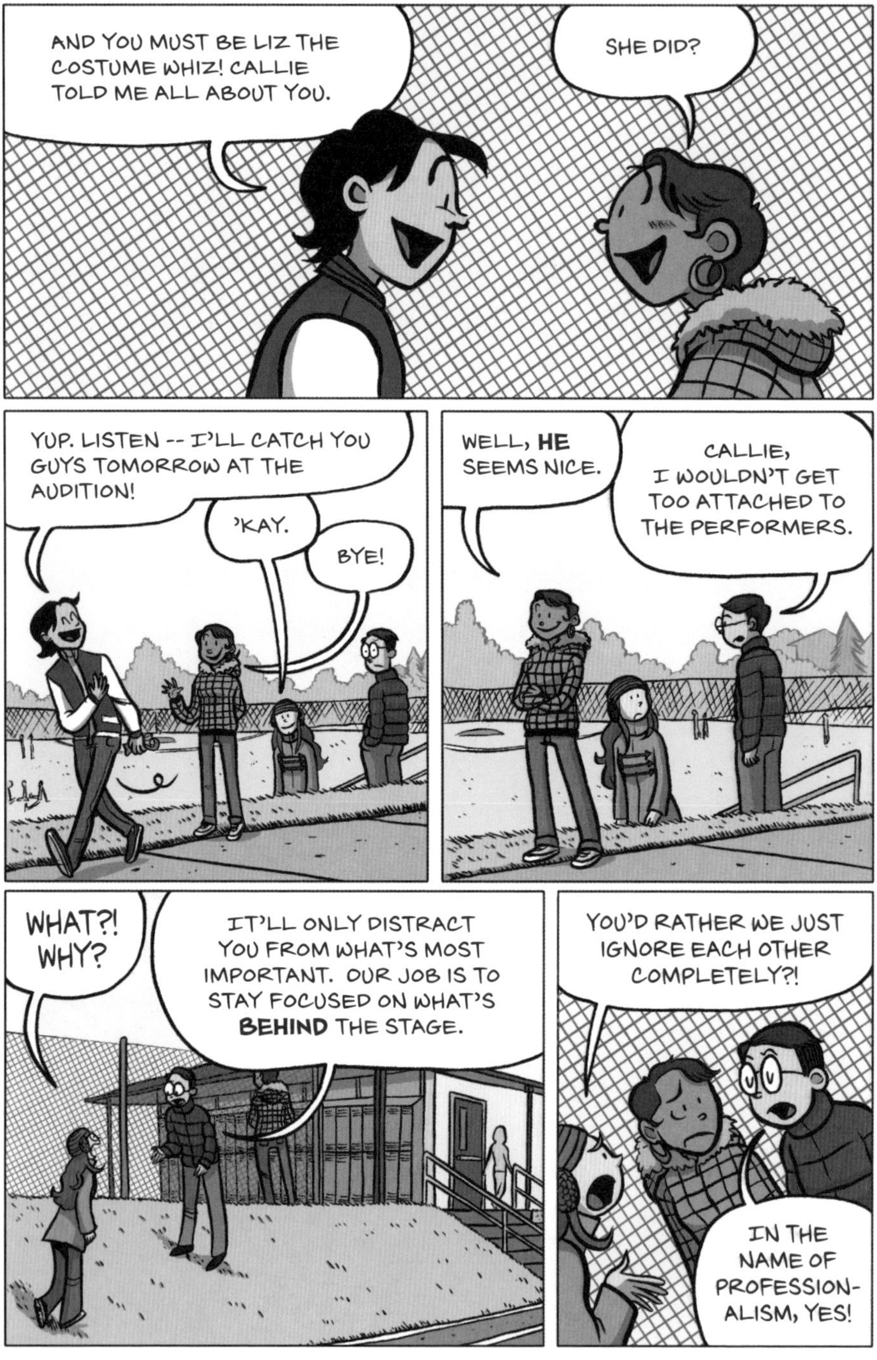
AND YOU MUST BE LIZ THE COSTUME WHIZ! CALLIE TOLD ME ALL ABOUT YOU.
SHE DID?
YUP. LISTEN -- I'LL CATCH YOU GUYS TOMORROW AT THE AUDITION!
'KAY.
BYE!
WELL, **HE** SEEMS NICE.
CALLIE, I WOULDN'T GET TOO ATTACHED TO THE PERFORMERS.
WHAT?! WHY?
IT'LL ONLY DISTRACT YOU FROM WHAT'S MOST IMPORTANT. OUR JOB IS TO STAY FOCUSED ON WHAT'S **BEHIND** THE STAGE.
YOU'D RATHER WE JUST IGNORE EACH OTHER COMPLETELY?!
IN THE NAME OF PROFESSION-ALISM, YES!

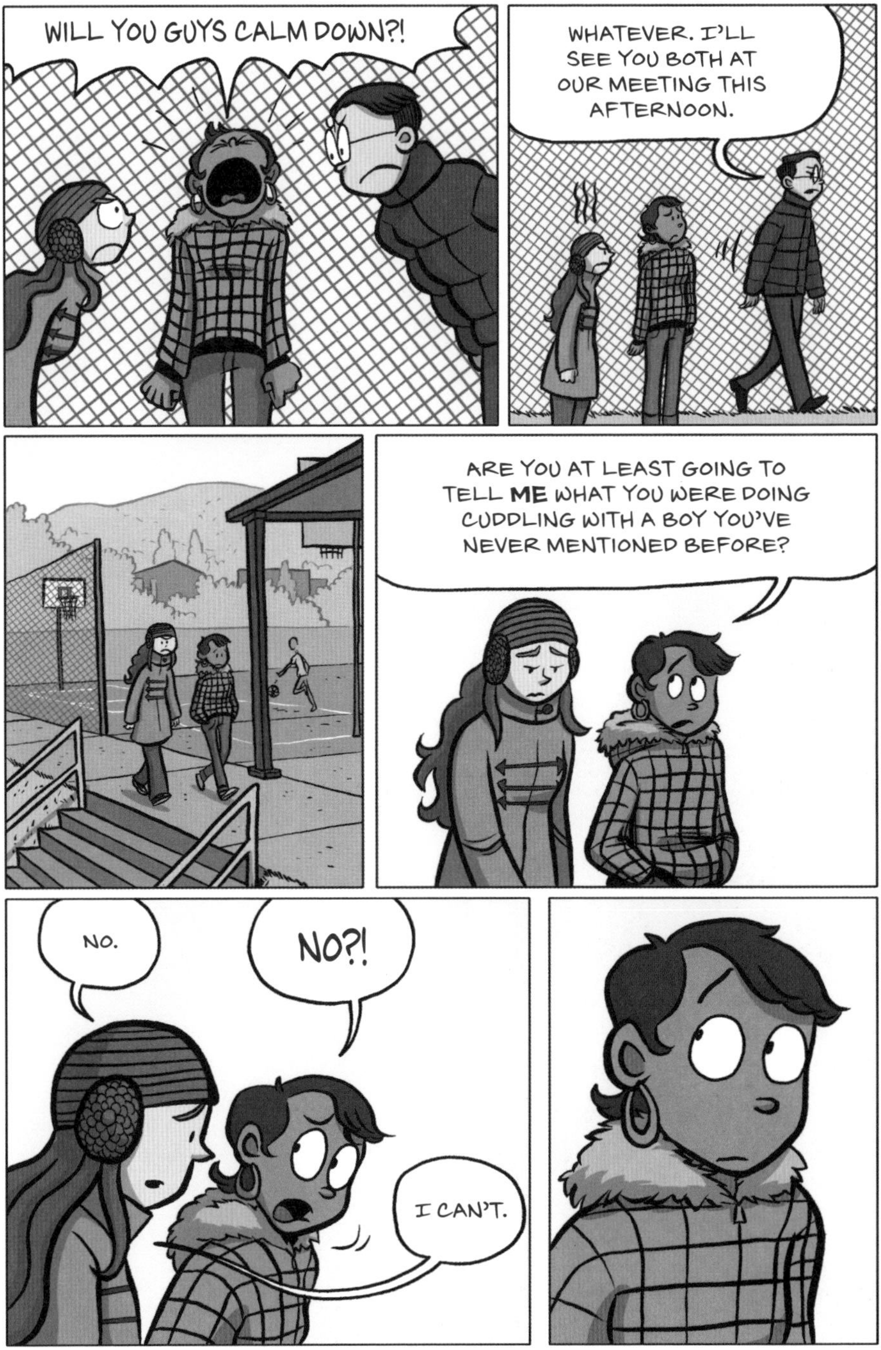
WILL YOU GUYS CALM DOWN?!
WHATEVER. I'LL SEE YOU BOTH AT OUR MEETING THIS AFTERNOON.
ARE YOU AT LEAST GOING TO TELL **ME** WHAT YOU WERE DOING CUDDLING WITH A BOY YOU'VE NEVER MENTIONED BEFORE?
NO.
NO?!
I CAN'T.

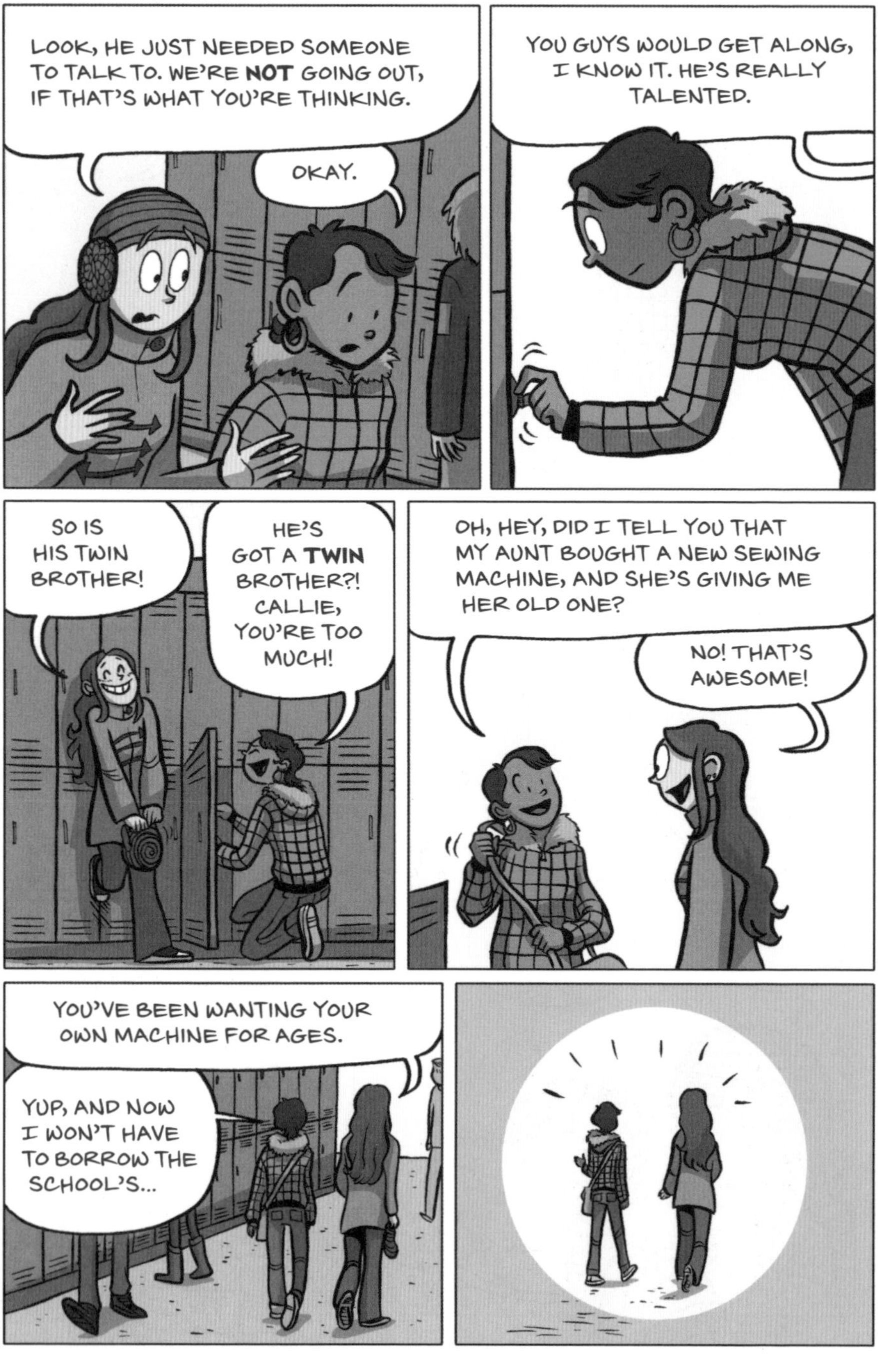
LOOK, HE JUST NEEDED SOMEONE TO TALK TO. WE'RE **NOT** GOING OUT, IF THAT'S WHAT YOU'RE THINKING.
OKAY.
YOU GUYS WOULD GET ALONG, I KNOW IT. HE'S REALLY TALENTED.
SO IS HIS TWIN BROTHER!
HE'S GOT A **TWIN** BROTHER?! CALLIE, YOU'RE TOO MUCH!
OH, HEY, DID I TELL YOU THAT MY AUNT BOUGHT A NEW SEWING MACHINE, AND SHE'S GIVING ME HER OLD ONE?
NO! THAT'S AWESOME!
YOU'VE BEEN WANTING YOUR OWN MACHINE FOR AGES.
YUP, AND NOW I WON'T HAVE TO BORROW THE SCHOOL'S...

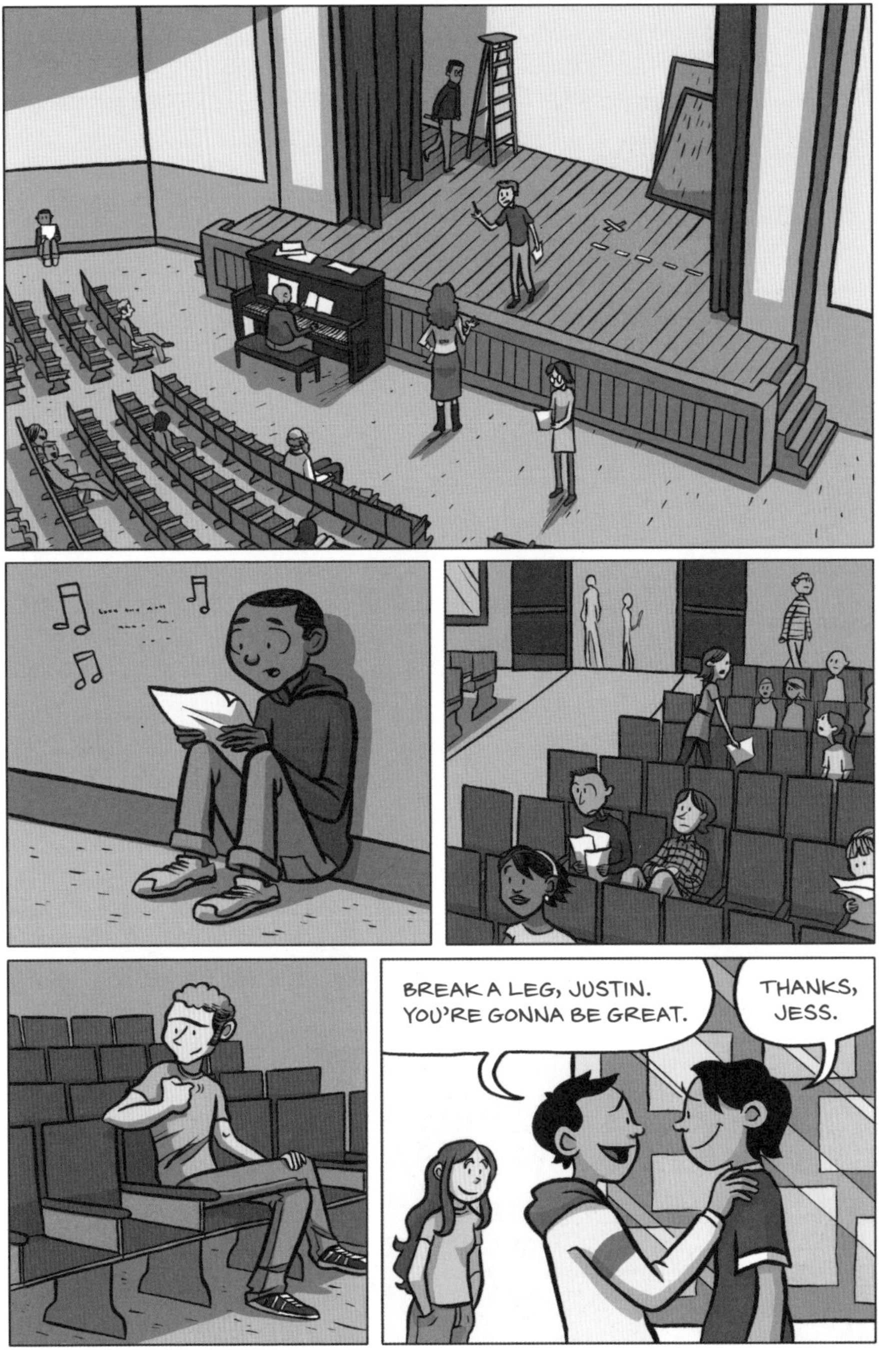
BREAK A LEG, JUSTIN. YOU'RE GONNA BE GREAT.
THANKS, JESS.

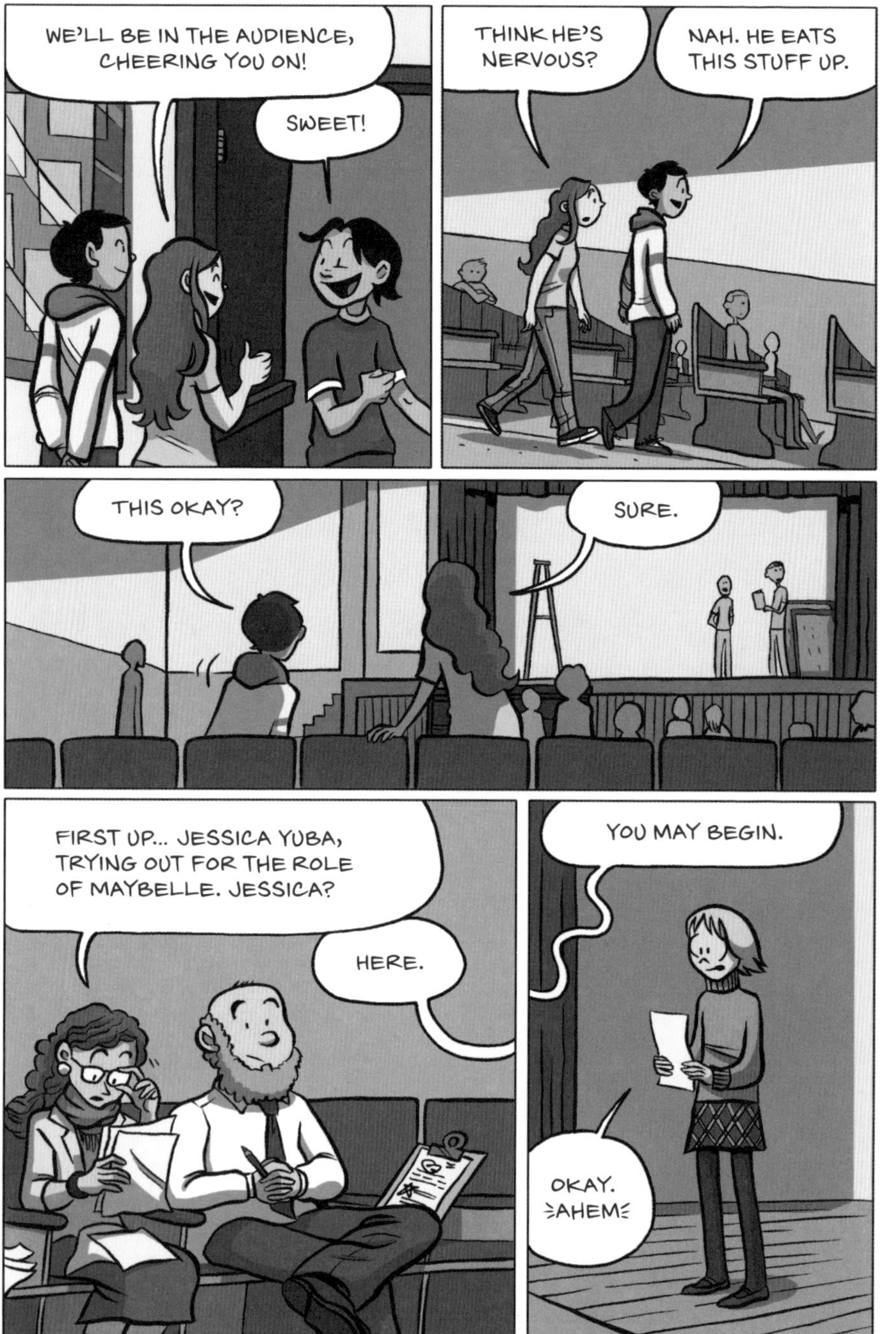
WE'LL BE IN THE AUDIENCE, CHEERING YOU ON!
SWEET!
THINK HE'S NERVOUS?
NAH. HE EATS THIS STUFF UP.
THIS OKAY?
SURE.
FIRST UP... JESSICA YUBA, TRYING OUT FOR THE ROLE OF MAYBELLE. JESSICA?
HERE.
YOU MAY BEGIN.
OKAY.
AHEM

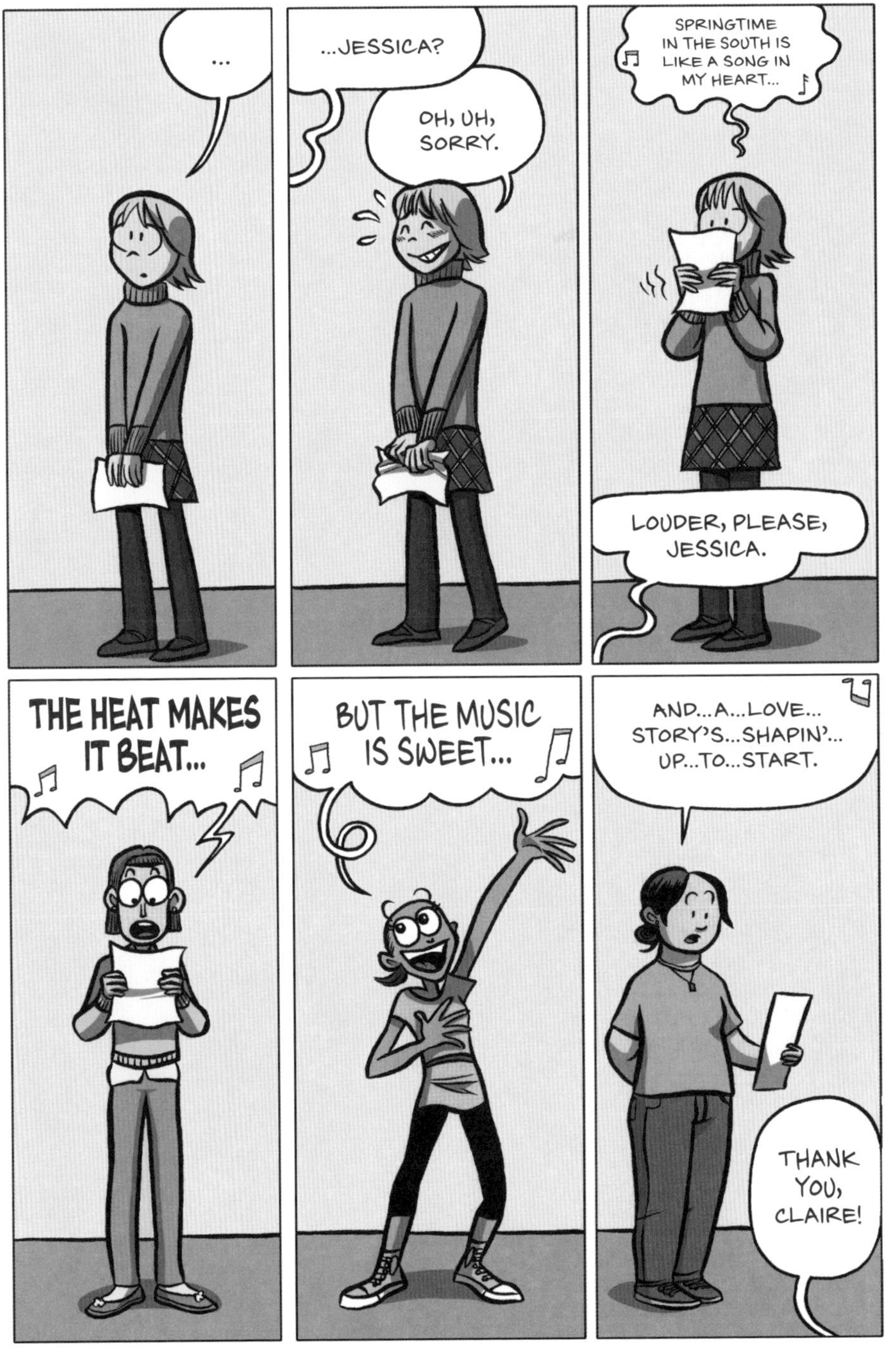
...
...JESSICA?
OH, UH, SORRY.
SPRINGTIME IN THE SOUTH IS LIKE A SONG IN MY HEART...
LOUDER, PLEASE, JESSICA.
THE HEAT MAKES IT BEAT...
BUT THE MUSIC IS SWEET...
AND...A...LOVE... STORY'S...SHAPIN'... UP...TO...START.
THANK YOU, CLAIRE!

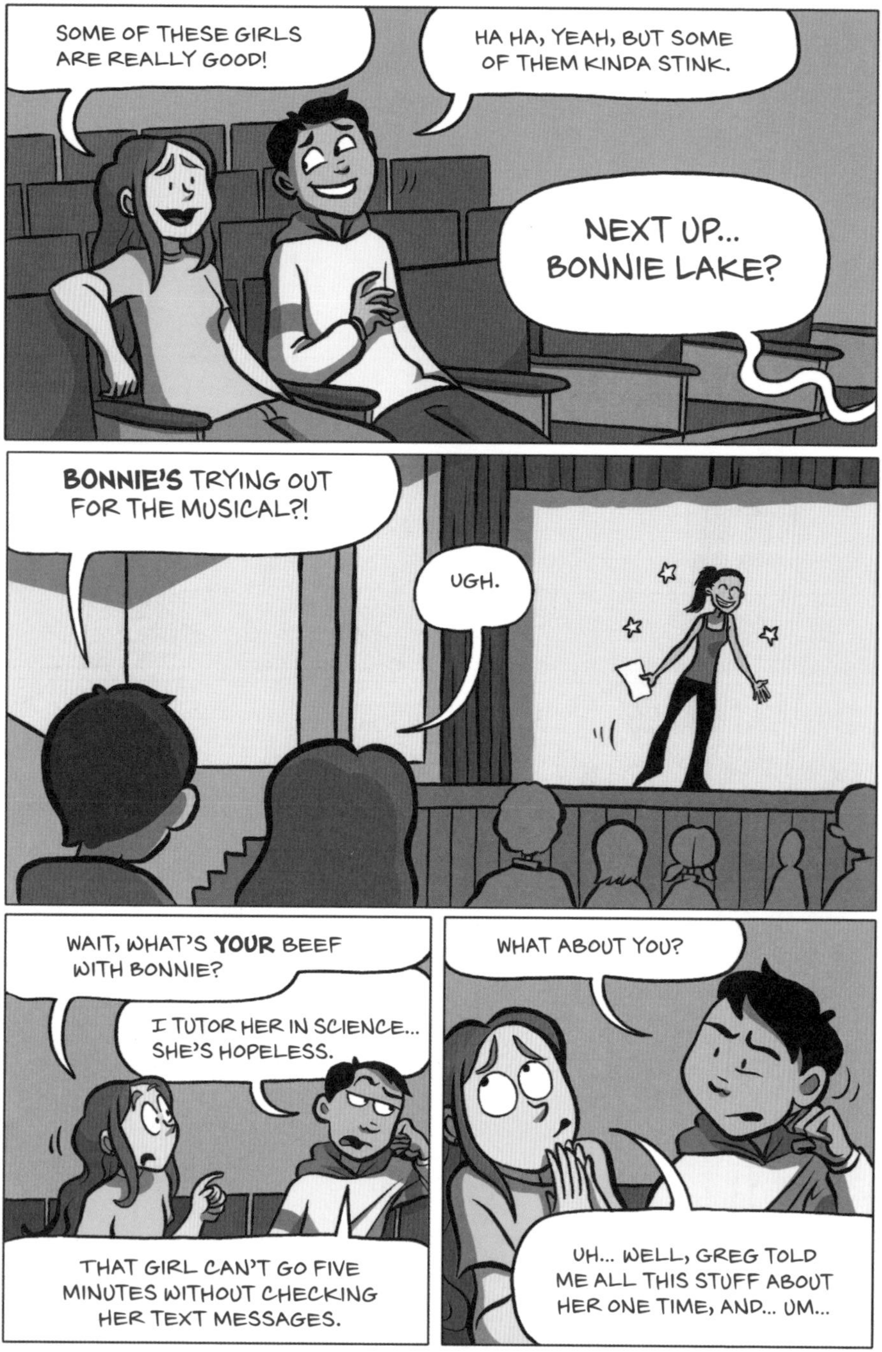
SOME OF THESE GIRLS ARE REALLY GOOD!
HA HA, YEAH, BUT SOME OF THEM KINDA STINK.
NEXT UP... BONNIE LAKE?
BONNIE'S TRYING OUT FOR THE MUSICAL?!
UGH.
WAIT, WHAT'S YOUR BEEF WITH BONNIE?
I TUTOR HER IN SCIENCE... SHE'S HOPELESS.
THAT GIRL CAN'T GO FIVE MINUTES WITHOUT CHECKING HER TEXT MESSAGES.
WHAT ABOUT YOU?
UH... WELL, GREG TOLD ME ALL THIS STUFF ABOUT HER ONE TIME, AND... UM...

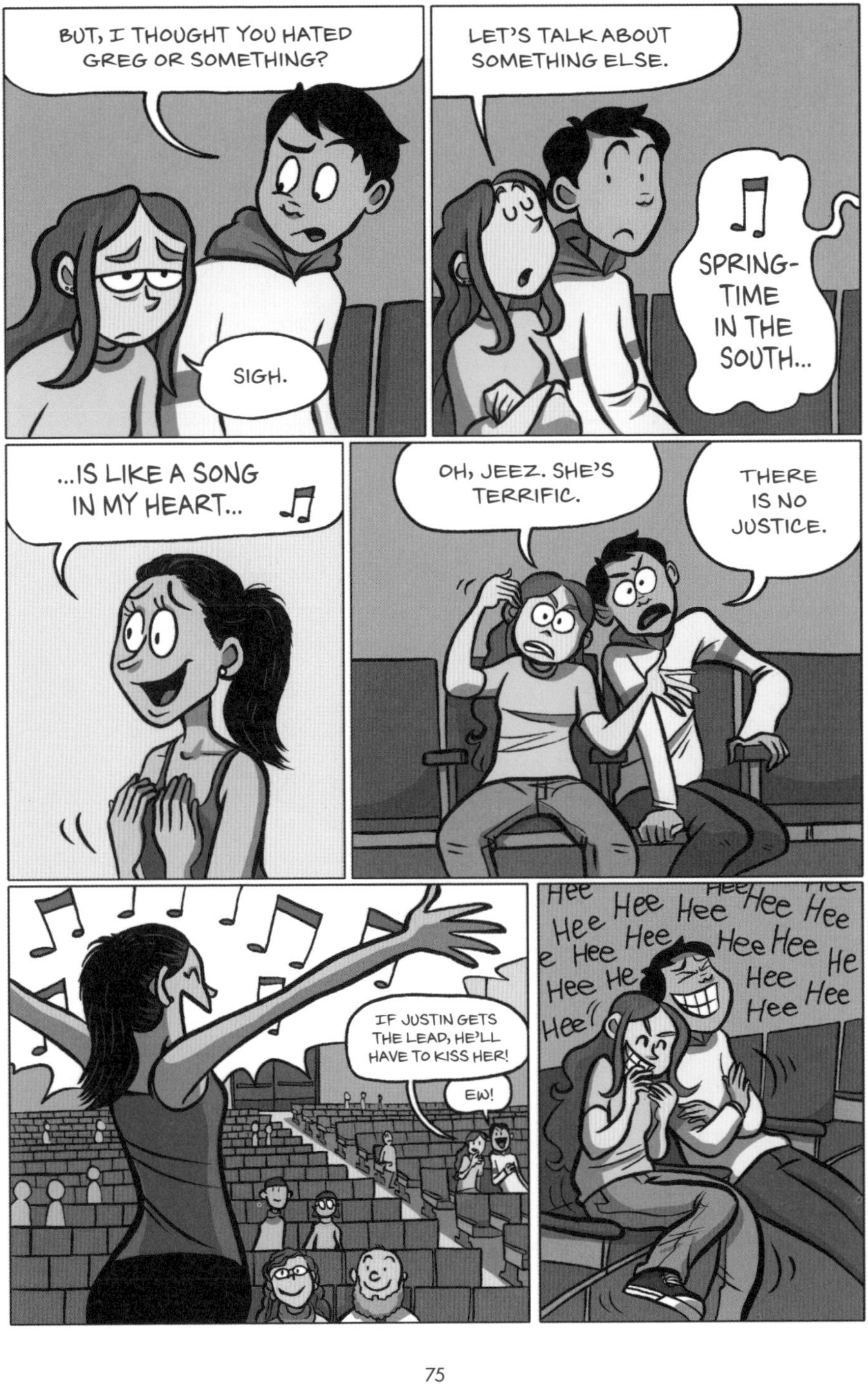
BUT, I THOUGHT YOU HATED GREG OR SOMETHING?
SIGH.
LET'S TALK ABOUT SOMETHING ELSE.
SPRING-TIME IN THE SOUTH...
...IS LIKE A SONG IN MY HEART...
OH, JEEZ. SHE'S TERRIFIC.
THERE IS NO JUSTICE.
IF JUSTIN GETS THE LEAD, HE'LL HAVE TO KISS HER!
EW!
Hee Hee Hee Hee Hee Hee Hee Hee Hee Hee Hee Hee Hee Hee Hee Hee

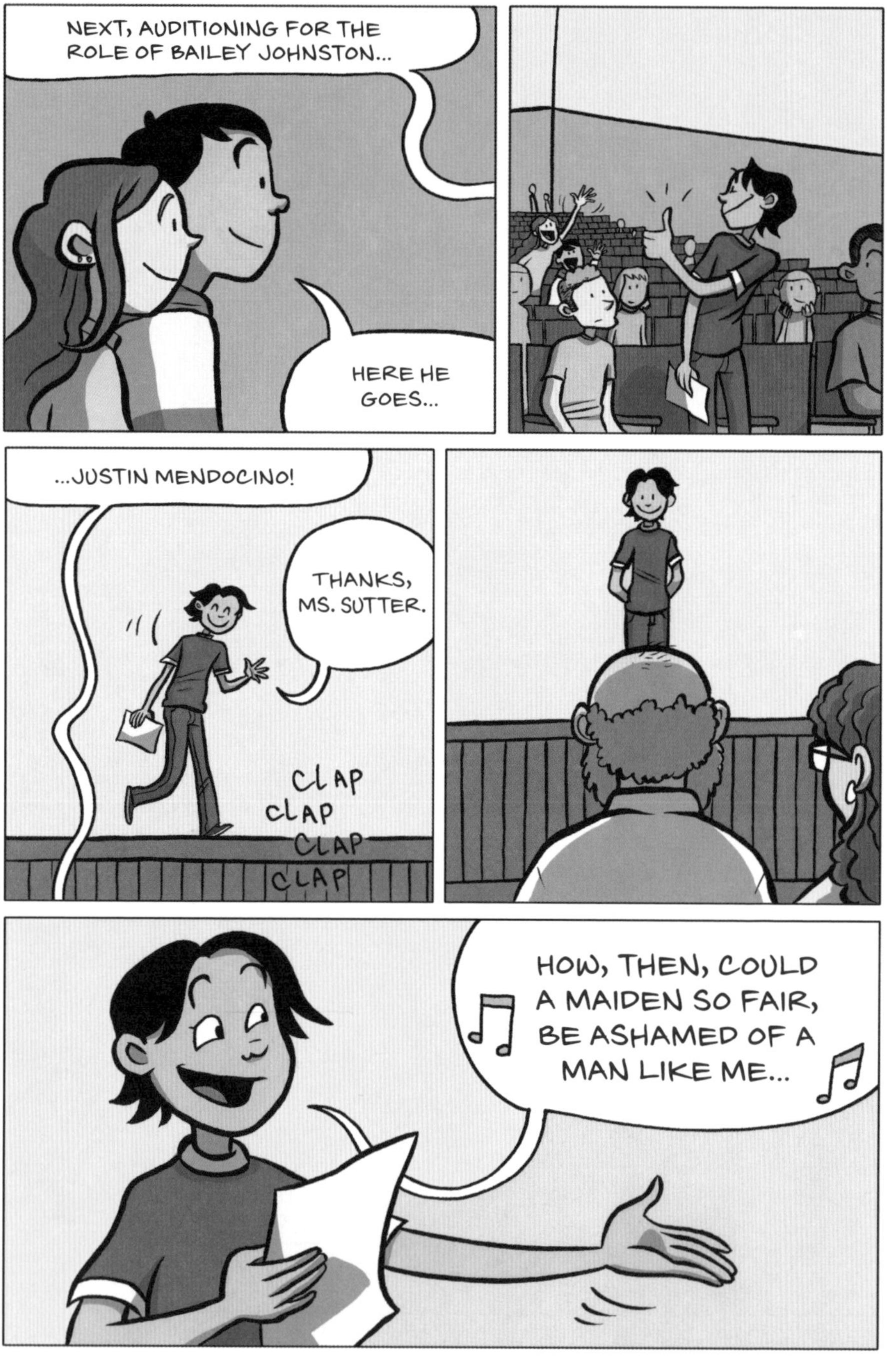
NEXT, AUDITIONING FOR THE ROLE OF BAILEY JOHNSTON...
HERE HE GOES...
...JUSTIN MENDOCINO!
THANKS, MS. SUTTER.
CLAP
CLAP
CLAP
CLAP
HOW, THEN, COULD A MAIDEN SO FAIR, BE ASHAMED OF A MAN LIKE ME...

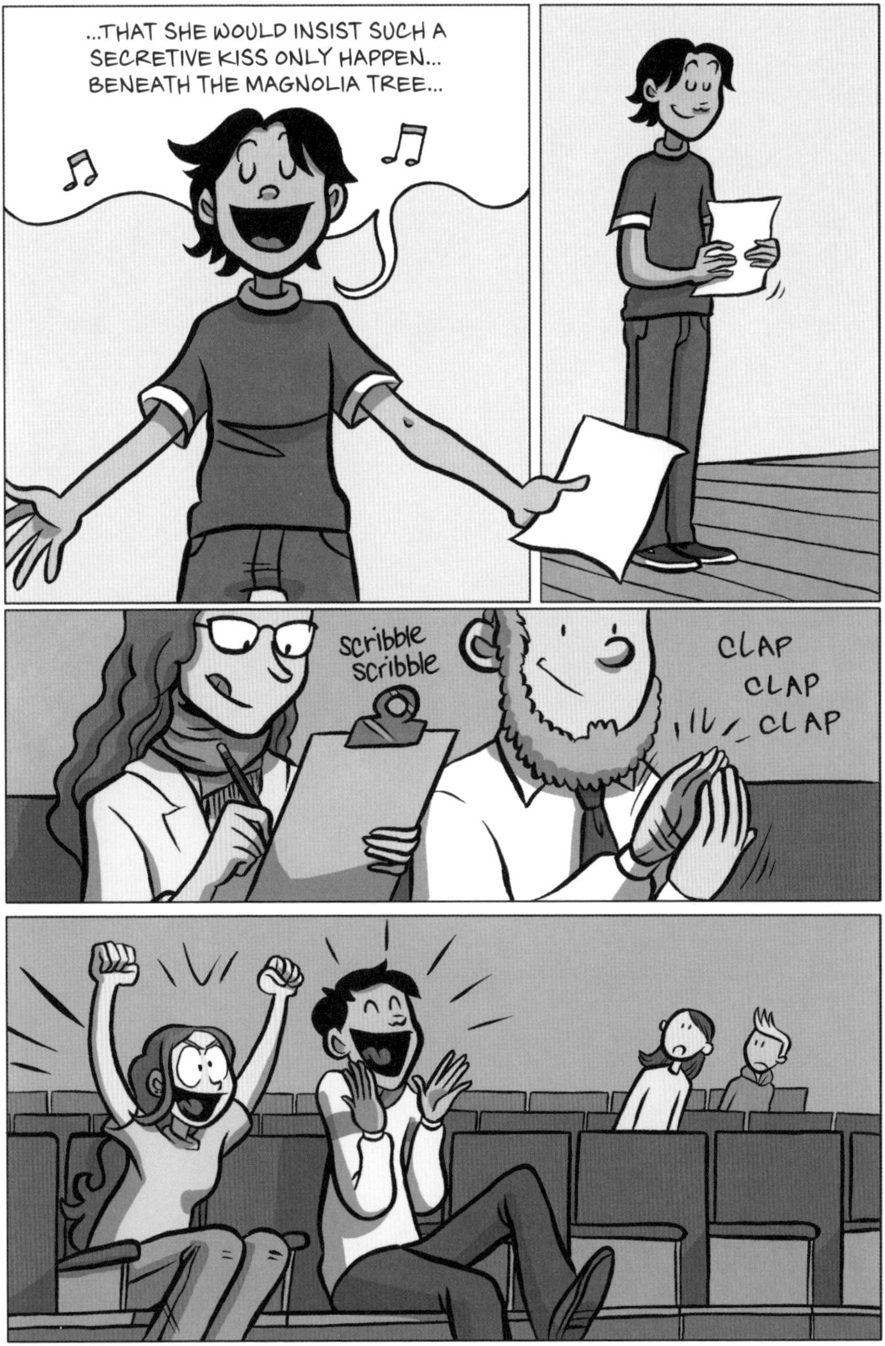
...THAT SHE WOULD INSIST SUCH A SECRETIVE KISS ONLY HAPPEN... BENEATH THE MAGNOLIA TREE...
scribble scribble
CLAP CLAP CLAP

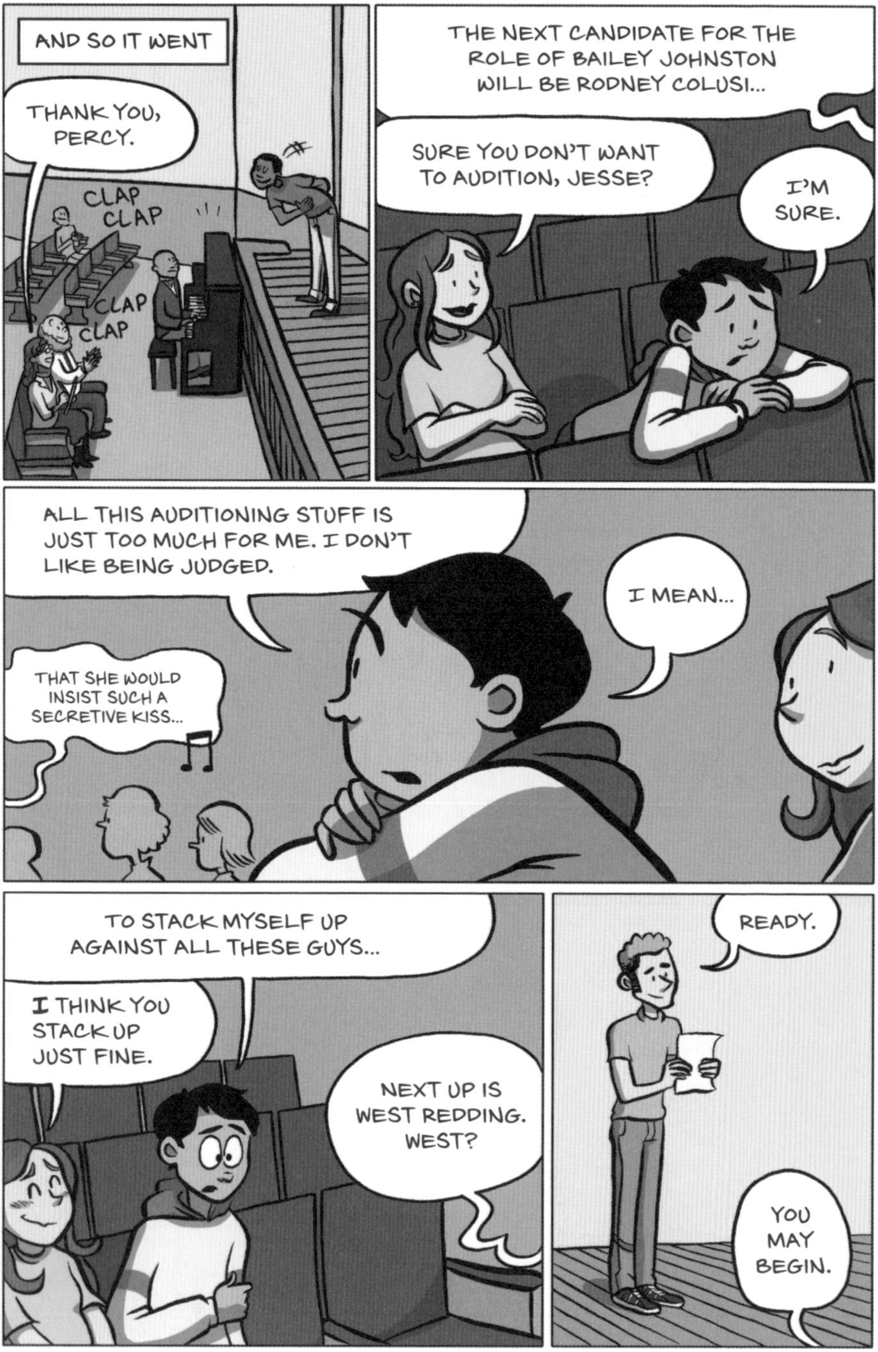
AND SO IT WENT
THANK YOU, PERCY.
CLAP CLAP
CLAP CLAP
THE NEXT CANDIDATE FOR THE ROLE OF BAILEY JOHNSTON WILL BE RODNEY COLUSI...
SURE YOU DON'T WANT TO AUDITION, JESSE?
I'M SURE.
ALL THIS AUDITIONING STUFF IS JUST TOO MUCH FOR ME. I DON'T LIKE BEING JUDGED.
I MEAN...
THAT SHE WOULD INSIST SUCH A SECRETIVE KISS...
TO STACK MYSELF UP AGAINST ALL THESE GUYS...
I THINK YOU STACK UP JUST FINE.
NEXT UP IS WEST REDDING. WEST?
READY.
YOU MAY BEGIN.

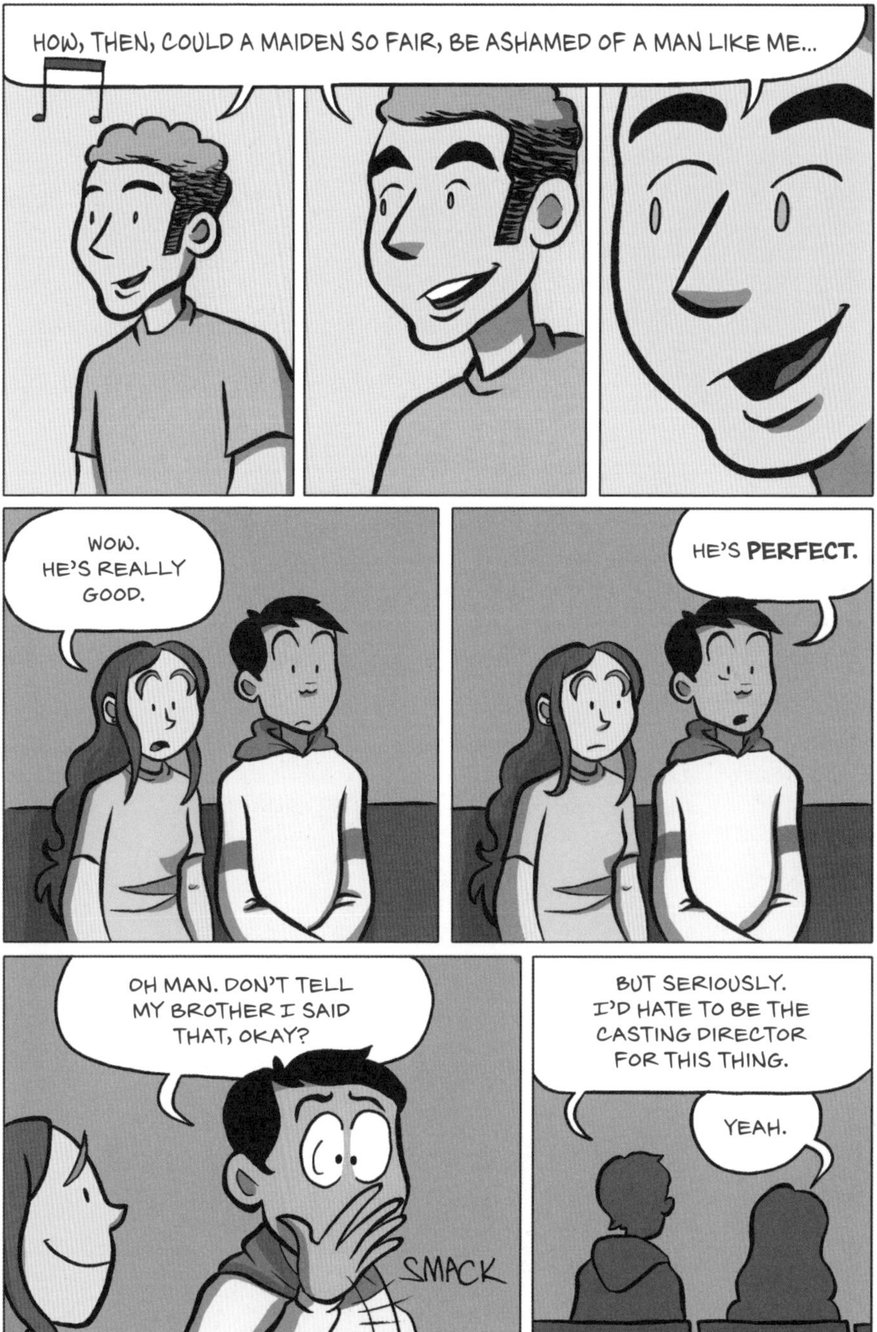

HOW, THEN, COULD A MAIDEN SO FAIR, BE ASHAMED OF A MAN LIKE ME...
WOW. HE'S REALLY GOOD.
HE'S **PERFECT.**
OH MAN. DON'T TELL MY BROTHER I SAID THAT, OKAY?
SMACK
BUT SERIOUSLY. I'D HATE TO BE THE CASTING DIRECTOR FOR THIS THING.
YEAH.

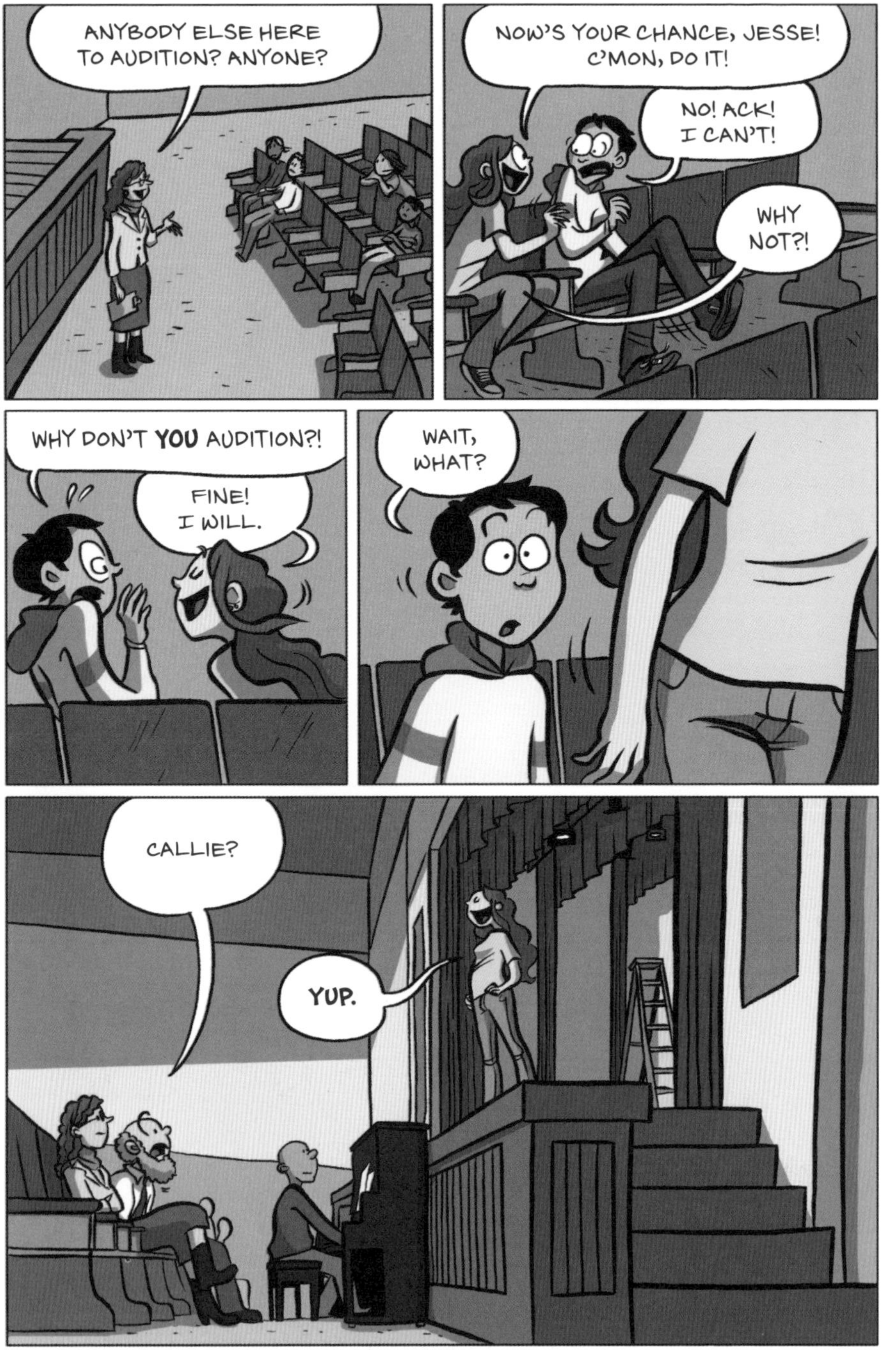
ANYBODY ELSE HERE TO AUDITION? ANYONE?
NOW'S YOUR CHANCE, JESSE! C'MON, DO IT!
NO! ACK! I CAN'T!
WHY NOT?!
WHY DON'T **YOU** AUDITION?!
FINE! I WILL.
WAIT, WHAT?
CALLIE?
YUP.

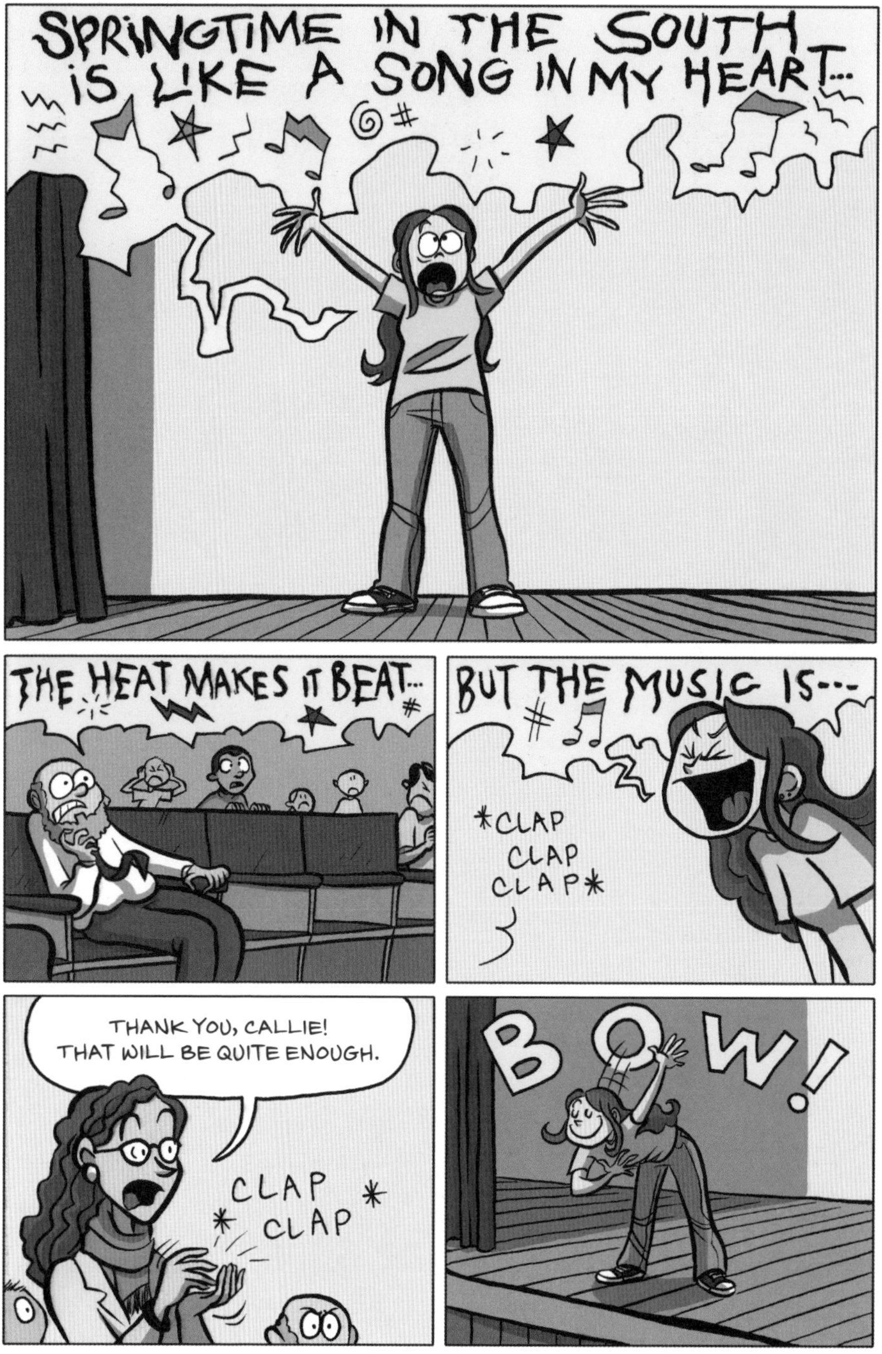
SPRINGTIME IN THE SOUTH IS LIKE A SONG IN MY HEART...
THE HEAT MAKES IT BEAT...
BUT THE MUSIC IS---
CLAP CLAP CLAP
THANK YOU, CALLIE! THAT WILL BE QUITE ENOUGH.
CLAP CLAP
BOW!

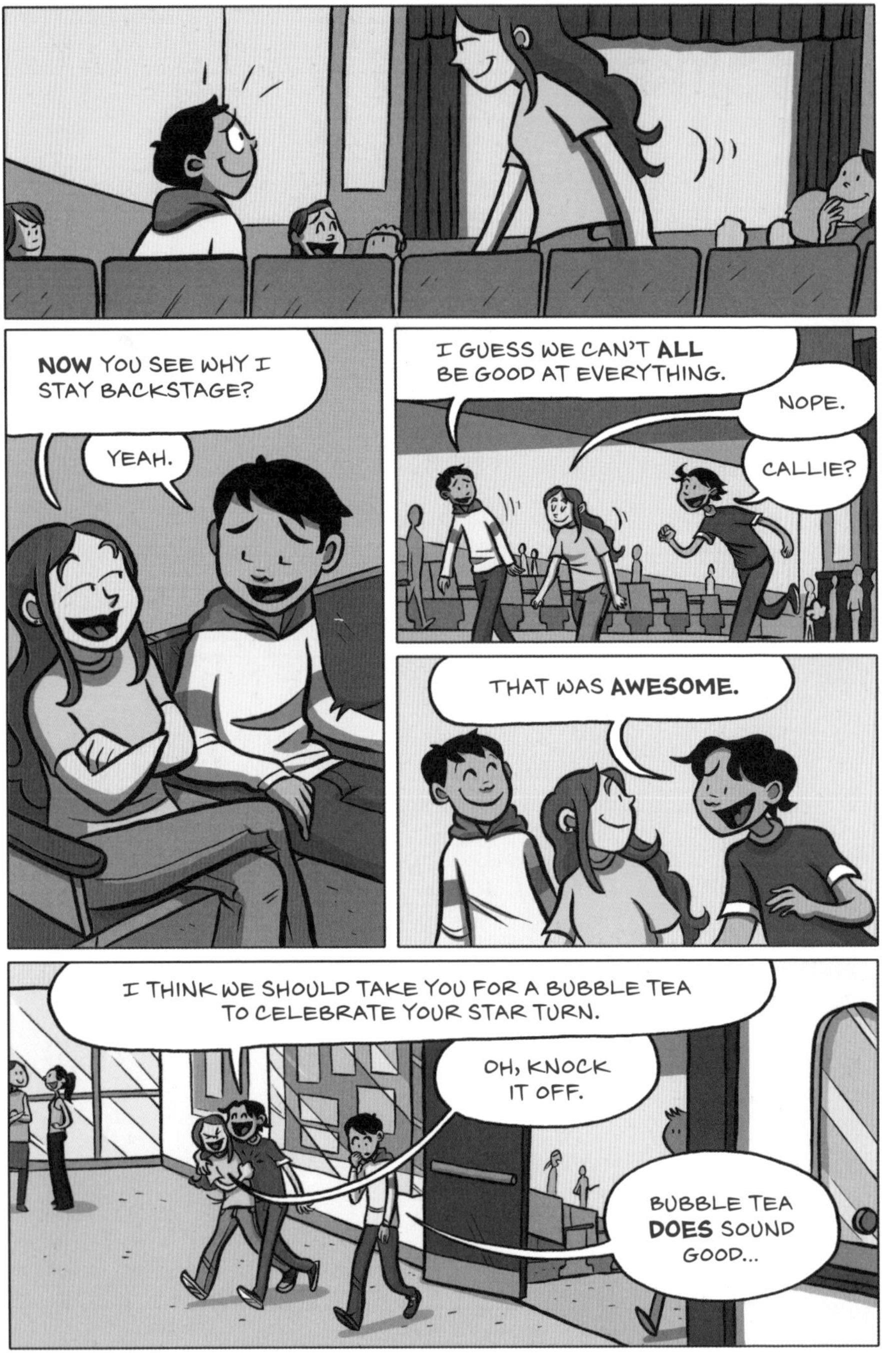
NOW YOU SEE WHY I STAY BACKSTAGE?
YEAH.
I GUESS WE CAN'T ALL BE GOOD AT EVERYTHING.
NOPE.
CALLIE?
THAT WAS AWESOME.
I THINK WE SHOULD TAKE YOU FOR A BUBBLE TEA TO CELEBRATE YOUR STAR TURN.
OH, KNOCK IT OFF.
BUBBLE TEA DOES SOUND GOOD...

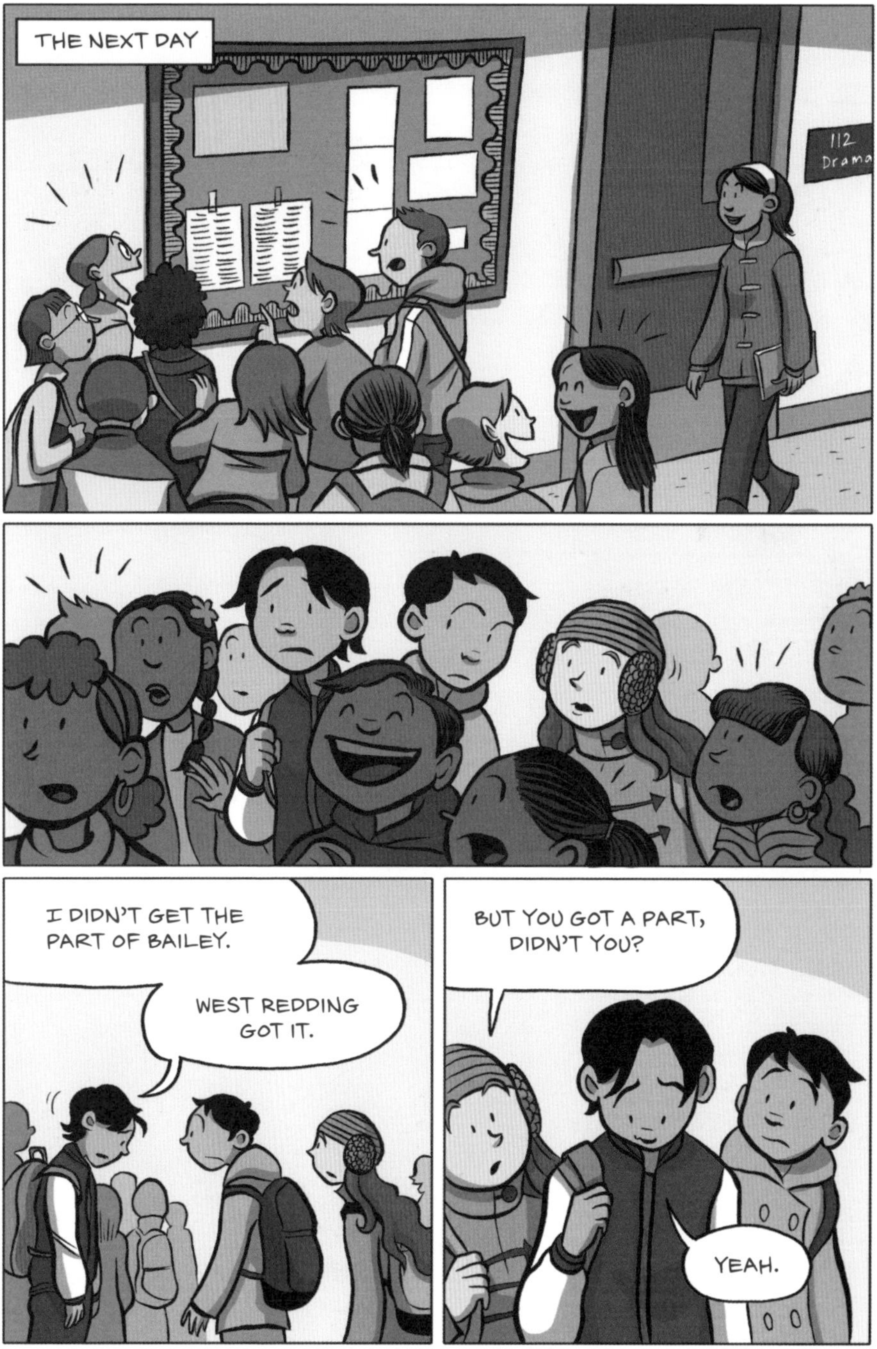
THE NEXT DAY
112
Drama
I DIDN'T GET THE PART OF BAILEY.
WEST REDDING GOT IT.
BUT YOU GOT A PART, DIDN'T YOU?
YEAH.

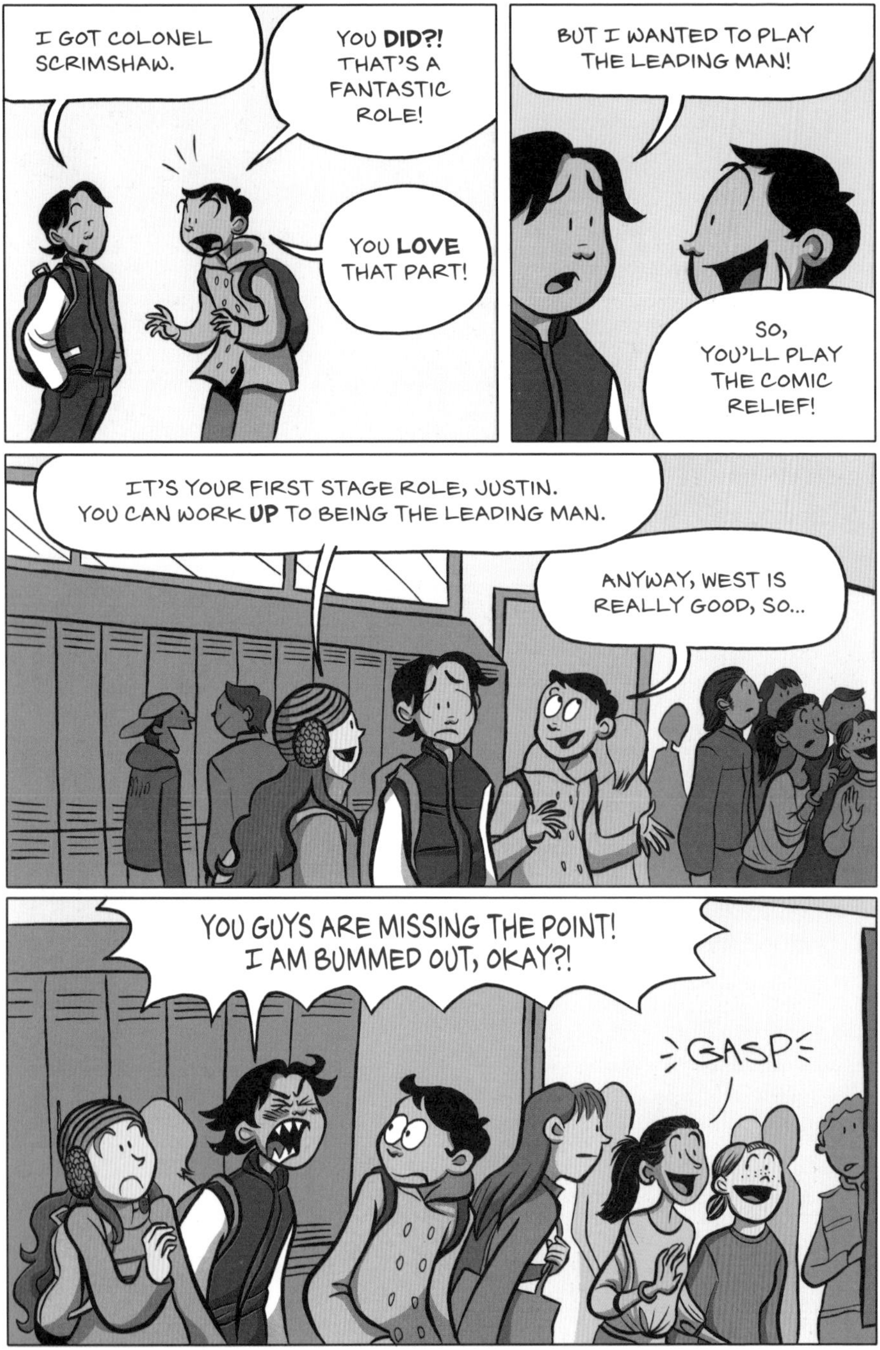
I GOT COLONEL SCRIMSHAW.
YOU **DID?!** THAT'S A FANTASTIC ROLE!
YOU **LOVE** THAT PART!
BUT I WANTED TO PLAY THE LEADING MAN!
SO, YOU'LL PLAY THE COMIC RELIEF!
IT'S YOUR FIRST STAGE ROLE, JUSTIN. YOU CAN WORK **UP** TO BEING THE LEADING MAN.
ANYWAY, WEST IS REALLY GOOD, SO...
YOU GUYS ARE MISSING THE POINT! I AM BUMMED OUT, OKAY?!
GASP

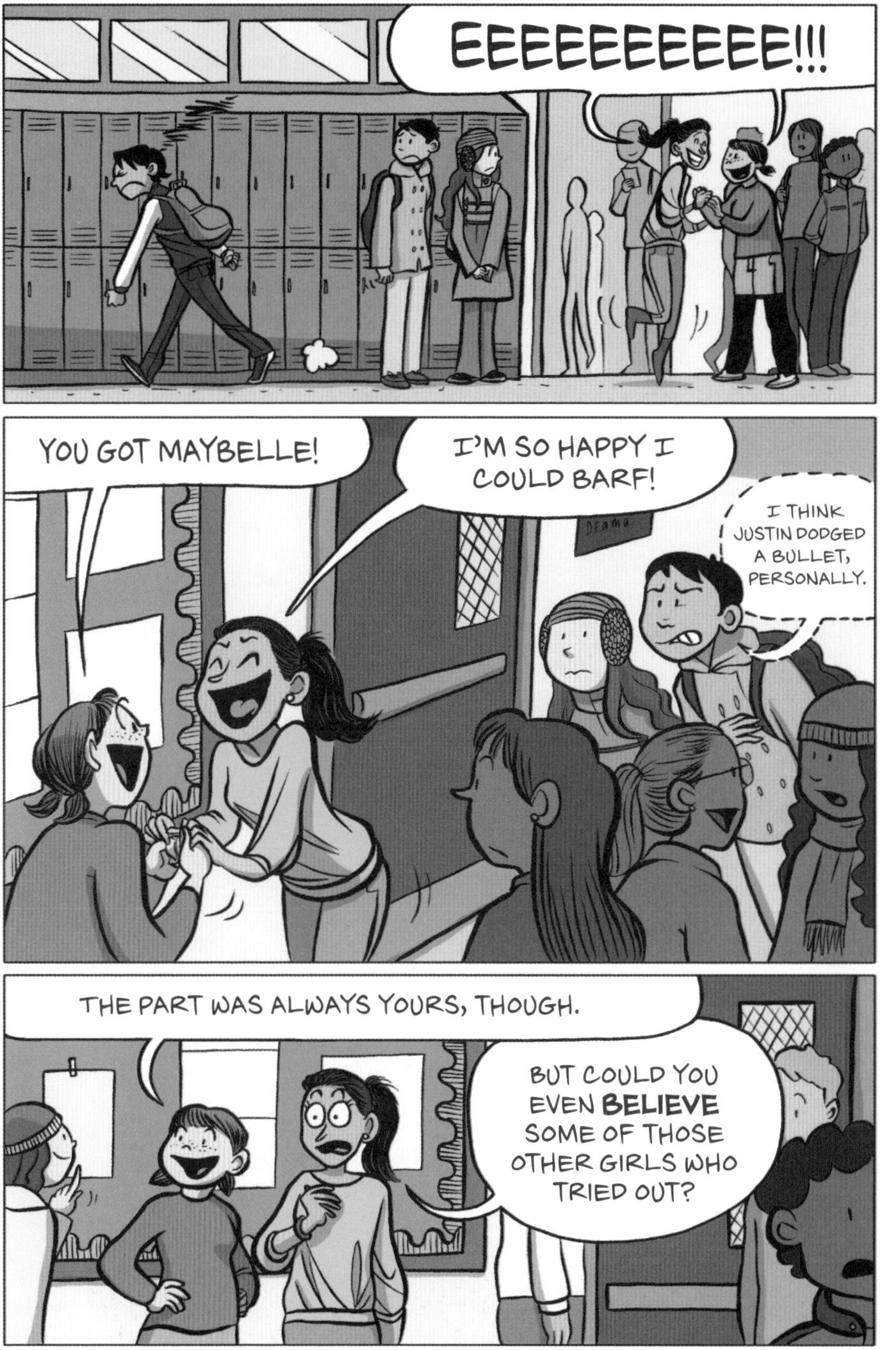
EEEEEEEEEEE!!!
YOU GOT MAYBELLE!
I'M SO HAPPY I COULD BARF!
I THINK JUSTIN DODGED A BULLET, PERSONALLY.
THE PART WAS ALWAYS YOURS, THOUGH.
BUT COULD YOU EVEN **BELIEVE** SOME OF THOSE OTHER GIRLS WHO TRIED OUT?

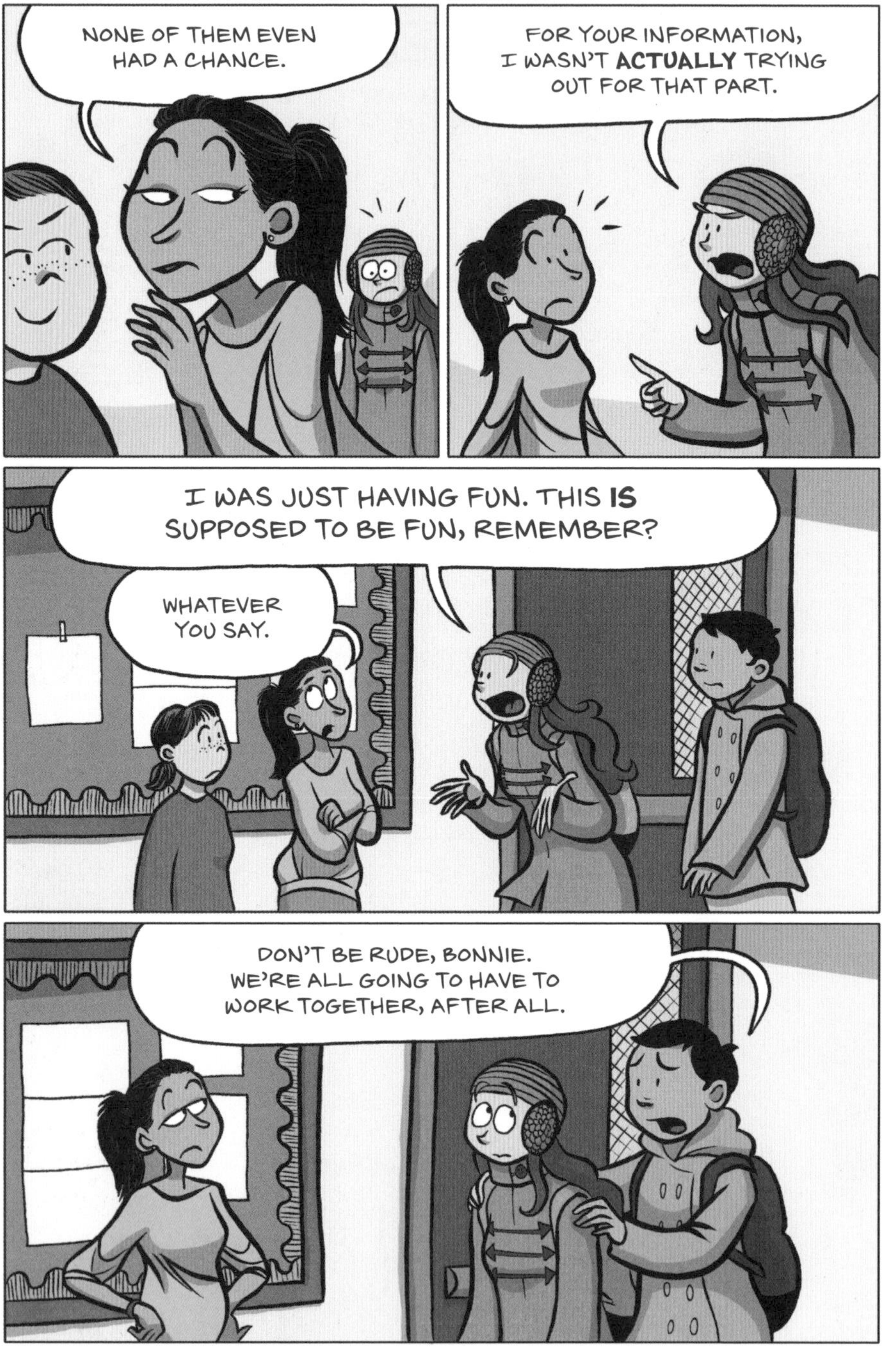
NONE OF THEM EVEN HAD A CHANCE.
FOR YOUR INFORMATION, I WASN'T ACTUALLY TRYING OUT FOR THAT PART.
I WAS JUST HAVING FUN. THIS IS SUPPOSED TO BE FUN, REMEMBER?
WHATEVER YOU SAY.
DON'T BE RUDE, BONNIE. WE'RE ALL GOING TO HAVE TO WORK TOGETHER, AFTER ALL.

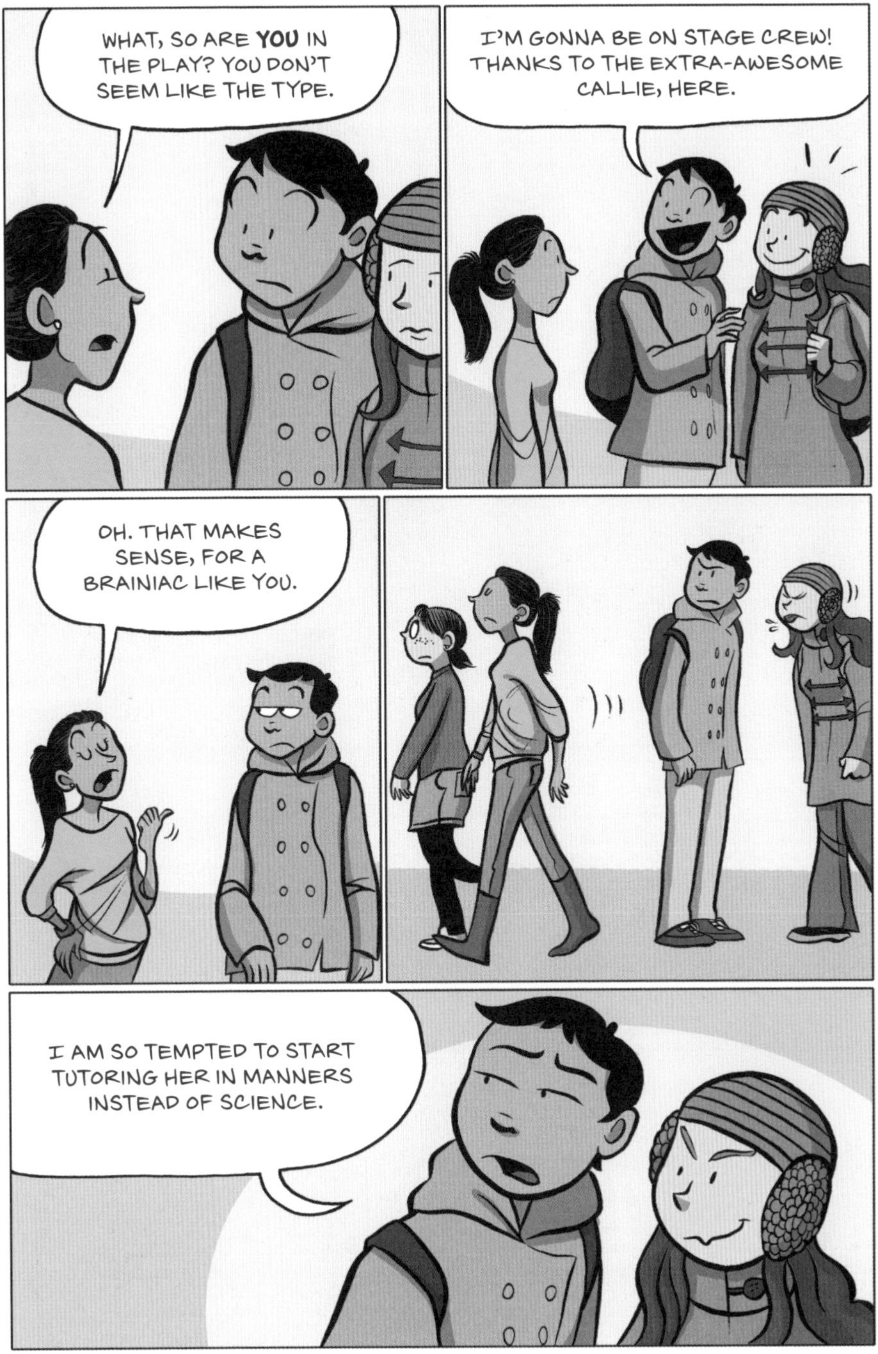
WHAT, SO ARE **YOU** IN THE PLAY? YOU DON'T SEEM LIKE THE TYPE.
I'M GONNA BE ON STAGE CREW! THANKS TO THE EXTRA-AWESOME CALLIE, HERE.
OH. THAT MAKES SENSE, FOR A BRAINIAC LIKE YOU.
I AM SO TEMPTED TO START TUTORING HER IN MANNERS INSTEAD OF SCIENCE.

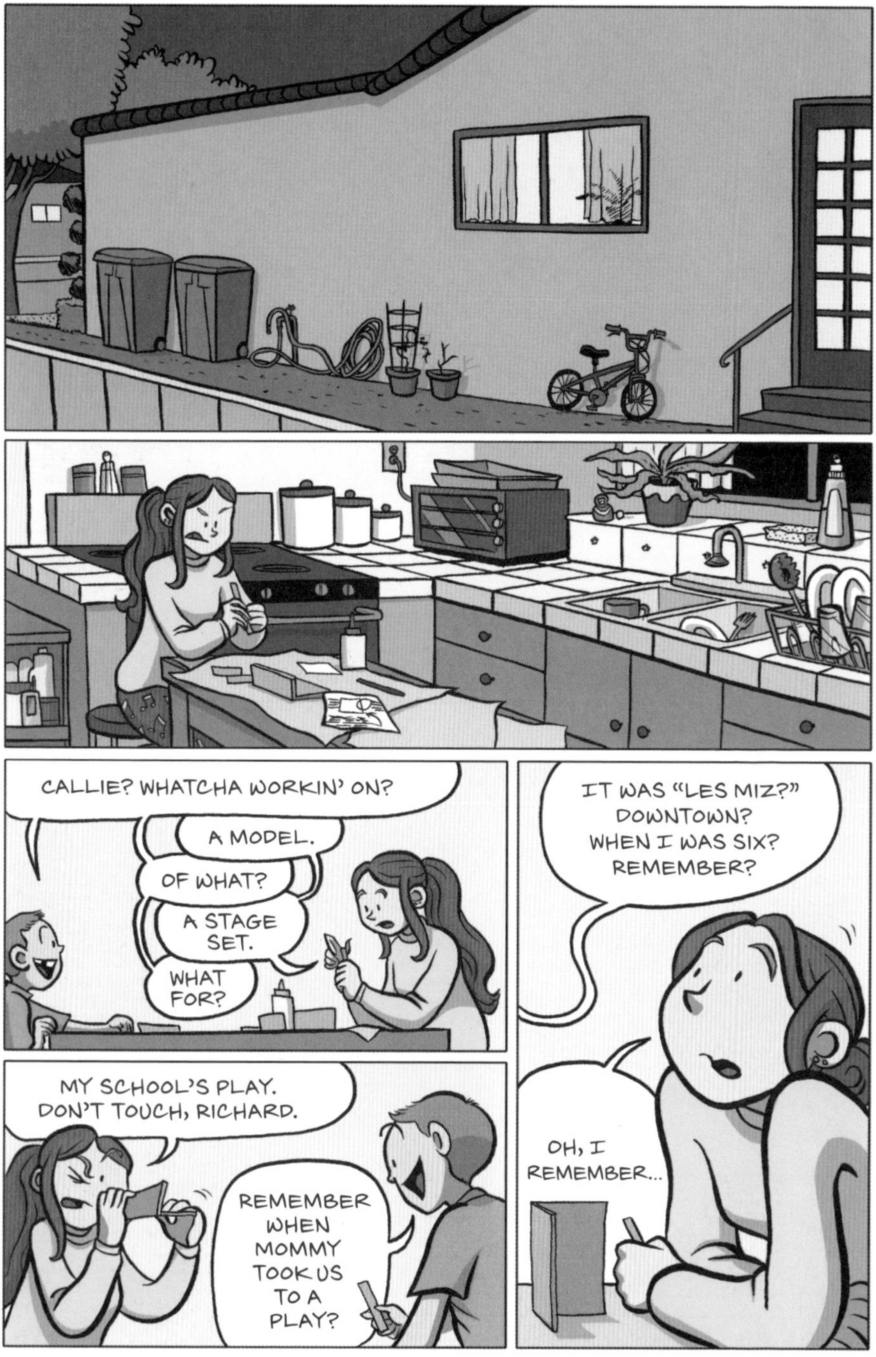
CALLIE? WHATCHA WORKIN' ON?
A MODEL.
OF WHAT?
A STAGE SET.
WHAT FOR?
IT WAS "LES MIZ?" DOWNTOWN? WHEN I WAS SIX? REMEMBER?
MY SCHOOL'S PLAY. DON'T TOUCH, RICHARD.
REMEMBER WHEN MOMMY TOOK US TO A PLAY?
OH, I REMEMBER...

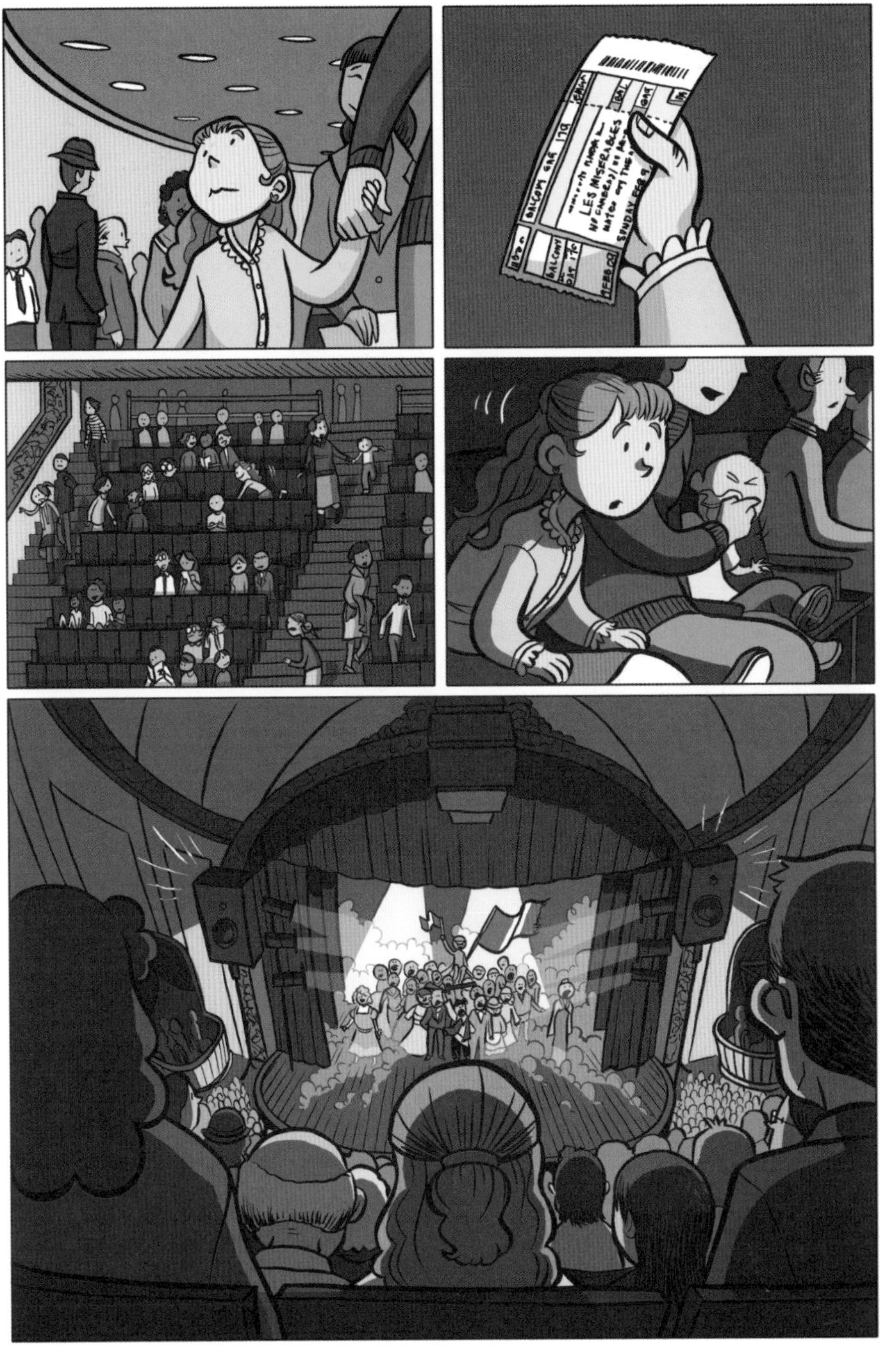
LES MISERABLES
BALCONY
SUNDAY FEB 9

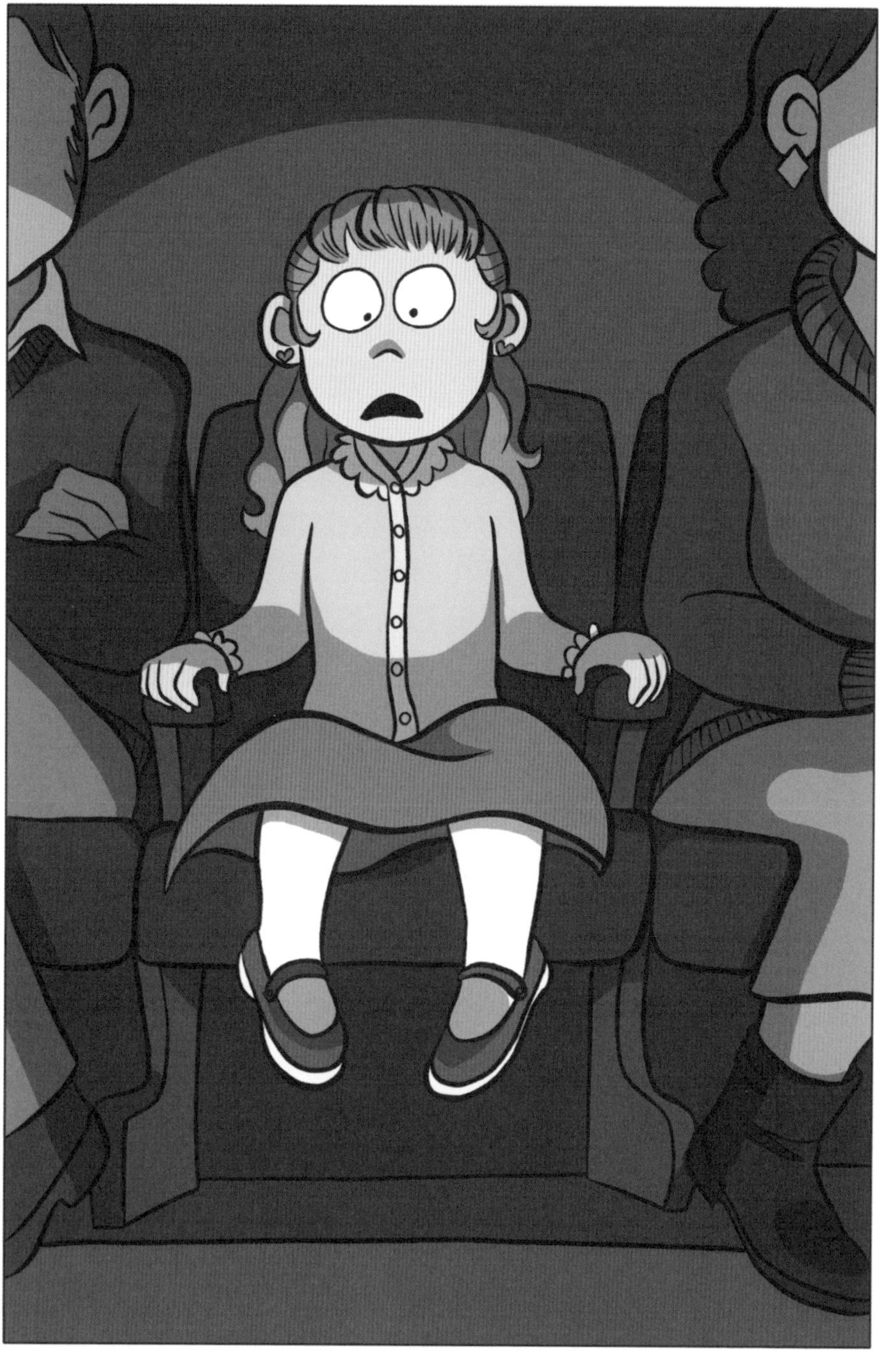

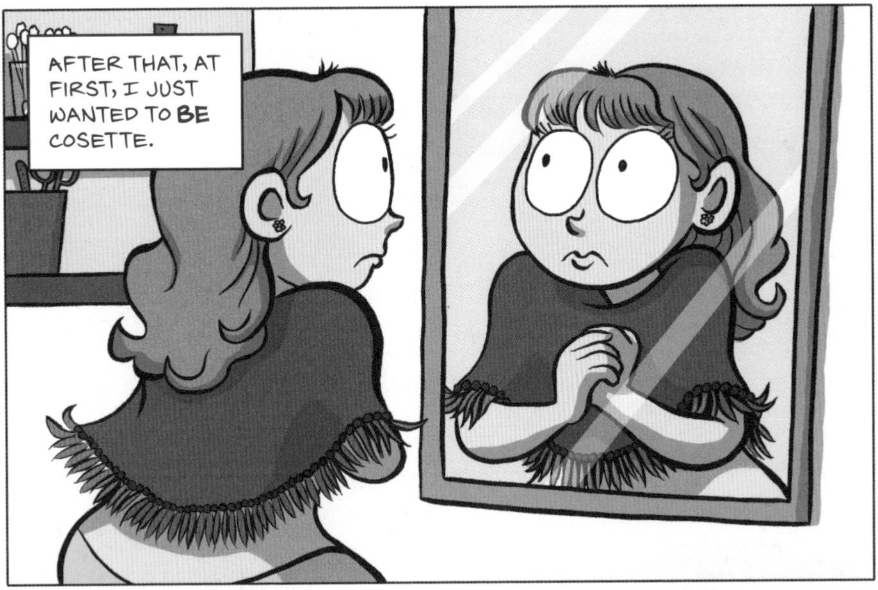
AFTER THAT, AT FIRST, I JUST WANTED TO **BE** COSETTE.

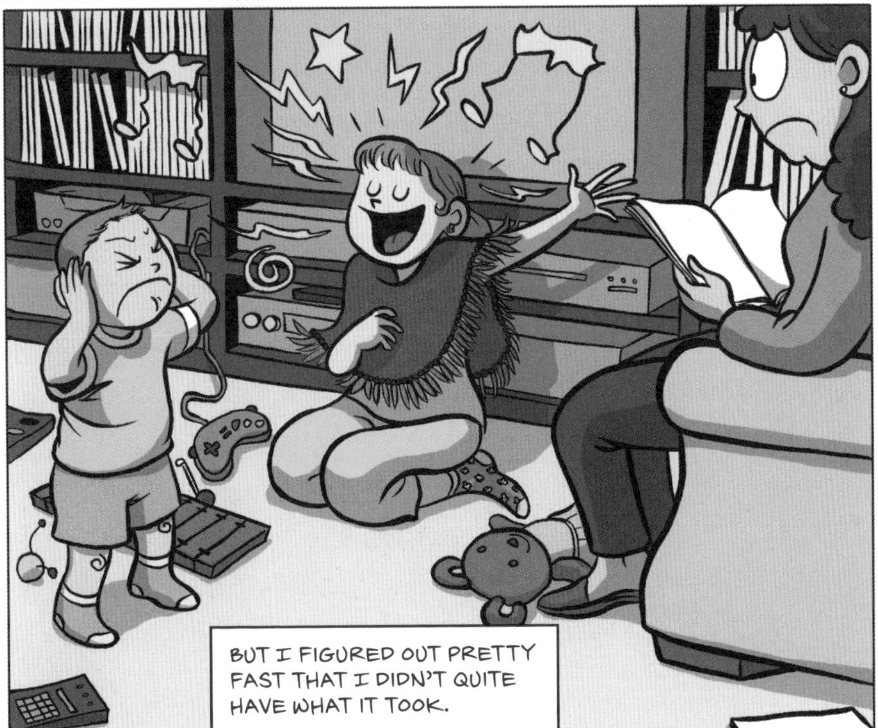
BUT I FIGURED OUT PRETTY FAST THAT I DIDN'T QUITE HAVE WHAT IT TOOK.

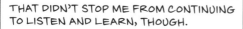
THAT DIDN'T STOP ME FROM CONTINUING TO LISTEN AND LEARN, THOUGH.

MY FIRST WEEK OF SIXTH GRADE, A MAGICAL FLYER APPEARED.

JOIN THE
EUCALYPTUS MIDDLE SCHOOL
STAGE CREW!!
★ make new friends! ★
★ learn new skills! ★
★ help make theater ★
   productions POSSIBLE!

See Mr. Madera in C-103 for more info. We meet M+W after school.

AND MY NEW LIFE BEGAN.

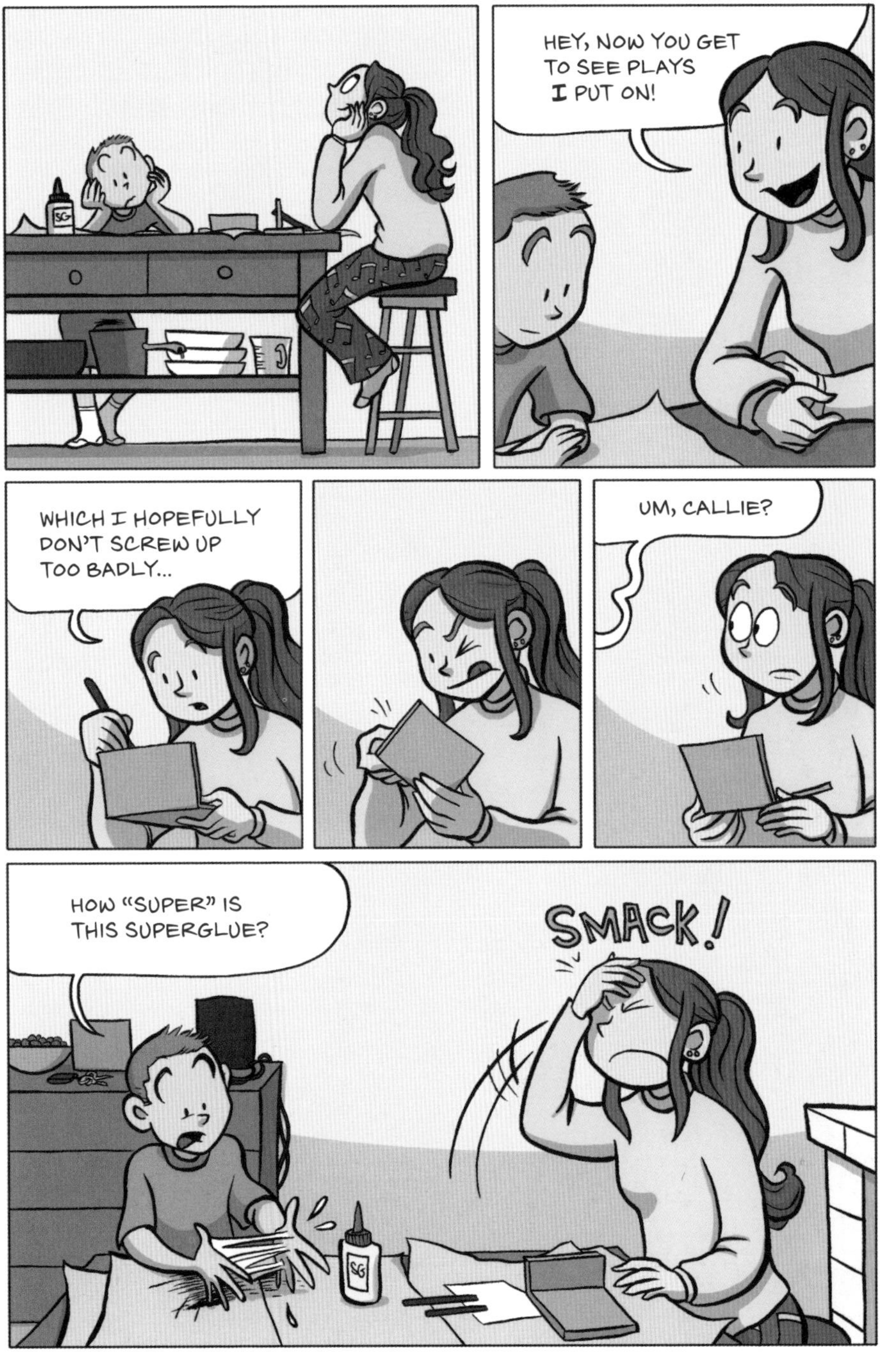
HEY, NOW YOU GET TO SEE PLAYS I PUT ON!
WHICH I HOPEFULLY DON'T SCREW UP TOO BADLY...
UM, CALLIE?
HOW "SUPER" IS THIS SUPERGLUE?
SMACK!

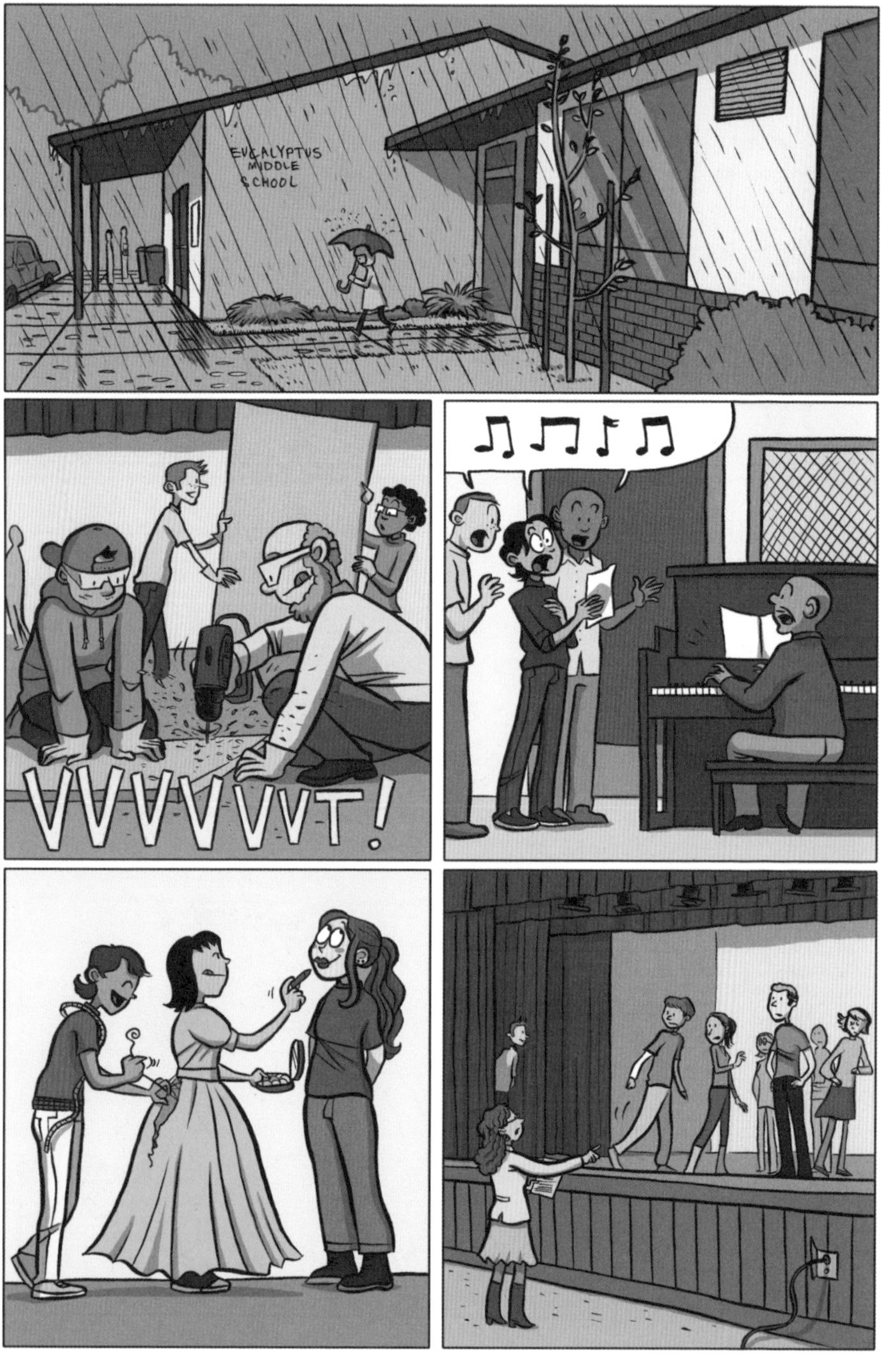
EUCALYPTUS MIDDLE SCHOOL
♫ ♫ ♪ ♫
VVVVVVT!

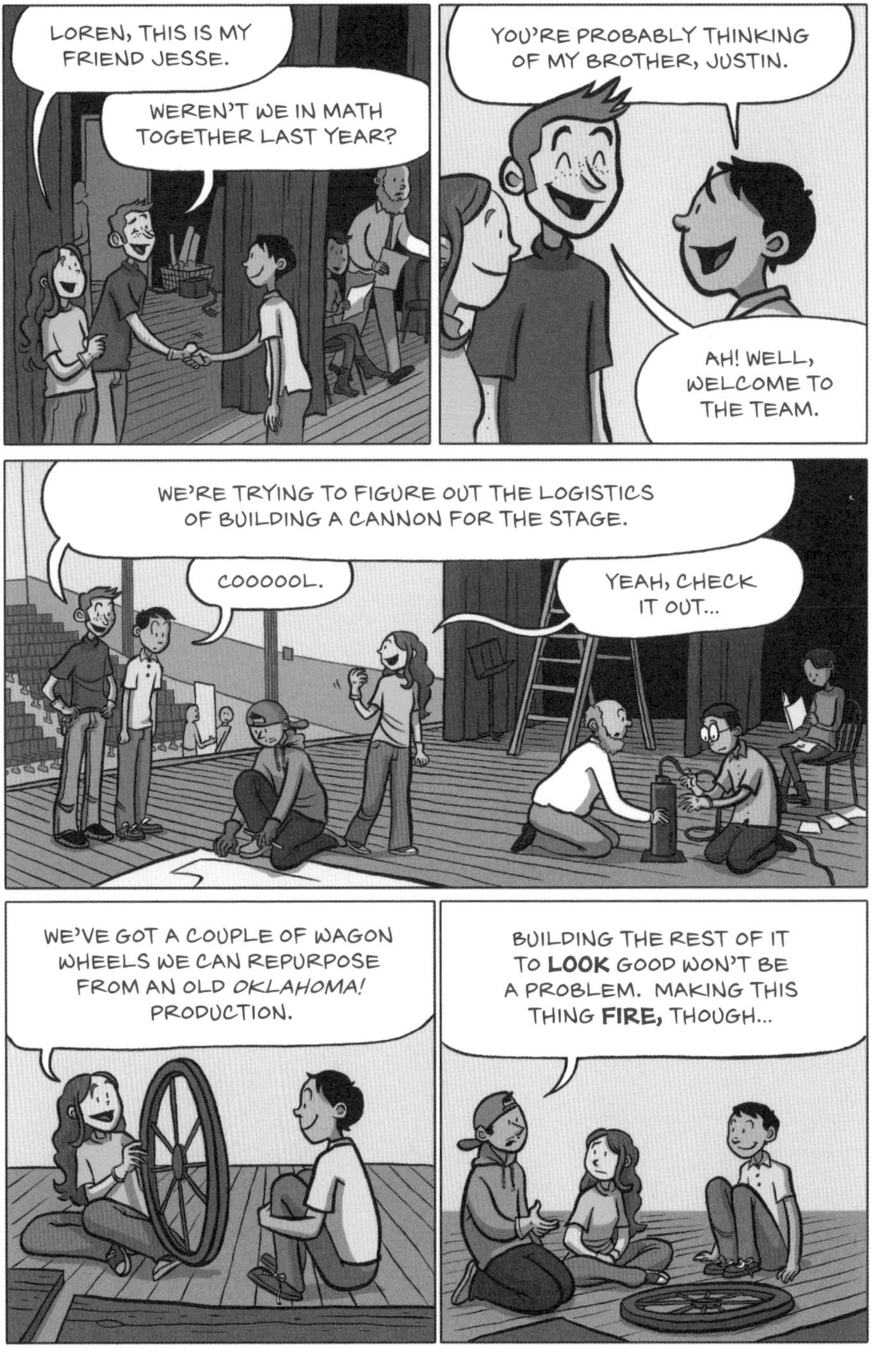
LOREN, THIS IS MY FRIEND JESSE.
WEREN'T WE IN MATH TOGETHER LAST YEAR?
YOU'RE PROBABLY THINKING OF MY BROTHER, JUSTIN.
AH! WELL, WELCOME TO THE TEAM.
WE'RE TRYING TO FIGURE OUT THE LOGISTICS OF BUILDING A CANNON FOR THE STAGE.
COOOOOL.
YEAH, CHECK IT OUT...
WE'VE GOT A COUPLE OF WAGON WHEELS WE CAN REPURPOSE FROM AN OLD *OKLAHOMA!* PRODUCTION.
BUILDING THE REST OF IT TO **LOOK** GOOD WON'T BE A PROBLEM. MAKING THIS THING **FIRE,** THOUGH...

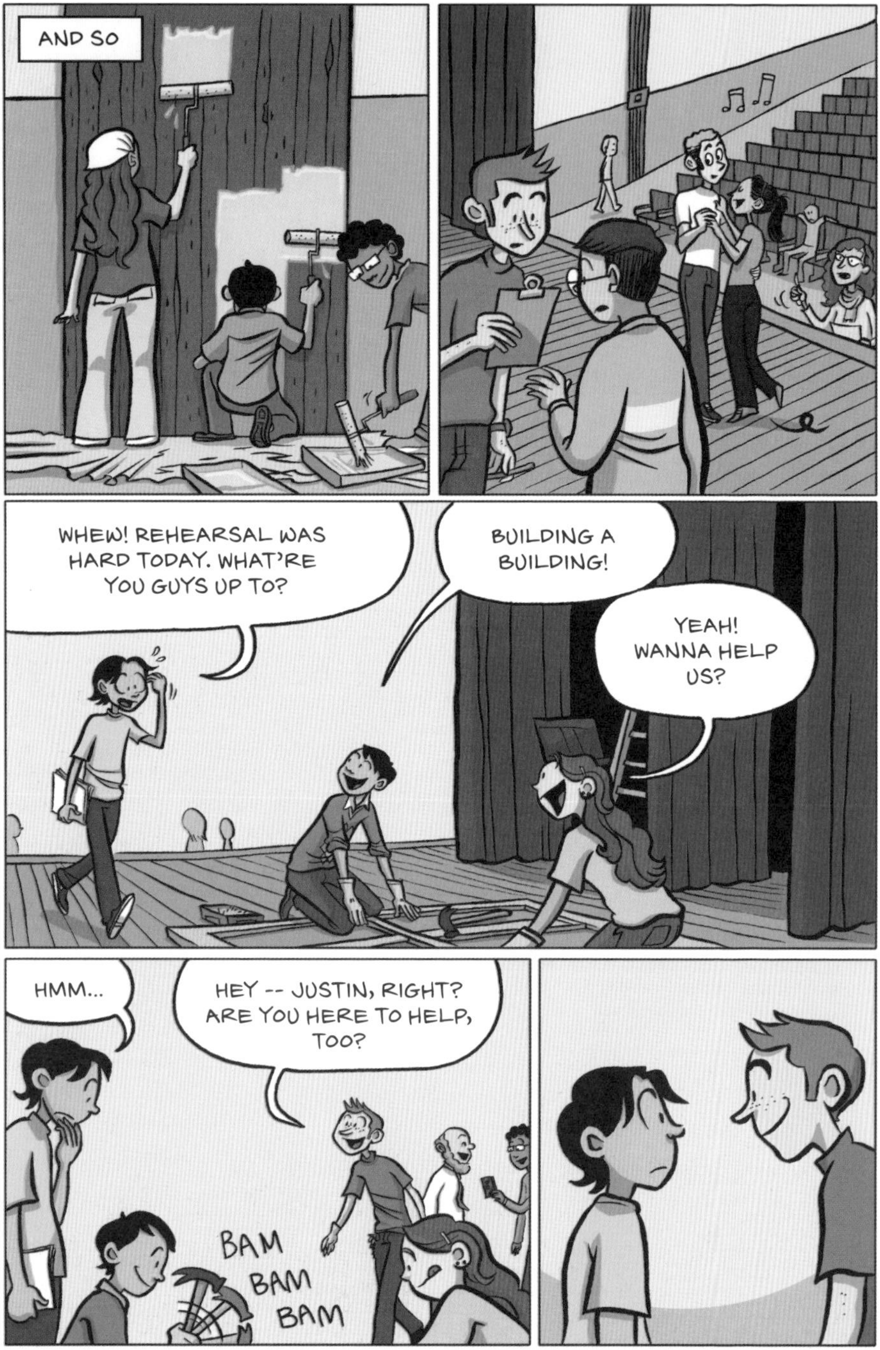

AND SO
WHEW! REHEARSAL WAS HARD TODAY. WHAT'RE YOU GUYS UP TO?
BUILDING A BUILDING!
YEAH! WANNA HELP US?
HMM...
HEY -- JUSTIN, RIGHT? ARE YOU HERE TO HELP, TOO?
BAM
BAM
BAM

YES. ♥

GREAT! THE MORE, THE MERRIER!

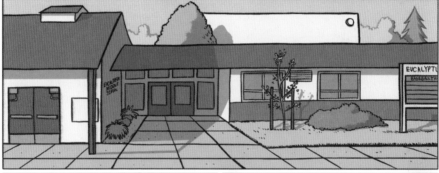

SO THIS SHOULD STAY TOGETHER FINE, WITH WOOD GLUE AND A FEW NAILS.

WHOA!

YOU DID A GREAT JOB WITH THAT, JESSE!

MAN, I'M STARVING.

SNACK RUN?

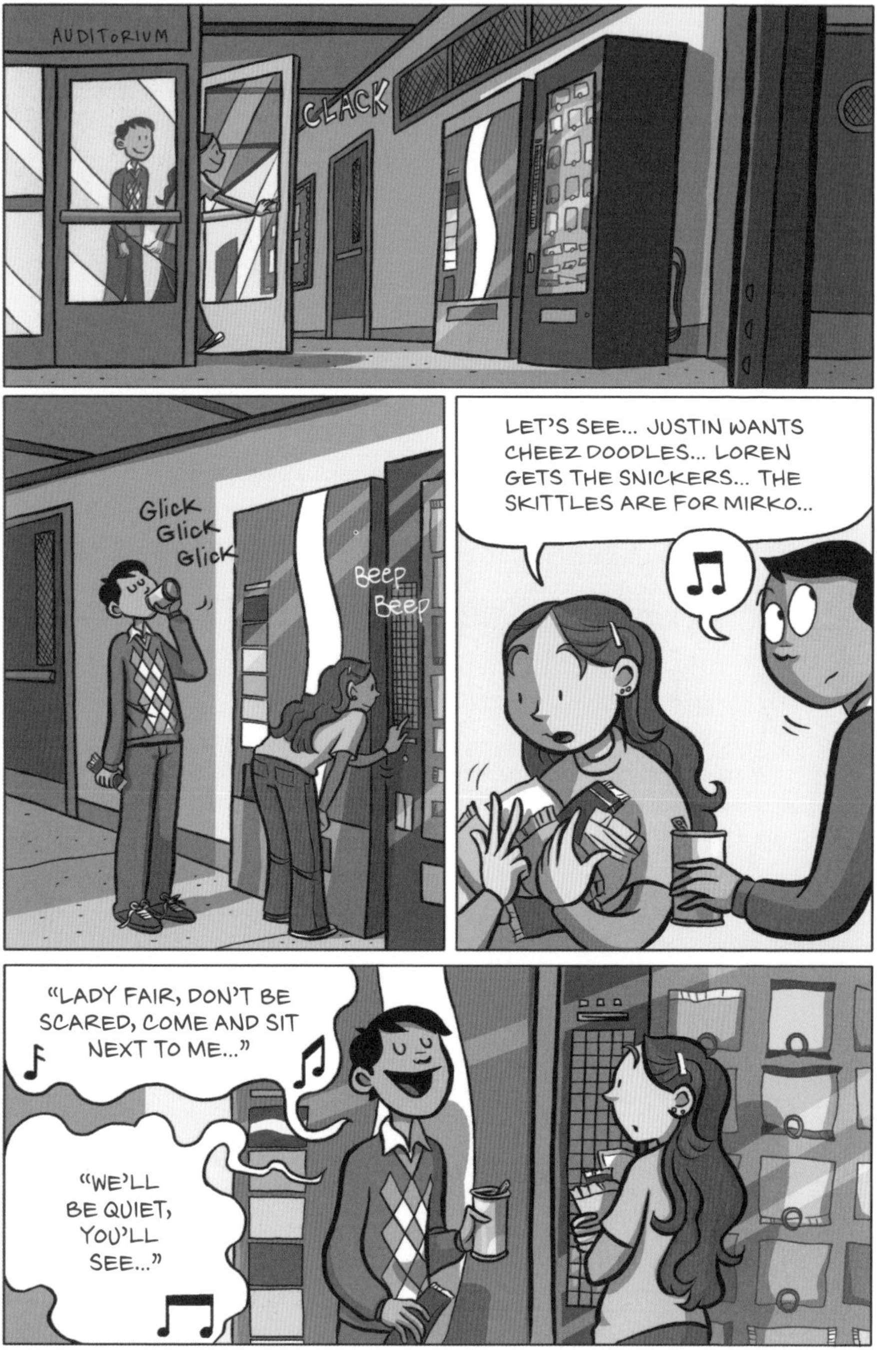
AUDITORIUM
CLACK
Glick
Glick
Glick
Beep
Beep
LET'S SEE... JUSTIN WANTS CHEEZ DOODLES... LOREN GETS THE SNICKERS... THE SKITTLES ARE FOR MIRKO...
"LADY FAIR, DON'T BE SCARED, COME AND SIT NEXT TO ME..."
"WE'LL BE QUIET, YOU'LL SEE..."

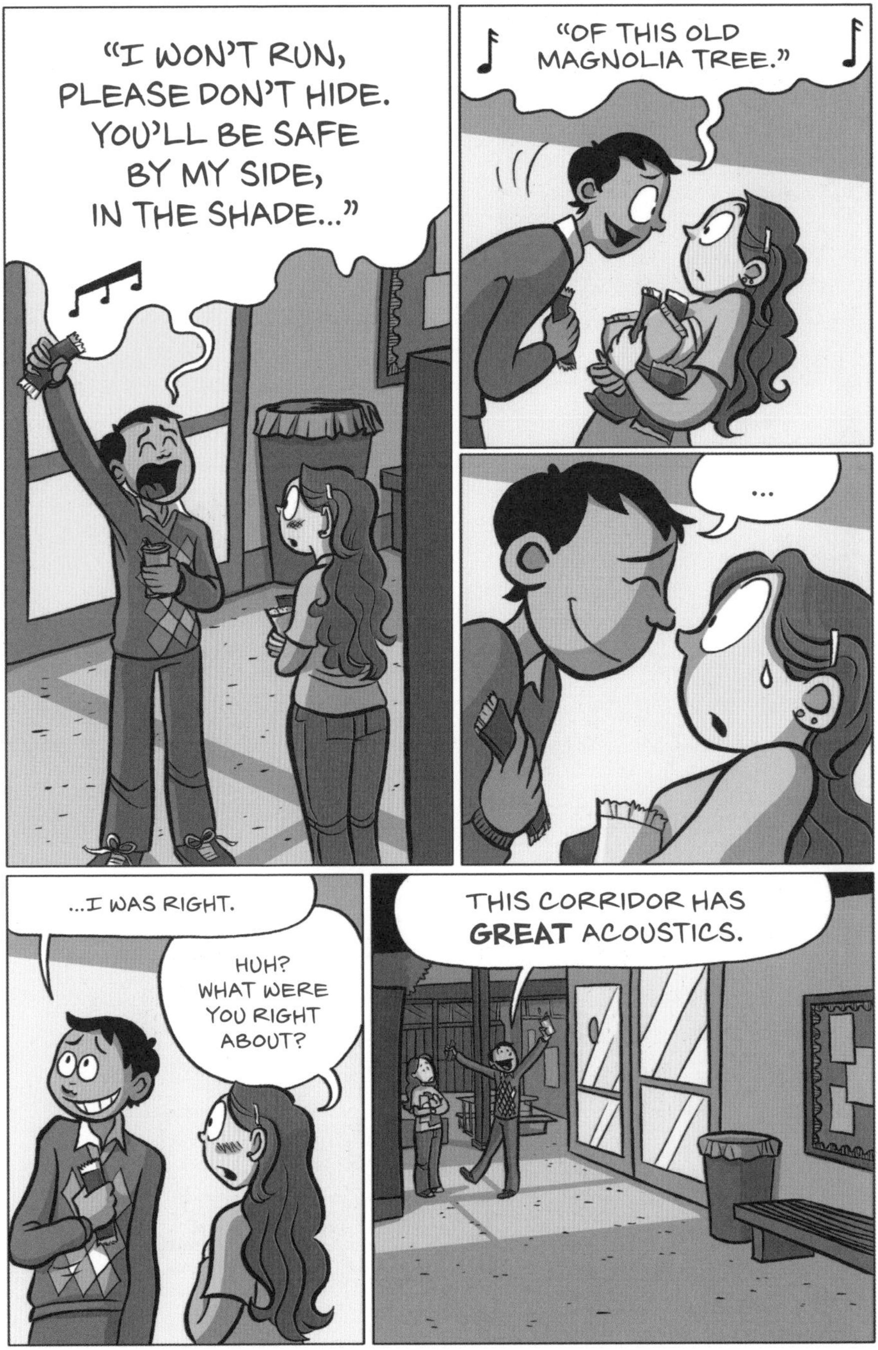
"I WON'T RUN, PLEASE DON'T HIDE. YOU'LL BE SAFE BY MY SIDE, IN THE SHADE..."
"OF THIS OLD MAGNOLIA TREE."
...
...I WAS RIGHT.
HUH? WHAT WERE YOU RIGHT ABOUT?
THIS CORRIDOR HAS **GREAT** ACOUSTICS.

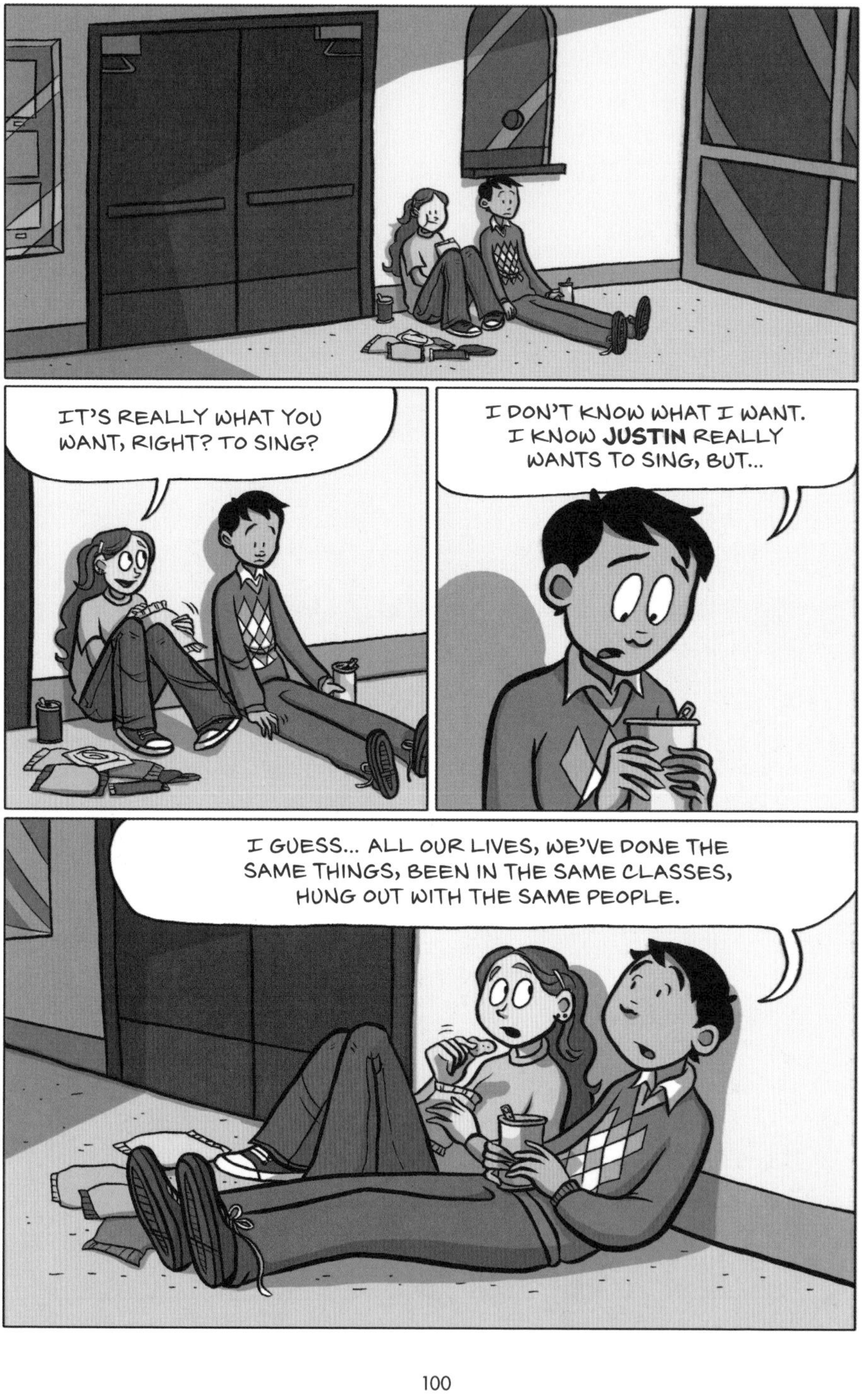
IT'S REALLY WHAT YOU WANT, RIGHT? TO SING?
I DON'T KNOW WHAT I WANT. I KNOW **JUSTIN** REALLY WANTS TO SING, BUT...
I GUESS... ALL OUR LIVES, WE'VE DONE THE SAME THINGS, BEEN IN THE SAME CLASSES, HUNG OUT WITH THE SAME PEOPLE.

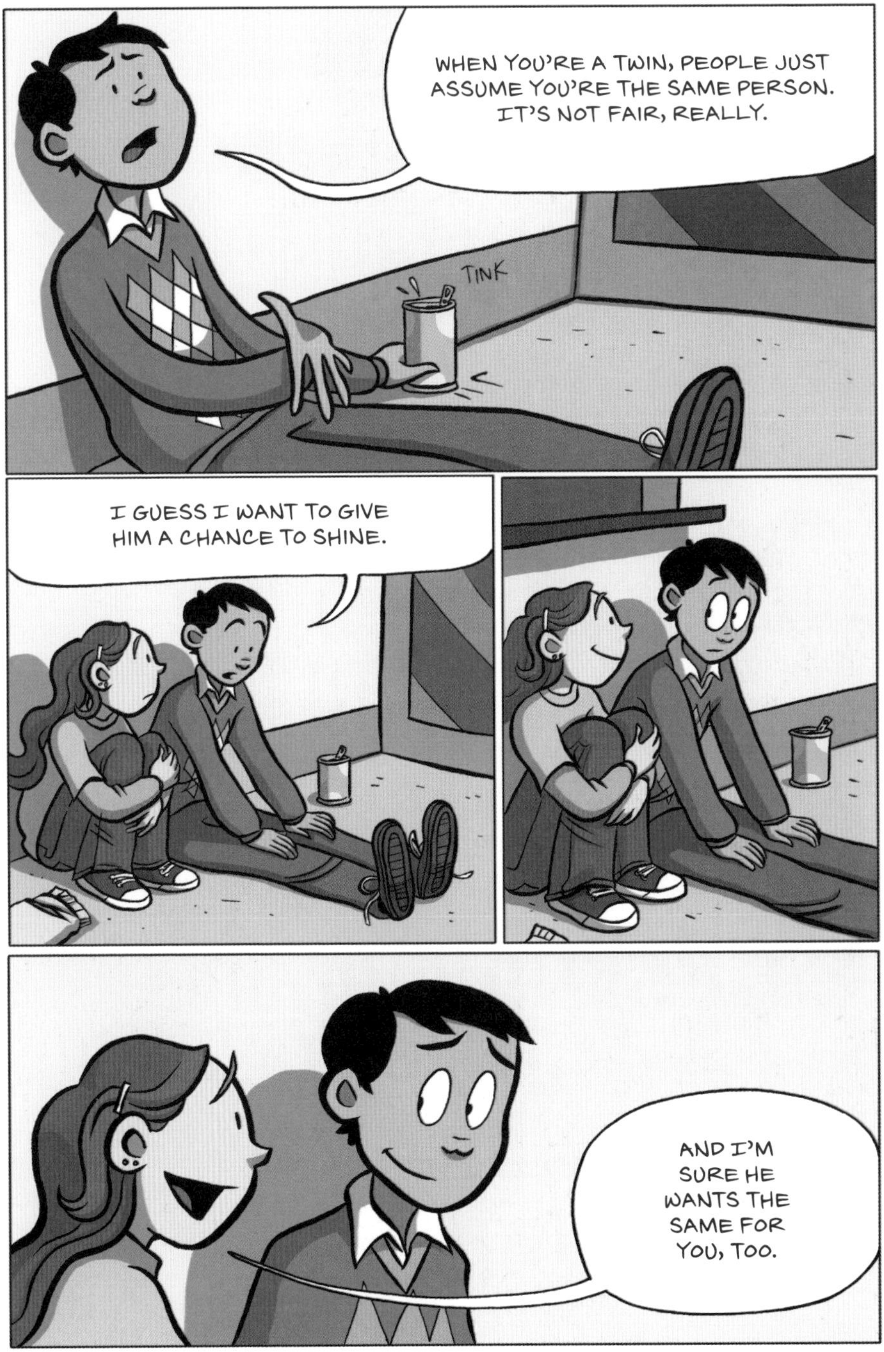
WHEN YOU'RE A TWIN, PEOPLE JUST ASSUME YOU'RE THE SAME PERSON. IT'S NOT FAIR, REALLY.
TINK
I GUESS I WANT TO GIVE HIM A CHANCE TO SHINE.
AND I'M SURE HE WANTS THE SAME FOR YOU, TOO.

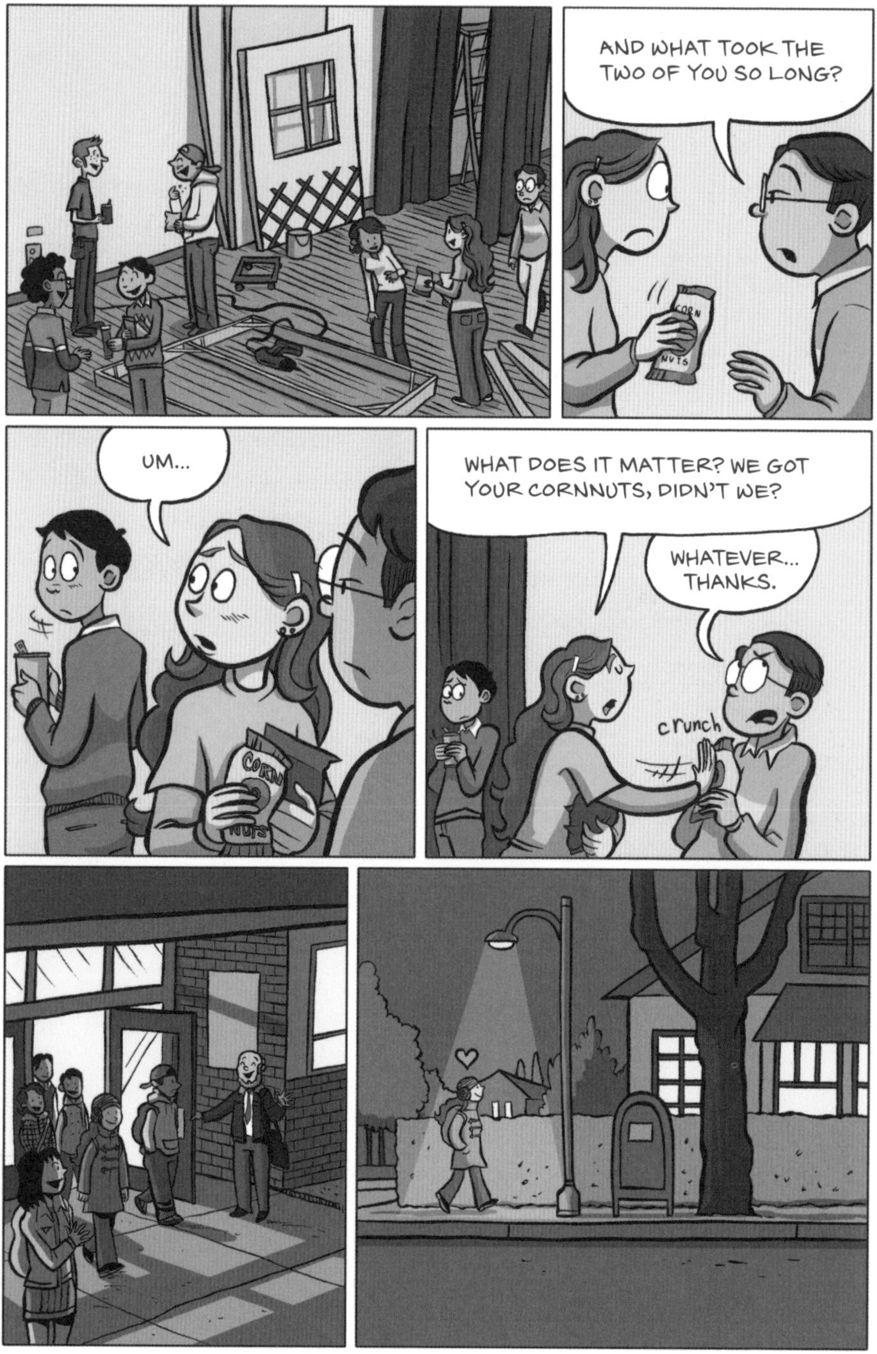
AND WHAT TOOK THE TWO OF YOU SO LONG?
CORN NUTS
UM...
CORN NUTS
WHAT DOES IT MATTER? WE GOT YOUR CORNNUTS, DIDN'T WE?
WHATEVER... THANKS.
crunch

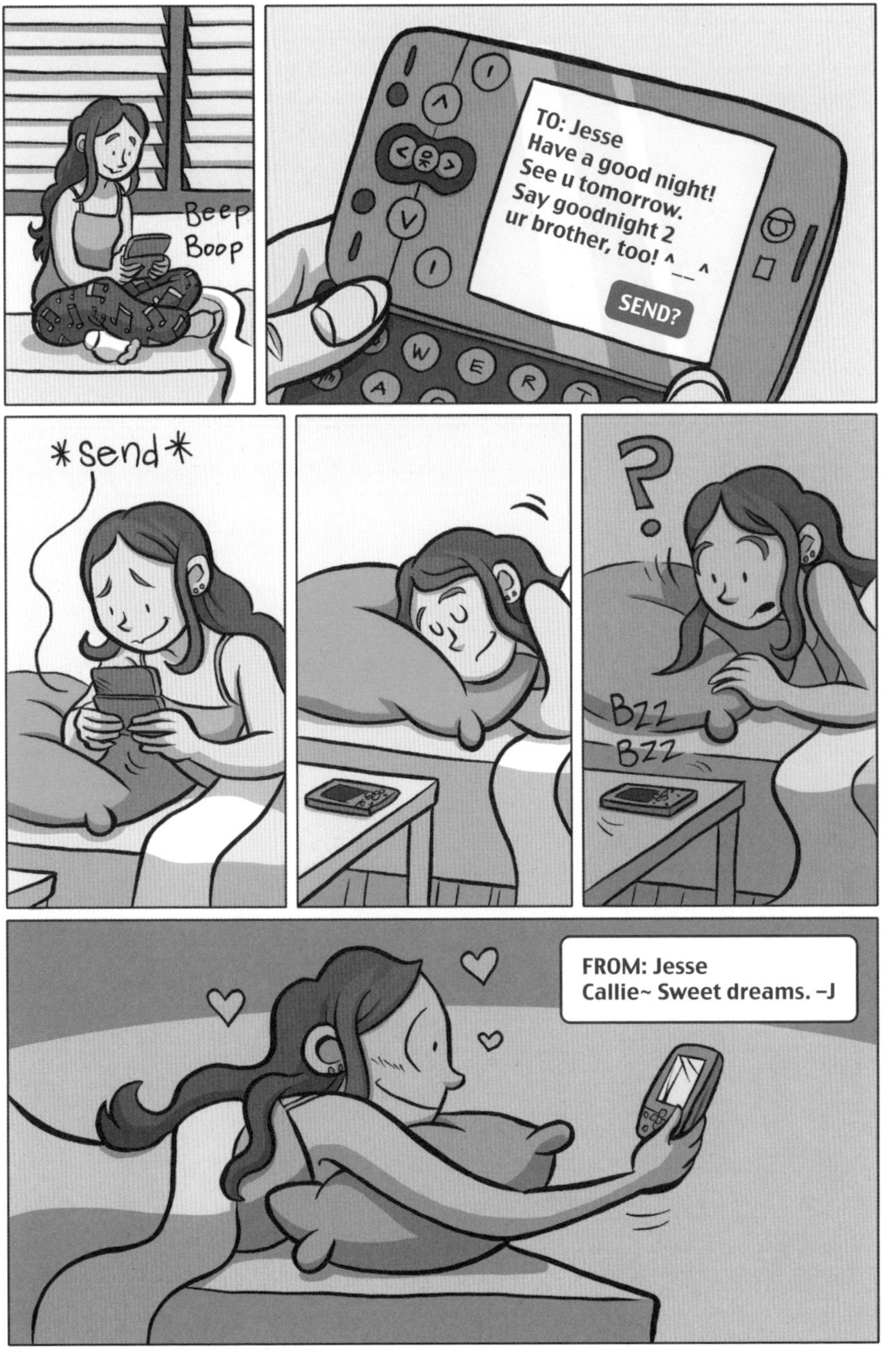

Beep
Boop
TO: Jesse
Have a good night!
See u tomorrow.
Say goodnight 2
ur brother, too! ^__^
SEND?
Send
?
BZZ
BZZ
FROM: Jesse
Callie~ Sweet dreams. -J

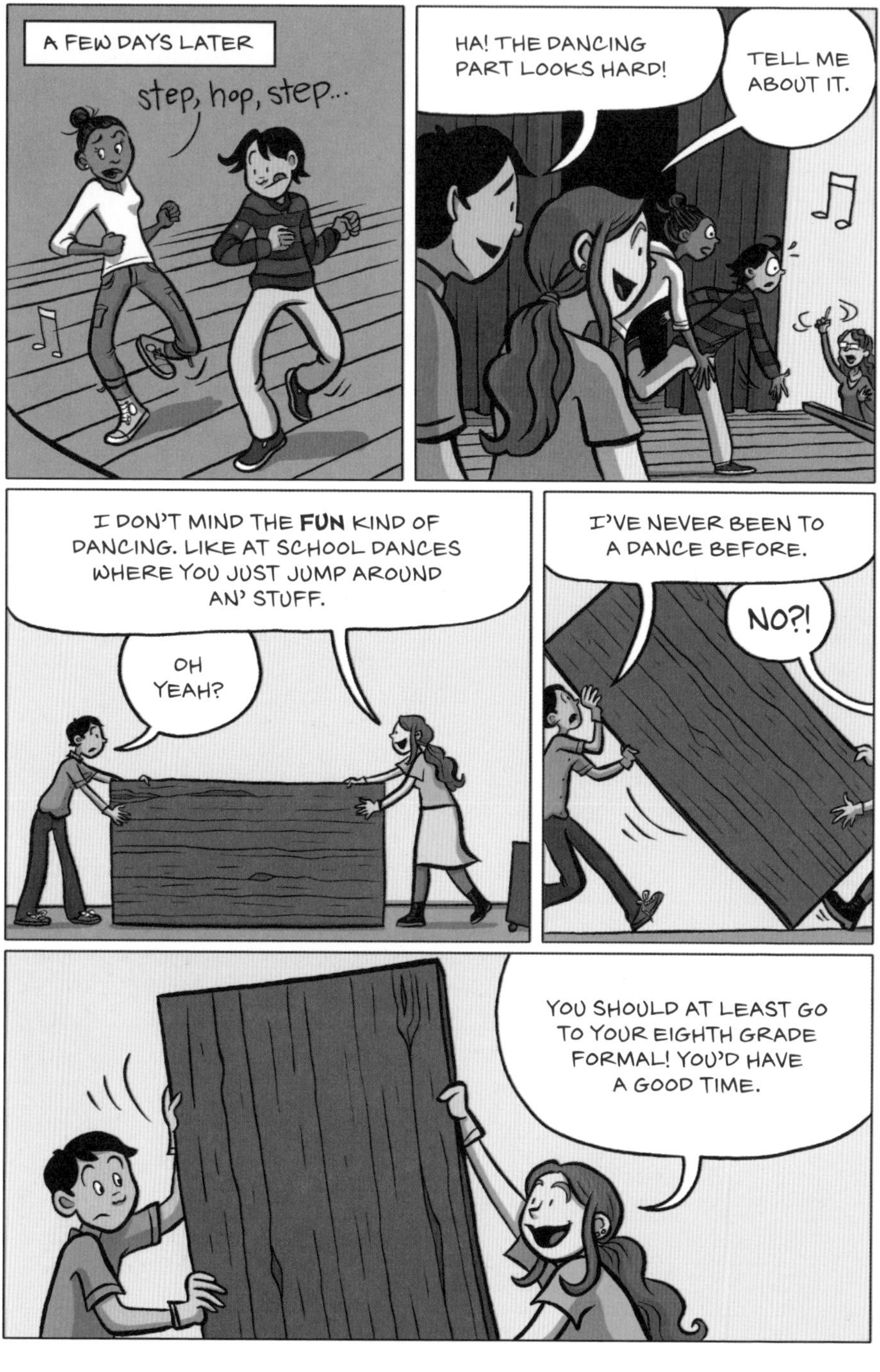
A FEW DAYS LATER
step, hop, step...
HA! THE DANCING PART LOOKS HARD!
TELL ME ABOUT IT.
I DON'T MIND THE **FUN** KIND OF DANCING. LIKE AT SCHOOL DANCES WHERE YOU JUST JUMP AROUND AN' STUFF.
OH YEAH?
I'VE NEVER BEEN TO A DANCE BEFORE.
NO?!
YOU SHOULD AT LEAST GO TO YOUR EIGHTH GRADE FORMAL! YOU'D HAVE A GOOD TIME.

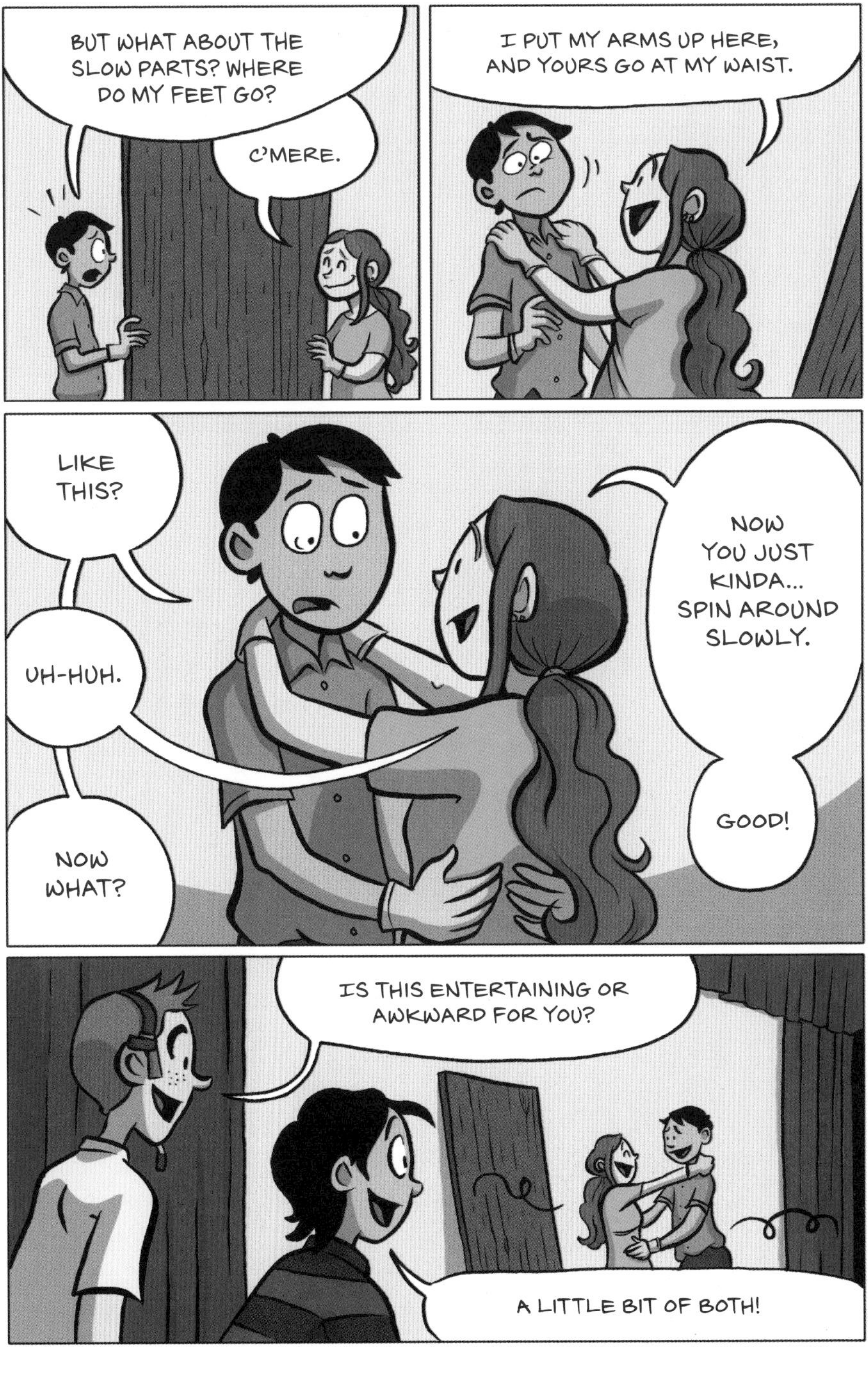
BUT WHAT ABOUT THE SLOW PARTS? WHERE DO MY FEET GO?
C'MERE.
I PUT MY ARMS UP HERE, AND YOURS GO AT MY WAIST.
LIKE THIS?
UH-HUH.
NOW WHAT?
NOW YOU JUST KINDA... SPIN AROUND SLOWLY.
GOOD!
IS THIS ENTERTAINING OR AWKWARD FOR YOU?
A LITTLE BIT OF BOTH!

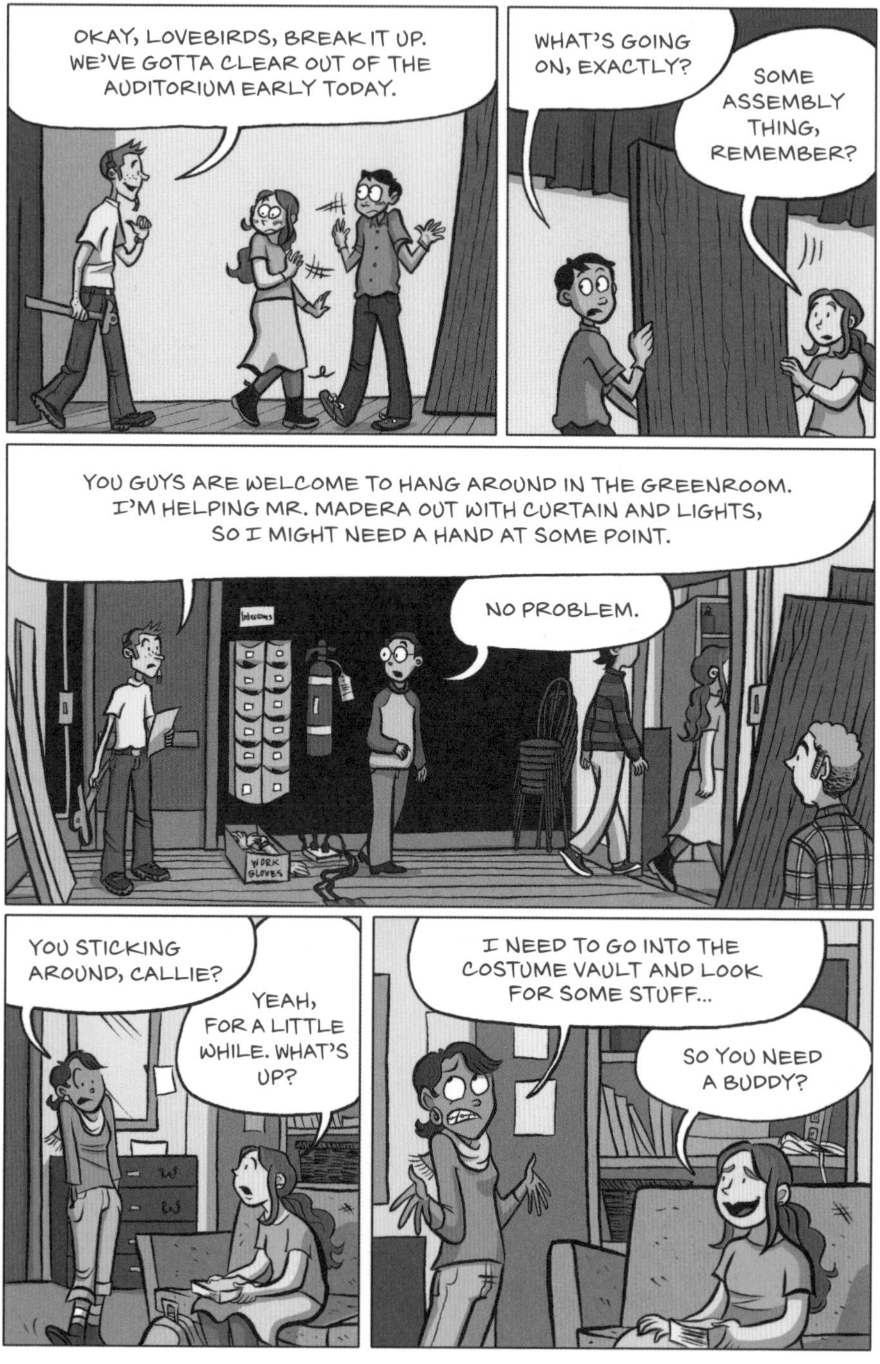
OKAY, LOVEBIRDS, BREAK IT UP. WE'VE GOTTA CLEAR OUT OF THE AUDITORIUM EARLY TODAY.
WHAT'S GOING ON, EXACTLY?
SOME ASSEMBLY THING, REMEMBER?
YOU GUYS ARE WELCOME TO HANG AROUND IN THE GREENROOM. I'M HELPING MR. MADERA OUT WITH CURTAIN AND LIGHTS, SO I MIGHT NEED A HAND AT SOME POINT.
NO PROBLEM.
WORK GLOVES
YOU STICKING AROUND, CALLIE?
YEAH, FOR A LITTLE WHILE. WHAT'S UP?
I NEED TO GO INTO THE COSTUME VAULT AND LOOK FOR SOME STUFF...
SO YOU NEED A BUDDY?

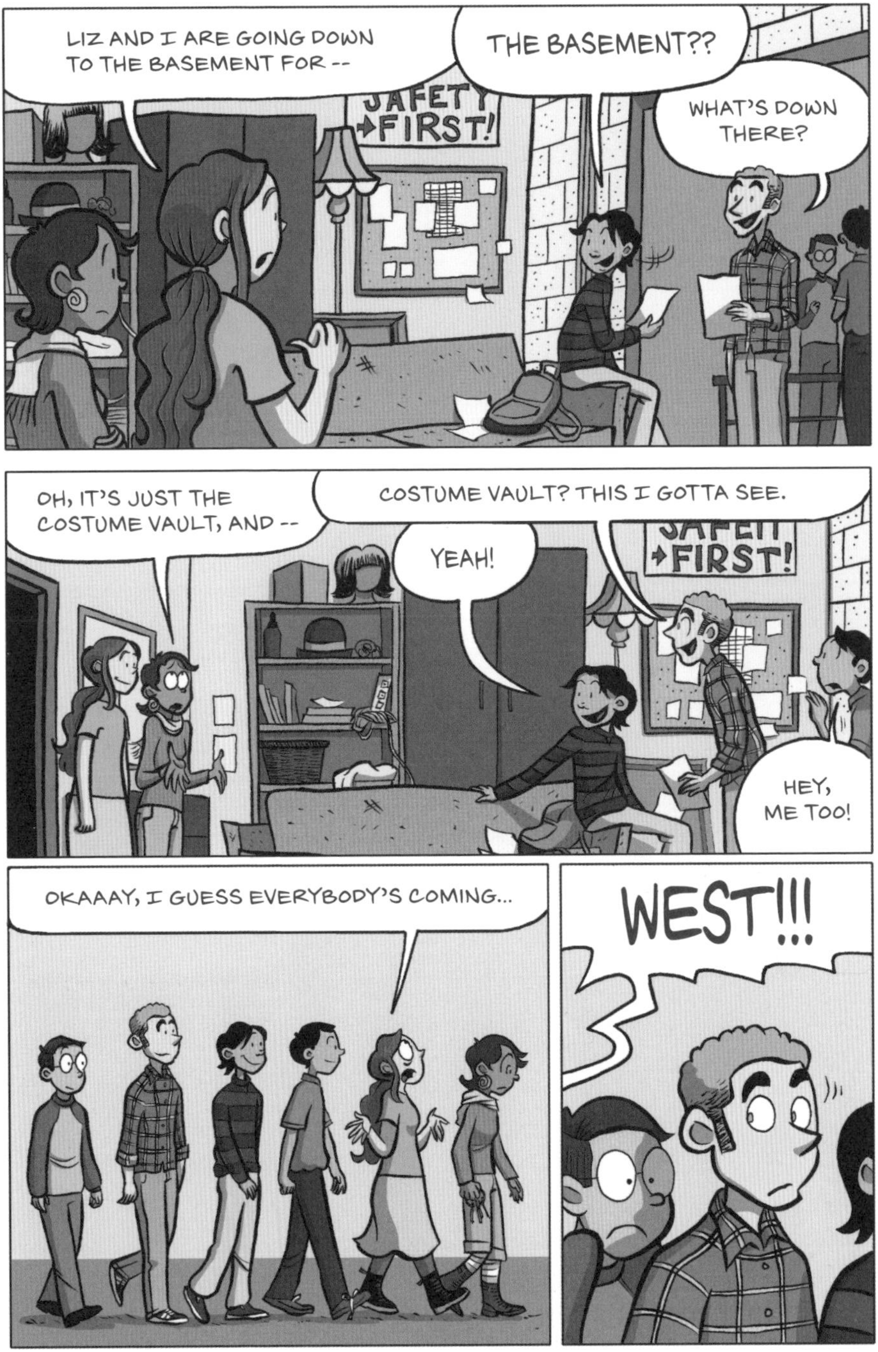
LIZ AND I ARE GOING DOWN TO THE BASEMENT FOR --
THE BASEMENT??
WHAT'S DOWN THERE?
SAFETY FIRST!
OH, IT'S JUST THE COSTUME VAULT, AND --
COSTUME VAULT? THIS I GOTTA SEE.
YEAH!
HEY, ME TOO!
OKAAAY, I GUESS EVERYBODY'S COMING...
WEST!!!

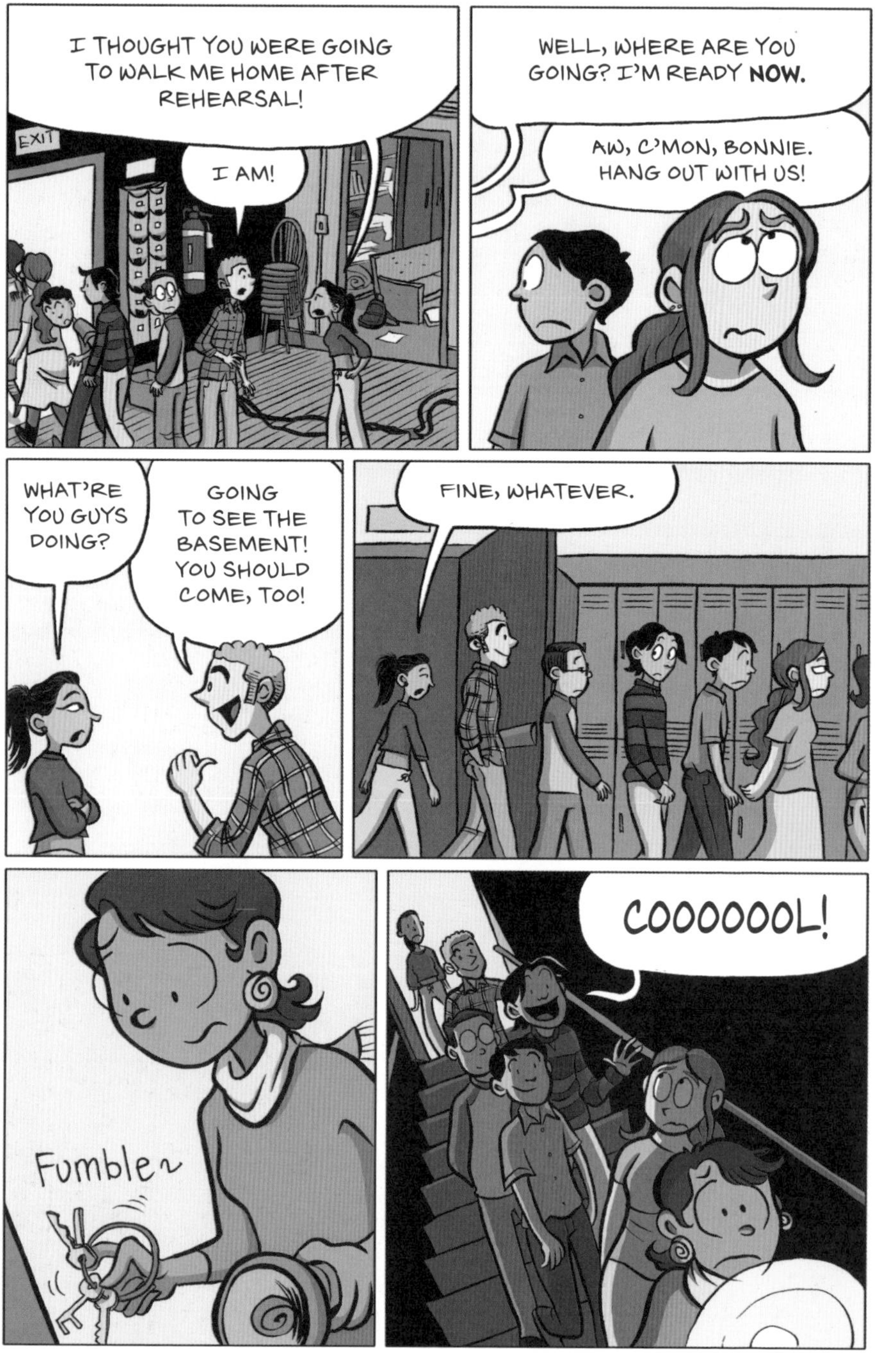

I THOUGHT YOU WERE GOING TO WALK ME HOME AFTER REHEARSAL!
EXIT
I AM!
WELL, WHERE ARE YOU GOING? I'M READY **NOW.**
AW, C'MON, BONNIE. HANG OUT WITH US!
WHAT'RE YOU GUYS DOING?
GOING TO SEE THE BASEMENT! YOU SHOULD COME, TOO!
FINE, WHATEVER.
Fumble~
COOOOOOL!

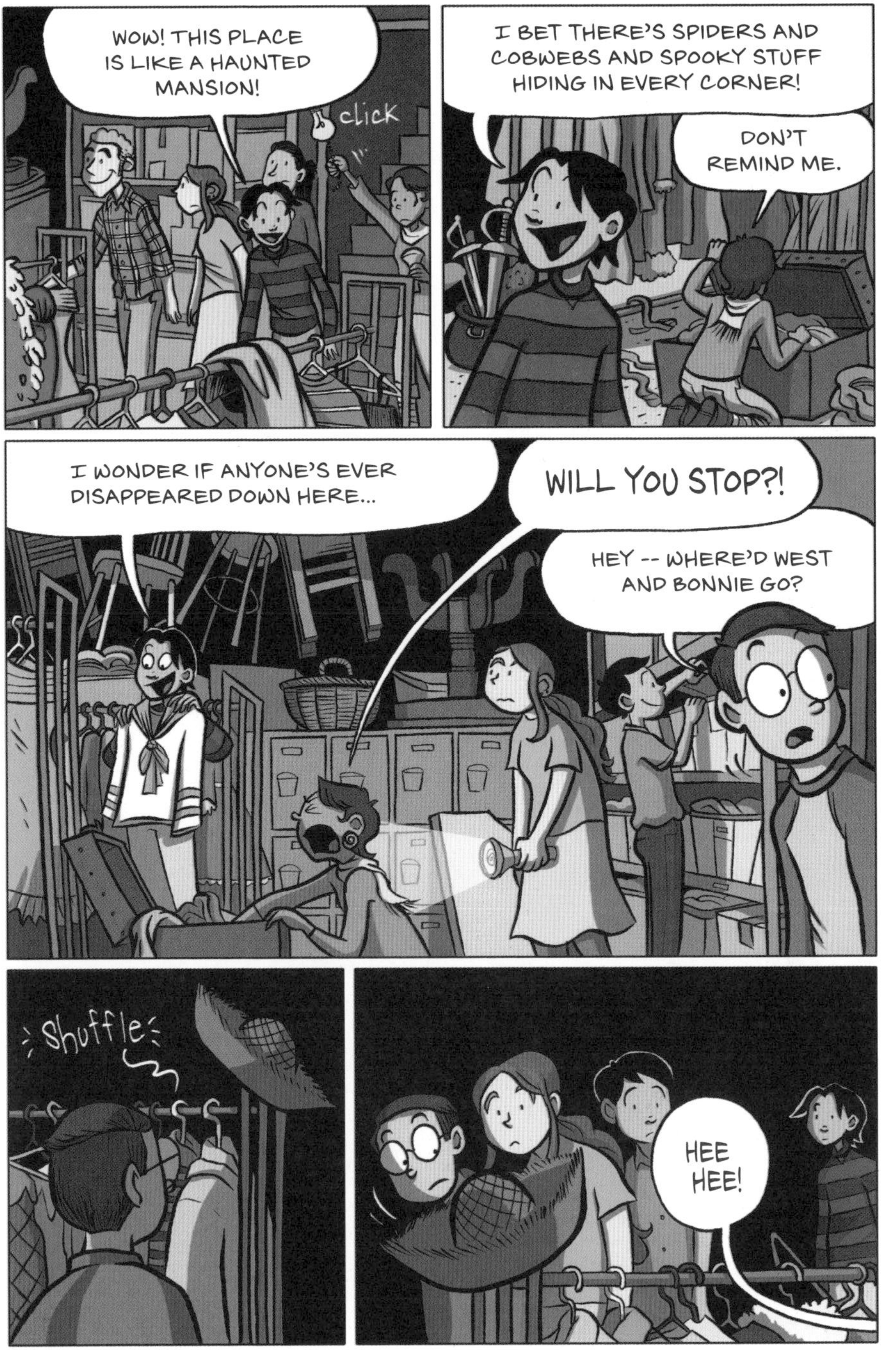
WOW! THIS PLACE IS LIKE A HAUNTED MANSION!
click
I BET THERE'S SPIDERS AND COBWEBS AND SPOOKY STUFF HIDING IN EVERY CORNER!
DON'T REMIND ME.
I WONDER IF ANYONE'S EVER DISAPPEARED DOWN HERE...
WILL YOU STOP?!
HEY -- WHERE'D WEST AND BONNIE GO?
shuffle
HEE HEE!

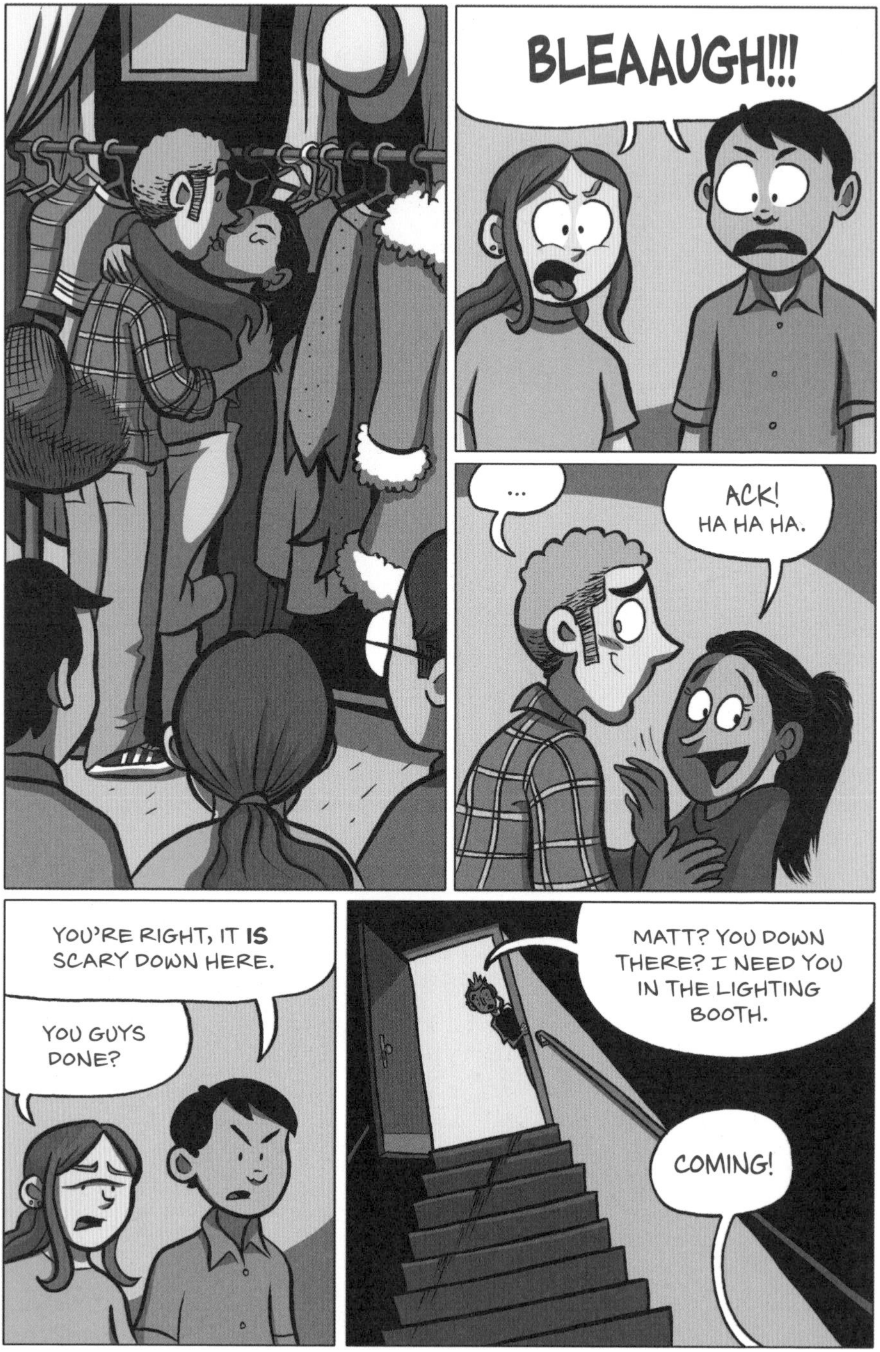
BLEAAUGH!!!
...
ACK! HA HA HA.
YOU'RE RIGHT, IT **IS** SCARY DOWN HERE.
YOU GUYS DONE?
MATT? YOU DOWN THERE? I NEED YOU IN THE LIGHTING BOOTH.
COMING!

DID YOU FIND WHAT YOU NEEDED, LIZ?

MOSTLY.

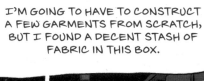

I'M GOING TO HAVE TO CONSTRUCT A FEW GARMENTS FROM SCRATCH, BUT I FOUND A DECENT STASH OF FABRIC IN THIS BOX.

GOOD!

BONNIE, CAN YOU MEET AT LUNCHTIME AGAIN TOMORROW?

UGH. DO WE **HAVE** TO??

NO, WE DON'T **HAVE** TO, BUT EIGHTH GRADE SCIENCE IS KIND OF IMPORTANT. IF YOU FAIL, YOU CAN'T GRADUATE IN JUNE.

FINE. I DON'T CARE, BUT FINE.

HOW CAN YOU NOT CARE?!

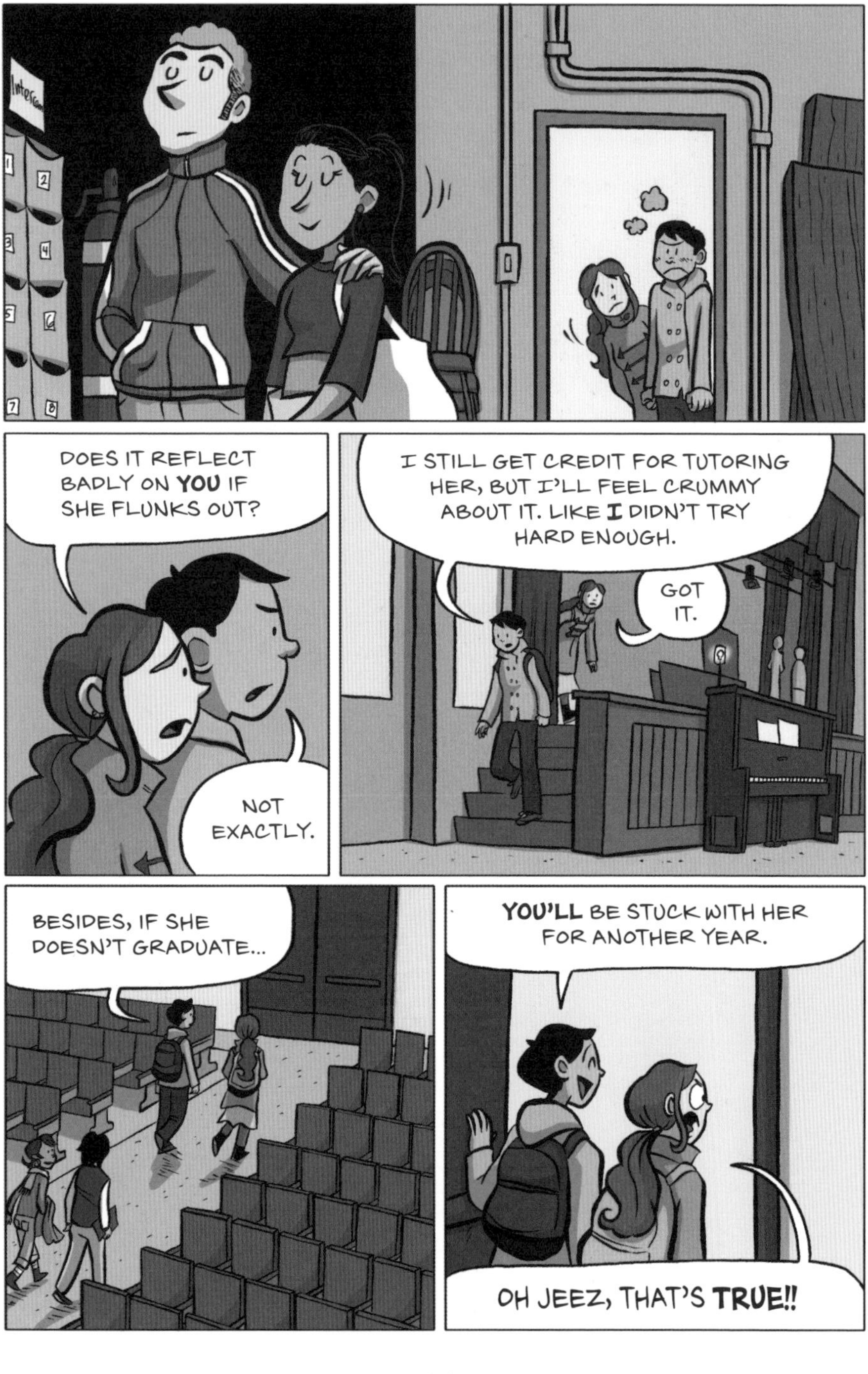
Intercom
1
2
3
4
5
6
7
8
DOES IT REFLECT BADLY ON **YOU** IF SHE FLUNKS OUT?
NOT EXACTLY.
I STILL GET CREDIT FOR TUTORING HER, BUT I'LL FEEL CRUMMY ABOUT IT. LIKE **I** DIDN'T TRY HARD ENOUGH.
GOT IT.
BESIDES, IF SHE DOESN'T GRADUATE...
YOU'LL BE STUCK WITH HER FOR ANOTHER YEAR.
OH JEEZ, THAT'S **TRUE!!**

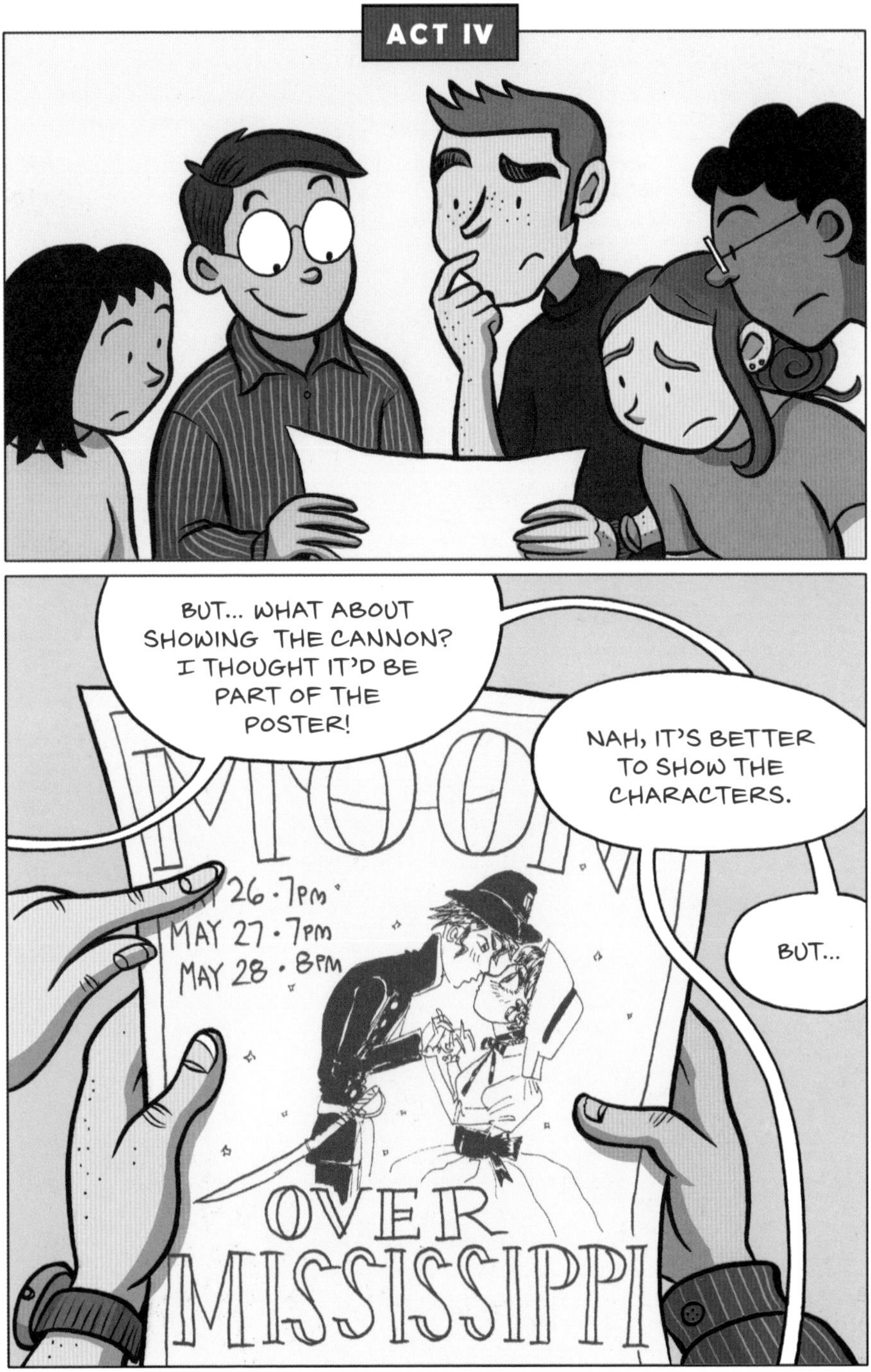
ACT IV
BUT... WHAT ABOUT SHOWING THE CANNON? I THOUGHT IT'D BE PART OF THE POSTER!
NAH, IT'S BETTER TO SHOW THE CHARACTERS.
BUT...
MAY 27 • 7PM
MAY 28 • 8PM
OVER MISSISSIPPI

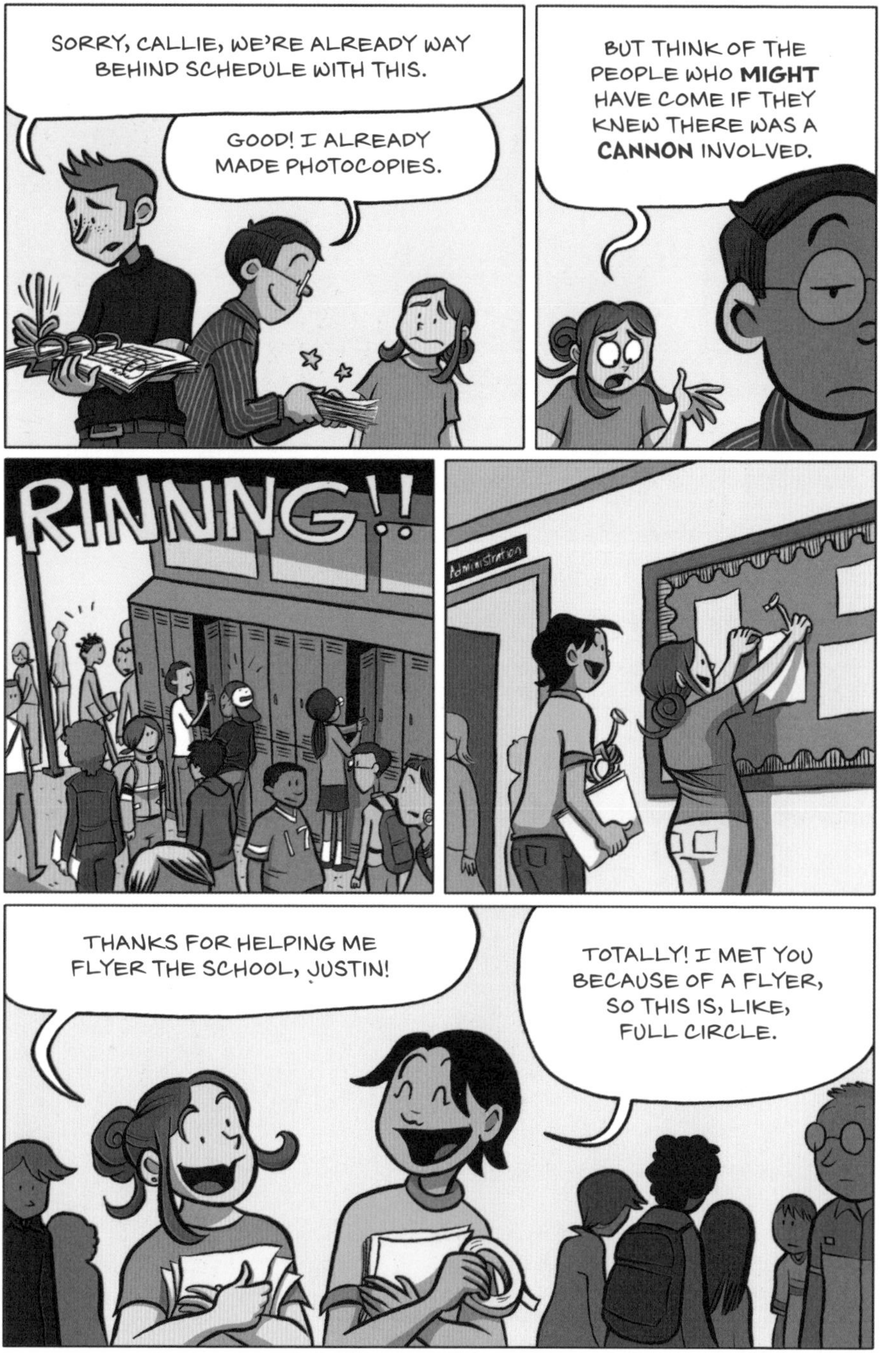
SORRY, CALLIE, WE'RE ALREADY WAY BEHIND SCHEDULE WITH THIS.
GOOD! I ALREADY MADE PHOTOCOPIES.
BUT THINK OF THE PEOPLE WHO **MIGHT** HAVE COME IF THEY KNEW THERE WAS A **CANNON** INVOLVED.
RINNNG!!
Administration
THANKS FOR HELPING ME FLYER THE SCHOOL, JUSTIN!
TOTALLY! I MET YOU BECAUSE OF A FLYER, SO THIS IS, LIKE, FULL CIRCLE.

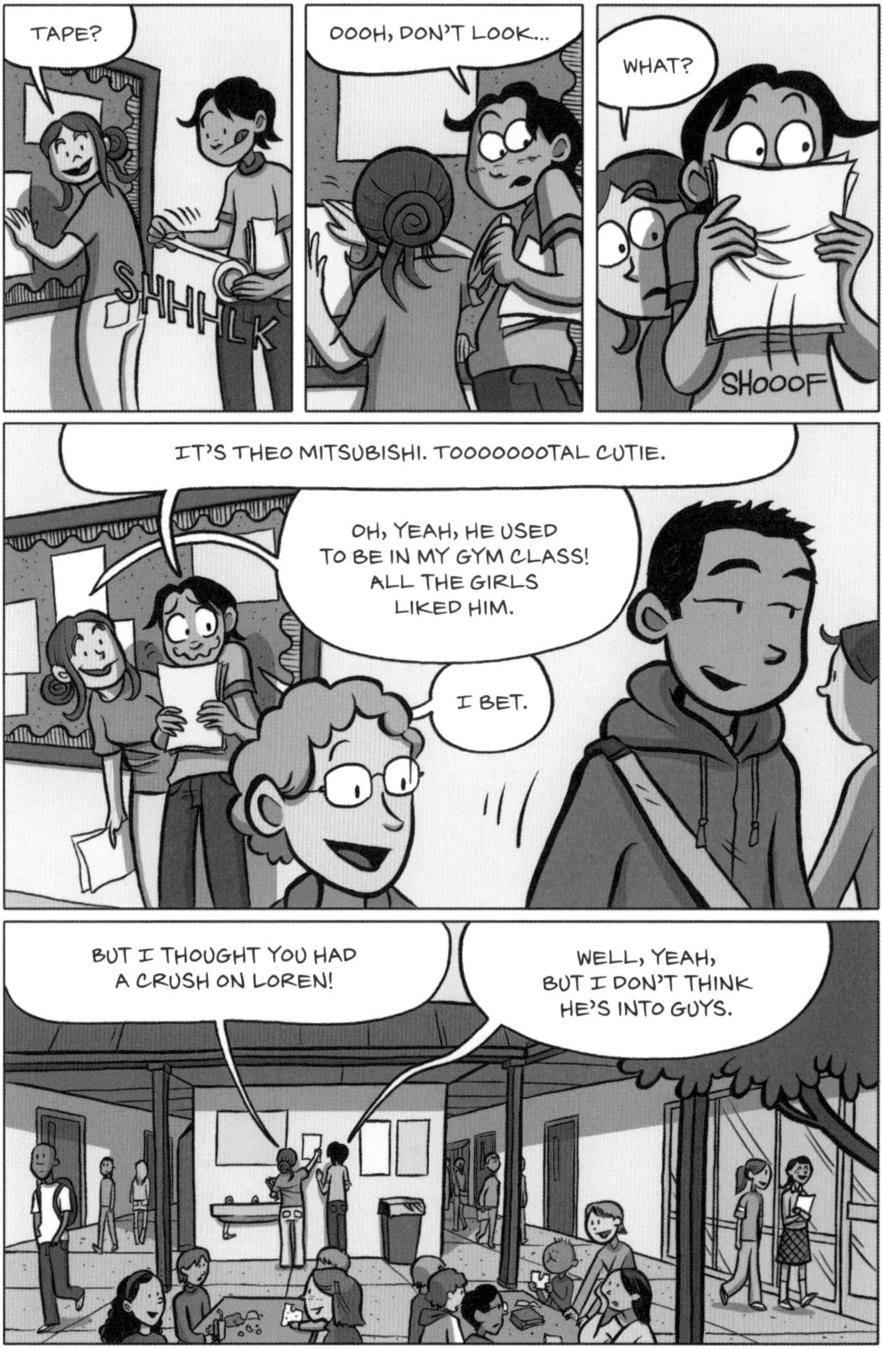
TAPE?
SHHHLK
OOOH, DON'T LOOK...
WHAT?
SHOOOF
IT'S THEO MITSUBISHI. TOOOOOOOTAL CUTIE.
OH, YEAH, HE USED TO BE IN MY GYM CLASS! ALL THE GIRLS LIKED HIM.
I BET.
BUT I THOUGHT YOU HAD A CRUSH ON LOREN!
WELL, YEAH, BUT I DON'T THINK HE'S INTO GUYS.

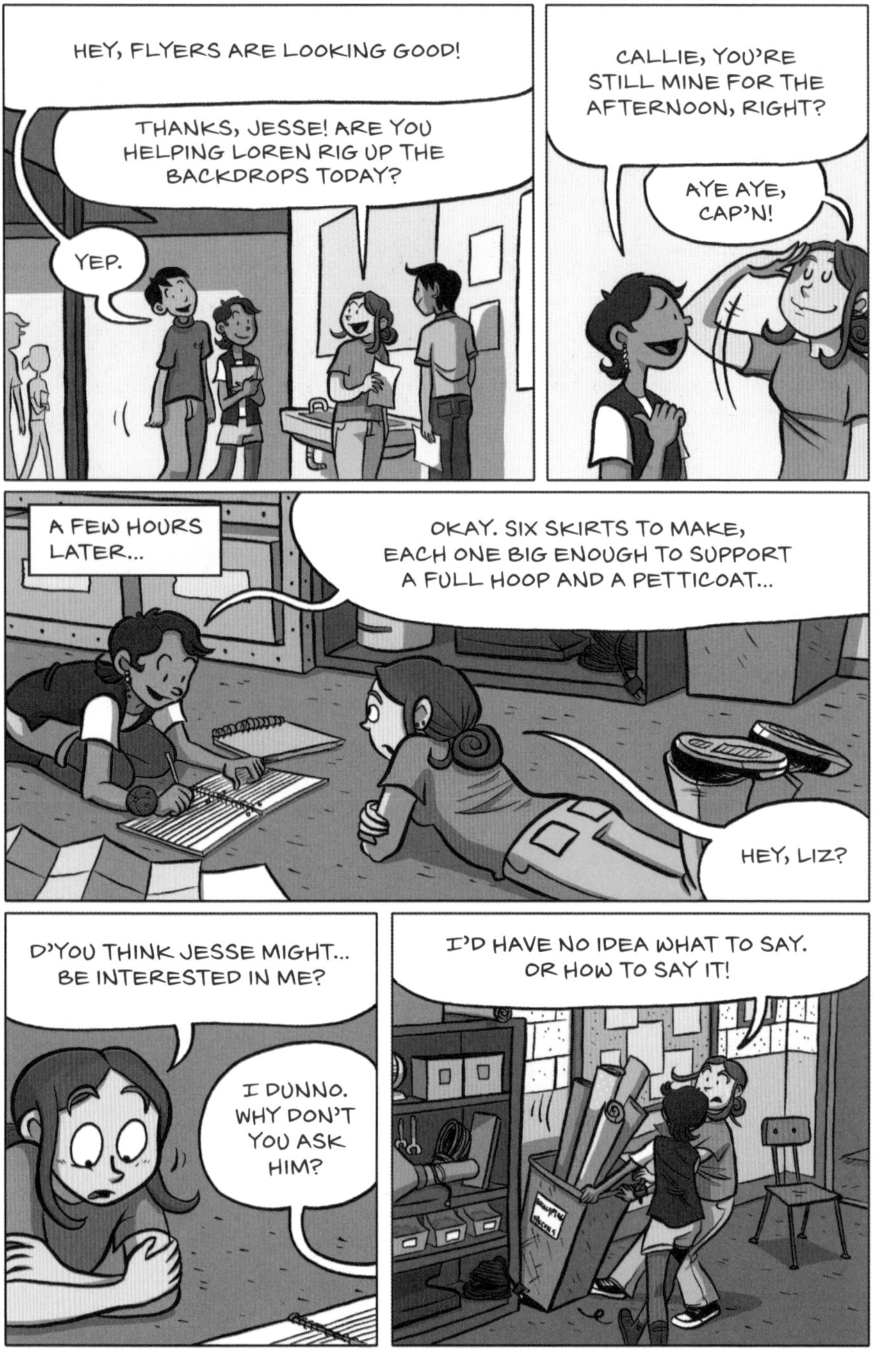
HEY, FLYERS ARE LOOKING GOOD!
THANKS, JESSE! ARE YOU HELPING LOREN RIG UP THE BACKDROPS TODAY?
YEP.
CALLIE, YOU'RE STILL MINE FOR THE AFTERNOON, RIGHT?
AYE AYE, CAP'N!
A FEW HOURS LATER...
OKAY. SIX SKIRTS TO MAKE, EACH ONE BIG ENOUGH TO SUPPORT A FULL HOOP AND A PETTICOAT...
HEY, LIZ?
D'YOU THINK JESSE MIGHT... BE INTERESTED IN ME?
I DUNNO. WHY DON'T YOU ASK HIM?
I'D HAVE NO IDEA WHAT TO SAY. OR HOW TO SAY IT!

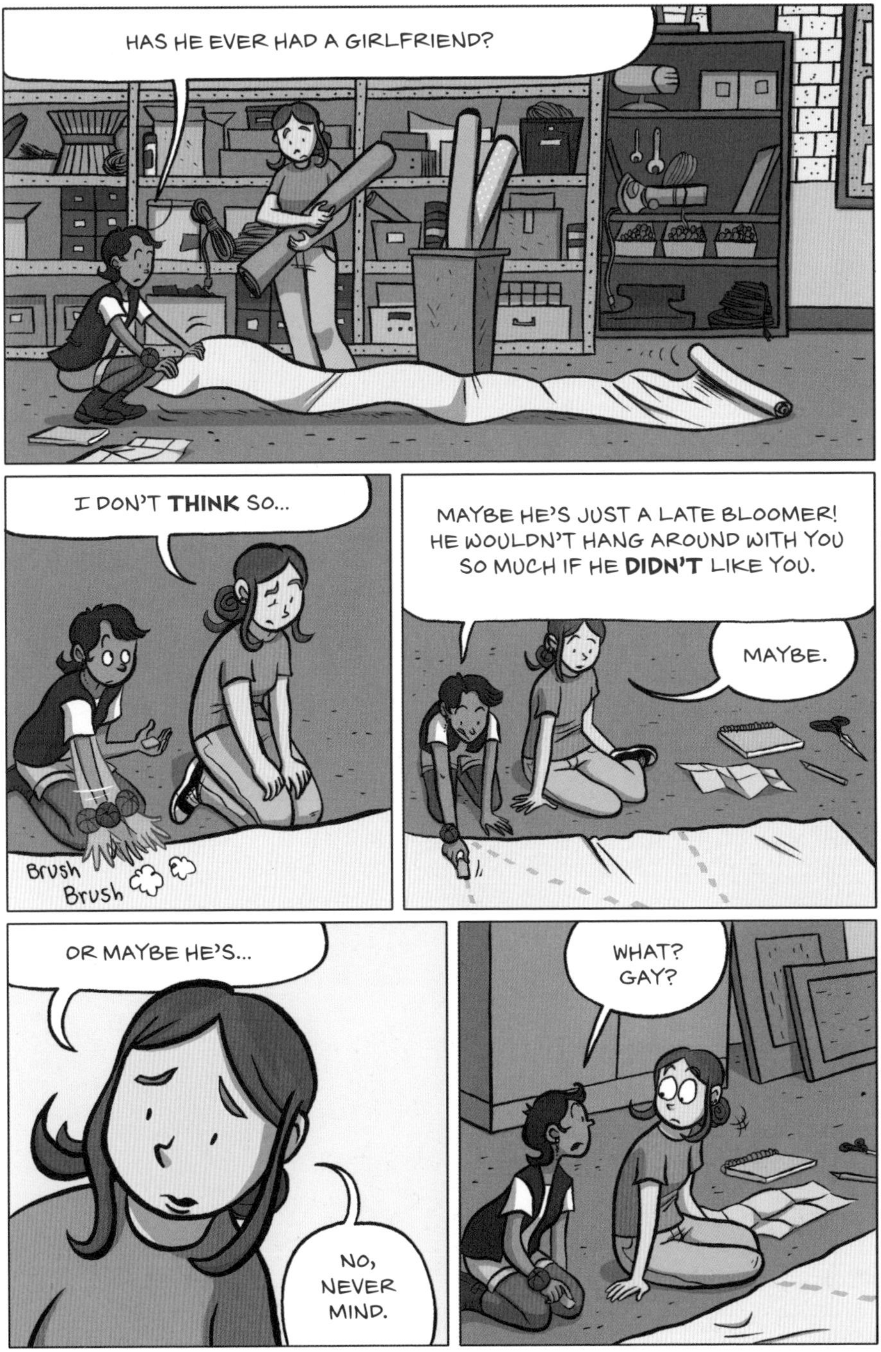
HAS HE EVER HAD A GIRLFRIEND?
I DON'T **THINK** SO...
Brush
Brush
MAYBE HE'S JUST A LATE BLOOMER! HE WOULDN'T HANG AROUND WITH YOU SO MUCH IF HE **DIDN'T** LIKE YOU.
MAYBE.
OR MAYBE HE'S...
NO, NEVER MIND.
WHAT? GAY?

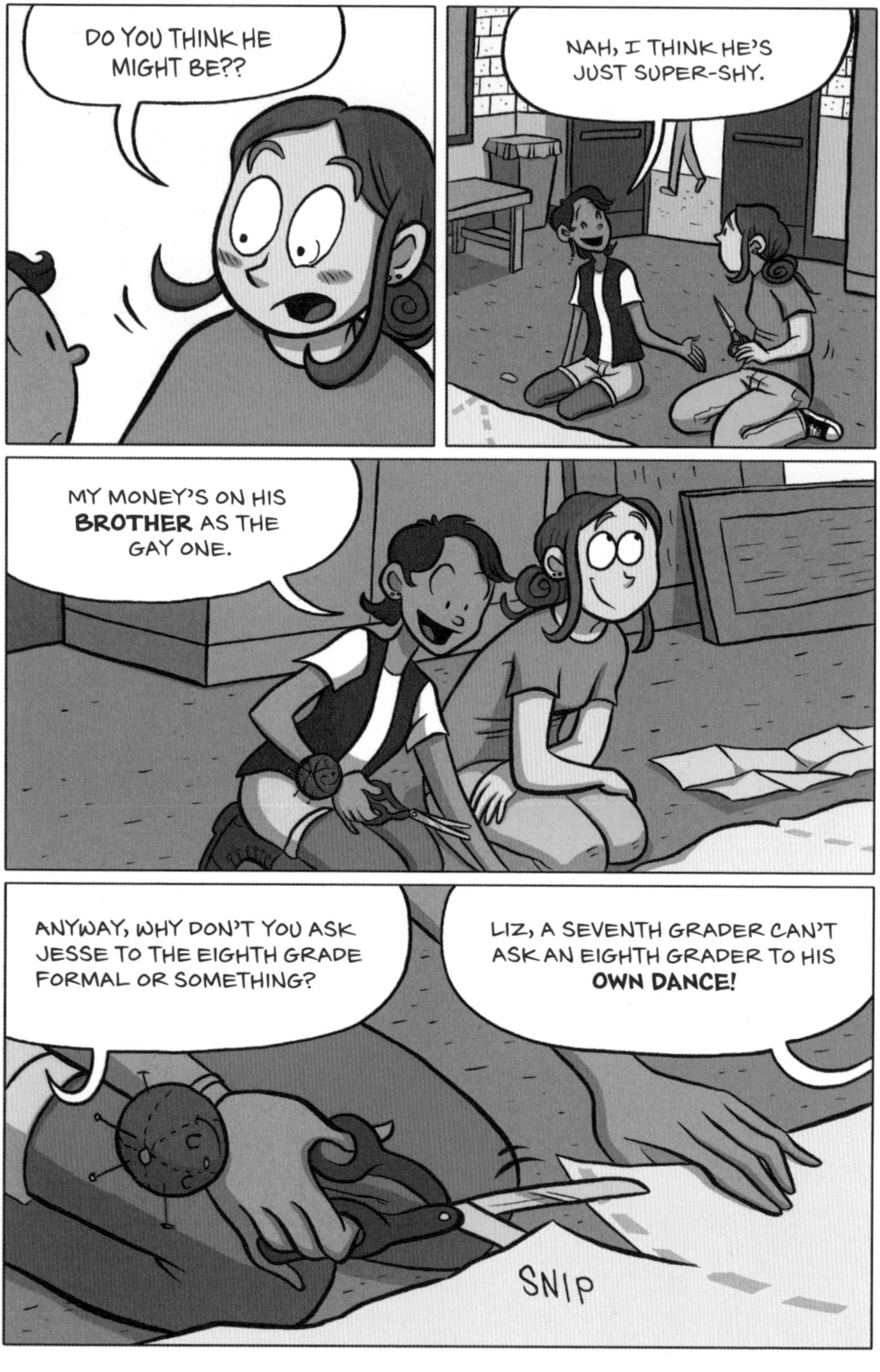
DO YOU THINK HE MIGHT BE??
NAH, I THINK HE'S JUST SUPER-SHY.
MY MONEY'S ON HIS **BROTHER** AS THE GAY ONE.
ANYWAY, WHY DON'T YOU ASK JESSE TO THE EIGHTH GRADE FORMAL OR SOMETHING?
LIZ, A SEVENTH GRADER CAN'T ASK AN EIGHTH GRADER TO HIS **OWN DANCE!**
SNIP

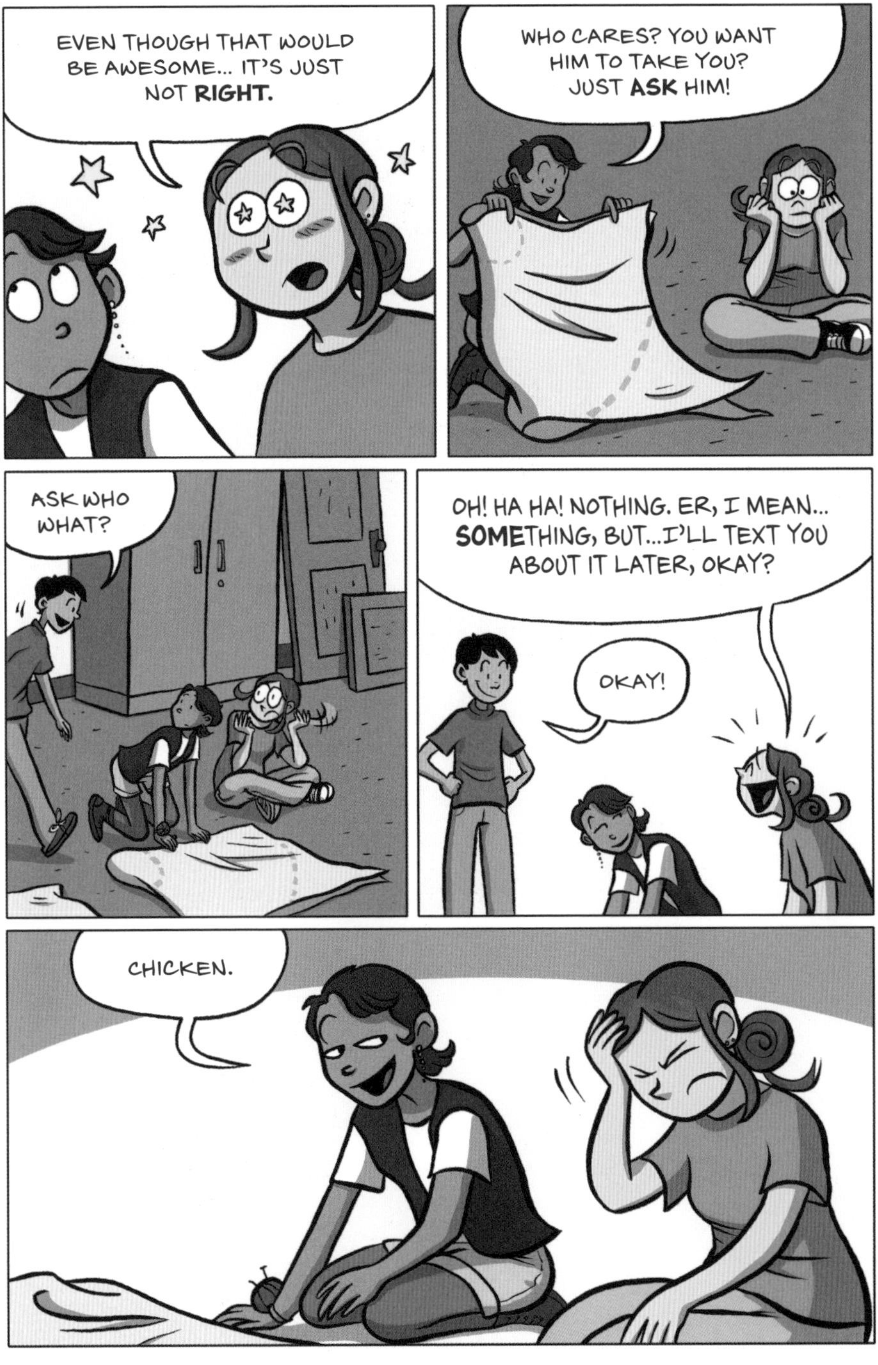
EVEN THOUGH THAT WOULD BE AWESOME... IT'S JUST NOT **RIGHT.**
WHO CARES? YOU WANT HIM TO TAKE YOU? JUST **ASK** HIM!
ASK WHO WHAT?
OH! HA HA! NOTHING. ER, I MEAN... **SOME**THING, BUT...I'LL TEXT YOU ABOUT IT LATER, OKAY?
OKAY!
CHICKEN.

TO: Jesse
Hey... do u

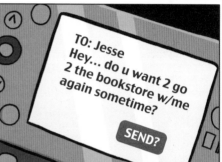

TO: Jesse
Hey... do u want 2 go 2 the bookstore w/me again sometime?

SEND?

send!

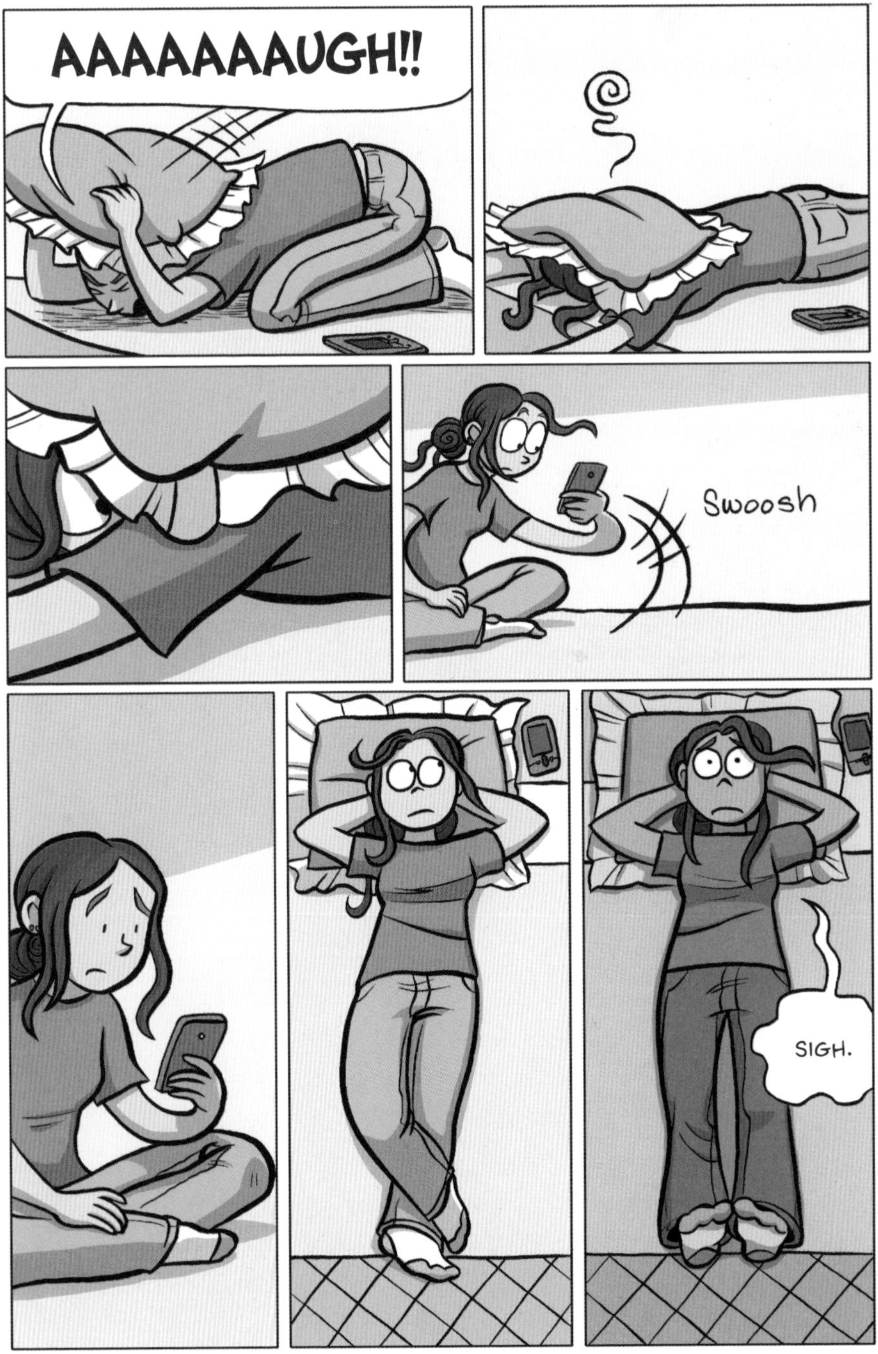
AAAAAAAUGH!!
Swoosh
SIGH.

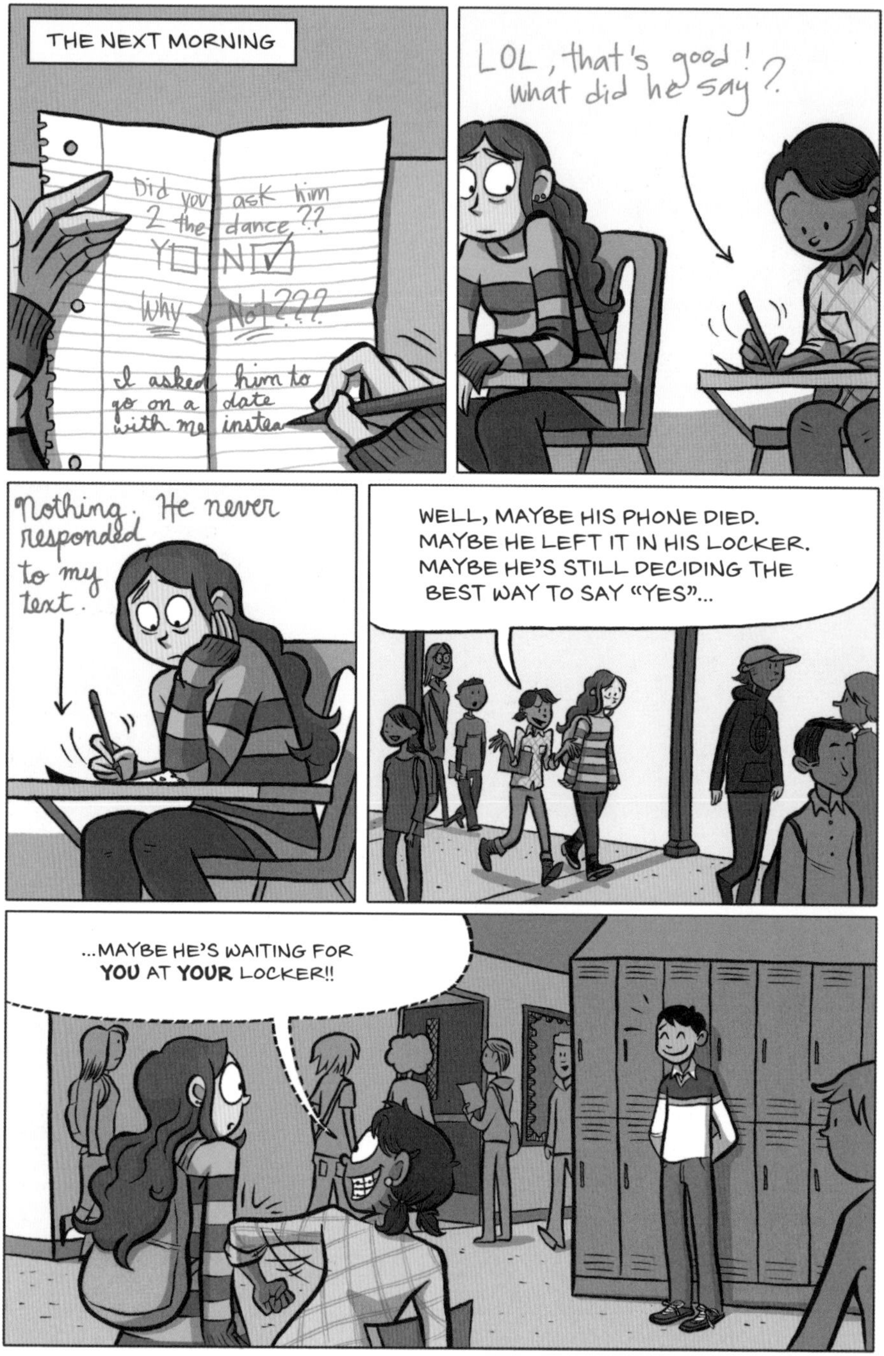
THE NEXT MORNING
Did you ask him 2 the dance??
Y N
Why Not???
I asked him to go on a date with me instea
LOL, that's good! what did he say?
Nothing. He never responded to my text.
WELL, MAYBE HIS PHONE DIED. MAYBE HE LEFT IT IN HIS LOCKER. MAYBE HE'S STILL DECIDING THE BEST WAY TO SAY "YES"...
...MAYBE HE'S WAITING FOR **YOU** AT **YOUR** LOCKER!!

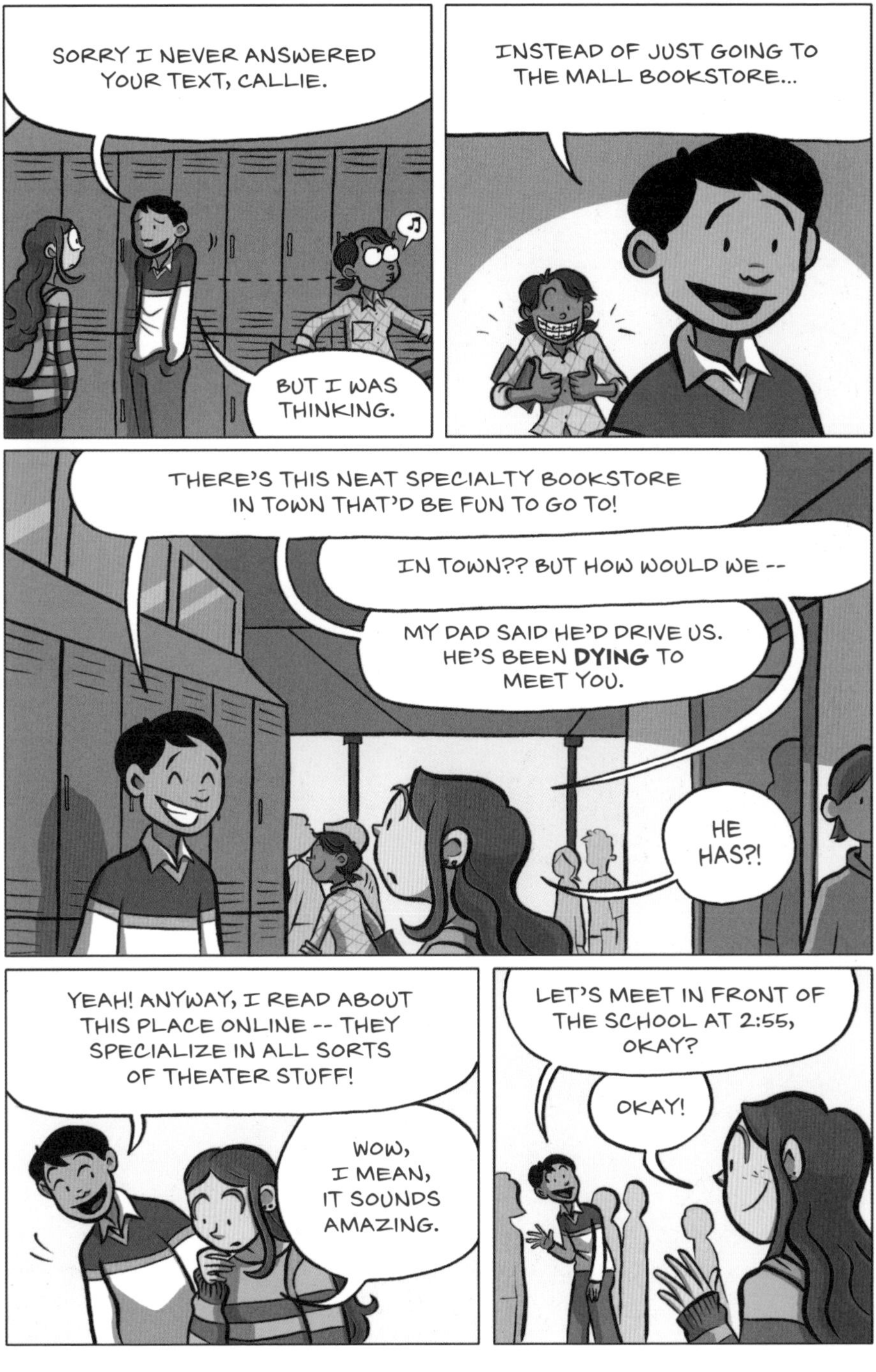
SORRY I NEVER ANSWERED YOUR TEXT, CALLIE.
BUT I WAS THINKING.
INSTEAD OF JUST GOING TO THE MALL BOOKSTORE...
THERE'S THIS NEAT SPECIALTY BOOKSTORE IN TOWN THAT'D BE FUN TO GO TO!
IN TOWN?? BUT HOW WOULD WE --
MY DAD SAID HE'D DRIVE US. HE'S BEEN **DYING** TO MEET YOU.
HE HAS?!
YEAH! ANYWAY, I READ ABOUT THIS PLACE ONLINE -- THEY SPECIALIZE IN ALL SORTS OF THEATER STUFF!
WOW, I MEAN, IT SOUNDS AMAZING.
LET'S MEET IN FRONT OF THE SCHOOL AT 2:55, OKAY?
OKAY!

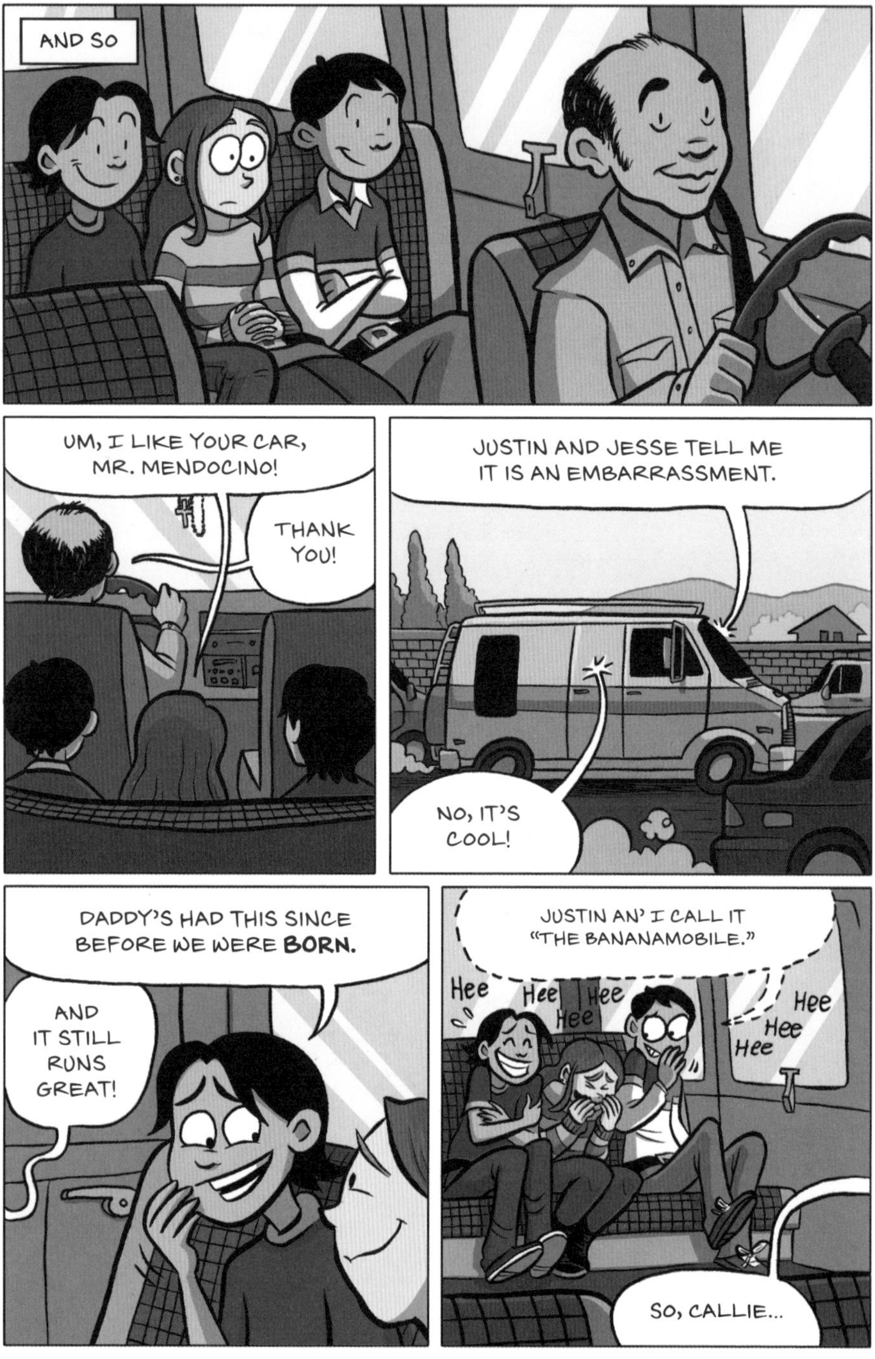
AND SO
UM, I LIKE YOUR CAR, MR. MENDOCINO!
THANK YOU!
JUSTIN AND JESSE TELL ME IT IS AN EMBARRASSMENT.
NO, IT'S COOL!
DADDY'S HAD THIS SINCE BEFORE WE WERE **BORN.**
AND IT STILL RUNS GREAT!
JUSTIN AN' I CALL IT "THE BANANAMOBILE."
Hee Hee Hee Hee
Hee Hee Hee
SO, CALLIE...

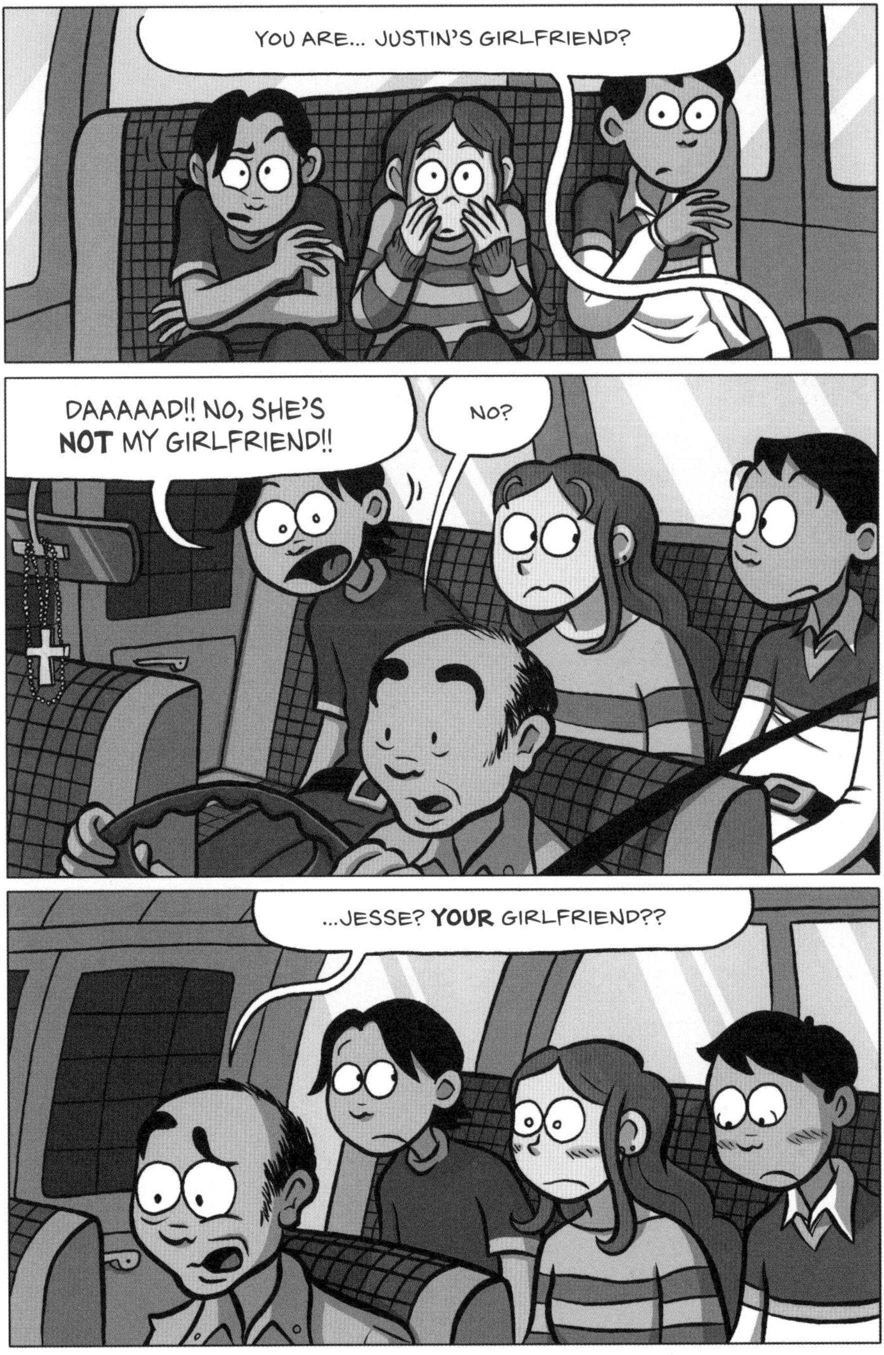

YOU ARE... JUSTIN'S GIRLFRIEND?
DAAAAAD!! NO, SHE'S **NOT** MY GIRLFRIEND!!
NO?
...JESSE? **YOUR** GIRLFRIEND??

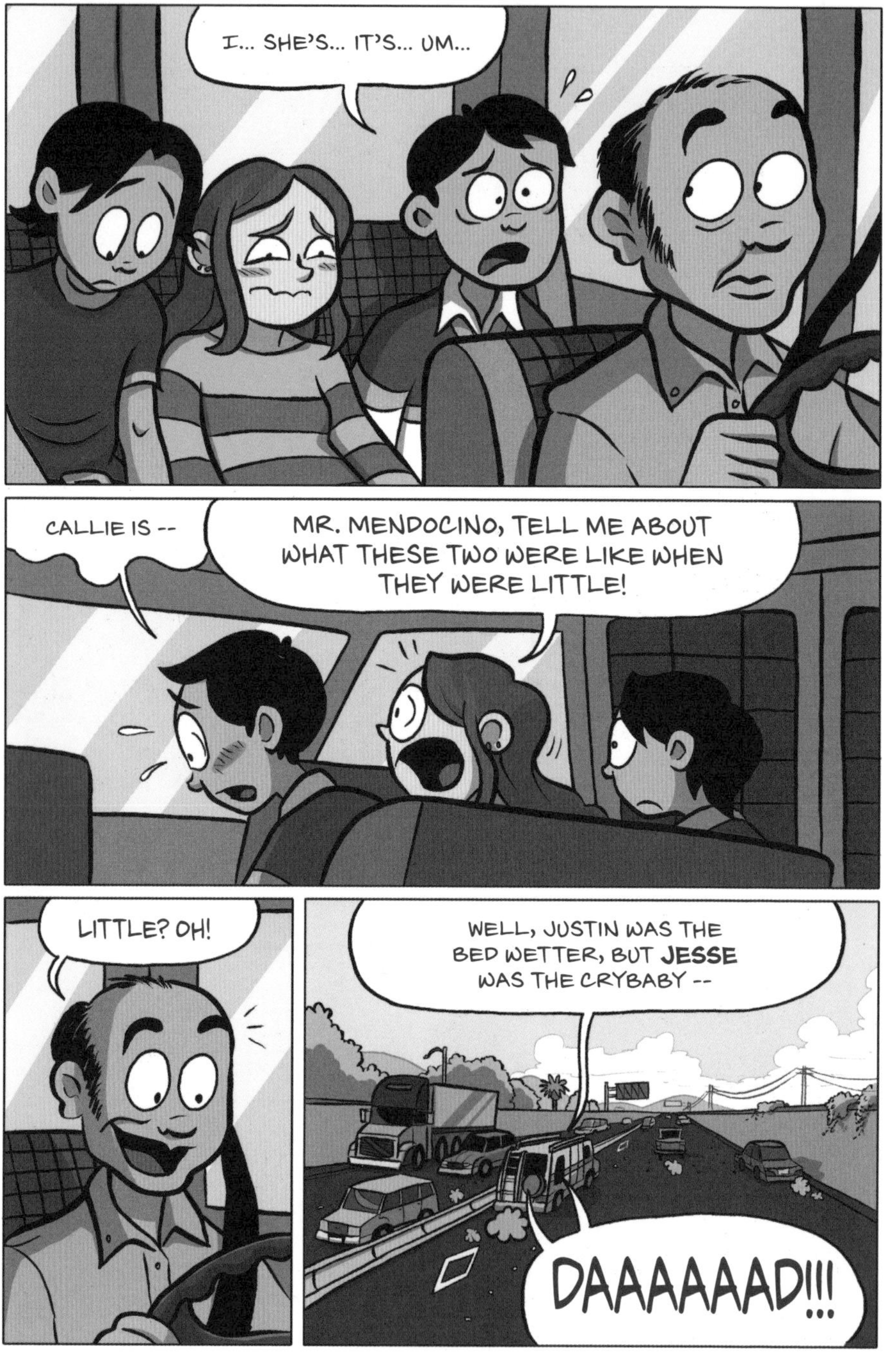
I... SHE'S... IT'S... UM...
CALLIE IS --
MR. MENDOCINO, TELL ME ABOUT WHAT THESE TWO WERE LIKE WHEN THEY WERE LITTLE!
LITTLE? OH!
WELL, JUSTIN WAS THE BED WETTER, BUT **JESSE** WAS THE CRYBABY --
DAAAAAAD!!!

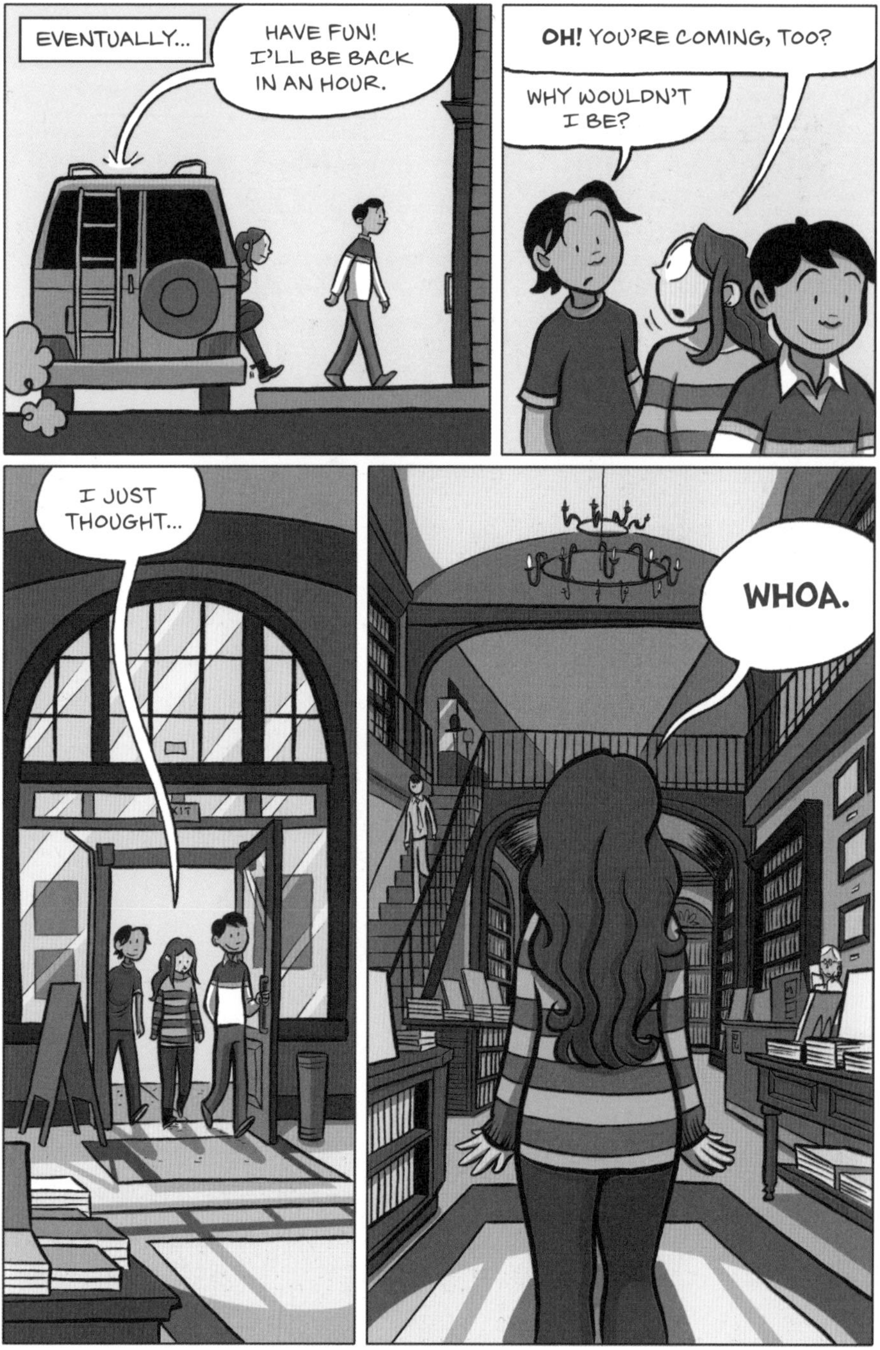
EVENTUALLY...
HAVE FUN! I'LL BE BACK IN AN HOUR.
OH! YOU'RE COMING, TOO?
WHY WOULDN'T I BE?
I JUST THOUGHT...
EXIT
WHOA.

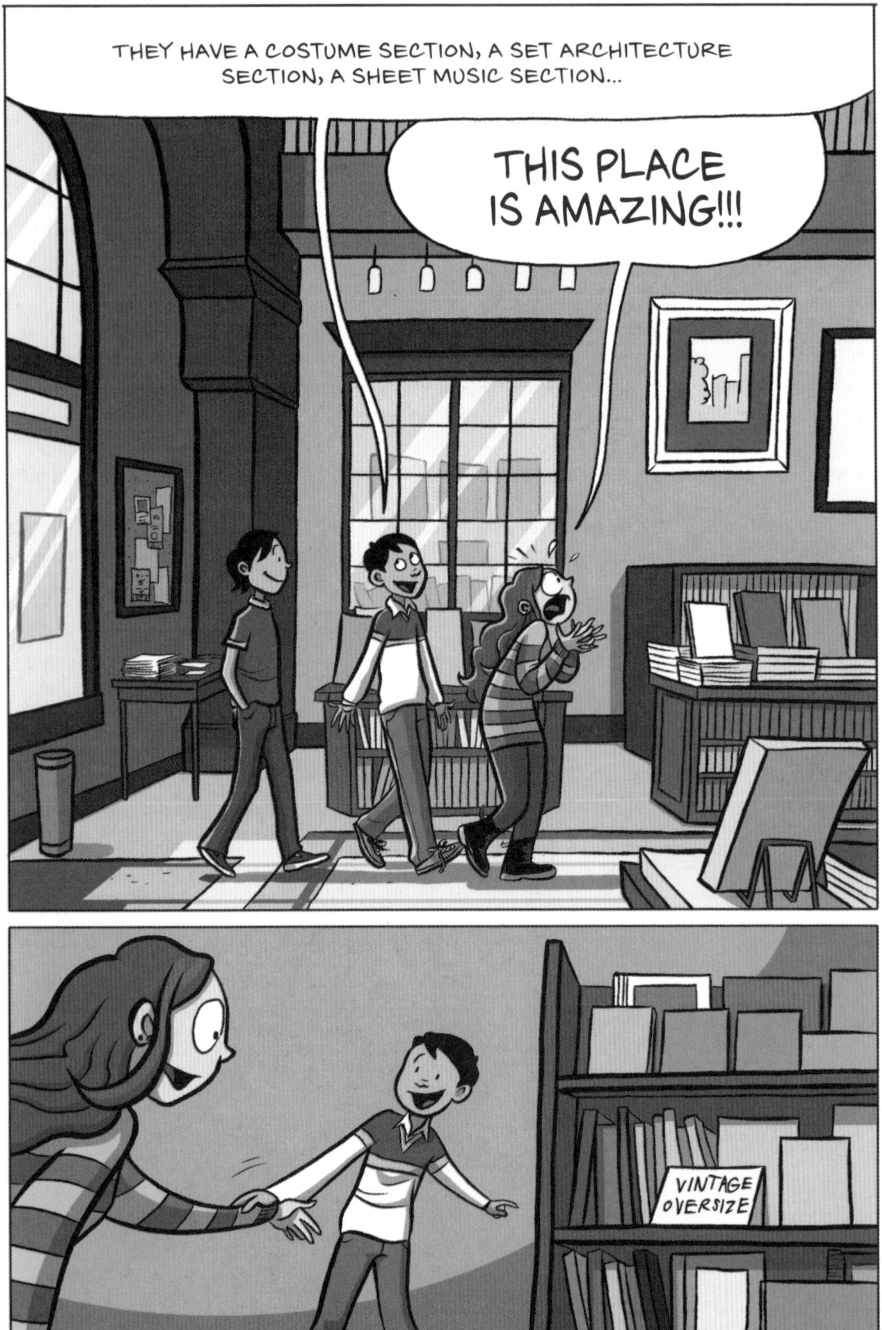
THEY HAVE A COSTUME SECTION, A SET ARCHITECTURE SECTION, A SHEET MUSIC SECTION...
THIS PLACE IS AMAZING!!!
VINTAGE OVERSIZE

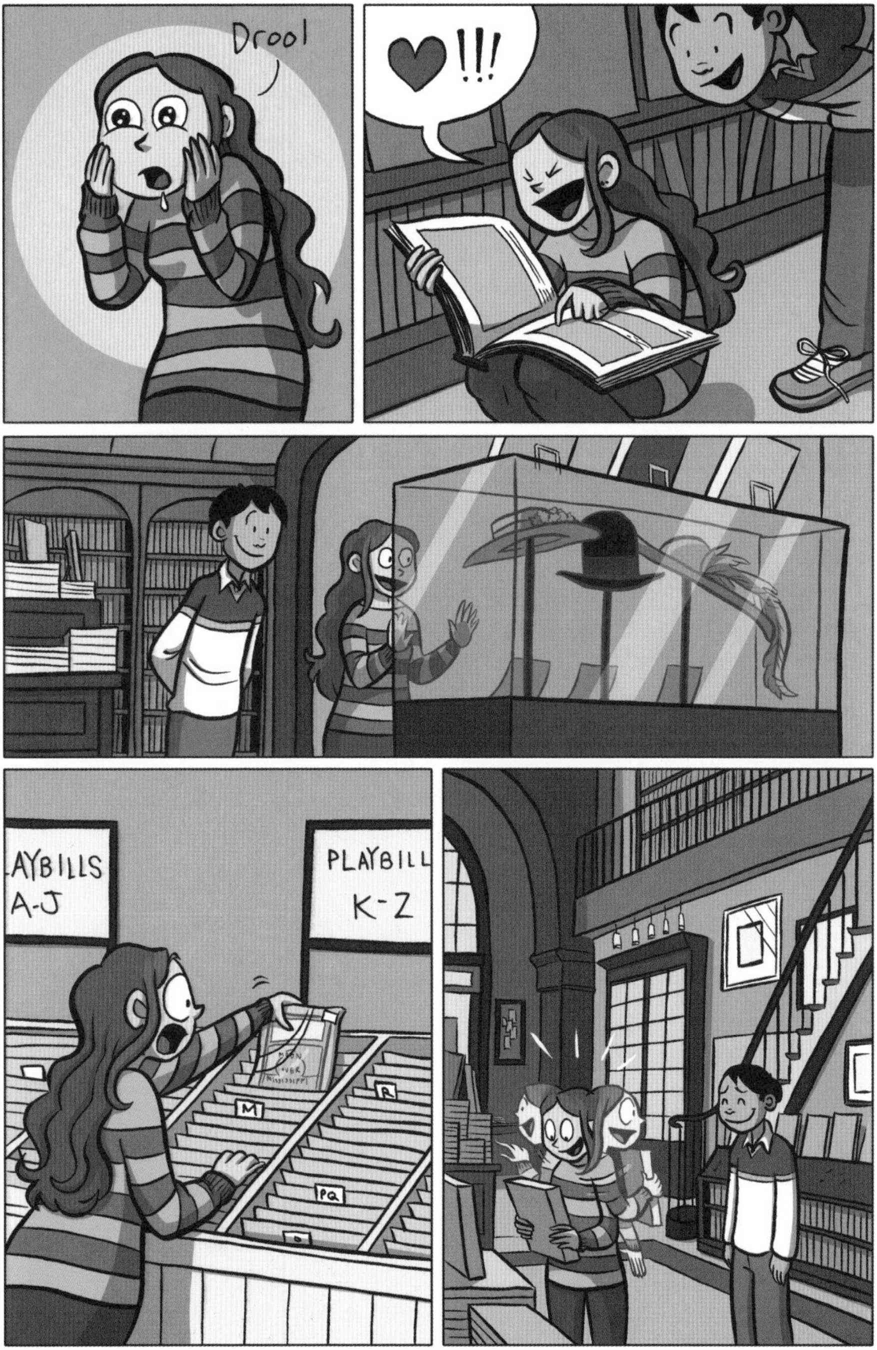
Drool
♥!!!
PLAYBILLS
A-J
PLAYBILL
K-Z
M
R
PQ

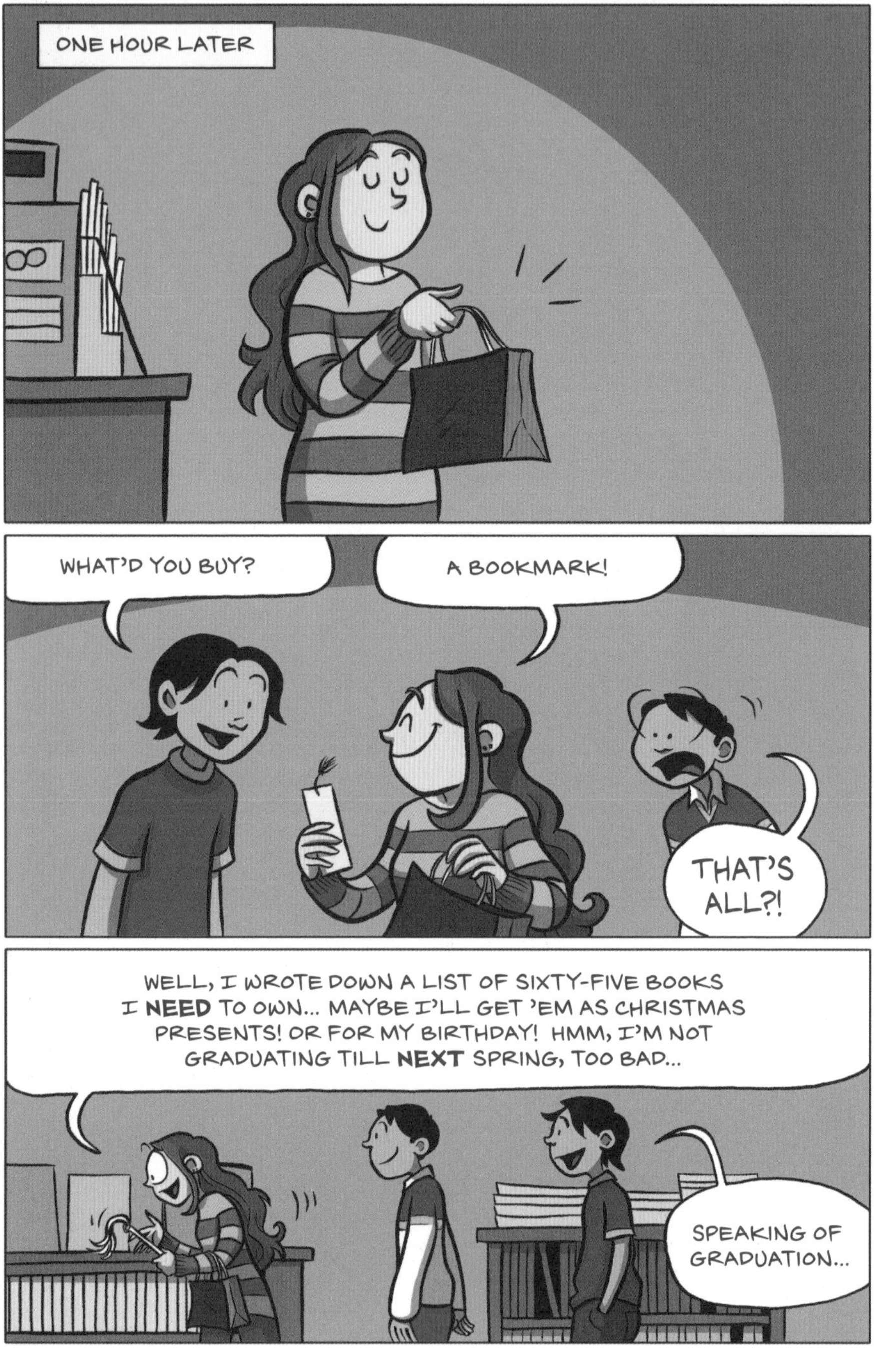
ONE HOUR LATER
WHAT'D YOU BUY?
A BOOKMARK!
THAT'S ALL?!
WELL, I WROTE DOWN A LIST OF SIXTY-FIVE BOOKS I **NEED** TO OWN... MAYBE I'LL GET 'EM AS CHRISTMAS PRESENTS! OR FOR MY BIRTHDAY! HMM, I'M NOT GRADUATING TILL **NEXT** SPRING, TOO BAD...
SPEAKING OF GRADUATION...

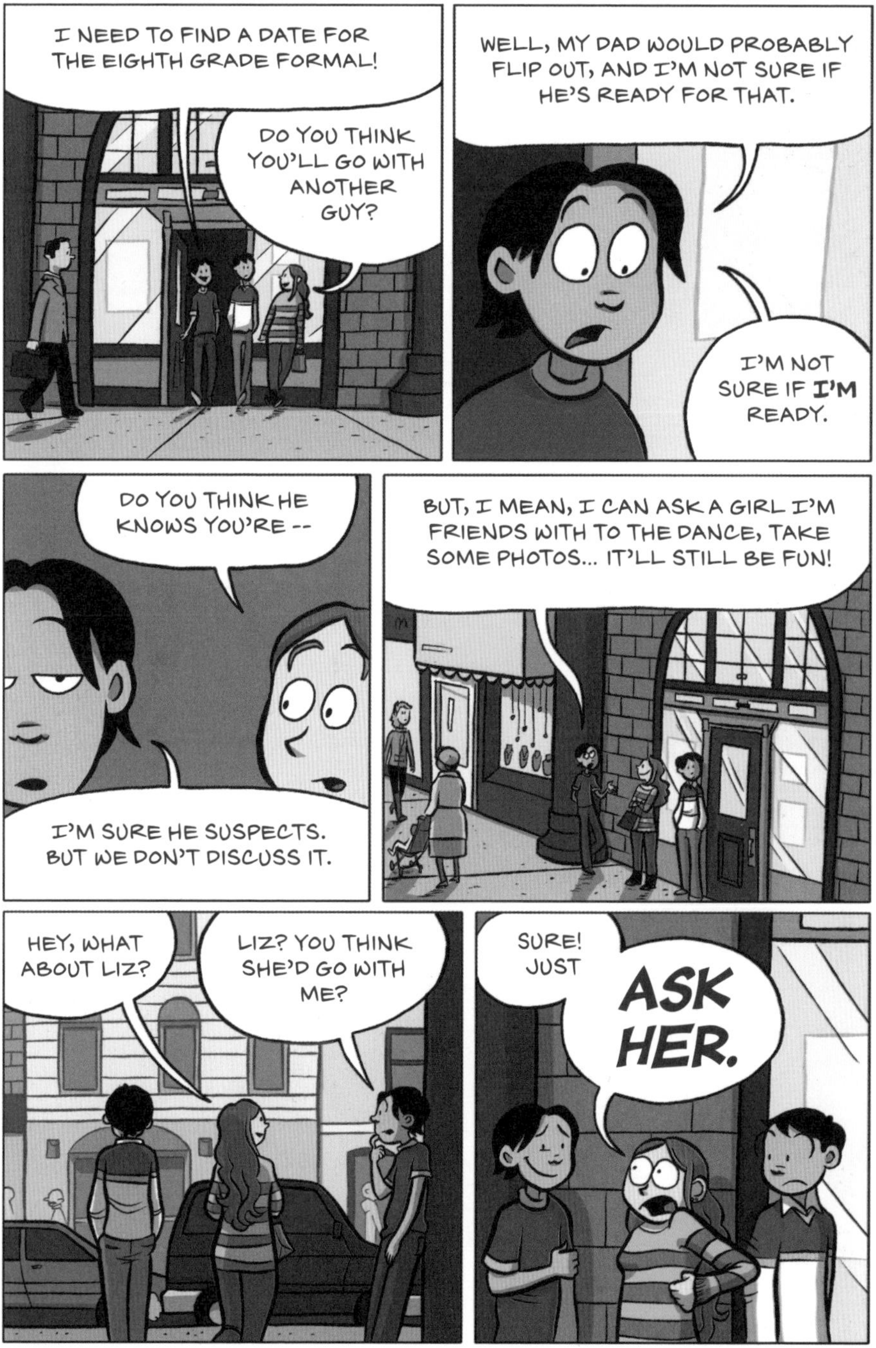
I NEED TO FIND A DATE FOR THE EIGHTH GRADE FORMAL!
DO YOU THINK YOU'LL GO WITH ANOTHER GUY?
WELL, MY DAD WOULD PROBABLY FLIP OUT, AND I'M NOT SURE IF HE'S READY FOR THAT.
I'M NOT SURE IF **I'M** READY.
DO YOU THINK HE KNOWS YOU'RE --
I'M SURE HE SUSPECTS. BUT WE DON'T DISCUSS IT.
BUT, I MEAN, I CAN ASK A GIRL I'M FRIENDS WITH TO THE DANCE, TAKE SOME PHOTOS... IT'LL STILL BE FUN!
HEY, WHAT ABOUT LIZ?
LIZ? YOU THINK SHE'D GO WITH ME?
SURE! JUST
ASK HER.

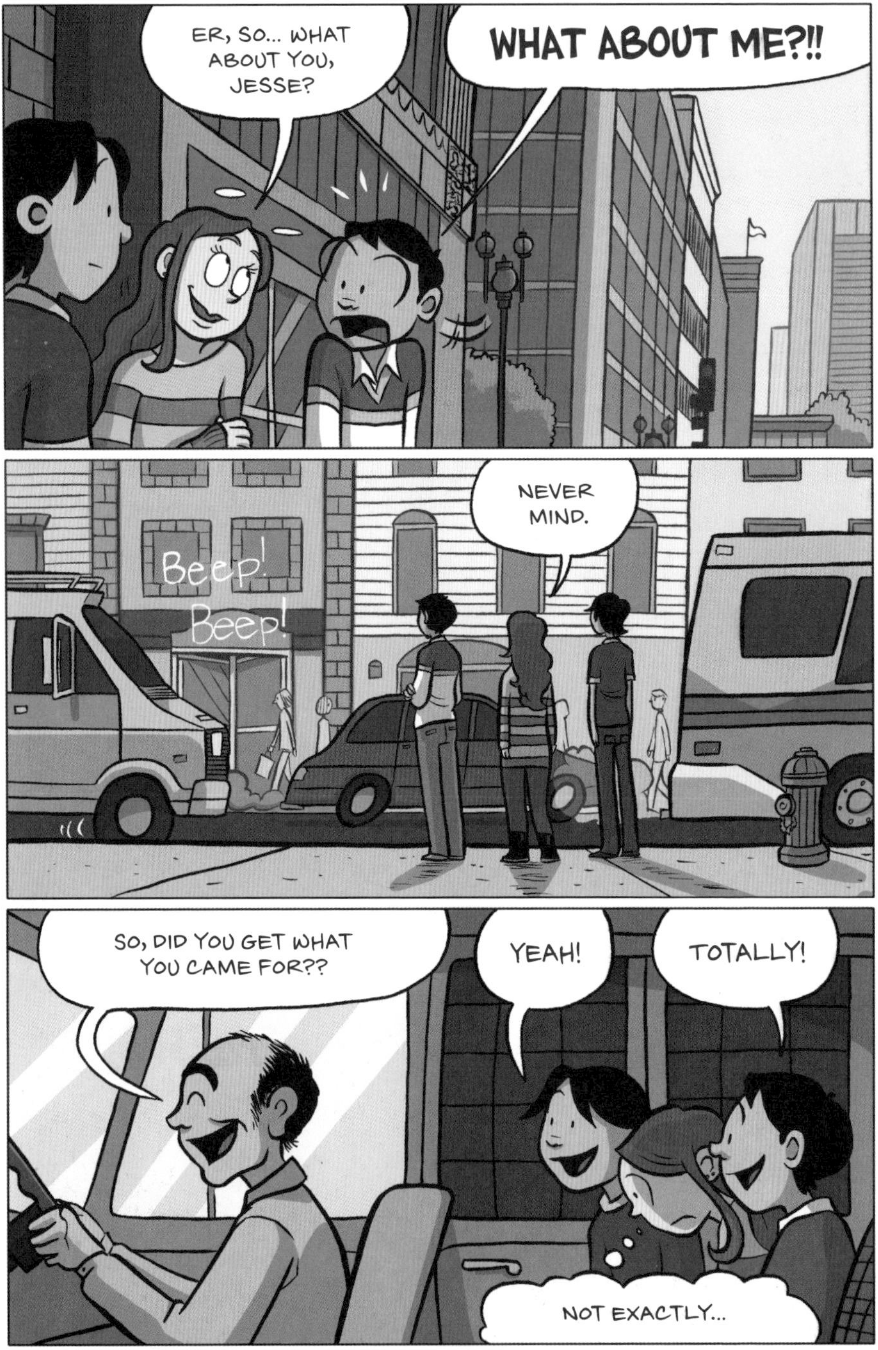
ER, SO... WHAT ABOUT YOU, JESSE?
WHAT ABOUT ME?!!
NEVER MIND.
Beep! Beep!
SO, DID YOU GET WHAT YOU CAME FOR??
YEAH!
TOTALLY!
NOT EXACTLY...

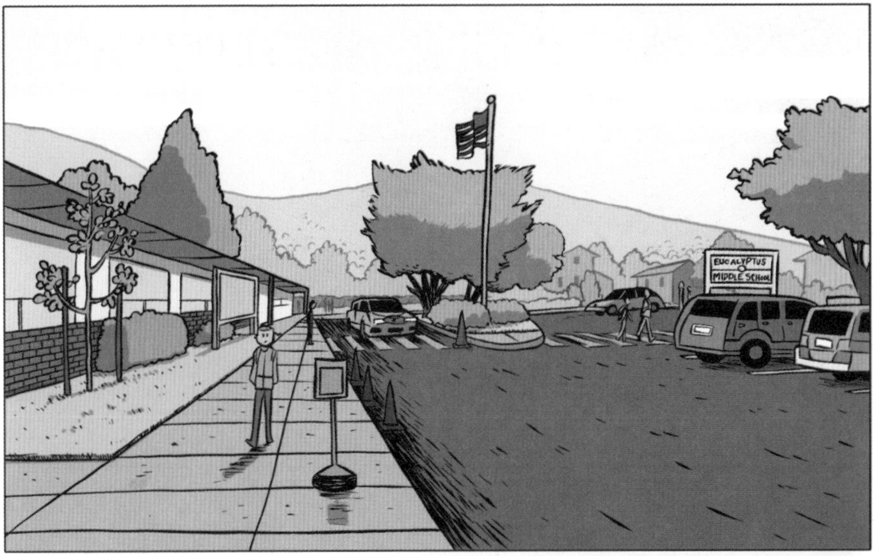
EUCALYPTUS MIDDLE SCHOOL

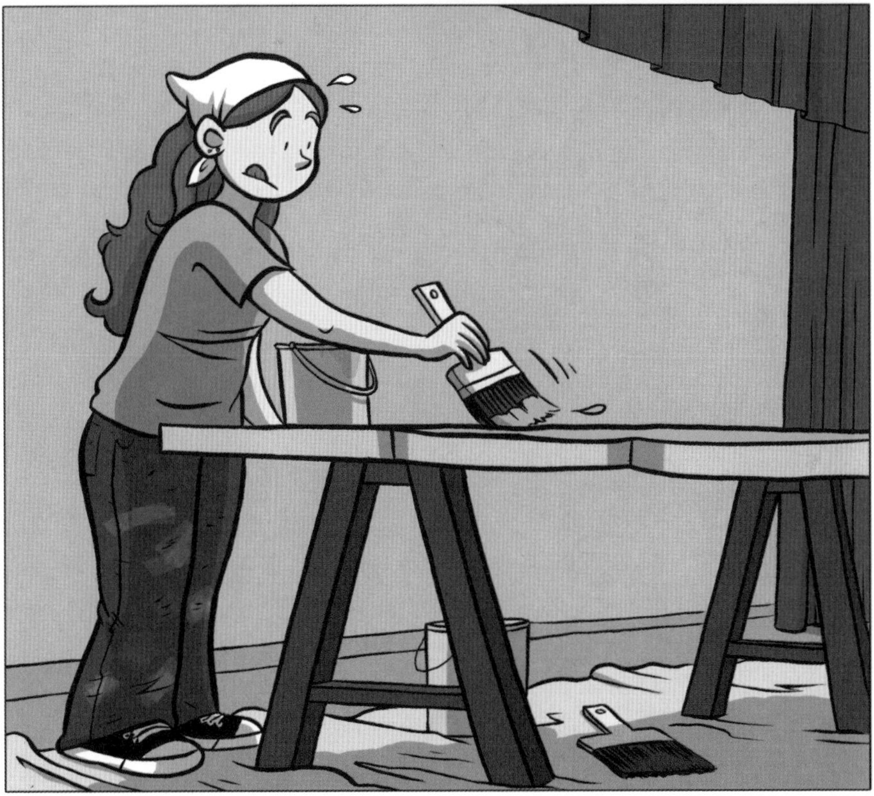

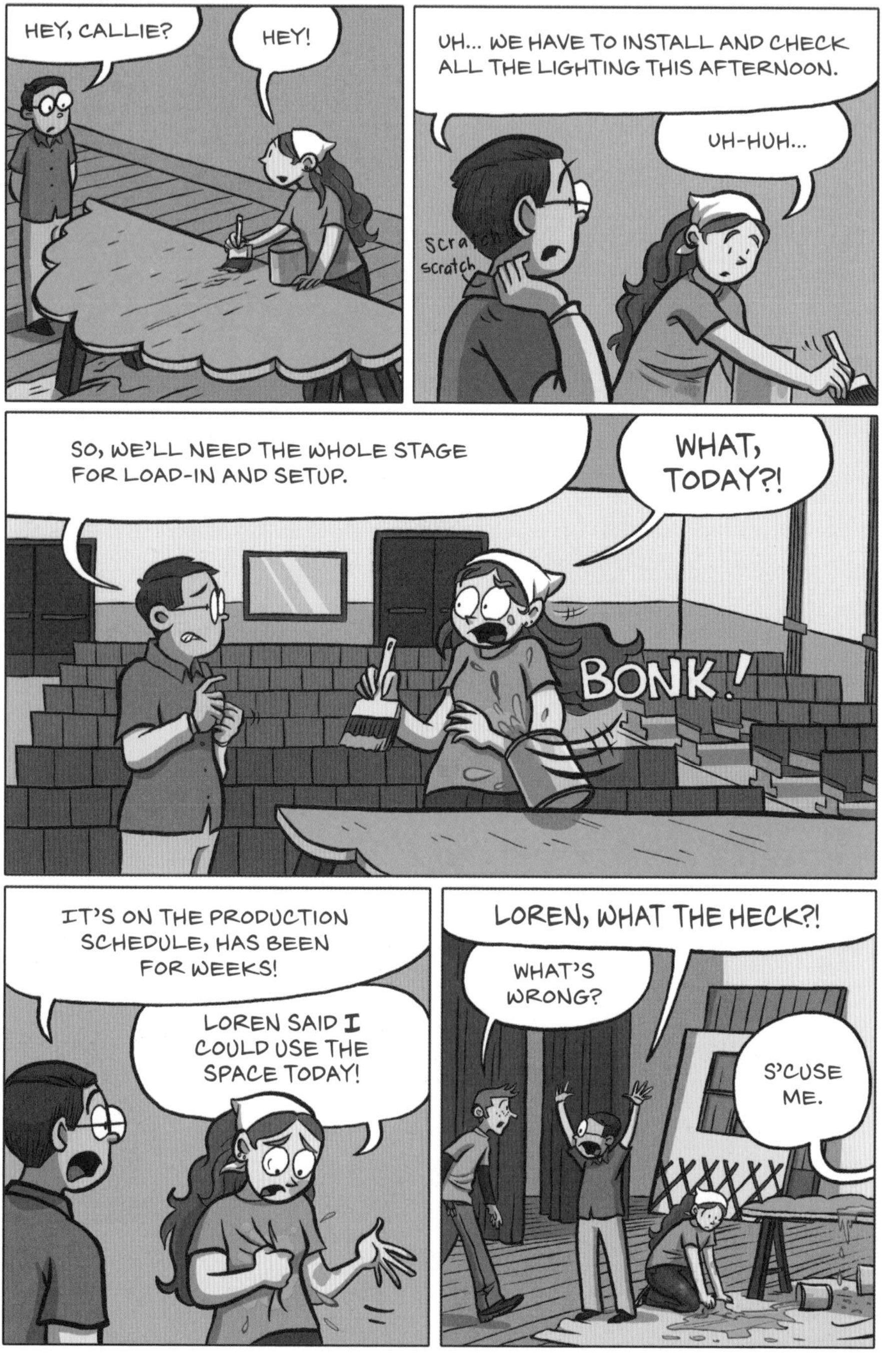
HEY, CALLIE?
HEY!
UH... WE HAVE TO INSTALL AND CHECK ALL THE LIGHTING THIS AFTERNOON.
UH-HUH...
scratch
scratch
SO, WE'LL NEED THE WHOLE STAGE FOR LOAD-IN AND SETUP.
WHAT, TODAY?!
BONK!
IT'S ON THE PRODUCTION SCHEDULE, HAS BEEN FOR WEEKS!
LOREN SAID I COULD USE THE SPACE TODAY!
LOREN, WHAT THE HECK?!
WHAT'S WRONG?
S'CUSE ME.

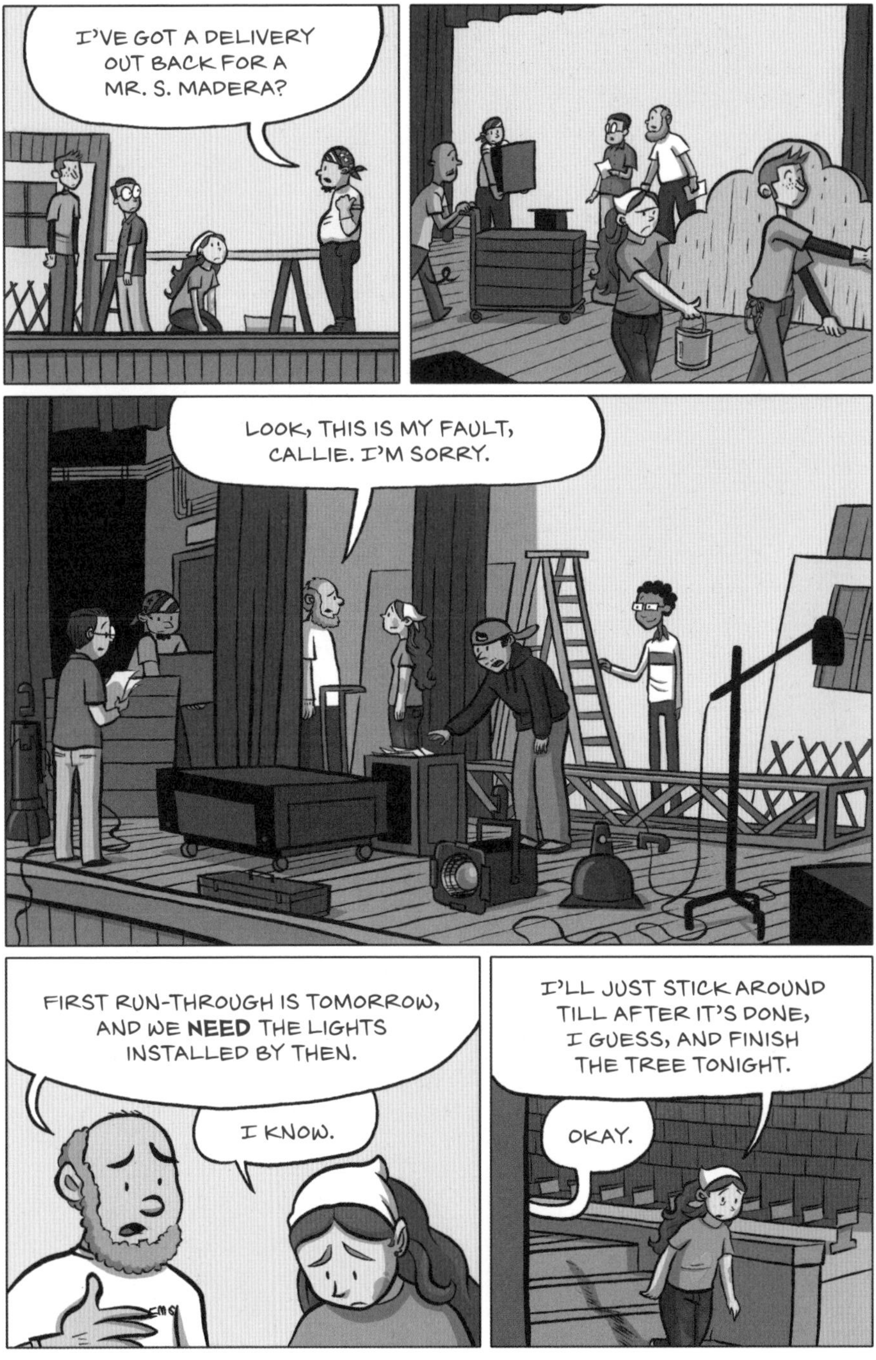
I'VE GOT A DELIVERY OUT BACK FOR A MR. S. MADERA?
LOOK, THIS IS MY FAULT, CALLIE. I'M SORRY.
FIRST RUN-THROUGH IS TOMORROW, AND WE **NEED** THE LIGHTS INSTALLED BY THEN.
I KNOW.
I'LL JUST STICK AROUND TILL AFTER IT'S DONE, I GUESS, AND FINISH THE TREE TONIGHT.
OKAY.

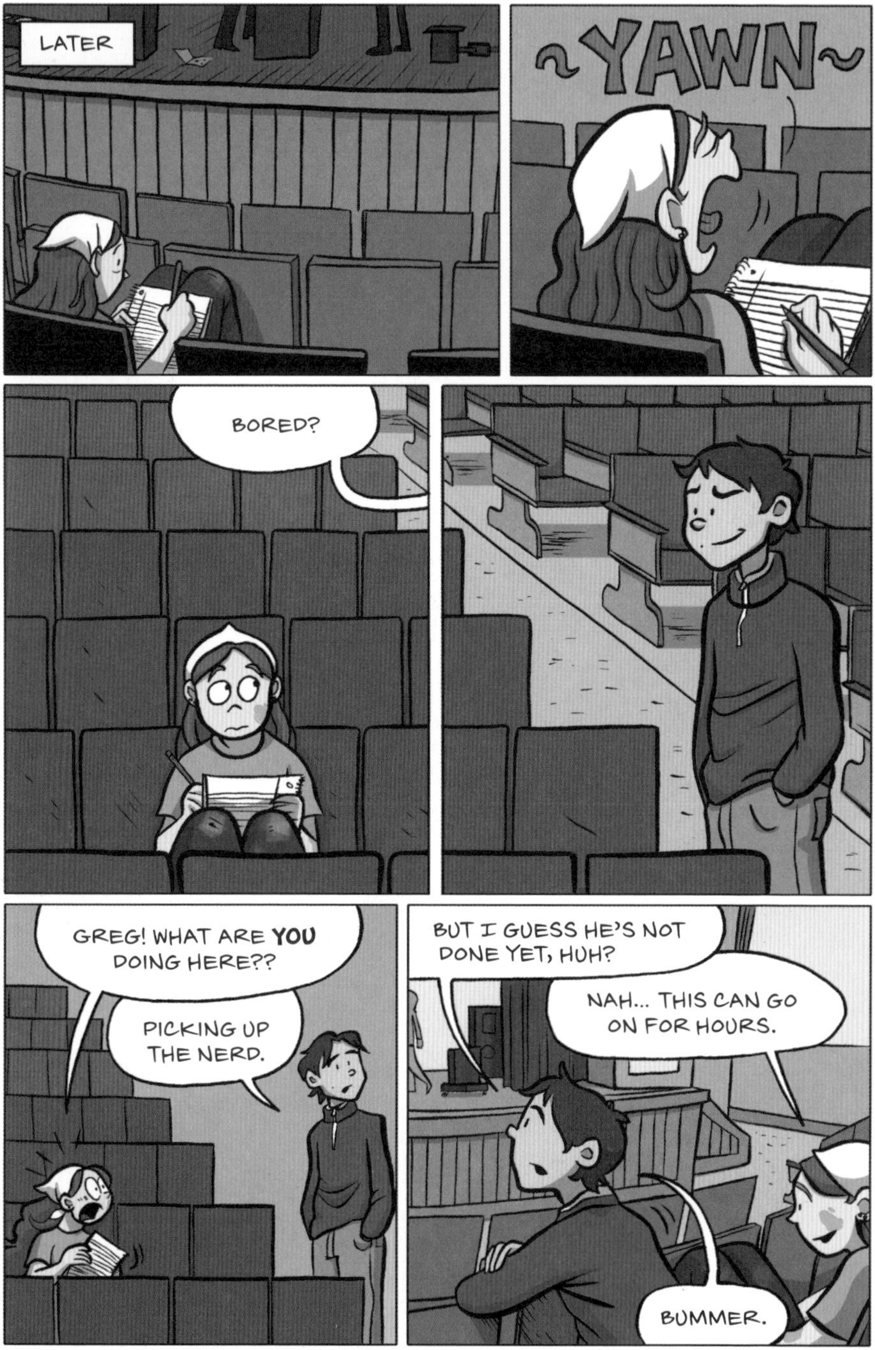
LATER
~YAWN~
BORED?
GREG! WHAT ARE **YOU** DOING HERE??
PICKING UP THE NERD.
BUT I GUESS HE'S NOT DONE YET, HUH?
NAH... THIS CAN GO ON FOR HOURS.
BUMMER.

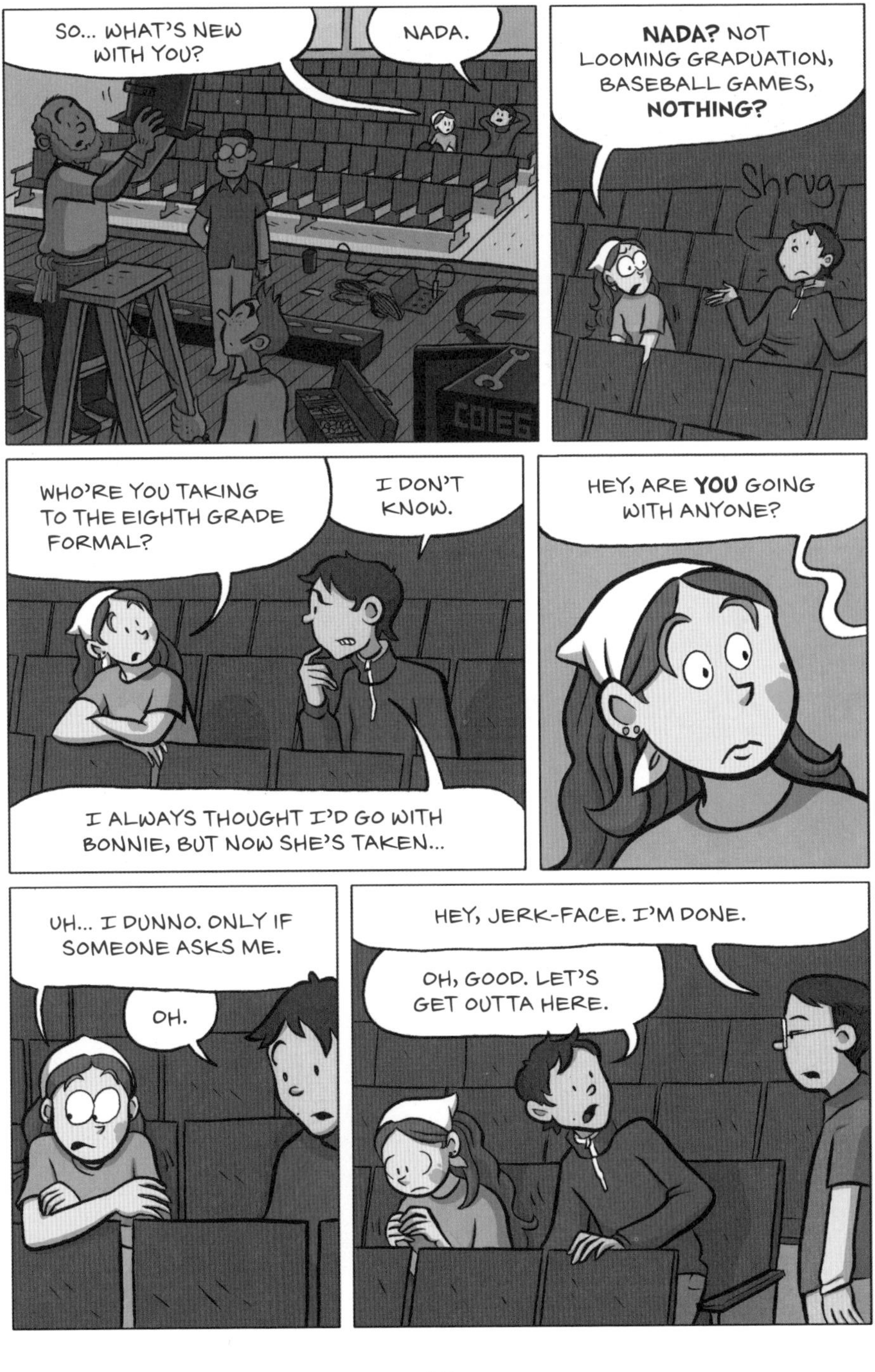
SO... WHAT'S NEW WITH YOU?
NADA.
NADA? NOT LOOMING GRADUATION, BASEBALL GAMES, NOTHING?
Shrug
WHO'RE YOU TAKING TO THE EIGHTH GRADE FORMAL?
I DON'T KNOW.
I ALWAYS THOUGHT I'D GO WITH BONNIE, BUT NOW SHE'S TAKEN...
HEY, ARE YOU GOING WITH ANYONE?
UH... I DUNNO. ONLY IF SOMEONE ASKS ME.
OH.
HEY, JERK-FACE. I'M DONE.
OH, GOOD. LET'S GET OUTTA HERE.

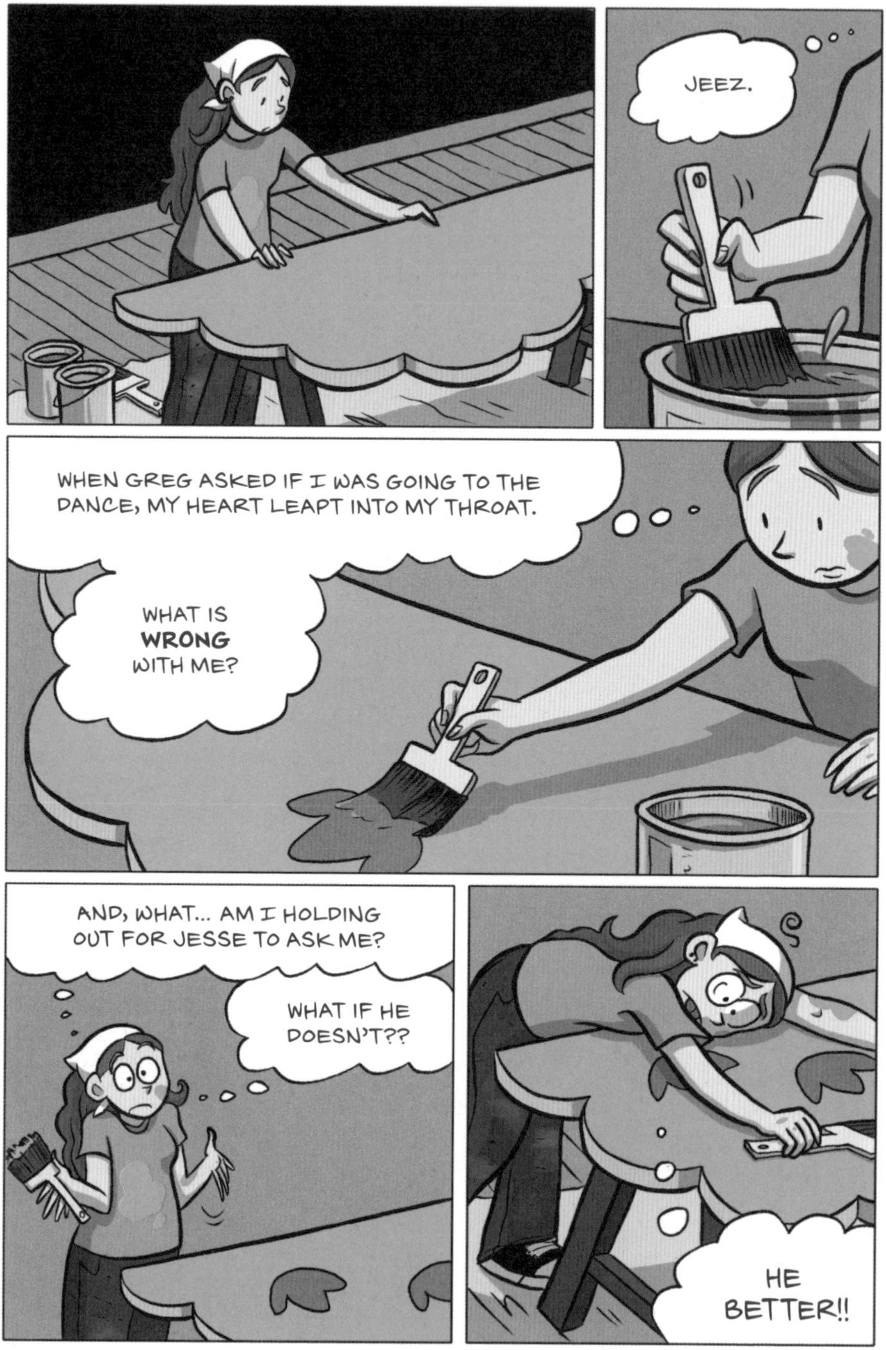
JEEZ.
WHEN GREG ASKED IF I WAS GOING TO THE DANCE, MY HEART LEAPT INTO MY THROAT.
WHAT IS **WRONG** WITH ME?
AND, WHAT... AM I HOLDING OUT FOR JESSE TO ASK ME?
WHAT IF HE DOESN'T??
HE BETTER!!

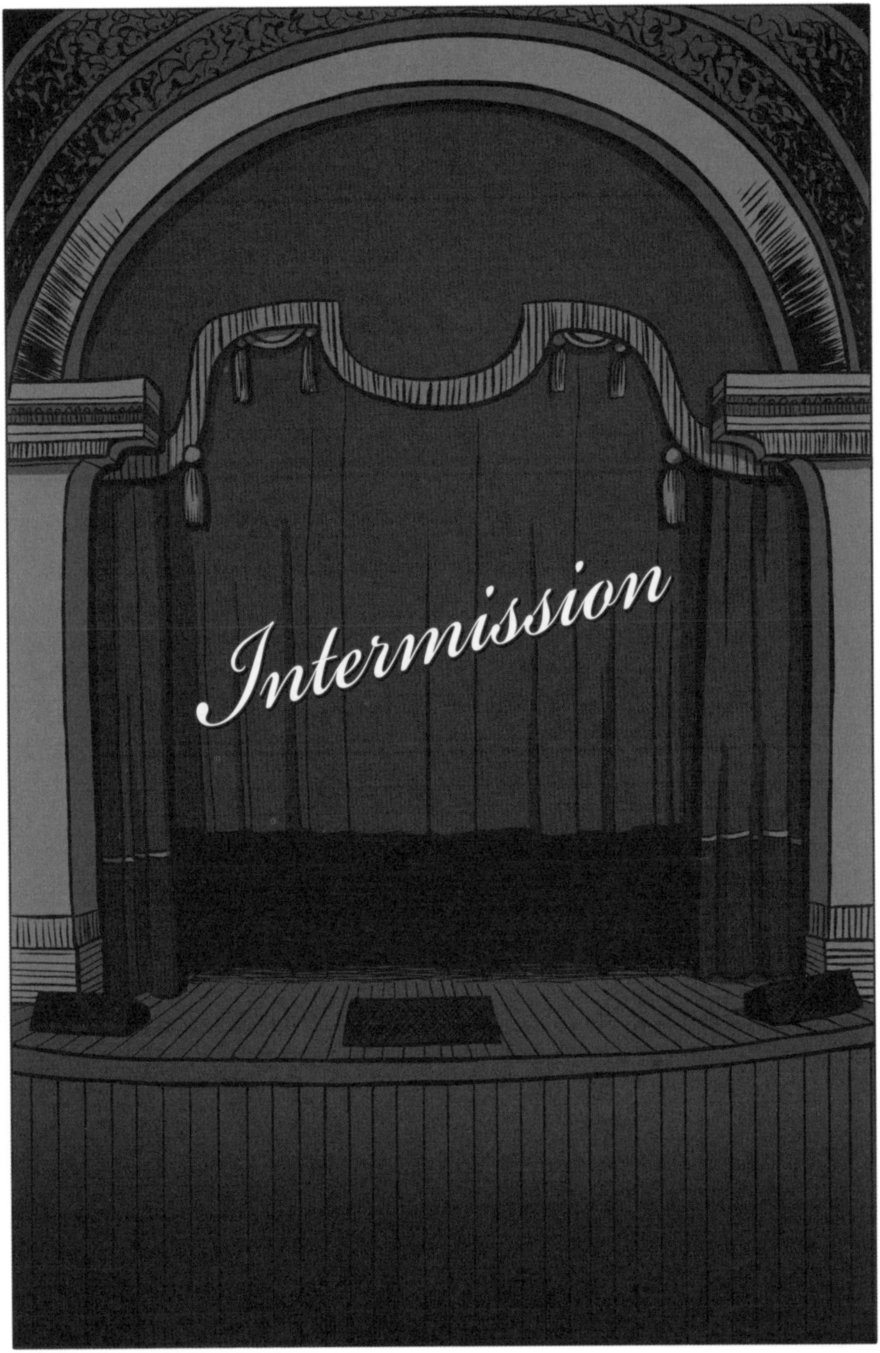
Intermission

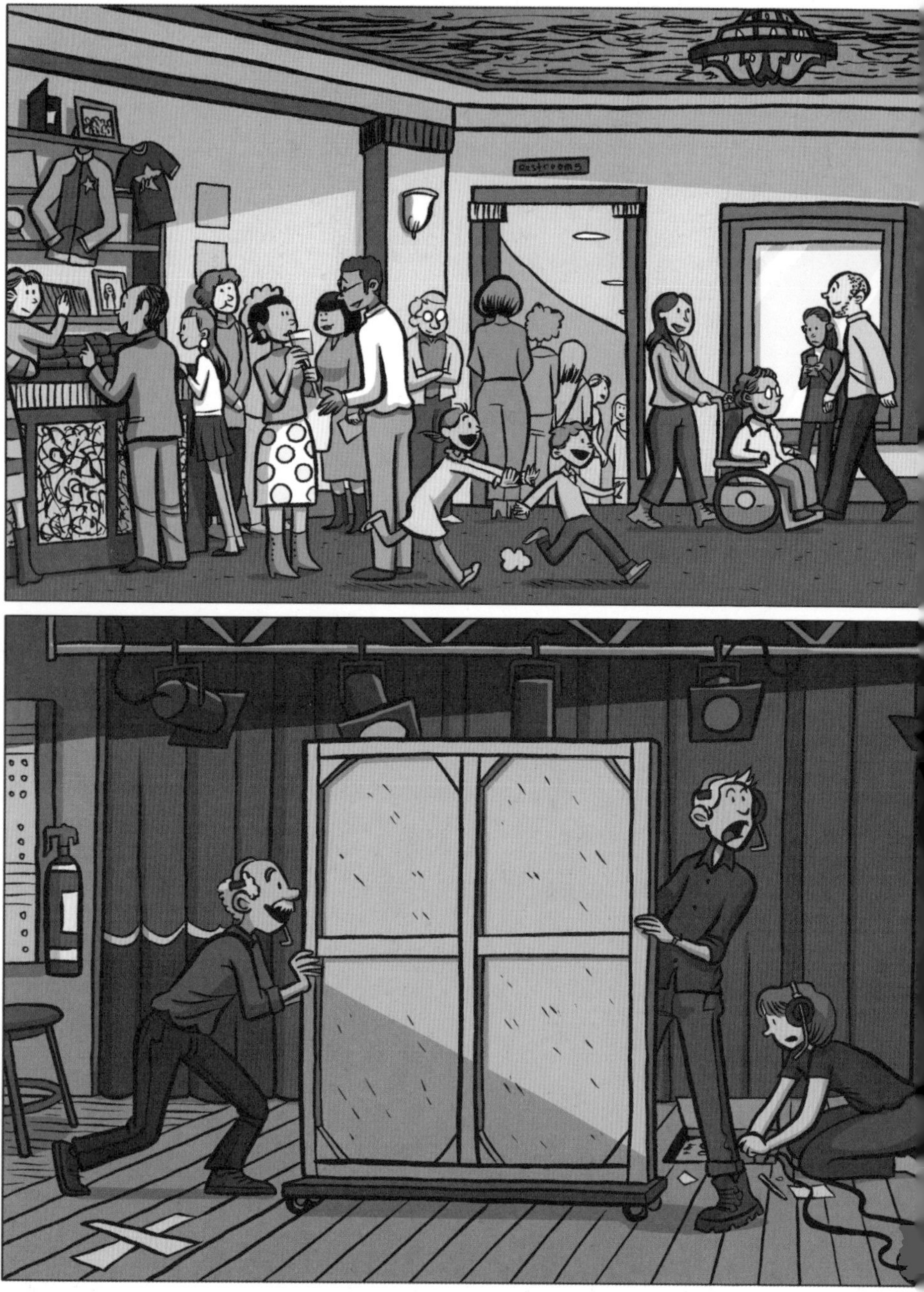
Restrooms

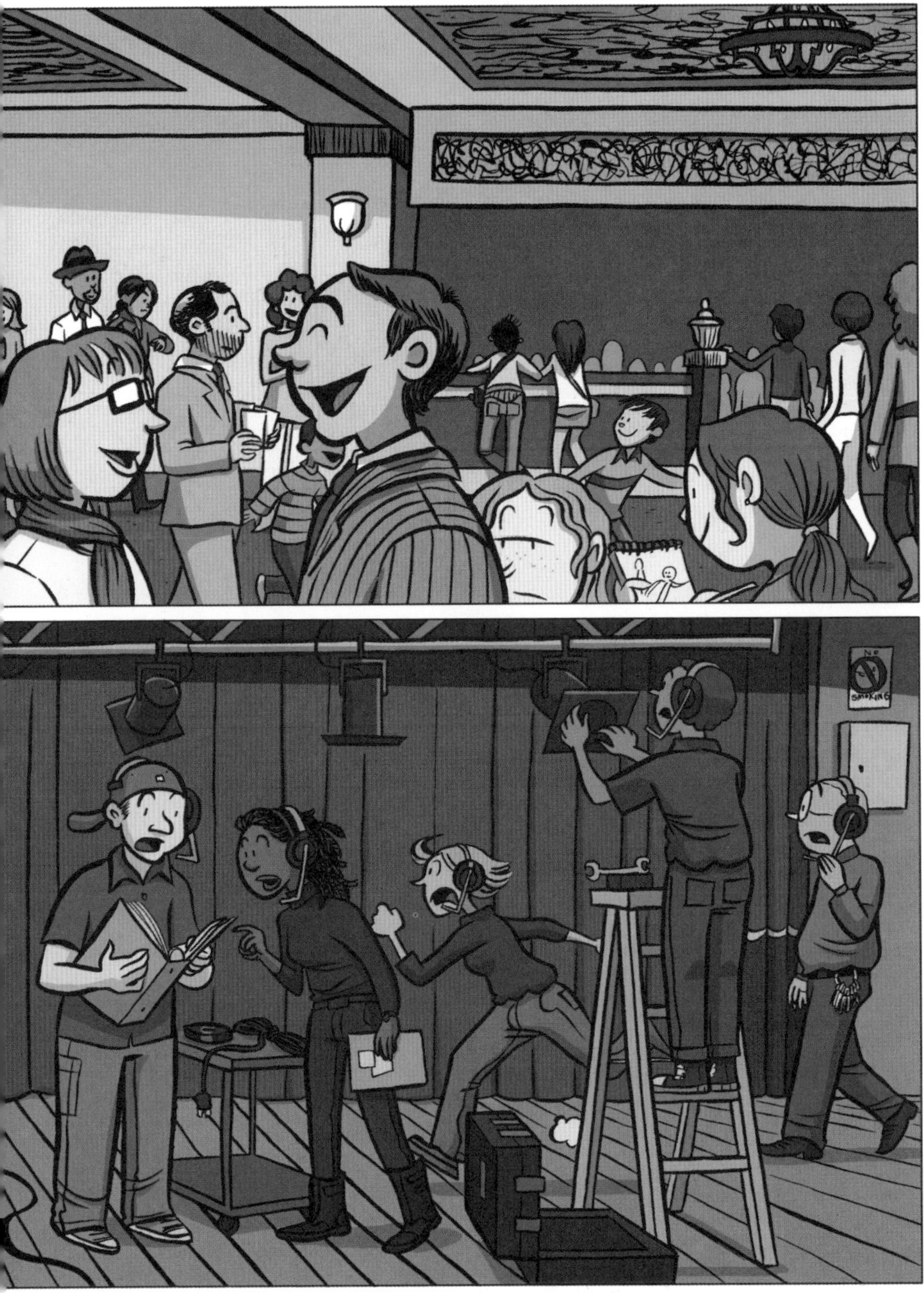
NO SMOKING

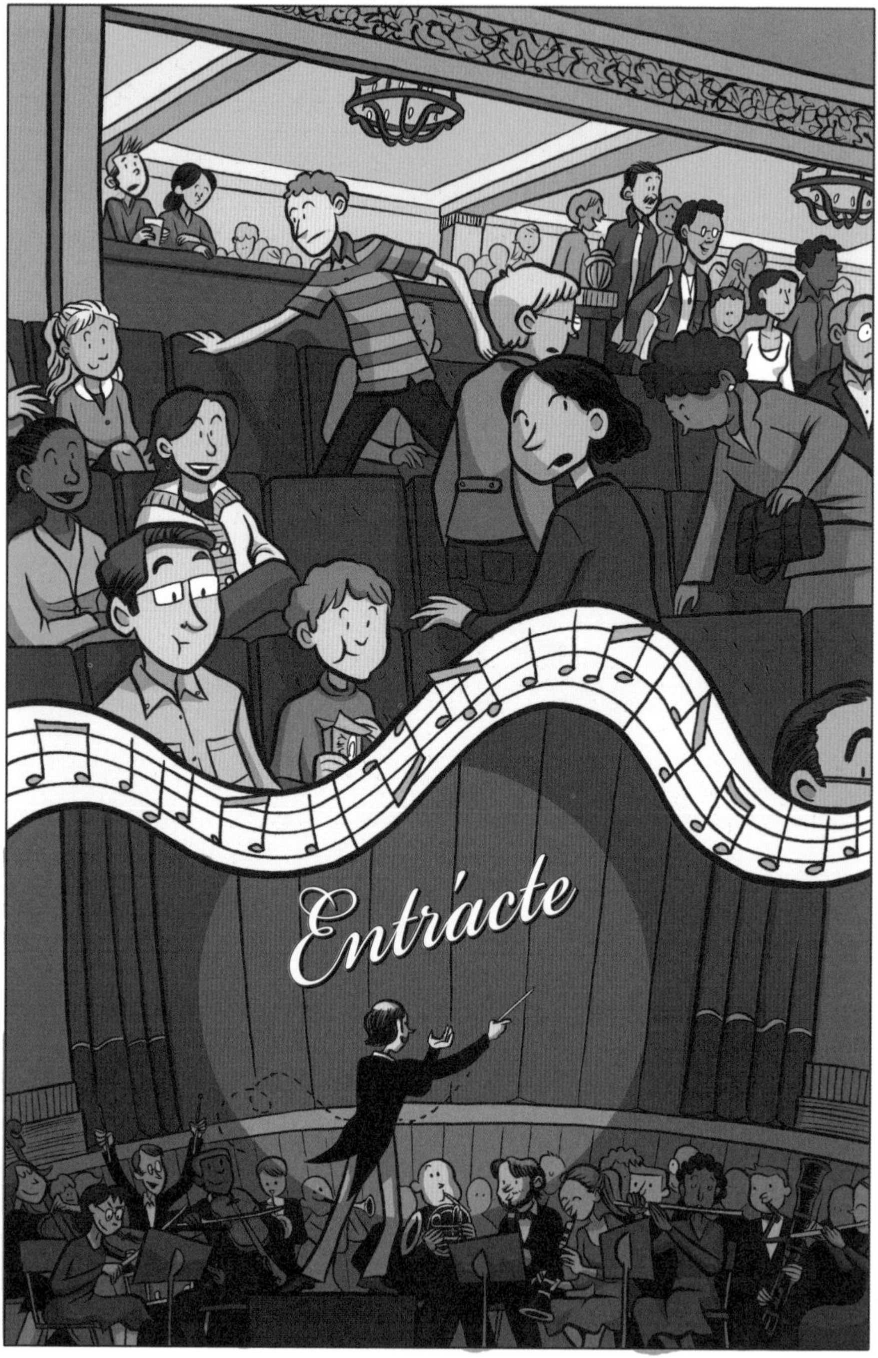
Entrácte

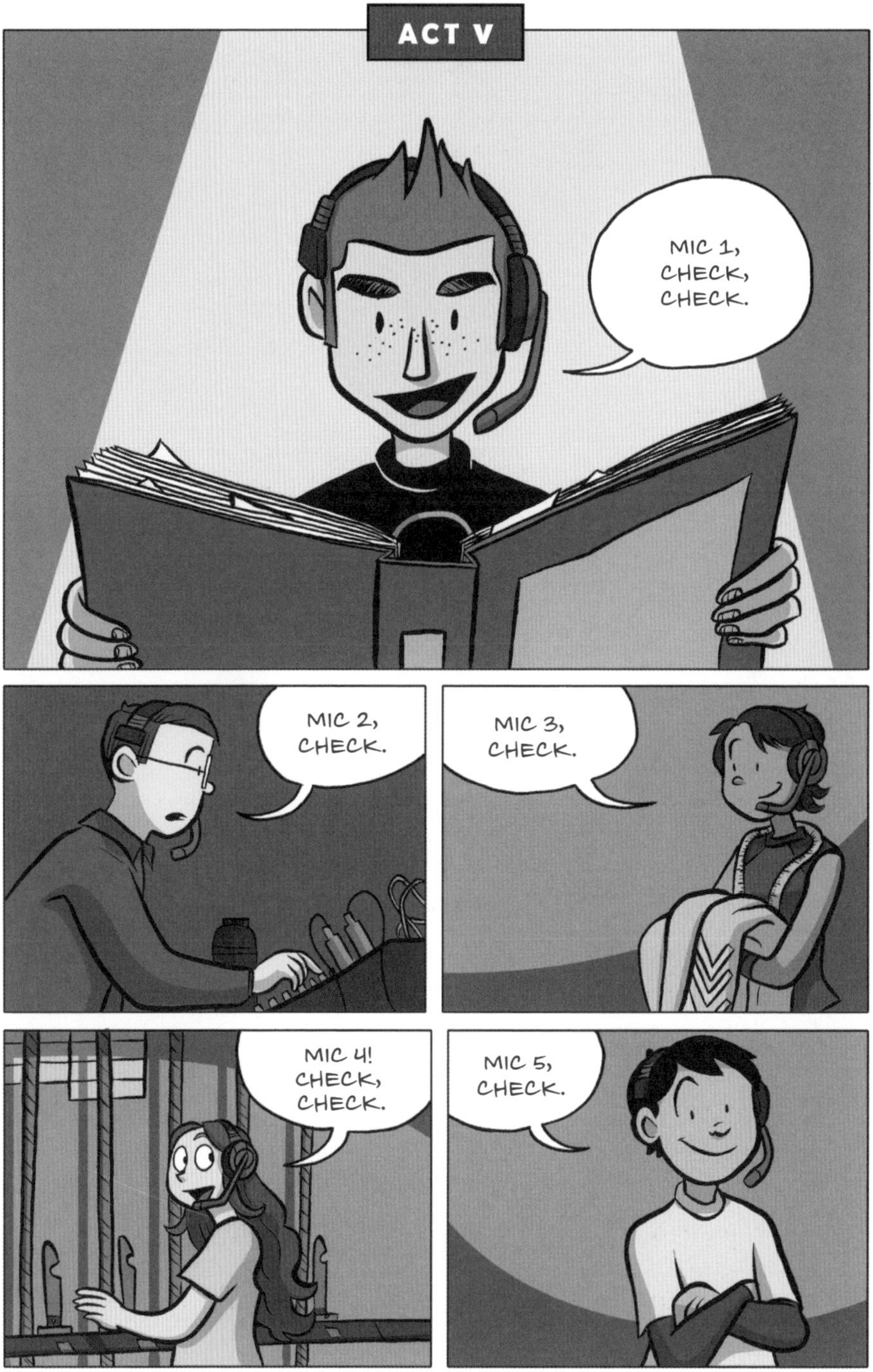
ACT V
MIC 1, CHECK, CHECK.
MIC 2, CHECK.
MIC 3, CHECK.
MIC 4! CHECK, CHECK.
MIC 5, CHECK.

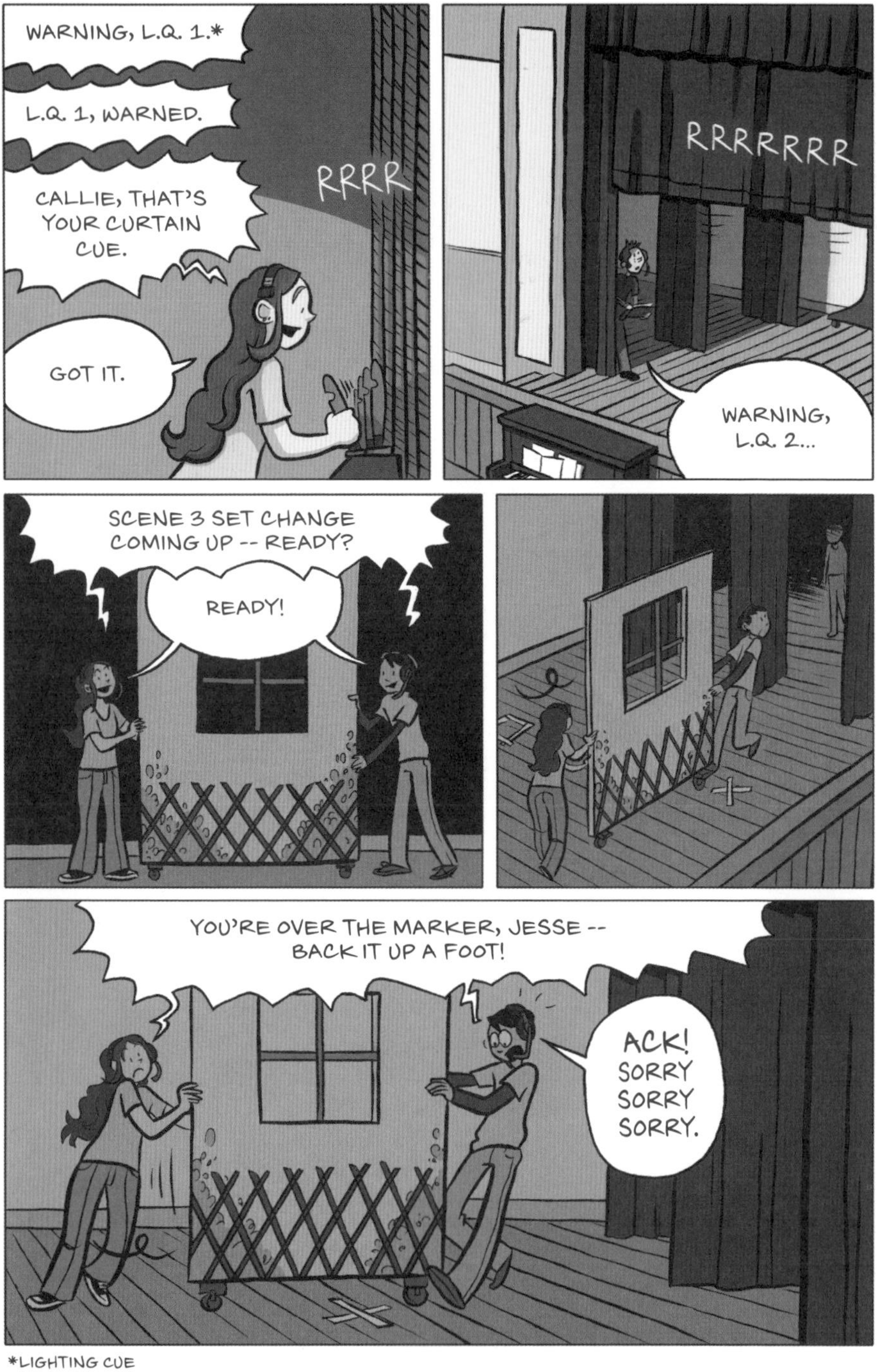
WARNING, L.Q. 1.*
L.Q. 1, WARNED.
CALLIE, THAT'S YOUR CURTAIN CUE.
RRRR
GOT IT.
RRRRRRR
WARNING, L.Q. 2...
SCENE 3 SET CHANGE COMING UP -- READY?
READY!
YOU'RE OVER THE MARKER, JESSE -- BACK IT UP A FOOT!
ACK! SORRY SORRY SORRY.

*LIGHTING CUE

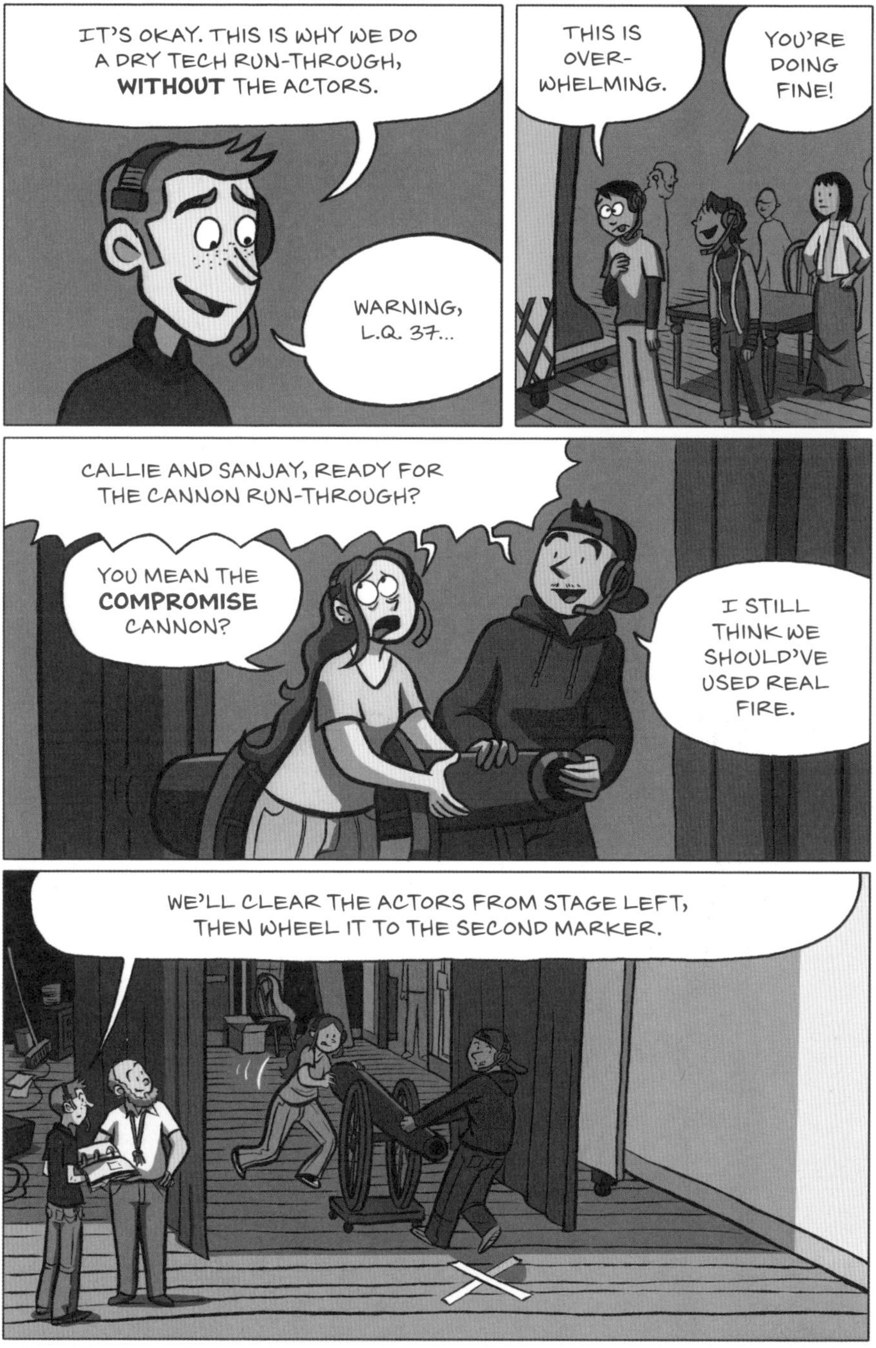
IT'S OKAY. THIS IS WHY WE DO A DRY TECH RUN-THROUGH, **WITHOUT** THE ACTORS.
WARNING, L.Q. 37...
THIS IS OVER-WHELMING.
YOU'RE DOING FINE!
CALLIE AND SANJAY, READY FOR THE CANNON RUN-THROUGH?
YOU MEAN THE **COMPROMISE** CANNON?
I STILL THINK WE SHOULD'VE USED REAL FIRE.
WE'LL CLEAR THE ACTORS FROM STAGE LEFT, THEN WHEEL IT TO THE SECOND MARKER.

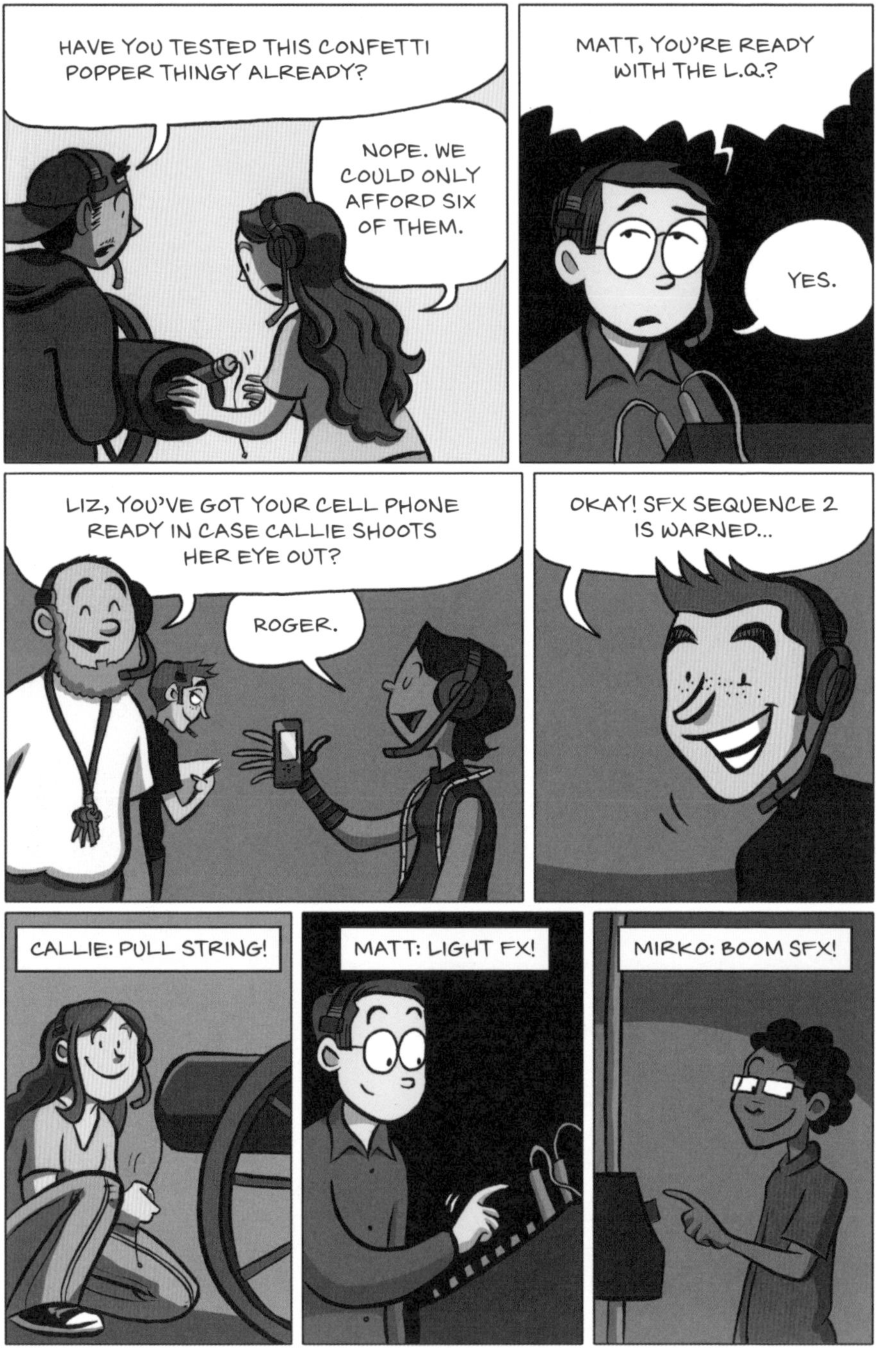
HAVE YOU TESTED THIS CONFETTI POPPER THINGY ALREADY?
NOPE. WE COULD ONLY AFFORD SIX OF THEM.
MATT, YOU'RE READY WITH THE L.Q.?
YES.
LIZ, YOU'VE GOT YOUR CELL PHONE READY IN CASE CALLIE SHOOTS HER EYE OUT?
ROGER.
OKAY! SFX SEQUENCE 2 IS WARNED...
CALLIE: PULL STRING!
MATT: LIGHT FX!
MIRKO: BOOM SFX!

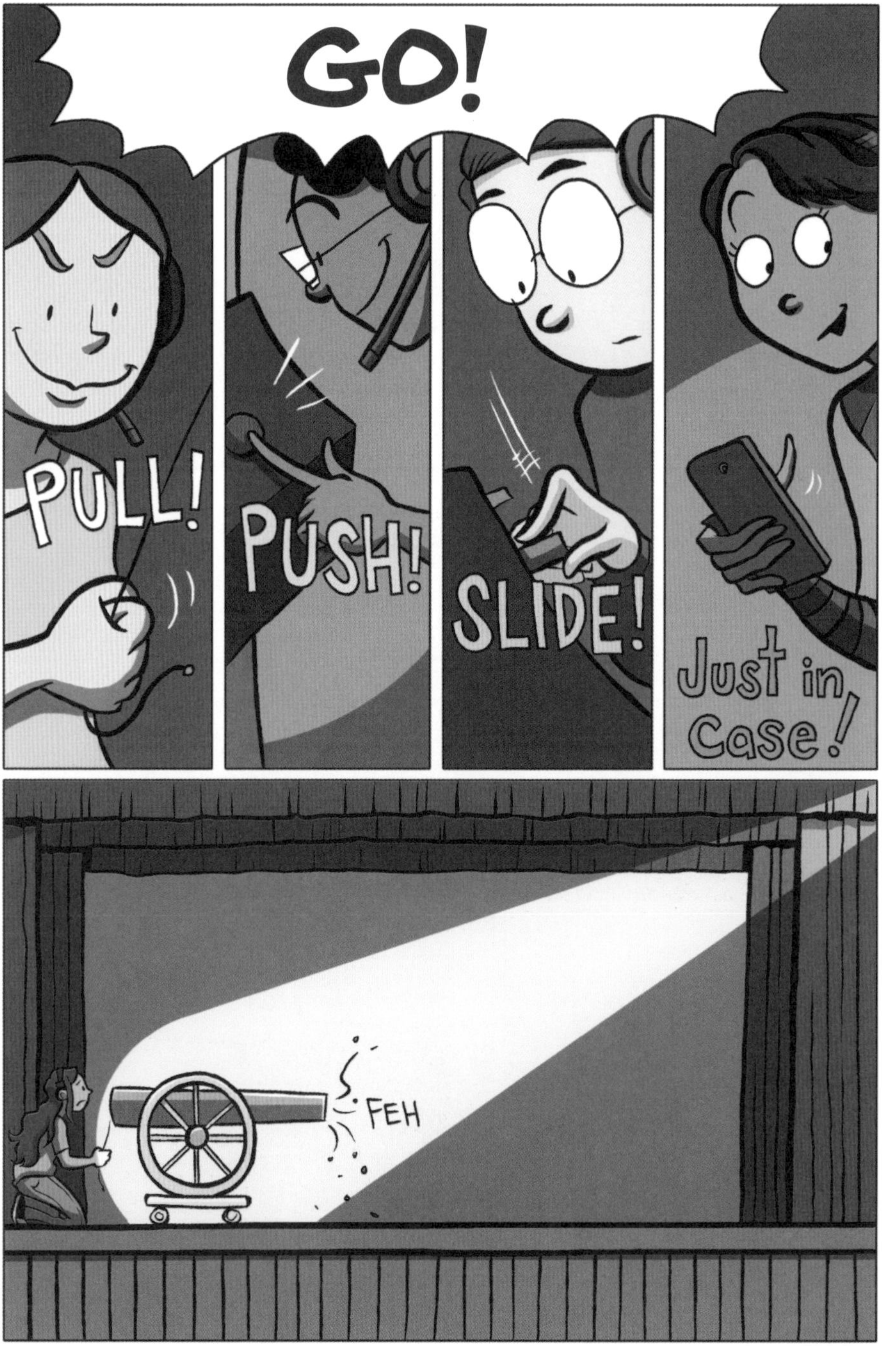
GO!
PULL!
PUSH!
SLIDE!
Just in Case!
FEH

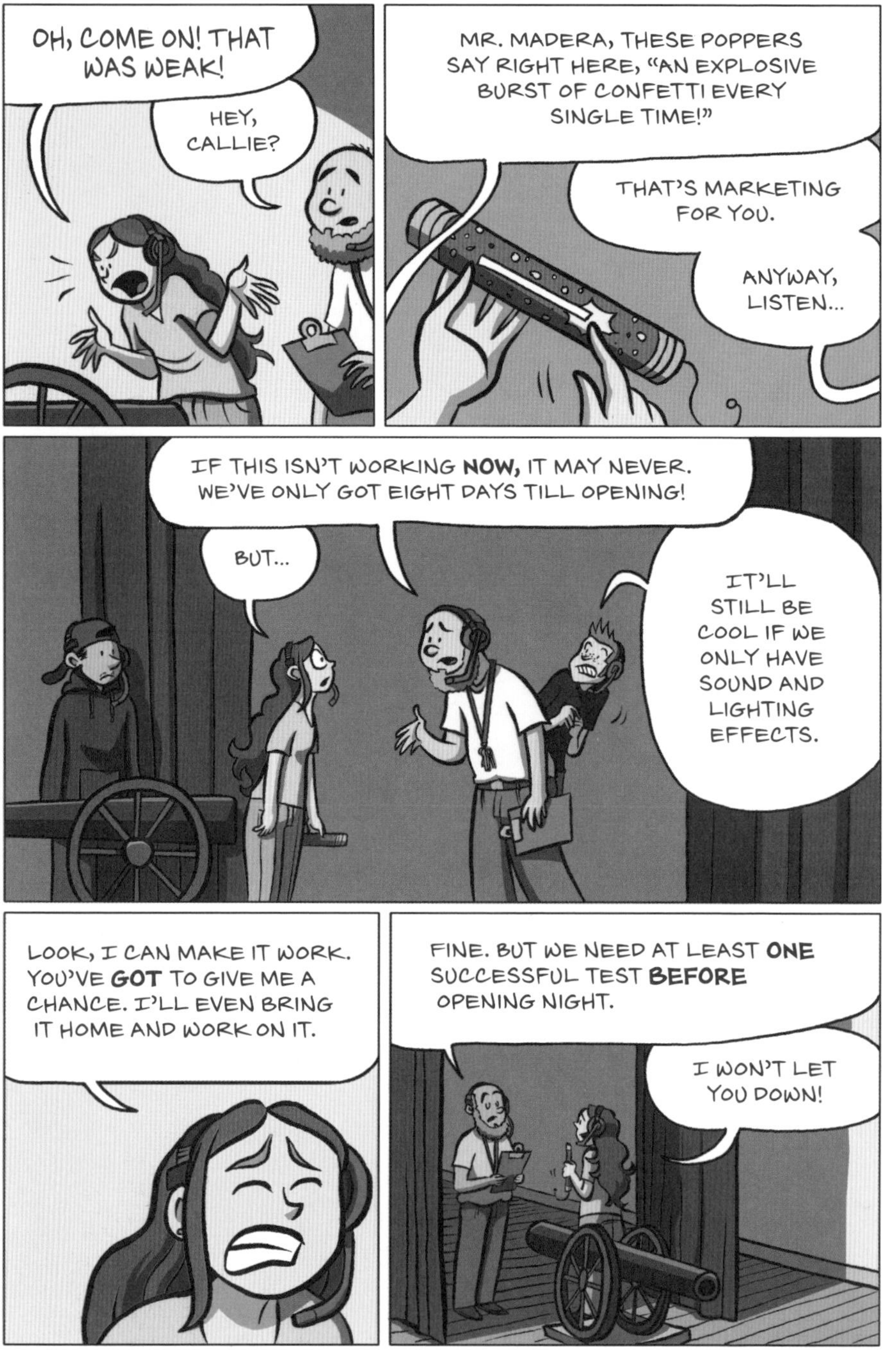
OH, COME ON! THAT WAS WEAK!
HEY, CALLIE?
MR. MADERA, THESE POPPERS SAY RIGHT HERE, "AN EXPLOSIVE BURST OF CONFETTI EVERY SINGLE TIME!"
THAT'S MARKETING FOR YOU.
ANYWAY, LISTEN...
IF THIS ISN'T WORKING **NOW,** IT MAY NEVER. WE'VE ONLY GOT EIGHT DAYS TILL OPENING!
BUT...
IT'LL STILL BE COOL IF WE ONLY HAVE SOUND AND LIGHTING EFFECTS.
LOOK, I CAN MAKE IT WORK. YOU'VE **GOT** TO GIVE ME A CHANCE. I'LL EVEN BRING IT HOME AND WORK ON IT.
FINE. BUT WE NEED AT LEAST **ONE** SUCCESSFUL TEST **BEFORE** OPENING NIGHT.
I WON'T LET YOU DOWN!

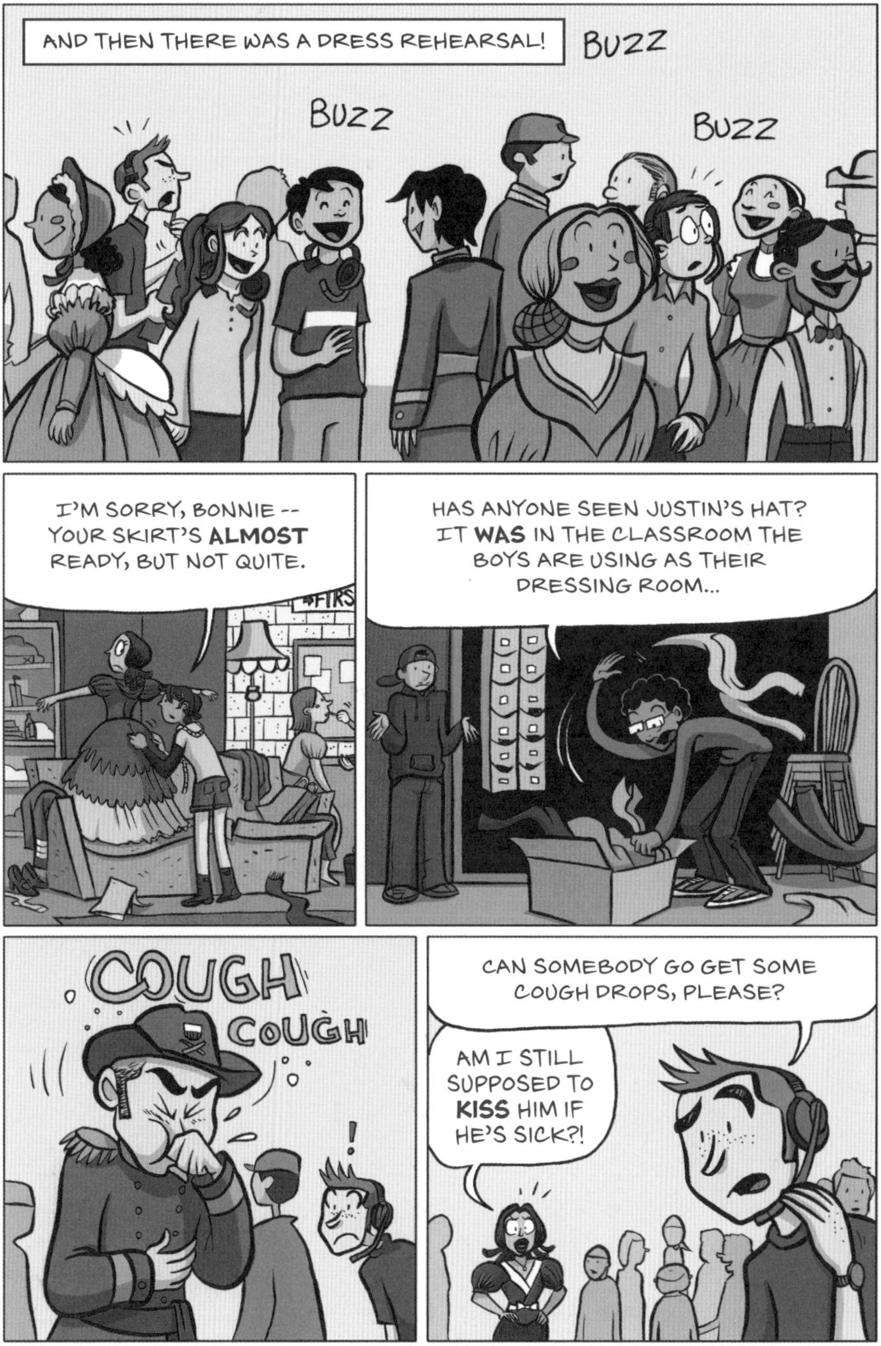
AND THEN THERE WAS A DRESS REHEARSAL!
BUZZ
BUZZ
BUZZ
I'M SORRY, BONNIE -- YOUR SKIRT'S **ALMOST** READY, BUT NOT QUITE.
HAS ANYONE SEEN JUSTIN'S HAT? IT **WAS** IN THE CLASSROOM THE BOYS ARE USING AS THEIR DRESSING ROOM...
COUGH
COUGH
!
CAN SOMEBODY GO GET SOME COUGH DROPS, PLEASE?
AM I STILL SUPPOSED TO **KISS** HIM IF HE'S SICK?!

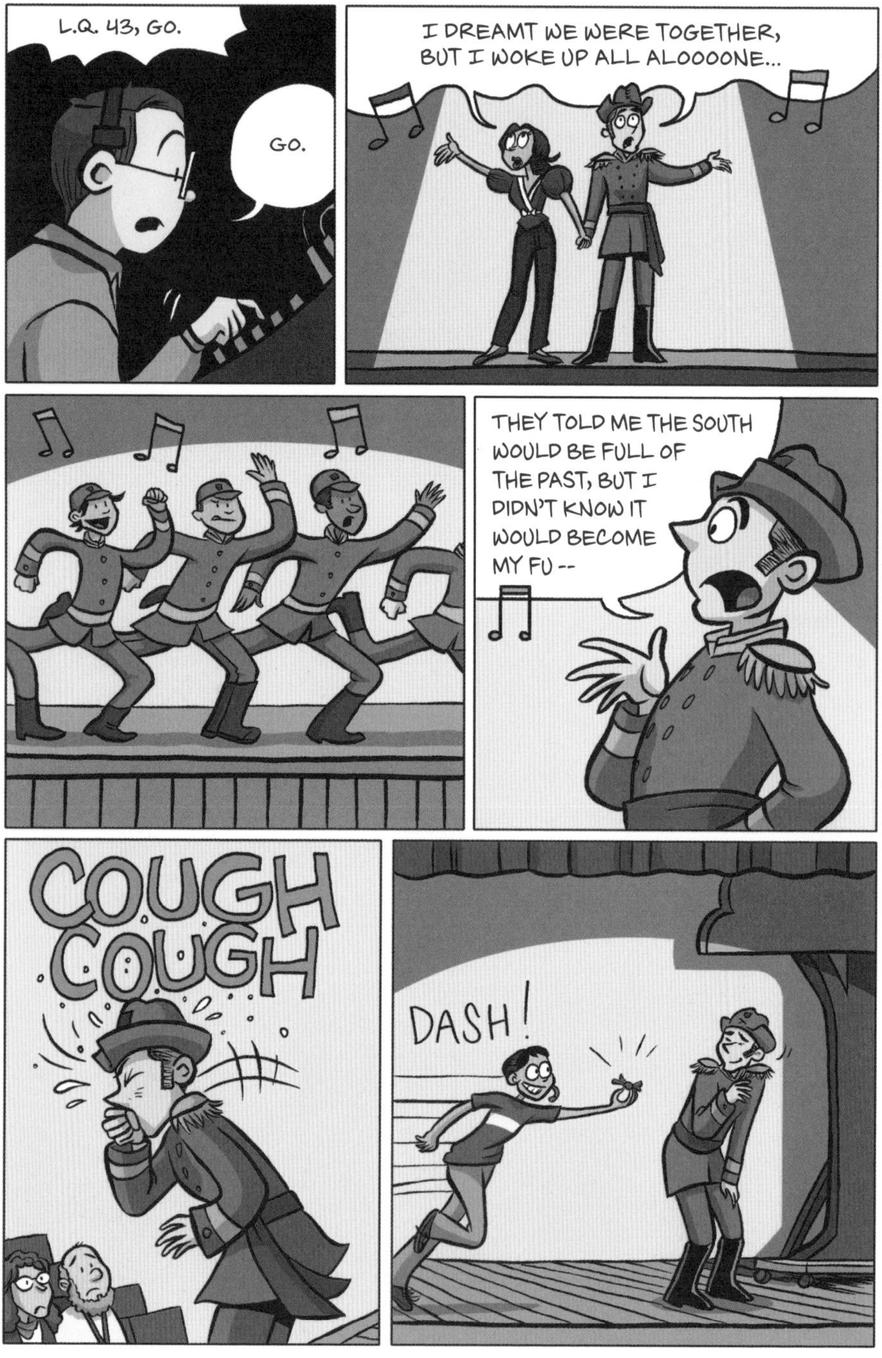
L.Q. 43, GO.
GO.
I DREAMT WE WERE TOGETHER, BUT I WOKE UP ALL ALOOOONE...
THEY TOLD ME THE SOUTH WOULD BE FULL OF THE PAST, BUT I DIDN'T KNOW IT WOULD BECOME MY FU --
COUGH COUGH
DASH!

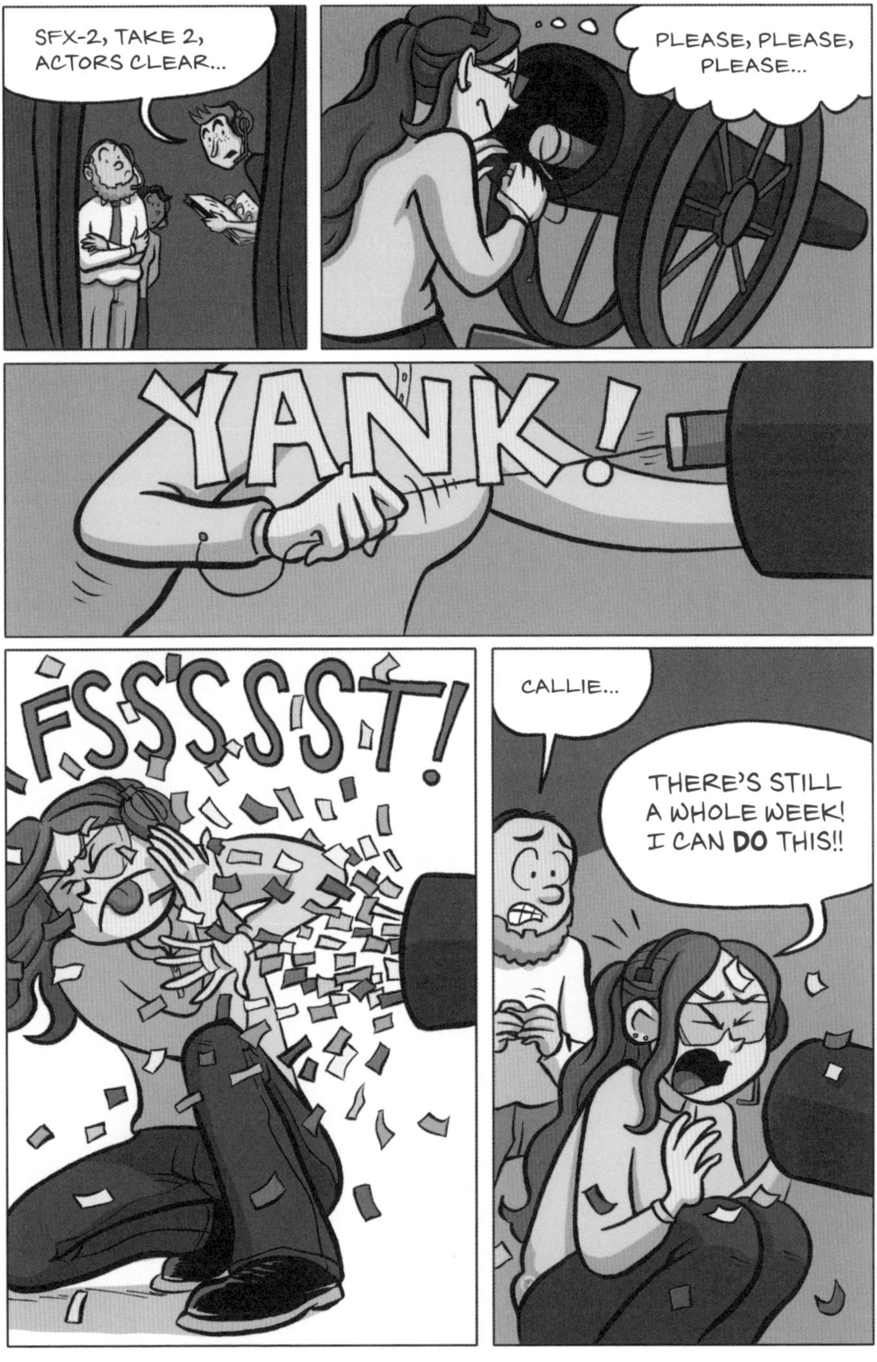
SFX-2, TAKE 2, ACTORS CLEAR...
PLEASE, PLEASE, PLEASE...
YANK!
FSSSSST!
CALLIE...
THERE'S STILL A WHOLE WEEK! I CAN **DO** THIS!!

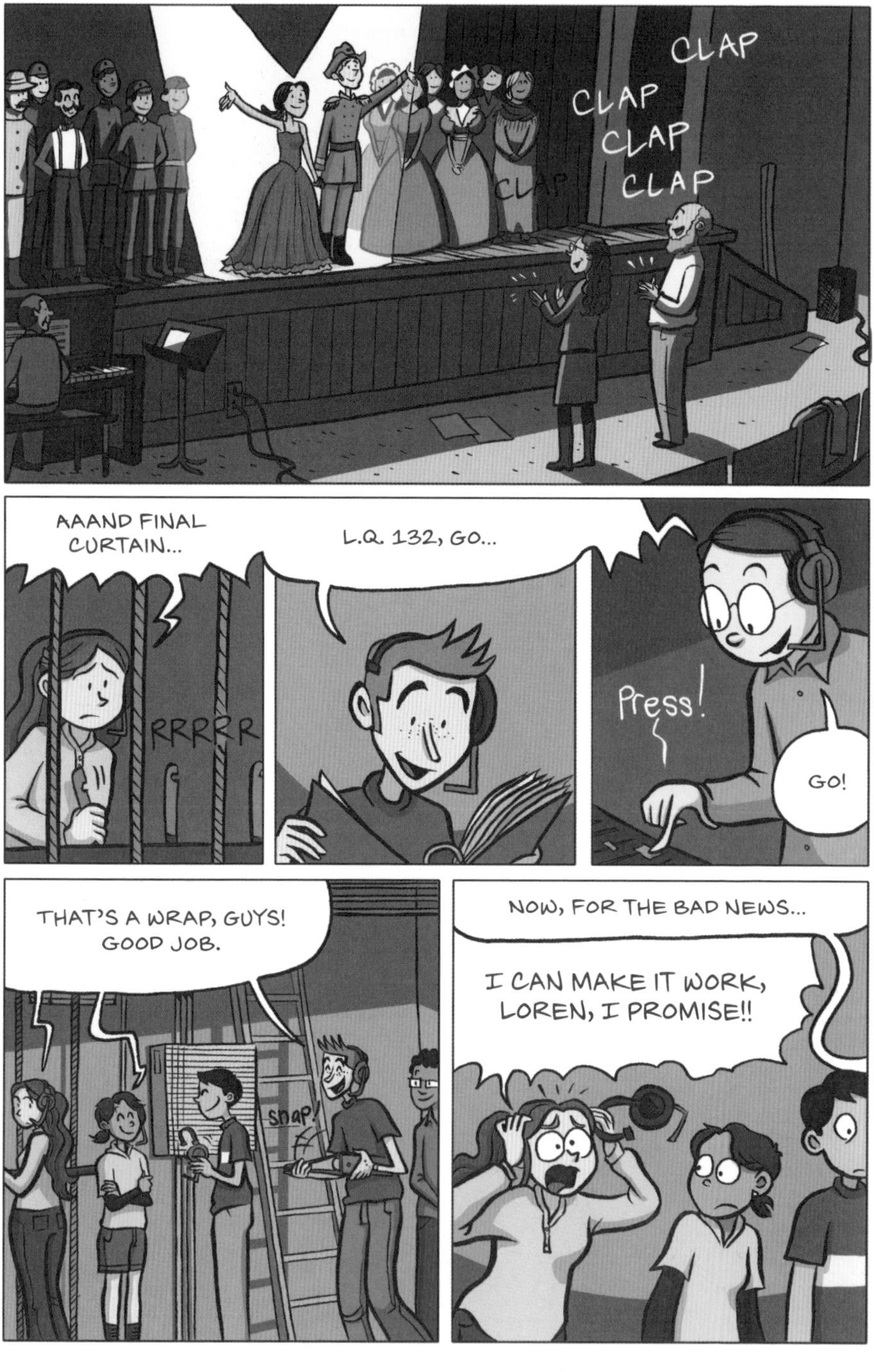
CLAP
CLAP
CLAP
CLAP
CLAP
AAAND FINAL CURTAIN...
RRRRR
L.Q. 132, GO...
Press!
GO!
THAT'S A WRAP, GUYS! GOOD JOB.
snap!
NOW, FOR THE BAD NEWS...
I CAN MAKE IT WORK, LOREN, I PROMISE!!

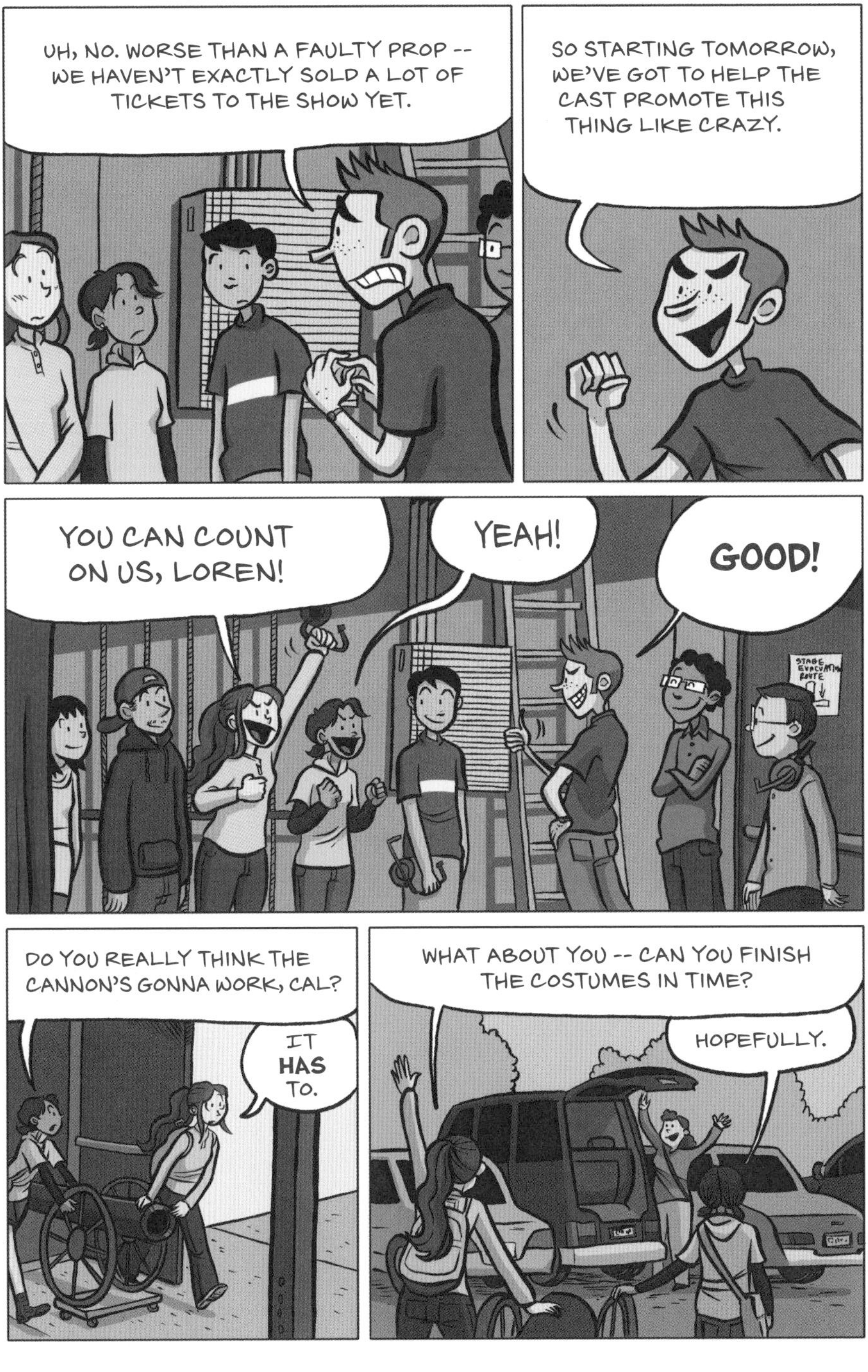
UH, NO. WORSE THAN A FAULTY PROP -- WE HAVEN'T EXACTLY SOLD A LOT OF TICKETS TO THE SHOW YET.
SO STARTING TOMORROW, WE'VE GOT TO HELP THE CAST PROMOTE THIS THING LIKE CRAZY.
YOU CAN COUNT ON US, LOREN!
YEAH!
GOOD!
STAGE EVACUATION ROUTE
DO YOU REALLY THINK THE CANNON'S GONNA WORK, CAL?
IT **HAS** TO.
WHAT ABOUT YOU -- CAN YOU FINISH THE COSTUMES IN TIME?
HOPEFULLY.

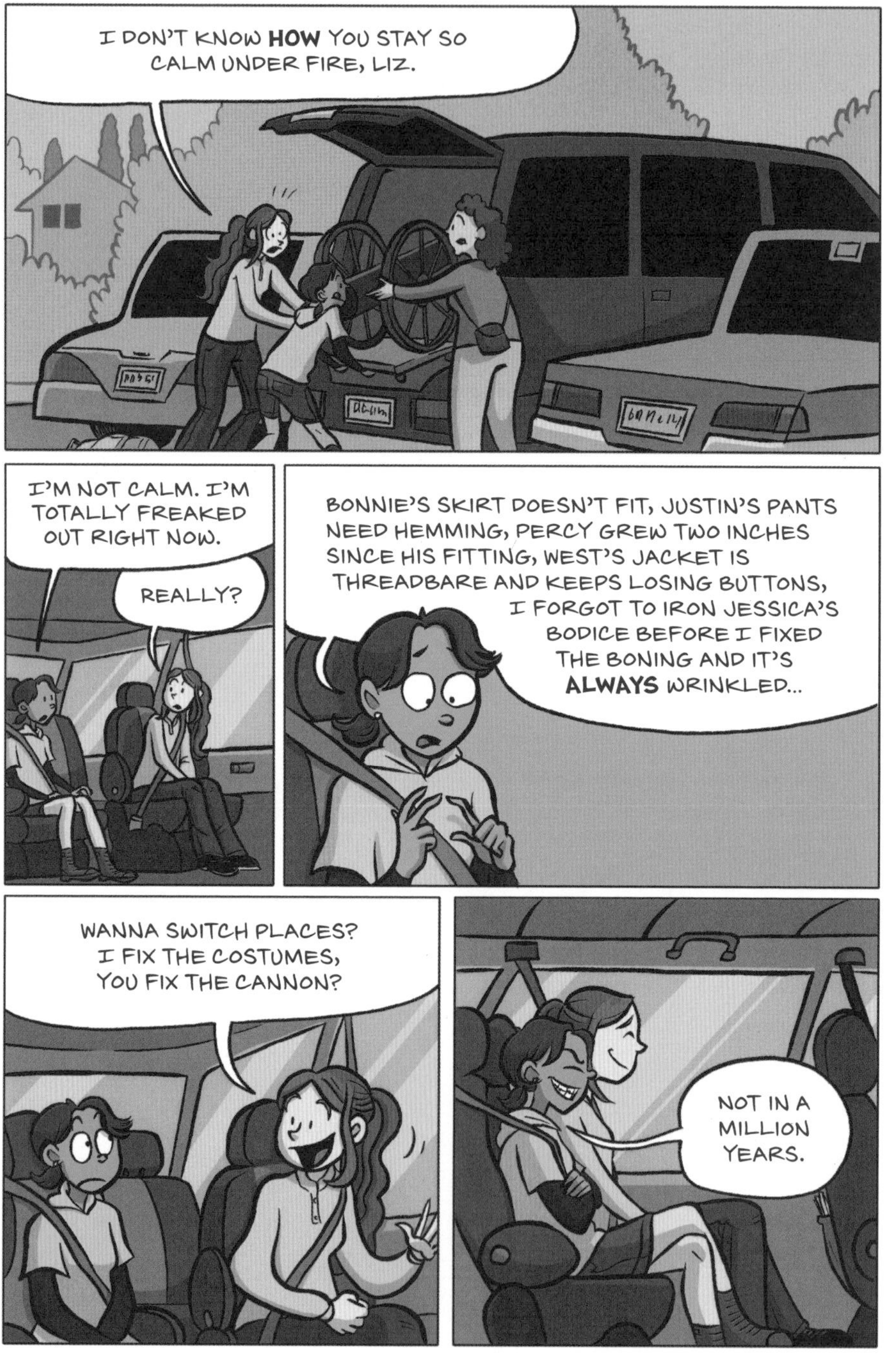
I DON'T KNOW **HOW** YOU STAY SO CALM UNDER FIRE, LIZ.
I'M NOT CALM. I'M TOTALLY FREAKED OUT RIGHT NOW.
REALLY?
BONNIE'S SKIRT DOESN'T FIT, JUSTIN'S PANTS NEED HEMMING, PERCY GREW TWO INCHES SINCE HIS FITTING, WEST'S JACKET IS THREADBARE AND KEEPS LOSING BUTTONS, I FORGOT TO IRON JESSICA'S BODICE BEFORE I FIXED THE BONING AND IT'S **ALWAYS** WRINKLED...
WANNA SWITCH PLACES? I FIX THE COSTUMES, YOU FIX THE CANNON?
NOT IN A MILLION YEARS.

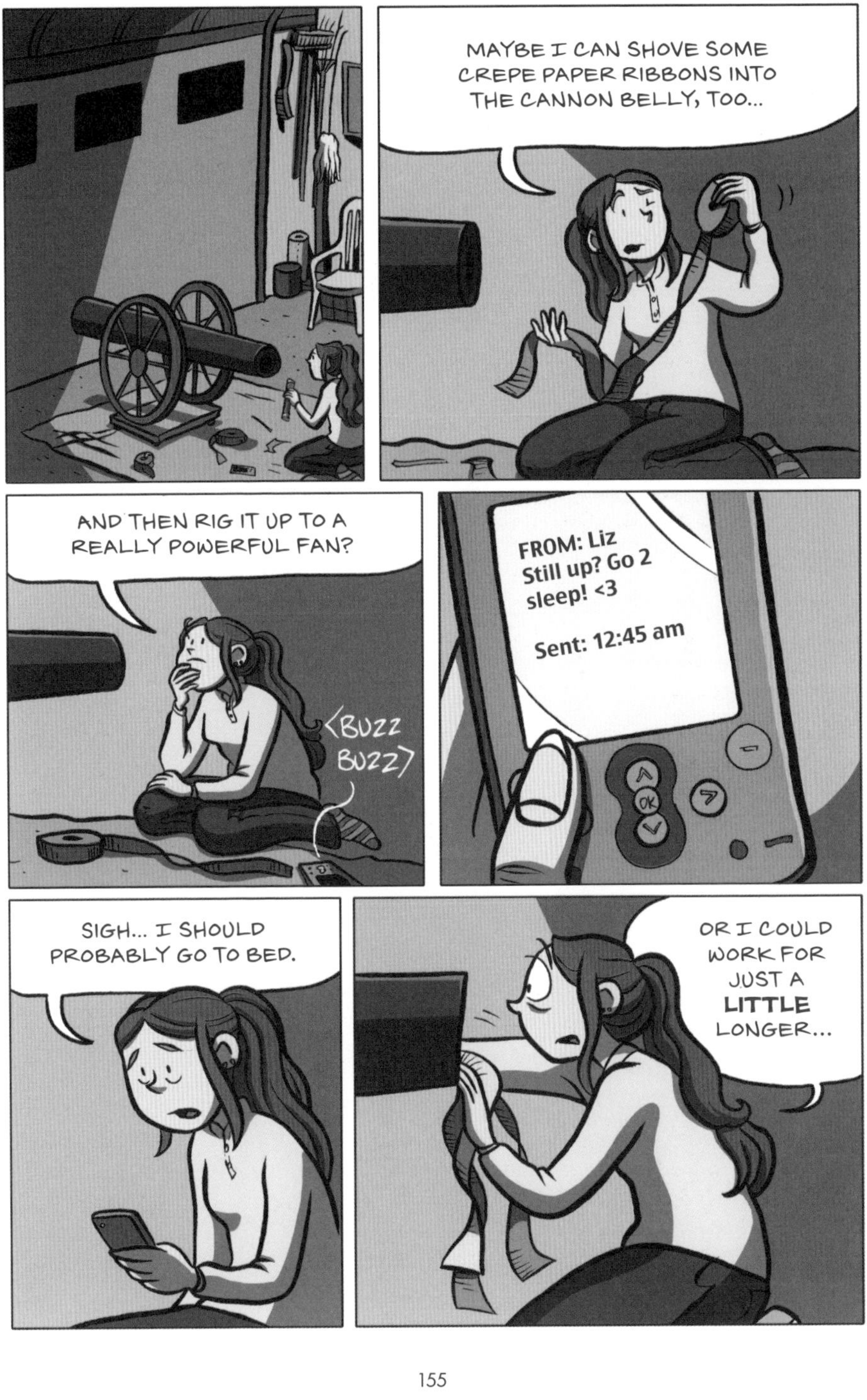
MAYBE I CAN SHOVE SOME CREPE PAPER RIBBONS INTO THE CANNON BELLY, TOO...
AND THEN RIG IT UP TO A REALLY POWERFUL FAN?
<BUZZ BUZZ>
FROM: Liz
Still up? Go 2 sleep! <3
Sent: 12:45 am
OK
SIGH... I SHOULD PROBABLY GO TO BED.
OR I COULD WORK FOR JUST A **LITTLE** LONGER...

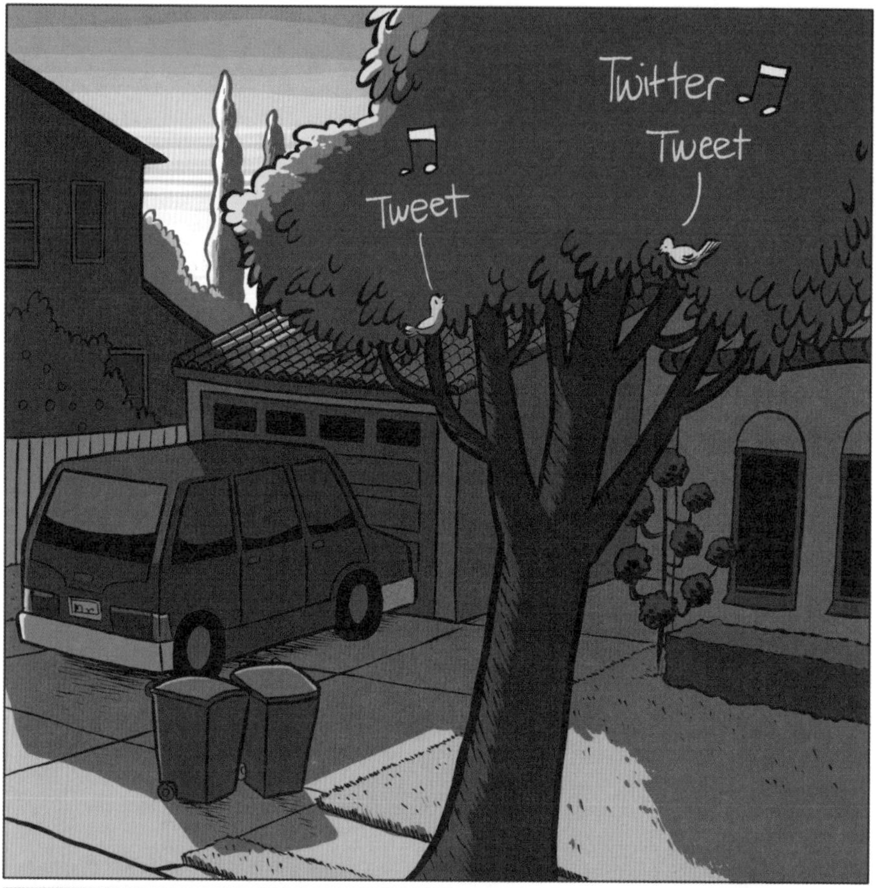
Twitter
Tweet
Tweet

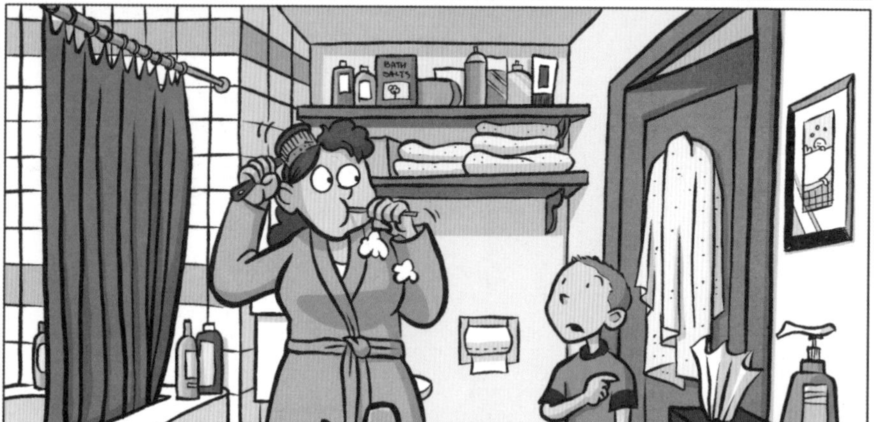
BATH SALTS

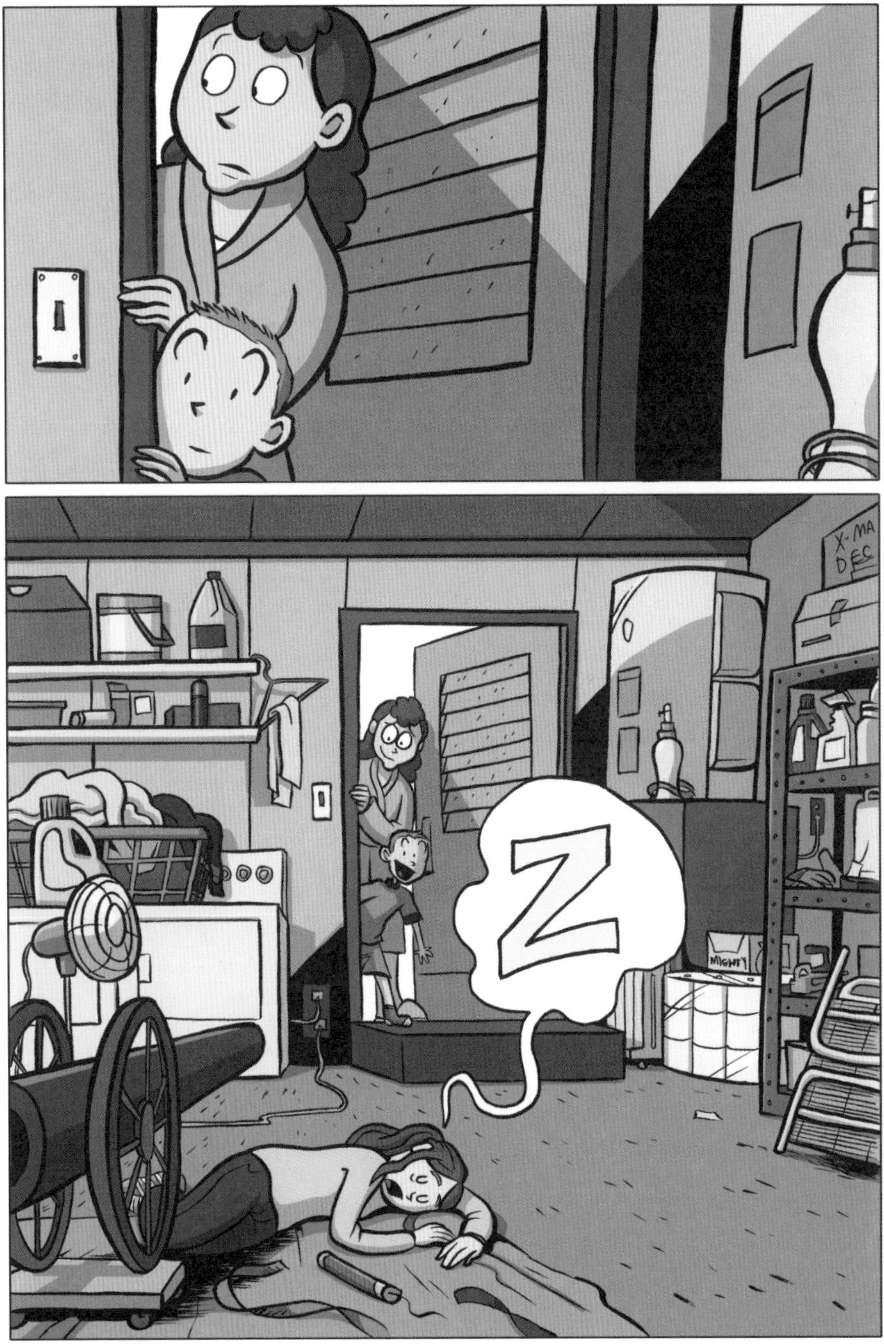
X-MA
DEC
MIGHTY
Z

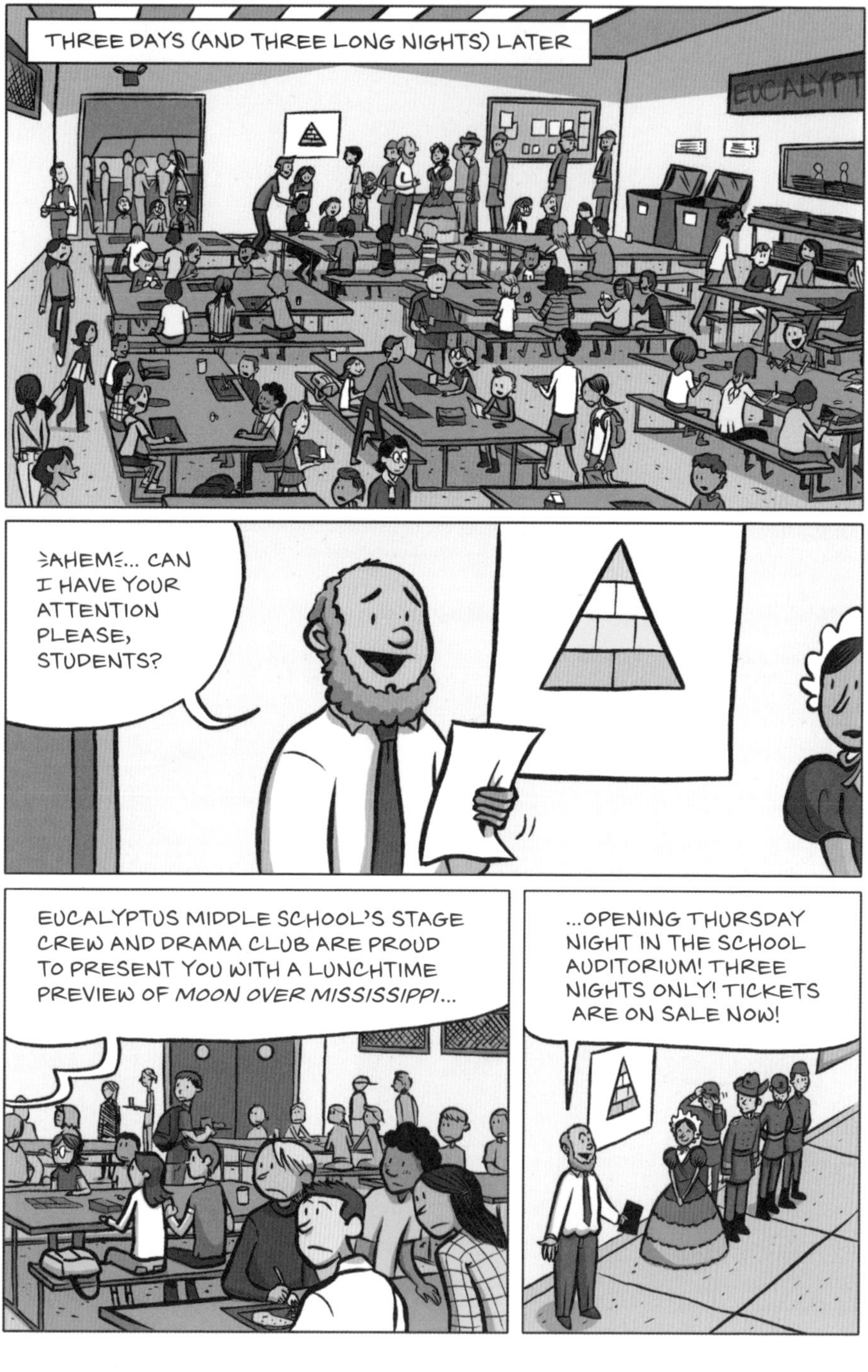
THREE DAYS (AND THREE LONG NIGHTS) LATER
EUCALYPT
≥AHEM≤... CAN I HAVE YOUR ATTENTION PLEASE, STUDENTS?
EUCALYPTUS MIDDLE SCHOOL'S STAGE CREW AND DRAMA CLUB ARE PROUD TO PRESENT YOU WITH A LUNCHTIME PREVIEW OF *MOON OVER MISSISSIPPI*...
...OPENING THURSDAY NIGHT IN THE SCHOOL AUDITORIUM! THREE NIGHTS ONLY! TICKETS ARE ON SALE NOW!

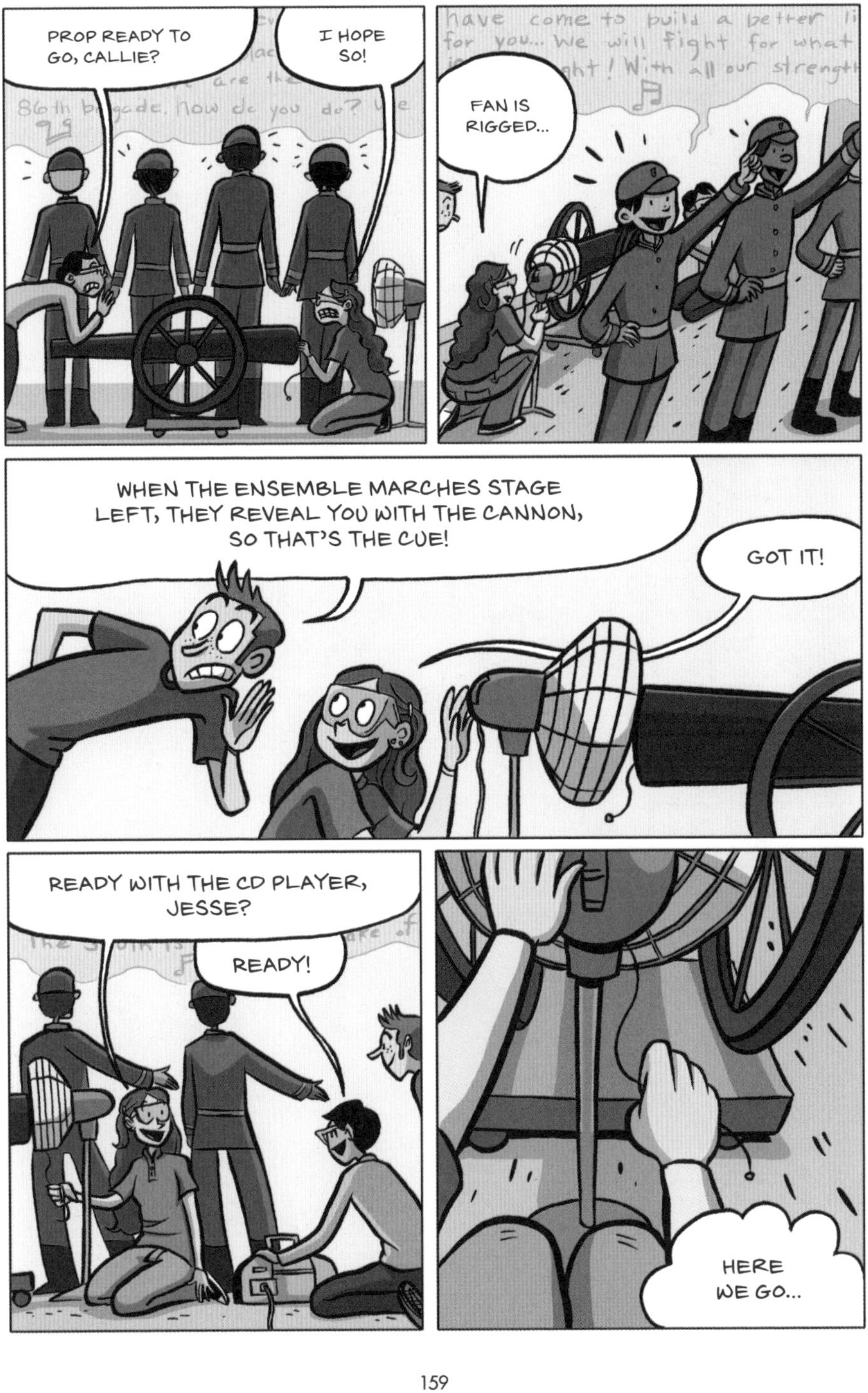
PROP READY TO GO, CALLIE?
I HOPE SO!
FAN IS RIGGED...
WHEN THE ENSEMBLE MARCHES STAGE LEFT, THEY REVEAL YOU WITH THE CANNON, SO THAT'S THE CUE!
GOT IT!
READY WITH THE CD PLAYER, JESSE?
READY!
HERE WE GO...

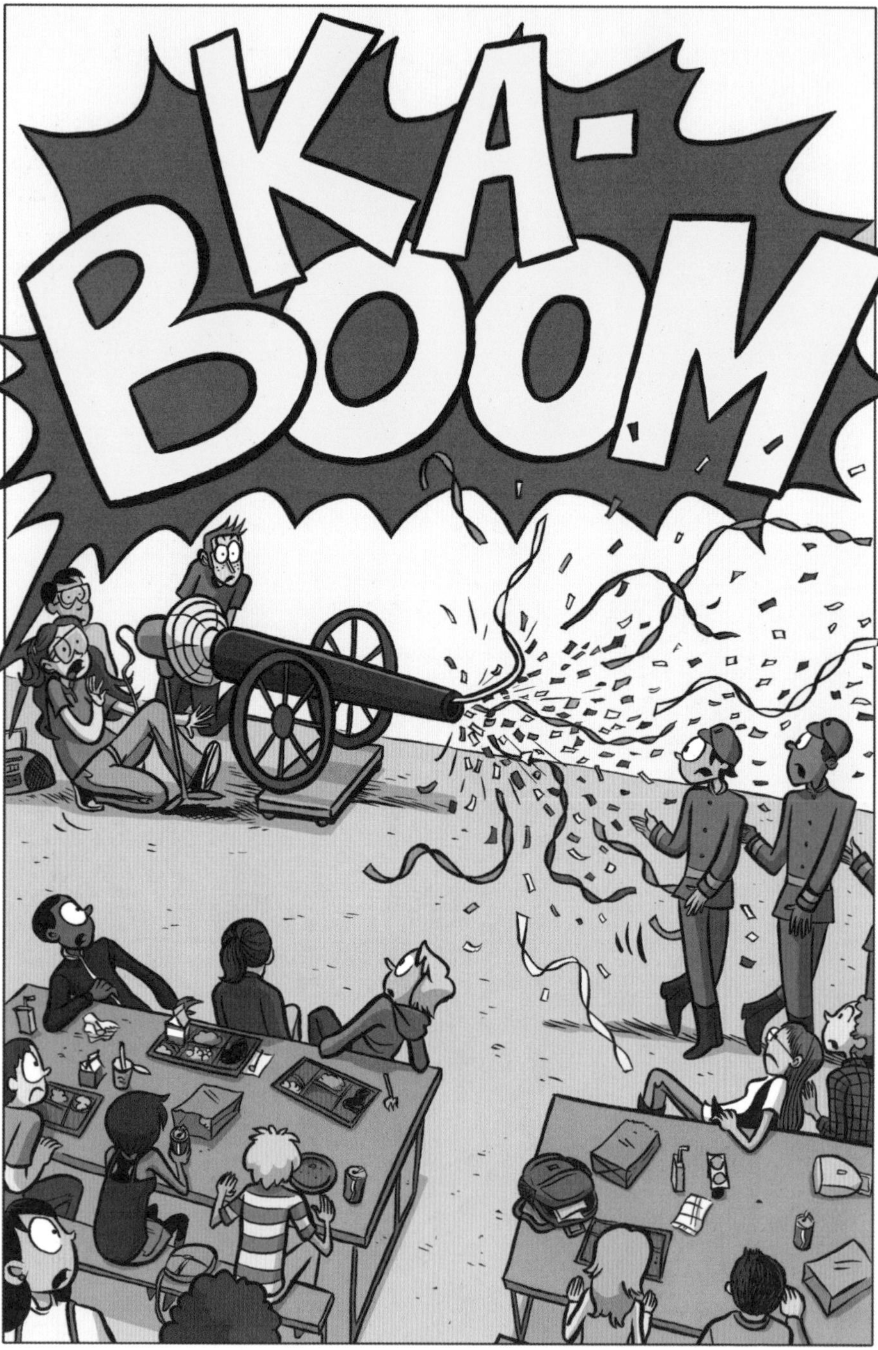
KA-BOOM

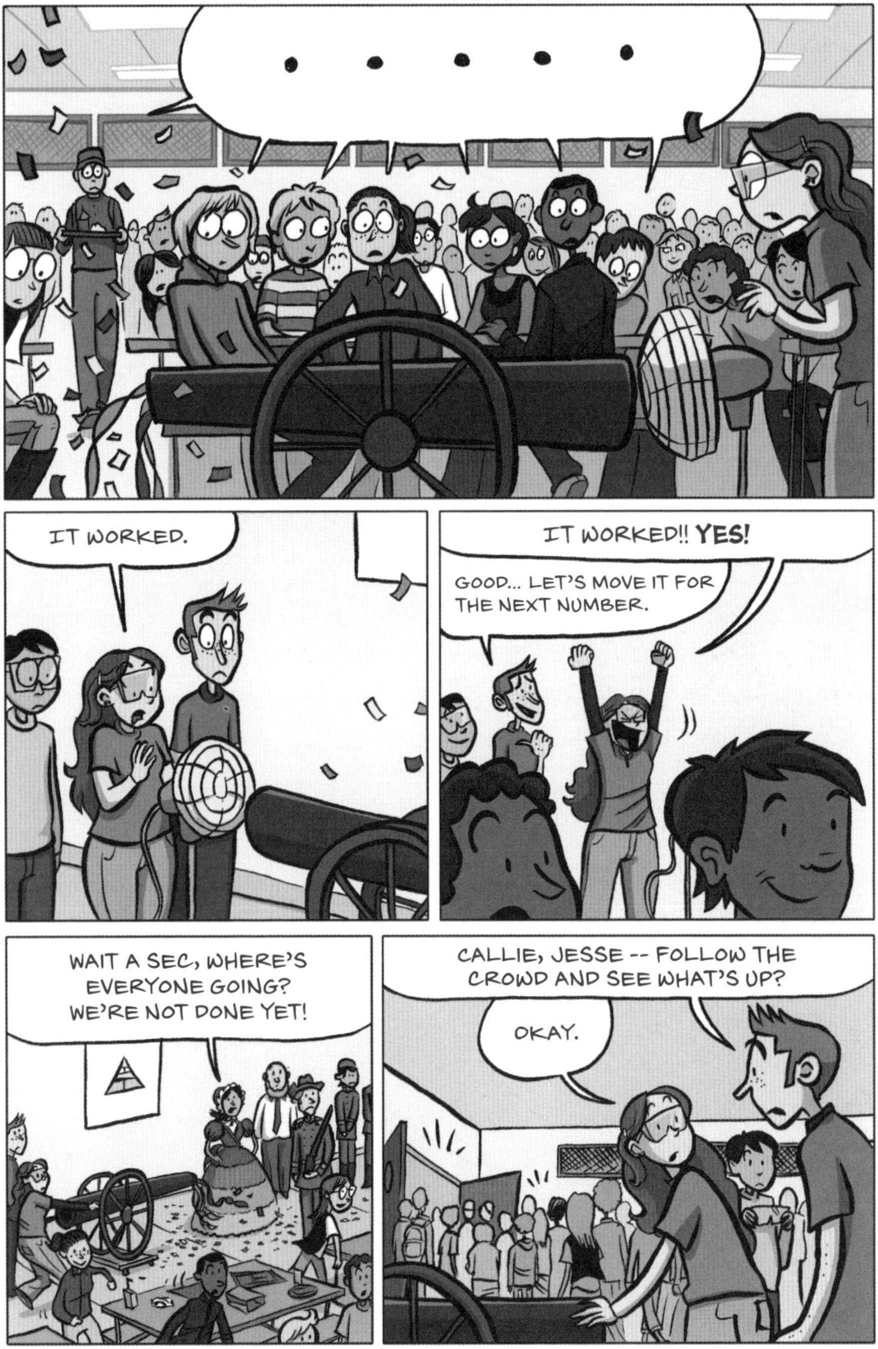
. . . . .
IT WORKED.
IT WORKED!! YES!
GOOD... LET'S MOVE IT FOR THE NEXT NUMBER.
WAIT A SEC, WHERE'S EVERYONE GOING? WE'RE NOT DONE YET!
CALLIE, JESSE -- FOLLOW THE CROWD AND SEE WHAT'S UP?
OKAY.

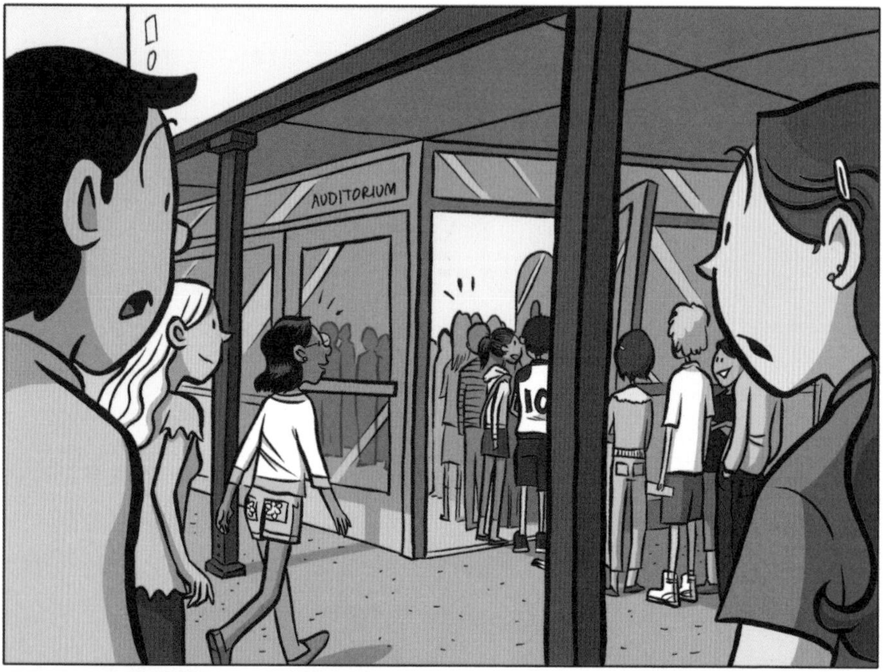
AUDITORIUM
10

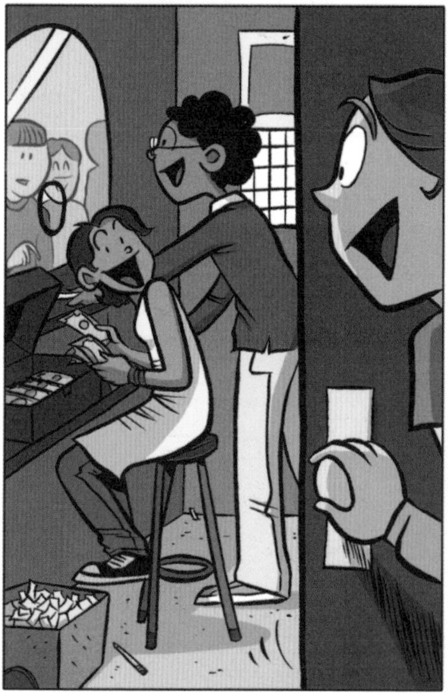

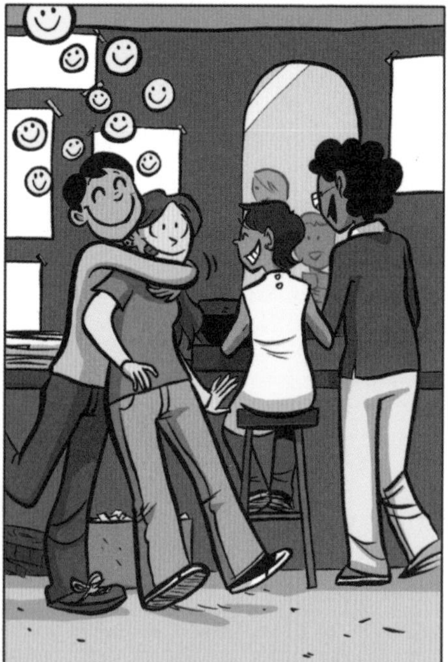

ACT VI

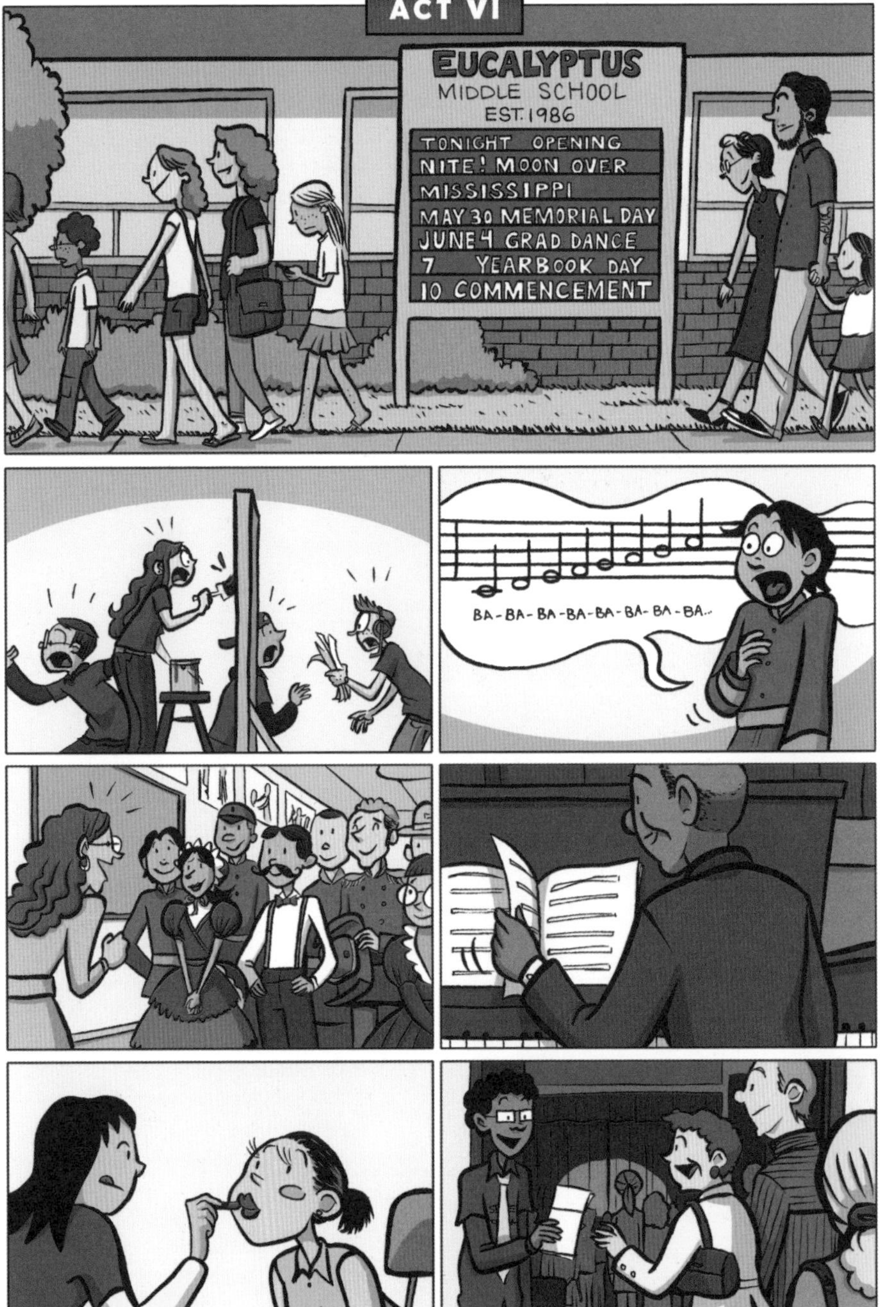
EUCALYPTUS
MIDDLE SCHOOL
EST. 1986
TONIGHT OPENING
NITE! MOON OVER
MISSISSIPPI
MAY 30 MEMORIAL DAY
JUNE 4 GRAD DANCE
7 YEARBOOK DAY
10 COMMENCEMENT
BA-BA-BA-BA-BA-BA-BA-BA...

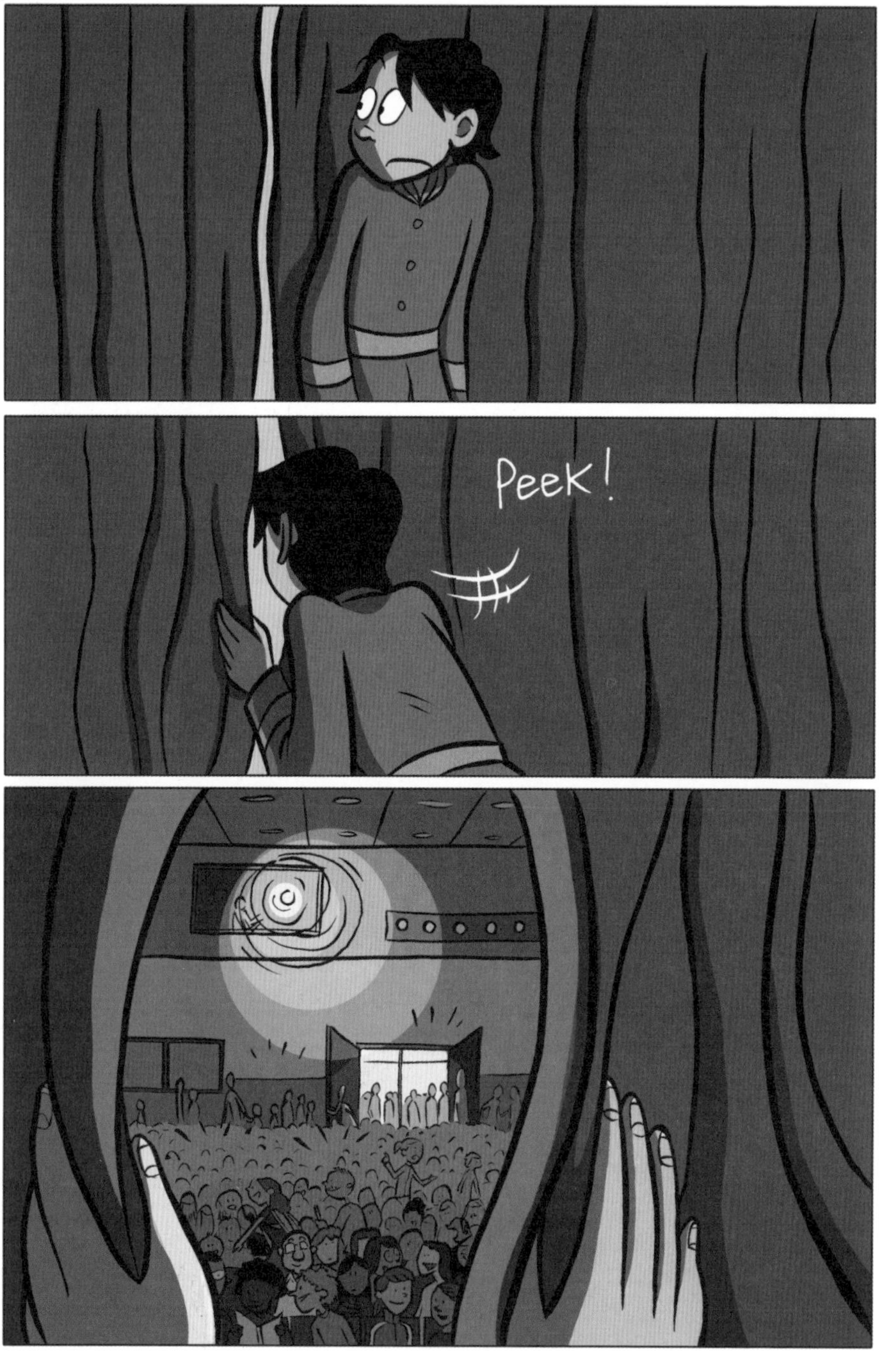
Peek!

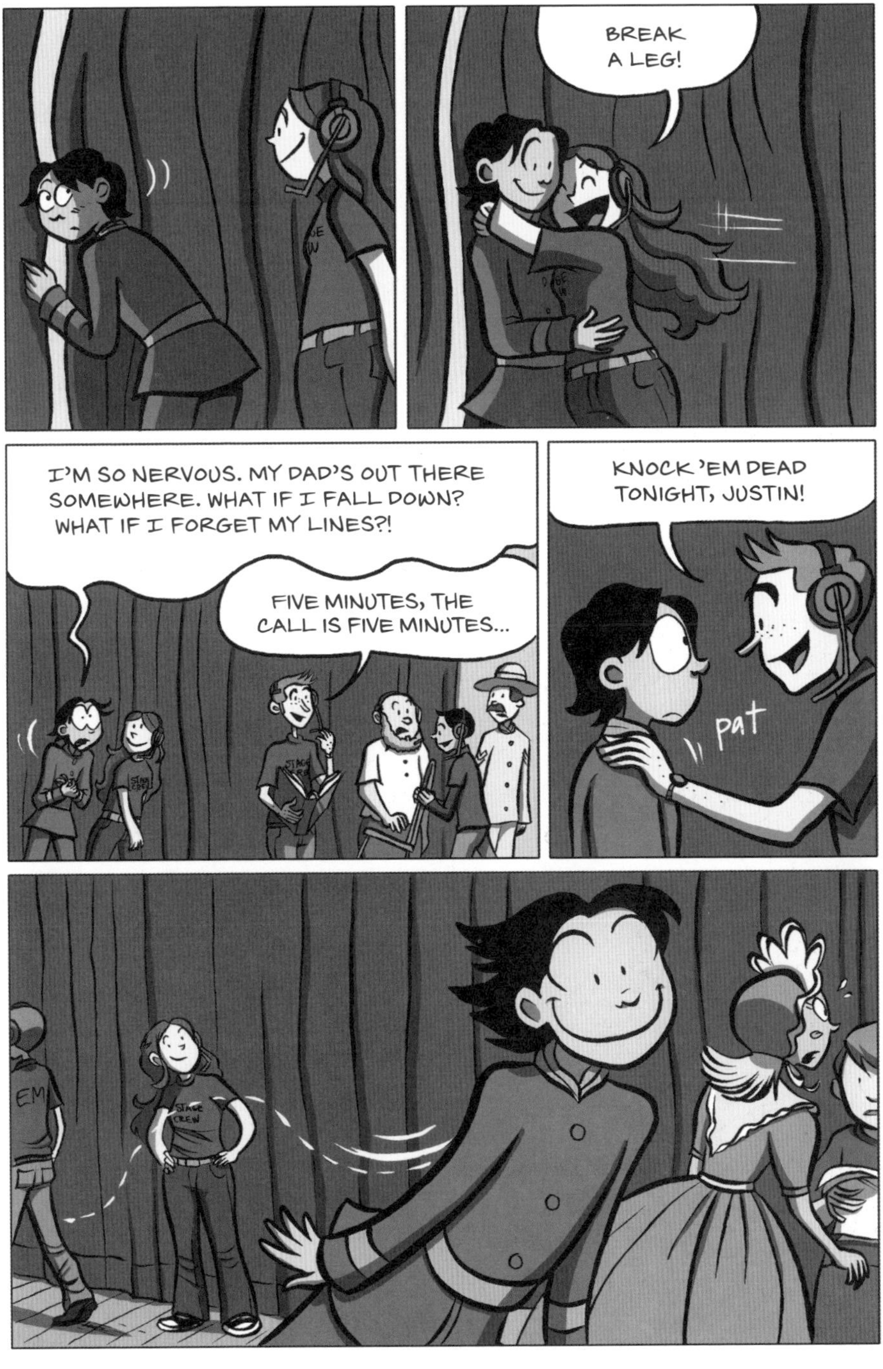

BREAK A LEG!
I'M SO NERVOUS. MY DAD'S OUT THERE SOMEWHERE. WHAT IF I FALL DOWN? WHAT IF I FORGET MY LINES?!
FIVE MINUTES, THE CALL IS FIVE MINUTES...
KNOCK 'EM DEAD TONIGHT, JUSTIN!
pat
STAGE CREW

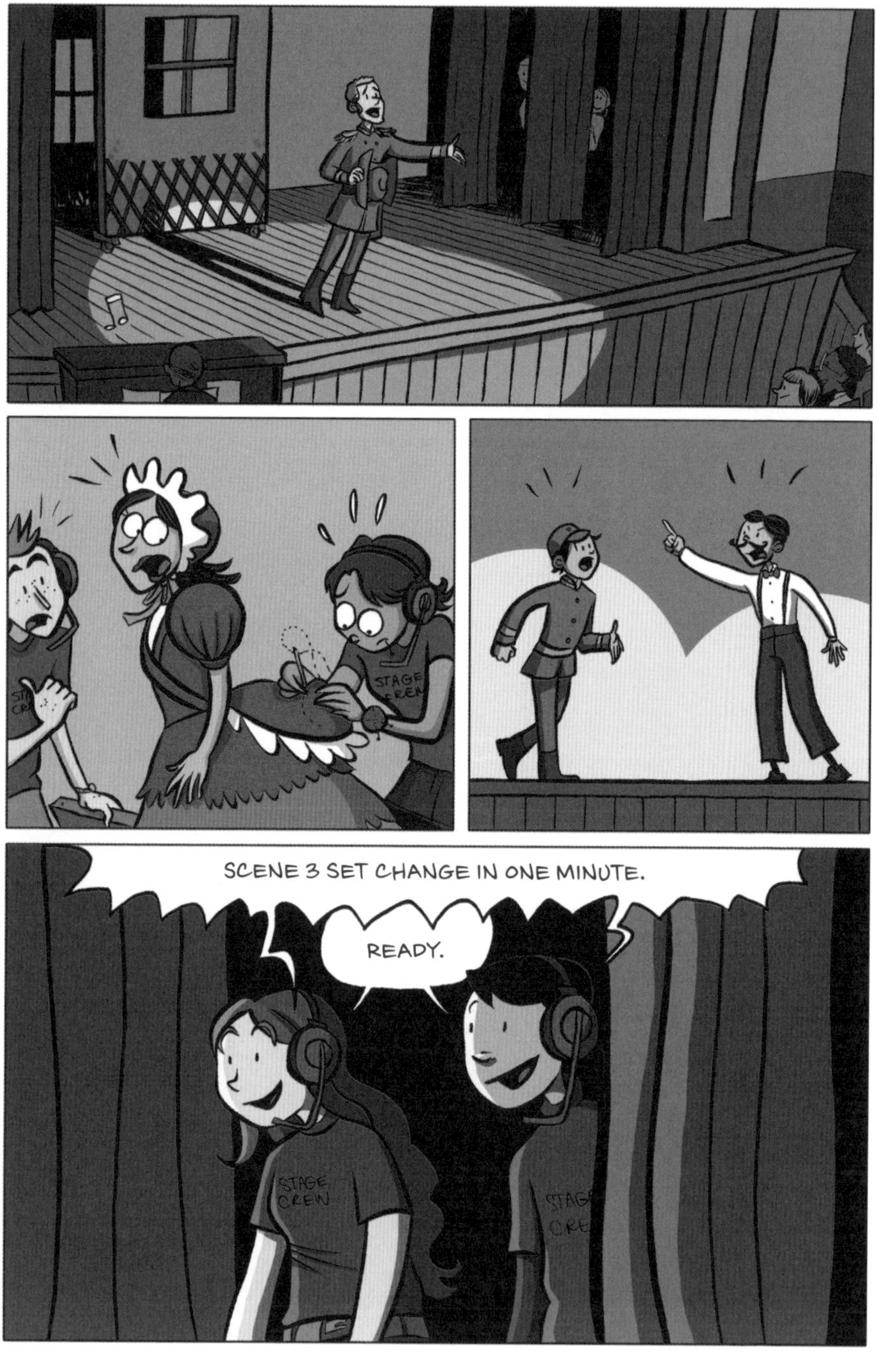
STAGE CREW
STAGE CREW
SCENE 3 SET CHANGE IN ONE MINUTE.
READY.
STAGE CREW
STAGE CREW

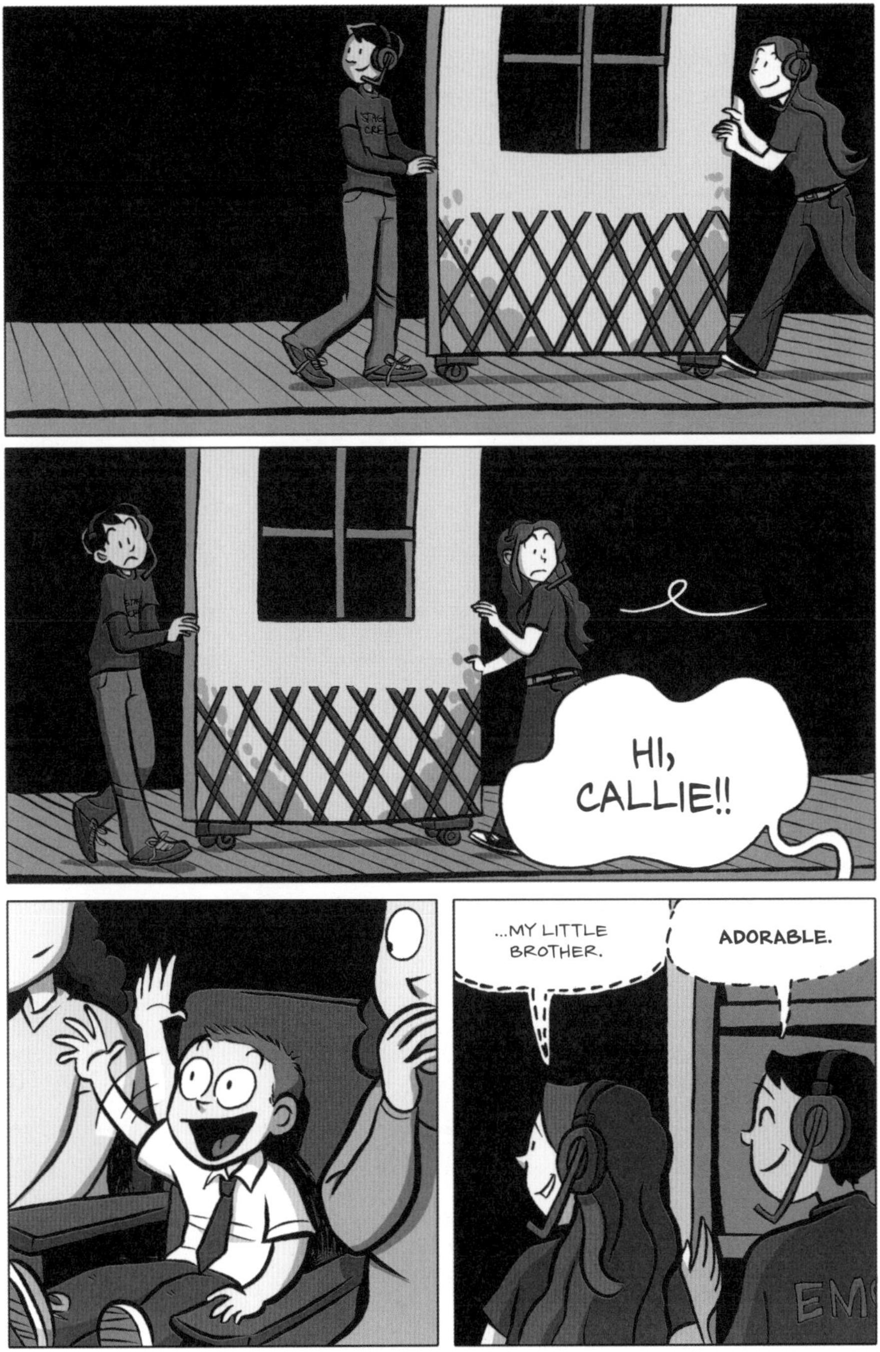
HI, CALLIE!!
...MY LITTLE BROTHER.
ADORABLE.

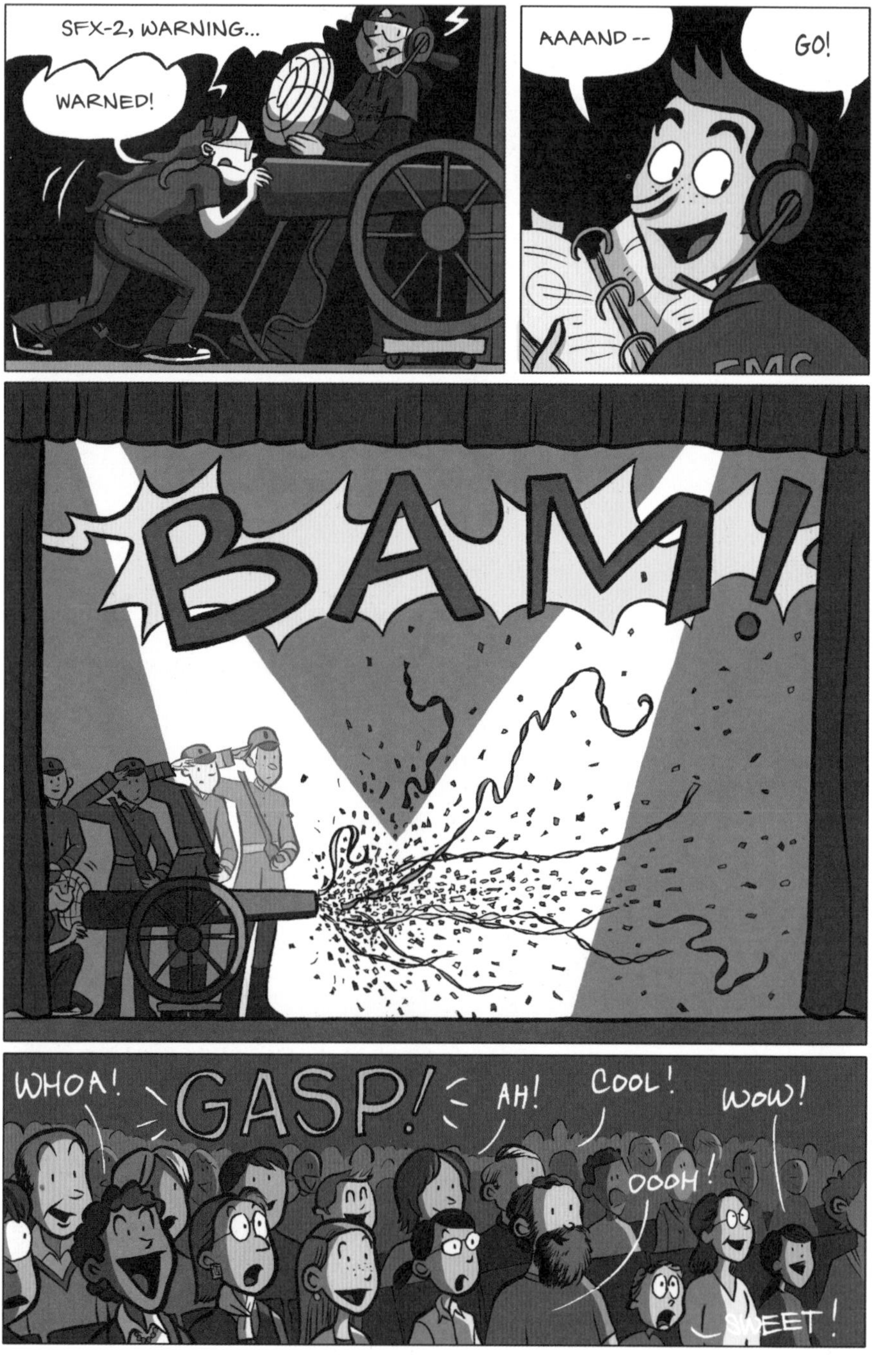
SFX-2, WARNING...
WARNED!
AAAAND --
GO!
BAM!
WHOA!
GASP!
AH!
COOL!
WOW!
OOOH!
SWEET!

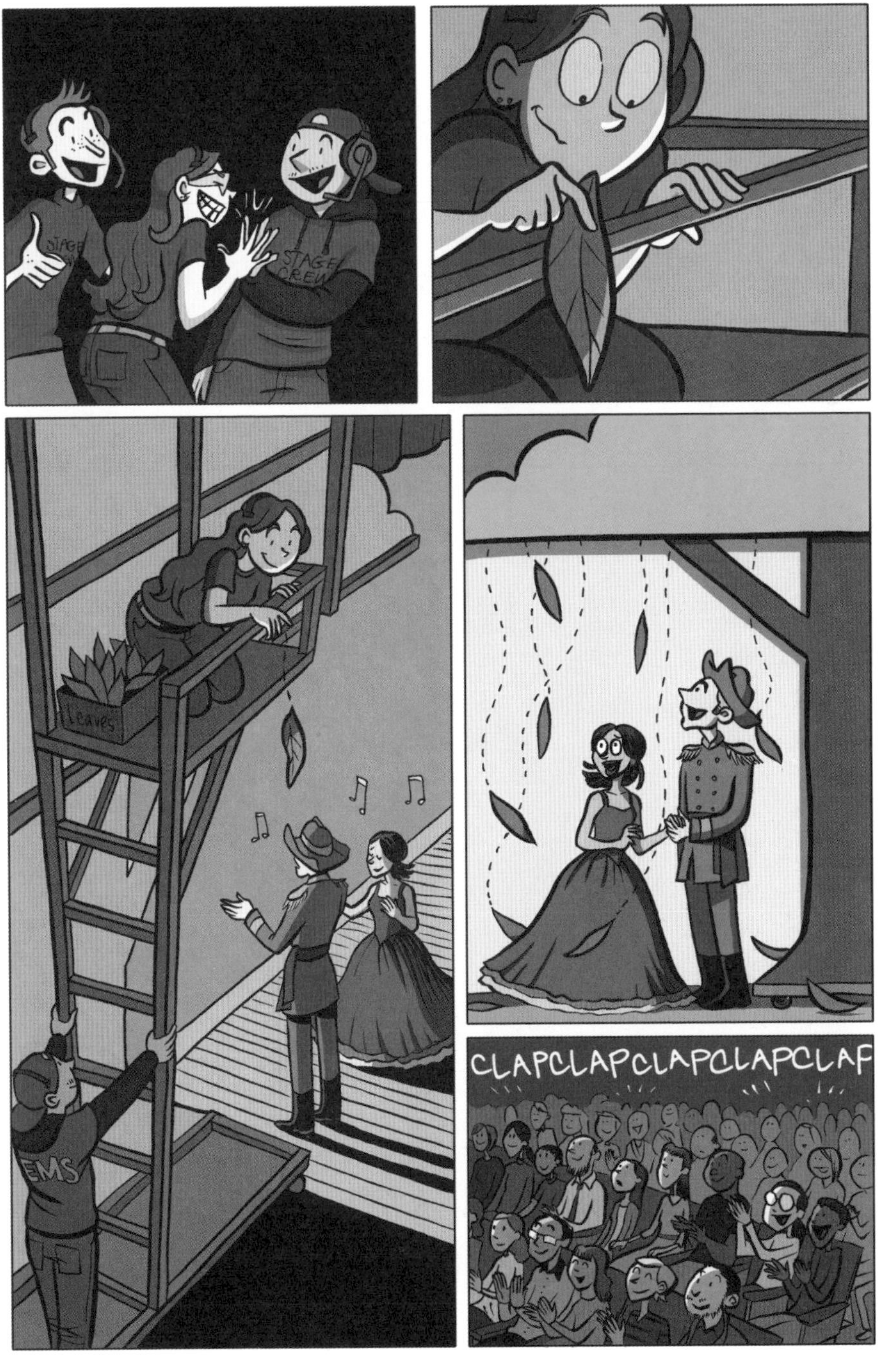
STAGE CREW
STAGE CREW
LEAVES
EMS
CLAPCLAPCLAPCLAPCLAP

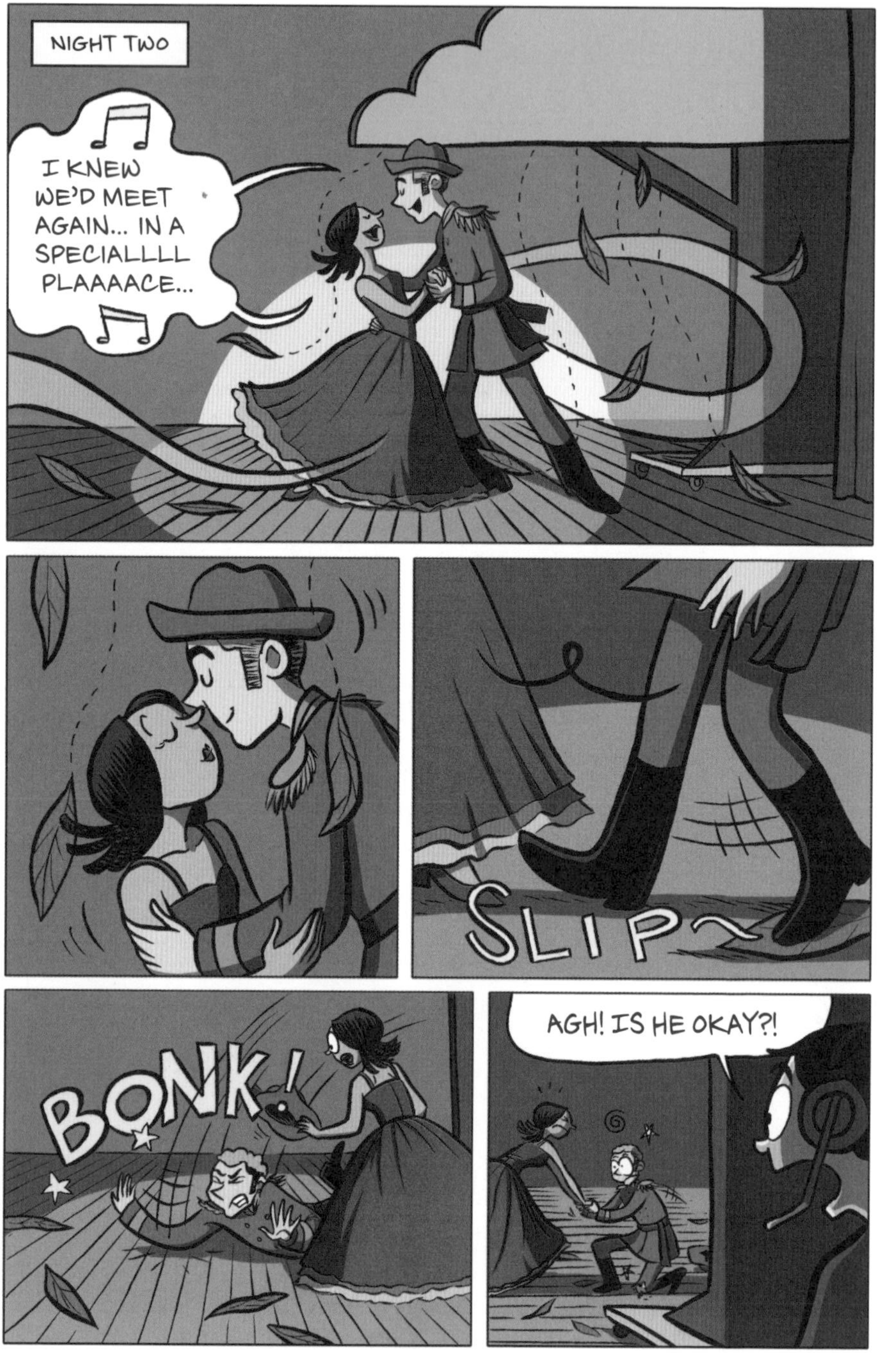
NIGHT TWO
I KNEW WE'D MEET AGAIN... IN A SPECIALLLL PLAAAACE...
SLIP~
BONK!
AGH! IS HE OKAY?!

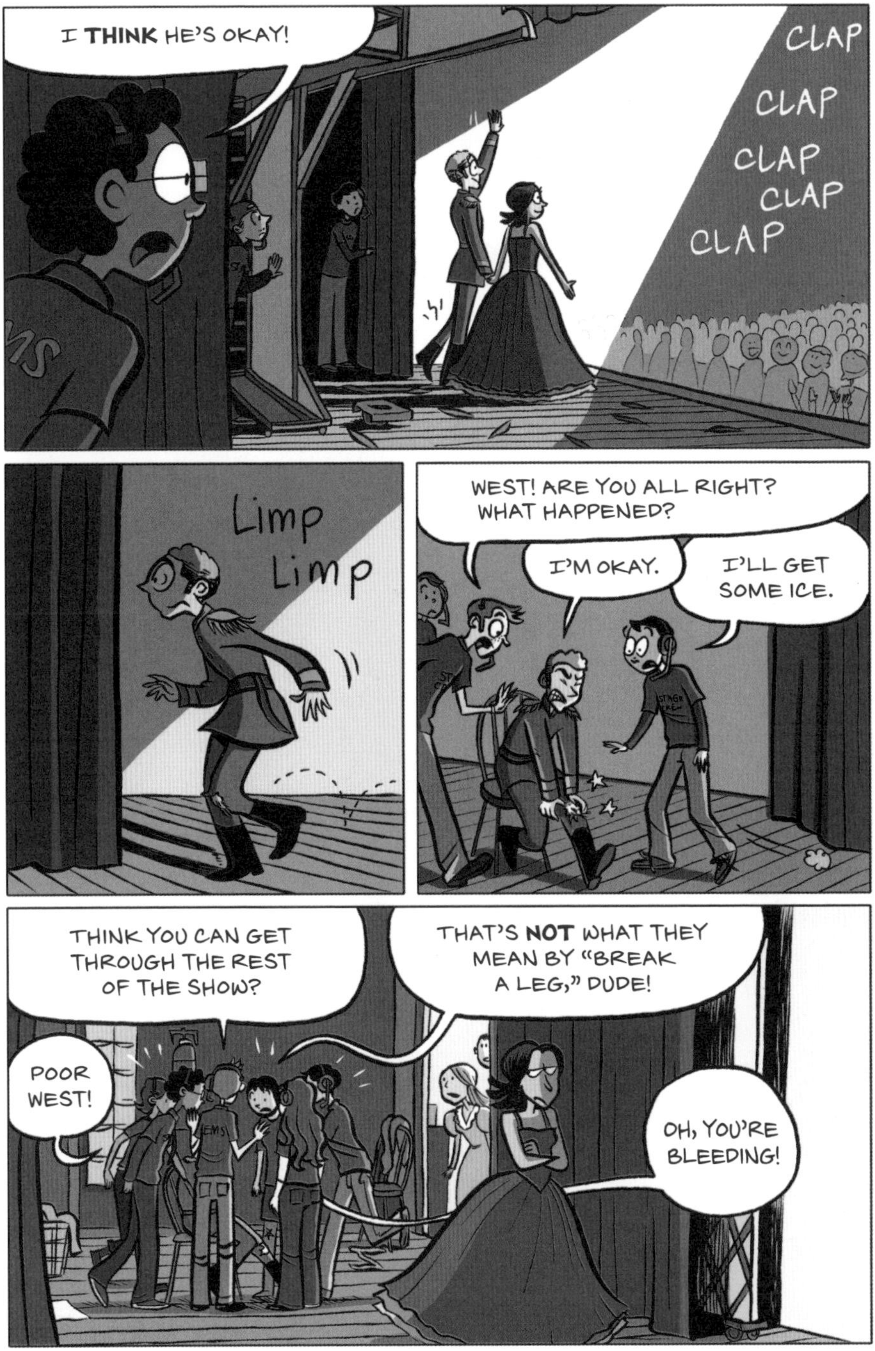

I **THINK** HE'S OKAY!
CLAP
CLAP
CLAP
CLAP
CLAP
Limp
Limp
WEST! ARE YOU ALL RIGHT? WHAT HAPPENED?
I'M OKAY.
I'LL GET SOME ICE.
THINK YOU CAN GET THROUGH THE REST OF THE SHOW?
THAT'S **NOT** WHAT THEY MEAN BY "BREAK A LEG," DUDE!
POOR WEST!
OH, YOU'RE BLEEDING!

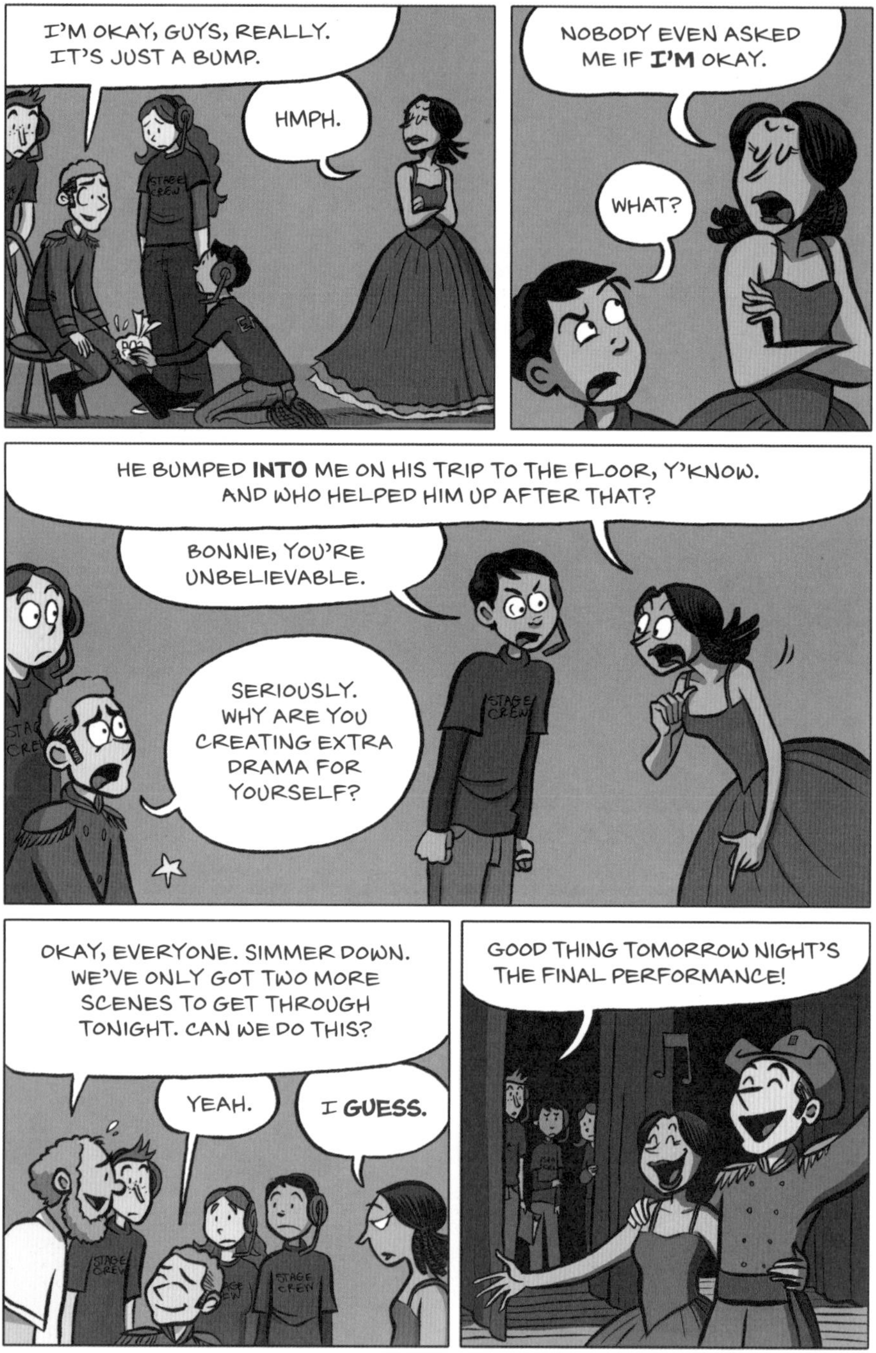
I'M OKAY, GUYS, REALLY. IT'S JUST A BUMP.
HMPH.
STAGE CREW
NOBODY EVEN ASKED ME IF **I'M** OKAY.
WHAT?
HE BUMPED **INTO** ME ON HIS TRIP TO THE FLOOR, Y'KNOW. AND WHO HELPED HIM UP AFTER THAT?
BONNIE, YOU'RE UNBELIEVABLE.
SERIOUSLY. WHY ARE YOU CREATING EXTRA DRAMA FOR YOURSELF?
STAGE CREW
OKAY, EVERYONE. SIMMER DOWN. WE'VE ONLY GOT TWO MORE SCENES TO GET THROUGH TONIGHT. CAN WE DO THIS?
YEAH.
I **GUESS.**
GOOD THING TOMORROW NIGHT'S THE FINAL PERFORMANCE!

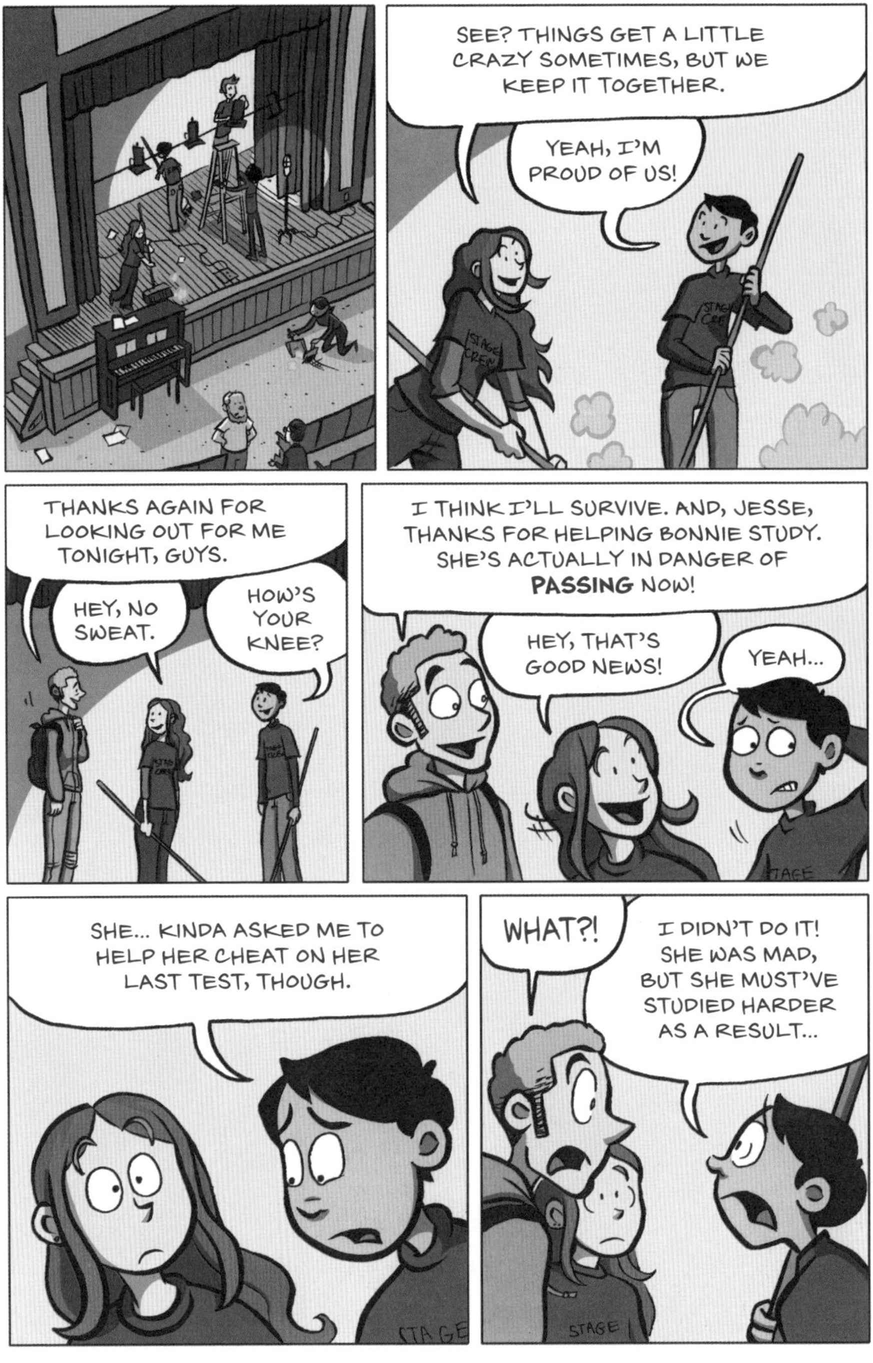
SEE? THINGS GET A LITTLE CRAZY SOMETIMES, BUT WE KEEP IT TOGETHER.
YEAH, I'M PROUD OF US!
STAGE CREW
THANKS AGAIN FOR LOOKING OUT FOR ME TONIGHT, GUYS.
HEY, NO SWEAT.
HOW'S YOUR KNEE?
I THINK I'LL SURVIVE. AND, JESSE, THANKS FOR HELPING BONNIE STUDY. SHE'S ACTUALLY IN DANGER OF **PASSING** NOW!
HEY, THAT'S GOOD NEWS!
YEAH...
SHE... KINDA ASKED ME TO HELP HER CHEAT ON HER LAST TEST, THOUGH.
WHAT?!
I DIDN'T DO IT! SHE WAS MAD, BUT SHE MUST'VE STUDIED HARDER AS A RESULT...

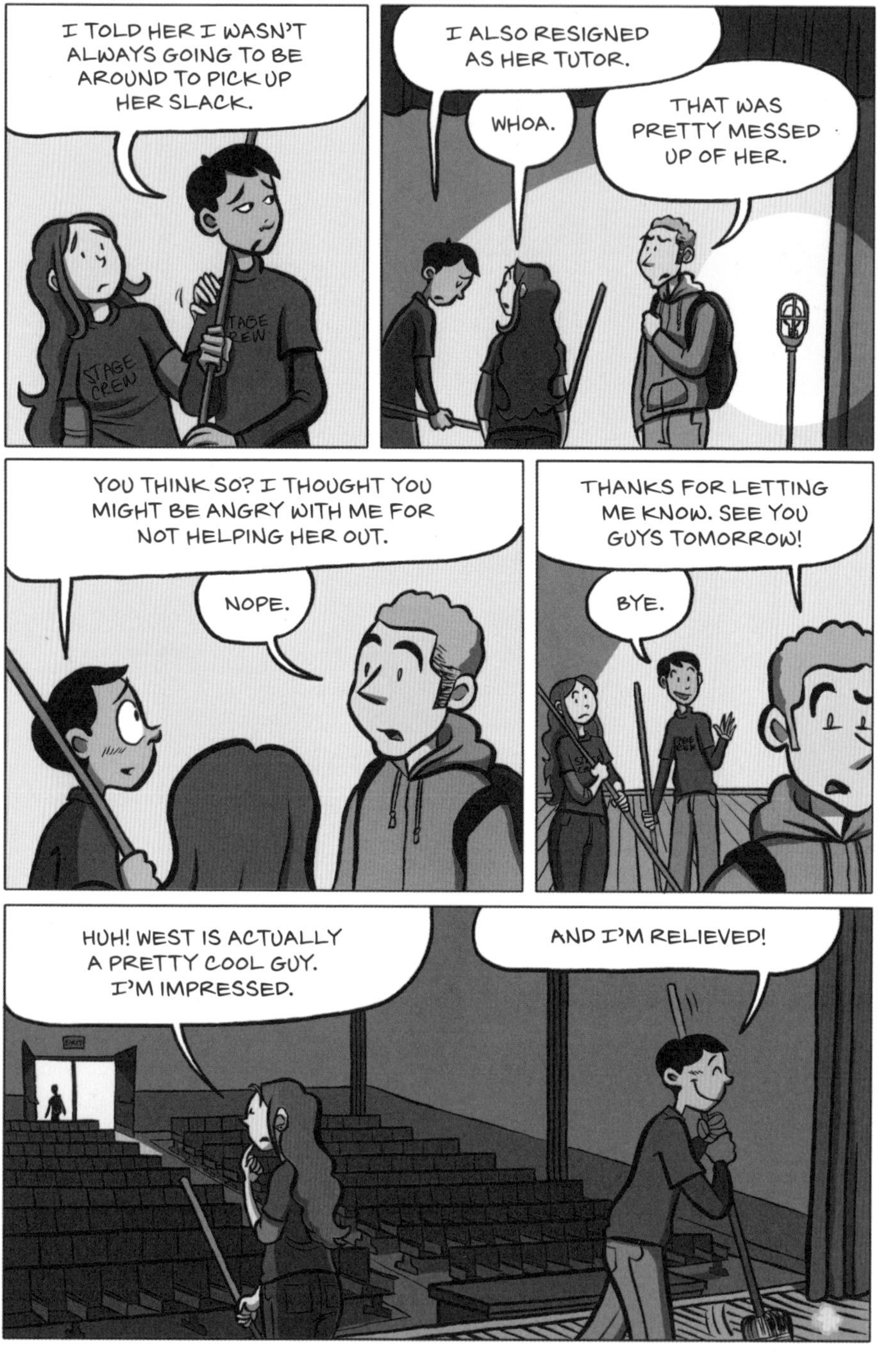

I TOLD HER I WASN'T ALWAYS GOING TO BE AROUND TO PICK UP HER SLACK.
STAGE CREW
STAGE CREW
I ALSO RESIGNED AS HER TUTOR.
WHOA.
THAT WAS PRETTY MESSED UP OF HER.
YOU THINK SO? I THOUGHT YOU MIGHT BE ANGRY WITH ME FOR NOT HELPING HER OUT.
NOPE.
THANKS FOR LETTING ME KNOW. SEE YOU GUYS TOMORROW!
BYE.
HUH! WEST IS ACTUALLY A PRETTY COOL GUY. I'M IMPRESSED.
AND I'M RELIEVED!

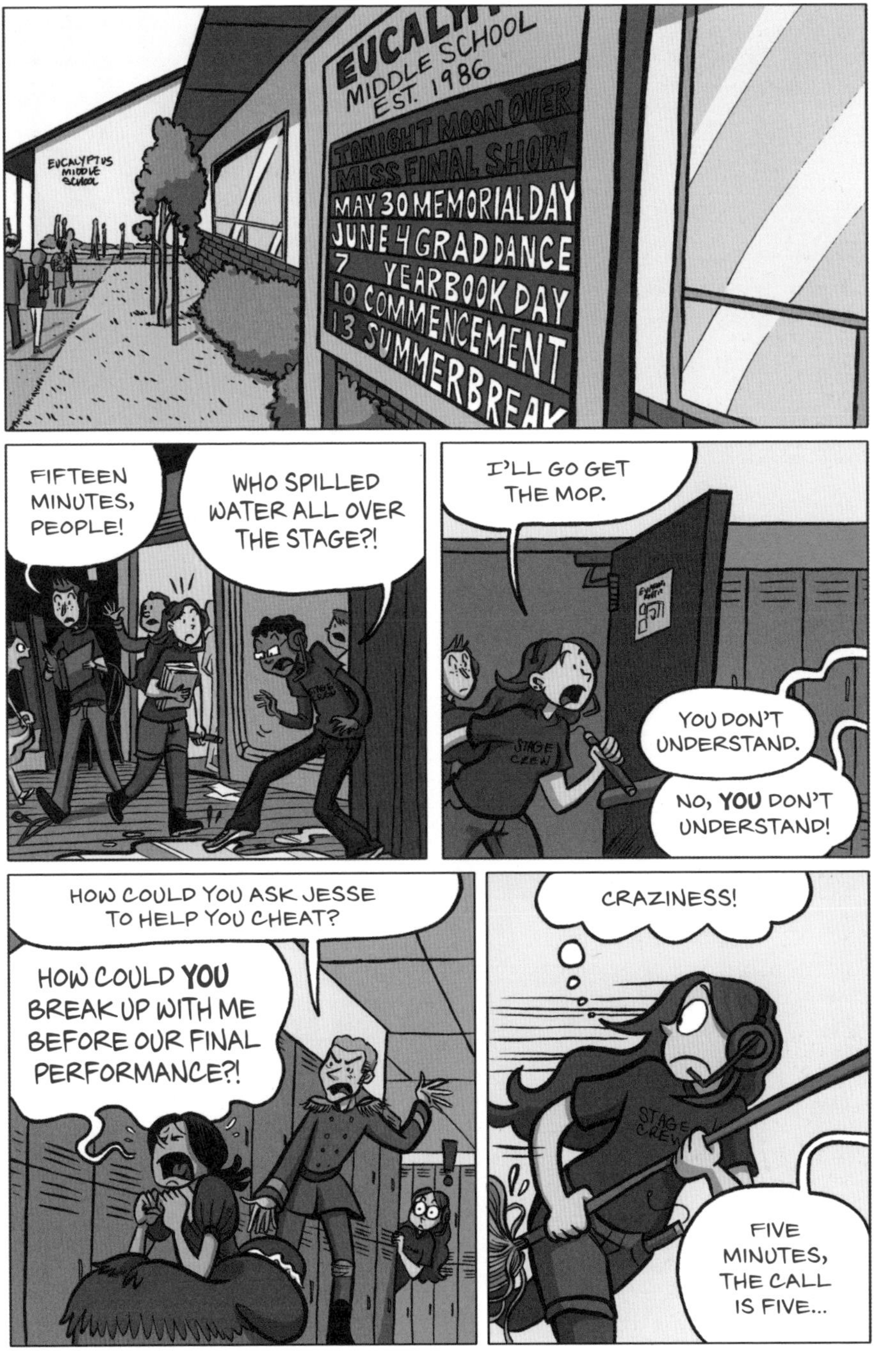
EUCALYPTUS MIDDLE SCHOOL
EUCAL... MIDDLE SCHOOL EST. 1986
TONIGHT MOON OVER MISS FINAL SHOW
MAY 30 MEMORIAL DAY
JUNE 4 GRAD DANCE
7 YEARBOOK DAY
10 COMMENCEMENT
13 SUMMERBREAK
FIFTEEN MINUTES, PEOPLE!
WHO SPILLED WATER ALL OVER THE STAGE?!
I'LL GO GET THE MOP.
YOU DON'T UNDERSTAND.
NO, YOU DON'T UNDERSTAND!
HOW COULD YOU ASK JESSE TO HELP YOU CHEAT?
HOW COULD YOU BREAK UP WITH ME BEFORE OUR FINAL PERFORMANCE?!
CRAZINESS!
FIVE MINUTES, THE CALL IS FIVE...

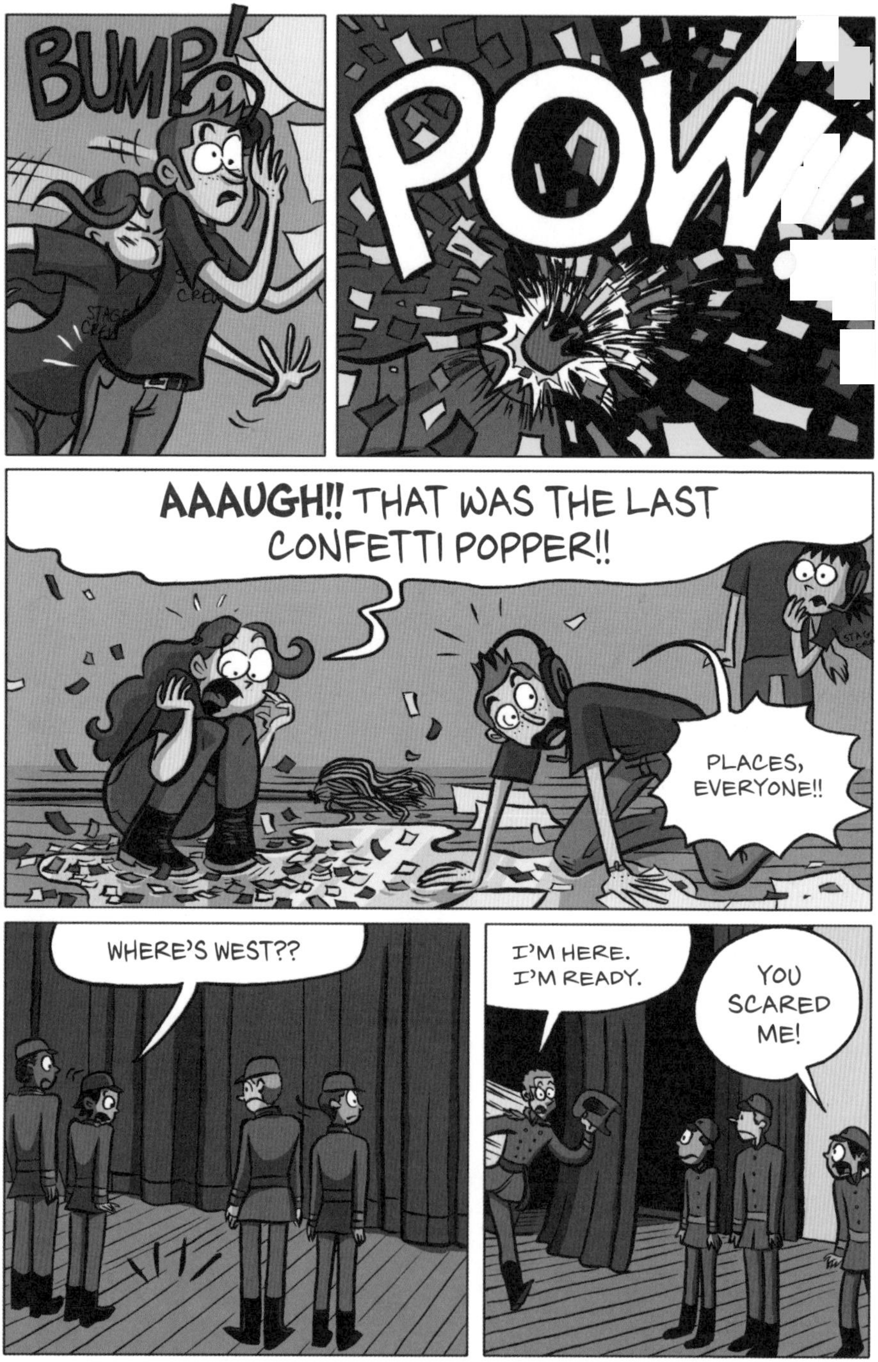
BUMP!
POW!!
AAAUGH!! THAT WAS THE LAST CONFETTI POPPER!!
PLACES, EVERYONE!!
WHERE'S WEST??
I'M HERE. I'M READY.
YOU SCARED ME!

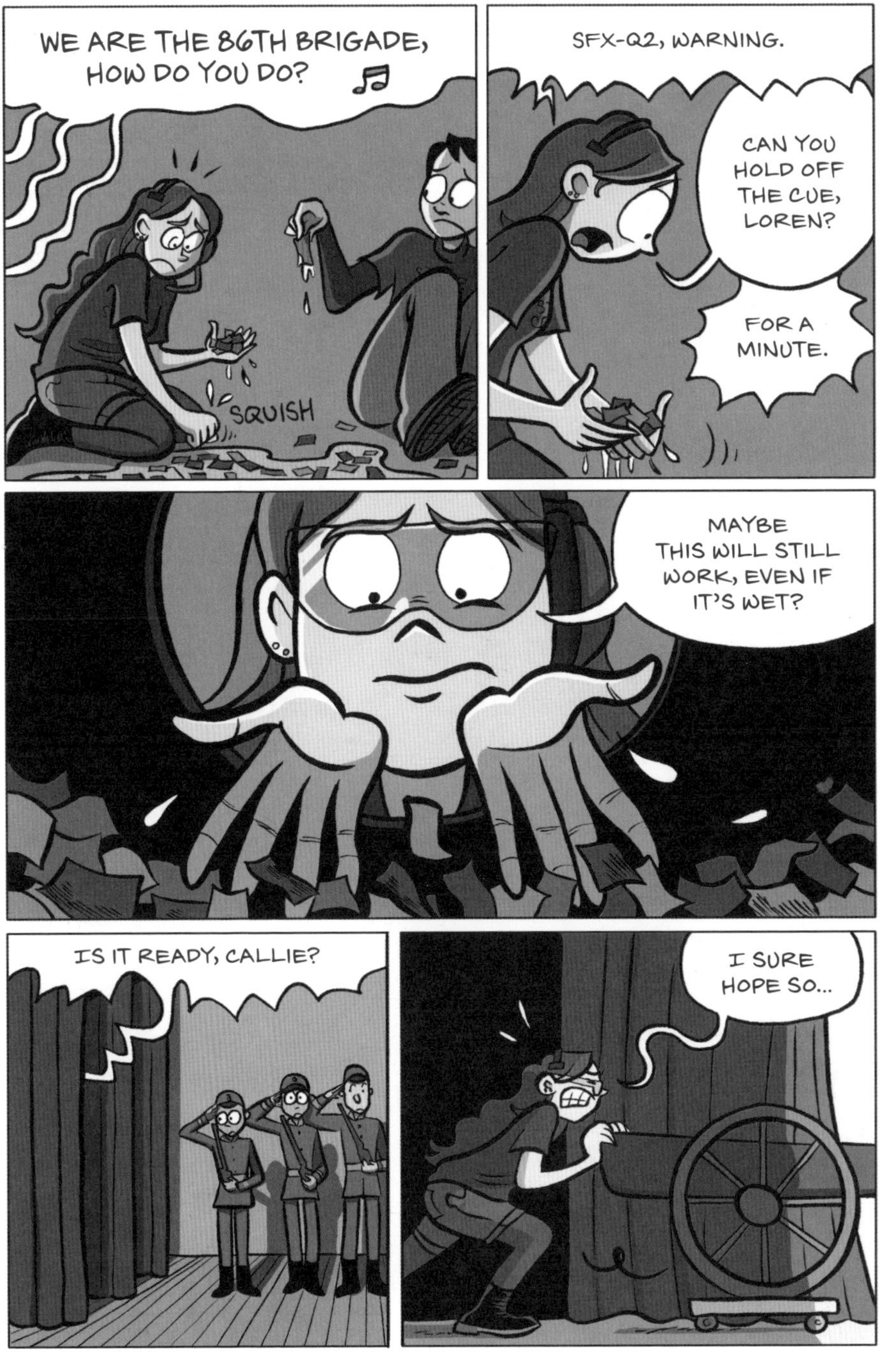
WE ARE THE 86TH BRIGADE, HOW DO YOU DO?
SQUISH
SFX-Q2, WARNING.
CAN YOU HOLD OFF THE CUE, LOREN?
FOR A MINUTE.
MAYBE THIS WILL STILL WORK, EVEN IF IT'S WET?
IS IT READY, CALLIE?
I SURE HOPE SO...

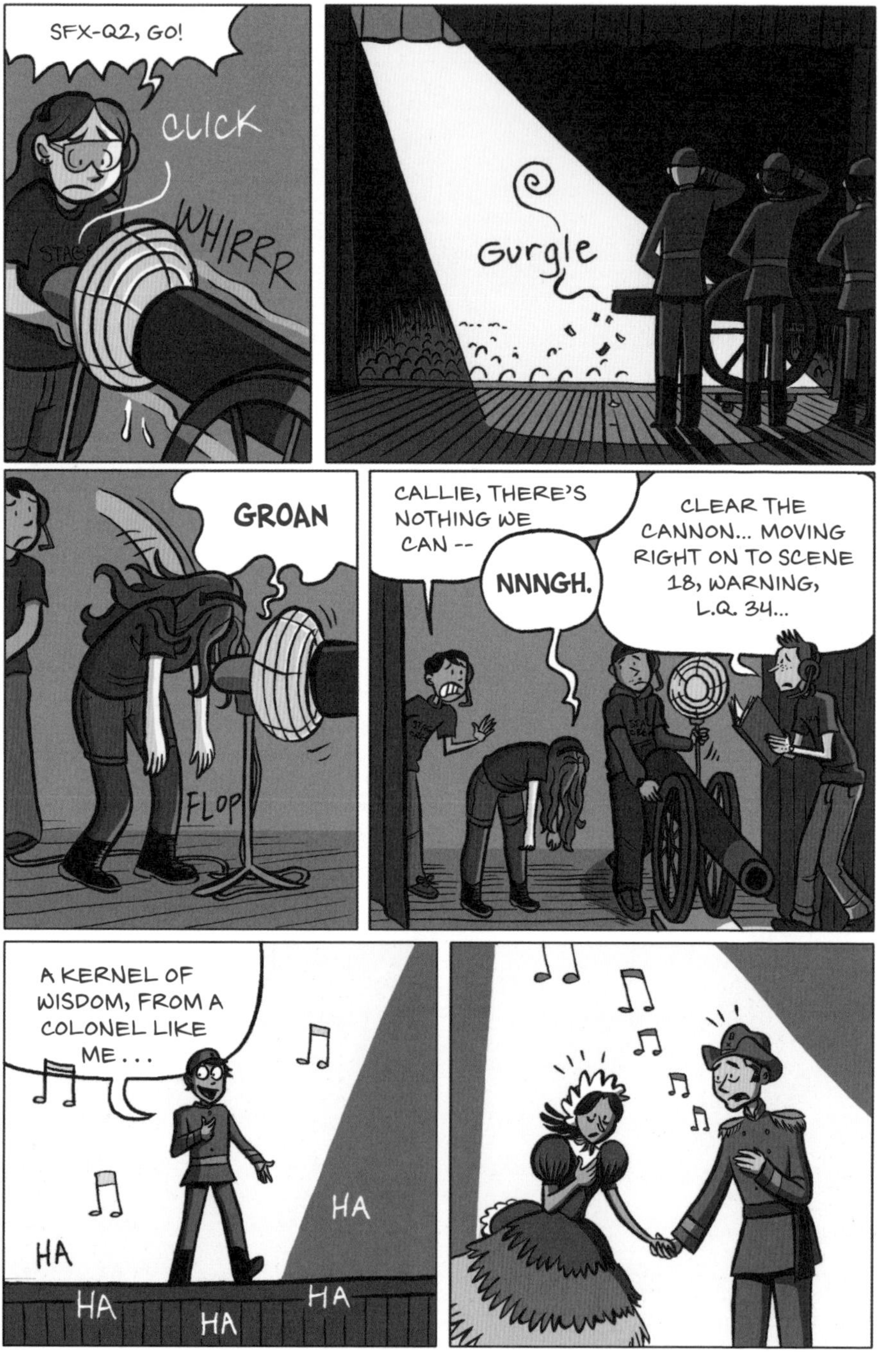
SFX-Q2, GO!
CLICK
WHIRRR
Gurgle
GROAN
FLOP
CALLIE, THERE'S NOTHING WE CAN --
NNNGH.
CLEAR THE CANNON... MOVING RIGHT ON TO SCENE 18, WARNING, L.Q. 34...
A KERNEL OF WISDOM, FROM A COLONEL LIKE ME . . .
HA
HA
HA
HA
HA

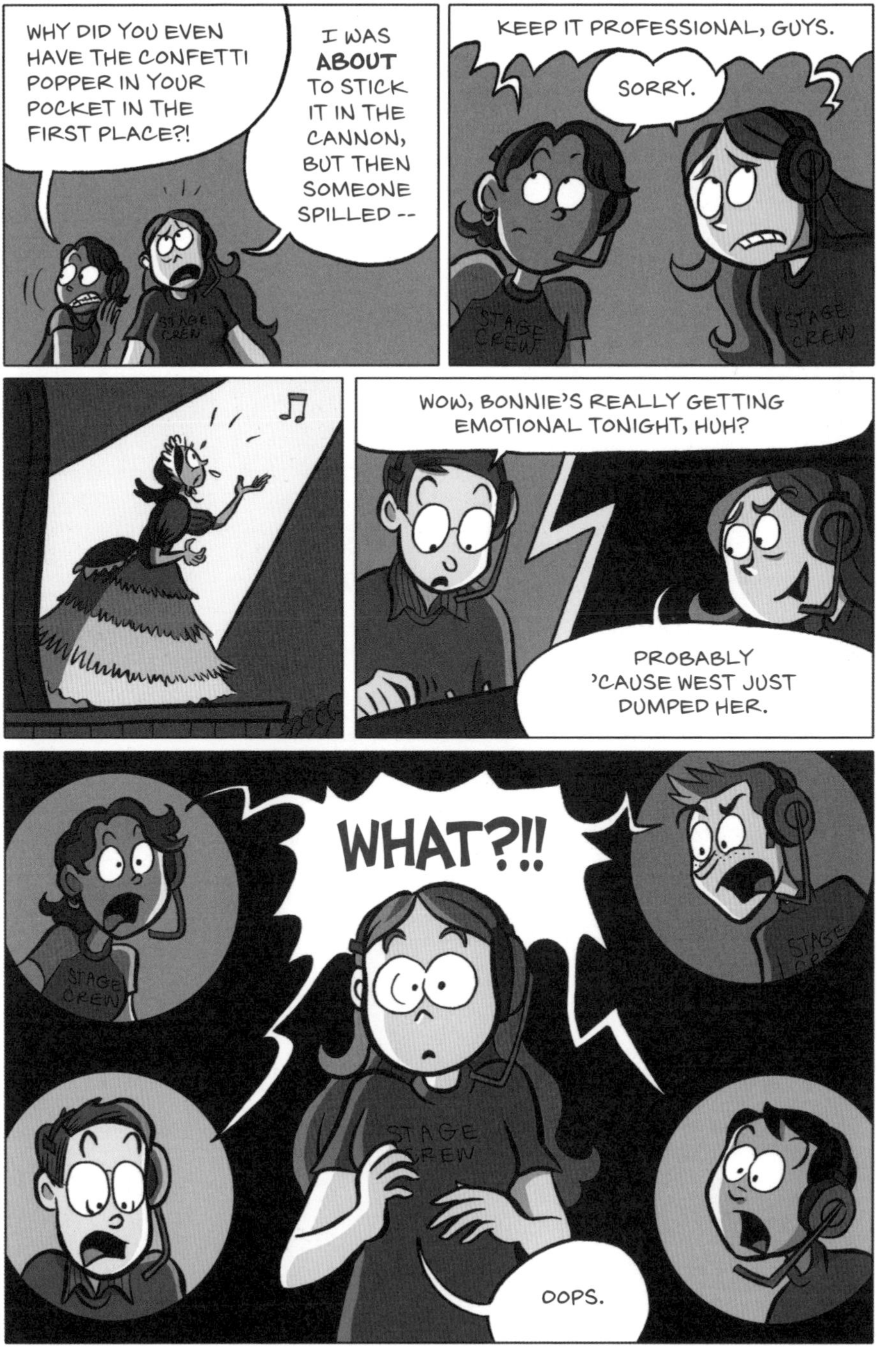
WHY DID YOU EVEN HAVE THE CONFETTI POPPER IN YOUR POCKET IN THE FIRST PLACE?!
I WAS **ABOUT** TO STICK IT IN THE CANNON, BUT THEN SOMEONE SPILLED --
STAGE CREW
KEEP IT PROFESSIONAL, GUYS.
SORRY.
STAGE CREW
STAGE CREW
WOW, BONNIE'S REALLY GETTING EMOTIONAL TONIGHT, HUH?
PROBABLY 'CAUSE WEST JUST DUMPED HER.
WHAT?!!
STAGE CREW
STAGE CREW
OOPS.

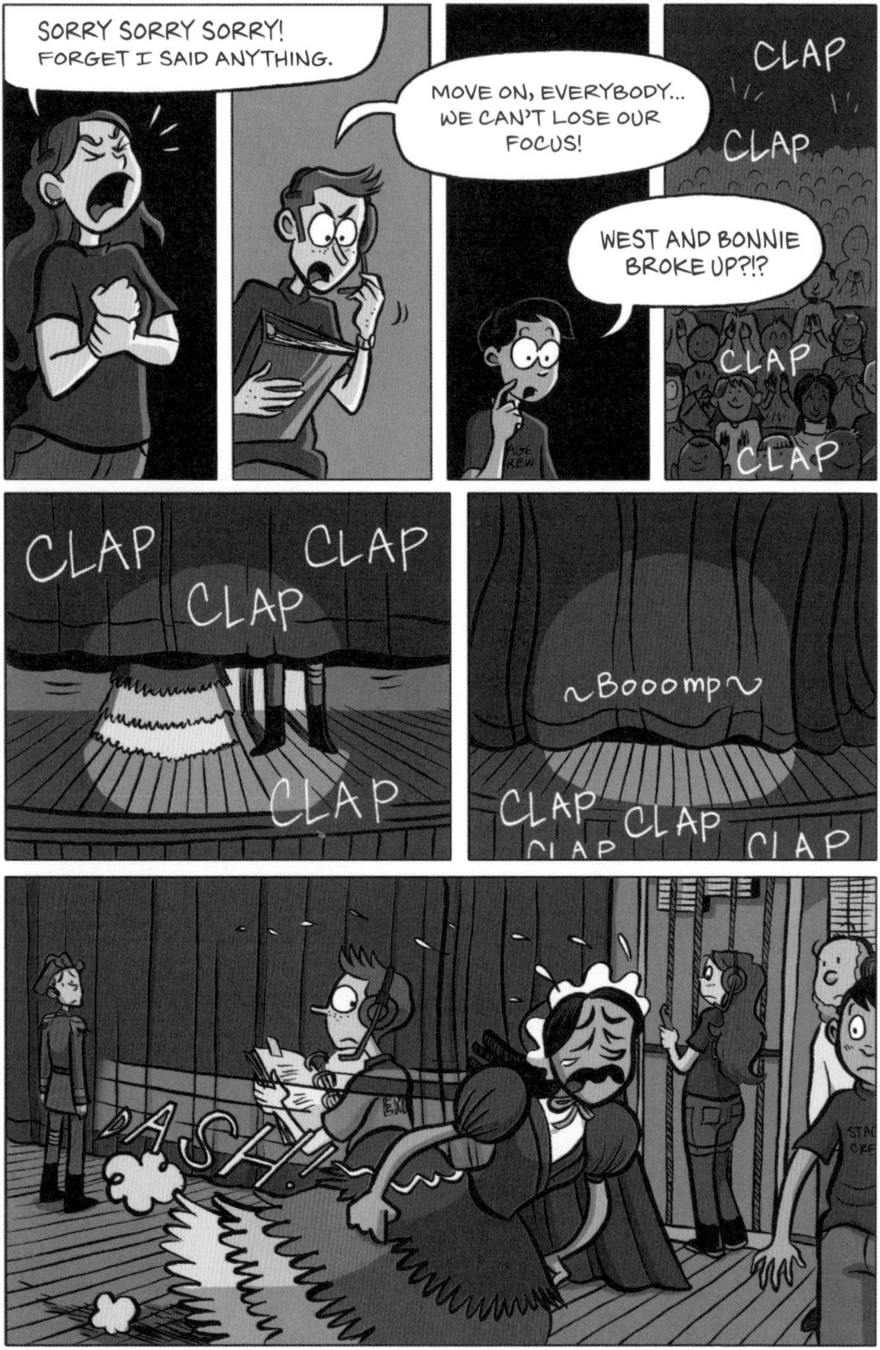
SORRY SORRY SORRY!
FORGET I SAID ANYTHING.
MOVE ON, EVERYBODY... WE CAN'T LOSE OUR FOCUS!
WEST AND BONNIE BROKE UP?!?
CLAP
CLAP
CLAP
CLAP
CLAP
CLAP
CLAP
CLAP
~Booomp~
CLAP
CLAP
CLAP
DASH!

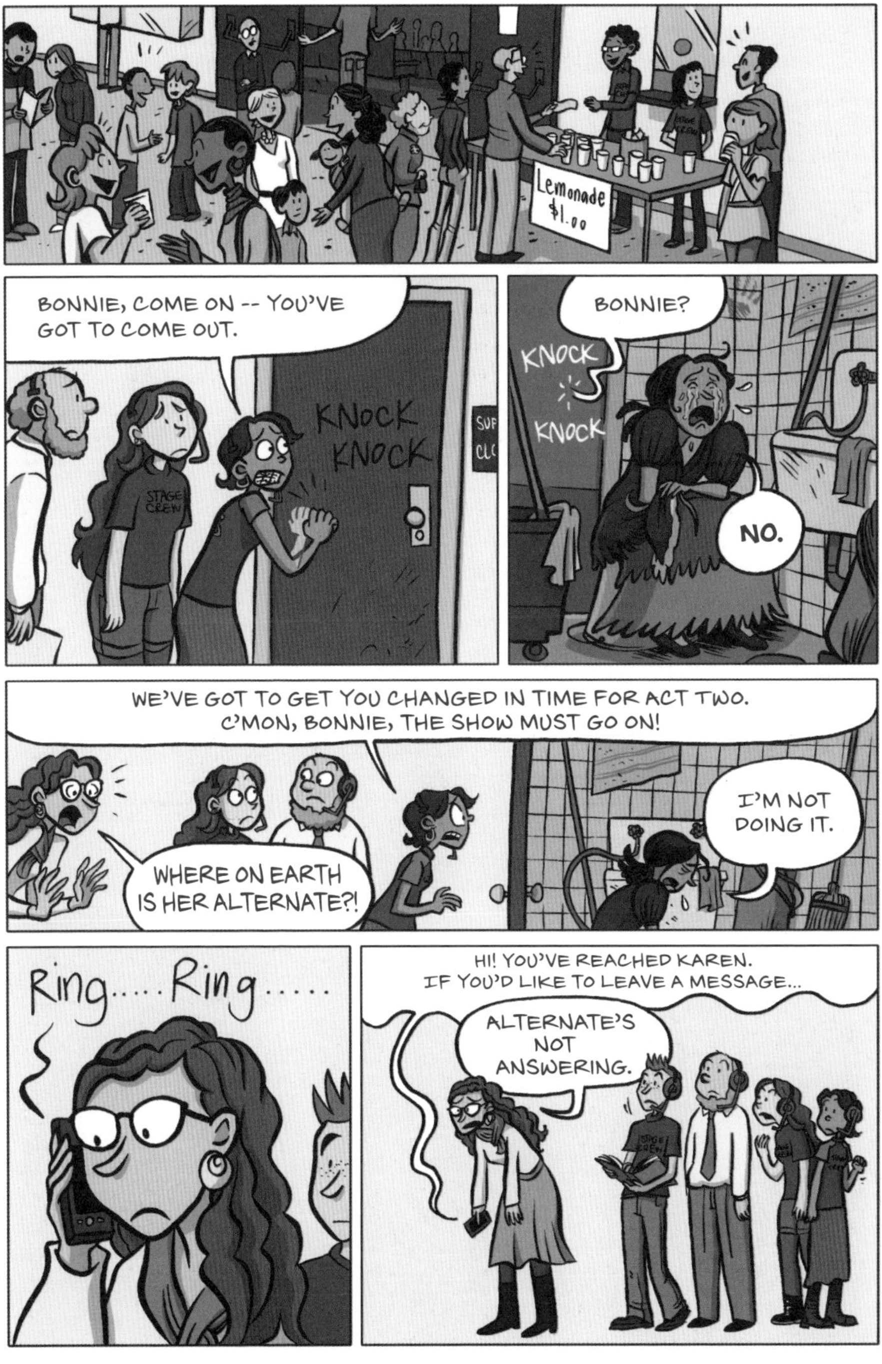

Lemonade $1.00
BONNIE, COME ON -- YOU'VE GOT TO COME OUT.
KNOCK KNOCK
BONNIE?
KNOCK KNOCK
NO.
WE'VE GOT TO GET YOU CHANGED IN TIME FOR ACT TWO. C'MON, BONNIE, THE SHOW MUST GO ON!
WHERE ON EARTH IS HER ALTERNATE?!
I'M NOT DOING IT.
Ring.....Ring.....
HI! YOU'VE REACHED KAREN. IF YOU'D LIKE TO LEAVE A MESSAGE...
ALTERNATE'S NOT ANSWERING.

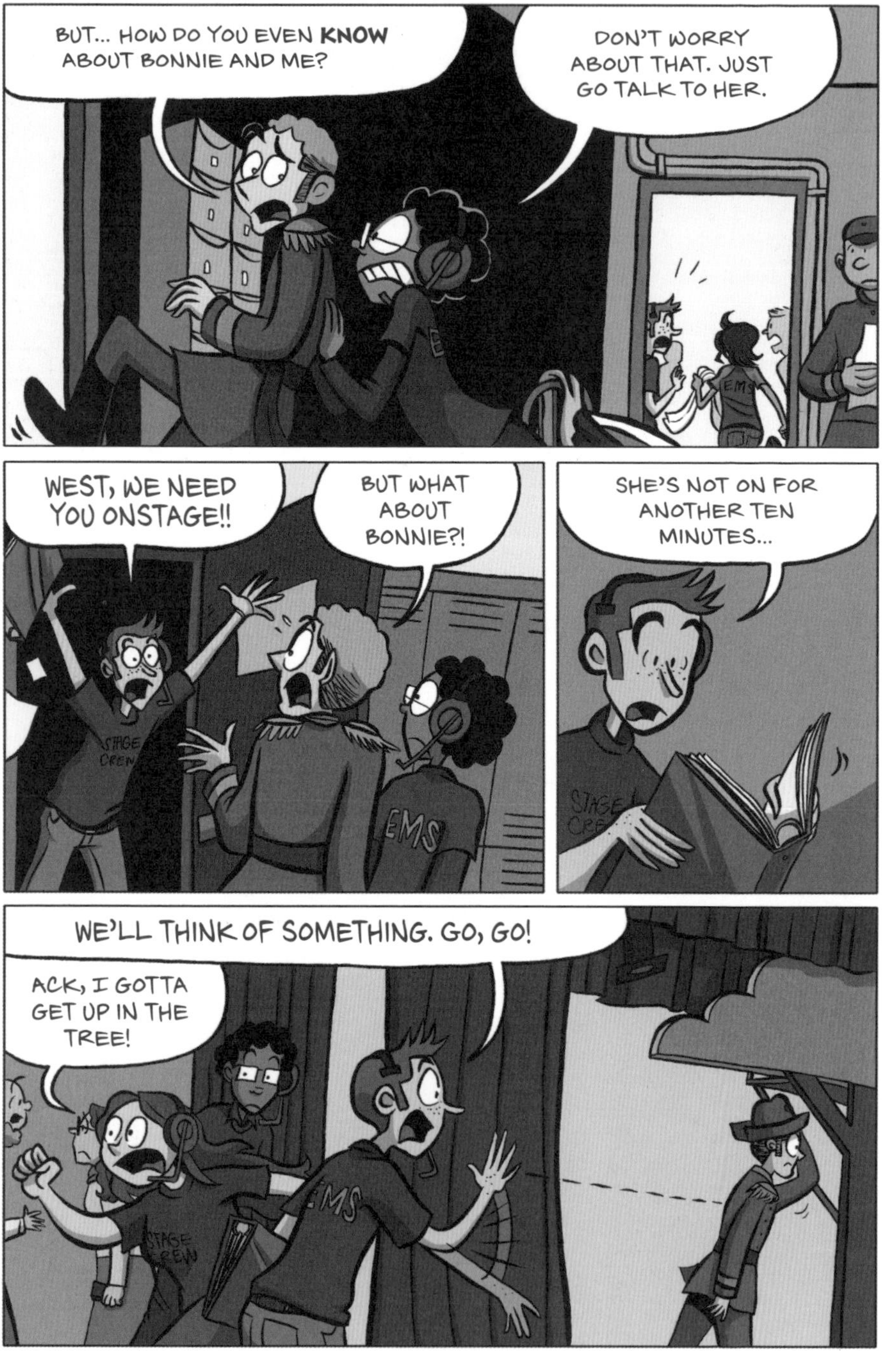
BUT... HOW DO YOU EVEN **KNOW** ABOUT BONNIE AND ME?
DON'T WORRY ABOUT THAT. JUST GO TALK TO HER.
EMS
WEST, WE NEED YOU ONSTAGE!!
BUT WHAT ABOUT BONNIE?!
STAGE CREW
EMS
SHE'S NOT ON FOR ANOTHER TEN MINUTES...
STAGE CREW
WE'LL THINK OF SOMETHING. GO, GO!
ACK, I GOTTA GET UP IN THE TREE!
STAGE CREW
EMS

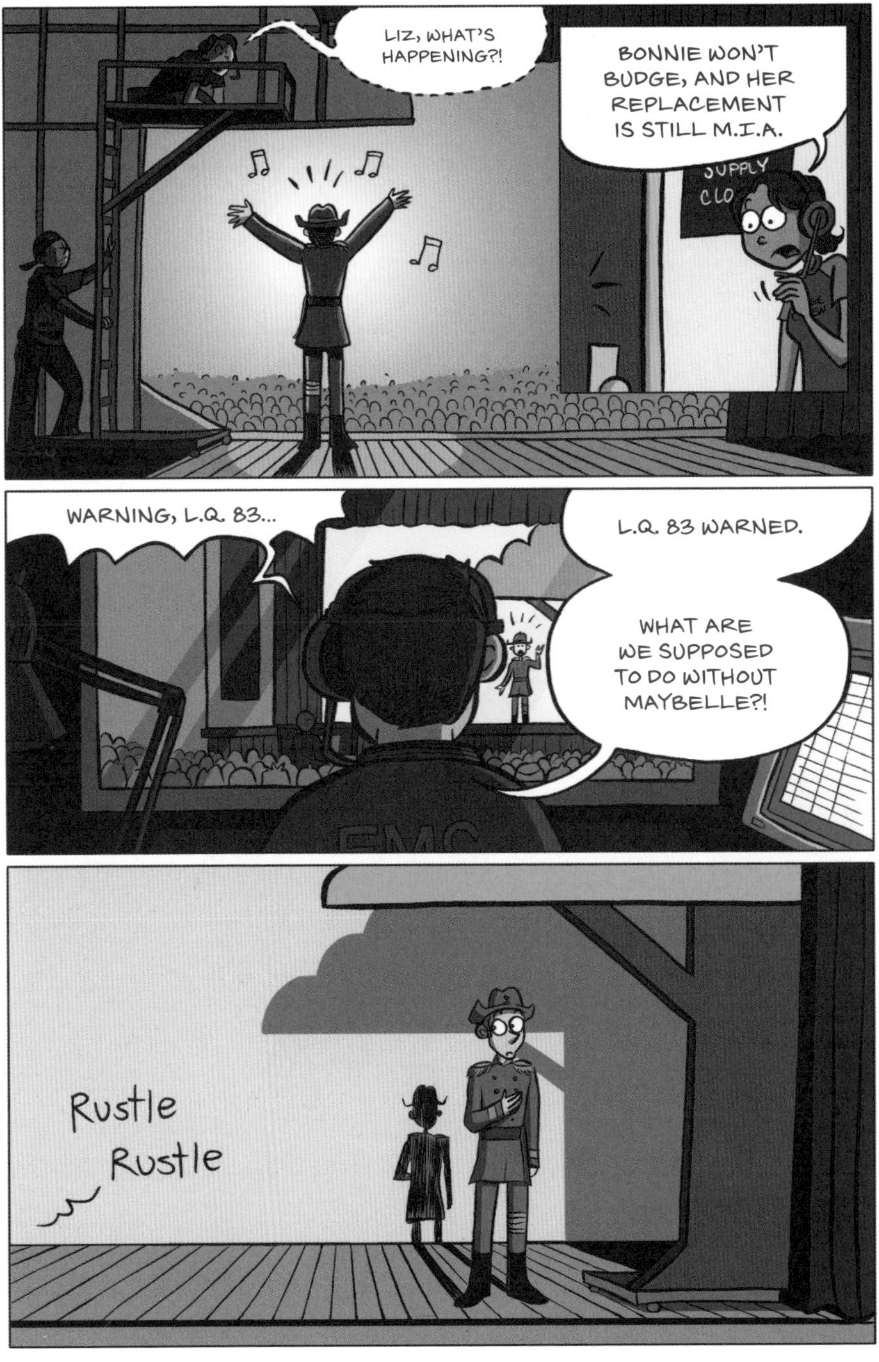
LIZ, WHAT'S HAPPENING?!
BONNIE WON'T BUDGE, AND HER REPLACEMENT IS STILL M.I.A.
SUPPLY CLO
WARNING, L.Q. 83...
L.Q. 83 WARNED.
WHAT ARE WE SUPPOSED TO DO WITHOUT MAYBELLE?!
Rustle
Rustle

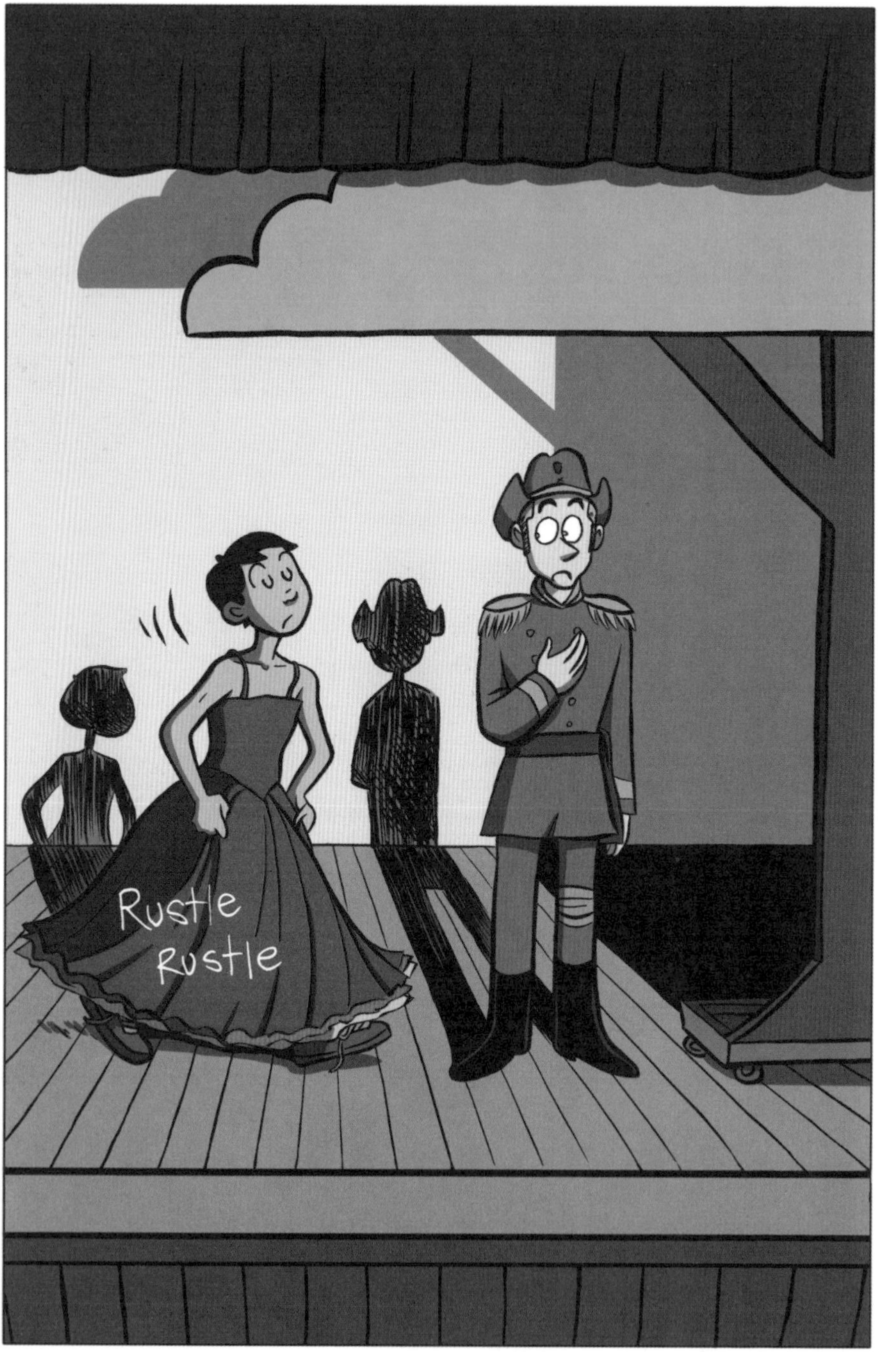
Rustle
Rustle

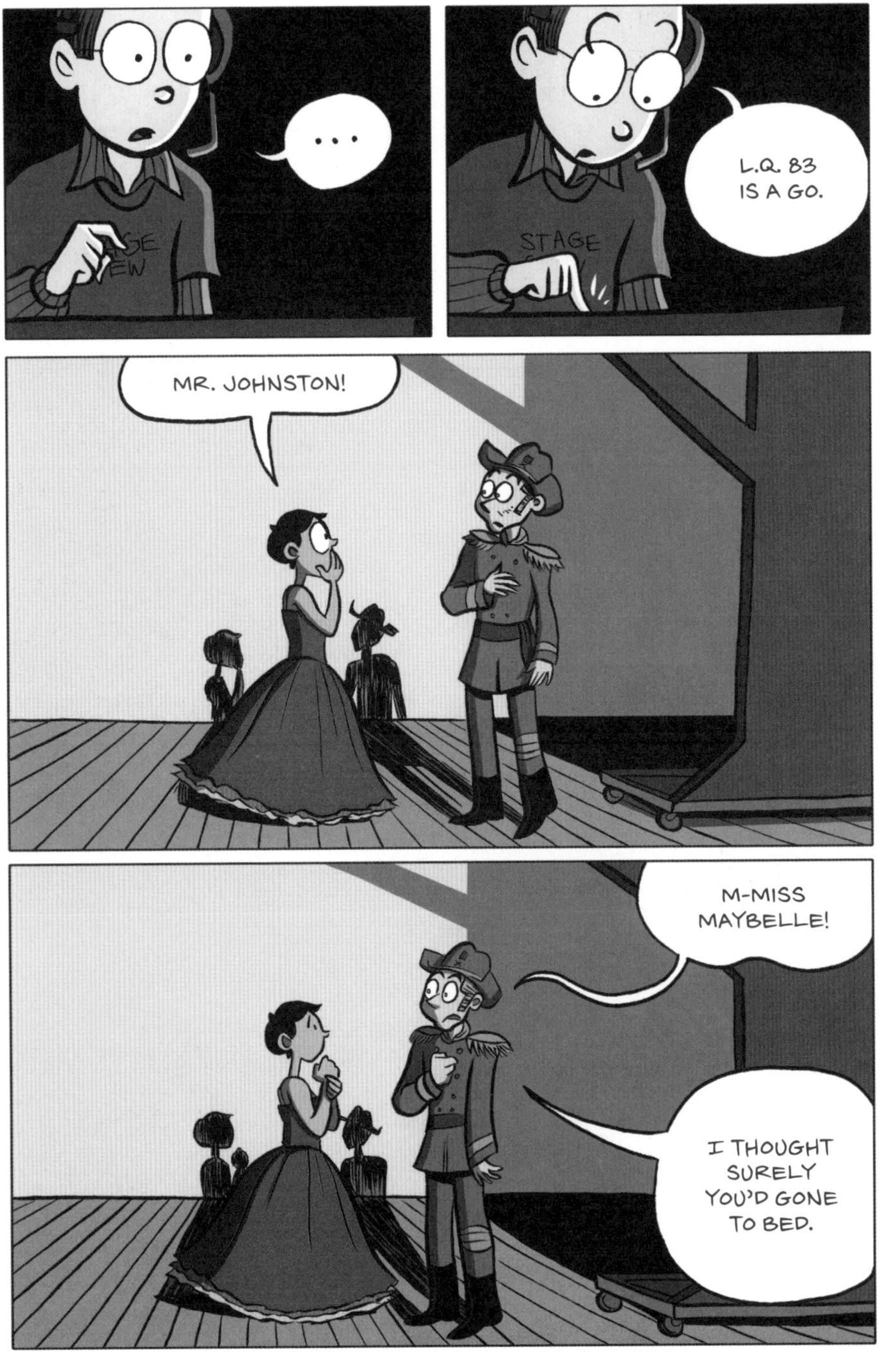
...
STAGE
L.Q. 83 IS A GO.
MR. JOHNSTON!
M-MISS MAYBELLE!
I THOUGHT SURELY YOU'D GONE TO BED.

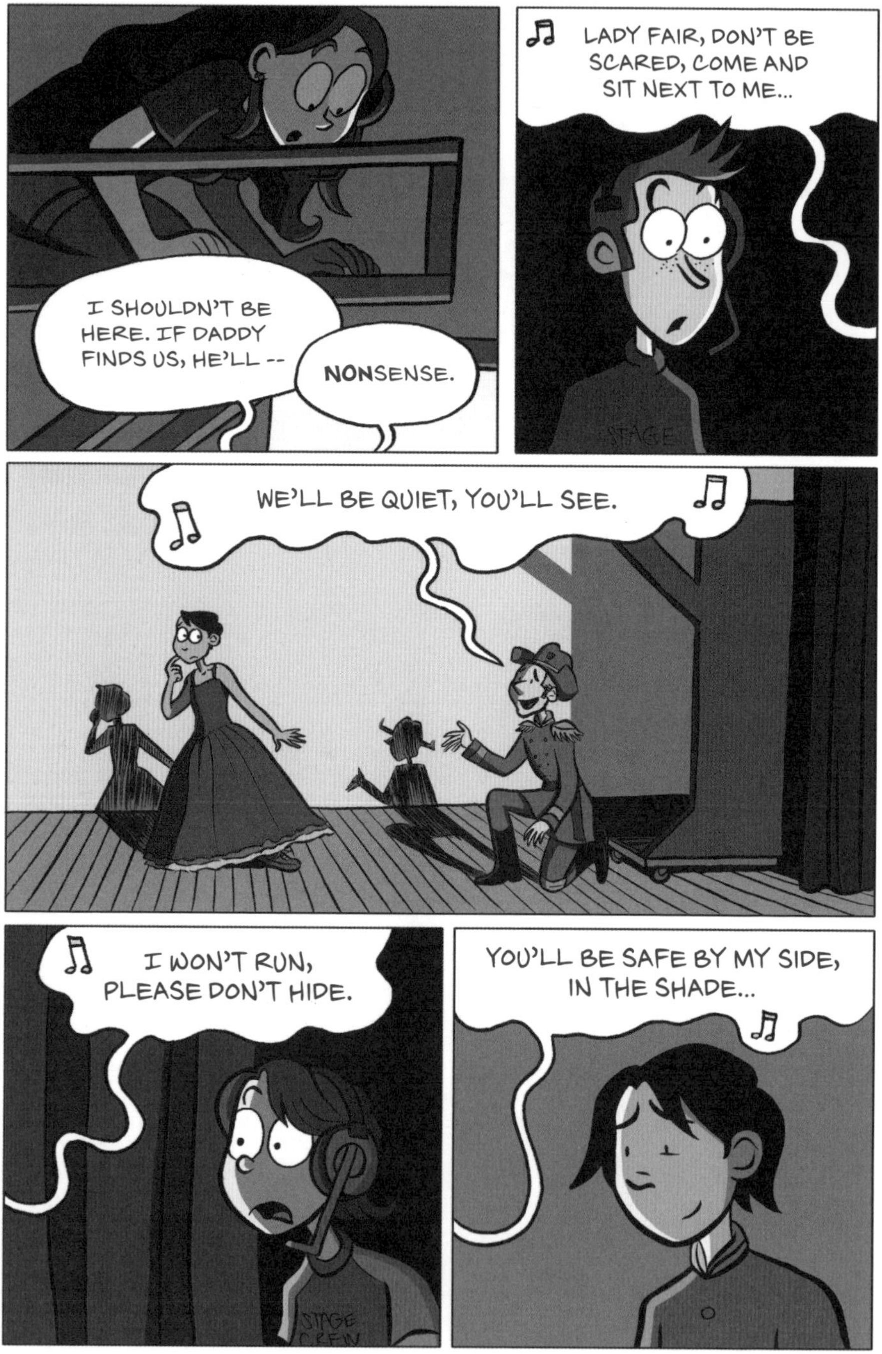
I SHOULDN'T BE HERE. IF DADDY FINDS US, HE'LL --
NONSENSE.
LADY FAIR, DON'T BE SCARED, COME AND SIT NEXT TO ME...
STAGE
WE'LL BE QUIET, YOU'LL SEE.
I WON'T RUN, PLEASE DON'T HIDE.
STAGE CREW
YOU'LL BE SAFE BY MY SIDE, IN THE SHADE...

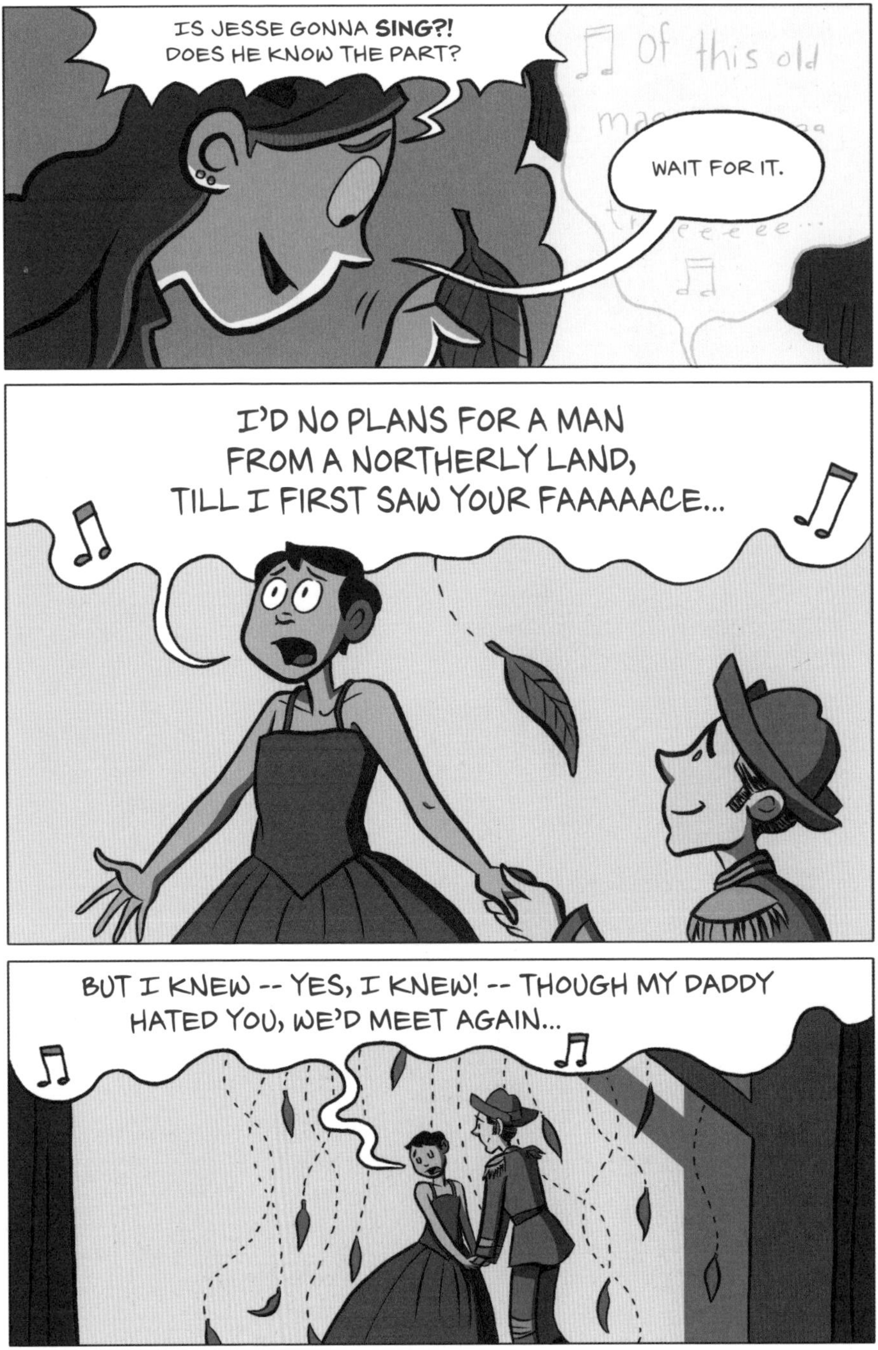
IS JESSE GONNA **SING?!** DOES HE KNOW THE PART?
Of this old
WAIT FOR IT.
I'D NO PLANS FOR A MAN FROM A NORTHERLY LAND, TILL I FIRST SAW YOUR FAAAAACE...
BUT I KNEW -- YES, I KNEW! -- THOUGH MY DADDY HATED YOU, WE'D MEET AGAIN...

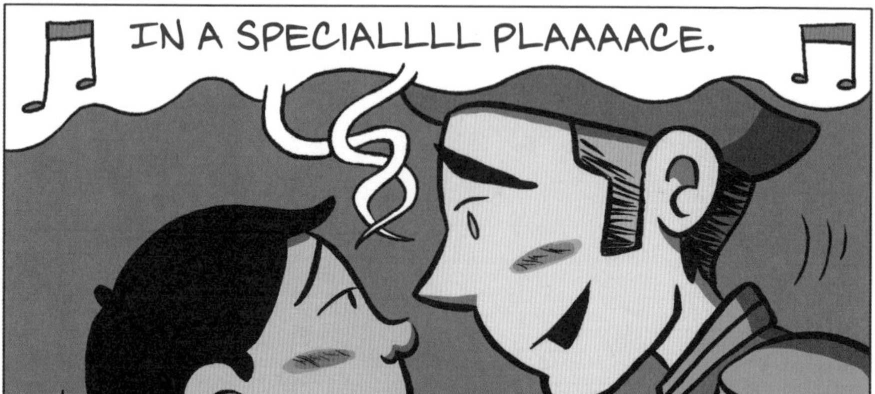
IN A SPECIALLLL PLAAAACE.

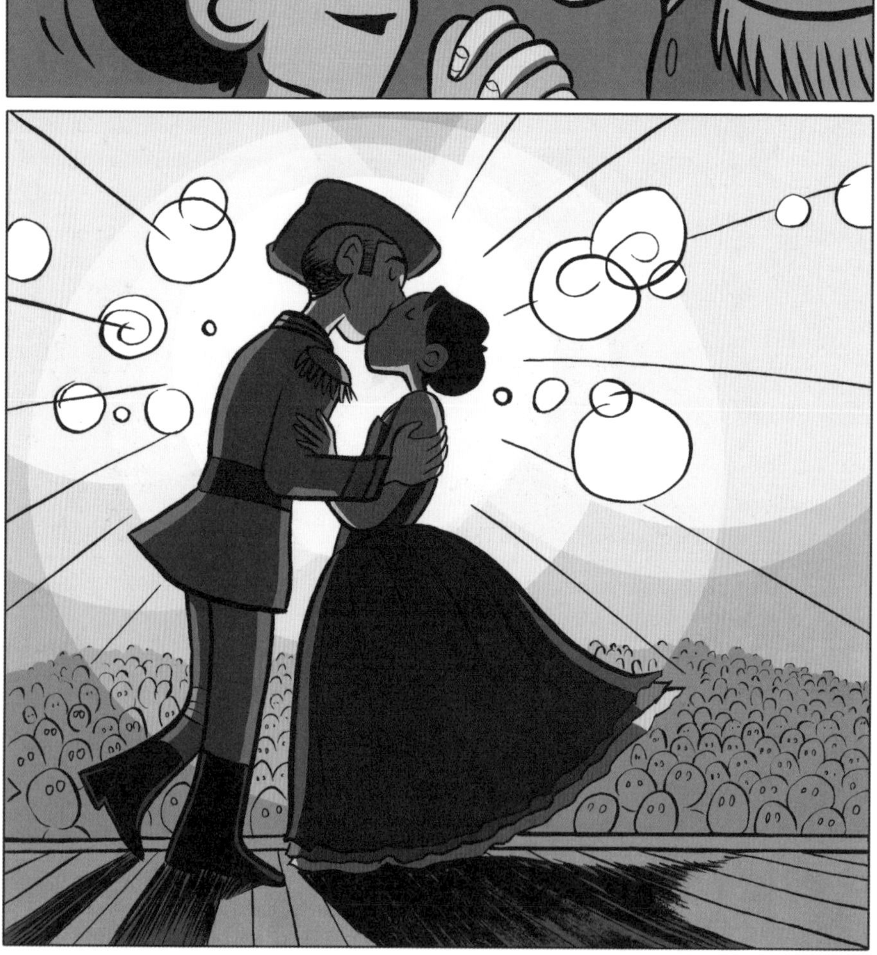

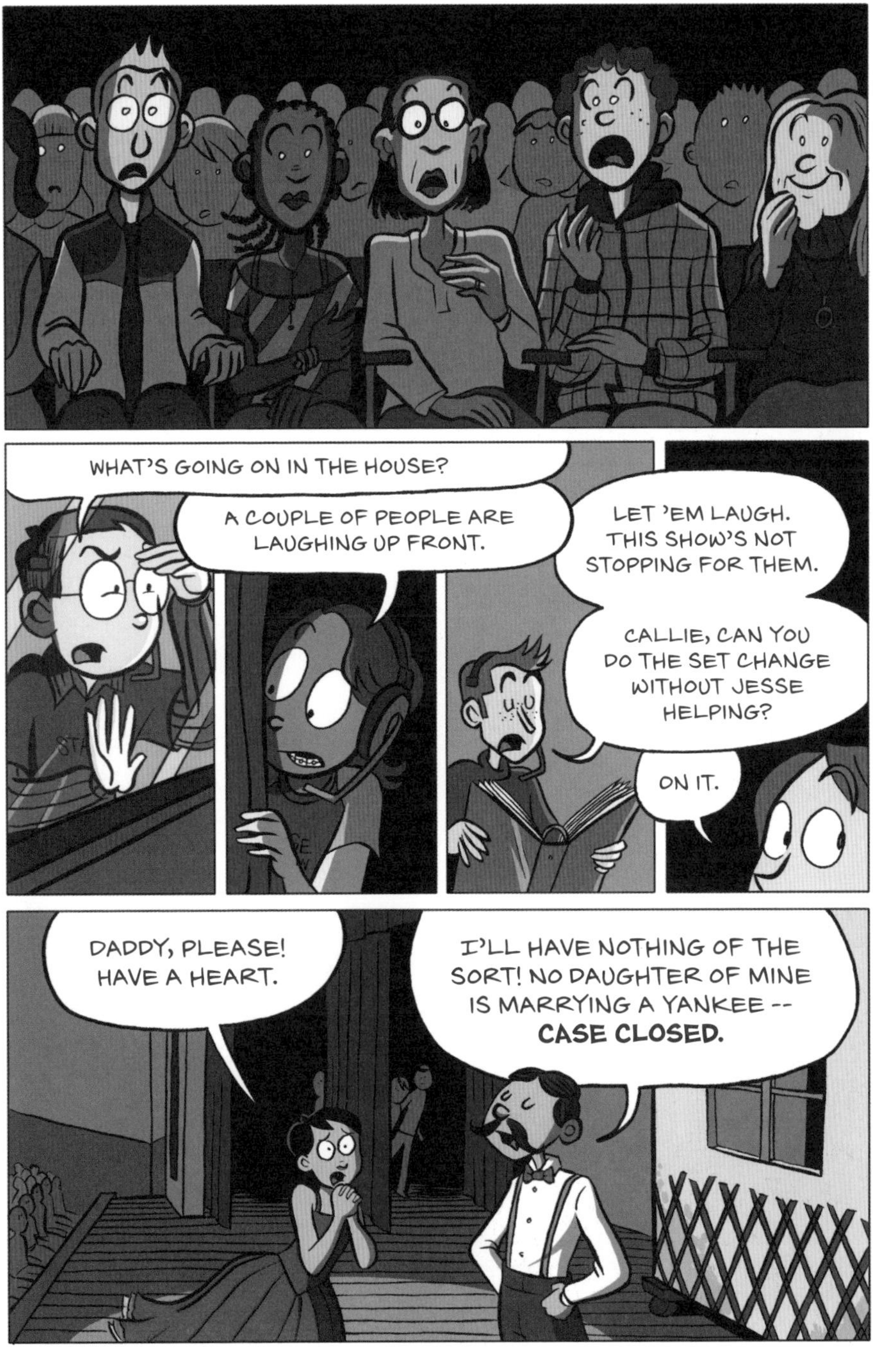
WHAT'S GOING ON IN THE HOUSE?
A COUPLE OF PEOPLE ARE LAUGHING UP FRONT.
LET 'EM LAUGH. THIS SHOW'S NOT STOPPING FOR THEM.
CALLIE, CAN YOU DO THE SET CHANGE WITHOUT JESSE HELPING?
ON IT.
DADDY, PLEASE! HAVE A HEART.
I'LL HAVE NOTHING OF THE SORT! NO DAUGHTER OF MINE IS MARRYING A YANKEE -- **CASE CLOSED.**

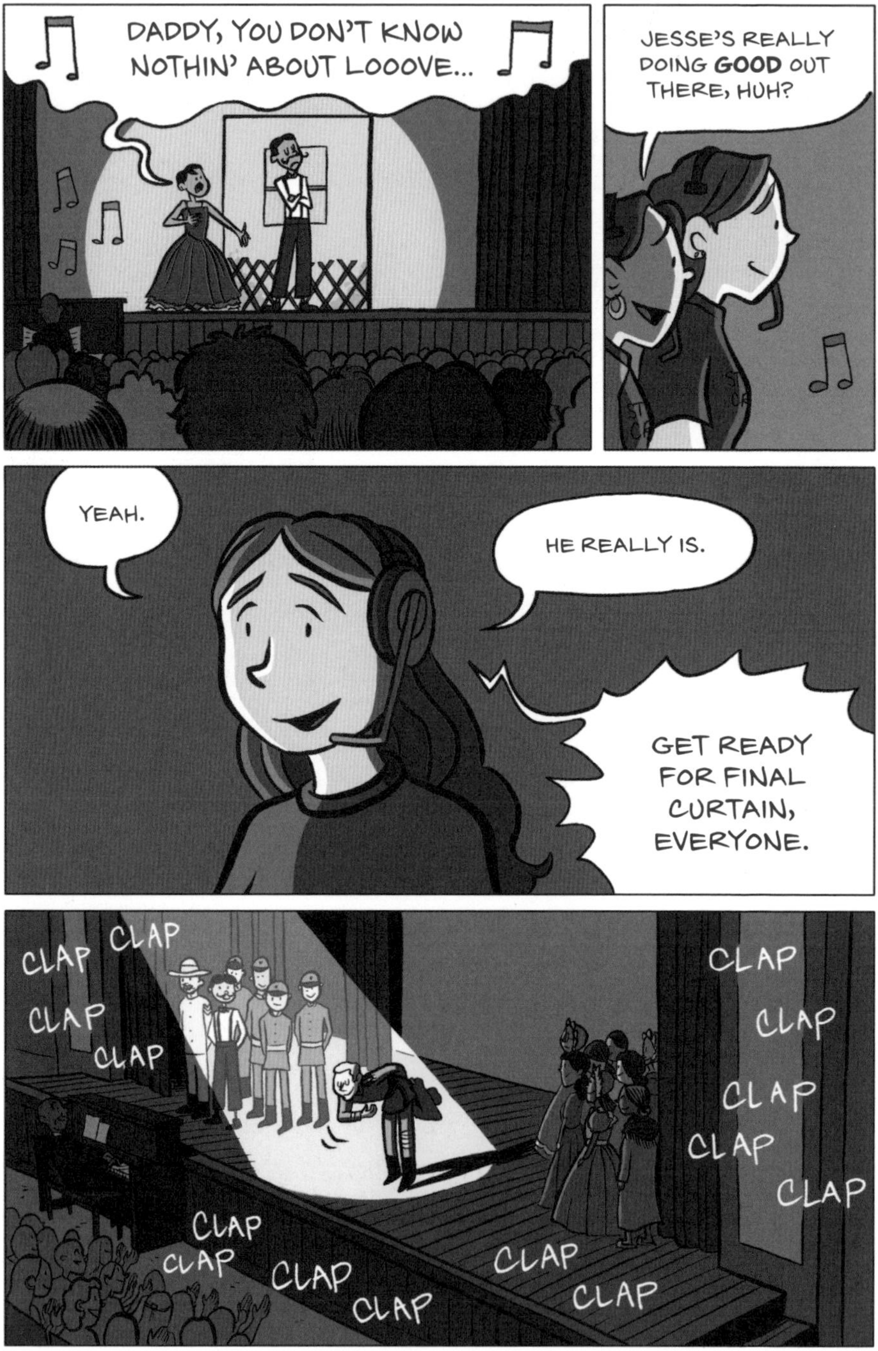
DADDY, YOU DON'T KNOW NOTHIN' ABOUT LOOOVE...
JESSE'S REALLY DOING **GOOD** OUT THERE, HUH?
YEAH.
HE REALLY IS.
GET READY FOR FINAL CURTAIN, EVERYONE.
CLAP CLAP
CLAP
CLAP
CLAP
CLAP
CLAP
CLAP
CLAP
CLAP
CLAP
CLAP
CLAP
CLAP
CLAP
CLAP

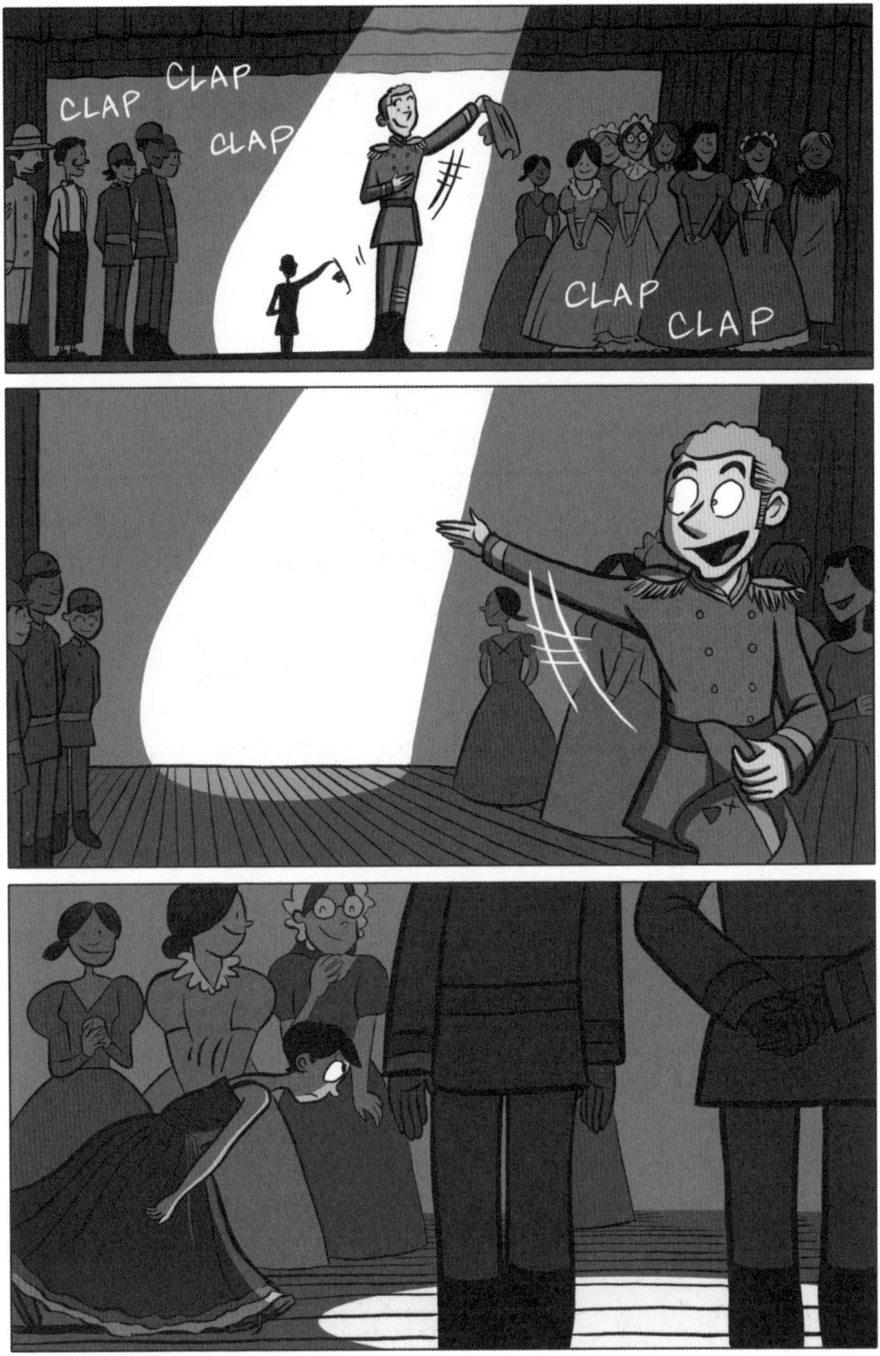
CLAP
CLAP
CLAP
CLAP
CLAP

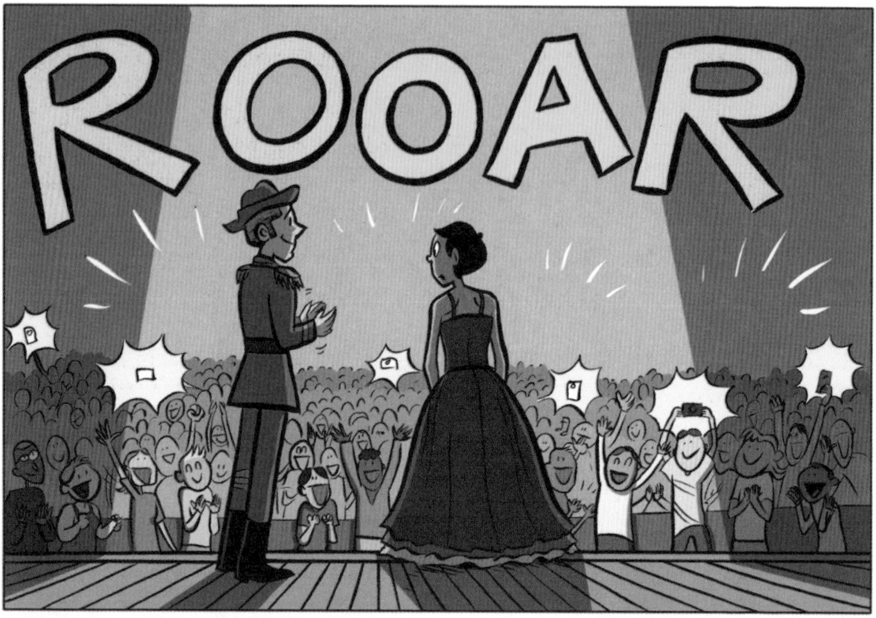
ROOAR

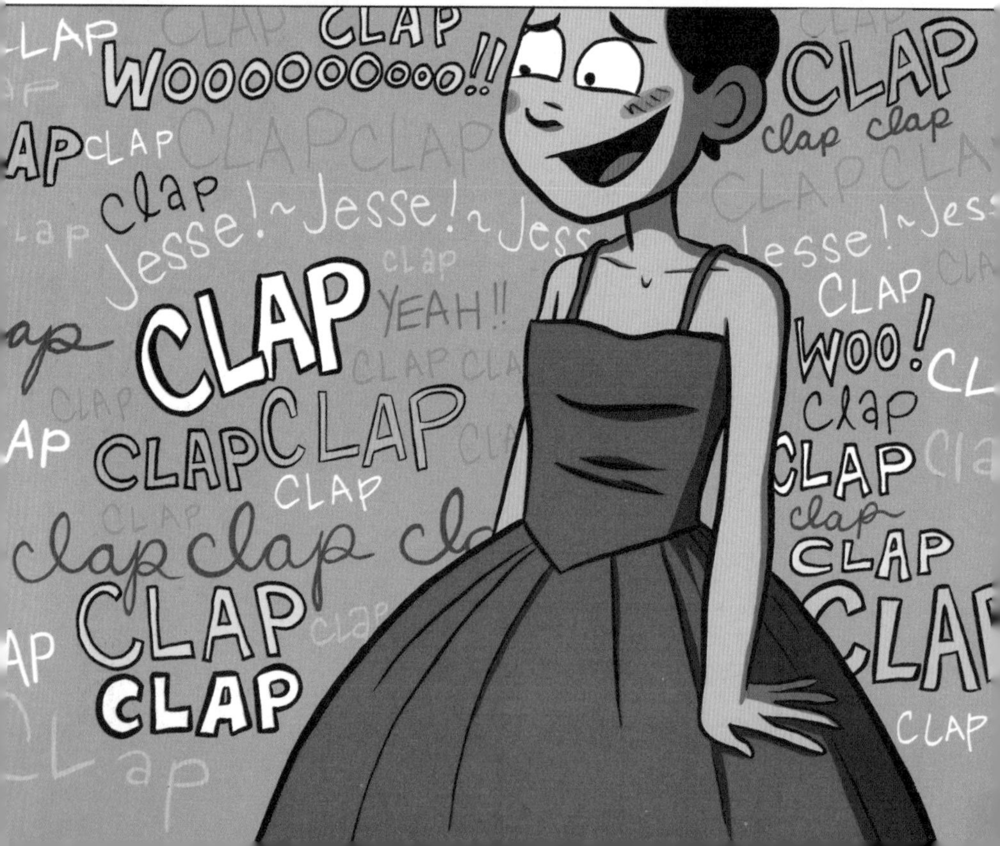
CLAP
WOOOOOOOooo!!
CLAP
clap clap
CLAP CLAP
clap
Jesse! ~ Jesse!
clap
CLAP
YEAH!!
CLAP
WOO!
clap
CLAP CLAP
CLAP
CLAP
clap clap
clap
CLAP
CLAP
CLAP
CLAP

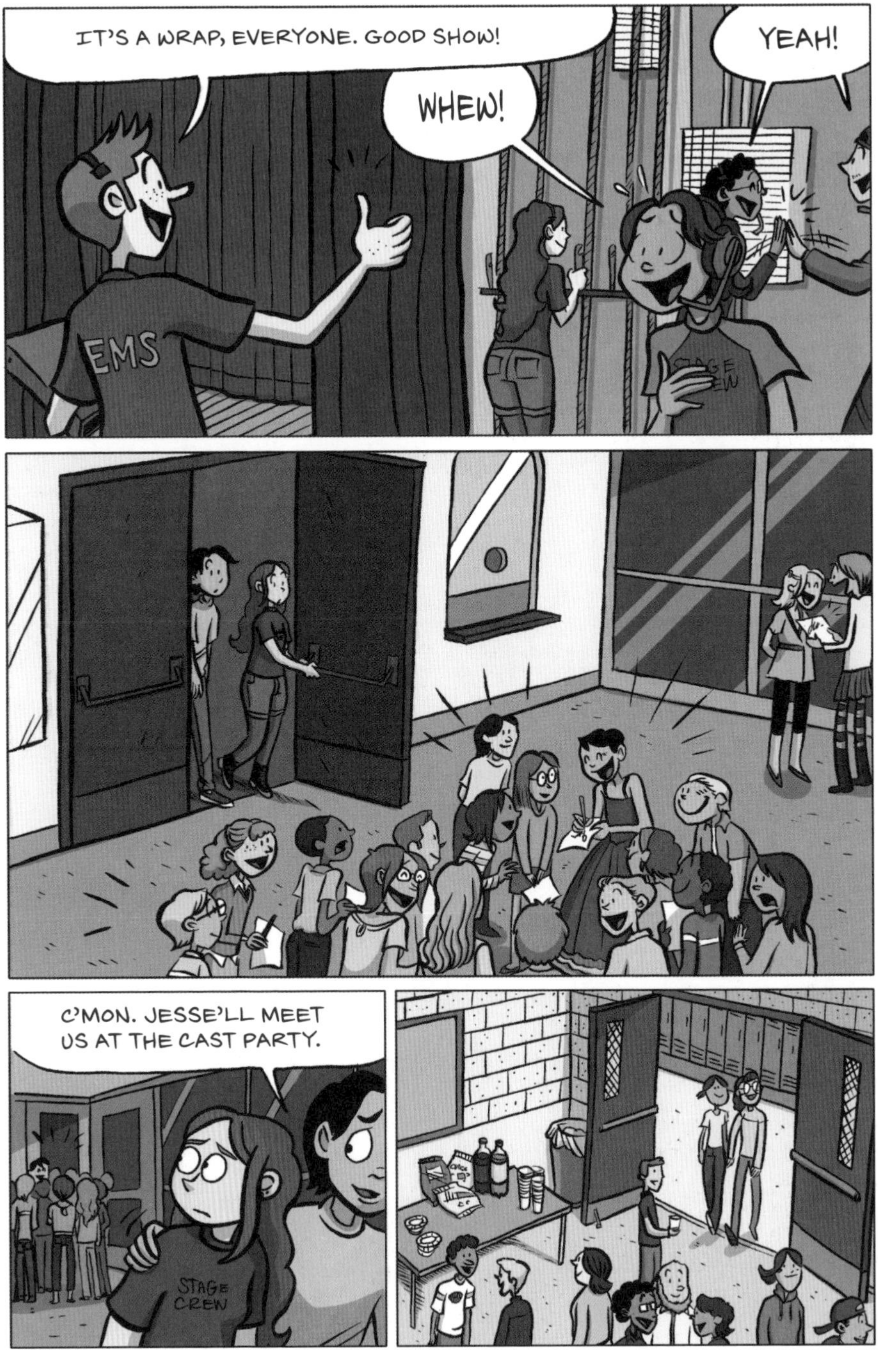
IT'S A WRAP, EVERYONE. GOOD SHOW!
WHEW!
YEAH!
EMS
STAGE CREW
C'MON. JESSE'LL MEET US AT THE CAST PARTY.
STAGE CREW

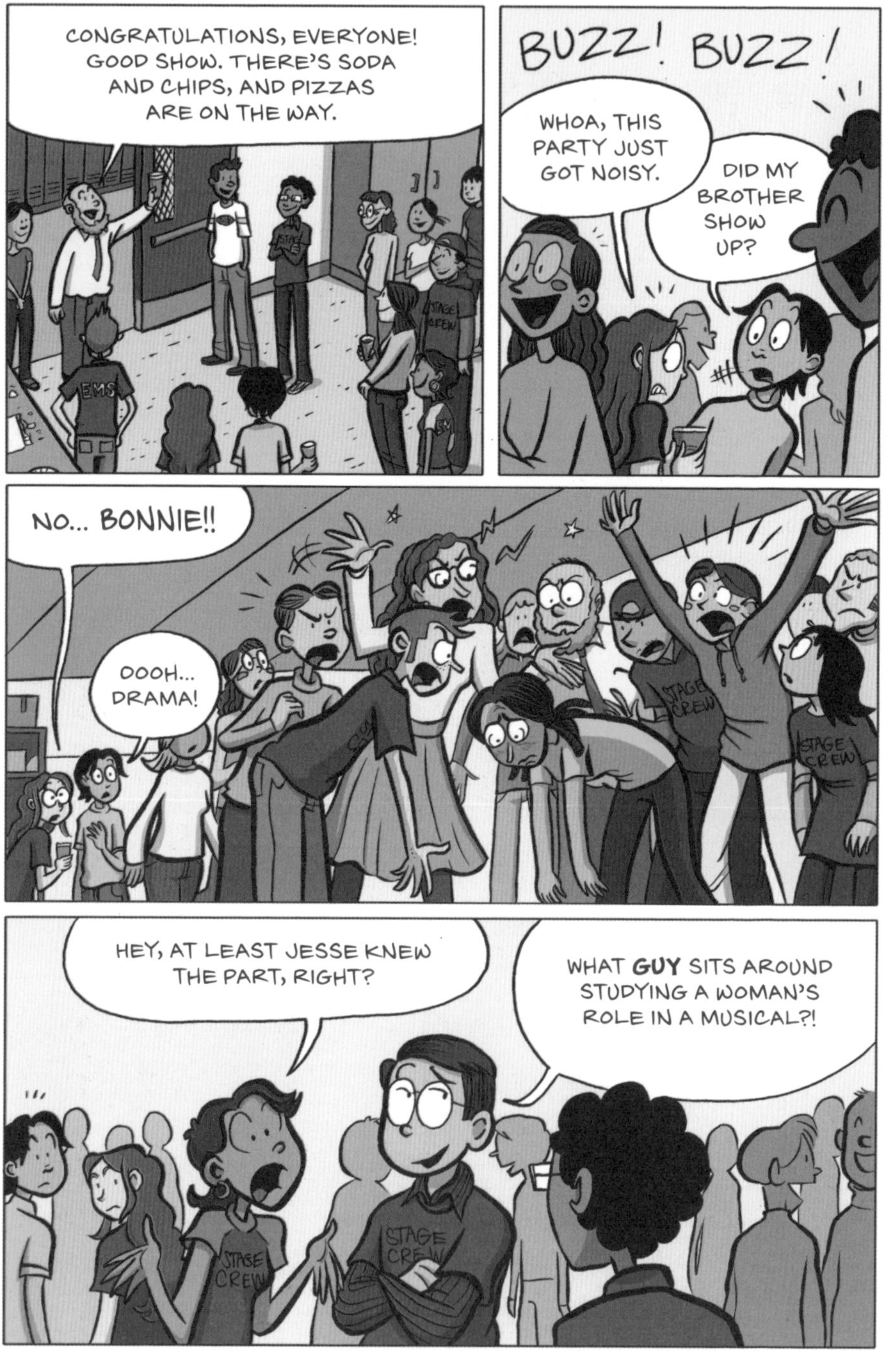
CONGRATULATIONS, EVERYONE! GOOD SHOW. THERE'S SODA AND CHIPS, AND PIZZAS ARE ON THE WAY.
BUZZ! BUZZ!
WHOA, THIS PARTY JUST GOT NOISY.
DID MY BROTHER SHOW UP?
NO... BONNIE!!
OOOH... DRAMA!
STAGE CREW
HEY, AT LEAST JESSE KNEW THE PART, RIGHT?
WHAT GUY SITS AROUND STUDYING A WOMAN'S ROLE IN A MUSICAL?!

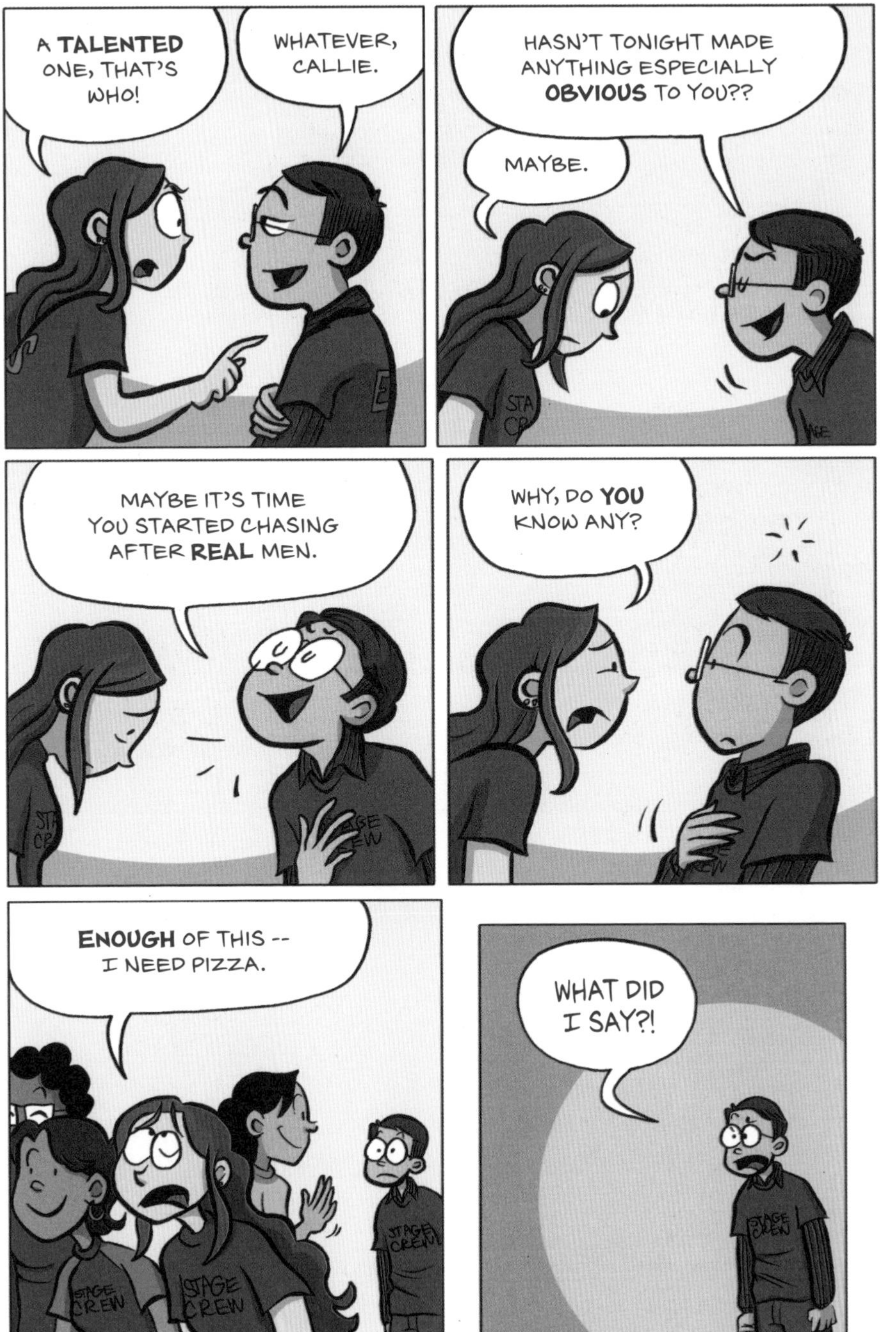
A TALENTED ONE, THAT'S WHO!
WHATEVER, CALLIE.
HASN'T TONIGHT MADE ANYTHING ESPECIALLY OBVIOUS TO YOU??
MAYBE.
MAYBE IT'S TIME YOU STARTED CHASING AFTER REAL MEN.
WHY, DO YOU KNOW ANY?
ENOUGH OF THIS -- I NEED PIZZA.
WHAT DID I SAY?!

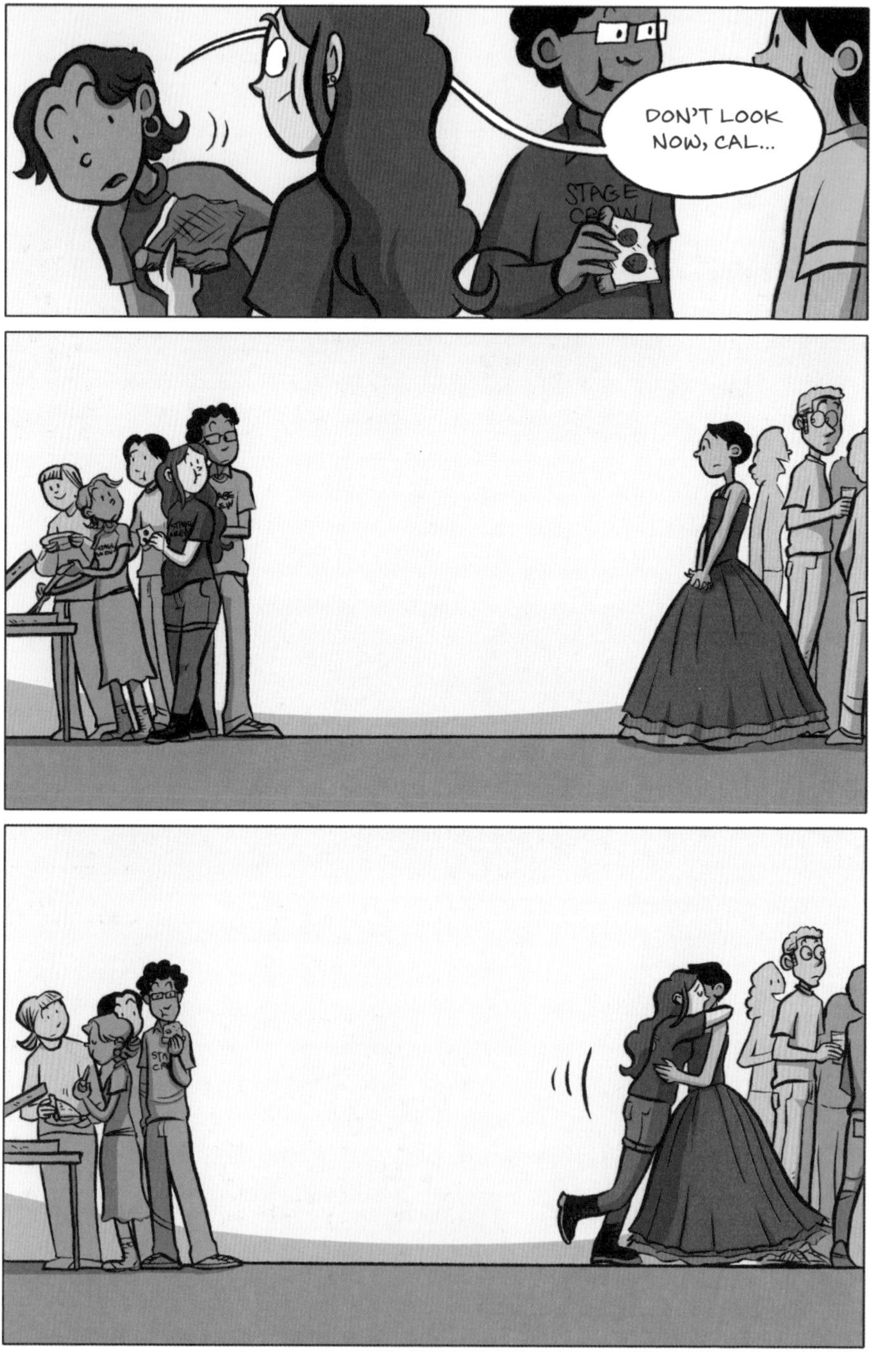
DON'T LOOK NOW, CAL...
STAGE CREW

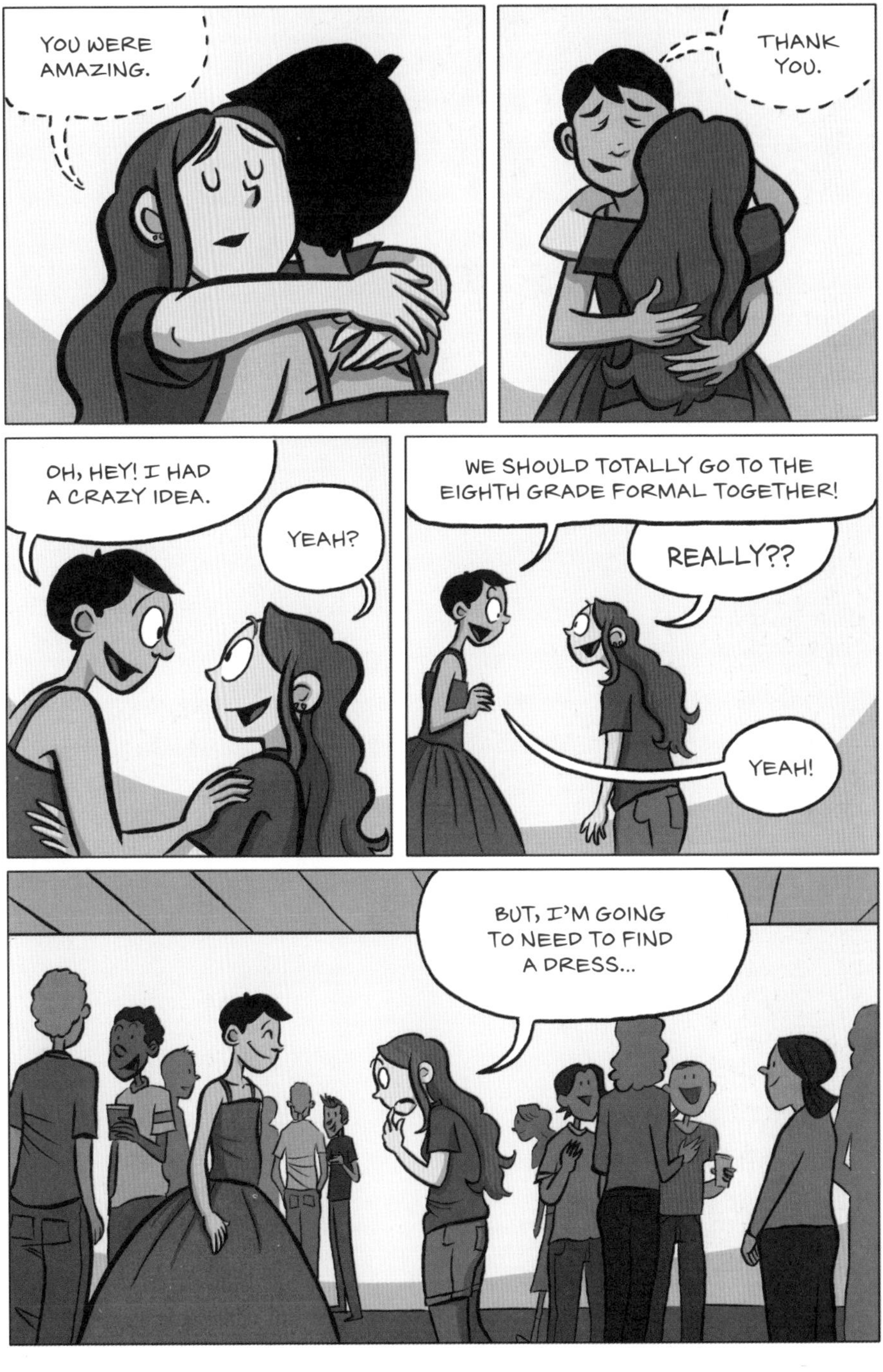
YOU WERE AMAZING.
THANK YOU.
OH, HEY! I HAD A CRAZY IDEA.
YEAH?
WE SHOULD TOTALLY GO TO THE EIGHTH GRADE FORMAL TOGETHER!
REALLY??
YEAH!
BUT, I'M GOING TO NEED TO FIND A DRESS...

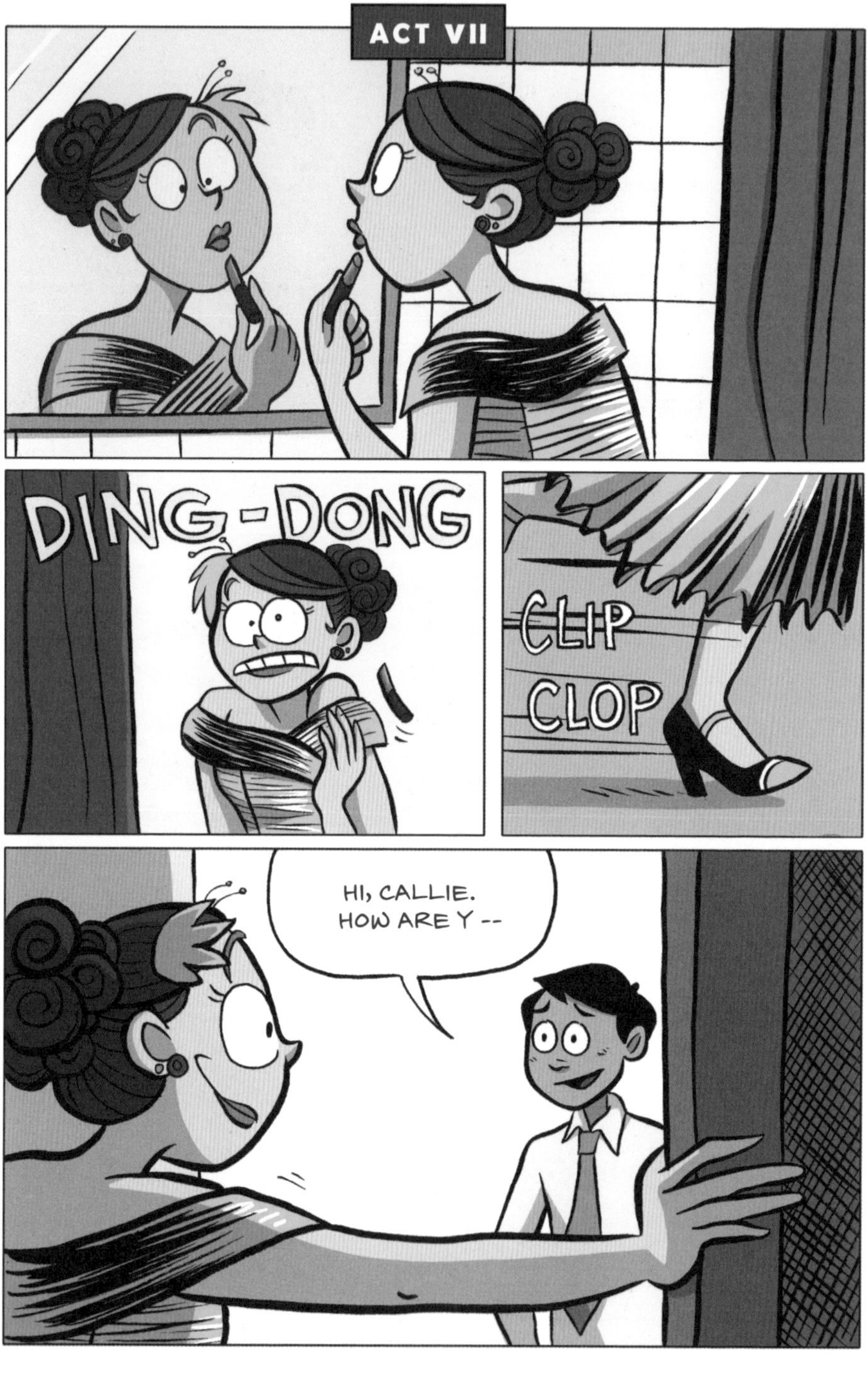
ACT VII
DING-DONG
CLIP
CLOP
HI, CALLIE.
HOW ARE Y --

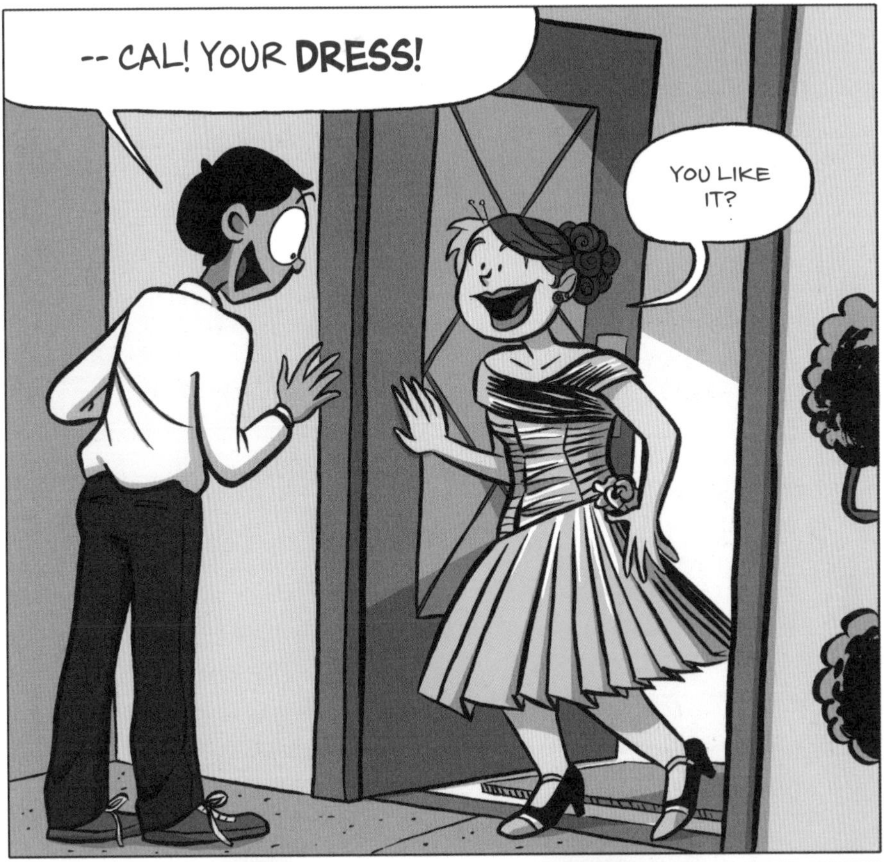
-- CAL! YOUR **DRESS**!
YOU LIKE IT?

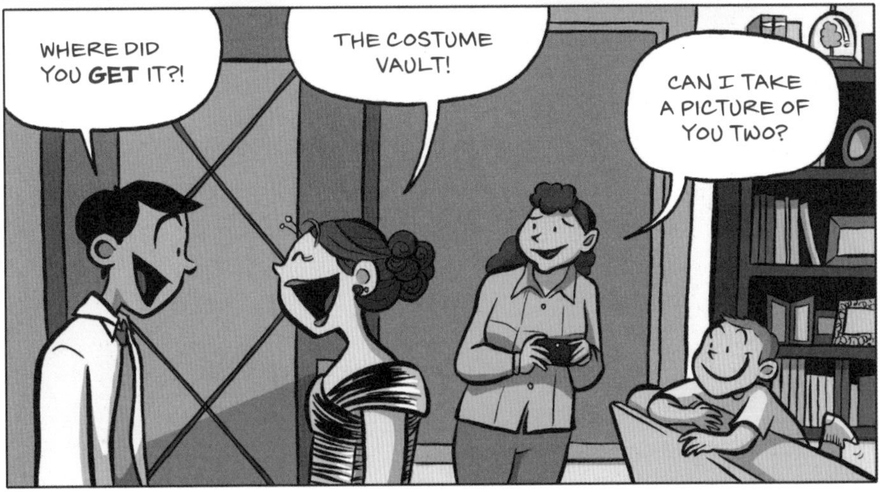
WHERE DID YOU **GET** IT?!
THE COSTUME VAULT!
CAN I TAKE A PICTURE OF YOU TWO?

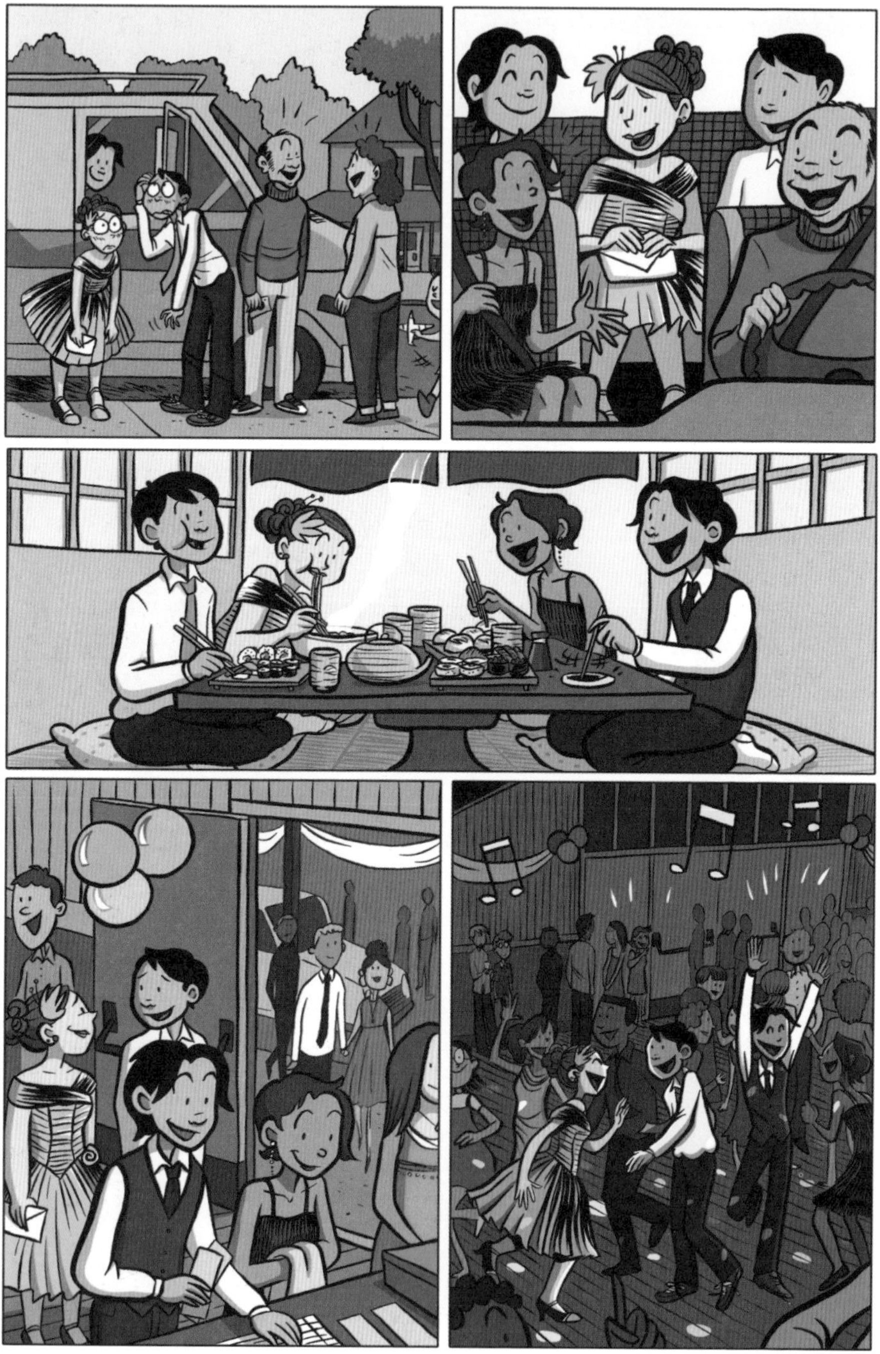

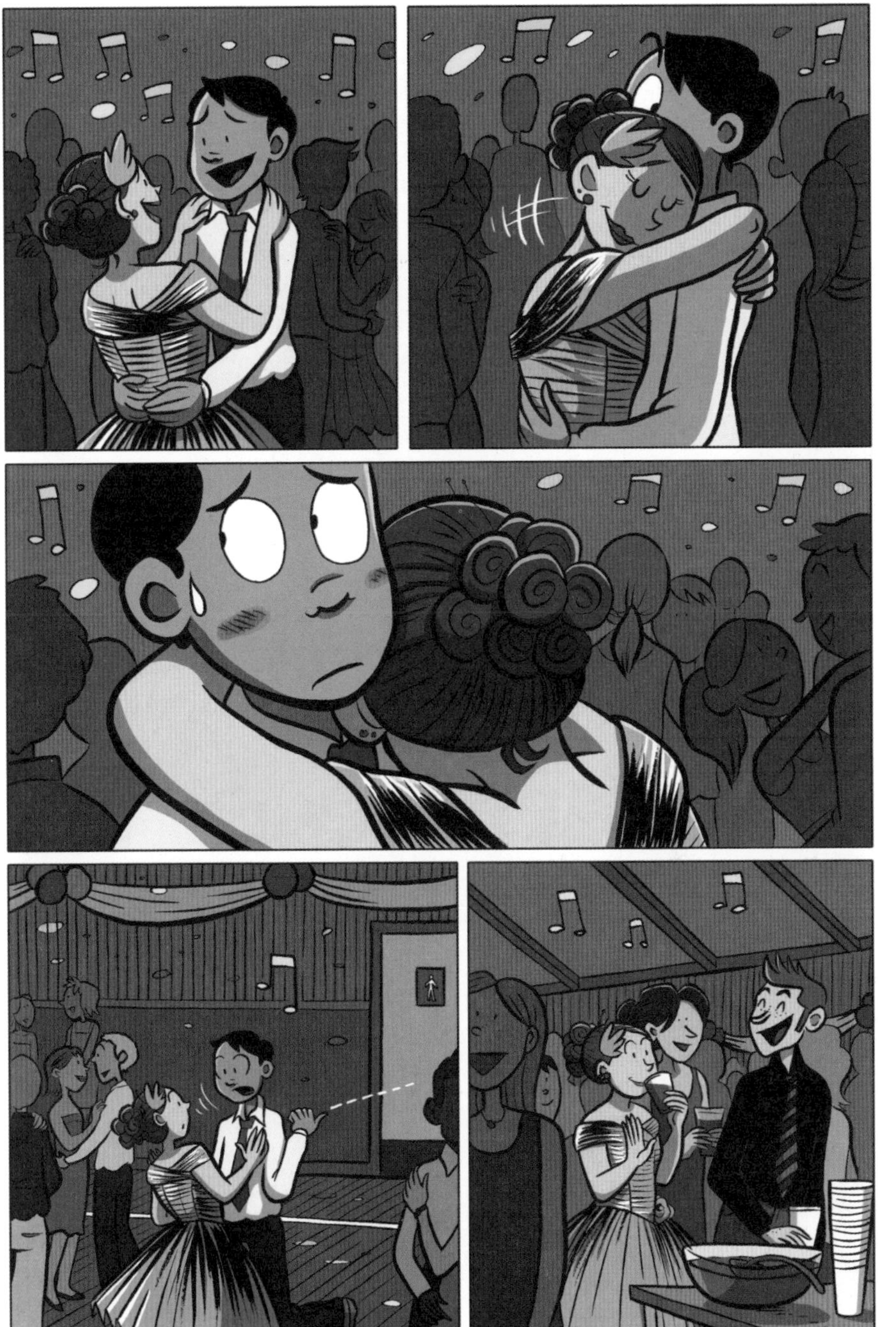

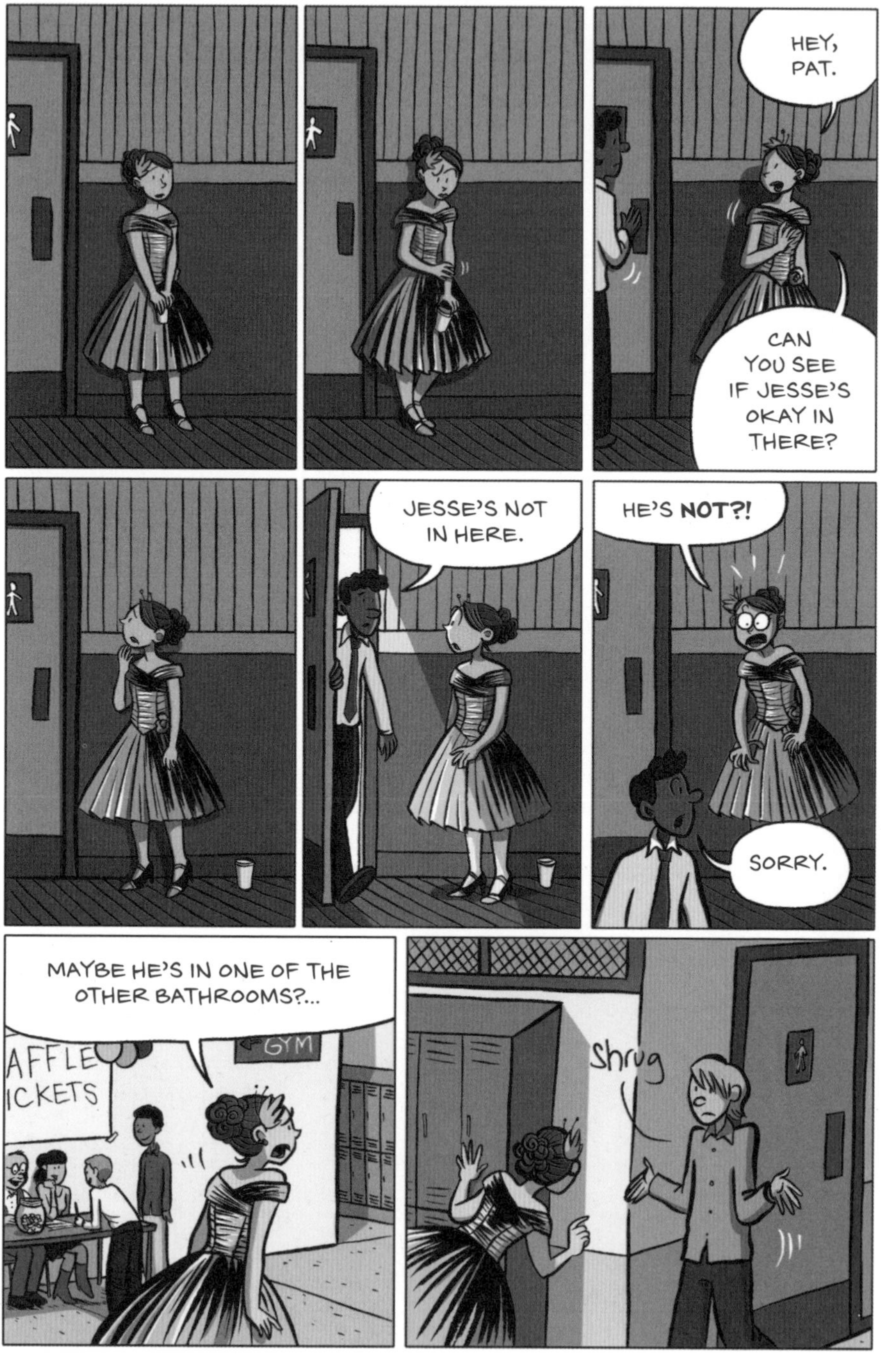
HEY, PAT.
CAN YOU SEE IF JESSE'S OKAY IN THERE?
JESSE'S NOT IN HERE.
HE'S **NOT?!**
SORRY.
MAYBE HE'S IN ONE OF THE OTHER BATHROOMS?...
AFFLE ICKETS
GYM
Shrug

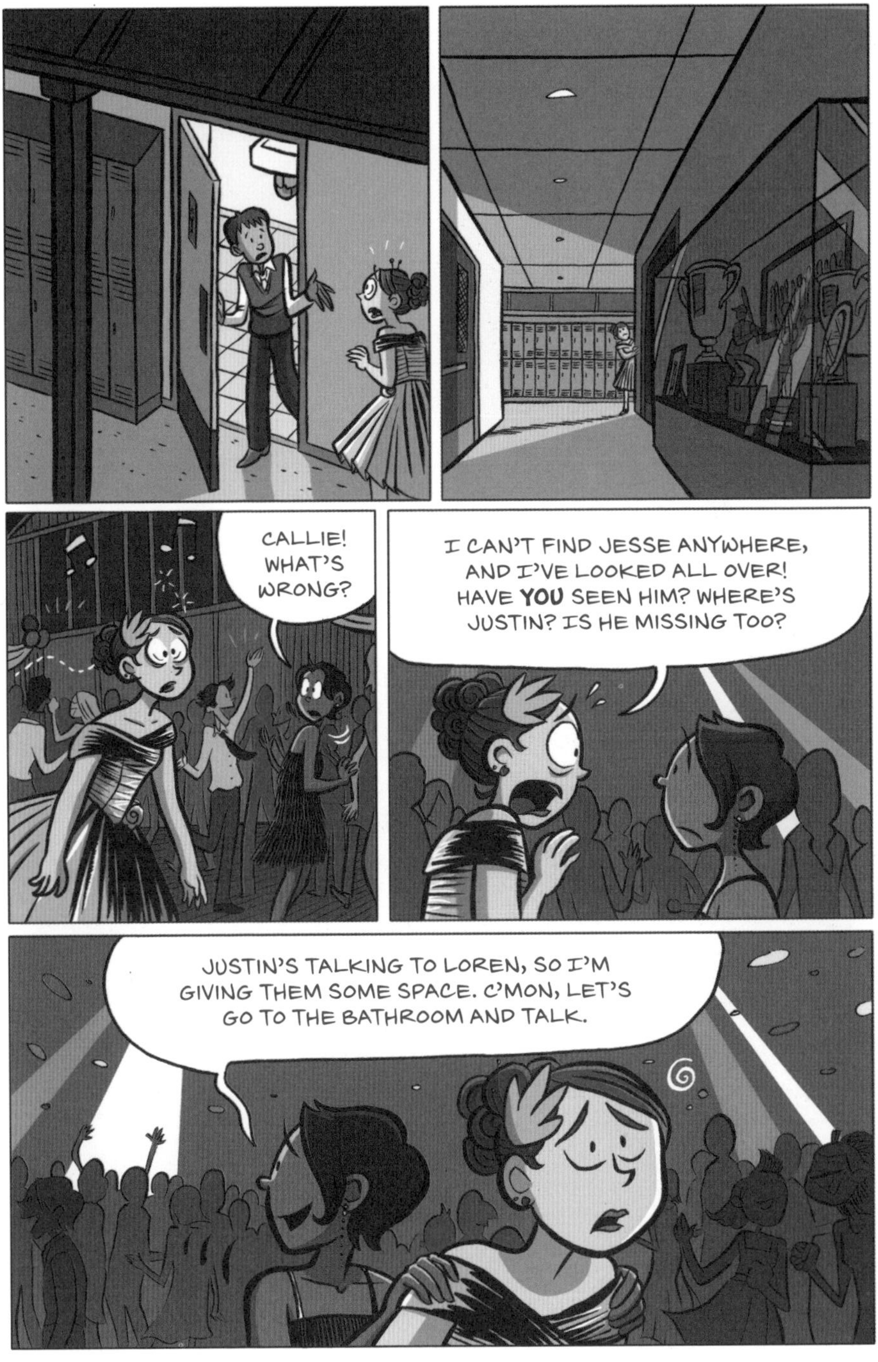
CALLIE! WHAT'S WRONG?
I CAN'T FIND JESSE ANYWHERE, AND I'VE LOOKED ALL OVER! HAVE **YOU** SEEN HIM? WHERE'S JUSTIN? IS HE MISSING TOO?
JUSTIN'S TALKING TO LOREN, SO I'M GIVING THEM SOME SPACE. C'MON, LET'S GO TO THE BATHROOM AND TALK.

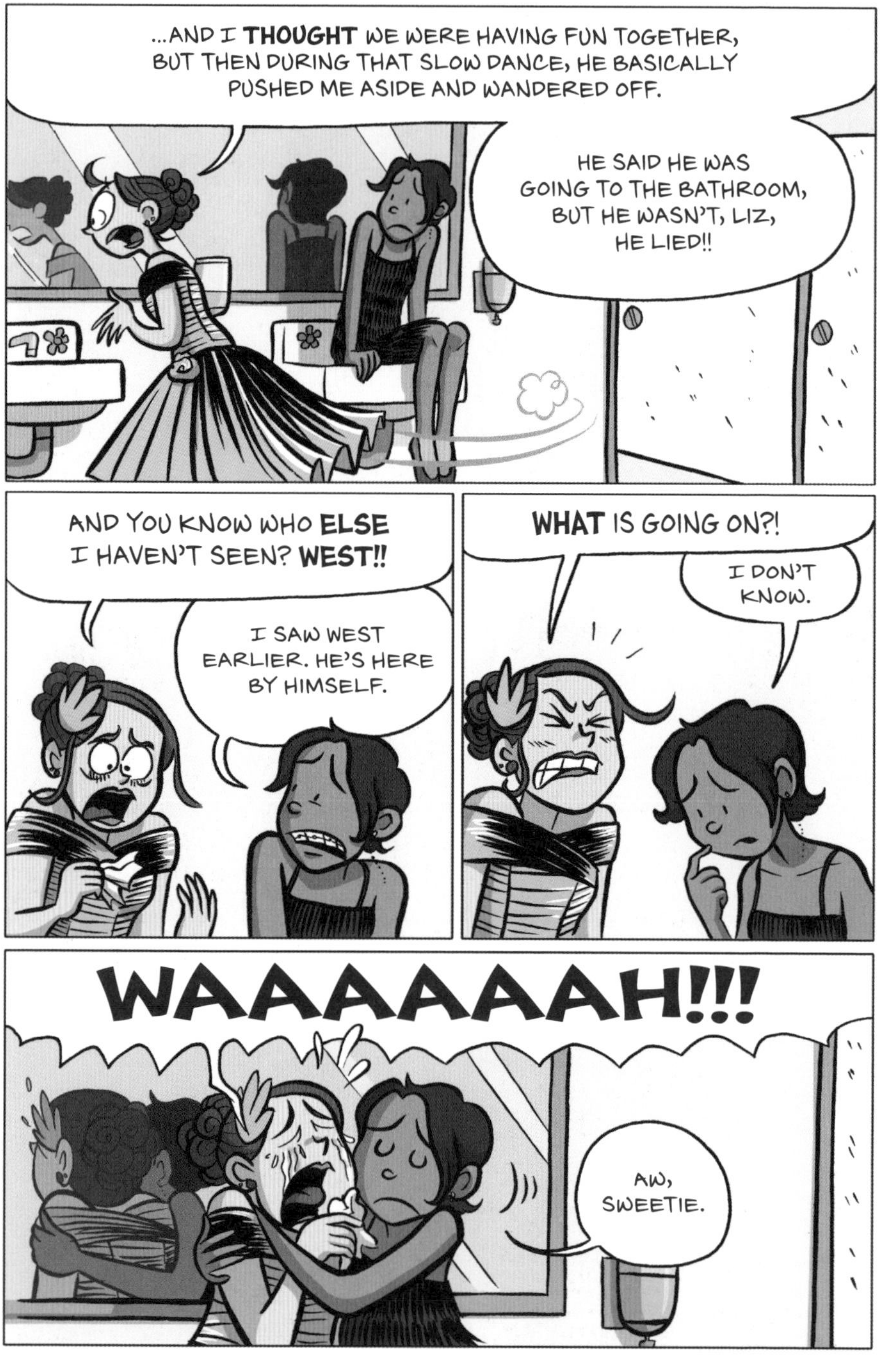
...AND I **THOUGHT** WE WERE HAVING FUN TOGETHER, BUT THEN DURING THAT SLOW DANCE, HE BASICALLY PUSHED ME ASIDE AND WANDERED OFF.
HE SAID HE WAS GOING TO THE BATHROOM, BUT HE WASN'T, LIZ, HE LIED!!
AND YOU KNOW WHO **ELSE** I HAVEN'T SEEN? **WEST!!**
I SAW WEST EARLIER. HE'S HERE BY HIMSELF.
WHAT IS GOING ON?!
I DON'T KNOW.
WAAAAAAH!!!
AW, SWEETIE.

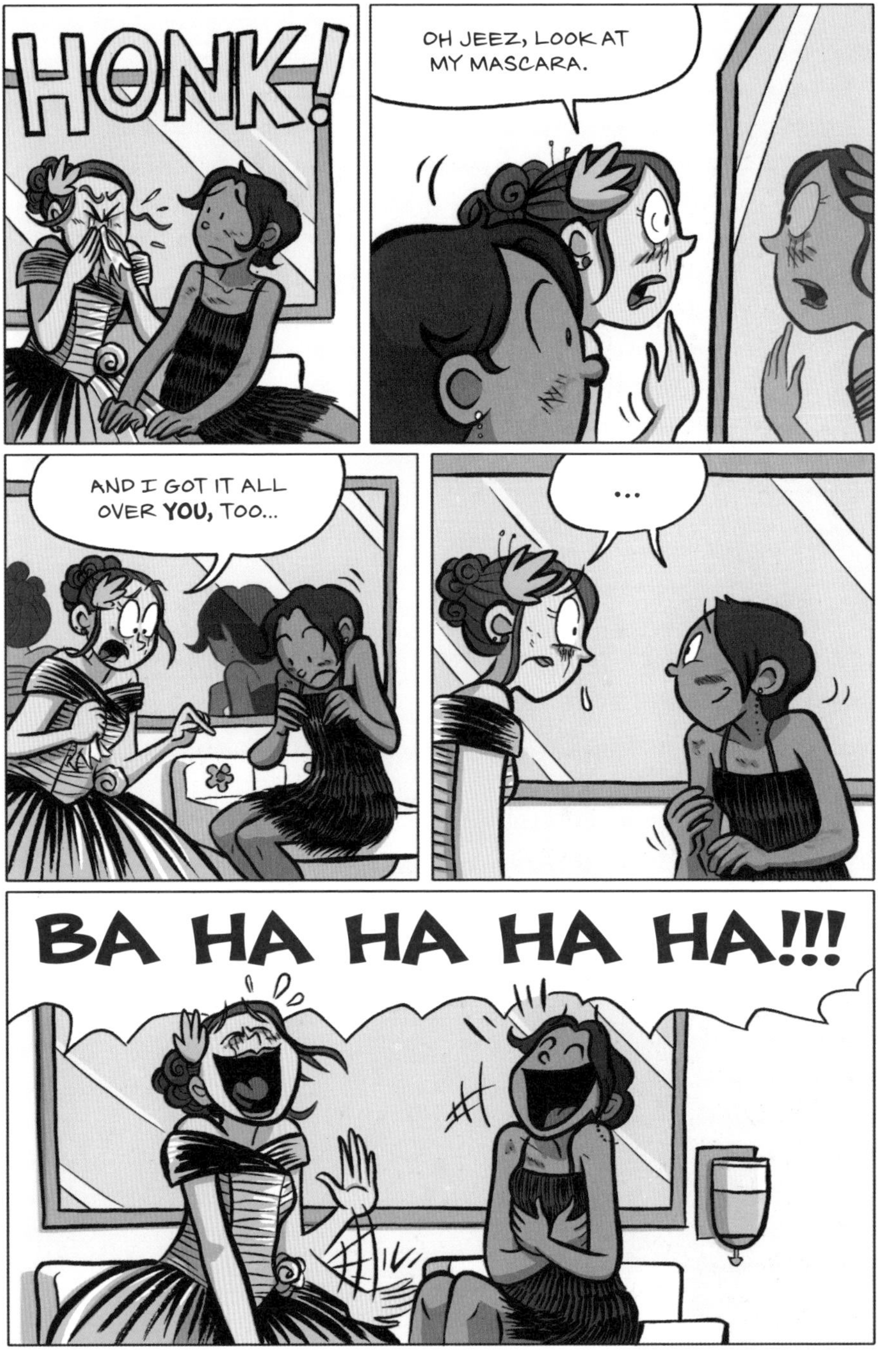
HONK!
OH JEEZ, LOOK AT MY MASCARA.
AND I GOT IT ALL OVER YOU, TOO...
...
BA HA HA HA HA!!!

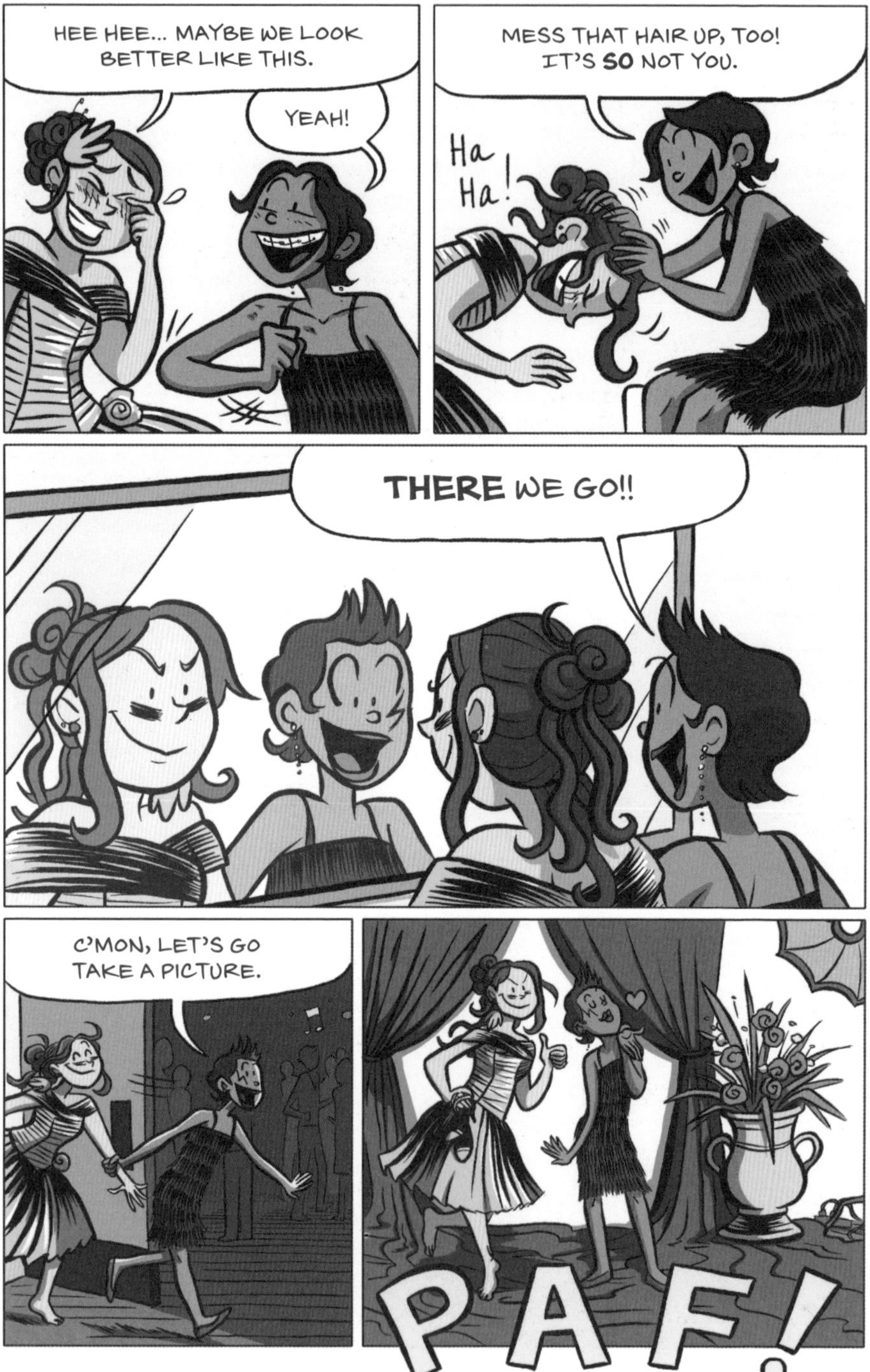
HEE HEE... MAYBE WE LOOK BETTER LIKE THIS.
YEAH!
MESS THAT HAIR UP, TOO! IT'S **SO** NOT YOU.
Ha Ha!
THERE WE GO!!
C'MON, LET'S GO TAKE A PICTURE.
PAF!

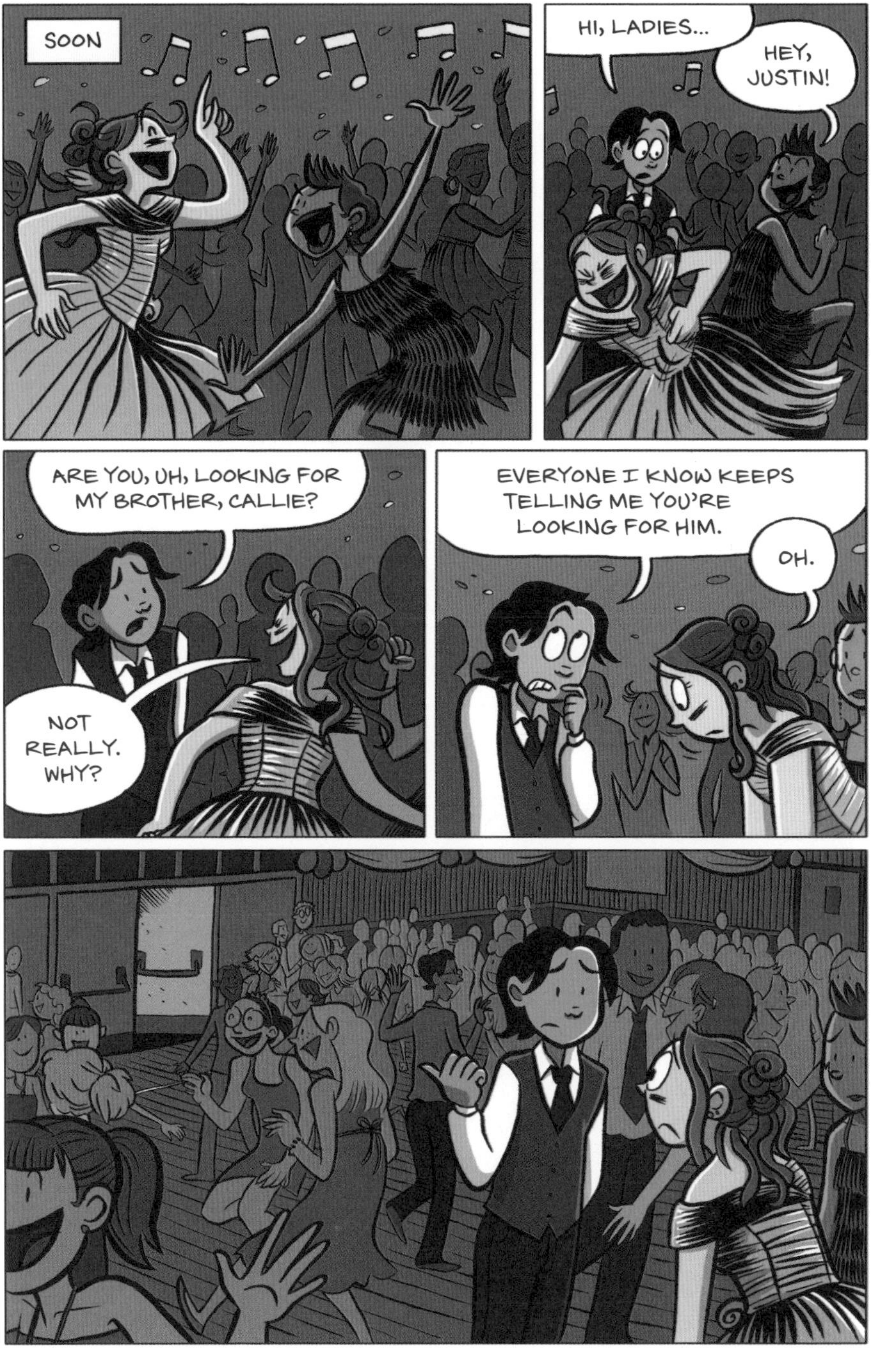
SOON
HI, LADIES...
HEY, JUSTIN!
ARE YOU, UH, LOOKING FOR MY BROTHER, CALLIE?
NOT REALLY. WHY?
EVERYONE I KNOW KEEPS TELLING ME YOU'RE LOOKING FOR HIM.
OH.

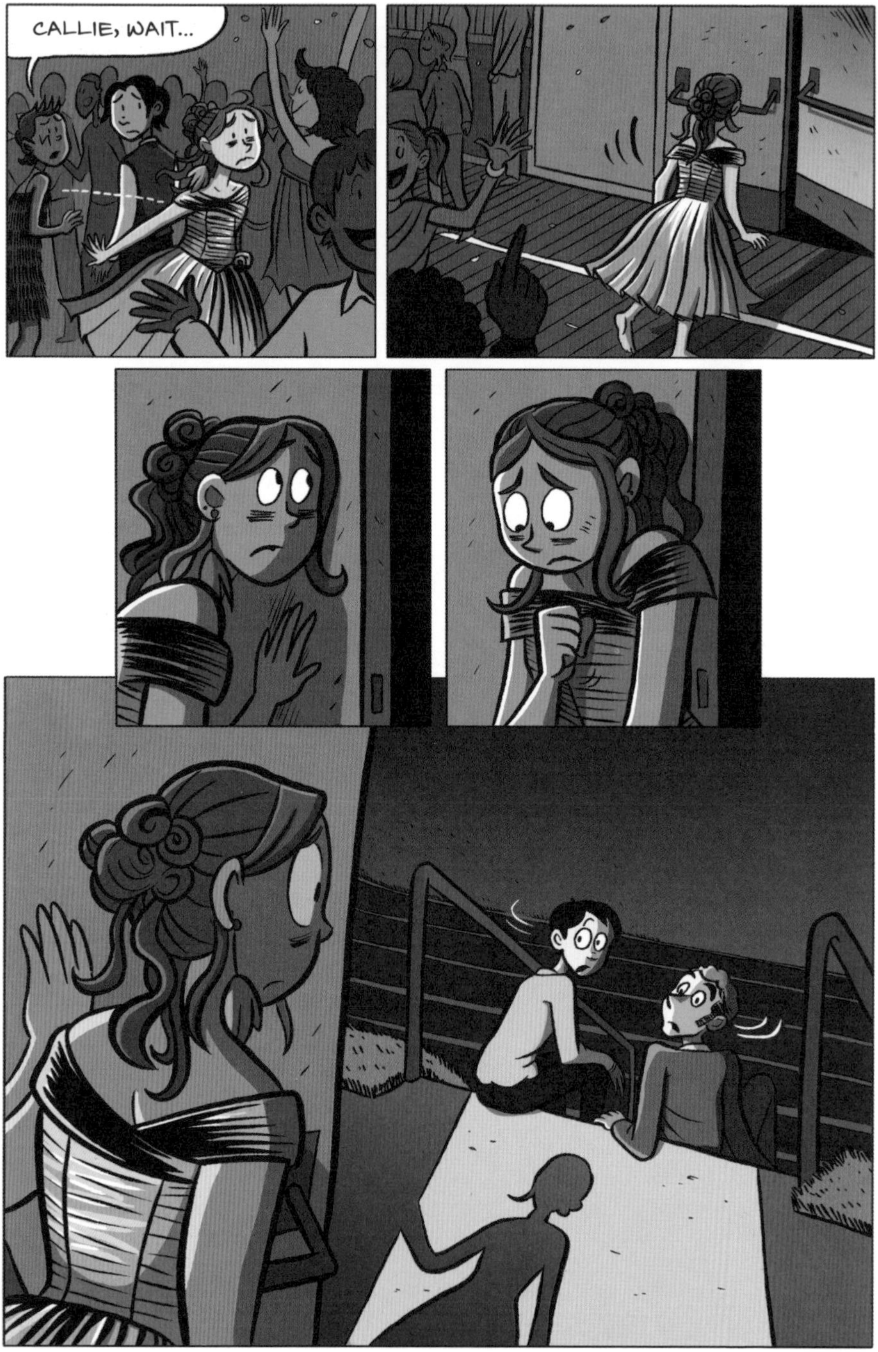
CALLIE, WAIT...

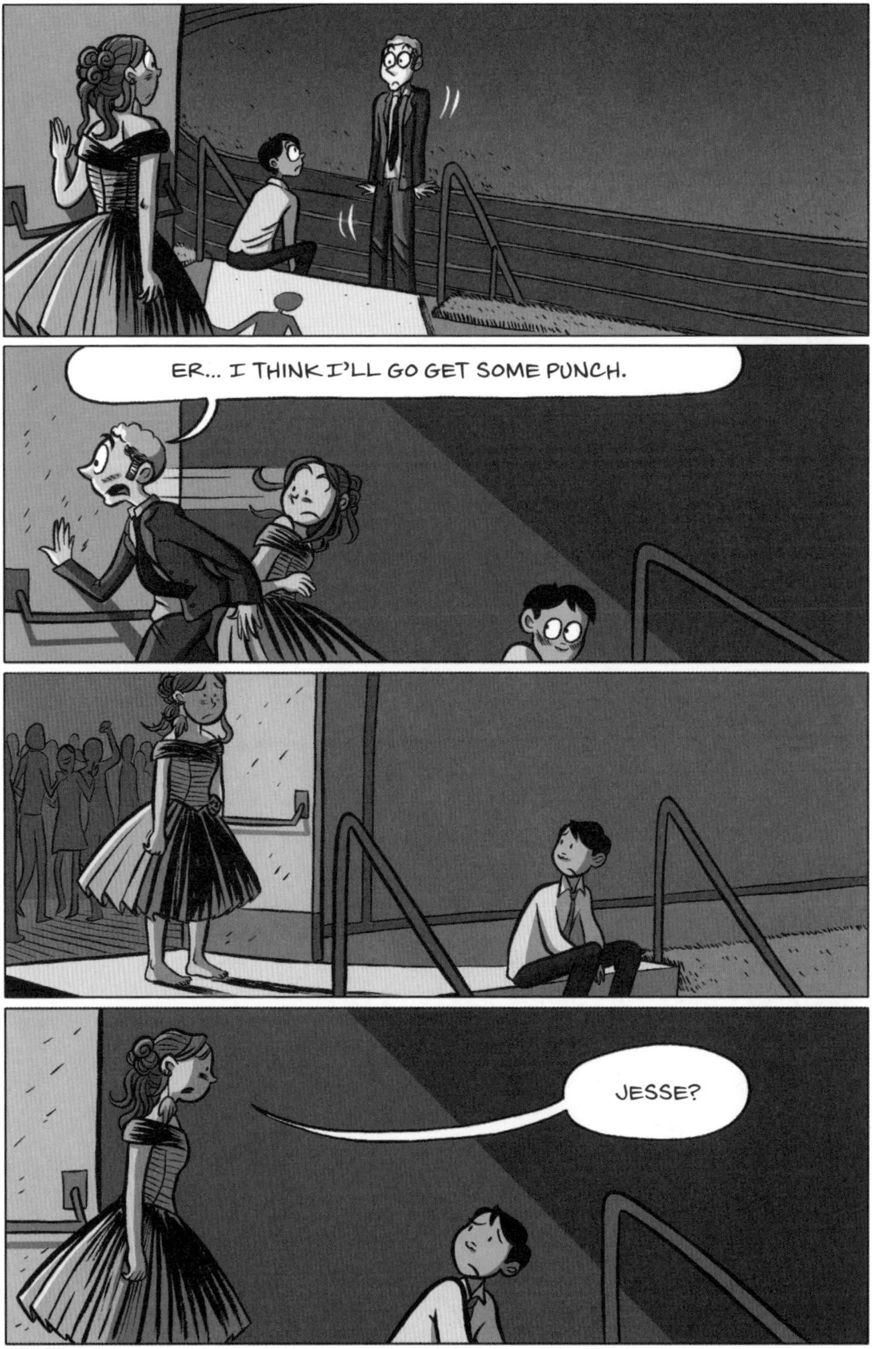
ER... I THINK I'LL GO GET SOME PUNCH.
JESSE?

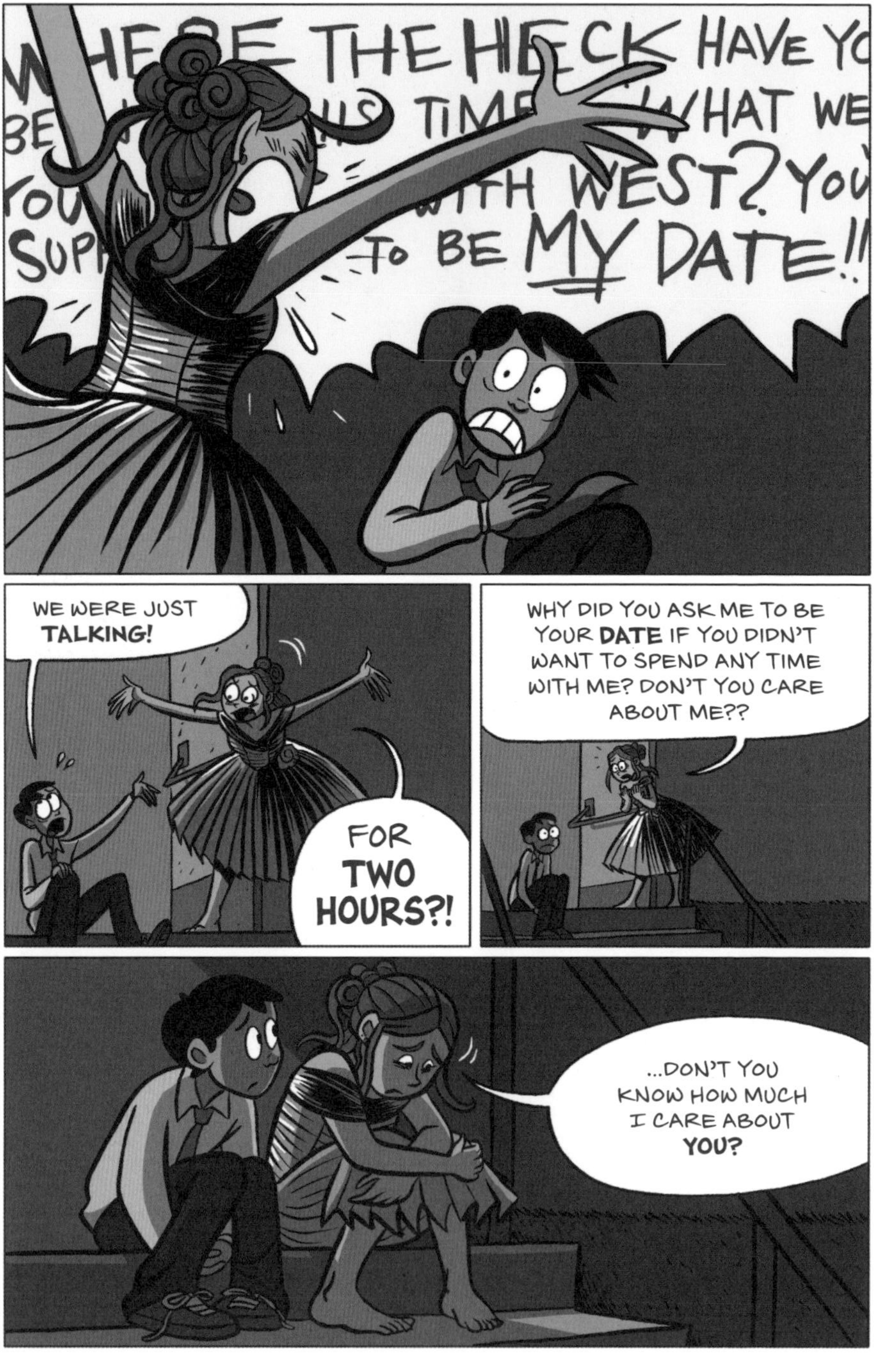
THE HECK HAVE YO
TIME WHAT WE
WITH WEST? YOU
TO BE MY DATE!!
WE WERE JUST TALKING!
FOR TWO HOURS?!
WHY DID YOU ASK ME TO BE YOUR DATE IF YOU DIDN'T WANT TO SPEND ANY TIME WITH ME? DON'T YOU CARE ABOUT ME??
...DON'T YOU KNOW HOW MUCH I CARE ABOUT YOU?

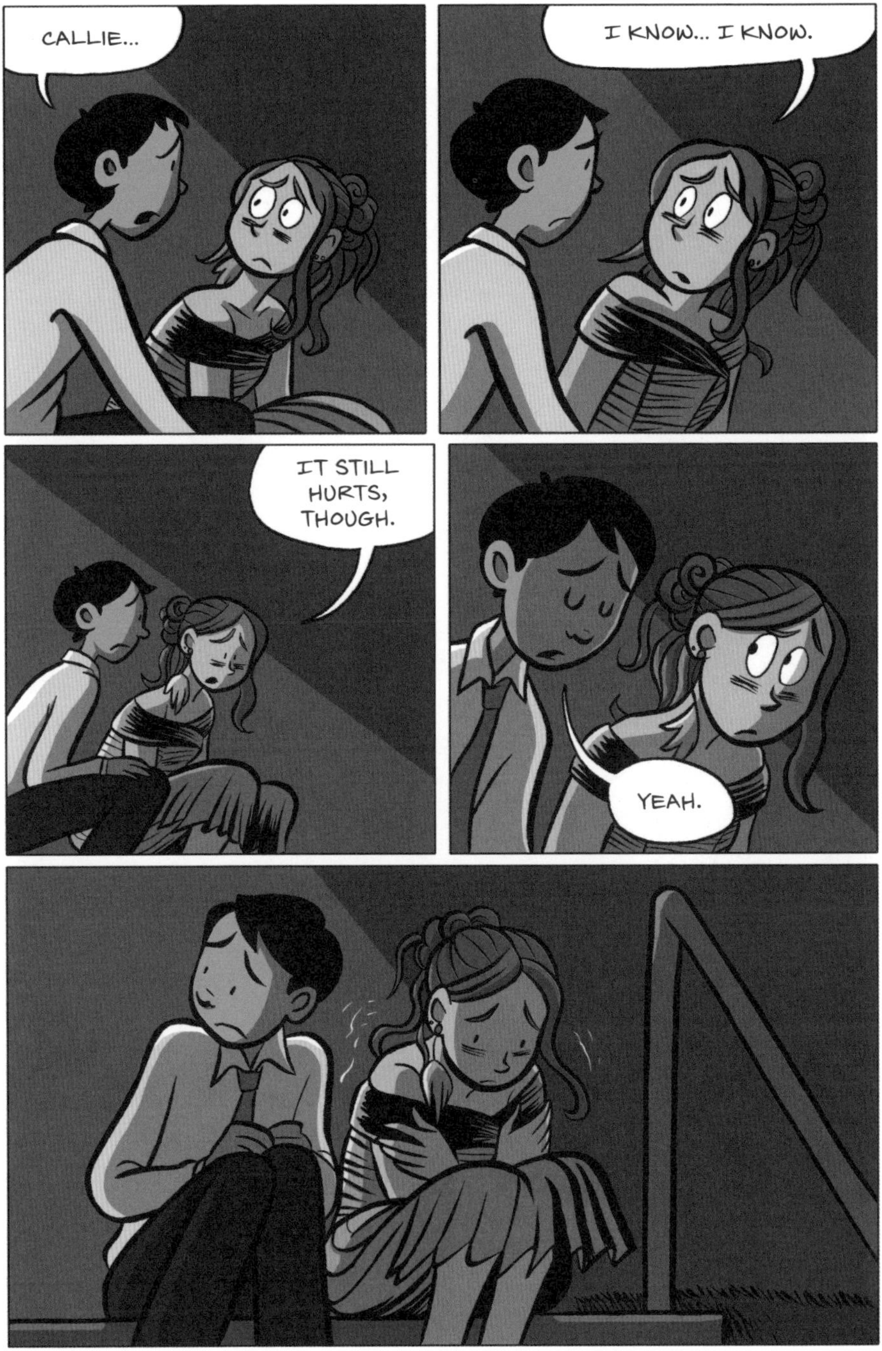
CALLIE...
I KNOW... I KNOW.
IT STILL HURTS, THOUGH.
YEAH.

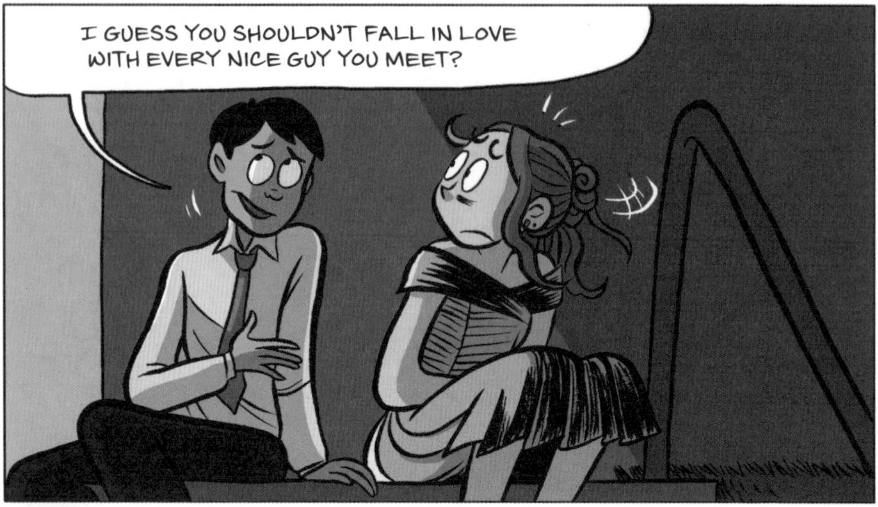
I GUESS YOU SHOULDN'T FALL IN LOVE WITH EVERY NICE GUY YOU MEET?

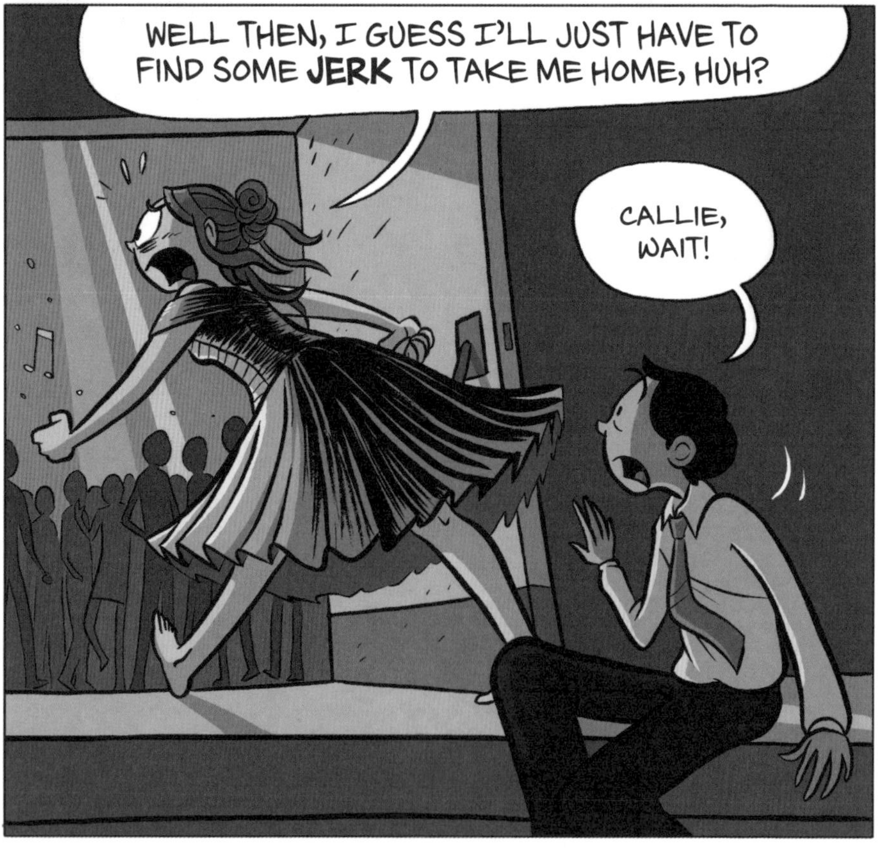
WELL THEN, I GUESS I'LL JUST HAVE TO FIND SOME JERK TO TAKE ME HOME, HUH?
CALLIE, WAIT!

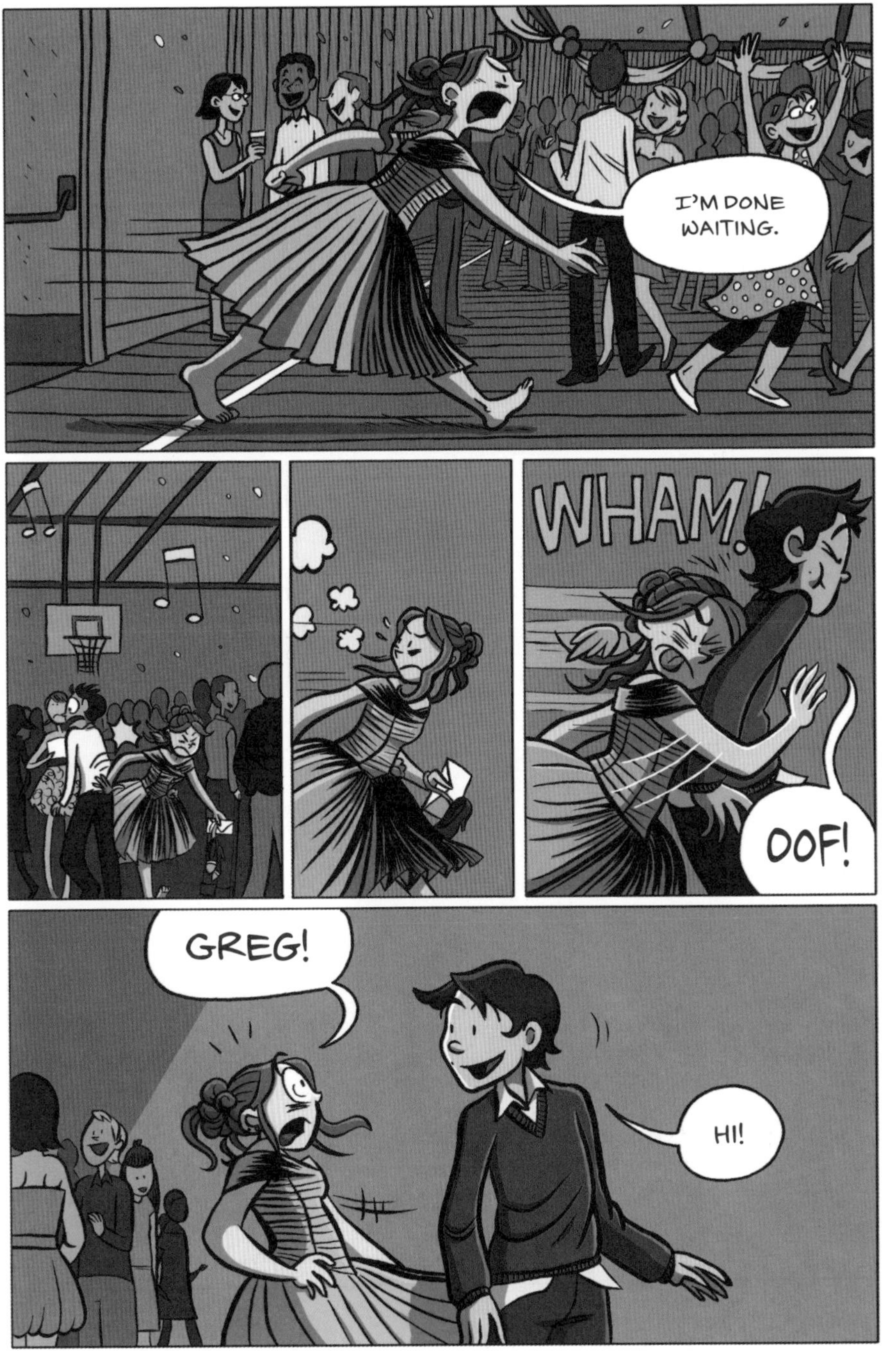
I'M DONE WAITING.
WHAM!
OOF!
GREG!
HI!

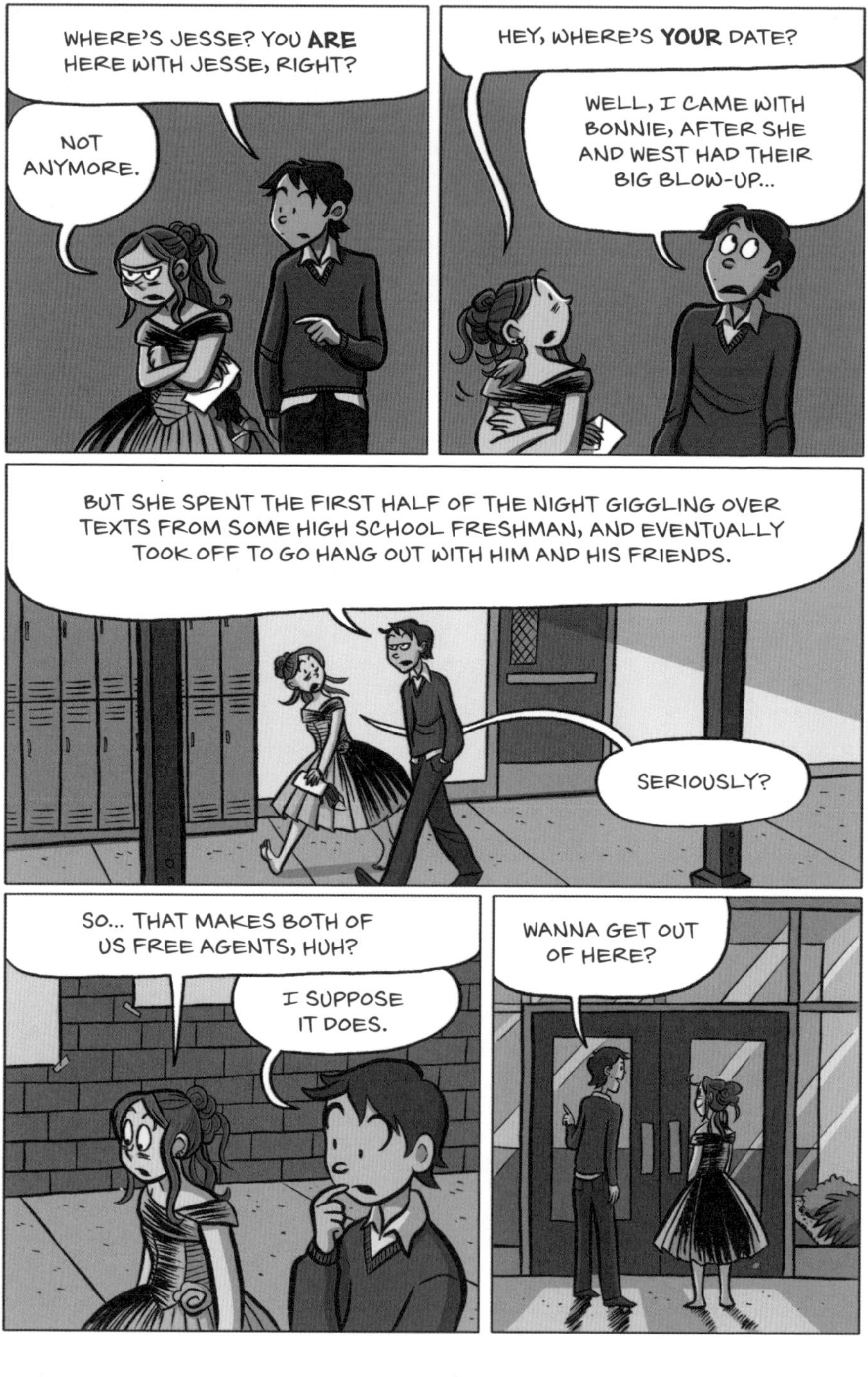
WHERE'S JESSE? YOU **ARE** HERE WITH JESSE, RIGHT?
NOT ANYMORE.
HEY, WHERE'S **YOUR** DATE?
WELL, I CAME WITH BONNIE, AFTER SHE AND WEST HAD THEIR BIG BLOW-UP...
BUT SHE SPENT THE FIRST HALF OF THE NIGHT GIGGLING OVER TEXTS FROM SOME HIGH SCHOOL FRESHMAN, AND EVENTUALLY TOOK OFF TO GO HANG OUT WITH HIM AND HIS FRIENDS.
SERIOUSLY?
SO... THAT MAKES BOTH OF US FREE AGENTS, HUH?
I SUPPOSE IT DOES.
WANNA GET OUT OF HERE?

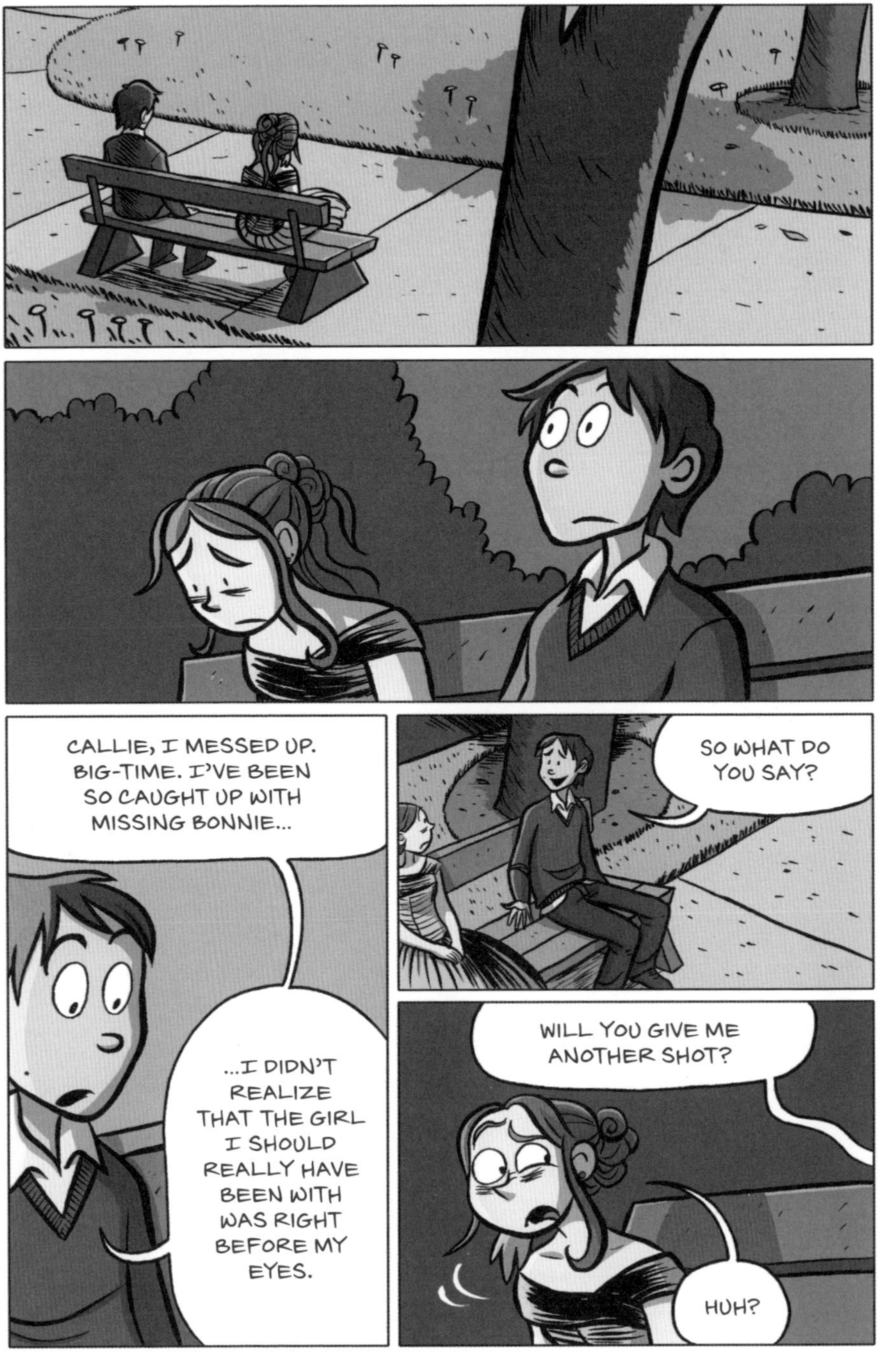
CALLIE, I MESSED UP. BIG-TIME. I'VE BEEN SO CAUGHT UP WITH MISSING BONNIE...
...I DIDN'T REALIZE THAT THE GIRL I SHOULD REALLY HAVE BEEN WITH WAS RIGHT BEFORE MY EYES.
SO WHAT DO YOU SAY?
WILL YOU GIVE ME ANOTHER SHOT?
HUH?

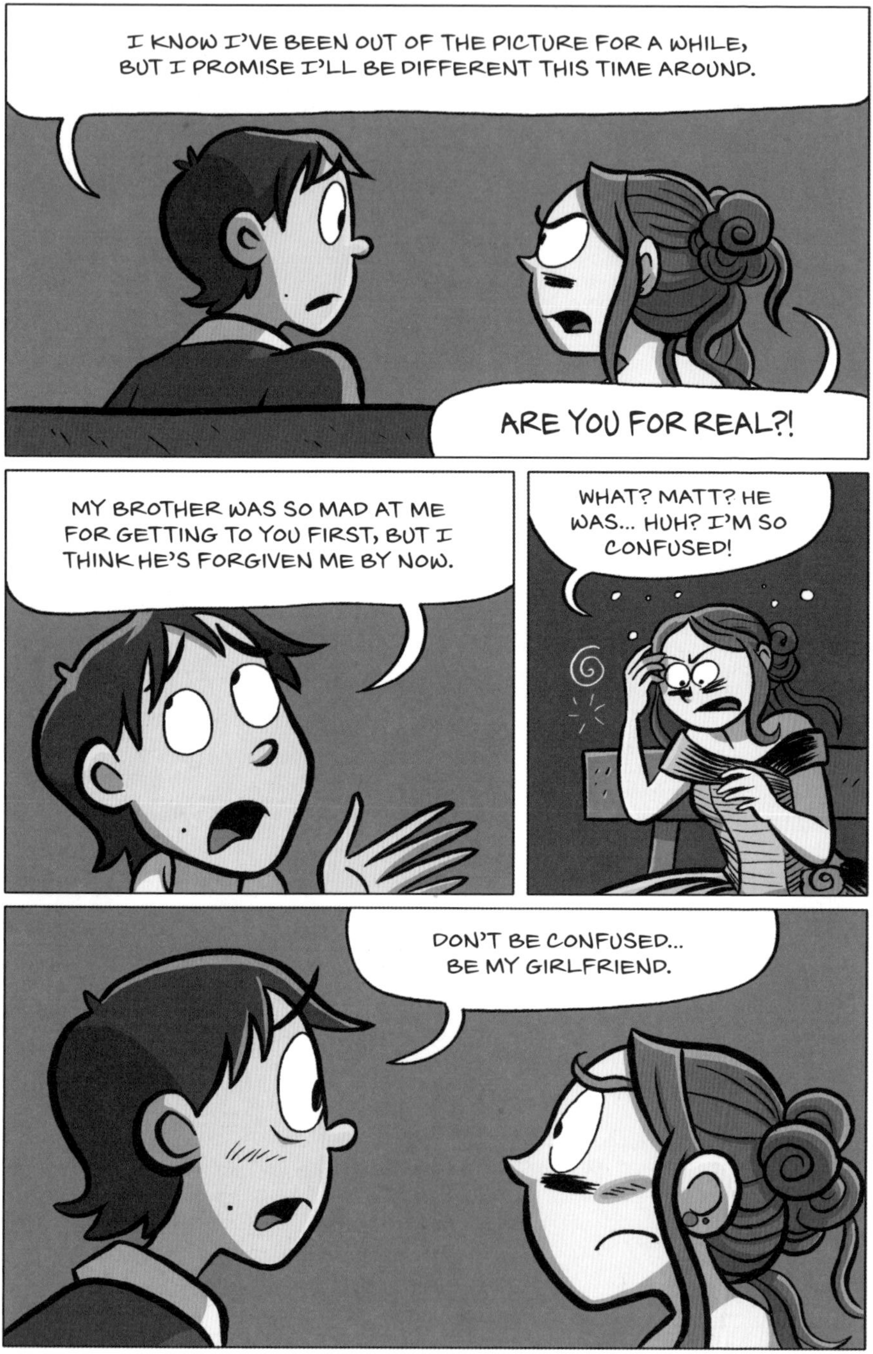
I KNOW I'VE BEEN OUT OF THE PICTURE FOR A WHILE, BUT I PROMISE I'LL BE DIFFERENT THIS TIME AROUND.
ARE YOU FOR REAL?!
MY BROTHER WAS SO MAD AT ME FOR GETTING TO YOU FIRST, BUT I THINK HE'S FORGIVEN ME BY NOW.
WHAT? MATT? HE WAS... HUH? I'M SO CONFUSED!
DON'T BE CONFUSED... BE MY GIRLFRIEND.

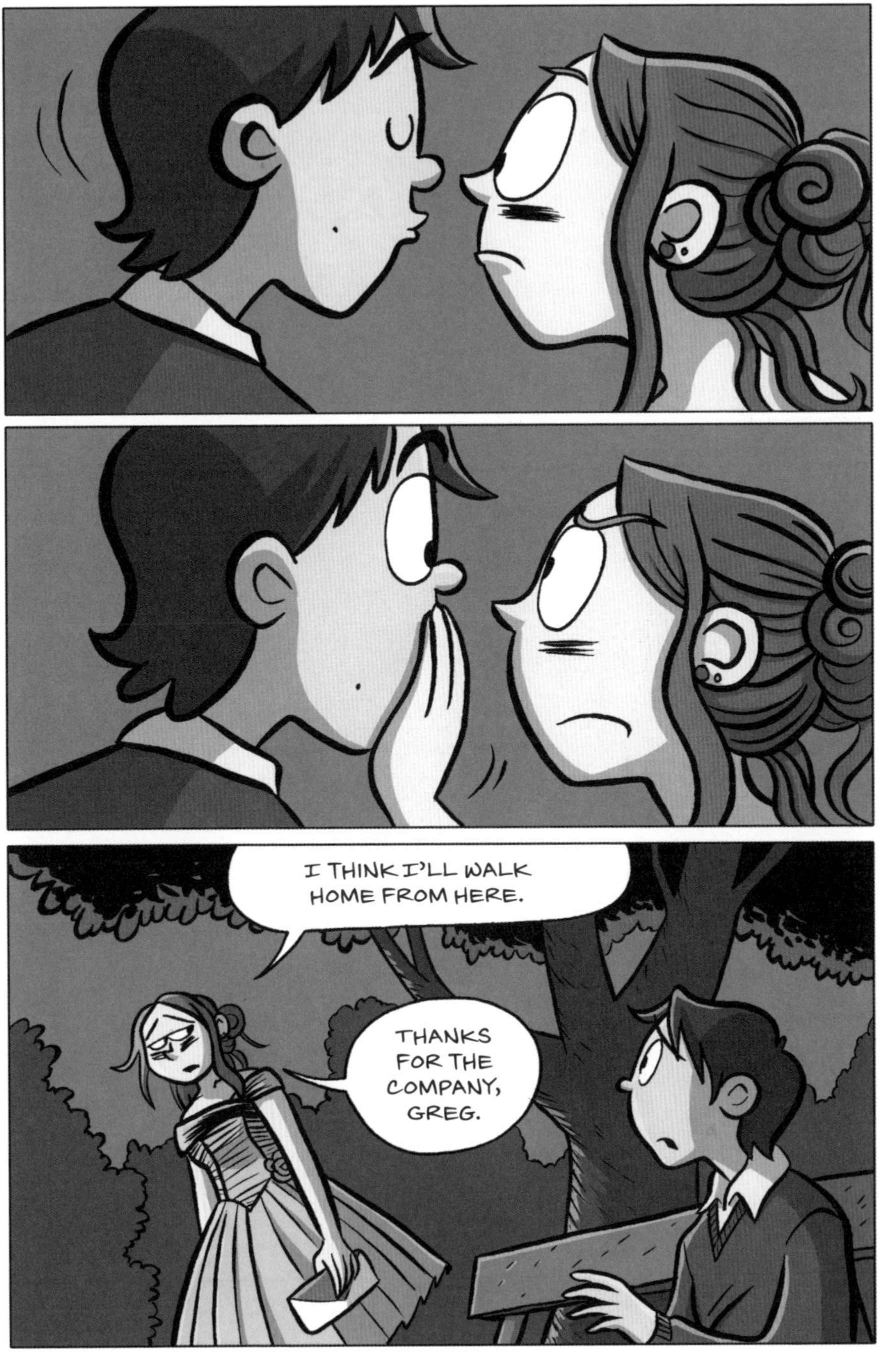
I THINK I'LL WALK HOME FROM HERE.
THANKS FOR THE COMPANY, GREG.

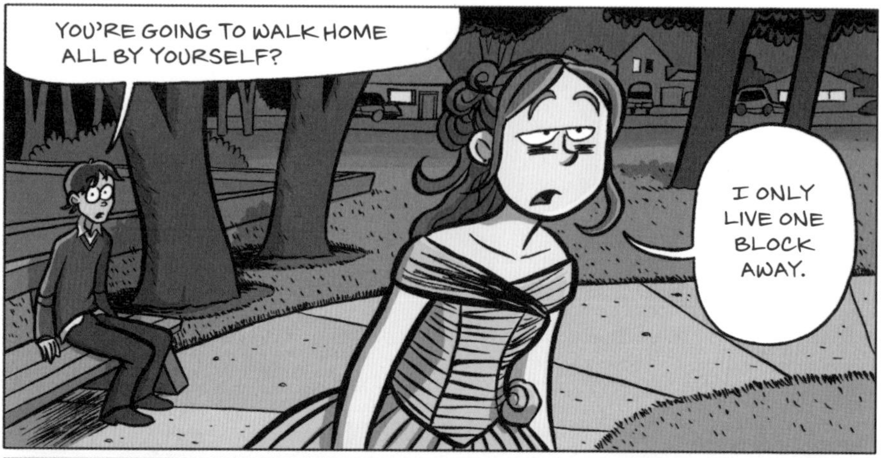
YOU'RE GOING TO WALK HOME ALL BY YOURSELF?
I ONLY LIVE ONE BLOCK AWAY.

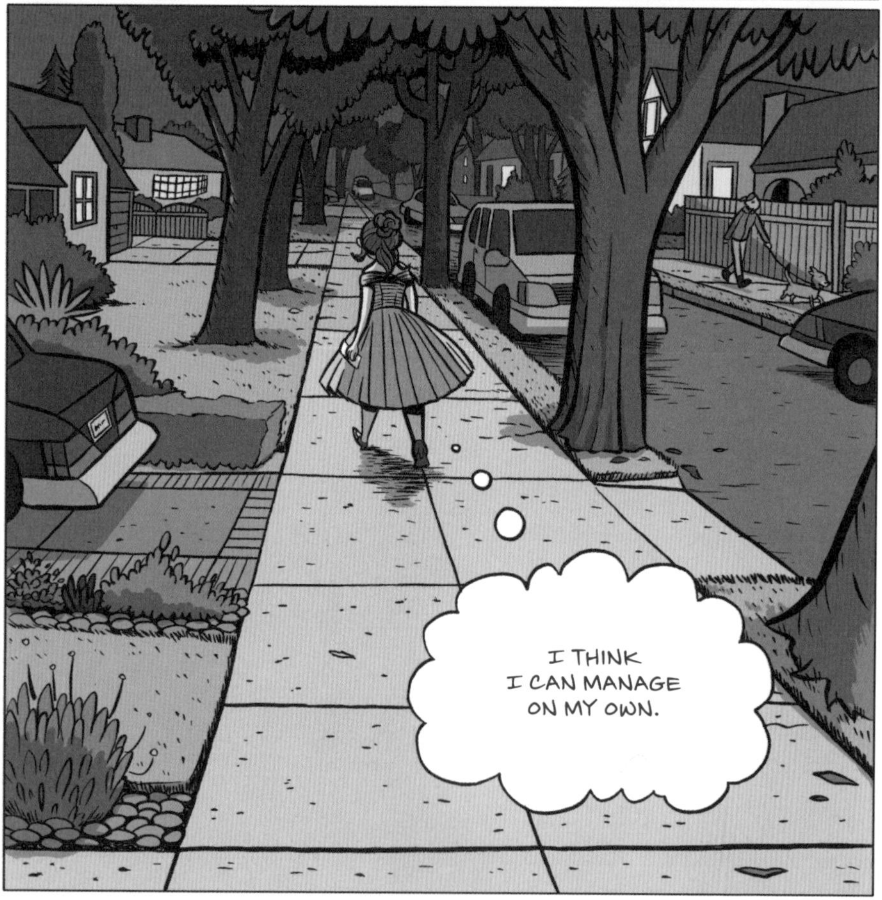
I THINK I CAN MANAGE ON MY OWN.

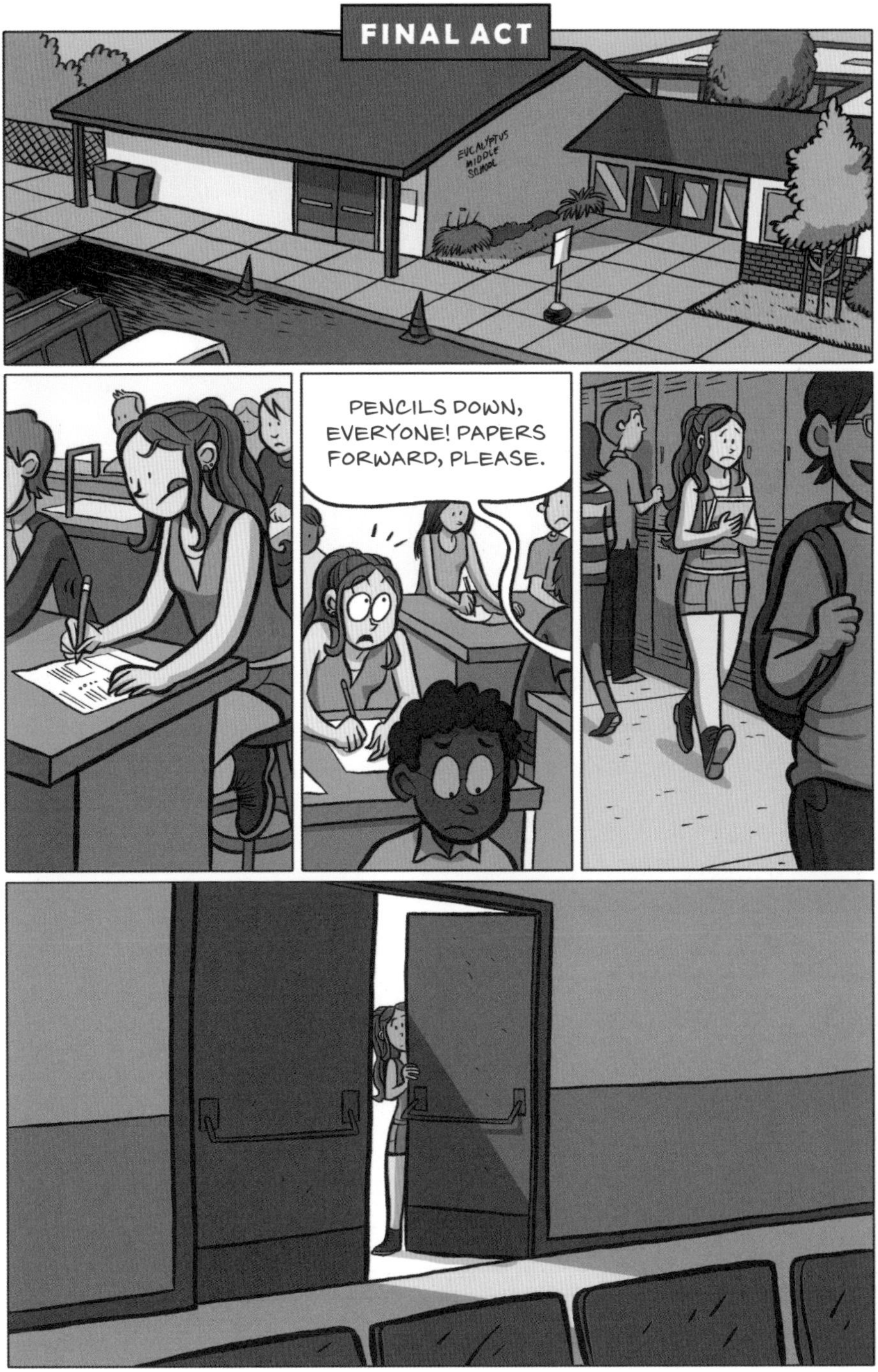
FINAL ACT
EUCALYPTUS MIDDLE SCHOOL
PENCILS DOWN, EVERYONE! PAPERS FORWARD, PLEASE.

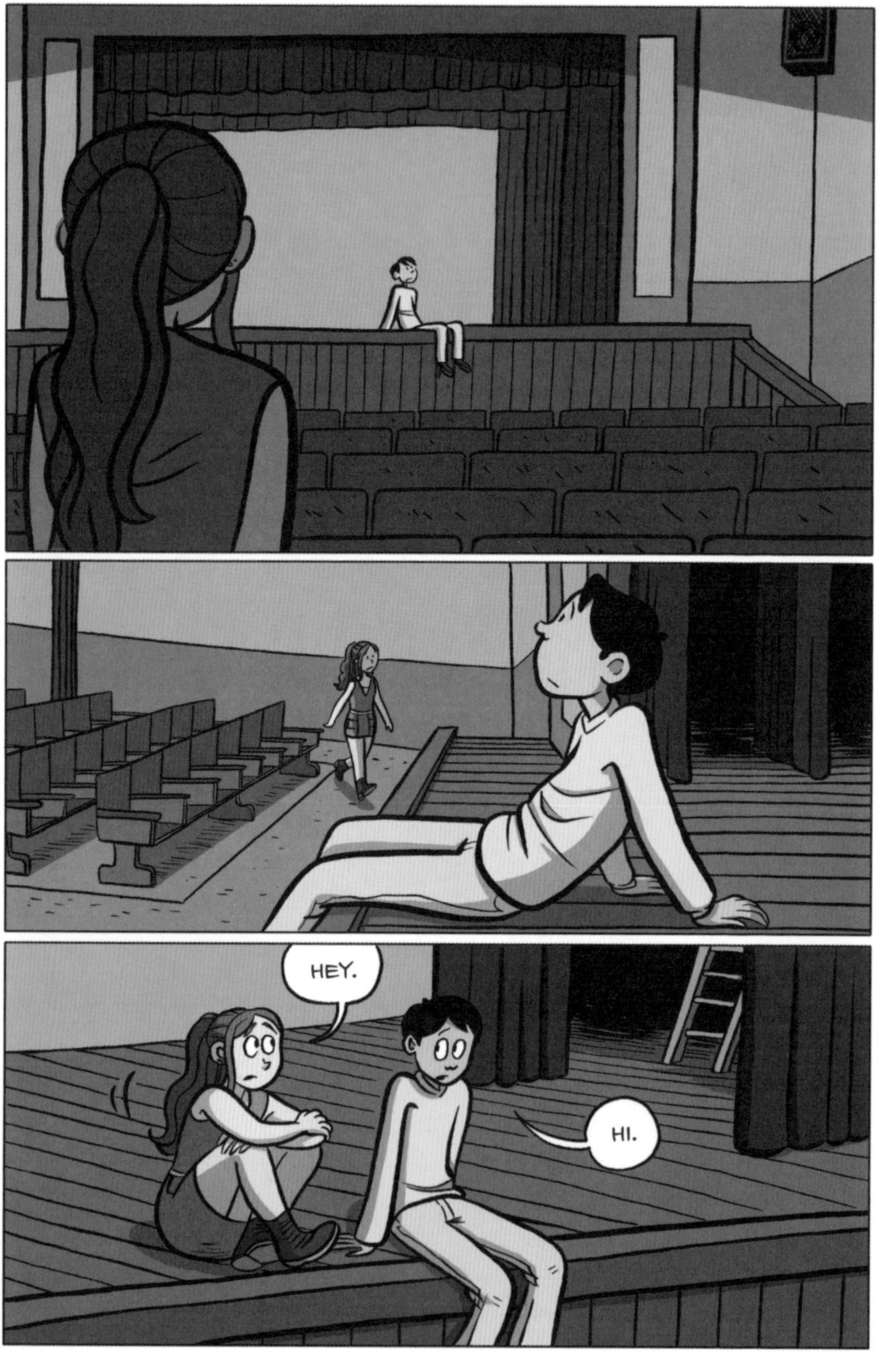
HEY.
HI.

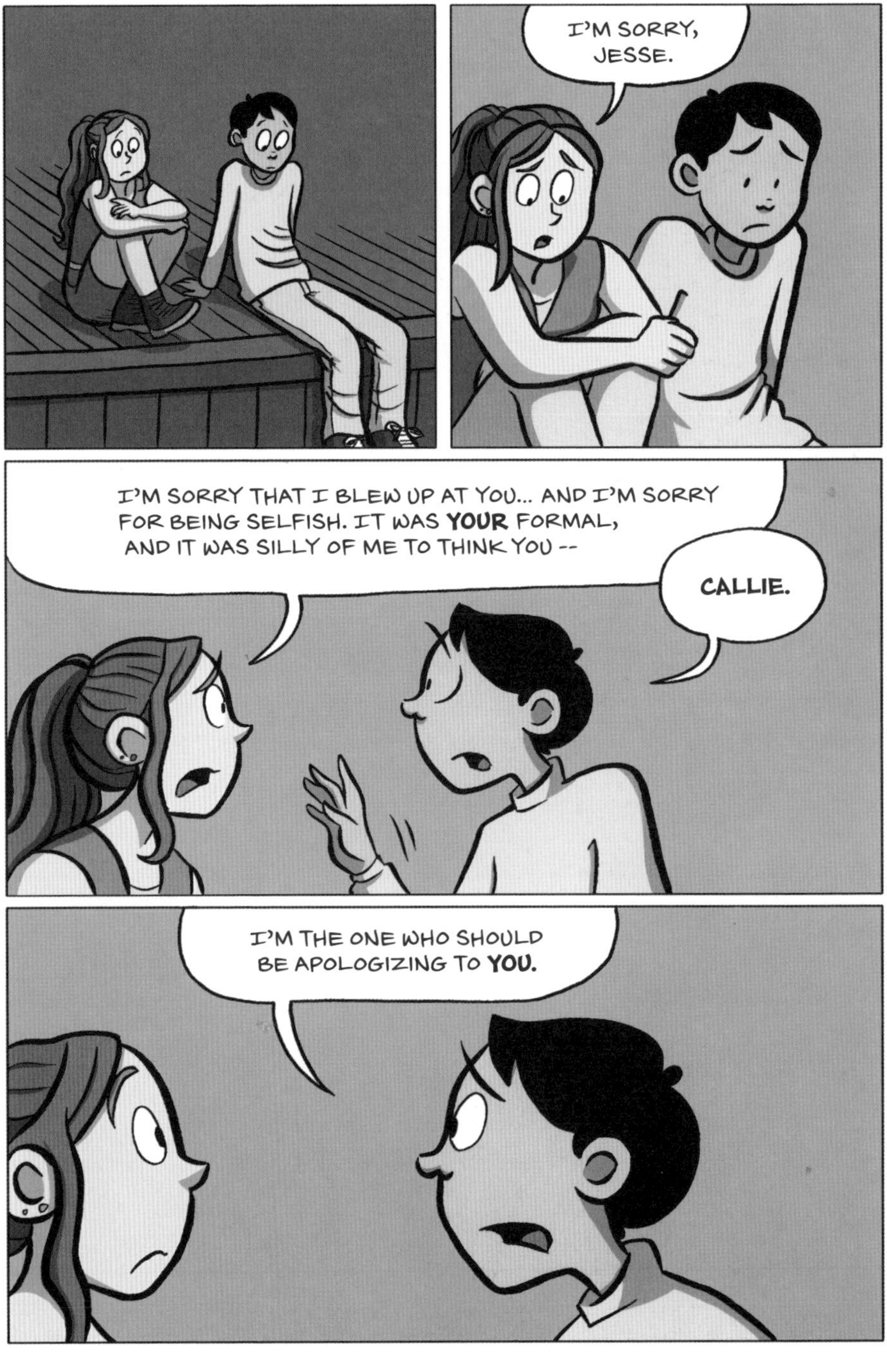
I'M SORRY, JESSE.
I'M SORRY THAT I BLEW UP AT YOU... AND I'M SORRY FOR BEING SELFISH. IT WAS **YOUR** FORMAL, AND IT WAS SILLY OF ME TO THINK YOU --
CALLIE.
I'M THE ONE WHO SHOULD BE APOLOGIZING TO **YOU.**

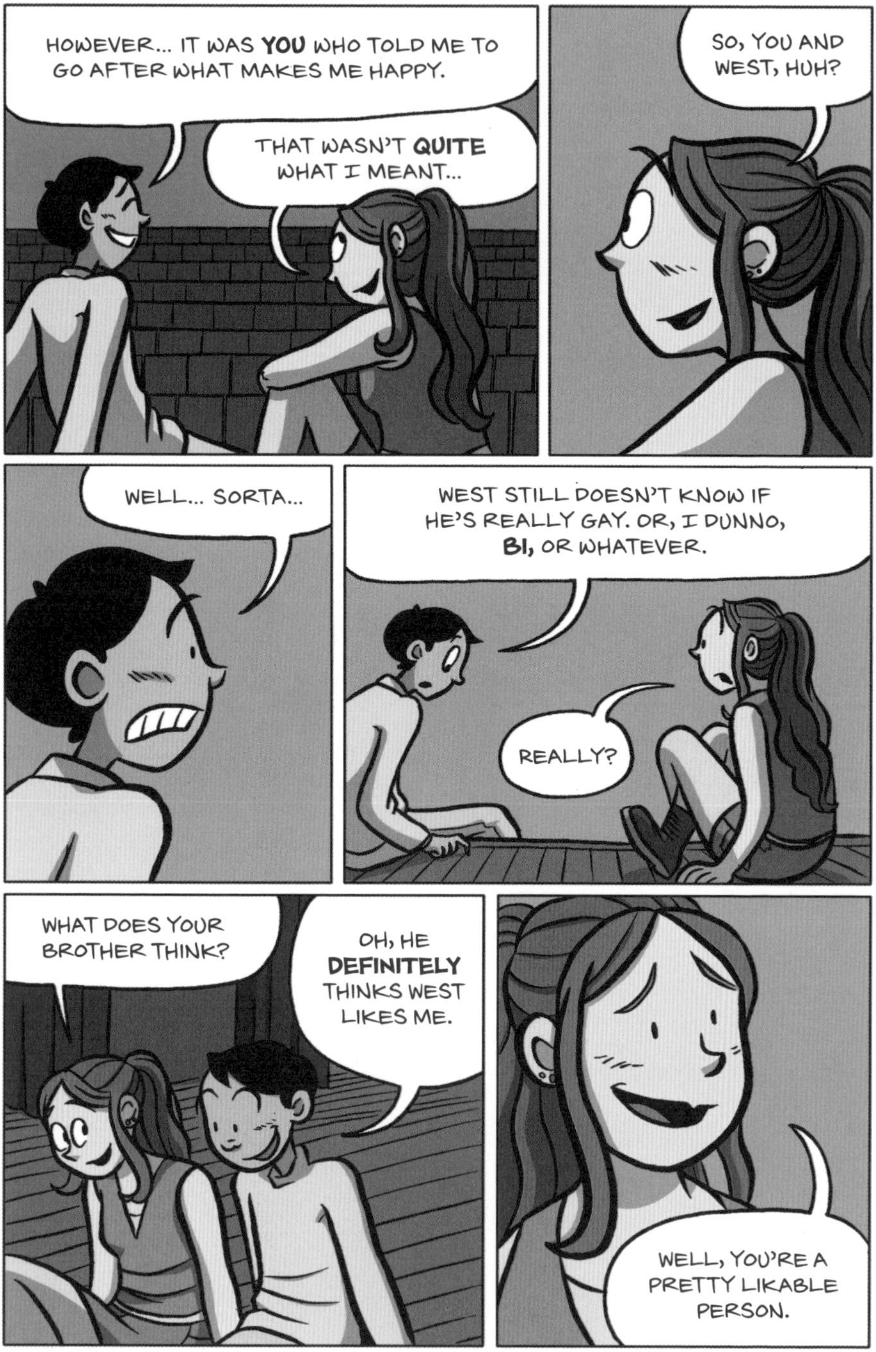

HOWEVER... IT WAS **YOU** WHO TOLD ME TO GO AFTER WHAT MAKES ME HAPPY.
THAT WASN'T **QUITE** WHAT I MEANT...
SO, YOU AND WEST, HUH?
WELL... SORTA...
WEST STILL DOESN'T KNOW IF HE'S REALLY GAY. OR, I DUNNO, **BI,** OR WHATEVER.
REALLY?
WHAT DOES YOUR BROTHER THINK?
OH, HE **DEFINITELY** THINKS WEST LIKES ME.
WELL, YOU'RE A PRETTY LIKABLE PERSON.

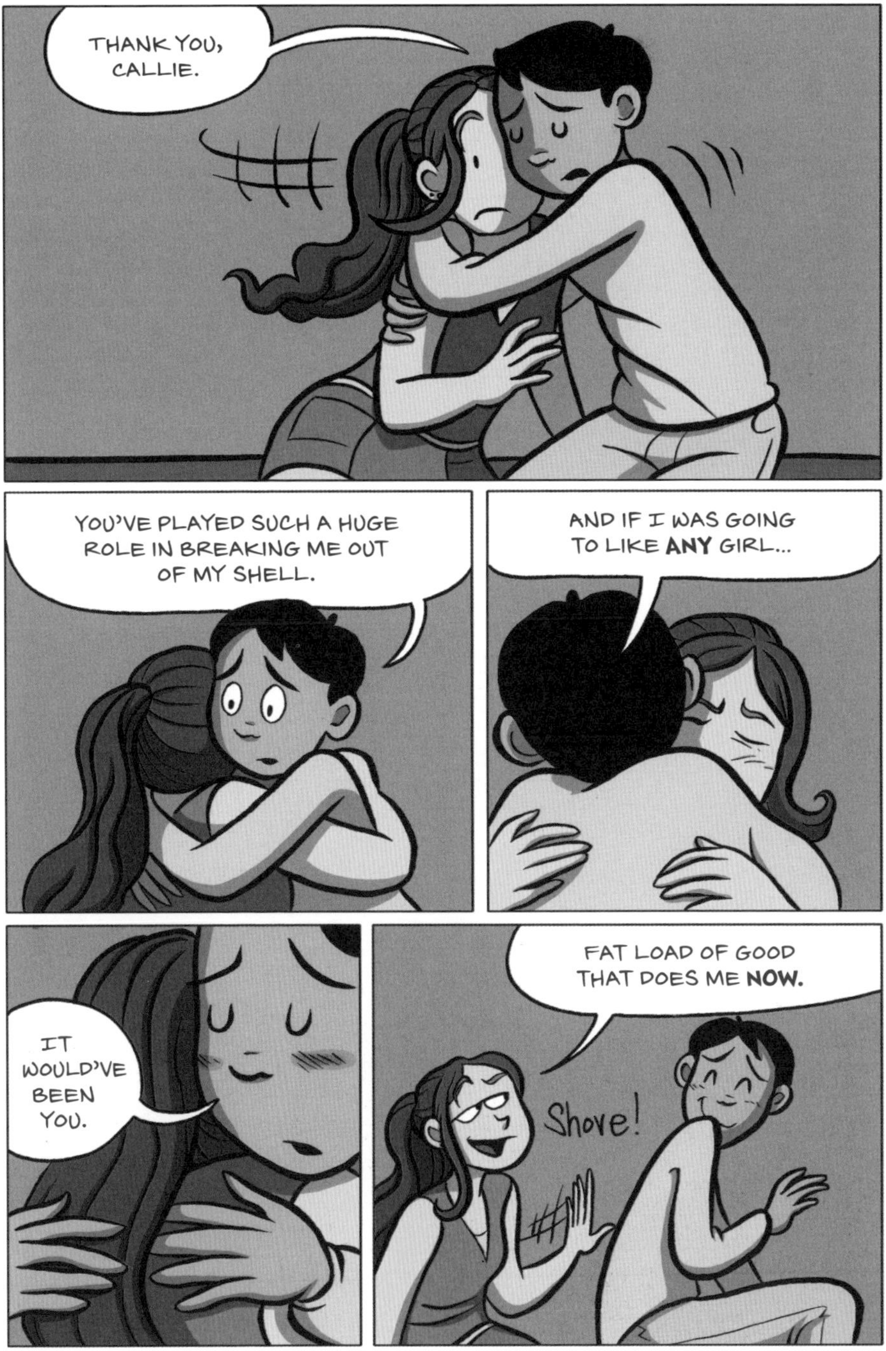
THANK YOU, CALLIE.
YOU'VE PLAYED SUCH A HUGE ROLE IN BREAKING ME OUT OF MY SHELL.
AND IF I WAS GOING TO LIKE **ANY** GIRL...
IT WOULD'VE BEEN YOU.
FAT LOAD OF GOOD THAT DOES ME **NOW.**
Shove!

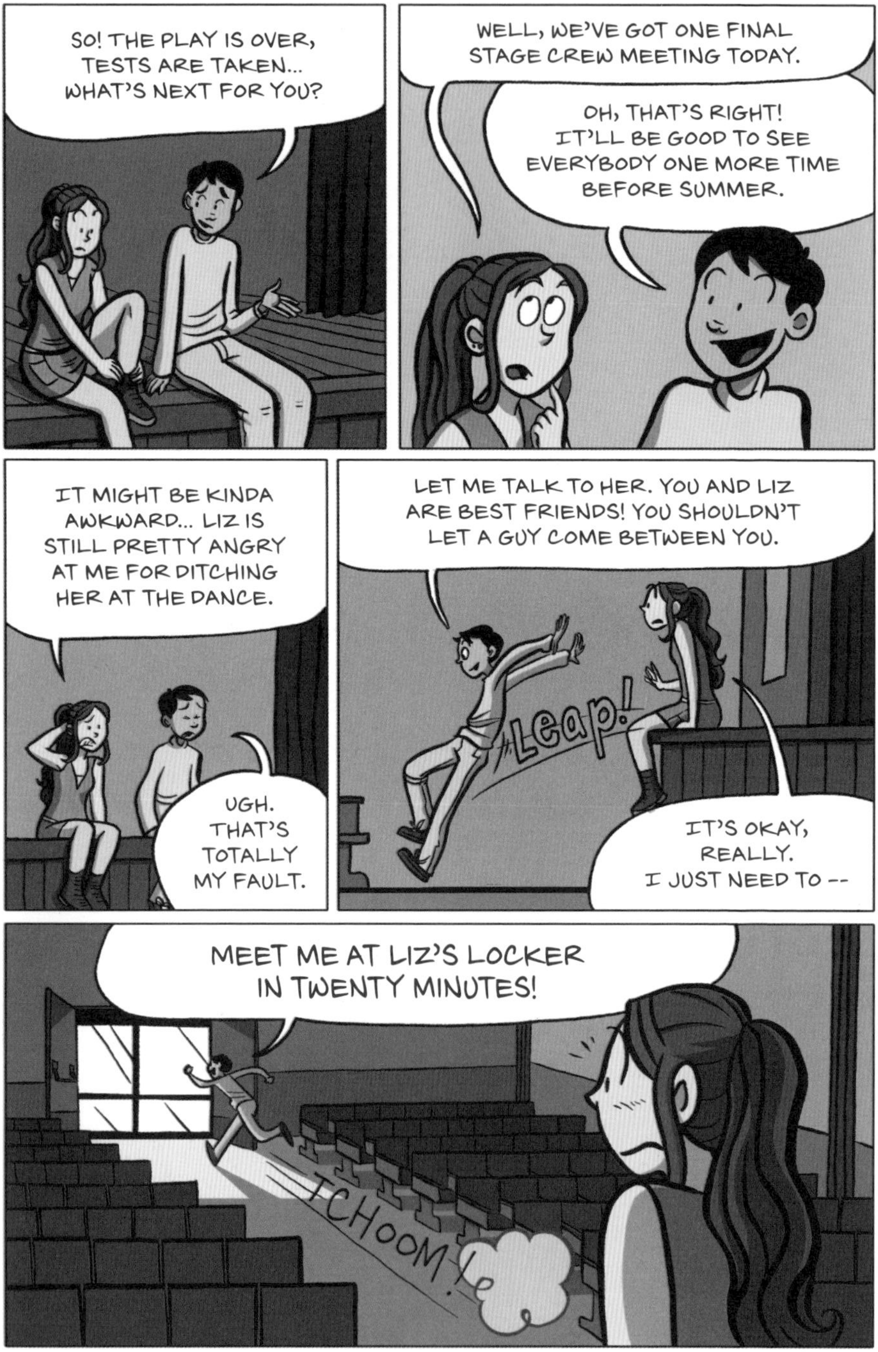
SO! THE PLAY IS OVER, TESTS ARE TAKEN... WHAT'S NEXT FOR YOU?
WELL, WE'VE GOT ONE FINAL STAGE CREW MEETING TODAY.
OH, THAT'S RIGHT! IT'LL BE GOOD TO SEE EVERYBODY ONE MORE TIME BEFORE SUMMER.
IT MIGHT BE KINDA AWKWARD... LIZ IS STILL PRETTY ANGRY AT ME FOR DITCHING HER AT THE DANCE.
UGH. THAT'S TOTALLY MY FAULT.
LET ME TALK TO HER. YOU AND LIZ ARE BEST FRIENDS! YOU SHOULDN'T LET A GUY COME BETWEEN YOU.
Leap!
IT'S OKAY, REALLY. I JUST NEED TO --
MEET ME AT LIZ'S LOCKER IN TWENTY MINUTES!
TCHOOM!

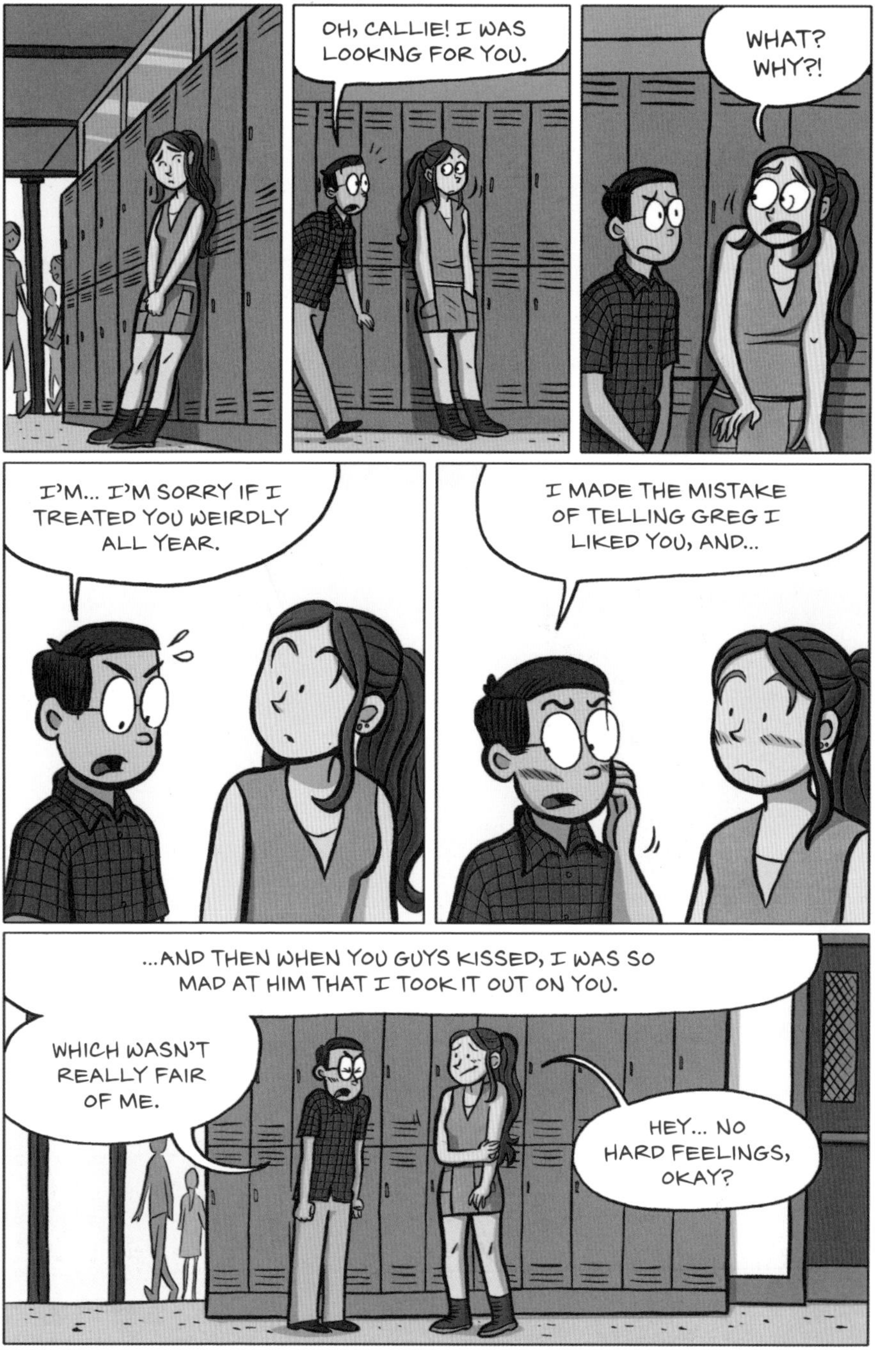
OH, CALLIE! I WAS LOOKING FOR YOU.
WHAT? WHY?!
I'M... I'M SORRY IF I TREATED YOU WEIRDLY ALL YEAR.
I MADE THE MISTAKE OF TELLING GREG I LIKED YOU, AND...
...AND THEN WHEN YOU GUYS KISSED, I WAS SO MAD AT HIM THAT I TOOK IT OUT ON YOU.
WHICH WASN'T REALLY FAIR OF ME.
HEY... NO HARD FEELINGS, OKAY?

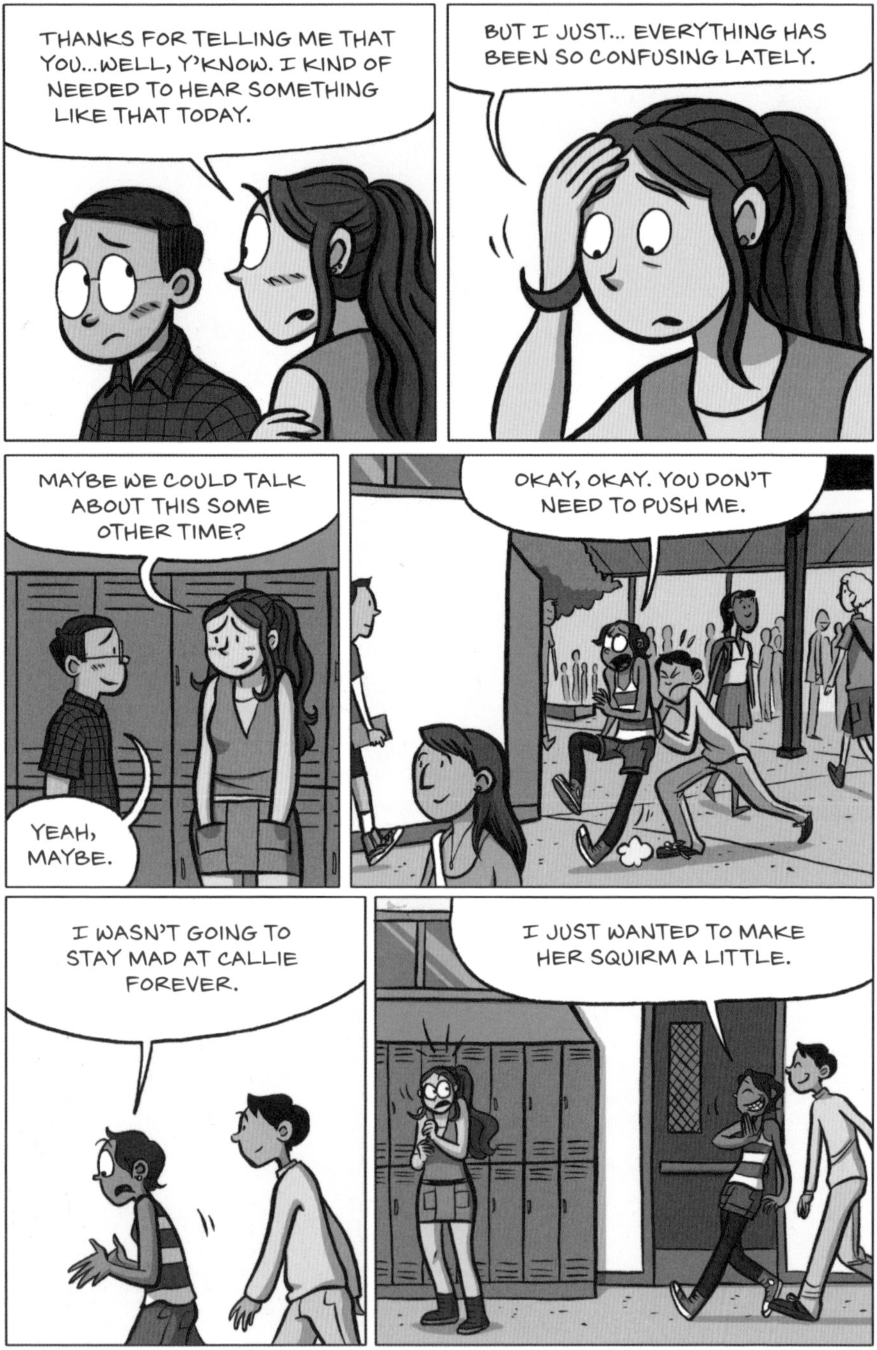
THANKS FOR TELLING ME THAT YOU...WELL, Y'KNOW. I KIND OF NEEDED TO HEAR SOMETHING LIKE THAT TODAY.
BUT I JUST... EVERYTHING HAS BEEN SO CONFUSING LATELY.
MAYBE WE COULD TALK ABOUT THIS SOME OTHER TIME?
YEAH, MAYBE.
OKAY, OKAY. YOU DON'T NEED TO PUSH ME.
I WASN'T GOING TO STAY MAD AT CALLIE FOREVER.
I JUST WANTED TO MAKE HER SQUIRM A LITTLE.

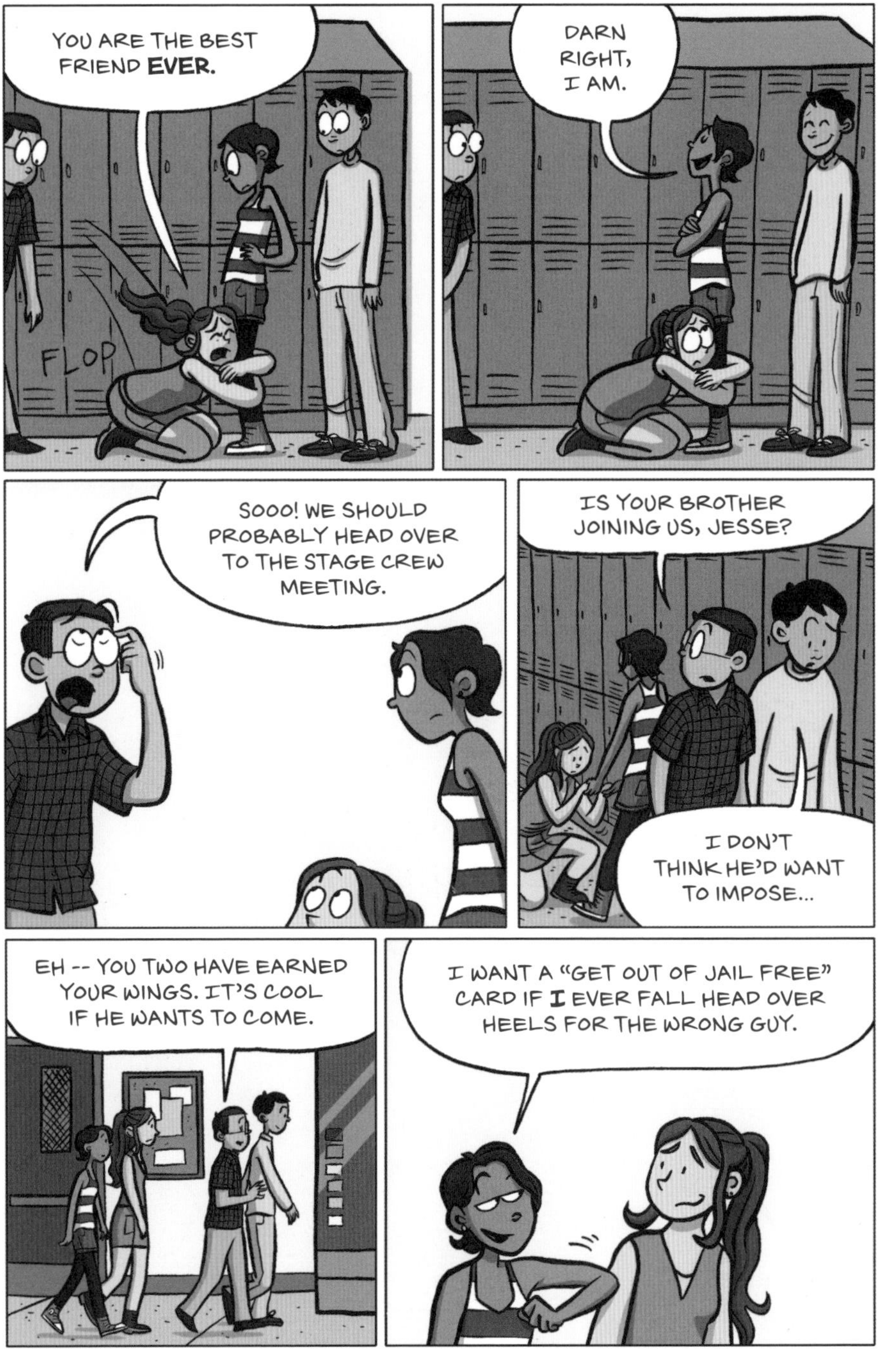
YOU ARE THE BEST FRIEND **EVER.**
FLOP
DARN RIGHT, I AM.
SOOO! WE SHOULD PROBABLY HEAD OVER TO THE STAGE CREW MEETING.
IS YOUR BROTHER JOINING US, JESSE?
I DON'T THINK HE'D WANT TO IMPOSE...
EH -- YOU TWO HAVE EARNED YOUR WINGS. IT'S COOL IF HE WANTS TO COME.
I WANT A "GET OUT OF JAIL FREE" CARD IF **I** EVER FALL HEAD OVER HEELS FOR THE WRONG GUY.

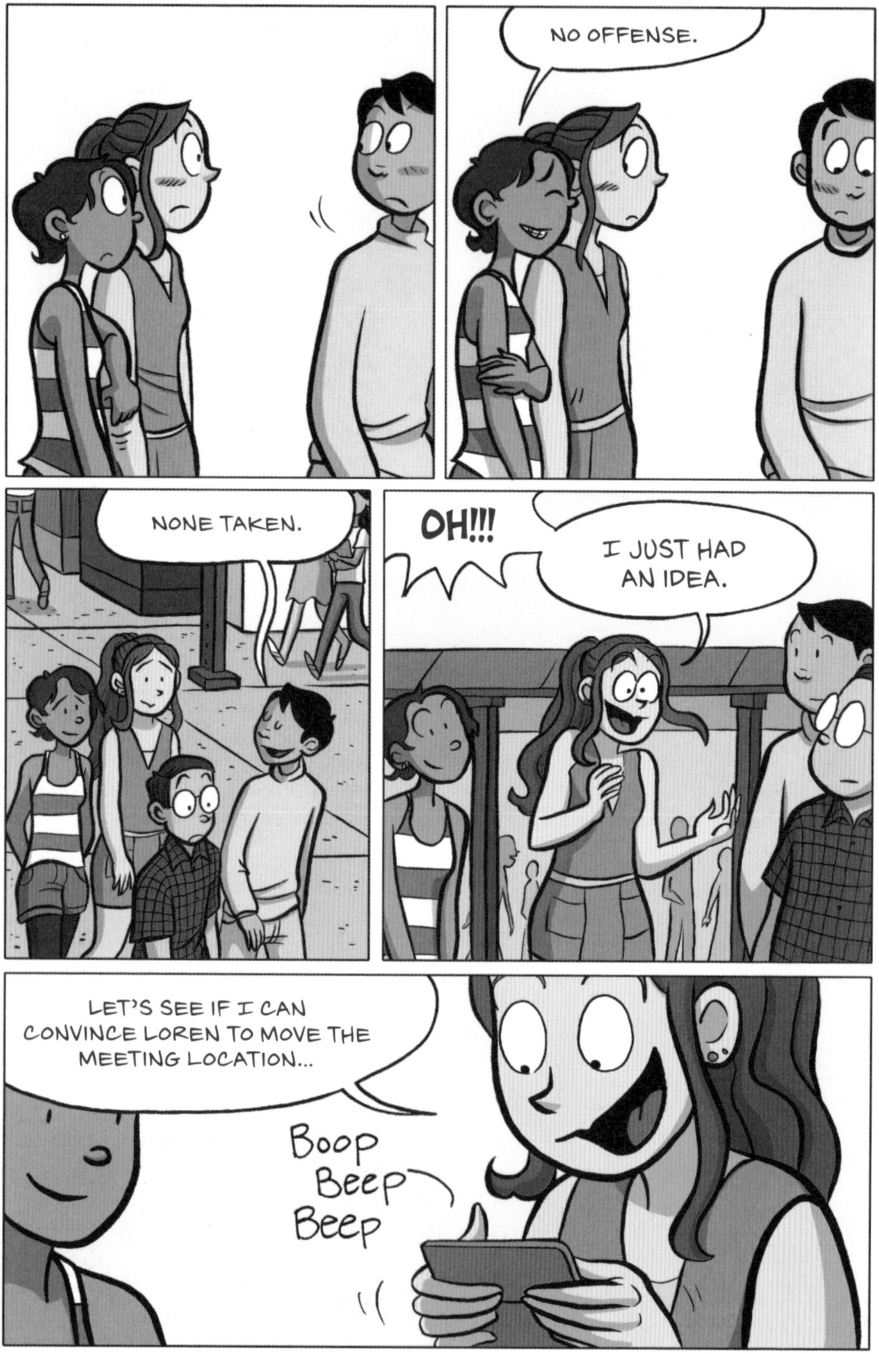
NO OFFENSE.
NONE TAKEN.
OH!!!
I JUST HAD AN IDEA.
LET'S SEE IF I CAN CONVINCE LOREN TO MOVE THE MEETING LOCATION...
Boop
Beep
Beep

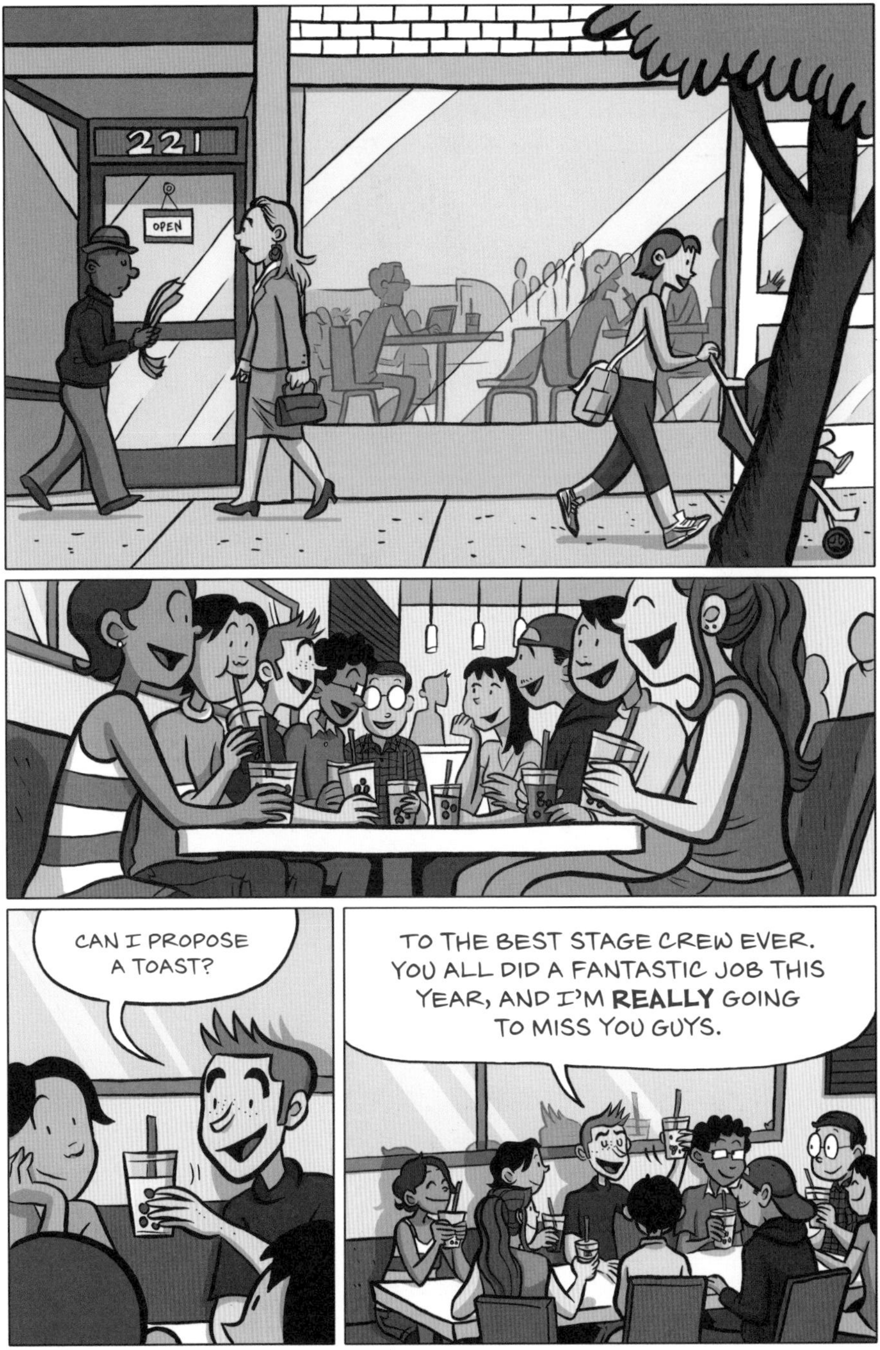
221
OPEN
CAN I PROPOSE A TOAST?
TO THE BEST STAGE CREW EVER. YOU ALL DID A FANTASTIC JOB THIS YEAR, AND I'M **REALLY** GOING TO MISS YOU GUYS.

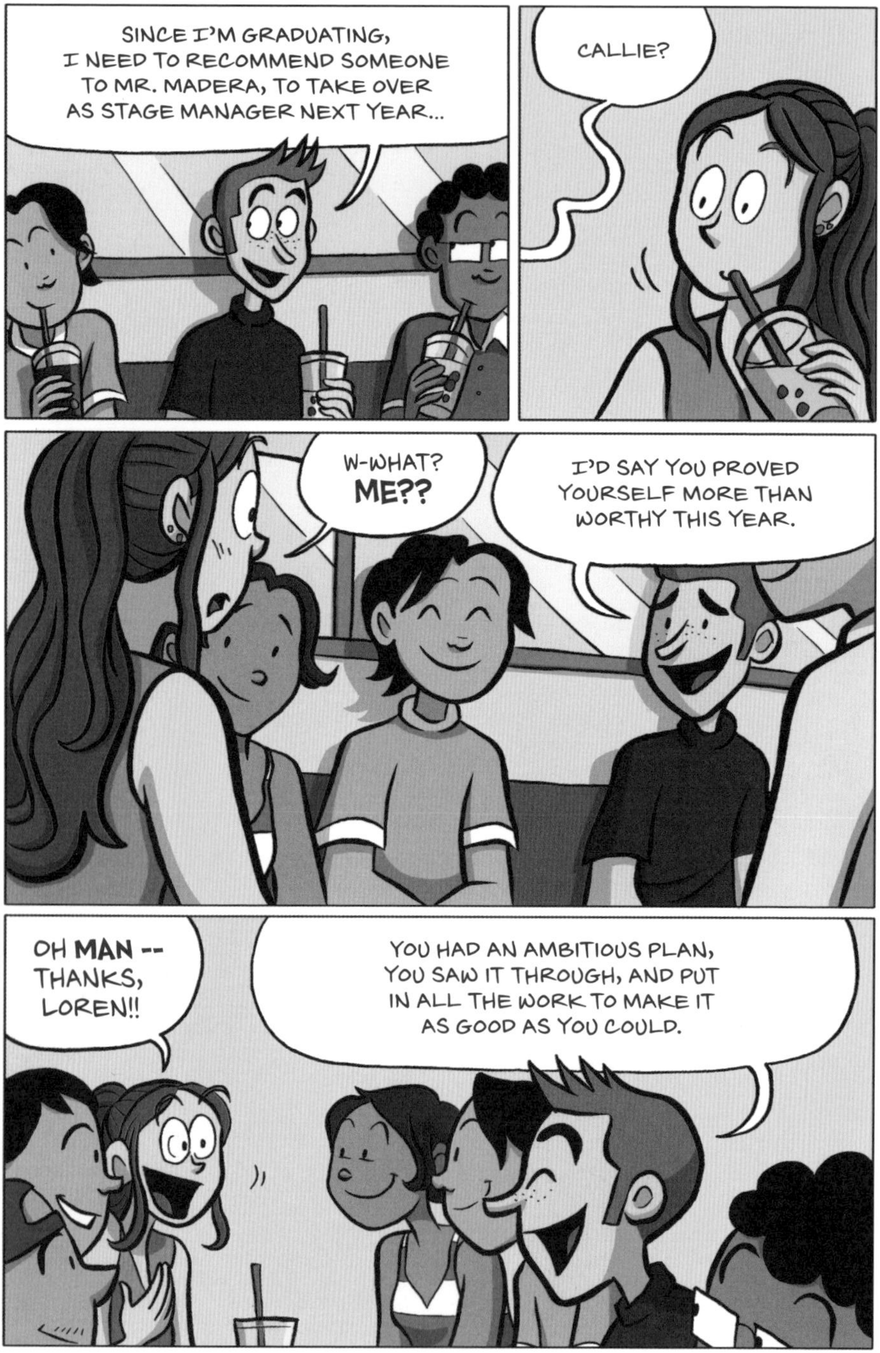
SINCE I'M GRADUATING, I NEED TO RECOMMEND SOMEONE TO MR. MADERA, TO TAKE OVER AS STAGE MANAGER NEXT YEAR...
CALLIE?
W-WHAT? **ME??**
I'D SAY YOU PROVED YOURSELF MORE THAN WORTHY THIS YEAR.
OH **MAN** -- THANKS, LOREN!!
YOU HAD AN AMBITIOUS PLAN, YOU SAW IT THROUGH, AND PUT IN ALL THE WORK TO MAKE IT AS GOOD AS YOU COULD.

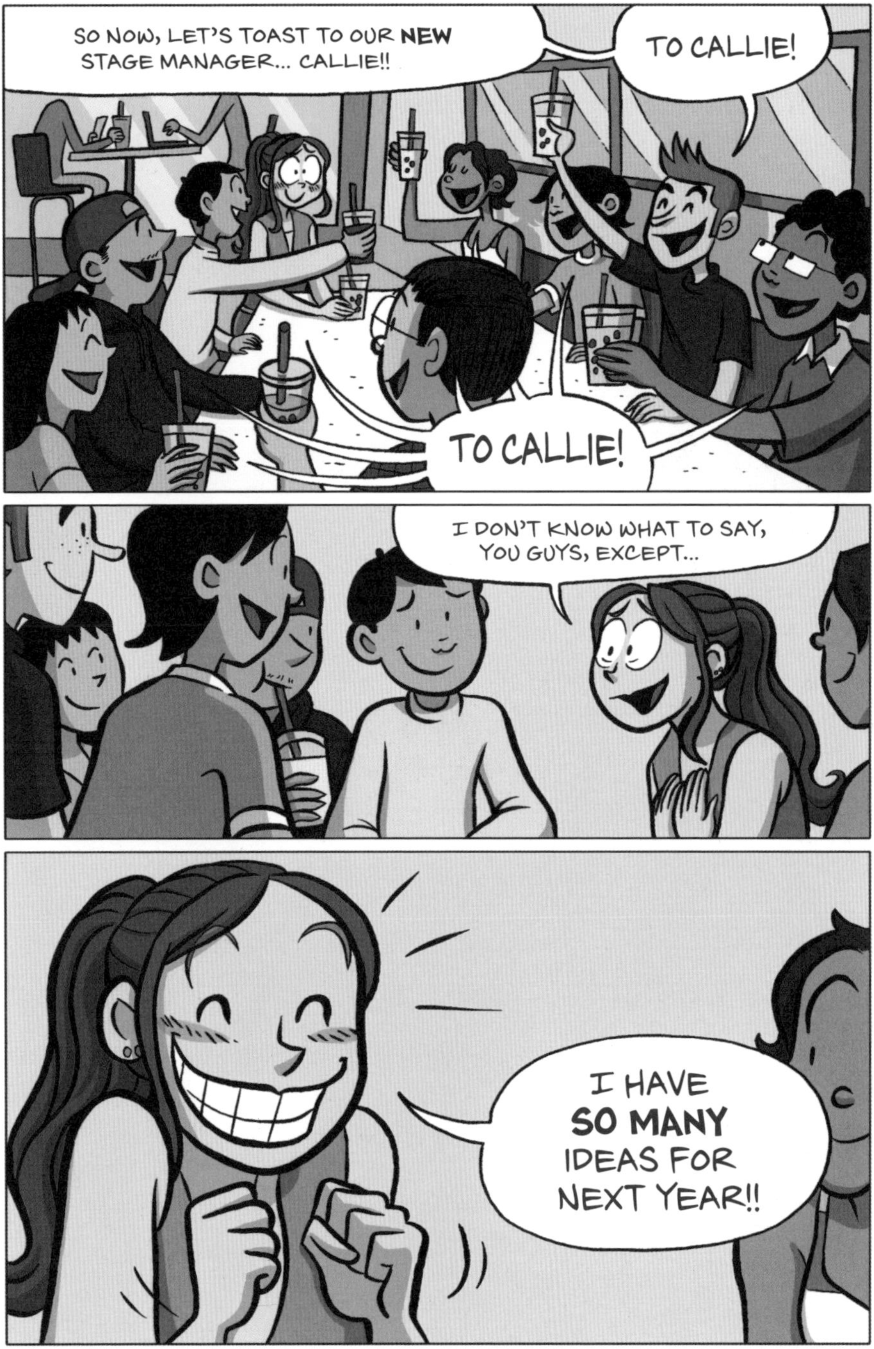
SO NOW, LET'S TOAST TO OUR **NEW** STAGE MANAGER... CALLIE!!
TO CALLIE!
TO CALLIE!
I DON'T KNOW WHAT TO SAY, YOU GUYS, EXCEPT...
I HAVE **SO MANY** IDEAS FOR NEXT YEAR!!

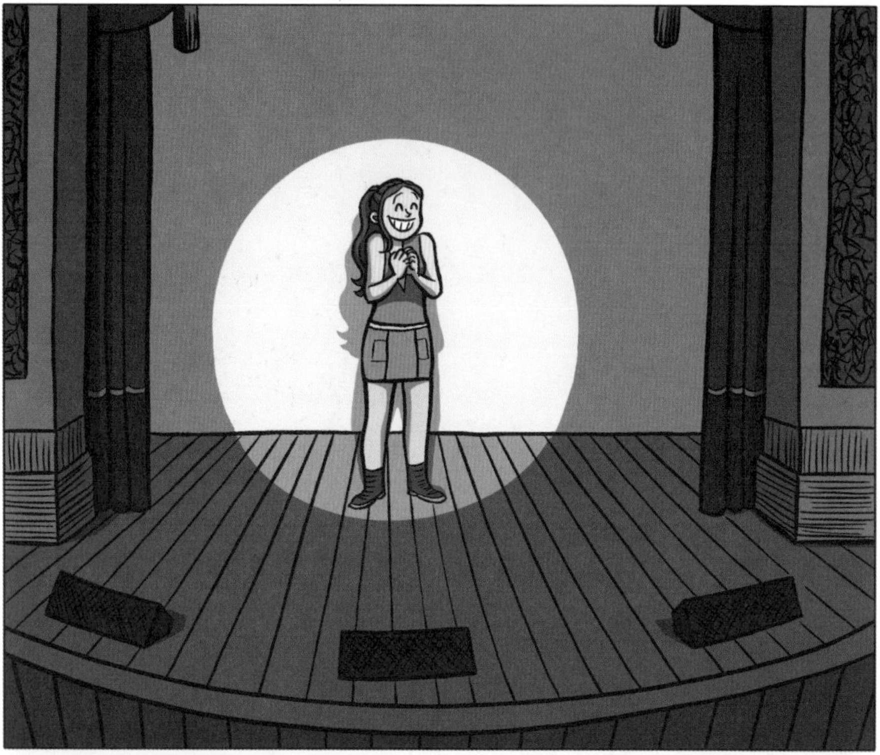

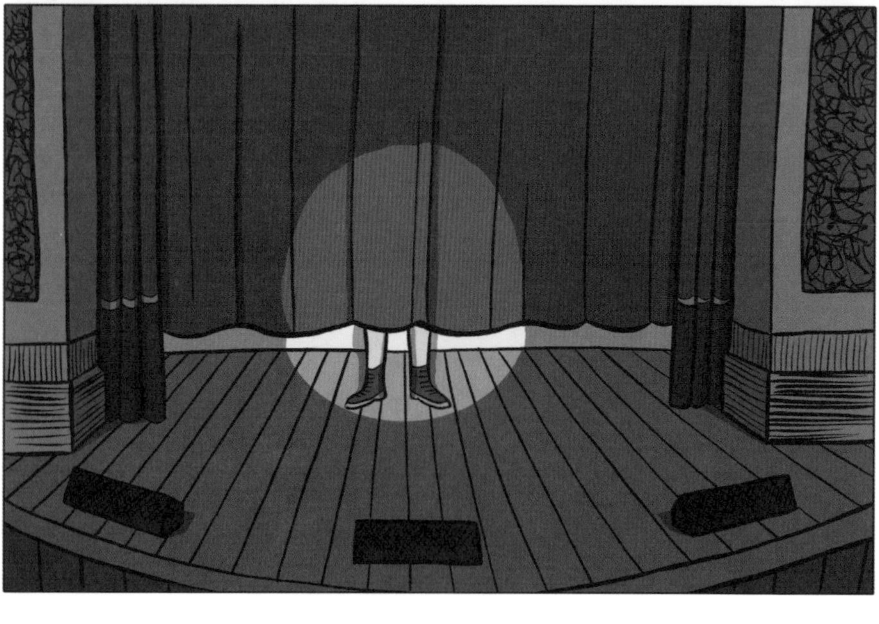

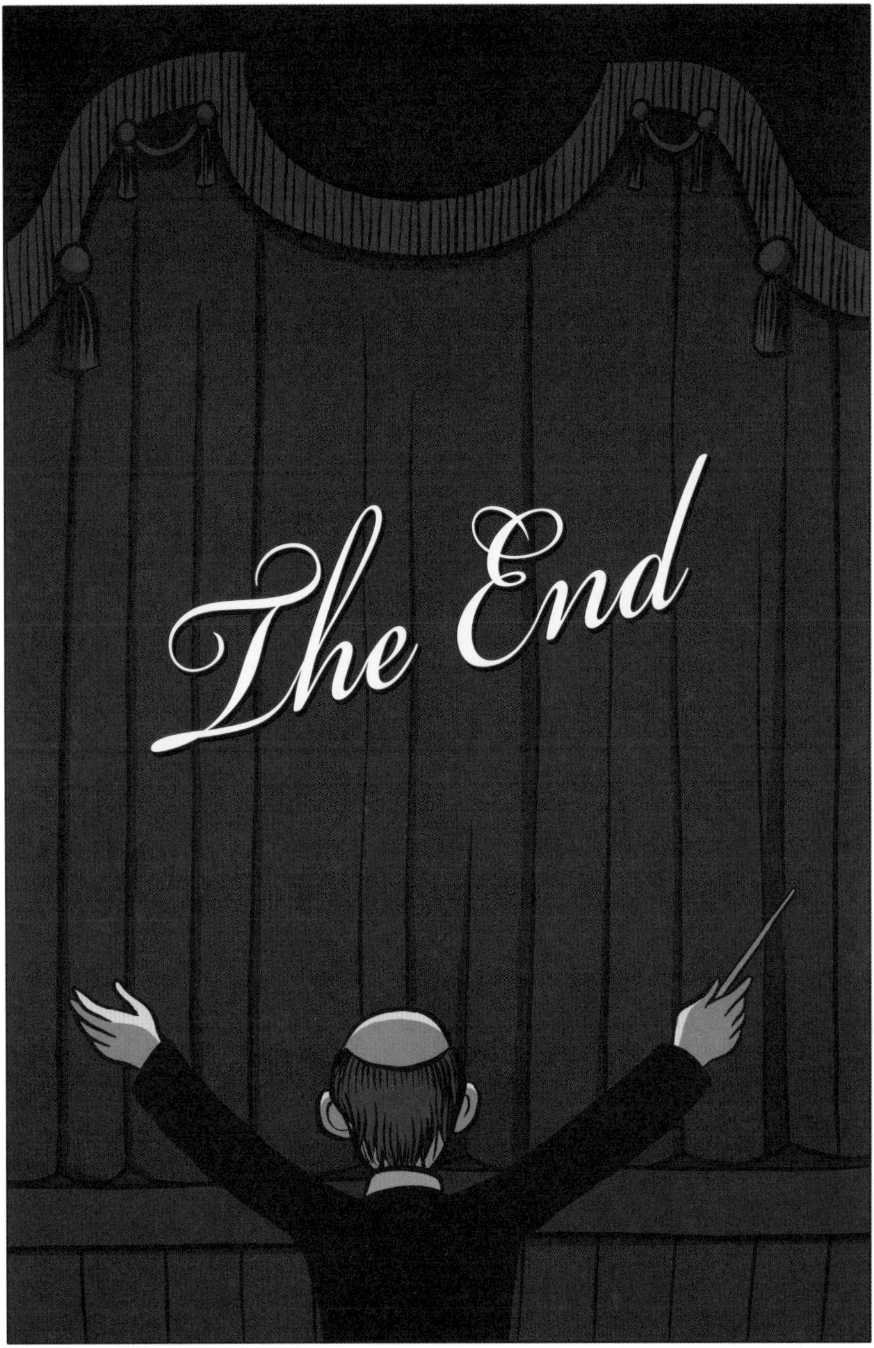
The End

AUTHOR'S NOTE

This book would not exist without my friends and instructors from the theater, choir, and stage crew communities in high school.

As a teenager, I took drama and choir classes, which led to small roles in school productions of *Guys and Dolls*, *Sweeney Todd*, *Evita*, and *City of Angels*. I sang exactly one solo line in my four years of high school, but enjoyed being part of the ensemble (singers who play lots of different characters, mostly in the background or crowd scenes) so much that I did it every chance I got.

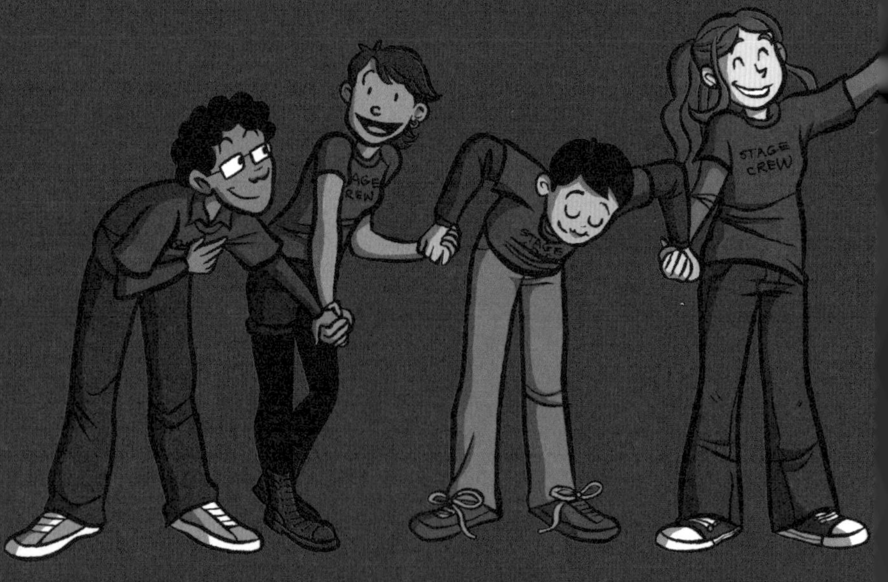
STAGE CREW

More important than any of the parts I sang were the people I met: singers, dancers, actors — many of them surprisingly modest or shy! — set designers, stage managers, directors, band members . . . every person on or behind the stage had an important role to play, and pulling off a live show together was thrilling.

In a way, those years of my life helped me to find my voice and gave me a wealth of artistic material to draw from. Callie's experiences are different from my own, but many of the characters and events in this story are inspired by things I was a part of. And the talent, courage, and dedication of my friends continue to inspire me every single day.

-Raina

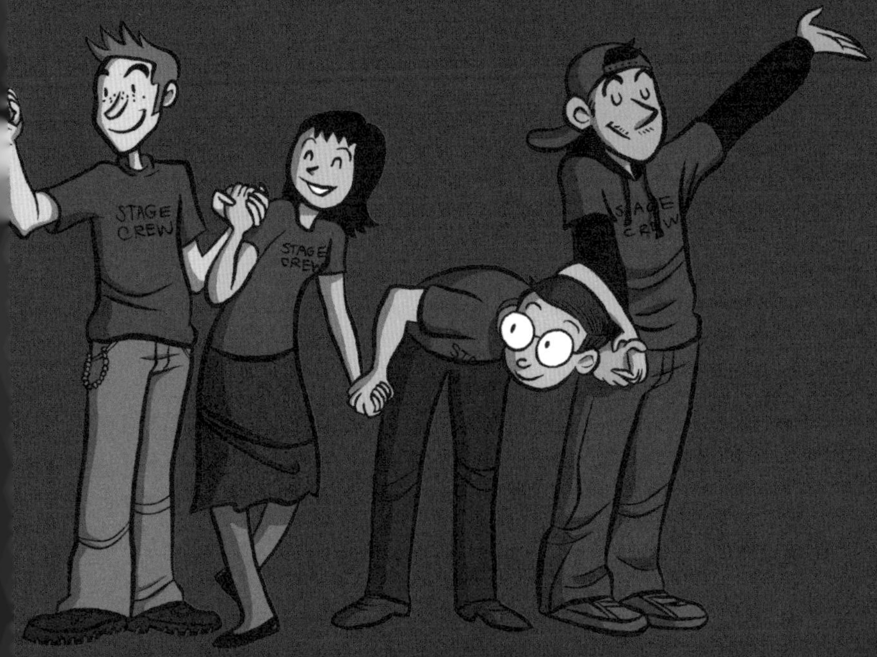
STAGE CREW
STAGE CREW
STAGE CREW

THANKS TO . . .

Jake and Jeff Manabat, for being two of my favorite people on the planet.

Cassandra Pelham, David Saylor, Phil Falco, Sheila Marie Everett, Lizette Serrano, Tracy van Straaten, Ed Masessa, and everyone at Scholastic. You are a joy to work with.

John Green, Gurihiru, and Aki Yanagi, my dedicated production team.

Megan Brennan and Gale Williams, my skilled production assistants.

The Riverdale Country School, who were kind enough to let me photograph their theater department.

Ivy Ratafia and Winter Mcleod, for their insightful notes on the manuscript.

Sara Ryan, Dylan Meconis, Faith Erin Hicks, Hope Larson, David Levithan, Kate Kubert Puls, Jerzy Drozd, Vera Brosgol, and Debbie Huey for their support, advice, and friendship during this book's creation.

Judy Hansen, my fabulous agent.

My family, who got me hooked on movie musicals when I was a kid.

And Dave Roman, who contributes so much of himself to my work, and cannot be thanked enough. I'm lucky to have him as my co-star.

BIBLIOGRAPHY

Appelbaum, Stanley, ed. *The New York Stage: Famous Productions in Photographs*. New York: Dover Publications, 1976.

Campbell, Drew. *Technical Theater for Nontechnical People*. New York: Allworth Press, 2004.

Carter, Paul. *Backstage Handbook: An Illustrated Almanac of Technical Information*. Louisville: Broadway Press, 1994.

RAINA TELGEMEIER is the #1 *New York Times* bestselling, multiple Eisner Award–winning creator of *Smile* and *Sisters*, which are both graphic memoirs based on her childhood. She is also the creator of *Drama*, which was named a Stonewall Honor Book and was selected for YALSA's Top Ten Great Graphic Novels for Teens. Raina lives in the San Francisco Bay Area. To learn more, visit her online at www.goRaina.com.